possible he speaks in his own words. As William McFee says, the book has "the authenticity of history and the readability and excitement of fiction."

Nelson is always the central figure — this is his story, not only of him in action, but of his relationship with his wife and his meeting with Lady Emma Hamilton in Italy. But the other actors in the drama — the middies, the servants, the army officers — are well drawn, too, all completely in character.

The story covers the years from 1793, when Nelson took command of his first battleship, *Agamemnon,* to the battle of the Nile in August 1798. It tells of the Siege of Corsica and the Battle of St. Vincent, after which Nelson became rear-admiral. Then at Santa Cruz de Teneriffe during the Blockade of Cadiz Nelson lost his arm and was invalided home for a time before the fierce pursuit of the French Fleet culminated in the Battle of the Nile. That battle, on which the fortunes of empires hung, was also a great climax in the life of Horatio Nelson.

Jacket design by Anton Otto Fischer

* * * * * *

PEARL FRYE (Mrs. Lowell Sanford Rau) is a talented artist as well as a novelist of remarkable versatility. One of her paintings has been purchased for the permanent collection of the Metropolitan Museum in New York. Born in California, she is the daughter of Dr. Alexis E. Frye, famed geographer and educator. She was married in 1940 and went with her husband to Hawaii in 1941. There she lived through the bombing, gave birth to her first child in April 1942, and returned home in June. She now lives in Connecticut with her husband and two children.

A Gam

A Game for Empires

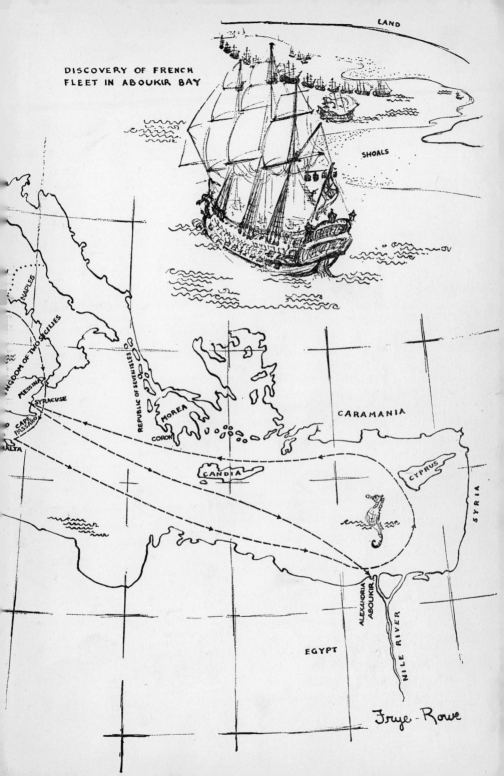

DISCOVERY OF FRENCH
FLEET IN ABOUKIR BAY

LAND

SHOALS

NAPLES

KINGDOM OF TWO SICILIES

MESSINA

SYRACUSE

CAPE PASSARO

MALTA

REPUBLIC OF SEVEN ISLES

MOREA

CORON

CANDIA

CARAMANIA

CYPRUS

SYRIA

ALEXANDRIA
ABOUKIR

EGYPT

NILE RIVER

Frye-Rowe

A Game for Empires

A Biographical Novel

(1793–1798)

BY PEARL FRYE

1950
Little, Brown and Company · *Boston*

As always,
to
Lowell Sanford Rowe

Contents

Contents

A Game for Empires

I. Overtures

DURING the waning years of the eighteenth century two ambitious but impoverished young men succeeded almost simultaneously in breaking through the norm of human obscurity to play the devil with each other's schemes and the lives of tens of thousands. The elder of the two became known to his people and their allies as the "savior of civilization"; the younger to his as "the champion of liberty."

They never met, nor exchanged so much as a scathing letter. The elder of the two, "the savior," would smile at the mention of the "champion," saying: "In the person of the Corsican, I can see but little difference between the name of Emperor, King, or Préfet, if his people perfectly obey his despotic orders." While the younger, "the champion," would shrug at the mention of the "savior," saying, "That sea wolf!"

Diametrically opposed in their philosophy, and the mediums in which they practiced their arts, they deprecated each other's mode of livelihood while each constantly crossed the other's masterfully arranged works.

They put on a dazzling as well as frightening duel for all of twelve years. The world still feels the repercussions of it.

This is the story of the elder during the first five years of the twelve; the time it took him to create his first masterpiece.

Though no one living in the winter of 1792–1793 could predict what was five years ahead, there was no shortage of political opinions and conflicting predictions shouted from all over the globe that if something drastic—and preferably violent—were not immediately done, the whole world would go to smash.

❈   ❈   ❈

A sudden December snowstorm howling down from the North Sea sent the villagers of Burnham Thorpe, in Norfolk, England, hurrying home. The main thoroughfare wound beyond the village, swept over the distant low hills across the sandy beaches of the Wash and ended at the sea. It was deserted except for two men approaching from opposite directions. One man suggested age in the heaviness of his step, though he was still too far away to recognize as he forced his slow way against the prevailing wind. The nearer, coming with the gale from the sea, was a slender, almost frail-looking young naval captain in his early thirties; the son of the village rector. There was a reedlike tenacity in his step as he blew before the North Sea storm—until a perverse blast buffeted him off his course, flattened him to a stone wall. He picked himself up, casting a heavenward glance of reproachful disgust at the downward swirling snowflakes. Suddenly he pivoted in his track and dove for the shelter of the local alehouse.

"Good evening, sir!" The keeper, who had leaped to serve him, peered uneasily toward the door, as if he had been expecting someone else.

"Good evening," the young Captain smiled as he finally stopped shivering, "for so custom demands we call it."

"'Tis a mean night, sir. Beer, Captain?"

As he nodded assent, the Captain's pleasant smile vanished. He drew off his gloves, unbuttoned his greatcoat, and took out the silver watch his ship's company had given to him for a wedding present. He studied it, calculating the time he knew it regularly lost against the hour it marked. It was late. His wife would be anxious, unless, and his smile returned faintly awry this time, she had gone to bed for the winter! Well, as soon as he thawed out a bit he would be off.

There was a searching restlessness in his face as he glanced about the dim room, nodding to the various eyes that met his with the careful respect of laborers for a gentleman. Most of the villagers were ragged, eternally hungry, trying to get warmth from the meager but costly fire on the hearth. Many were on their way home to cottages that could not afford fires. England was a shabby discontented isle this winter, but for all that she was at peace with the entire world! In some respects then, a promising place: there were the new factories which people said were the signs of a new era. There were immense advances in the looms to weave rich India's cotton harvest. New machinery of all kinds. Yet the factories struck terror in the hearts of these laborers who swore the machines would replace their two hands, take their only means of livelihood from them. There were open frenzies: mobs broke in and smashed the crazy inventions of the devil with sticks and axes. And King George III, who distrusted the rising power of industrialism, sided with his people against the progressive, predominantly Whig nobility which hoped to curb the crown's power, loosen the centralization of England's government.

Even so there was talk from the scientific laboratories of greater uses for the diabolically dangerous, but interesting little stationary steam engine, and rumors that electricity, now a medicinal "shock" stimulant, would actually prove to have other uses. Talk of communicating by electrical impulses sent from stations set several *miles* apart! Though horses and heliograph were still more dependable, the Captain relished the idea of faster communication, more work accomplished, time saved. Life was short and ambition long.

So, in spite of the King's suspicion of industrialism, and the people's real misery, the majority of Englishmen with next to nothing were better off than their fellow laborers across the Channel: the French without pants—the sans-culottes!

The Captain shook his head as now and then the voices of the laborers in the tavern paused and some lone voice would growl their oppression and hint 'twas about time they heeded the French. But the majority of voices would drown it in laughter. And the Captain felt easier, although he wondered as the keeper could be heard to mutter in a low voice, "Any minute now, 'e'll come and 'e'll talk!"

Only a man like the Captain, who had seen war, could appreciate how well off these Englishmen were even in these hard times. For seven hundred years England had successfully fought off all threats of invasion from foreign conquerors. He had a sudden vision of palm-thatched huts filled with English soldiers and seamen in three stages—sick, dying and decomposed; of a lonely fort rearing out of a rain-soaked Nicaraguan jungle; of months of fighting for an objective that high army and navy chiefs had quarreled over so long the rainy season had begun before the attack was launched, and the government had already given it up as a useless project, but because communications were slow . . . such things are. Oh, if men could communicate faster, act sooner, surely then there would be an end to such hideous mortal misunderstandings. . . . He rubbed his forehead. His hair had turned white from that expedition and the months of fever following it.

So his hair was white. He smiled wryly again. It saved having to powder it as other men did. And he could blame himself for having gone at all. He had been ordered merely to sail up the San Juan River, land the troops, not to lead them. But the fort had proved to be farther inland than their maps showed, the San Juan River shallow and unnavigable. Was he to abandon an army to struggle through sickly jungle? He had wrangled with the Indians for canoes to transport them upriver; helped them make camp; led the first attack in his stocking feet—shoes lost in knee-deep mud—and finally pointed their cannon for them. Until the navy had at last tracked him down; ordered him to report back to his base, and the army stayed on to die.

Good God! It took memories like that to make him remember his blessings, for all the way down the street just now even he had been chafing against the government, musing moodily over his premature retirement from just such activity! Yet he wouldn't have missed that campaign for anything so long as there was a campaign to be fought. There had been the satisfaction of making seemingly insurmountable obstacles crumble before him; hearing a hard-bitten old army colonel say he was a born leader, and recommend him to the government as a credit to England. Even the treacherous Indians had come to treat him with awed superstition, saying he was empowered by the gods because he had survived their attempts to poison him, and had not been bitten by a venomous serpent coiled in his hammock. Nothing like a miracle to top off his carefully conciliating manners when having to deal with diseased, suspicious, fetish-bound savages. Now if the army and navy had co-ordinated so that the attack could have been made in the dry season . . . The memory of that highhanded stupidity made him ill. Oh, what couldn't he do if they would give him the chance!

Of course, if he had money he could bribe an election, or buy a seat in Parliament as Prime Minister Pitt's father had done for him. The only snag there was that he shied from bribery, though it was customary, for to deal as a thief among thieves . . . anyway, he had no money, and if he were in Parliament he would have to give up being a Whig and a Tory both, which he would not do. That was that.

Restless once more he listened to the rising gale knocking the tavern sign against the trembling house. And his soul grew stormier as he foresaw years on end and every path upward closed to him. He had served his country too well while stationed in the West Indies. He had dared to take issue with his commander in chief; refused to close his eyes to the powerful English and Yankee businessmen who were smuggling in order to avoid the tariff. He, a junior captain of a small frigate, had calmly read the text of England's Navigation Acts to his commander in chief. When the commander in chief, Admiral Hughes, warned him to mind his own business, he had disobeyed the Admiral's orders. He had stopped the smuggling in the West Indies, but had he been promoted or praised for saving his country hundreds of thousands of pounds?

The Captain gulped his beer to calm his sudden uprising anger. He signed to the keeper to bring him another. He sat staring moodily into the small fire that did not even light the hewn rafters; and again his thoughts were interrupted by that strange muttering of the keeper, " 'E'll come—be patient, can't ye—" The Captain frowned; whatever it meant he did not like the tone, nor the way the keeper looked from him toward the door. The Captain suddenly caught sight of a familiar black forelock hanging over beady eyes which were fastened like leeches on the Captain's face, as if hoping for a word from him. The Captain smiled, but shook his head, warning the eyes to keep their distance, and the black-haired man mingled back in the crowd while the Captain sat aloof, plunged in thought.

Oh, no, he had not been praised for enforcing English law. The Admiralty had coolly thanked his commander in chief for stopping the smuggling, while he, the real hero who had staked his career on being right, had been quietly beached and hounded by lawsuits for the last five years ashore. That was public gratitude. He had made plans with his wife to flee to Paris as the lawsuits mounted. But the government had finally shouldered his lawsuits; the Treasury was grateful to him, but he had never had another ship.

He was doomed to retirement on a captain's meager half pay. He who had been made a post captain, with his own frigate, in line for an admiral's flag rank, at twenty-one. The only patronage he had ever had had been his uncle's, but his uncle had died soon after he had been made a lieutenant, and he had risen in the navy by his own wits. He had been called a genius, a profound student, the best tactician in the navy, by Admiral Lord Hood, at the age of twenty-four. He had been made tutor to the Duke of Clarence, third son of George III, when the Duke was stationed in the West Indies. Those had seemed promising years for a young man not even thirty. Now . . .

he was beached like a rotten old hulk. He sighed deeply—and again met the determined eye of the black-haired man. He signed to the man not to bother him now.

As his first beer began to take effect and the keeper brought him the second he looked about him at the laborers with a quickened sympathy. His mind eased its grip on his worries. He could be worse off, he supposed. And the howling of wind reminded him at last not so much of rage, but of shelter. Finishing the second beer, he sat forward, thankful he was still alive, and enjoying the warmth of the fire that had finally permeated his frozen bones. Well. Someday, by God, he would still show—

His eyes suddenly focused on the door. The traveler he had seen in the street was also turning in at the alehouse, stamping the snow from his feet, slamming the door against the strong wind. The stranger, having jerked off his outer wrappings, held up his hands and in a deep voice proclaimed:

"I am the martyr of Birmingham. All you who are oppressed cast off your chains! England will achieve the new paradise! Why should you not be as free as the noble savage roaming his jungle? Your brothers in France yearn to liberate you as they have liberated their own! Do not pay taxes to the Pilate in London wresting the food from your little ones! The food you toiled to earn . . ."

The young Captain's white head came up, his bright eyes narrowed. Good God! A revolutionist! So this was the notorious Priestley, clergyman and scientist! He felt his hackles rise, recoiling from Priestley as if he were the serpent in Eden.

England was weakened by troubles enough without these blind, mental Samsons trying to wreck her foundations: deliver her into the hands of a foreign government!

But the laborers in the alehouse who had been joking together in spite of their poverty, talking crops and boxing, and grousing a bit, as everyone did, about the idiots in Parliament ruining England, now gazed at Priestley with hypnotized faces, their eyes almost ecstatic as he told them the meaning of liberty and equality and fraternity. They tossed a few more pennies on the counter; ordered more beer.

At that, the Captain rose, and with a quiet, crackling, " 'Tis a false fire this incendiary kindles to warm you good men!" stalked out.

The alehouse keeper rolled up his eyes and let out a long breath that ended in an abrupt soft whistle. Yet, seeing the Captain leave, some of the men grinned and followed him out the door. One especially, the squat mass of brawn, about nineteen years old, with black hair falling in his eyes and the smug self-assurance in his smile of a total illiterate.

As for the Captain, the moment he had closed the door he was chilled to the marrow. But he would rather freeze in this storm than remain under the same roof with that scoundrel Priestley. He coughed and shivered, made up his mind that the cursed ague was attacking him again—probably fatally—and at that, his momentarily chilled temper began to heat him once more; while the Caliban monster from the alehouse followed him doggedly, though the Captain seemed totally unaware of the man.

Puffing frost like a high-spirited war horse the Captain turned up his collar and fairly pranced down the road. Why, this Priestley was not representative of the people, even though Priestley in his reputed well-meaning might think so, but the tool of a rich and powerful movement seeking to overthrow the King of England! To a man like himself, trained since he was twelve years old to defend his King and Country, Priestley was speaking rank treason! Paradise indeed! Jungles and savages was it! He could tell them what that meant. And revolution meant *war*—war in these fields: these villages would be burned by one side or the other; these, the common people, would be the ones to suffer, not their leaders! And as the Captain tramped through the still, peaceful village, he sighed, "Oh, God keep it so."

Indeed, Priestley sounded very wise, perhaps, with all his book learning. He was the author of the *History of Electricity*. That was all right, but what of his heretical publication, *The Corruption of Christianity?* The High Church Captain snorted. And as for Priestley's "martyrdom"? The outraged common people of Birmingham had burned Priestley's chapel and sacked his house for celebrating the Fall of the Bastile; given him a taste of what he was asking them to do. As far as the Captain was concerned, Botany Bay was where Priestley belonged!

He came to an abrupt halt, his shadow nearly plowed into him. The Captain stood, getting his bearings in the thickening snowfall; then paced on, faster than ever.

He had traveled in France, he had seen the depravity of the nobility and the poverty of the peasants which made England—harsh though she was in the treatment of her people crawling on hands and knees, naked as mules, through her coal mines—still look like heaven by comparison. He had seen whole French villages where there was not one house, except the surrounding châteaux, fit to keep English pigs in! That had been several years ago, and he had sworn even then that the disparity of wealth in France was too acute to continue: miles of beautiful wheat fields tended by wretches grateful for a penny for a brace of partridges. In those days everyone in France had been aping the English, wishing for a parliamentary government. But now! He snorted again and snowflakes went up his nose. He began to cough hard and that made him more miserable.

So far, England had remained aloof of continental trouble, but she was finding it increasingly difficult to remain neutral, although just a few months ago Prime Minister Pitt, who willingly recognized the revolution for the sake of peace, had put himself on record: "There never was a time when, from the situation of Europe, we might more reasonably expect peace than we may at the present moment."

After four years of revolution and declarations of atheism the French had finally alarmed the world by confiscating the territories of Avignon and Venaissin from the Pope. Prussian and Austrian leaders had been exploding for a year with proclamations damning the revolution. Now they had begun to march on France. As the tension in Europe increased, each side in England became more and more fearful, dissatisfied and suspicious of the other. They should have been drawing together, searching for some peaceful economic solution of their most dangerous immediate problem: physical hunger.

The Captain's deep-set, gray-blue eyes became meditative, his prematurely lined and weathered face that marked him forever as one who had roughed it in far-off colonies grew white with cold. His full lower lip was thrust out when it was not quivering with chills. He paced the crisp snow back to his father's rambling parsonage, lopping off corners and taking short cuts. He made a straight wake through the swiftly deepening snow as he closed on his objective with its five tall chimneys and rounded dormer windows just coming in sight. Behind him tramped the black-haired creature shaped like an ape.

The Captain cursed Priestley for making trouble for the ignorant poor who had troubles enough already. They were cold this winter, these poor brother Englishmen. He had known these villagers since birth. He had even helped his parson father record their vital records. They were good patient people on the whole, and when it came to giving to the poor of the parish he would give blankets, not inflammatory words!

As the Captain and the monster stalked on, a middle-aged man dashed out of a side lane, blinded by the milky flying snow, and bent double against the wind. The Captain leaped to one side, laughing.

"Good evening, Mr. Fielding!"

The middle-aged man straightened. "Ahoy, Captain! You sail along smartly but a landlubber like me can't keep his course in this gale. What brings you out? Good wife not ill again?"

The Captain pointed back down the road right through his Caliban. "That blackguard Priestley—here again!"

The middle-aged man nodded. "Well, as my good uncle would have to admit, were he here, his Tom Joneses are full of Tom Foolery nowadays. But here's my house! Bless us! I thought I was lost. Won't you drop in and chat while you thaw by the fire? Nights like this one would swear the devil himself had risen out of the North Sea maelstrom—"

"Mebbe he has—" rumbled the black-haired man behind them, but neither the Captain nor Mr. Fielding paid any attention.

"Thank you, Mr. Fielding, I must get home," the Captain smiled. "My tropical wife will go into hibernation if I stay away too long. And I'm half dead with a chill. I've been all afternoon listening to our good neighbor Dr. Poyntz's theories on the cultivation of nut trees." There was a hint of boredom in the Captain's voice. "This storm caught me aback, though why anything this ungrateful climate does should surprise me . . . But as to that Priestley! He's talking to Englishmen, not to Frenchmen!"

"Oh, I think we can give him as good as they gave him in Birmingham, Captain."

"Yow tell 'em!" the shadow from the alehouse rumbled. "Cap'n he coon do ut."

Neither the Captain nor Mr. Fielding appeared to hear the man, as the Captain said, "I hope so, Mr. Fielding. Indeed, I would like to chat, tell you what I think of our cringing justices, but my wife—and this chill, Mr. Fielding . . . You will give my regards to your family, sir."

"And mine to your wife. Is the Reverend still at Bath for the winter?"

"Aye, we're all alone—except for our boy home for the holidays."

"Yes, I—ah—saw the youngster. . . ." Mr. Fielding seemed to be masking dislike under a grim smile. "Grown husky."

"Oh, pray, and what was he into?" the Captain asked wearily.

"Into? Not a thing!"

"No, he weren't *into* nothing, 'e was just knocking the tar outa some little fella 'alf as big," mused the shadow. "Packs a smart upper cut, 'e does."

"Not at all!" Mr. Fielding tried to drown the truth from off stage. "Well, take care of that cold, Captain. Pitch and beeswax in a blister plaster should break up that cough. Good night."

"Ah, thank you. Good night. . . . I'll have a heart-to-heart talk with our boy. Means well, poor lad. . . ." But the Captain's lip had curled at the mention of blister plasters. Mr. Fielding waved his hand, nodding and walking away.

"Now yow never hark to nobody. But him was telling yow true about the plaster." The shadow came closer. The creature's black hair was frosted with snow; the gale blew through the holes in his clothes, but he was not shivering.

"What brings you here, Thomas Allen?" the Captain had paced on, throwing the question out casually over his shoulder.

"How do. Good evening." The man beamed at recognition. "I been thinking."

"Indeed?" The words brought the Captain about.

"I been thinking when yow get a ship it'll be lonesome 'ere. I been thinking now the Captain's a smart man but who's to look after him?"

"When I get a *ship?*" The Captain gave a short laugh. Yet something in the other man's big ugly face suddenly touched him. "Well?" he said more kindly, trying not to see the browbeaten upward glances of a cur that was trying to find a master. "You have a good right arm, Tom, but I have *no ship.*"

"Got to lick them incen'ries, ain't we?"

"War? Good God, I pray not!"

"Well, yow better get home. Yow're shivering like a pup," Thomas Allen growled suddenly, turning on his heel. "G'night."

The Captain stood leaning into the wind, momentarily paralyzed at being dismissed by that—that yokel! Then the man's stupidity began to amuse him more than it annoyed him.

"Yow get home to bed!" Tom Allen had stopped a few paces down the road, shooing him on with a violent waving of arms. He turned and plodded away again.

The Captain smiled, murmuring, "Beast . . ." and the vision of trying to make a disciplined seaman of Tom Allen struck him as infinitely more difficult than fighting a battle. He shook his head slowly. Poor Tom had been bitten with sea fever; but the man was impossible. He dismissed the whole incident; put Tom in the same category with his rowdy young stepson who also wanted to go to sea. Unfortunately his stepson was backed by his mother who would not and could not cope with her twelve-year-old boy. Anyway, he did not have a ship. . . .

By the time he reached home, the storm was shrieking, his cold was much worse, and his temper no better. Dear God in heaven, he knew what it was to feel oppressed, to fawn as Tom Allen had in his clumsy way. Hadn't he, a captain in the King's navy, faithfully served his King for seventeen years only to find himself at the age of thirty-four left to rot in obscurity?

He pounded on the door for what seemed an age before his wife finally opened it a crack and made him squeeze in like a draft. She slammed the door on his coattail and fled back to the fire before he could speak. Huddled in her chair once more, she raised her cheek for a kiss, saying tensely while he struggled out of his coat, "You are very late, dear. The housekeeper's gone to bed. Your supper is cold, dear."

Her softly challenging tone did not soothe him as he kissed her shivering jawbone. He was still cursing fate and Priestley as he announced: "Not being a man of fortune is a crime which I cannot get over, and therefore none of the Great care about me!"

"My dear?" His wife, who was holding his greatcoat to the fire, turned about in sudden alarm.

"No!" he went on as he kicked off his shoes, and would have peeled stark naked still expounding his woes if his wife had not snatched up a candle, thrust it in his hand and modestly sent him upstairs to the freezing cold, but decorous bedroom, while she dried his coat and then put it on, crouching by the fire.

Shivering in the drafty dark stair hall, her husband groped on, wet clothes freezing to his body. He finally found the bedroom, crashed into his dressing stand and set the candle down, eyeing himself gloomily in the dim mirror. He had written to the Admiralty time and again for a ship; the last time he'd told them he would be happy to command even a cockleboat. True, during peacetime the navy kept very few ships in commission, and he had to be content with that excuse, but it was his life, his mortal years passing by, and though he was not physically hungry, he was starving for action—but not for revolution.

He had fought his way out of his clinging damp clothes and into a battered but beloved dressing gown. The dry warmth soothed him somewhat and as he caught a glimpse of the huge bed piled with quilts in the shadows, his never long dormant humor began to nibble away rancor. Anyway, a beached sailor could sleep with his wife, and did not have to dream about dark rooms full of virgins!

Smiling to himself, he studied the remains of his afternoon call on Dr. Poyntz: a heap of soggy clothes on the floor. They would be there in the morning—perhaps even till next week—until the housekeeper found them. His smile faded. Let them stay! Let his wife lift her skirts and her eyebrows stepping over them . . . a cold supper, was it? Ah, never mind, he was used to foul weather mess. These West Indian ladies were accustomed to black slaves unfortunately, and his wife had once commanded an army of them. He had met her during his martyrdom, when everyone hated him, especially the ladies belonging to the West Indian businessmen indulging in the lucrative smuggling. Fanny had come into his life when the one lady he had adored, as did all the rest of the navy, Mrs. Moutray, had gone back home to England with her kindly but incompetent husband. At that, the most dismal hour in his personal and public life, he who was by nature demonstratively affectionate had met the attractive Mrs. Nisbet, and she had spoken civilly to him . . . pressed him to bring His Royal Highness, King George's son, to call.

He snatched up his candle, spilling hot tallow on his fingers, and started back down the old protesting stairway.

Hearing a snore, he remembered he must speak to his stepson. He retraced his steps and crossed the hall, peeking into the little dormered room where the boy lay with bruised and blackened eyelids quivering slightly to the candle beam flickering over his pillow. The Captain closed the door again softly. He could not understand the boy. He was not a wicked boy, not all the time. Sometimes he was loving. No, he couldn't punish a poor wild lad whose very own father had been a lunatic . . . Let his wife swear her husband died of sunstroke, he knew what the West Indians had said about his predecessor, the surgeon. He must have been crazy, how else explain his wife's strange hysteria? Ah . . . Suddenly, he went back and picked up his wet clothes and started once again down the stairs. This time he was washed of all sins, beaming virtue, as he sat down to a cold, cold supper and watched his wife begin to feel a little sorry for him.

Having regained the mastery of his own castle, and having very pleasantly kissed his wife and thanked her ceremoniously for his evening meal, he felt so much better he did not go straight to bed, nurse his cold or recurrence of ague, whatever it was that plagued him. Instead he sat down to write out his troubles as well as the people's to the highest man he knew: to his former student, His Royal Highness, the Duke of Clarence.

There was an ironic incongruity in the small homely study furnished with the most ordinary essentials, and a few grim ancestral portraits sneering at the fallen fortunes of a family, where he sat trying to invoke the lords of England. Only a small silver frigate, another gift, from his officers, reminded the eye of any life but this.

His dark-eyed wife sat by the fire watching him. She was shivering in spite of the blaze and the layers of flannel underwear that her husband abhorred, but which she wore anyway. Her thin face with its regular and positive features was sharpened and petulant. It was a proud face that said bitterly it had been almost beautiful once.

Out in the West Indies she had been the niece of the President of the Council in Nevis, Mr. Herbert, a man whose slaves and cattle alone were worth sixty thousand pounds! And she had ruled his household.

She had expected to take her second marriage with the guarded philosophy born of a nightmare experience: her first marriage had ended within eighteen months in a lonely English town, a strange graveyard, leaving her with the remains—the terror of an empty purse in a death-empty hotel room, and a husky baby boy. She had fled back to her uncle's roof wanting nothing more to do with emotions, and willing to accept a second marriage of propriety and common sense.

But back in the West Indies, her captain had seemed a different man. Before she had ever met him, her uncle had come bursting in to tell her that *the* Captain Nelson, of whom everyone was afraid, had just been discovered on all fours peering out from under the library table! When a second pair of eyes had appeared under the table the shock had been mitigated. Captain Nelson was playing bear with her little son. Her uncle had gone off muttering, "Good God!" And even previous to that a friend had meowed to Fanny that she had met the admittedly brilliant and courageous, but highly unpopular, Captain Nelson of the *Boreas* frigate, and added that "if you, Fanny, had been there, we think you would have made something of him, for you have been in the habit of attending to these odd sort of people."

And Fanny, four years widowed and twenty-six years old, had discreetly knocked four years off her age, to make herself four years junior instead of four months senior to Nelson, and gently encouraged the restrained, but charming, advances of this grandson of the Prebendary of Westminster, and close relative of Lord Walpole, Earl of Orford. Even the Duke of Clarence had sensed the elevated plane of their relationship, saying their marriage promised to be one of "esteem" rather than "vulgar love."

She had known Captain Nelson was poor as Job—he had made no pretense of hiding it; but her uncle had laughingly clapped Nelson on the shoulder and promised them twenty thousand pounds when he died, as well as an inheritance for her son. He had died without willing anything to them, though he had not forgotten her son. The boy would have money in a few years. But the fact that neither her husband nor the impressive Duke of Clarence had any political influence, Fanny had learned too late.

She stabbed her embroidery. And she stabbed her finger. She screamed for her husband and waited for the blood to flow. Her husband's pen spluttered, ink blotted his letter as he leaped up.

He eyed the one drop of blood on her finger. "That's too bad, my dear . . ." he gritted, choosing a new quill to resume his writing.

Fanny stared at him, simmering with insult. The room had grown deathly chill, the fire dwindling low. The gale had found the crack where the old door did not square with the sill and was whistling softly across the worn flagstone floor.

Her husband did not appear to notice it. He was happy just writing that letter. And as he finally pushed back his chair, waving the last paper dry, Fanny felt very lonely.

"Listen to this, my dear," he said, and took his stand before the fire. Fanny smiled at last, as he began to read between coughs and sniffles:

To his Royal Highness the Duke of Clarence

BURNHAM, *December 10, 1792*

SIR:

I was honored by your Royal Highness's letter last night: and it shall ever be my pride to deserve your Royal Highness's kindness. Respecting my present situation with Admiral Lord Hood, I can readily and truly answer. We have not for a long time had any communication with each other. Our familiar correspondence ceased on a difference of opinion . . . when almost the whole service were called forth, I asked Lord Hood to interest himself with First Lord Chatham, that I might be appointed to a ship, and Lord Hood made a speech never to be effaced from my memory, viz. *that the King was impressed with an unfavorable opinion of me!*

The Captain's voice faltered, and his pale face turned slowly white, his eyes burned. "Fanny, I didn't deserve that!"

"Leave it out, Horace, it's partly His Highness's fault."

He nodded slowly, and going to the table slashed his pen through the lines from the word "ship."

"I will have to copy the letter anyway." He began to read again:

His Lordship having declined doing it, has prevented my troubling him again for his interest or influence. However, in consideration of our former intimacy, whenever I have gone to London, I have hitherto thought it right to leave my name at his Lordship's door. I certainly cannot look on Lord Hood as my friend; but I have the satisfaction of knowing, that I never gave his Lordship just cause to be my enemy.

His face regained some color as he laid that sheet down and began the next. Now he came to the point that had troubled him all the way home through the storm—the cries of paradise by revolution ringing in his ears:

Our Lord Lieutenant has summoned a meeting of the Norfolk Justices on Tuesday next; and I have no doubt that they will resolve to do collectively, what none of them chose to do individually—to take away the licenses from those public houses who allow of improper Societies meeting at them, and to take up those incendiaries who go from ale-house to ale-house, advising the poor to pay no taxes, etc. In this neighborhood, a person of the name of Priestley, a clergyman, has held this language to a circle of ten miles round him; and, a few days past, I asked a Justice of the Peace, "Why, as such a man's conduct was known, that he was not taken up?" His answer was, "that no Justice would render himself unpopular at this time, by being singular: *for that his life and property were gone, if the mob rose:* but that when the Justices all agreed to act in a uniform manner, this man should certainly be taken hold of, if he went on with such conduct."

That the poor laborer should have been seduced by promises and hopes of better times, your Royal Highness will not wonder at, when I assure you, that they really are in want of everything to make life comfortable. Hunger is a sharp thorn, and they are not only in want of food sufficient, but of clothes and firing.

And again he came to a halt. His voice had grown impassioned. Once again he took up his pen. "That's pretty strong—for His Highness's ear. . . ." And again he drew a line through the last sentence. "I think the rest explains it anyway":

Part of their wants, perhaps, were unavoidable, from the dearness of every article of life; but much has arose from the neglect of the Country Gentlemen, in not making their farmers raise their wages in some small proportion, as the prices of necessaries increased. The enclosed paper will give your Royal Highness an idea of their situation. It is most favorable; but I have been careful that no Country Gentleman should have it in his power to say, I had pointed out wants of the poor greater than they really are. Their wages have been raised within these three weeks, pretty generally, one shilling a week: had it been done some time past they would not have been discontented, for want of loyalty is not amongst their faults; and many of their superiors, in many instances, might have imitated their conduct with advantage. The wise precautions of Government have certainly given a vigor to the loyal of the Nation, who are most undoubtedly by far the majority; and the disaffected join them at present, for fear of being suspected; therefore I have no doubt but our tranquillity will be restored.

> I am, as ever,
> Your most attached and faithful,
> Horatio Nelson

Enclosure:
An Account of the Earnings and Expenses of a Laborer in Norfolk, with a Wife and three Children, Supposing that he is Not to be One Day Kept from Labor in the Whole Year.

	£	s.	d.

One pair of Man's shoes, 7s., one pair of Woman's,
   4s. 6d., one pair for each of the three Children,
   10s. 6d., and £1 1s. for mending.

	£	s.	d.
Shoes and Mending	2	3	0
Shirts, two	0	10	0
Breeches or Jacket	0	3	0
Woman's and Children's clothes	1	6	0
Soap, 12 lbs.	0	8	10
Candles, 6 lbs.	0	4	0
Coals, one chaldron and a half	1	19	0
House Rent	2	0	0
	£8	13s.	10d.

The Advanced Prices

	£	s.	d.
From Oct. 10th to March 31st at 9s. per week	11	14	0
From March 31st to June 30th, at 8s. per week	5	4	0
From June 30th to Aug. 24th, turnip-hoeing and hay harvest	3	0	0
Harvest	2	2	0
Woman's gleaning	1	1	0
Total earnings	£23	1s.	0d.
Earnings	23	1	0
Clothes, etc.	8	13	10
For food, five people	£14	7s.	2d.

Not quite twopence a day for each person; and to drink nothing but
water, for beer our poor laborers never taste, unless they are tempted,
which is too often the case, to go to the Ale-house.

When he had finished he waited for his wife to give him enthusiastic applause. She never had, but he always hoped. . . . At last as
she knotted a fresh thread, took an invisible stitch, she said, "I am
glad you did not tell His Highness of the King's speech, and really,
Horace, should you trouble His Highness with any other problems?
After all he is retired, in disgrace with the King for not having stayed
with his squadron going to Canada. Don't you think the King must
feel that if *you* were his tutor years ago—and, dear, you did go to that
wild party His Highness gave when the Admiralty punished him by

ordering him to stay on his ship at anchor. Sometimes I wonder if you both weren't just a little too impulsive—" She cringed at his searing glance.

Speechless, he paced up and down. She had criticized every word! He made a motion of throwing his letter into the fire; thought better of it, as he slowly drew his chair around facing her and sat down on it. He began to speak slowly and distinctly. "It was not a *wild* party, Fanny. The Duke is my friend. His invitations are Royal Commands. I could not possibly have influenced his decision to disobey orders when he was halfway across the Atlantic. Even if I had been there, I cannot control a King's son any more than Lord Hood could when he laid the blame at my door. . . . Now. It would be criminal not to warn His Highness of what is going on in this country. Do you think anyone else will risk his displeasure to tell him the God's truth? All they want are his favors. It's my duty to—"

His wife put down her sewing. "Oh, very well, my dear, you know best. But I only thought that if His Highness would not make me a lady in waiting to his Duchess after His Highness insisted upon naming our wedding day, standing as father to me, *giving* me to you in marriage . . . well, what can you expect him to do for the mob?"

"For the *mob?*" Captain Nelson fell back in his chair, clapping his hands to his eyes, "Oh, my God, Fanny! I am for the King!"

His wife put down her embroidery and folded her hands, saying stiffly, "The Lord's name in vain again! For shame, Horace!" Her use of his boyhood nickname sharpened her reproof.

He had stalked from the fire to the table and back again. Now he spun on her.

"Pray"—his tone became bland, almost a whisper—"how is it you always endeavor to misunderstand? How could you suspect *me* of disloyalty?"

Fanny gasped. Tears started to her eyes. "My dear, I didn't, I mean— I assure you—I—"

"As a man, as an officer, as an Englishman! My one purpose, my whole plan of existence has always been, and always will be, that it is better for an officer to serve an ungrateful country than to give up his own fame. Posterity will do him justice; a uniform conduct of honor and integrity seldom fails of bringing a man to—" He gazed hopelessly about the shabby room, conscious of her bleak stare.

"Of course, Horace," Fanny said placatingly.

"That was a sermon." He went back to his table. "Forgive me and God bless you, my dear!"

❋   ❋   ❋

When His Royal Highness, the Duke, answered Captain Nelson's letter, he found that Fanny had unfortunately been only too right. The Duke, while roundly damning the Admiralty, disliked his having criticized Country Gentlemen. The Duke replied with an evasive half-truth reminiscent of Marie Antoinette's recent and equally inane bread versus cake: if the poor had more money they would buy gin.

At this point, many young Englishmen tucked a tricolor cockade in their hats and took off for the revolution in Paris, swearing they could no longer live like Englishmen in England. Some went, as poet Wordsworth did, because they were high-minded and had never seen bloodshed. Most threatened but did not travel. And some were like poet Coleridge, who had craved the adventure of starting Utopia in America with his friend Southey, only to fall in love and anchor himself to a nice girl before he discovered babies did not eat poetry; who stayed home, "wept at Britain's name," relied on Southey for shelter and food, sought financial pensions from his King, a newer Utopia in the revolutionary spirit—and took opium.

Rebuffed, Captain Nelson shook his head sadly, raised his eyebrows and went back to cursing the cold damp English climate. He mulled over his charts, refighting history, lost himself in his volumes of voyages, or when the weather permitted galloped Tycho, his pony, over the countryside. And so he whiled away December and most of January, 1793. His wife shivered and amused herself by painting anemic water colors and worrying aimlessly; taking to her bed whenever the cold or her hot-tempered son threatened to force her to some decision.

Yet, if Captain Nelson were willing to yield to the Duke and refrain from revolution, though blocked in his own career, many other men who did not go to France, and who had purchased power and hoped for more of it, did not give in, but clamored the loudest for an English mob to rise. To these Englishmen who took as myopic a view of their brother countrymen as the Duke of Clarence had in his way, France offered the assistance they needed to set up the republic of England. Still neither side in England appeared willing to compromise. But toward the last of January, 1793, something happened that turned the faces of the Duke of Clarence and George III white, and caused the

Royal Scientific Society to disown one of its most scholarly and distinguished colleagues—Dr. Priestley.

During the first days of February a black-bordered newspaper finally reached Burnham Thorpe. Captain Nelson was the first, as always, to unfold it. "Fanny!" And as his wife rushed into the study, he caught her up in his arms. "They have guillotined King Louis XVI!"

"Oh, no—" Fanny's hand went to her own throat. "Oh, stop smiling, Horace!"

"I'm not smiling! I'm shocked—I'm grieved, I'm—oh, my God, don't you realize, Fanny?" But he was smiling. "I'm going to London. It's —I'm going to get a ship!" And suddenly he was grave. "I hope."

But Fanny had swooned.

Captain Nelson began the one-hundred-and-fifty-mile wintry trip from Burnham to London, by post chaise, through snow and mud and sickening weather. Surely now . . . and as he saw the parsonage receding and Fanny's handkerchief disappear like a snowflake into the winter landscape, he turned away, pinning his hopes, his life, on the shapeless intangible future. And he felt like the child Horace, peering tearfully back at his father who had handed him into the post chaise and told the driver to see that the lad got off at Chatham where his uncle's *Raisonnable* waited for him. Only the child Horace had been fleeing from interminable sermons, mediocre schools, a motherless home, and he had been oh, so sure of the future! He had dried his eyes and known he would capture a rich Spanish galleon no later than the day after he sailed, and that he would come home quickly an admiral.

He had not done either, but he had gone from boyhood to manhood in the few days that it took him to reach Chatham, and find his midshipman's berth.

And as Captain Nelson stared at the white countryside stretched out as far as he could see, blank as the morrow, he realized it was not that first parting he was thinking of, but the anguish of a later day. As he sat in his corner something came to him—receded—illusive. The hubbub of conversation of the other travelers in the coach died out of his consciousness, and at last he saw it again, clearly: a soft mellow light, like an orb before his mind's eye. He had first seen it when he was paralyzed with that strange fever in India; known he was going to die, and wanted desperately to live. Yet life had seemed insupportably hard, and death at least bearable. Out of that struggle, as if he had wrestled with an angel, made a covenant, had come peace. His life for his King; the reward, immortality. At last he looked about him at the other passengers, and the length of his journey seemed to lead so much farther than theirs. . . .

His heart grew lighter, though he could not quite tell why, and then again heavier, for if he did not get a ship now on the verge of war . . .

At the first stop the post chaise made, he leaped out to purchase another newspaper; buried himself behind it while the other passengers ate basket lunches and spilled ale on each other, flirted and argued and talked of death and taxes and clicked their tongues over the Prince of Wales's debts and the Duke of Clarence's mistress. But Captain Nelson read his paper, advertisements and all. Some lucky captains, he read, were already posting for crews to man ships of war, for across the Channel, Danton had cried out:

"The King challenges us. We hurl at their feet as the gage of battle, the head of a King!" To the rest of Europe it was like a knife across the throat of that sleepy continent.

Captain Nelson's chaise jolted on. He counted each slippery hill the horses plodded, each stop for more passengers—all of whom seemed so terribly oblivious of the fact that England was at a crisis, though they shook their heads over Louis—as time lost.

France, goaded by the challenges of Prussia and Austria, had begun to march wholeheartedly on Holland. The French were puncturing Pitt's dreams of neutrality, peace, prosperity and a balanced budget, for England had a treaty of mutual support with Holland to protect the neutrality of the Scheldt and maintain a balance of commercial power on the Continent. It began to appear stupid to sympathize with anything French. Dr. Priestley had gone back to preaching in churches for a living, pondering gases and electricity. He denied ever having had anything to do with plotting actual overthrow of his government. But he still harped on the corruption of Christianity. . . .

And as Captain Nelson stared from his window, pulling his coat up to his ears trying to escape the drafts, his breathing clouded the pane, evaporated, clouded again just as his thoughts clouded and cleared over and over again. As the countryside inched past his coach window, or stood still while harnesses were repaired, or he tossed restlessly in some strange inn, trying to sleep and listening to the rioting before the fire downstairs, he sometimes felt as confident as David be-

fore Goliath. And when he rose in the black pre-dawn to climb into
the coach again, sometimes he only hoped that God did mark His
littlest sparrow. . . . And as the post chaise lurched on, gaining speed
as it left the quiet snows of northern England, nearing London, his
hopes soared higher and fell lower. One bitterly humbled, obscure
young man in a noisy public conveyance pondering his world should
England go to war.

Russia was at present ruled by Catherine II, who would soon leave
Russia's enslaved serfs and barbaric nobles to an absolute and maniac
Czar: Paul. George III of England was not a maniac; his periods of
"illness," requiring a regency, came and went. Often he was apparently
a well-meaning old man, moral, kind when not crossed, with a healthy
interest in farming. Captain Nelson had been presented to him once
by old Admiral Lord Howe, before Captain Nelson met the Duke of
Clarence. Unfortunately, in spite of periodic lunacy, George III remembered the presentation as well as later incidents. Leaving that
impasse, Captain Nelson could ponder the fact that Austria was ruled
by Francis, a weak man about par for an emperor. Spain was already
senile after her long and dissolute life as ruler of the world, upon
whose flag the sun never used to set. Spain was cautiously and suspiciously following whoever she believed was likely to prove most
powerful in thwarting her enemies. Her enemies were England,
France, Austria and Prussia. While Prussia's Frederick William II
was trying to rule a discontented country that wanted to be left alone,
preferably without Frederick. The Italian states were bickering among
themselves in their eternal triangular wars for internal domination:
the Kings or Doges or Dukes, all titular heads, against the nobility,
both seeking the intervention of the Papal State to sway the balance of
power . . . so Italy was festering of the same sores that it had suffered
for some five hundred years.

Overseas, South America was enslaved, closed to any but Spanish
trade, and the United States, as that suspiciously republican group
called itself, was surprisingly neutral, having won what it set out to
obtain. But unofficially the United States was at war with France, for
the French who had, under Lafayette, gallantly helped America to
spite England were now, still under Lafayette, plundering American
merchant ships. It gave a slight respite to English fears that the United
States and France would unite to drive the British out of Canada;
prove the death of General Wolfe at Quebec had been futile.

Down in the Mediterranean, the Barbary pirates were raking in tribute for not pirating indiscriminately.

But something had happened in England when Louis died. The loyal majority of Englishmen on both sides quietly took a thoughtful second look at the scars of their own Great Rebellion and the execution of Charles I—one hundred and fifty years before. And England invited the French Ambassador to leave London.

At the last stop before the post chaise reached London, Captain Nelson bought his last newspaper.

The French, still hearing only the minority promises of an English uprising, had declared war on England, confident of insurrection. That had been on February 3, 1793.

And England had declared war on France the following week—February 11. There was no mass insurrection in England.

The passengers in the post chaise suddenly brought their minds into focus.

"War?"

And they stared at each other as if it had happened out of a clear sky, without rhyme or reason.

"War *again* between France and England!"

In the midst of the furor, Captain Nelson's post chaise began to rattle over cobbled city streets; London's smoke and fog swallowed him. He crawled stiffly out of his corner, took a room in a small hotel and prepared to present himself physically whole and of a sound mind to the High Lords of the Admiralty; asking only that he might fight for the King who had a poor opinion of him.

A few days after Captain Nelson vanished through the haughty doorway of the Admiralty, the post from London arrived in Burnham Thorpe, and before the villagers had time to exhaust the possibilities of what Mrs. Nelson's London letter contained, they saw the outdoor man who did odd jobs at the parsonage gallop past on the Captain's pony. Before they could close their mouths, digest that, the doctor flew by on his horse, clutching his hat with the hand that held his bag, nearly losing his wig as he reined up before the parsonage door.

"Flighty sort," Tom Allen spoke for the villagers, "one'd think she'd learn not to swoon on that hard stone floor."

The villagers nodded, and the women's eyebrows went up in unison.

"Contrary, she is. Nothing to do but look pretty and never brought to bed with one baby in all these five years. 'Tain't right. She's queer. And her husband what loves children so plays with any he sees."

"That boy of hers is enough for a lifetime! Don't give me no more like him!"

While the villagers watched, the doctor had gone inside, applied smelling salts and comforted Fanny by reaffirming the delicacy of her constitution. Weeping, she told him that her husband, no classical scholar, had lost his mind, written to her in Latin! And she held up the wrinkled letter:

Post nublia Phoebus: Your son will explain the motto. After clouds comes sunshine. The Admiralty so smile upon me, that really I am as much surprised as when they frowned. First Lord Chatham yesterday made many apologies for not having given me a ship before this time, and said, that if I chose to take a Sixty-four to begin with, I should be appointed to one as soon as she was ready; and whenever it was in his power, I should be removed into a Seventy-four. Everything indicates War. One of our ships looking into Brest has been fired into. . . .

So! The last five years of peaceful retirement in her company had nearly bored him to death compared to the prospects of commanding his very first battleship, a small Third Rate at that, with the salary of about 13*s.* 6*d.* per day. Fanny made up her mind to score her point: her son must go with him.

Thus Fanny sobbed her resignation to being robbed of husband and son, while Captain Nelson, prancing on air, visualized laurels raining down on his head, and tackled the work of manning and supplying and painting the *Agamemnon* 64—until he had to borrow money to pay for the privilege of going to war with a shorthanded crew made up mostly of Norfolk men. He said they were as good as two of any other kind.

He bade good-by to his father and took his farewell of his wife a little too eagerly.

Agamemnon, his new love, his sea wife, reeked of the fresh blood-red paint on her insides, as her new masts were set high into the spring sky. The port women swarmed aboard in boatloads to swear by all that was unholy they were the honest wives of the men. The port women got exhilaratingly drunk, made overtures to the sullen impressed men nursing skulls that had split to belaying pins. The women screeched epithets at the officers who dared not answer back for fear of clawed eyes, and the women climbed the rigging with wind-blown immodesty to "yoo-hoo" to friends. Until at last, all was in utter disorder; the Captain exhausted; his stepson, Josiah Nisbet, grinning bug-eyed; another midshipman, William Hoste, lip quivering, shocked; the officers raging: the ship was ready for sea.

But the wind blew foul. The port women who had been routed stood and yelled obscenities from the shore, or tried to climb up the cables, squeeze through the deadeyes, while the men lay lashed in their hammocks, dead drunk; one night of stupor permitted before they were read the Articles of War, learned the honor of being in the King's navy.

Shut off in his cabin, guarded from low life by a sentry with sword unsheathed, the Captain was writing to his wife. The ship was cleared of unseemly creatures and he had been looking for her every minute to come and say good-by to him and her son for the last time before they sailed off to war. The wind blew foul long enough for her reply to reach him: there was no certainty in winds or tides to compensate for the tedious journey.

With that, the wind blew fair, the Captain's spirits rose and he sailed away. His Caliban from Burnham Thorpe, Thomas Allen, had been appointed a waister, a rank higher than a ship's rat.

❋   ❋   ❋

But the war began slowly, like a cancer on Europe. By midsummer, England had been at war with revolutionary France nearly half a year and the only action Captain Nelson, who did not like being trifled with, had seen occurred at Cádiz, Spain, where the Spanish fleet entertained the officers of the English Mediterranean fleet under Admiral Lord Hood. Spain was allied. But Captain Nelson made careful mental notes of Cádiz's vulnerability, her fleet and her arsenal.

It was a point of some irritation that the Spanish and French built by far the biggest and most splendid ships in the world, and the English some of the crankiest tubs afloat. Some English ships were known to be rotten and ready for drydock the day of launching. As to the manning of ships, the English boasted they were the best seamen—they had to be. The French boasted they were the best artillerymen. Who was which this war, no one had as yet had an opportunity to prove. Captain Nelson admitted of the allied Spanish that "the Dons may make fine ships—they cannot however make men," as he went to dine aboard the giant Spanish First Rate, the *Concepción* 120. That was just the intellect at work on an empty stomach. After dinner the Dons escorted him to a bullfight. It was a sultry hot day. Cádiz stank as usual for it was built so close to sea level it could not drain. The crowds had been munching garlic.

And there came the bull. . . .

When Captain Nelson made his shaken way back to his ship, his face still green, he wrote Fanny: "It turned us sick, and we could hardly go through it: the dead mangled horses with their entrails torn out, and the bulls covered with blood were too much. . . ."

But with the spring and summer, Fanny had shaken the dust of Burnham from her feet to go visiting his relatives and various resorts for her health. Nelson's reverend father had announced he would see to it that she had enough money to live as befitted a lady.

Still no shooting. The English and Spanish continued inactive. The Spanish put to sea in a massive glory of wood and sail; soon announced they were going home. The sea made them sick. Captain Nelson laughed and laughed in high humor once more.

Still no action.

At last his commander in chief, who neither was his friend nor had just cause to be his enemy, and who had once said Captain Nelson was the best tactician in the navy, but who now treated him very stiffly, Admiral Lord Hood in H.M.S. *Victory*, 100 guns, sailed his fleet into the Mediterranean Sea.

Captain Nelson was delighted with the milder climate. His thoughts turned on his wife and his first meetings with her in the warm West Indies; she became the perfect wife again in memory.

While she, slower of mind, had suddenly realized that her husband and her only son had gone to *war;* and grew wan and haggard as if a Promethean vulture tore eternally at her vitals.

Still no shooting. . . .

Meanwhile, Lord Hood, who had seen enough shooting in his day, very skillfully arranged with French Royalists still resisting the revolution in southern France to allow the English fleet to move into Toulon, the best French naval base in the Mediterranean Sea! It was nearly landlocked, heavily fortified, invulnerable to attacks from the sea. Captain Nelson approved this measure—in his letters to his wife.

Lord Hood took over the whole French Mediterranean fleet, including the immense ship of the line, the *Sans Culottes* 120, in the most incredible bloodless coup of the century. Triumphant, Lord Hood waited for a large army to be sent from England, to push on to Paris, meet the Duke of York's army from the north, and thus assist the Royalists in reconquering France by not any later than next Christmas. The revolutionists, encamped behind Toulon, sniped at the English, but day after day went by without their hitting anything. Rumor had it that a drunken musician had wangled the post of revolutionary general to recapture Toulon. Captain Nelson wrote home to start fattening the Norfolk turkeys for his Christmas dinner.

Even before Lord Hood had completely finished taking over Toulon and posting garrisons, he sent Captain Nelson, upon whom he was perhaps beginning to smile again, to the Kingdom of the Two Sicilies—to Naples with instructions to procure Neapolitan troops. The Captain's assignment was pleasant; though he regretted not witnessing the final glory at the fall of Toulon to the English, he carried the news of it: England's first victory!

He sailed into Naples late at night, and stood awe-struck, unable to take his eyes from the slowly smoldering Vesuvius. The next morning, the spell of the earth's molten core dispelled by the greater blaze of the sun, he went ashore to pay his official respects to the English Ambassador, Sir William Hamilton.

The Ambassador received him in a welter of scientific pamphlets, for he was an authority on Vesuvius and an avid rummager about Pompeii, as well as a dabbler in Attic curios. He was only passingly interested in diplomacy, and this war that was interfering with his hobbies. Captain Nelson saw the withering, elderly man that Goethe on his Italian journey had marveled upon, calling Sir William a "man of universal culture"; the kind of man young Goethe hoped to become. Even Captain Nelson knew the rest about Sir William: he had cut a dashing swath among the ladies of his day, leaving his faithful and adoring first wife to comfort his pet dog.

The Ambassador shook hands cordially with Captain Nelson and began pointing out some of the finer charms of a small bronze, trying very hard to interest this interruption in the form of a sailor in anything but business. Slowly, the Ambassador set the bronze back on the desk, feeling himself being drawn forcibly from his curios. . . . He peered more closely at the Captain who was reciting an official and routine speech with spritely enthusiasm; compelling the Ambassador to listen!

The Ambassador stared. The outer aspects of the Captain could be dismissed; his looks were neither here nor there except for his blazing bright eyes—then what was it? The Ambassador lost the thread of Captain Nelson's speech utterly, for he found himself more engrossed in the enigma of this specimen of humanity than he had been a moment before in contemplating the commercial possibilities of reproducing his Portland vase. A man who could draw Sir William from his vases to face the reality of war was a scene stealer empowered by the gods! Without thinking twice, the Ambassador excused himself to write a note to his wife.

Emma, Lady Hamilton soon read his instructions, and willingly did as her husband bade her. She opened her boudoir door and hollered down the cool tall corridor, "Mother! Maw-ther! *Momma!*"

Her mother, closeted in her own suite of rooms, cocked her ear to the shouts. Quickly she tucked her forbidden gin bottle into her sewing basket, gave a twitch to her expensive and conservative morning cap and walked sedately into her daughter's apartment. Her face was jolly, used to rolling a blacksmith husband's punches, as she said:

"Em! Stop squealing like one of Grannie's pigs! Tut! You who was offered a contract at La Scala, straining your voice again."

Lady Hamilton laughed, hugging her mother. "Sir Will'am has a genius. That means the suite we just decorated for Prince Augustus."

"And where, I should like to know, do we sleep the Prince if 'e comes?"

Lady Hamilton shrugged, and shouted above the yaps and howls of a pack of mongrel and purebred dogs that came bursting in, "The Prince'll be too stupid to know the difference."

Together, Lady Hamilton, née Lyon, or Emily Hart, and Mrs. Cadogan, formerly Mrs. Lyon and secondly Mrs. Dugan, soon had the Embassy as perfectly ordered, and themselves as presentable, as Sir William could want them; perhaps because the servants loved the Ambassador's breezy ménage, and perhaps because Lady Hamilton did have a warm spot in her heart for geniuses, whoever they might be.

Geniuses had found her at sixteen, painted her, tossed her from one man to another. She had been a maidservant to a doctor, and mistress to a young naval captain, and once, down-and-out, she had taken a job as a "Goddess of Health" in a dubious salon where she sat on a stage to illustrate a quack's lectures, with only her modest head and shoulders poked out of a mud bath. But what she could do with only her eyes showing would have been enough to cause a riot.

Drifting from here to there she had galloped to hounds with a man afflicted from birth with the name of Sir Harry Featherstonehaugh, who gave her a baby—for a girl had to eat—and then turned her out when she grew rebellious. Besides she began to look her part too obviously. Pregnant, scared to tell her good mother, homeless, she recalled having met another man, Greville, at a party. She fastened on him; for the first time in her life humbly grateful for shelter. He was Sir William's nephew. After her baby was born she had told Greville how happy she was to have her child and her man all under one roof. So help her God, she was reformed.

She kept his house neat and economical, made dresses for her baby and fell in love with Greville. But Greville very respectably refused to keep someone else's bastard in his own mistress's house. Emma burst into tears, she felt married to Greville although they were not married. So, with a belief that anyone who moved in such lofty respectable society as he did must be wise, she gave in. The baby was sent away. It was not sold. Greville supported it for her. Emma kept track of it surreptitiously. She had instincts if no education, and she could not have supported it without Greville.

Greville had saved her life. He was a really kind gentleman, and he readily allowed her to keep her mother in the house. She had met Sir William when he came to visit Greville in London, and Emma thought him very kind, too, and let the good elderly man steal a kiss now and then, which she scrupulously reported to Greville. But Sir William with that lightning perception of his had recognized something unique in his nephew's lovely illiterate. If only he could work with her! Sir William had an immense sense of humor. At first he suggested Greville marry her and all three live in Naples together, for Sir William wondered if at his age he could make her happy alone. Emma was not consulted. But Greville said no, and named a price for his *objet d'art*: Greville must be made heir to Sir William's estate. As for the girl, she had natural wits, if no soul, and her future was no one's concern when Sir William chose to die.

Emma was told she was going to Naples to learn to be a lady. And

Emma believed it was Greville's promise of marriage. He said yes, yes of course, he would come to Naples for her eventually.

It had been a long time before the girl, who had only one reason in her mind for learning to be a lady in Naples, and that was to please Greville, began to realize that Greville had sold her—body and soul— like a horse or a dog. At first she pleaded for only one letter of explanation, some word. What had she done to offend him? She groveled, she implored. Why, she had been faithful to Greville for five mortal years! Sir William bided his time.

At last she blew up. The Embassy rocked, as she wrote Greville:

I wou'd murder you and myself boath. . . . If it is not to be, I will except of nothing. I will go to London, their I will go into every excess of vice till I dye, a miserable broken hearted wretch, and leave my fate as a warning to young whomen never to be two good; for now you have made me love you, you made me good, you have abbandoned me.

Greville carefully corrected her spelling and righteously reminded her that ladylike submissiveness to Sir William was infinitely more becoming than low-class temper. Had she no gratitude? Emma, who thought with her heart, tried to fathom the ways of the intellect.

Sir William, whose patience equaled his humor, was somehow remarkably understanding and brotherly, through all her heartbreak. She came to her senses. Greville had been just another man after all. She eyed English society very closely and applied herself once more to her studies: the art of being a lady. And she honestly was still too humbly grateful for all Greville had done for her to hate him very long. She obeyed him, and submitted to the calm Sir William of whom she was truly immensely fond. He did not preach as much as Greville. Sir William had not been mistaken in her. She was a genius.

She soon convinced Sir William that in order that she might graduate in her studies, he must marry her. He took her to London and made her his legal wife under English law. She now sang and spoke two or three languages better than her native English; made bosom friends with the Queen of the Two Sicilies; landed on her feet—an Ambassadress.

And her mother, whose native astuteness combined with a sense of humor delighted Sir William, was one of the leaders of the more genteel older members of the more conservative Neapolitan society.

No one suspected that fun-loving Sir William felt he had played his final immense joke on society. He was such a scholarly, polite man, no one dreamed that one of his greatest amusements was to sit back while Emma, a born mimic, comically impersonated everyone from visiting Bishops to King Ferdinand of the Two Sicilies trying to sing duets with the English Ambassadress. She caught the unconscious idiosyncrasies that made even the dignified Englishman, Sir John Acton, Prime Minister of the Two Sicilies, appear an utter fool. She did not mimic friends; for them she "wou'd dye."

Only Greville was unhappy over the match. His mistress was now his respected aunt. She wrote him friendly letters of advice. But the original agreement stood: Greville, not Emma, was Sir William's principal heir.

Emma had learned the art of keeping still like a lady. Beyond the bad enough facts that she had been an artist model to Sir Joshua Reynolds and George Romney, been "jilted" in her "engagement" to Greville, and formerly Sir William's "protégée," her past was as neatly buried as a cat's mess. Sometimes some boor did recall seeing her billed in London as a "Goddess," but as gentlemen had never frequented that place, she could turn up her beautiful nose to their "Haven't we met . . . ?" And she could sweep away from an overly amorous Neapolitan duke, saying, with all the dignity of a duchess, "Where was you brought up?" Sir William gently persisted and nearly eradicated grammatical errors.

So it was she who stood, framed in a columned doorway, finger tips extended, eyes warmly shining, this particular morning when Sir William dragged home his latest find. Captain Nelson was still talking war. Josiah Nisbet brought up the rear, frowzy and surly.

Captain Nelson's own throat choked off his own words before his mind reacted to what his eyes were beholding. He saw a tall creature, so simply dressed that nothing distracted his eyes from contemplating a voluptuous woman moving toward him with the grace of a goddess. She had a face as mobile and sympathetic as it was haunting and mischievous. Her features dovetailed toward perfection. If her upper lip was a little too short, it only made her smile curl more readily. If there was an intriguing brown fleck in one eye, it was only a perfecting detail, otherwise she would have been inhumanly beautiful. The devil himself must have designed her.

She gave her hand to the Captain and he inwardly quivered, then quickly presented his stepson and groped back to the safety of Sir

William's conversation. He even listened to Sir William's speeches on vases, and fought to keep his eyes on them. Sir William was delighted.

And after a while Captain Nelson, who was gifted with excellent will power, reminded himself of his wife, his stepchild, his *career,* and thus marshaling his defenses was able to look at Lady Hamilton and think straight. After all, he was used to having people, even dukes and those most formidable of all creatures, admirals, like him on sight (all except West Indians—and even there he had found a bride) so he took the hospitality of the Hamiltons philosophically. And he had heard all about *her* as soon as he had come into the Mediterranean, and already made up his mind that she was disreputable, and Sir William a senile old fool to marry his mistress. Obviously such a situation might be acceptable in a heathenish place like Naples which was made up of nothing but foreigners and wintering English nobility. Captain Nelson, the parson's son, already knew what that kind of woman would be called back in Burnham Thorpe! But until now he had not *seen* her. . . .

To see was to forgive all. Lady Hamilton was a man's woman. He could not blame Sir William for marrying her; what man would hesitate if he were a bachelor and found her unattached? Beyond that he could not waste time moralizing. His mission was important, and he was absorbed in a round of diplomatic interviews, for he brought wonderful news when he brought the news of Lord Hood's victory at Toulon, to Naples in particular.

"Only two years ago," Sir William told him, "after Emma and I were married in London, we stopped in Paris on our way back to Naples. Emma visited Queen Marie Antoinette; had a heart-to-heart chat—you know women! Emma brought one of Marie Antoinette's last 'farewells' to Her Majesty, Queen Maria Carolina of the Two Sicilies. Both Queens are daughters of the late Maria Theresa of Austria, so you see how Emma's sentimental heart has entangled her in their troubles. In a way, it is convenient to have the English Ambassadress in the Queen's confidence."

"I would die for them!" Emma said, rising like a goddess of vengeance.

"Damned but I *know* she would, Nelson! Sir William laughed. "She'd stick that pretty head in a guillotine just for the glory of it! But calm down, my precious, Marie Antoinette's still alive and with Captain Nelson's good news of victory—"

The Ambassadress waved him silent; shaking back her long chestnut hair, laughing and clapping her hands, she danced about the room. " 'Twill be the end of the revolution!"

Sir William turned to Nelson, saying dryly, "Emma's patriotism is sincere if a bit cockney. She really loves the Queen of Naples like a sister."

"More, dear Sir William," Emma laughed mischievously, "with all my soul—next to you—and England," and she curtsied to the Captain. "Think how my dear Queen's heart bleeds for her sister in France, Captain Nelson, threatened night and day with the guillotine!" And tears suddenly brimmed the Ambassadress's magnificent eyes.

Captain Nelson's face flushed. He had sisters, too, and how would he feel if someone tried to chop the head off his beloved Kitty—or even Susanna? "Dear lady, pray tell Her Majesty that no one could feel more deeply than I the terrible misfortunes that have fallen on these two lovely daughters of the immortal Maria Theresa."

Emma listened intensely, like a man, but as he finished she smiled gratefully and flew to Josiah, who had lounged to the window to stare wide-eyed at the great foreign city below. "Dear boy"—Emma straightened Josiah's cravat and smoothed his hair before he had time to defend himself. Arm circling Josiah, she turned back to Nelson. "Josiah and I shall celebrate the victory of Toulon while you wise men attend to business. Pray may we, Captain Nelson? May I pretend he's mine for today? I have no boy, and his mother must be weeping for hers, so pray give me leave? We will explore all the funny little places I know boys would like—I'll take him everywhere—please—?"

Captain Nelson felt an upsurge of gratitude and erased all bad marks from her character. "Your ladyship is wonderfully kind. I shall be eternally grateful, madam. . . . Behave yourself, son, *try* to act like a gentleman."

"I shall cuff him like a good mother if he does not. But he will," Emma laughed, lightly pulling Josiah's ear.

"Yaaa—yes, ma'am—aye, sir!" Josiah looked conquered for once.

And that was almost the last Captain Nelson saw of either his stepson or Lady Hamilton for the next three days. All Naples turned out to celebrate the fall of Toulon to the English. The bay glowed with lantern-lit barges and boatloads of serenaders. They cheered Captain Nelson like a conquering hero—though he had not fired one shot at the French this war. But it was a refreshing contrast to five years buried at Burnham. He wished Fanny could see it and enjoy the milder climate. Fanny would love Lady Hamilton's amiable manners.

When Sir William insisted they snatch an hour to see Lady Hamilton's noted "Attitudes," Captain Nelson sank into his chair ready to catch a wink of sleep while Sir William fussed with the limelights and Lady Hamilton, suddenly all art and silence, slipped behind a screen to select the scarves she would wear with her simple Grecian gown. Captain Nelson sat restlessly wondering what on earth would happen next, wanting to sleep, but distracted, mulling over the interviews he had accomplished, calculating what he must say in his next; worrying about his ship's company nearly all sick and exhausted, having fagged for nineteen weeks on nothing but honor and salt beef. This was the first time he had been ashore since Cádiz. His men were not too happy. They wanted action for their pains; a chance to earn some prize money. So did he, but he wanted glory.

When he looked up to the soft "Ah's" of the other guests whom Sir William had invited for the hour, he saw a vision. Not the lush and almost loud Emma Hart, nor lighthearted Lady Hamilton, but an intense dramatic actress with a thousand personalities. There was not a sound in the roomful of notoriously blasé guests around the Captain who had thought *he* would snatch a nap only to have his eyes opened. This was the talk of the Continent, and in some opinions she was as great as Mrs. Siddons.

There was soft music off somewhere, but it wasn't necessary, as from moment to moment, by the twist of a scarf, she was totally transformed by the character she assumed, metamorphoses so complete, yet flowing one into the other, the young poet Goethe had groped for some description, finally said she was a "masterpiece of the arch artist." She went from role to role: a Greek slave, a Judith, a Circe, a Diana, even a Madonna without seeming sacrilege.

One even forgot to grope for words, until the esthetic, enthusiastic figure of Sir William doused the lights and signaled for the draperies to be flung back.

As the sun flowed once more into the room he turned beaming for praises of his "find," his wife, just as he had beamed over his curios, his volcano and vases, with the light of an insatiable hunter in his eye; just as he had "found" Captain Nelson.

Someone of the English colony had mused, "Bewitching."

And Captain Nelson remembered there was a siege at Toulon and

a war not won. He had not even won his own spurs yet, but was
basking in Lord Hood's glory! This had been a pleasant diversion, but
it belonged at the end and not at the beginning of a campaign.

He took out his watch, feeling as if he had been compelled to
something against his will, like having to stop, arrested by a picture
in a shop window when he was in a hurry, did not want to stop,
didn't have time! But he had been spun about anyway, impatiently
admiring for a moment the object he did not want to see. Hurried on,
forgetting, or at the least putting more important things in the foremost portion of his thoughts. He was not a connoisseur of art, but
he had always had a natural eye for beauty, and a haunting mood for
tragedy.

"The Death of Wolfe at Quebec," he told someone, "that is a picture I cannot pass by." It was not apropos, for Lady Hamilton could
not have played the role, and if eyebrows went up, he did not notice.
The hour had wrung a strange confession.

That was the last afternoon.

On the third morning Captain Nelson purchased a boatload of
flowers and reciprocated. His stepson was polished and strangely
subdued for the first time in his life: he had seen a reason for learning
to act like a gentleman as he rode about Naples sight-seeing with
Lady Hamilton. But he managed a snarl when his stepfather raised
an amused eyebrow to the metamorphosis, proving he was still his
normal nasty self.

Captain Nelson had invited the Hamiltons and the foremost of
English Neapolitan society to breakfast aboard his ship: the Bishop
of Winchester, Lord and Lady Plymouth, Earl Grandison and a
half dozen more, all governed by an Englishwoman whose former
easy virtue seemed modesty itself compared to the smart lewdness of
Naples's own *crème de la crème*.

After breakfast in the Captain's dining room, they stood on the
quarter-deck as the boatswain piped attention.

"All hands man ship, ahoy!"

The order echoed and re-echoed from deck to deck. And three
hundred men with the light topmen in advance leaped into the rigging.

"Away aloft!"

While Lady Hamilton gasped her excitement—here was a new
stage for her! And her face assumed the role of a Viking's woman,

but very careful not to ruin the act, steal the whole show from a very proud young Captain.

Sir William, watching them, marveled at how easily they kept the stage without clashing, or getting lost in the background gyrations of three hundred seamen.

The men leaped to their posts. The weathered boatswain, gold anchor buttons flashing on his blue coat, silver whistle with its silver chain swinging, piped, "Lay out." The exactingly squared black yards were covered with men wearing slick cues or artful lovelocks; their white trousers cut to show a gaudily silk-stockinged ankle (if they could buy or steal silk), their blinding polka-dotted shirts, or striped jerseys—whatever appealed to their artistic taste—vibrating and jeering at the blood red or canary yellow of their jackets; their black japanned hats and an occasional brilliant bandana and earring dazzling against the Neapolitan blue sky.

While Lady Hamilton stood, blown by the wind, friendly, notorious, an insinuating bit of Adam's earth grit had found its way into the sensitive oysterlike enclosure of the Captain's immaculate soul. Annoyed, he began the slow and laborious process of turning it into a comfortable pearl. While behind them both, the cone of Vesuvius, a sybarite reclining on the circular shore, was blowing towers of smoke, pondering as they disappeared.

Forward of the Captain and the Lady on the quarter-deck was the open waist with its long springy gangways of plank, and through it could be glimpsed the lashed guns of the main deck, with red tompions plugged into their muzzles like so many tongues. On the gangways of the waist the men sprang like crickets, one eye on duty, one on their superiors. Suddenly, Captain Nelson uttered a soft, almost soundless groan—"That yokel . . ." as his lowly waister, Tom Allen, poked his head through a hatch to see the show. Fascinated, he climbed up on the gangways, in every man's way, looking about him.

The next instant an officious Midshipman Nisbet was bawling, "Start that man!" And a boatswain's mate leaped like a cat, and swinging a knotted cord lashed the waister below. He disappeared, grinning apologetically.

A flicker of rage had flashed through the eyes of a once lowly blacksmith's daughter. "Oh, what a pity," her ladyship pouted, and shook her finger at Josiah Nisbet.

Captain Nelson had a fleeting desire to knock Tom's and Josiah's heads together. Both had broken discipline. A waister was something that walked and talked, but beyond that, the scum of the earth. And "starting" a man was illegal, though quite customary; like spurring a horse.

"Mistakes can endanger the lives of everyone." He turned apologetically to the Hamiltons.

"He didn't *do* anything, did he?"

"I'll have a talk with my boy," the Captain promised, and her ladyship's face was bright again. And Sir William was laughing. Hardly any of the other guests, craning their necks skyward, had noticed the incident.

"My dear Nelson." Sir William shook his head. "Emma would have your ship turned all about in no time."

"Think what a wonderful ball one could give on this quarter-deck." Lady Hamilton's eyes grew pensive, the way women's eyes do when they suddenly visualize moving the furniture and hanging new curtains.

Captain Nelson did not answer. He liked his ship the way she was.

Sir William went on: "And you saw that pack of mongrel dogs in my house? They're all Emma's children. They'll go mad one of these days and bite us in gratitude."

Now a boat alongside, a breathless messenger from Sir John Acton, the Sicilies' strange English-born Prime Minister: a French man-of-war and three sail were at sea!

The three days were done.

Under the scarlet line of marines, taut at attention above them on the poop, Captain Nelson made his apologies to his guests; guns saluted the Ambassador as he rowed ashore, bearing Captain Nelson's regrets to King Ferdinand of the Two Sicilies who had been promised lunch on a battleship. Duty was duty.

Before noon, Captain Nelson had sailed away, still slightly dizzy from the biggest reception he had ever had in his life, and more than grateful to be alone in the sanctuary of his hard bare cabin, with its cot, washbasin and rack of arms; master of his own; God or the Devil to his crew, whichever he chose. All was his, right or wrong. And as his ship rose and fell, rolling on through the water, he was priding himself on the fact he had raised six thousand troops for Toulon while sitting next to a King who had expressed *very friendly* opinions of him.

It was with mingled relief and disgust that he heard his 1st Lieutenant Hinton reporting no French man-of-war on the rendezvous
Sir John Acton had named, for his ship was no match for four enemy
battleships, though honor had demanded he seek them out. He felt
a wave of dislike for the Sicilies—decadent and hysterically afraid.
But he did like the King and the Hamiltons, and, of course, the poor
dear Queen.

I I. Toulon: *Enfants Perdus*

December, 1793

THAT HAD BEEN last summer. The gaiety of the Neapolitan entr'acte
was finished. Marie Antoinette was dead; her sister at Naples, once
intelligently democratic, growing tyrannical in her fear. The French,
unconquered, were fighting to retake Toulon from the English.

Today Captain Nelson's ship was moored in the internationally free
port of Leghorn; the best place in the Mediterranean for buying supplies. Captain Nelson was busy, and when he was busy his spirits
were high, and he was happy. He had been sitting for some time
in his cabin at his writing table making out meticulous reports and
checking the various officers' reports of the ship's needs; calculating
whether or not he had taken on an honest purser or, what was most
common, a thief, who perhaps hoped in time to persuade the Captain
to go halves on whatever was stolen from the crew. Satisfied that this
was not the case, Captain Nelson heaved a sigh of relief and a hot
qualm of seasickness suddenly hit him. Even here, in the lofty poop
cabin with its open stern windows, he smelled the ship, in spite of
fumigating her only this week. The boatswain was disturbing old
stores in order to keep them on top, to be eaten first. Though there
was little distinction between salt beef four and salt beef five years old
. . . And the cheese had rotted; someone had been into last week's
catch of salt fish. But more insidious than these, or even the musty
smell of rotten timber, were the habits of the rats. In their death throes
they hid themselves only God knew where. Sometimes men suspected
the shipwrights deliberately made secret catacombs, known only to
them and to the rats.

Yet the ship had been fumigated, scrubbed, as she was scrubbed
every day from poop to hold; been sprinkled with vinegar water. He
stood up. When judged on a comparative scale he knew she smelled

positively sweet. But he could not convince his stomach, even after all these years.

He ran on deck for a breath of fresh air and his lieutenants automatically shifted to the lee side of the quarter-deck and went on with their work. He had stopped, scowled at the sky; at the wind blowing straight shoreward. "Oh God! Still dead foul!" His mood changing, he stalked rather wearily to the side where the bulwark curved up and over, higher than his head, hopped on a gun and leaning over the netting where the hammocks were stowed for airing and sun eyed the work in progress.

For the impartial wind blew fresh westerly into the free port of Leghorn, pinning the small fishing boats, masts aslant, like wooden buttresses to the sea walls, though the bay swarmed with Jew merchants bartering trinkets. And this, His Britannic Majesty King George III's battleship lying along the mole was trapped by the same December wind that tossed the skirts of the fishermen's uglier daughters who had not been invited to live aboard with the crew, and who strolled the line of seamen taking on stores, trying to draw their attention. But the seamen saw the flash of the marines' bayonets and only grinned. It was too bad that British jacks had such a low opinion of patriotism they would desert if given shore leave. Even the ones who had been given the honor of choosing between the navy or going to the gallows; but hardened criminals had no sense of gratitude: some had been known to choose hanging. They were considered effeminate.

Captain Nelson prided himself on having mostly volunteers aboard. Some of them were from the first little ship he ever commanded, the *Lowestoffe,* which, when she was paid off after the American war, the men said had been so well handled, every officer and man aboard had petitioned him to let them sign on again, whenever he went to sea. As a matter of fact, he prided himself on understanding his men, for he thought that men or nations, all were alike, few would act infamously if it were shown them there was no profit in it. It was not easy to prove that to them always, but as he was not blind to the fact that the merchant marine was preferable to the navy, he tried applying merchant marine practices on his ship. He had come back from the merchant marine himself with a swagger and the boast "Aft the most honor and forward the better man." But his uncle had soon knocked such nonsense out of his own mind. Even so, he still despised sadistic power as indicative of little minds: flogging was his very last resort. And it wasn't entirely due to his weak stomach, though the vision of backs flayed to the bone day after day after breakfast may have had something to do with it.

He was watching the herd of cattle, sheep and pigs moaning along the mole. Tom Allen caught his eye: talking homesick sweet nothings to a pig. Once or twice on inspection he'd spied Tom hanging over the "manger" which served to catch the water shipped through the deadeyes at anchorage, and as a pigsty. Tom tended it.

Now the gusts of wind carried the blessed fresh oily tang of lemons, and the strength-giving miasma of onions, the tear-jerking earth damp of the baskets of greens. And there came the cursed oatmeal the cook— everyone swore—boiled in the bilge water. And the molasses, for Captain Nelson was decent enough to realize that a man could hardly "force the stuff down his throat"—the oatmeal—without molasses. And there came more salt junk—labeled beef. Though men also told sensitive newcomers it was ground up of stray black men, full of horseshoes, and that around the slaughterhouses could be heard mysterious meowings and barkings. Captain Nelson had lived on it, and it alone, for seventeen weeks once on a voyage to Canada—and got scurvy. He knew exactly what they meant. And there came the tons of flour, and the biscuits that would not get soft until the weevils did their share; like earthworms in the soil. And there—lovingly handled— came "Miss Taylor," a perfect bitch of a white wine from Spain, and, less kindly handled, the "black strap" or customary Mediterranean red wine.

"Easy, blast you!" a lieutenant howled, for there came a sacred case: the Captain's own favorite Florentine wine.

"Belay that hog! He slipped his hawser!" The boatswain blew the whistle that seemed a natural part of his weathered shrewd face, as away went a pig down the mole among the bare feet, till honor was avenged by two jacks tackling the creature fore and aft. The Captain, his humor restored, went back to his desk work, passing under the projection of the poop deck, past the huge double wheel, past the smart sentries, while his lieutenants coughed, and brought up the profanity they had swallowed on his first appearance.

The Captain was in a great hurry to finish supplying his ship. Since that flying visit to Naples he had been given the command of a small squadron of frigate cruisers to blockade the French who governed the island of Corsica, lying just out there, next to Italy and France. He was also acting as an aide in the negotiations between his commander in chief, Lord Hood, and the Corsican patriot, Pasquale Paoli, who was inviting the English to come in and drive out the hated French. Paoli had turned down an offer from a young Corsican, son of one of Paoli's former aides, who was serving with the French army in Corsica. The lieutenant had offered to instigate an insurrection within the French garrison in Corsica, set up a Corsican government. A lieutenant! Paoli had sent the small, eagle-eyed Corsican packing to France.

In return for liberating Corsica, England would have a good naval base for her Mediterranean fleet—as well as Toulon. Paoli's offer was being seriously considered. The war, like a patient who appears at first to have only a slight fever, was taking a turn for the worse. Besides the guillotining of Marie Antoinette, there had been the news that an English army under the Duke of York, in conjunction with the Allies, had *failed* to push across France to Paris. The army promised for the southern push from Toulon had never arrived from England. The French were still surprisingly vigorous. And still Captain Nelson had scarcely heard one shot fired this war!

❋   ❋   ❋

While the Captain struggled on through his desk work, which in the opinion of the jacks was about the equivalent of sneaking a nap, his ship took on stores remarkably fast, stowing her victuals greedily.

With the Captain out of sight, the men stole a word now and then behind officers' backs.

"That's Nel for ye! Wind's foul but he never took a chance of missing a fair wind!" And up went a bundle of bread on a sun-blackened back.

"Easy with that bread. Nel'll have ye fishing it outa the harbor like a tunny; hanging it up to dry. . . ."

"Aye, he's strict but there ain't a cussed bone in 'im."

"Give me a captain that's a bit of a tartar; not one of yer lazy slobs, weak as a woman, who don't care if he's got a killer of a first luff or a drunken sot of a bosun. Nel's luffs gotta leap."

"Yer signed on a smart ship," an old hand from the days of the *Boreas* frigate nodded. "Less flogging. I won't say *ye* might not be flogged through the fleet, but—" He winked at other old hands while a boy, who had been beguiled by a smooth-tongued recruiting officer into thinking there was romance in the sea, gulped.

"Ever seen a man flogged through the fleet?" the old hand growled. "I seen 'em. The last ship's boats flaying the last scrap of flesh off the backbone of a corpse—still warm—mind ye, but nothing but jelly left."

"Aye," from another oldster. "I served under Jervis, once."

"But there ain't been so much 'starting' lately," the youngster said eagerly, his face covered with cold sweat.

"Just the lull before the storm," the old hand nodded. "Don't cross the younker's hawse or he'll devil ye till ye die. It don't matter if he's only thirteen years old—he's an officer by the God of War!"

"Aye, the younker will be breaking his neck or the Captain's 'eart soon enough."

"No man—or officer and touch yer 'at—not even Nel can keep an eye on what happens below alla time. Any more than God sees a stinking waister carting sewage, or a holder cringing closer to the rats than to men. . . ."

"Well, give me a ship that ain't idle, like them at Toulon; the heroes taking their ease and the jacks playing soljer in all the forts . . . and let me give you a tip, lad—" the oldster grinned—"you see them Johnny-toe-the-lines"—he jerked an earring at the marines. "When ye have musket drill, quit swallowing them bullets. Bite the cartridge neat. 'At's what makes *'em* so stiff. Full of lead, couldn't learn to load proper without swallowing a handful for each one they got in their muskets."

"Deck there! Strange sail to westward!" A voice ringing down from the tops.

And a blast of blasphemy from the boatswain's mate who had spied the men idling; while as he turned his back, someone muttered, "Avast! Look at Nel now tumbling up. Larkin' aloft like a mid!"

❀   ❀   ❀

And there the Captain clung, lean and quick as his midshipmen, glass pasted to his eye, swinging about in the nautical trapeze with the ease and abandon of a nerveless child. As far above the jacks laboring under the stores, straining on the windlass, hoisting stores in, as the screaming gulls and impersonal winds.

"Well, Mr. Hoste?" The Captain turned on a midshipman swinging at his elbow.

"Frigates and—ah—transports, sir?" the boy blurted, blushed.

"Come, I was asking you, William . . ." the Captain urged in his patient, his bland voice. Yet his eyes flashed back at the ships almost angrily.

"Three frigates and four transports, sir!" The midshipman was a good-looking boy, neither churlish nor slyly vicious. And although his eyes were reverently on his Captain he was making faces as if biting chunks out of his cheeks to keep from laughing.

"They haven't let fly their topgallant sheets, sir. They aren't merchants in convoy, sir. There now! They're answering our signal, sir. Oh, and they're English—" Hoste added what should have been mentioned in the first place.

"Aye . . ." the Captain said slowly. He was scanning the sea again, his mind working three spheres at once: training the babies of his brood of some thirteen mids; seeing his ship victualed as fast as possible in order to get back to his small squadron blockading Corsica; *and* contemplating the fate of his country. The last was not strictly within his sphere as a Captain, but he made it his interest just the same.

Clinging below him in the rigging was another youngster with a rudely impudent eye, a swarthy bearlike face. He was trying to dislodge young Hoste from his spar by rapping him across the shins.

"Order my boat, Mr. Hoste."

"Aye, aye, sir!" Hoste shouted, kicking at his tormentor, but craftily, all behind the Captain's back. "Meet me in the hold and we'll settle, Mr. Nisbet," he whispered as he slid past, down a stay.

"That will do, Mr. Nisbet!" the Captain snapped without looking around. "I'll knock you off your perch, you rascal!"

"Oh? Aye, aye, aye, sir!" The boy laughed, not the least worried. "I say, Father, can Hoste and me go ashore—to buy a present for Mother?"

Hoste was now out of earshot.

"No, my dear child, you cannot." The Captain still did not look around, though the thought of two boys exposed to the rampant syphilis of Italian ports made his voice gently paternal. The Black Lion was the curse of the Mediterranean seamen.

"Oh, and why the devil not?" Nisbet's face darkened.

"What has come over you, Josiah? You must learn to obey orders willingly and unquestioningly, dear child. . . . Go below!"

As his stepson scrambled down, the Captain's mind snapped back to the question at hand, and his heavy-lidded, thoughtful eyes shifted from the far-off sails to the adverse wind and adverse tide that pinned his ship helplessly in the harbor.

Again he peered into his glass as if it were a crystal ball, relaying news from beyond the horizon, into a framework of skull armoring a delicate magnetized brain that was always seeking some pole, some ultimate answer.

He rested his glass a moment. Had the English capture of Toulon been a foothold or a trap? His heart pounded as he questioned his glass again, while the scent of fresh stores rose up to him; the squalling of livestock, cries of his minuscule men.

Within the encircling dark of his glass, half sea and half air, lean masts—like pins—on three frigates had thrust up through the water, casting threadlike shadows before them, growing taller, sprouting up everywhere; until the horizon was thick with the spars and the membranes of sails stretched before the wind—the sun diving red into the Mediterranean behind them. Now the whole glass reflected the red winter sky and heaving sea as one pool of blood.

"Your boat, sir!" Hoste again.

And down the rigging the Captain skittered, leaving his mid gaping after him until he was no more than a speck below. His blue coat threading the naked backs of his seamen, where the masts seemed to converge from the tops into toothpicks stuck in the deck; the whole ship suspended from the sky in the net of her rigging.

Hoste saw the officers drawing up, heard the pipe of the boatswain's omnipresent whistle, while the side boys ran out the side ropes on the gangway, the red, cloth-covered ones for the Captain; the marine sentry, red coat and white knee breeches, snapped to attention—and the Captain was gone.

In another moment his boat was pulling away from the bulging yellow-brown sides of his ship; now bobbing away in the bay like a fisherman's cork. The lean oars cut the bronze waves, flashed gold, cut again, in haste to meet the ships that bore down, all sails set, skudding for doubtful haven in Leghorn. A boatload of Leghornese shook their heads at him—an Englishman in port had no business rowing out to a ship that had not been cleared. It would do no good to complain; these English were very good customers and they usually did as they thought fit.

But the Captain's boat crew grinned and bent with a will on their oars. They were picked men, and it would please the Captain to swim along smartly. He finally answered their efforts with a good-natured nod.

There was a long pull ahead, and the wind struck into his face as his boat crept from under the wall of his battleship, which lay with her port lids yawned for air, showing the blood red of her insides: square patches on the two yellow stripes of the gun tiers. The brown of her side ended in a black band at her waterline which made the copper of her bottom gleam in contrast. As the Captain passed under her sternworks, she flashed her sky-blue, red and gold encrustations of cherubs and garlands like mammoth barnacles. She was massive and clumsy as she lay at anchor, bare-poled. Yet the rakish set of her masts and her upstarting bowsprit gave a hint of her glory under full sail. At last she was left astern.

A light mist showered the boat crew's backs, dampened the Captain's old undress coat, and a shabby-looking coat it was after years of service and five years in storage. The spray spotted his clean white stockings and buckled shoes. He disregarded it utterly as he sat forward; intense, attenuated, yet somehow giving the impression of calm reserve within him. He reflected a great deal of heart in his large eyes, still . . . there was that pistol shot abruptness in his gestures.

His face glistened, wet, as he squinted slightly, peering into the sunset. His nose was long, straight and positive. His straight white hair was brushed straight back from his high broad forehead and tied indifferently at the nape of his neck. Here among seamen his face seemed supersensitive, full of peculiar, striking contrasts. Why should such a forthright nose be given to wed such a wide, ironic mouth that smiled easily, but looked rather sad in repose; and such large, almost feminine eyes be set in such a brooding frame? All in all he was an arresting paradox, neither handsome nor homely. He didn't look like a sailor and he didn't look like a landsman. He looked like himself; something of a round peg whittled to fit a square hole.

"Steer for the first frigate, Sykes," he ordered his coxswain, a young man with a surprisingly intelligent eye that was quick to foresee the Captain's moods.

"Aye, aye, sir."

At last the steep dark hulls rose before them, the sails bellied out in tier upon tier. From their fish-eye view on the water it seemed the topmasts would rend the clouds. The convoy of transports, square-rigged brigs and fore-and-aft ketches yawed here and there exasperatingly out of line with the protecting frigates.

He heard them at last, humming before the wind. The strange human groans of the masts straining against the hulls, the harping in the taut rigging, the creaking protests of planks trying to burst the seams; the arrogant bowsprits dipping and rising like fantastic beaks sipping the swell rolling in toward the land. Their massive, gaudily painted figureheads leaning toward him, their upcast wooden eyes blind to horizons.

He hailed the first frigate bearing down on him. Her topsails were already shivering, reducing her speed, until with a spring the Captain was swinging between wind and water, hand over hand up the gangway. His boat made fast, playing out astern. The frigates were bringing to, sails furling, to await pratique into Leghorn.

But as Captain Nelson ran up the side he sensed something was wrong. The boatswain had been late to pipe him. As his foot touched the deck he saw the ship swarmed with women and children and men all disheveled. Some were weeping, some staring blankly at him. He caught the word, "Terror. . . ." Then many French words, but his French was halting.

"Dear merciful God!" he gasped, staring at these French refugees on this English frigate.

The thin wail of a newborn infant seemed to hang in the air; a woman was groaning. While the faces that stared back at his were like the faces of lunatics, maskers. Chalky. Blood-streaked.

Mauled, half-drowned, half-crazed human beings with back-breaking bundles of what looked like rag pickings. So much flotsam and jetsam heaped on the deck. Tatters of cloth, waterlogged trunks, bleeding adults clutching hysterical children. He glanced about for the officers. Saw a gaunt captain making his way toward him, and the sight stunned him: he knew this young French nobleman from Toulon. As the frigate captain came toward him through the nightmarish sea of flesh, something tugged at Captain Nelson's sleeve.

"Hello. . . ." He looked down, his face brightened, until he saw the terror again, reflected in the blank eyes and quivering mouth of a boy.

The Captain swallowed, and put out his hand to pat the youngster's head, but the child leaped away; hid behind others.

A stout bourgeois face came so close it blotted out everything else. "The terror! The terror has swept Toulon!"

And a dark-haired woman, her pretty face stupid with shock, sat stroking the bright enamel of a small clock in her lap, now and then wearily trying to pull her torn skirt over her nakedness.

Then they all lunged at him and the frigate captain, screaming their wants.

"Where will we go?"

"Have you news of my wife?"

"We are paupers—nothing left—"

"My husband blew his brains out! God! Why didn't he take us too?"

"See my skirt." The young woman with the clock suddenly began to laugh as the tears started to her eyes. "I dragged it through blood. Puddles—puddles of blood. They sing. Oh, they sing. And they dance. They laugh and laugh! Have comedies every hour—on the guillotine. Right on the guillotine! Entr'acte—comedy—between killings!"

The cries and the hands clung to him as he followed the frigate captain below, down the narrow companion, to the cramped beamed cabin. He still could hear the tramping and shuffling, the sighing on deck, smell the stench of filth and sickness seeping right through the beams.

He stood there stunned, his face white and pained, staring at the frigate captain. "My dear sir, what can I do?"

The frigate captain clenched his hands hopelessly. He was young Comte de Grasse who had joined the English and Spanish alliance to overthrow the French Revolution from Toulon.

"What can anyone do, Captain Nelson! My wife—my family—I can't find them—left behind—or—"

"At Toulon?"

The Frenchman nodded as he poured out two glasses of brandy, pushed one slowly toward Captain Nelson. His sleeve was blackened with dried blood, an epaulet torn from his coat.

Captain Nelson stared at his glass, his face still white, eyes round.

The Frenchman leaned forward, clasping his hands, while his long well-bred face sagged.

"Ever since Lord Hood detached your squadron to Corsica, the sans-culottes have been reinforcing the heights around Toulon. At first, as you know, their guns were so badly aimed they hit nothing, and apparently had nothing to fight with. In town we waited for the army promised from England—" The Frenchman's eyes snapped. "It did not come. The Spaniards swaggered and cut our throats. Everyone hated everyone! The English said hold out. Some of the merchants wanted to set up a new republic. Some still said hold out, we'd restore the monarchy. We prayed for Austria to remember their murdered daughter, our Queen, only two months dead, and they forgot us as they forgot her. May God forget them! Some said declare for the revolution—save ourselves! Madness. The sans-culottes did not want us to declare—they wanted our money—our lives—our shops!

"Everyone began to go mad. And something happened up on the heights. The sans-culottes' fire grew heavier, they began to hit us. At last Admiral Lord Hood issued a warning: Probable evacuation! That was all that was needed. Spies in town. Spies on the heights. Four months we lived in hope—hope! And there lay the French fleet. The most beautiful ships in the world. . . ."

Captain Nelson sat up with a jerk. He had been too slack in his pity. This man was flying English colors. "Exactly what happened?"

"A week ago on the seventeenth, at eight o'clock at night, the revolutionists' army attacked Toulon."

"Where?"

"Everywhere!" The Frenchman swept the cabin with his arm.

"The main blow? Did we hold L'Aiguillette fort guarding the roadstead?"

"The main blow? It fell *there*."

Captain Nelson sat back, his hands fell on his knees.

Comte de Grasse continued: "They took the fort. It was hard fought."

"Took it! *We* surrendered?"

"Wiped out."

"Oh, God!"

"And the next day the Allies were flying. Lord Hood himself went ashore, tried to rally the troops. He was great, but the Neapolitans— the Spanish—the English—all mixed up outnumbered were running —swimming for ships! That night, *the mob rose!*"

Captain Nelson was shaking his head while the Frenchman took a breath, covered his face with his hands, looked up again. He was not weeping. He was past that.

"Then *everyone* fled for the bay—for the ships. The town was in flames. Murder and plunder and rape! One—two—three guillotines working all day and all night and all day. There are only two kinds of people left in France: one mad and drunk, the other with horror in their faces. . . . There were not enough boats. Some overturned. Hundreds drowned, or were dragged back, cut to pieces. . . . And here are wives without husbands, children without fathers, husbands without their . . ." He broke off. "That is *liberté* and—"

Captain Nelson had risen, was pacing as the Comte spoke. He could see everything and especially that one little frightened boy—like an animal—running away from him. . . . And at last he was conscious of the stuffy little cabin, the oppressive tramping overhead, the shifting and crying. Nauseated, he asked, "And the French fleet in the harbor?"

A resentful shadow crossed de Grasse's face. After all, it had only been ten years since his admiral father had been defeated off Dominica by Admiral Lord Rodney and his second in command, then Rear Admiral, Hood. Only ten years since he'd hated the English for shaming his family. . . .

"Lord Hood ordered Captain Sir Sidney Smith to—to destroy those twenty beautiful French ships of the line and all the smaller ships—everything—destroyed at anchor!"

"Was it done?" Captain Nelson had nodded approvingly. "If so, we've crippled their navy for good."

"I'm afraid—we don't know. . . ." the Frenchman said slowly, remembering his place, his sworn alliance to England. "There was not time. . . ."

"Where is Lord Hood—the fleet—have you dispatches for me?"

"No, sir. Lord Hood is cruising off Toulon—off Hyères—all along the Riviera. But where, Captain Nelson, are the English ships to anchor?"

❋ ❋ ❋

When they came on deck the Leghorn waterfront loomed before them: the grim palaces of dead princes; ancient fortifications frowning down. Yet the distant hills seemed to be singing, re-echoing the cathedral bells ringing out sweetly across the water. The mole and the shore were thick with the townspeople peering out at the English ships hauled up in the roadstead, awaiting permission to send the refugees on shore.

A boat alongside. A flurry of petty Leghornese officials with big swords, moustachios, and frowns. A message from the Governor: The

Internationally recognized Free Port of Leghorn faces her own food shortages and would be greatly embarrassed by an increase of occupants—especially those without funds.

Captain Nelson and the Frenchman exchanged tired glances. It was the old story. Refugees were never wanted. Spanish Jews had once starved and died aboard ships anchored at the mouths of Italian ports. So for hundreds and hundreds of years . . . Stepping aside, Captain Nelson said thoughtfully: "I am pretty sure they will only protest this time. Their Governor has served with our navy. He's friendly to us. But what the free port of Leghorn will do later will depend on what we do in these seas. It's obvious that these poor homeless souls are about as welcome as the plague. Let me know if the town gives you any real trouble. I'll have a talk with the Governor."

They shook hands, and the cathedral bells seemed to sing louder through the dark evening.

"*C'est le Noël, Maman!*" cried a child.

"Sssssh! Be still! Never mind!"

Noël! Captain Nelson swung overside. Why couldn't a little child mention it? What had she done? As he clung to the swaying ladder, getting his bearings, tears came in his eyes. But it was dark. No one could see his tears on this Christmas Eve of 1793: discipline would not be demoralized. And tomorrow . . . Christmas was the day when the jacks got drunk, dead drunk. It was their holiday.

Once in his boat he pulled his coat about him and sat forward, as if the gesture lent speed to the oars. He closed his eyes, suddenly exhausted, listening to the steady splash of the oars, the breathing of his crew—and the wild, the joyous bells!

"Sykes." He took a deep breath. "There's an avenging angel to record all this. . . ."

"Aye, aye, sir," Sykes nodded. His face, too, was stony; all of them in the boat reflected something of outraged surprise. And in the mood and confidence of the moment, Sykes said, "And a blacklist he keeps, sir!"

Captain Nelson nodded, and his thought began to turn on his profession. Theoretically, as an officer, he had realized for some time that without a strong active army on shore England was wasting her time and her money on Toulon. Sooner or later the city would have to fall to the besieging army. Didn't he live tactics because they were the paramount art of his profession? He dreamed of evolving tactics so shrewd, so deadly, war would end in one blow. And there would be peace on earth: good will toward men!

Theoretically then, the English defeat at Toulon was not a shock. The surprise had been that they ever got in there at all! As Lord Hood's favorite courier when he carried the news to Naples, was feted by the English Ambassador and his lady, proudly showed them his fighting ship. . . . A fiasco? England's defeat smote him personally. He was proud. And suddenly the screams of terrified people fleeing like animals before the terror . . . he could not remember ever feeling so sick or so stunned!

He forced his mind to look ahead. Where would the fleet anchor? In Corsica! England would not leave the Mediterranean Sea to the French. England must keep her trade routes open to Turkey, Egypt and the desert caravan routes to Suez—to India.

England must liberate the island of Corsica, as Paoli had asked, and in return her ships would have harbors. Strategically then, England was not too badly off in this war. This war that he, in his boredom, had been writing to Fanny ought to stop, "for what are we fighting for?"

Now those hopeless faces haunted him. For the first time in his thirty-five years he had seen a new kind of war. This was murder and it was Christmas—and again he remembered the jacks expected their right to get raving drunk. And he thought of the child . . . *"C'est le Noël. . . ."* Perhaps she was the one whose father blew his brains out rather than go on a pauper . . . ? Murder and Christmas and a drunk crew tomorrow and Divine Services besides. As a parson's son—as a fighting man his mind leaped from one to the other and back again. And pity and hate, killing hate, seemed for the first time compatible: the French were in league with the devil!

He heard his boatswain piping his arrival, and looking up found himself just rowing under the high square stern of his ship. A glimmer of moonlight was wreathing the scrollwork around his own cabin windows; toying over the gold of the classical warlike name:

H.M.S. *Agamemnon.*

I I I. Bastia

Spring, 1794

GENERAL PASQUALE PAOLI, father of Corsican independence, was brooding in his island palace. It stood high among plaster huts braced by arches over the streets that toppled up slope and down. Winding alleyways led to grass-grown highways no better than footpads' trails. He was eyeing without seeing the snow-capped Corsican peaks, the fallow untilled fields, the fever-ridden marshes, the olive trees, like puffs of gray smoke on the slopes. The groves that rendered lemons and oranges were broken down, grown scraggly. Over it all Paoli brooded with a dream in his heart, a brain in his head—but no artillery.

The tall windows through which he stared were drizzled with rain, creaking as if to burst. In the distance, beyond the tumbling hills, rock cliffs dove swift from peak to bottom of the sea. Through the gusty mists on the shifting waves was the English fleet with the English army of liberation, all knocked about like children's paper boats. Now and then a long streamer of white broke from a boom; storm staysails shredded in the wind. Tossed up; tossed down. Wave piling over wave, pitch, stern skyward; roll, bow down.

And slowly one by one the ships and their transports, with their unseen souls, and two thousand British soldiers, green as gangrene, seasick, were swept out of sight. The English army of liberation scudding before the storm.

Paoli turned from the window as from a picture on the wall. His dark, well-bred face, its passion whetted to keen subtlety, was trained by a lifetime of defeat to seek the hidden channels rather than the open field. He smiled at the English gentlemen and his own fair weather generals seated around the conference table.

"We are now to our country like the prophet Elisha, stretched over the dead child of the Shulamite widow—eye to eye, nose to nose, mouth to mouth. It begins to recover warmth . . . for," he waved toward the stormy sea, "so through the gales the great soul of mankind remains confident of his ultimate good." He bowed himself into his chair and waited for an interpreter to mangle his prophecies.

The three Englishmen were: a former member of Parliament, Colonel John Moore, barely into his thirties; an army major, Kohler, both men in dazzling red coats. The third man, a near-middle-aged Scot, was Sir Gilbert Elliot, the appointed Viceroy to Corsica. He was wearing diplomatic black. He was a man who had been educated in France, studied with Hume and been friendly with Mirabeau; had his fling at trying to reform England, and become quite astute.

The three Englishmen had been sent to sound the political shoals of intrigue as first roughly charted by a Commodore Linzee and more recently, just before the fall of Toulon, by young Captain Nelson.

They twiddled the quills, squared the inkstands mathematically and shuffled their portfolios. And they reluctantly sipped execrable cognac served by a porter trailing a rusty musket in his left hand. He was barefooted, insect-bitten, probably diseased, and dangled a gold earring under his long black hair. There was a knife tucked in his sash. The musket was for the French, the knife for the revenge of family blood feuds. He was so obviously a scoundrel, Colonel Moore watched fascinated, exchanging amused glances with the Major, who kept shaking his head at the table. But it was not comedy, this was not *opéra bouffe;* this was the stuff of the Corsican army that two generations of Paolis, first father, now aging son, had tried to train.

Across from the Englishmen sat two generals: Franconcetti and Brogio, and a lesser man who did active fighting for Paoli—Frediani.

Meantime the interpreter for Paoli hemmed. He was a sharp-witted little Corsican merchant ruined by the French ban on Corsican exports. And while he ruminated, his eye watched a big blue fly walking sedately along rows of elegantly bound books: *The History of Corsica* or seven hundred years of bloodshed, divisioned off under different headings: the liberation of Corsica by Sardinia; the liberation of ditto by Spain; the liberation at the hands of the banking houses of Genoa and fostering of the incipient blood feuds to maintain balance of power; the liberation by Paoli, or the united Corsican Government, a short pamphlet ending in the liberation of Corsica by France through high-handed purchase from Genoa; Paoli exiled, seeking refuge and aid for twenty long years in England, followed by Paoli recognized by the French Revolution! Paoli returned. Paoli made puppet of revolution. Paoli denouncing the revolution. Paoli in revolt negotiating with the English . . . the fly had reached the end of the publications. The interpreter blinked.

"General Paoli has said that Corsica rises as one man to embrace the English Convention of deliverance. Throughout the length and breadth of Corsica men stand alerted, muskets—"

"The Convention as negotiated with Lord Hood is satisfactory." Sir Gilbert Elliot bluntly silenced the interpreter as he mopped his forehead under his elegantly yet manly powdered wig. "And in return, Paoli has agreed to cede the governing of Corsica to England. All very satisfactory. However we must know, will he lead his troops?"

Paoli bowed as the interpreter spoke. He smiled in the affirmative, yet his eyes sought and seemed to commune with one general, avoiding the eyes of the other. "Of course, from my heart—till it stops beating—I will direct my men that Corsica may prosper by your generous agreement."

Sir Gilbert Elliot bowed too, but his eyes had met those of the general whom Paoli avoided—Brogio.

"Ah—ask General Paoli, what's the meaning of the threats to blow up the two major towns, Bastia and Calvi, should the English attempt to land there?" Colonel Moore drawled out his request, for while Paoli and Sir Gilbert Elliot had been speaking, Moore had been eyeing Paoli's favorite general with an invitation to explore the question— *entre nous*—after the indispensable display of diplomacy ended.

Sir Gilbert had, however, caught the glance. Frowned. There was a great deal going on at this table today.

"Purely a French gasconade!" Paoli had answered Moore.

"We have driven the French into those towns," the interpreter hastily apologized.

Paoli began to speak again: "From what I have heard from Captain Nelson he sees no difficulty in taking those two towns. He is a great soul full of confidence and inspiration." Paoli smiled unreservedly, for the first time.

And the army smiled out of the other side of their mouths. "He is a sailor, not a soldier," Moore shrugged, as Paoli's words were translated. "And he doesn't know a damn thing about a siege"—to the Major.

Sir Gilbert however had brightened. "A splendid fellow—Nelson."
"He don't care if he gets blown up," mused the Major.

Colonel Moore ahemed for attention; though army commissions
were purchased, once attained they automatically gave the possessor
immense authority. Moore's voice had stiffened. "Tell General Paoli
that when the English have landed and the Corsican army comes out
from behind the bush and rocks, the responsibility for further progress
of this campaign must lie with the naval commander in chief, Lord
Hood, who signed the Convention!"

Sir Gilbert turned slowly, faced Moore. As they were both Scotch-
men and economical of words, Sir Gilbert made no comment and
Moore did not waste any looks of explanation as he went on: "You
can tell the General that the English army, once encamped in the harbor of San Fiorenzo, will act after taking due consideration of all
problems involved, and that includes the hearty co-operation of the
Corsican army."

Sir Gilbert turned Moore's words over in his mind while the interpreter swallowed them whole and regurgitated them in Italian.

"That shall be as you say." Paoli rose, and with a cool bow to the
English Viceroy and not so much as a nod for the army, expanded
with another graceful wave of his hand: "Yonder is the winter gale,
yet we cannot judge all life by one season's storm. It will disperse, and
the spring shall come upon Corsica. Our problem is only a transient
cloud passing through the hemisphere, which will soon be dissipated
and the sun break forth again with his usual splendor!" He bowed,
this time to all. The audience was over, the eagle of Corsica about to
withdraw to his eyrie. "Until dinner, gentlemen . . ."

Left alone, the English delegation stared gloomily for their ships.
"Hmmm . . . Machiavelli reincarnate. . . ." Sir Gilbert said after a
while. "By the way, gentlemen, have you read the latest book on Dr.
Johnson?"

Colonel Moore and the Major looked as if he had offered them a
mildewed lemon to sweeten their problems.

"I find that Dr. Johnson chastened Boswell, who had come to Corsica and caught a bit of the 'liberation' fever at one time. Dr. Johnson said of Boswell's enthusiasm and apropos of our General Paoli:
'I wish there were some cure, like the lover's leap, for all heads of
which some single idea has obtained an unreasonable and irregular
possession.' He went on to say that in these last twenty years the Cor-

sicans have had time to knock down the fortified cities—even crumble
the rocks with their teeth. . . . In short, I believe Dr. Johnson suspected a lack of sincerity. Of course, as Boswell pointed out in his
rebuttal, artillery is advantageous. . . ."

Colonel Moore nodded abruptly. "Those towns are impregnable, Sir
Gilbert, with our present means."

"But here is my point. General Brogio has never thought so. Paoli
distrusts him."

"Brogio?"

"Corsica!" The Major sneered softly. "On the last day of creation
the weary Lord must have been left with one rock in his hand. He
dropped it here."

"Very strategic," Sir Gilbert mused. "Anyone who holds Corsica can
blockade the ports of four or five nations. . . ."

And again they stared from the windows where the winter gales
swept the seas clean and pure of all ships; of H.M.S. *Victory,* of H.M.S.
Agamemnon, and all the other battleships of the Mediterranean fleet.
Now and then one appeared, disappeared, still stubbornly determined
that England should have anchorage; that Corsica should be liberated

❊   ❊   ❊

But the winter gales did abate, as Paoli had promised, though in
France Danton had tried to stem the Terror he had helped create—
gone to the guillotine himself, by order of Robespierre. The Terror
swept methodically on, preparing France for the new paradise. So a
thousand Parisians were guillotined in one month.

While in Corsica it was a quiet spring. Swinging along ahead of
his seamen, Captain Nelson smiled to himself. He had landed in Corsica ahead of the army, and without being ordered to!

The mat of thyme and rosemary under the bare horned feet of the
seamen cushioned their rolling gait, and made the fresh bright afternoon one for frolicking leave. The *Agamemnon's* marines marched in
stiff soldierly fashion that never ceased to amuse the seamen. Yet
even they sniffed the air. It was a beautiful day.

The sun seemed to be testing the razorlike edges of the newly
ground cutlasses, dancing on the tips of the murderously pointed pikes,
examining the pistols tucked in at the seamen's belts, then rippling
away across the small field of marine muskets, as if they were so many
stalks of grain. The small sword at the Captain's side meant business

as usual. There was no larking in the ranks, or even the free calling back and forth of a watering party. The Captain had an appointment.

Cues bristling, sun-scorched arms shoved aside the tangle of scrub oaks. The seamen grinned and nodded now and then toward their jaunty Captain flanked by three of his lieutenants: Hinton and Andrews and Weatherhead. The marines were under Marine Lieutenant Clarke. Now and then the Captain cocked his head listening, and peered ahead through the leaves.

They had pushed back from a cove, through the woods, leaving *Agamemnon* anchored just out of sight of the town of Bastia; hidden by the rough projections of the coast.

Captain Nelson pulled a small map from his pocket, matched it to the small compass Lieutenant Hinton held. They studied the map's hurried scrawls, the Captain nodded to Hinton and tucked the map back in his vest. At the top of a rise he signaled halt, and motioned to Weatherhead. "Better sound ahead."

Lieutenant Weatherhead crept forward slowly, from tree to tree.

"Paoli!"

The word whistled past his ear. He dropped back, hand on his pistol, as a sliver of sunlight started from a rock ten paces away.

"Hood," he answered the musket leveled at him.

"*Signore!* Admiral! This way!" Bare feet first, a ragged Corsican scrambled down the rock; and another and another as if the stones and the trees were turning to men.

"Well met," Captain Nelson nodded to the guerrilla guides.

"All friends of Paoli here, Admiral Nelson!"

"Captain," he corrected.

"*Signore* Admiral, pardon, Captain Admiral!" The guide, a starved little fellow, with big greenish teeth and black hair that looked as if it had been dipped in grease, hitched his ragged pants and adjusted his dagger by way of salute.

"How long you been friends of Paoli?" Captain Nelson asked cheerfully, quite offhand.

The Corsican laughed, and before answering turned to tell his comrades the Captain's question. Then they all laughed and nodded at Captain Nelson while gesturing to the guide to go on, go on, Joe—tell him.

"Ever since *you* land under French nose—last week—and cut down their liberty tree yourself with own ax! Ever since your ship put in and burn French flour mill . . . No?" The Corsican waxed chummy, winked.

The Captain nodded, continuing to smile trustfully. But his eyes grew suddenly wiser. And a recent cut on his back still smarted from a hand-to-hand tussle—but that French swordsman was silenced. Aye, he had been busy in a small way, harassing the remnants of French pocketed along the Corsican coast; enough perhaps to impress these people who, he began to suspect, would cry, "Long live the conqueror!" to all conquerors. His smile gradually faded.

The guide was leading him down an almost invisible path. A herd of wild sheep started, lifting their heads with their sweeping curled horns; flashed away.

"There," the guide pointed ahead, as they broke through the maquis, opened a plain with a tower set on it. The base of the tower flared outward as did the crenelated wall around the top where a cannon, mounted on a wooden swivel, was aimed seaward away from their landward approach. Beyond the tower, which looked like a lost chess piece accidentally dropped on the plain, was the walled town of Bastia: the French stronghold, approximately three miles farther on.

Captain Nelson spun around, motioning his lieutenants to come out of the brush.

"Mr. Andrews, order the men to keep hulls down starboard of this ridge, weather that open wheat field and wear for the tower only when we range within half pistol shot."

"Aye, aye, sir," and Andrews, wheeling smartly, thrust his foot in a vine as he lurched under the branches. There was a crash.

"Stove boat!" A voice from nowhere, but it sounded suspiciously like a volunteer from the village of Burnham Thorpe.

"Silence!" Weatherhead barked as Lieutenant Andrews picked himself up out of the entangling honeysuckle; glared at the faces of the men, all soberly gazing skyward.

"March!" snapped Andrews. "March, you sons of bitches, and bedamned!"

Captain Nelson appeared as outwardly unmoved as the mountains; his humor had to be divided. Andrews was the brother of a girl he had met in France and would have married—except she refused to be the wife of a pauper. The best of lieutenants, Andrews, but he had cut a monstrous caper over that vine. Without a word, the Captain followed the Corsican guides.

They were nimble as billy goats and almost as rank. They held their muskets high. The seamen and marines followed in good order. Lieutenant Andrews limped beside Captain Nelson, who was constantly eyeing the tower and the walled town beyond it, outstepping his lieutenant.

"Now, Meester George," he smiled, "we shall see if Paoli is their leader." He turned to young Andrews, who, still smarting from his fall, brightened under confidence. He had been the Captain's aide to Paoli who after all these months still called George Andrews by the habit of a first error, Meester George, until Captain Nelson had picked it up.

"Aye, aye, sir." Andrews decided the Captain's suddenly tense face did not invite any other answer, as cautiously now, with the Corsicans leading the way, they pushed toward a tiny village surrounding the tower.

The white houses cast intense black shadows on the field. Out of the shadows a knife would flash, or a musket, as Corsicans joined the English and the little army swelled.

Keeping the houses between them and the high stone tower they crept within yards of their objective. The French Tricolor flying from the tower was the only bit of animation in the village. The houses were shuttered. No one was to be seen.

Captain Nelson drew his 1st Lieutenant Hinton and Marine Lieutenant Clarke aside: "The marines must carry the tower and spike the cannon; the seamen, equally divided, will move on the wing of the marines . . . advance silently. . . ."

They were almost in the shadow of the tower. The men were watching their Captain. His sword flashed a white streak above his head.

"Huzza!" And with a bawling of lungs that would have rocked Jericho, they rushed in.

The tower spat musketry once from its embrasures, raising dust and chinking plaster. Then a silence.

"There!" A Corsican leaped up and down upon a rooftop, pointing at the fields. He leveled his musket, fired, as young Weatherhead scrambling up beside him yelled, "The French have abandoned the tower, sir! They're sprinting for Bastia!"

"Down with their rag!"

"And after them!"

While Captain Nelson and Lieutenant Clarke and the handful of marines shoved into the dark tower, ran up the circling stairs, hauled down the flag, Hinton and Andrews led the others after the French, darting from cover to cover. The seamen had fired their pistols one volley, hurled them down, and making their cutlasses whistle through the air took after the flying cockades. And all over the countryside the rocks and the bushes turned to Corsicans, running down to the village, chanting the name of "Paoli!"

Captain Nelson sheathed his sword, his eyes shining. His heart was hammering. Here was an outpost freed for the Corsicans. A countryside roused.

"*Signore!* Admiral!" A crowd circled him. The houses had burst their shutters with Corsicans, men, women and babes, tumbling out, crying and laughing like children. Some caught his hands; kissed them.

"Paoli! Paoli!" The magic mysterious name: "Paoli!" And they took chains from their necks, held up Paoli's miniature. Kissed it. Sank down on their knees; tears choked their whispers:

"*Nostro liberatore!* Paoli!"

The English seamen leaned on their pikes, slowly chewing their quids of tobacco. One had the French Tricolor wadded under his arm. While their young Captain watched the wild homage, the men shook their heads, grinned at one another, pointed out the prettiest girls, but the Captain with his heart and his brain still afire was thinking of *glory!*

He shook his head. This had been just another sortie on the shore. An afternoon's work. But the name they cried was "Paoli. . . ."

And if he had died in the skirmish, dying unknown by an unknown tower . . . "What's the name of this tower?"

"Miomo, *Signore* Captain Admiral!"

"Miomo." He spoke it distinctly, and his full, rather morbid lower lip drooped. "March," he muttered to Hinton. To the Corsican guerrillas: "Miomo is yours. Soon the English will have the big town of Bastia—for Paoli!" And the rafters of Miomo echoed their cheers and their laughter.

Marching back to his ship, he was conscious of being exhausted, yet so alerted as to start at a bird. It was dark, which was just as well. The day's work was done.

"Look, sir!" Andrews pointed west, stopping in his tracks.

A glow was springing up behind the far hills, like a false dawn. There was distant thunder.

"Our fleet's taken it! Lord Hood has moved in, landed the army in San Fiorenzo!" Captain Nelson caught Andrews's hand, wrung it. "Congratulations, Meester George, on the arrival of our army!"

"Nel's full of pranks," grunted one of the seamen.

The *Agamemnon* loomed welcome from the beach as the boats shoved off to her, gritting down the sands.

"The Captain's thanks to you, my lads!"

"May we cheer, sir?"

"Aye."

And they cheered.

❋   ❋   ❋

Captain Nelson was pacing off his quarter-deck, back and forth past the skylight midships that winked facetiously at the sun, unmindful of Captain's moods. On his other hand, marking the limits to the breadth of his walk, were the cannon lashed parallel to the bulwarks. Above them was the sandy-colored line of hammocks carefully stowed in the nettings. The bulwarks made a tunnel of shadow where, through the open ports, he caught glimpses of the sea dashing away, scintillating blue sparks of waves; as if the sea were scurrying, the ship suspended motionless above it. Then the shift of the shadows revealing a flash of red: the cheeks of the gun carriages, the sudden heave of the horizon up, then down again, set all aright. The illusion of suspension in space was gone: *Agamemnon* was on the sea, cleaving it, her rigging a-hum, her great wheel creaking as the master shifted it, and the squeaking of the heavy leather thongs that guided her rudder—all was motion and movement. A restless man could find peace in it.

So Captain Nelson was thinking: One stroke, the countryside around the fortified town of Bastia on the northeast coast of Corsica was roused and declaring for Paoli. The French bottled up.

Second stroke: Admiral Lord Hood had sailed into San Fiorenzo on the other side, the west side, of the island, and landed two thousand troops. Well? The English now had a port from which to maneuver against the French mainland, provided they could drive the French from the main strongholds of Corsica, clear the Corsican coast of their ships.

Captain Nelson, who wanted to get ahead in his profession this war, was very well pleased, so far. Not that what pleased him made a ha'pence worth of difference to anyone on earth, except to his wife and his aging father. It was unfortunate that his career upset her, kept her in nervous hysteria by day and by night—so she said—lest anything happen to him or her son. And that displeased him, for he had never witnessed any such lavish demonstration of affection when he was home although, come to think of it, those five years of peace with nothing on his mind, no worries, no cares, just five quiet years of domestic joy, had been the happiest years of his life—now looking back on them. Poor Fanny, she just did not realize that a poor man could not rise to the top in his profession and still try to dodge shot! And he intended to rise this war!

His face grew harassed as he walked, the grooves around his mouth deepened. At present he was about fiftieth captain in line for promotion to flag rank. Before his name could come up for lowest ranking rear admiral in the navy there must be fifty promotions, either singly or in groups. And then, if he did get his promotion, chances were he would merely get it—and be immediately retired on half pay —so that someone below him with more patronage could have the rank of active rear admiral!

And here he was thirty-five years old! Practically one foot in the grave, half his life, more likely nine tenths of his life gone! And still fiftieth in line! At that dear Fanny would have comforted him that he was better off than most of his contemporaries because he had been posted for flag rank at an early age. But fourteen years a post-captain! Life was too short. He could hear Fanny now: "But old Mr. Marlinspike was sixty years a midshipman, dear, before he was made lieutenant. You know we can't all be great folk. . . ." And that homely bit of philosophy would be enough to goad him into trying!

His eyes had been on the enemy town of Bastia as he ruminated. Now they snapped into focus.

He spun on Lieutenant Hinton, who leaped to attention expecting some sharp reprimand, but the Captain only said, "Set all the sail she will carry, if you please, Mr. Hinton," and to the master, "Keep her course as it is. We will run in on Bastia, Mr. Wilson."

"Aye, aye, sir." The master squared his shoulders. Never a dull moment on *Agamemnon*.

And down through the ranks: "All hands make sail ahoy!" And

the almighty boatswain piped. Though not a gentleman, a boatswain was a petty officer and along with the ship's carpenter one of the most important men on the ship. The boatswain rated a private cabin, and could carry a supple cane to punctuate his commands. Now he flexed it as he piped.

The Captain took another turn as his ship bore down on her objective, while his lieutenants and master bawled his orders. And there went his stepson, Josiah, skipping aloft to his post on the foremast to cheer the hands making sail, encourage them to set a record. As the boy achieved his post in smart time his stepfather smiled. The salt air would cure the lad eventually.

"Set studding sails below and aloft, Mr. Hinton!" His voice soared impatiently, for he had felt a slackening in the wind; the driver sail just above his head had luffed suspiciously. It was a great fore-and-aft sail, left over from Drake's time, and it narrowly missed Mr. Wilson's taller head as he steered.

Hinton was shouting: "Trim sails! Set topgallant studding sails, topmast studdings to hand—rig out the booms—"

Captain Nelson to Mr. Wilson once more: "Keep her as she is *now,* if you *please!* Let her carry the wind down with her."

As *Agamemnon* pushed on under her press of sail he could see a smoother, sluggish patch of water ahead just beginning to ripple, as if a child were blowing on a bowl of milk. The ripples danced higher, cupped and dashed into peaks, and the calm vanished as *Agamemnon* rushed in, a wild sprite teasing the wind to follow her.

Captain Nelson nodded his approval to no one in particular and his thoughts became more peaceful. Lord Hood was a good admiral, if not an overly friendly one. He felt he had the chance of a lifetime here off Bastia, unless Lord Hood allowed one of those innumerable rear admirals basking in the Bay of San Fiorenzo just around the north end of the island to decide it was his spot for glory.

"Opening the town to larboard, sir."

The Captain only nodded in reply and Mr. Wilson reminded himself that the Captain always saw first with those two blue-gray beacons peering every which way!

As *Agamemnon* bore down, ranging daringly close to the shore, Captain Nelson ran up on the poop, peered over the taffrail where the ensign, as big as a sail, flapped and her sternlight swung over her wake like a small glass castle. Captain Nelson was studying his "fleet":

one small frigate, *Romulus* 36, Captain Sutton, and one smaller frigate, *Tartar* 28, Captain Freemantle.

To a lieutenant: "Make signal to *Romulus* and *Tartar* to keep in company to reconnoiter the battery southward of the town."

He was scanning for a place to land the army and besiege Bastia as soon as Lord Hood gave him the sign to go ahead, As he left the poop, he gave his ship a quick over-all glance. From here he could sight, from taffrail to bowsprit. A column of greasy smoke poured out of the galley chimney on the forecastle, close to the carved belfry where the timekeeper was preparing to swing the clapper on the ship's bell. And just aft of the forecastle, his seamen were running along the companions of the waist. As he started down the ladder to the quarter-deck *Agamemnon* rang with the bawling of orders from Captain straight down to the cook's cat, the only member of the crew that kept his mouth shut.

Captain Nelson stayed on the companion overlooking the quarter-deck, where he could see Bastia the better.

Before him, the town, with its tall dazzling white houses ranged like an audience in an amphitheater, terrace on terrace, was backed against the black-green mountains. The ancient citadel stood square in the center, sweeping down and out with a stone keep, like a skirt, that could ricochet balls at crazy angles. The town wall reared higher as the *Agamemnon,* a 64-gun ship, cut a straight wake with a brisk southerly breeze on her stern. She was hauling abreast the first battery south of the town: a halfmoon breastwork of earth and sandbags.

A sudden flash from the shore battery guns splashed orange against green trees. A geyser of water shot up, sprayed *Agamemnon.*

Captain Nelson dropped to the quarter-deck, leaped on a cannon and rested his telescope across the hammocks.

"Back the mizzen topsail! Beat to quarters! The devils are asking for trouble!"

The *Agamemnon* nosed up, and her wake idled from froth to ripples. Captain Nelson hopped down from the gun which must be unlashed and went back to his lookout on the companion. It was unfortunate that God had not made him a taller man, for he was always having to climb up to see out of his ship.

Now to the quickening beat of *Agamemnon's* drums the men scattered to their posts, a helter-skelter mad turmoil resolving into perfect order. The guns were unlashed and cursed and pried around into position, the breechings run through the ring on the pommelion made fast to the bulwarks to keep the crazy things from leaping clear across the deck on the recoil. Up came the pale little boys with cartridges hugged inside their jackets; the buckets of painted shot, unrusted, were set by, the tubs full of sand and water held the long twine matches, soaked in lye, that burned for hours. The Captain sent the keys to the magazines in the hold, deep below the waterline, and up came the powder and more shot. The gunlocks were fitted into the cannon, the tompions wrenched out of the muzzles.

Another flash from shore. A whine and an explosive smack.

The eight men in each gun crew redoubled their efforts as a shower of splinters rained down from aloft, and the black shadows of the sails on the deck were suddenly dotted with flashes of sunlight. A gunner, knotting his silk neckerchief about his ears, glanced aloft, grinned at the sky, blue-black through the shot holes in canvas.

Agamemnon still had not answered. Below in her copper-lined magazines, men in slippers ran about on the felt floor, among the kegs of powder and the chests of cartridges, lighted by lanterns hung behind double glass windows; passed the ammunition into the hands of the big-eyed powder monkeys, mere children who darted up, past the midshipmen whose duty it was to shoot them if they tried to hide. Only the hatches to the magazines were left open. Deck by deck the ship was sealed off. *Agamemnon's* lieutenants, Hinton, Andrews, Spicer, Noble, Weatherhead, strode their stations, worked their crews like cogs in one machine.

Below the gangways of the waist where part of the crew must still tend sails with no protection from shot but a thickness of canvas was the main deck with her long rows of guns. Below that was the lower deck where the ports had just been yawned, and the lanterns set by each gun.

Now the captain of the gun crews ladled the powder, each handling his copper shovel with the deftness of an artist; dropping the cartridge into the hollow handle it fell into position right on top the powder. Next the wads of yarn driven home by the rammer. Then the shot with a loose wad on top of that.

The cannon was loaded, the running tackle had run the gun out of the port. The captain of a cannon took his priming iron, stabbed it into the touchhole, cutting the cartridge; next the quill filled with a paste of powder and wine. The cannon was ready to fire.

A lieutenant running by stopped, eyed the elevation, adjusted the triangular wooden quoin under its breech a notch to depress the muzzle by a degree, gave the nod to the gun captain of the gun crew who was swearing like a sergeant of marines, "Stand clear, you jack-headed skunks!" And with one eye on the powder in the touchhole, his lighted match in hand, the other eye on the roll of the ship . . . he blew his match brighter and brighter, and all along the gun decks other captains did the same. As *Agamemnon* began a slow upward roll of her larboard side . . . "Fire!" The gun captains touched the match to powder, leaped back for their lives as, *flash!* a torch shot up, then blast and the cannon recoiled, thrown back on her breechings.

Agamemnon's broadside had answered. She heeled slightly, as thirty-two of her cannon weighing from a ton to two and a half tons leaped from the deck on the recoil and thudded heavily down. Her sails shivered, and she rolled steady. Captain Nelson peered at the town as she went through the routine again. As the cannons grew hot they leaped higher, fell to the deck with tremendous force that kept the gun crews guessing which way the recoil would veer.

A brown cloud puffed up on the shore. Through the dust came another flash and a shot thudded into *Agamemnon's* hull, creaking the mainmast. A powder monkey hugging his load of explosive cartridges sank to his knees in stark fright, staggered up to the bawling for more cartridges from the crews, grinned sheepishly when he saw he was really alive.

"Carpenter reports the shot was above water, sir."

"Very well." The Captain smiled as men ran by with oakum and wooden plugs to stop shot holes.

And *Agamemnon* answered, her smoke streaming forward with the wind, leaving the shore clear to her sights. And again a brown cloud—but no shore battery. Only small men streaming for cover. A chunk of their cannon falling out of the clouds, shearing them down.

Captain Nelson glanced at the town. The mean black embrasures cut in the wall were beginning to spit. As *Agamemnon* slowly ranged abreast they opened full and from farther back in the town he caught the particular thunder of squat mortars, shelling her.

Now blast and recoil, the *Agamemnon* edged forward, laying her shots in the town. Her wooden walls against stone walls. Wounds cracked open in the faces of houses, corners crumbled, and austere white clouds moved slowly over the hills, sailing indifferently through the blinding blue sky.

And no visible bloodshed. Not a scratch on the seamen.

A doll figure fell on the town wall, and a thin streak crawled down the dazzling stone, as ball after ball scored, pockmarking the wall.

A patch of town went sailing skyward, roared a moment later. Walls buckled out, collapsed. The gun crews shouted cheers to the crashing recoil of their guns. *Agamemnon* had hit a town magazine!

"Something's on the hills, sir!" Young Hoste was screaming though his words sounded like whispers through the blast and recoil.

"What's something?" Captain Nelson raised his glass.

"Redcoats, sir! Looks like."

Here and there on the high green slopes above Bastia appeared strange red dots moving in order.

"It is! It's our army come overland from San Fiorenzo!"

Another cheer carried along the decks. And *Agamemnon* kicked harder against the town wall till her hot cannon on the lower deck began to strike the beams of the main on the recoil and the guardian breechings, reining the guns in position, strained to the limit. And again and again at the insolent Tricolor stiff in the wind, crowning the enemy citadel.

The frigates astern were laying down their shot, so that the broadsides from the battleship and her cruisers struck the town with a pagan syncopation.

"If I had five hundred men I'd storm Bastia!" Captain Nelson muttered, and passed the word for Lieutenant Clarke, whose marines were drawn up like so many red tenpins on the poop. They were momentarily useless, for the range was too great for their musketry. "Scatter your men, Clarke," Captain Nelson snapped, disgusted with useless parade.

Clarke gave the order, returned.

"With a quick blow, storming the town from seaward and two thousand men on their rear . . ." Captain Nelson clapped his hands; rubbed them together.

"They don't seem to be going forward, sir!" Lieutenant Clarke scowled through a glass at the redcoats.

"What a sight they behold from up there!" Captain Nelson laughed, visualizing his fine fighting ship, until he eyed them again.

There the English army stood, like exotic bloom on the crest overlooking the town; a thin scarlet edge on the green.

And there they remained as the wind changed, blew a squally easterly, causing Captain Nelson to cease fire, order his squadron offshore for the night.

❀   ❀   ❀

The red line was there in the morning as a Corsican boat rowed out of a cove toward the English, cheering and hailing.

Up the side came the Corsican guide of a few days before. He was beaming. "You kill good!" He laughed. "The town will rise. They no stand fire. They ready to kill Le Combe St. Michel, the French Commissioner. They massacre him!"

"Bravo! Already?" Captain Nelson was gleeful.

"Soon." The Corsican nodded. "That coward, he hide in the citadel. Say he blow up the town if they rise—otherwise—"

"Otherwise," the Captain nodded, beginning to understand these people.

"We see army above town. All Corsica rise. You kill good. Plenty die. Killed all over Bastia!"

"We aim at the French, not at innocent inhabitants." The parson's son came stiffly to the surface.

The Corsican shrugged. "Maggiore and Corrio no better than French."

"I understood you to say the Corsicans were ready to give up the city to us."

"But true, Admiral! But true. I mean we do not care if you kill Maggiore and Corrio—"

"And Saleri!" boomed a short, even greasier bandit clothed in a badly cured sheepskin. He rattled along in a bastard Italian.

"What's he saying?" from Captain Nelson.

"He say his family kill Saleri. My family kill Maggiore. Maggiore kill—"

"Ah . . ." The Captain's face grew somewhat drawn. War made peculiar allies. "And the French?"

"First we kill French, then—"

"I see."

"Oh, but sad! You kill young girl just seventeen years beautiful.

A Roberti—they kill Maggiore. Too bad. Many people rise. They kill French in citadel some night—perhaps. Yes?"

But the man's words shocked the Captain. He had never killed an innocent noncombatant—a girl—before! "We're sorry about that girl." Tears had surprised his eyes. He frowned, face aging slightly, and brought out the eternal, "Horrors of war . . . You people holding your position above town?"

The Corsican eyed him in amazement. "The French make new batteries. Big one. They push us back unless you land guns. Then all Corsica rise with you. No?"

For a moment their eyes turned on the thin line of redcoats back of the town. They had not moved.

Dismissing the Corsicans, Captain Nelson ordered his ship to close once more on Bastia. On enemy French and Corsican townsmen alike. But ironically, war was legal, recognized by French Terrorists or Englishmen, all nations, as a sure-fire catalytic. "So the sooner the poor devils understand they are doomed to surrender, the better!" the Captain said finally.

The bombardment began again. This time *Agamemnon* ran in closer, until the rush of her hull cutting water echoed against the town wall that was spouting its constantly changing rosettes of bright fire and shreds of black smoke.

Still the Tricolor taunted them over the citadel, and the English army beyond seemed to have rooted to the hilltops.

"The army moves slowly. . . ." Captain Nelson was pacing with 1st Lieutenant Hinton, whose neat uniform and great height made him look more like a captain at first glance. "We could have Bastia in no time at all. These generals have their methods"—the Captain paused to allow the crash of recoil to pass before going on—"but damned if they'll take a town at that rate!"

"They were at Gibraltar when they should have been at Toulon, now they're on the heights—at least they're in the vicinity of war, sir." Lieutenant Hinton grinned.

"That may be enough for them," the Captain smiled.

Agamemnon had made the slow run of the wall.

"Wear ship!" the Captain sang out. He'd give Bastia a taste of his starboard guns now. But *Agamemnon* shivered, disobeyed, hovering neither here nor there. Her sails sagged slowly. The wind was failing.

"Down helm! Bring her round!"

Agamemnon sulked, and her sails drooped as listlessly as dying hands.

"Damn," Captain Nelson said with remarkable restraint. *Agamemnon's* broadsides could not bear on the town. Neither could her stern chasers. As to her bow guns, they pointed at a lone sea gull soaring and dipping, nothing more.

Now Bastia opened up. Shells soared over and shot smacked under the ship. A cloud of spray rolled over the deck. *Agamemnon* shuddered, but budge she would not.

Stark calm.

And from their grand encampment on the hilltop, the English army never sallied, while *Agamemnon* wallowed like an old sow with her feet in her trough and could not answer one enemy shot.

Inwardly seething, Captain Nelson ran down the ladder to the main deck, to cheer his men.

"We'll save our shot," he called out to the whine of a shell careening over their heads, "and give them double tomorrow."

The men cheered. Forward on the main deck the captain of a gun crew, his face pimpled with "grog blossoms," was creeping toward a cannon while his crew stood back watching him tensely. The silence traveled along the deck, in spite of the enemy fire. Captain Nelson stopped in his tracks, waiting.

The gun captain had reached the cannon and with set jaw was lifting a powder quill out of the gun's touchhole. With fingers as sensitive as a thief's he retrieved it and leaped back. Still nothing happened. The men suddenly grinned and whistled relief. It wouldn't have attracted so much attention in battle—cannon often misfired; but now in a lull it would have been rather messy to see the gun captain smashed to a pulp by a stray spark taking a notion to light after all.

Captain Nelson had turned away after giving the gun captain a congratulatory nod. He had seen the new flintlocks for cannon that would fire by pulling a lanyard at a safe distance. It would be some time before he or anyone else in the navy could persuade his gunners to forgo the glory of being blown up; use what they sneeringly considered a lazy invention of the devil. It would save men. . . . He had stooped to peer from the open port toward the town. He caught a flashing of bayonets.

"What the devil . . . ?"

A long line of French soldiers was moving out from the town of Bastia. Captain Nelson went back to the quarter-deck. He wanted a better view, and to crane one's head from a port was giving the enemy a soft target.

Within half an hour a wave of flame licked over the countryside, while *Agamemnon's* sails still hung lifeless, and now and then bits of rope and canvas showered down on her deck. So far the French had not given her one smart shot, but the French army in Bastia had taken advantage of her position to make a sortie.

"Miomo still stands, sir!"—hollered down from the tops.

"And that is where we will land," Captain Nelson gritted, "when this siege commences."

But his eyes narrowed, running the red line on the hilltops. An English army had not moved to stop the French.

On the third day, the redcoats were still on the heights, and the Tricolor flew jauntily over Bastia's citadel. But with a fresh friendly breeze, *Agamemnon* was back, behaving like a lady, running the gantlet of sea wall again: puffing and roaring and knocking down the French batteries thrown up during yesterday's calm.

"Deck there, Admiral Lord Hood with five sail in sight to leeward, sir!"

For a moment Captain Nelson's hopes rose. This was it! The joint land-sea attack. "Masthead, keep your eyes peeled for Admiral's signals!"

Though he itched to join the Admiral, find out the latest news, he dogged the shore, keeping Bastia under fire. A low mist hid the heights when the sun went down. Lord Hood's *Victory* was still just in sight, hull down, topsails like pink shells floating on the water.

❅   ❅   ❅

Captain Nelson was in his cabin making out a report. There had been an odd sideways slipping of his ship when he got up a little earlier than his usual four o'clock—an hour that was cursed even by an early rising navy, cursed by everyone except sprightly Captain Nelson, who liked to make the most of time. Instead of his servant, Frank Lepee, waking him, proffering coffee to soothe the pain of rising, the Captain would be up, fresh as a daisy, when Frank staggered in, bleary-eyed, and sullenly went about breakfast.

Now while the Captain very delicately and thoughtfully waited for

Frank to shake off his morning gloom, he studied the boatswain's and carpenter's reports: fuel, wine, beef, pork, flour, water—foul—and way down. Ropes, nails, hoops. *Agamemnon* had run out of everything, down again to her last biscuit. There had been a long thin red worm in the cheese yesterday.

But the worst of it was, with stores consumed, *Agamemnon* was growing light, riding too high, a little more and a little more each day. She would be difficult to handle inshore soon, for she would not hold her side to the wind. He would have to apply for leave to run in to Leghorn just when things were beginning to look up here off Bastia. He'd postpone it as long as he could.

There was a smart rap on the door. Josiah's rap.

"Lord Hood making your signal to come aboard—got any newspapers for me to read?"

"Acknowledge the signal, Josiah. And tell Hoste to be ready to go with me."

Josiah ducked out, was back in a few moments. He sank down in a chair, picked up a three-month-old *London Mirror*. He thumbed it, turning from news to the section *Memoranda Dramatica,* to see what was going on in the London theaters. Josiah had certain privileges in private. "Why can't I go with you to see that old fuddy-duddy?"

The Captain laughed before he could stop himself, then coughed sternly. "Don't be disrespectful. It's Hoste's turn. After all, other mids think it an honor also."

"You can skip the honor, just set me down at the Admiral's dinner. Aren't I your family? Haven't I any rights?"

Captain Nelson tried to overlook these sudden flares of jealousy. "Oh, come, take your turn like a sport."

"Listen to this." Josiah was turning the pages of the gazette, refusing to answer or to back down. "At Drury Lane: 'Terpsichore's Return—a ballet. Mademoiselle Parisot certainly astonishes us as an Attitudinarian, but does not afford much delight as a dancer. Pan is called in to make love to Terpsichore, the constitutional warmth of that Deity is well known, and on the stage his amours are generally rendered offen—' "

"Josiah!" Captain Nelson had taken his uncle's sword from its rack, hardly heeding, while Frank came in flicking the last speck of dust from his full dress coat and scowling at the tarnished gold braid that nothing would brighten.

Josiah read on to himself, grinning. "Haw! Haw!" He tossed the gazette across the cabin. "It says, 'The goat, too, was disgusting!'"

"Don't you have watch, my dear boy, at this moment?" His stepfather had slid out of his dressing gown and stood for a moment in his shirt sleeves eyeing his stepson. Frank Lepee appeared to notice nothing; he moved like a zombi. It took practice to be a captain's manservant.

Josiah only yawned, stamped his stepfather's seal on the palm of his hand. Tossed it aside, picked up a stick of sealing wax. Snapped it in two. "I'm going with you to Lord Hood."

Captain Nelson waited till Frank withdrew for a moment, before losing his temper. "Go to your post!"

Josiah looked up amazed. He could no longer recognize the man who had always been willing to humor and coax his every mood. And suddenly he hated him. "Go on, take Hoste, and I hope to God you break your damn neck. Go to hell! Hell! Hell!" For an instant he threatened to throw himself down, kick and scream. His stepfather was staring at him aghast.

Both were white.

"You'd better take a perch aloft, Josiah, cool off." His stepfather's voice was hard as flint, but not loud. He started past the boy toward the door.

Josiah suddenly burst into tears, his face purple. "Aye, aye, sir." He was swallowing, his voice broken. "I—I—" He caught his stepfather's arm. His face was hopelessly bewildered. "I didn't mean that! Honest I didn't. It's—you're all I've got—Mother never—I'm sorry, *Father?*"

His stepfather smiled slowly. "Run along. . . ."

The Captain shook his head wearily as Josiah went out. He honestly loved the boy, but . . . and he'd borrowed money, when he was already in debt to his ears, to fill out Josiah's pay. So! By God! Josiah would get ahead in the navy if it killed them both!

❋   ❋   ❋

Josiah was watching from his perch astride a spar when the Captain, with young William Hoste, who rose hourly in the Captain's eyes by comparison to his stepson, pulled away, rowing for H.M.S. *Victory.*

At last Josiah slid down a stay, avoiding any lieutenant who might give him an order, and made for the Captain's cabin. The sentry, who dreaded the possibility of making trouble with the Captain's protégé, let him pass. Josiah found Frank putting the Captain's effects in order.

"Damn you, Frank, come here!" Josiah yelled.

"Aye, aye, sir." Frank straightened. He had been the Captain's servant in the West Indies and knew this boy from way back. Frank had nursed the Captain through fever, fought off mosquitoes, watched the Captain fall in love with that Commissioner Moutray's wife, hopelessly in love like a gentleman, and knowing the whole situation was impossible, break his heart because she and her husband went back to England. . . . Frank looked straight at Josiah, who was standing without saying a word, forcing Frank to stay at attention, apparently trying to cow him.

So the Captain had to fall in love with Mrs. Nisbet on the rebound, Frank, who was worldly, had suspected. Not that Frank disliked *her*. She was a lady, but her brat . . . used to lording it over black slaves . . . Frank continued to stare unblinking at the cocky youngster in front of him.

"Sing that song, Frank, you used to sing," Josiah hissed. "The one about 'Come join . . .' Sing it, damn you!"

Frank sang woodenly:

> All you that have bad masters,
> And cannot get your due,
> Come, come, my brave boys,
> And join our ship's crew!

And when he finished Josiah hit him across the face. "Sing it again!"

"Aye, aye, sir." Frank's eyes flickered but he held himself in check. "Beggin' pardon, sir," he coughed.

"Sing!"

"My throat, sir, may I oil it, sir?" Frank slid a bottle out from under his coat.

Josiah held out his hand. "Give me half or I'll report you for having it and see you flogged."

"Aye, aye, sir." Frank handed him the bottle. Josiah uncorked it and swallowed his half on the spot. Frank was grinning slyly. Rum was illegal for boys, but a man had to protect himself somehow.

Josiah walked rather unsteadily to his stepfather's cot.

"Sit down, Frank." He waved his hand toward a chair.

"Aye, aye, sir." Frank sat gingerly.

"Now we will both sing," Josiah announced.

And they sang till Lieutenant Hinton routed them, sent Josiah aloft and ordered Frank's grog stopped for a week for behaving disrespectfully, sitting in the presence of a midshipman. Hinton didn't feel too hard on Frank, but he would have liked to lash Josiah spread-eagle to the shrouds. But even he felt a certain diffidence toward the Captain's protégé.

The word got about the ship, however, that Josiah could be had.

❅   ❅   ❅

Captain Nelson, rowing closer to the *Victory,* was reminded just how small *Agamemnon* was. A fine old ship, *Victory,* a favorite of admirals for nearly thirty years, with her comfortable officers' quarters, her hundred guns: everything a captain might dream of in a ship.

The sight of Lord Hood's red flag flying over her, bright against the early morning sky, casting a rippling pool of red in the water lapping her copper bottom, reminded Captain Nelson he could reconcile himself, thanks to Lord Hood's speech, never to expect the King of England's favor!

He had learned two things the hard way: that patronage could be but an empty keg for a poor young man, and to undertake to enforce English law against powerful English merchants and in spite of cautious admirals was to bring down the wrath of all officialdom on his young head.

"William," he said very soberly to his midshipman, lifting his head to the sea breeze, squinting over the silver tips of the waves at the dark side of *Victory,* "there are three things which you are constantly to bear in mind."

Young Hoste had been chattering to the Captain about all his studies, now he sat up very straight. "Aye, aye, sir?" Remembering that perhaps he should not have been talking so much. Hoste's father was a parson, just as Weatherhead's, and Hoste appreciated his chance to go to sea, entered as a mid, for he pitied the other boys aboard ship, just his own age, the powder monkeys and the like whom the government saved from starving in the streets by herding them into the navy.

"First, William, you must *always implicitly obey orders, without attempting to form any opinion of your own respecting their propriety.*"

"Aye, aye, sir."

"As a matter of fact, you're doing very well. Secondly, you must consider every man your enemy who speaks ill of your King; and thirdly, you must hate a Frenchman as you do the devil."

"Aye, aye, sir."

And the sound of Hoste's answer, neither servile nor surly, was a balm to Captain Nelson's spirits.

✻   ✻   ✻

The moment Captain Nelson's foot touched the *Victory's* deck and he saluted the quarter-deck, he felt her massive weight, settled comfortably in the water. Her steadiness, her three gun decks, all reminded him of how high and long the climb must be from captain of a small third-rate battleship to commander in chief of a fleet. It had taken him twenty-three years to reach *Agamemnon!*

Summoned to go to Lord Hood, he descended the ladder and turning aft on the deck below the captain's poop cabin, passed between sentries down a narrow corridor, past various staterooms, to the suite of the Commander in Chief. Coming out of the dark corridor with its canvas-covered decks painted like blocks of black and white marble, he entered the grand cabin, where the morning sun, flashing on the long row of *Victory's* stern windows, nearly blinded him. He made his bow to the dark silhouette of Lord Hood.

Lord Hood received him distractedly, barely muttering a "Good morning," as he motioned Captain Nelson to sit down in one of the heavy chairs by the stationary table.

Something was afoot, for not a rear admiral's inquisitive nose was to be seen. Not even a senior captain's. That meant more than courtesy, it was an acknowledgment that Captain Nelson was considered to be in sole command of his station off Bastia.

He waited for the Admiral to speak, knowing too well that it was useless to try to breach this bastion with anything but the utmost respect.

The Admiral was a big man, about seventy, florid in the well-fed naval tradition, white-haired. He had determined eyes and the unexpressive, somewhat stubborn face of a bird of prey.

He had a long career behind him, not inglorious. Beside his work as second in command under Rodney at Dominica when they defeated de Grasse and then had a legal battle with each other, Hood accusing Rodney of gross negligence and greed for prize money rather than a complete victory, Hood swearing he'd rather collect goat droppings than serve Rodney! Hood had fought one battle of his very own in his day. While not a complete victory exactly, it had been a fairly "smart action." And to command one battle in a lifetime in these modern eighteenth-century days of civilized warfare was enough to make a man immortal and titled as well. As Captain Nelson had never seen a major battle, Hood's career seemed enviable.

"Well, Captain Nelson? How goes Bastia?" Lord Hood lifted his unpowdered head, and the light crowned his hair with a silver halo. Though he was not smiling, his glance was favorable.

"We have done considerable damage, my lord, and from accounts brought out by Corsicans the city is in a turmoil. Indeed, my lord"— Captain Nelson edged forward in his chair—"if the army were to attack, I have no doubt Bastia would be ours. Last Sunday when our reconnoitering turned into a brush with them, I was ready and willing, had I five hundred men, to storm the wall. And by all accounts they expected us!"

Lord Hood smiled, priding himself that his early recognition of this young man's intellect had not guttered out, and feeling certain that having left Captain Nelson with his face to the wall without a ship for five years had tamed him. A tight rein was all this Nelson needed. He was straight, pathetically honest, eager, but stubbornly and naïvely indifferent to his own best interests when it came to politics!

"I have a few letters for you to read." The Admiral held them out. "Our army has marched back over the island to San Fiorenzo."

"My lord!" Captain Nelson stared at Hood, then raced through the letters; gazed up, his face mingling perplexity and utter disgust. He put his finger on a paragraph. "Our *brave* General Dundas says: 'after mature consideration, and personal inspection for several days of all circumstances, local as well as others, he considers the siege of Bastia, with our present means and force, to be a most *visionary and rash* attempt, such as no Officer could be justified in undertaking—' He's— he's—*wrong!*" Captain Nelson, who had sadly written his report to Hood of killing a girl, was on his feet, eyes blazing. "What the General could have seen to make him retreat—my lord, what would the immortal Wolfe have done? As he did, beat the enemy, if he perished in the attempt!" He paced from the starboard to the larboard cannon and back again.

"You read the other letter? Paoli says, 'Captain Nelson will be in

Bastia before the army has pitched its tents!'" Lord Hood grunted. "And *I* resent Dundas's opinion! Being given neither to rash nor to visionary judgments!"

"My lord"—Captain Nelson sat down again in his chair, leaned toward the Admiral. "With *Agamemnon* and her frigates lying against the town wall for a few hours, and with five hundred troops—our own marines—ready to land when we had battered down the sea wall, we could certainly carry the place!"

"My dear Nelson, I appreciate your zeal, but with an army of two thousand men sent here for that purpose, now lying idle, it would be too great a sacrifice in trained seamen and ships, of which you know we have none too many!"

Captain Nelson listened politely, then burst out again. "If your lordship will pardon my mentioning it, my men mind shot no more than peas. We have had miraculous luck and are ready to serve. And as far as Bastia is concerned, though the enemy still retained the heights, we, holding the town, could soon force them to surrender by cutting them off to starve."

Lord Hood nodded, not too pleased to have Captain Nelson trying to influence him. . . . "We must be patient. Our gallant General Dundas has announced he is going home. That may take care of his statement, 'circumstances, local as well as others'—possibly."

"And meantime, my lord—"

"Meantime we will wait for the new general, d'Aubant. I expect him hourly from Gibraltar."

"Pray, if your lordship will—"

"However—" Lord Hood held the floor, in spite of all Captain Nelson's maneuvers—"certain officers still remain with the army who no doubt influenced General Dundas. Still, I hope for more from General d'Aubant."

Their eyes met. "God knows what it all means!" Captain Nelson muttered and let it go at that.

"By the way, how's your ship?"

"Splendid, my lord, a bit light, but we'll manage somehow until we find an opportunity to run to Leghorn."

"She's only a sixty-four, of course." Lord Hood eyed Captain Nelson shrewdly.

"But very fast, if your lordship will pardon my mentioning it. And my officers and jacks are the best in the world."

"In the world? All of them. Well, that is unusual."

"I wouldn't trade any of them, my lord."

Lord Hood smiled. This Nelson always praised his geese as if they were swans. "You could use a larger ship, say a seventy-four? There'll be a vacancy."

"Your lordship does me great honor. . . ." The Captain hesitated. He knew the ship Lord Hood had in mind; and its faults. *Agamemnon* had grown like an instrument in his hands. He might have to give up all his officers and men. A larger ship would have nothing to do with his promotion, that was a matter of time and subtraction. He framed his answer carefully. "If your lordship will forgive me, and if it will in no way compromise your plans, thank you, but I shall stay with *Agamemnon*."

Lord Hood nodded. He was not pleased. "As you will, of course. Perhaps you are right." Yet there was an edge in his tone, a definite disappointment. He had a frigate captain, Hunt, who had just lost a ship and he had hoped to juggle the fleet a bit, give him another opportunity, as well as a boost to a battleship. He could not insist. The *Agamemnon* was Nelson's by commission from the Admiralty, and a shipwreck, such as Captain Hunt's, was a black mark against a man. So he must do what he could for his favorite subtly. "*Agamemnon* is a deadly little toy. You will dine with me, my dear Nelson?"

"Thank you, my lord, with pleasure." Captain Nelson rose at the same moment as the Admiral, alert to the minutest details of his deportment now that he sensed Lord Hood was not too happy about the ships.

"You'll continue blockading Bastia, Captain Nelson. Perhaps we can starve the devils. And we'll hope for a fighting heart in the new general."

"Aye, my lord." Captain Nelson stepped nimbly out of his way, bowing his Admiral ahead of him. "And if we had a few gunboats, my lord," he pleaded to the receding back of the Commander in Chief, "the town would not only starve, it would not sleep nights!"

This finally wrung a chuckle from Hood. "We shall see what may be done to keep you from being bored."

❈   ❈   ❈

General d'Aubant expected hourly. Weeks went by. *Agamemnon* had time to go to Leghorn and back again. And then the hourly expected hour: General d'Aubant arrived and hurriedly consulted with the English army officers already stationed in Corsica.

An announcement expected hourly. *Agamemnon* frisked around the north end of the island into San Fiorenzo. Captain Nelson had been summoned to witness the decision.

Below deck in the handsome cabins of *Victory,* Lord Hood, Sir Gilbert Elliot, and Captain Nelson received Colonel John Moore, the General's aide.

After two months' delay, two months' starvation and bombardment of Bastia, the Colonel read the army's announcement: " 'General d'Aubant will not entangle himself in any co-operation,' my lord."

"Sir!" Lord Hood came up like a harpooned whale, thrashing his flukes, blowing high to the delight of Captain Nelson basking in the sudden spray of action. "Sir!" And down came Hood's fist; feathered quills fluttered in the inkstand. "I am ready and willing to undertake the reduction of Bastia at my own risk, with the force and means at present here! Indeed, sir, I am strongly impressed with the necessity of it. Unless we have Corsica for a base, our country must resign the Mediterranean Sea to the enemy. Our commercial convoys will be harassed and plundered by French privateers as well as by the whole French fleet lying at anchor in Toulon!" Lord Hood sat down again.

A bow from Colonel Moore and a rather amused smile. Perhaps it pleased him to wring an admission from Hood: the French fleet had not been destroyed at the evacuation of Toulon! Sir Sidney Smith had boasted and having told his story first, it stuck, and the world had hailed him, only to learn the firing of the French fleet, once in Hood's possession, was really superficial and quickly extinguished by the revolutionists. The world was puzzled; the army guffawing; the navy embarrassed.

Whatever it was that amused Moore, the smile was polite. Moore, as everyone knew, had strong political backing from the days when his own special patrons, among them H.R.H. the Duke of York, the elder and more astute brother of Captain Nelson's gay and blundering Duke of Clarence, saw fit to push Moore into Parliament. To Captain Nelson, eyeing Colonel Moore hostilely, this brother Englishman sent here to fight showed nothing but a cold-blooded will to break the naval Commander in Chief, or was it the new Viceroy? It did not appear to matter if the delay added years to the war; apparently there were more advantageous stakes to be gained. Perhaps time and the seas and other battlefields would decide the issue. But Captain Nelson had made up his mind: he loathed and distrusted Colonel John Moore.

With an utterly unperturbed bow, Moore withdrew and Captain Nelson leaped to his feet to congratulate his commander.

"Forgive me, my lord, but we can land to the north of Bastia. I walked that Colonel all over the ground last week, and though he wouldn't speak, his other officers did. My lord, they agreed Miomo is exactly the spot to land!"

And in his corner sat Sir Gilbert Elliot, nodding thoughtfully, sizing up the various officers, still waiting for the hour when he would be proclaimed Viceroy of Corsica.

"I am convinced," he said dryly, "that the people of Corsica are loyal to us, more so, I might say, than some Englishmen."

There was an awkward pause. He went on thoughtfully, "I have already been led to suspect that certain negotiations between our recently departed messenger and certain Corsicans are going on."

"Paoli?" Hood asked bluntly. "I don't trust him either. Not since I heard that he turned down an offer by a young Corsican friend of his who swore he could lead an uprising right within the French garrisons. Free Corsica in a day!"

Sir Gilbert nodded. "Paoli, I hear, made one of his usual speeches about mankind moving away from dreams of world domination— away from the times of Plutarch! That young officer, I hear, was too brilliant. No, I don't trust Paoli."

Captain Nelson glanced up amazed, remembering the cries of "Paoli . . ." and the kind letter from Paoli to Hood just a few weeks ago, praising Nelson. He kept very still. This was beyond his depth, supposedly, as a subordinate. But he listened.

"To be perfectly frank, my lord"—Sir Gilbert turned to Hood— "there is a three-cornered play for power right under our noses. Two generals have refused to carry out the commands of their country and only an all-powerful motive could persuade such an action. As to Paoli. He plays a lone hand. He wants to be King of Corsica and is the natural enemy of any young Corsican officer—lieutenant or General Brogio—and of our King, His Majesty George III."

Well. Captain Nelson was turning it all in his mind, from this angle and that. All he wanted out of the tangle was a victorious peace for

England. That seemed to be logical, but he was beginning to think it was peculiar only to himself to ask so little.

"I have made my decision," Lord Hood said. "We will act, Captain Nelson?"

He came out of his musings with a start of delight. "All or nothing, my lord!"

Lord Hood nodded. "Oh, and my dear Nelson." He spoke in that inspired tone of a man who pretends he has just remembered something that has really been weighing on his mind. While Sir Gilbert sat back, watching the two very astutely as Lord Hood said, "You will have complete naval command on shore, of course, jointly with Colonel Villettes of our naval marines, but I'll send young Captain Hunt along with you. Since losing his frigate he has been anxious for action. He will be entirely under your orders, but I will be eternally obliged, my dear Nelson, if you will give him all the opportunity for advancement he deserves. You do me a great favor, Nelson."

"With pleasure, my lord!" Captain Nelson smiled, though he didn't feel like it. Hunt had entered the service four years ago as a midshipman. He was not popular, nor very smart, and though it usually took four years for a mid to be made lieutenant, Hunt was already a post-captain with a shipwreck on his record, so he was being pushed on— toward what? The safety of an Admiralty post?

From Frediani, Corsican officer in command of guerrillas, to Captain Nelson: "I arrived at camp extremely fatigued and found myself overwhelmed with difficulties; but the arrival of my secretary with the news, that you were to command the squadron, and the seamen who are landed, set all right again, and I seemed to have suffered nothing; for I shall now have the comfort of being associated with you and Mr. George in the assault: victory is in consequence certain. . . . It is the first of my wishes to learn under the auspices of your courage, the art of making war. . . ."

Bastia had starved by day, lain sleepless through long nights while English longboats rowed guard, oars muffled in canvas, to prevent any French reinforcements from landing; any but English gunboats closing under the wall. And in the dark the English gunboat mortars squatted like monstrous green frogs, all encrusted with arabesques of lovingly wrought artistry, their wide mouths coughing shells into the town.

Under cover of this bombardment, through the thick dark lying languidly over the heaving black sea, Nelson's ships sailed close to the shore, and just before dawn disgorged boatload after boatload of the navy's marines, eight hundred in all, and four hundred seamen.

The Corsicans were watching anxiously from the rocks as the surf drained from their ankles. And Corsicans sent the whispered word through the trackless island: the English had landed by Miomo Tower!

By daybreak sweat had already streaked the arched backs of the seamen dragging their cannon on sledges. Captain Nelson, his face relaxed and contented, was eyeing the slopes that challenged his guns.

Hinton saluting: "May I suggest we secure straps round those rocks, sir, fasten the straps to our most powerful tackle, and with the cannon on the sledge pointed uphill at one end of the tackle and the jacks on the other end, pulling downhill . . ."

"Very good."

And the cannon slowly edged forward.

Axes rang through the woods, and from a rock overlooking the camp site, naval Captain Nelson and naval marine Colonel Villettes eyed the enemy French and calculated the sites for batteries in the first parallel. Little by little these parallel lines of batteries would close on the town.

Below them the seamen were felling trees in a great circle around the camp, for an abatis: the branches thrust outward, the tip of each branch hacked to a spear point. Tree piled upon tree until the locked mass presented a giant bramble around the camp that an enemy would hesitate to storm. All day and all night the trees fell, and the ship cannons, each weighing as much as two and a half tons, lurched and screeched an inch at a time to the muscle-torn wrenching and hauling of the jacks.

An army lieutenant watched a gun teetering over a rocky embankment, backsliding, hauled up again. "So that's the way the navy moves on land! And not a horse or a mule to be had!"

"Oh, we seamen take things as they come," Captain Nelson beamed. "Including you army volunteers who have our heartfelt thanks, Mr. Duncan."

"Oh, I wouldn't have missed it for all the whist and pipes of a quiet afternoon back in camp—not even for Rosita the queen of the camp women!"

"Right!" Captain Nelson nodded. "This is the field for glory."

Lieutenant Duncan mulled the last rather whimsically smiling; nevertheless he had been one of the officers who had accepted Captain Nelson's invitation to reconnoiter Bastia along with Colonel Moore, and after studying the situation was one of fifty officers and men out of the army's two thousand who had volunteered to assist the navy. Moore, it seemed, preferred to sulk in his tent over in San Fiorenzo.

So this was a sailor's siege, with a handful of red-coated red-blooded English army men thrown in. Spars and sails were stretched into tents for stores. Every moment was worked. For while as yet no shot had been fired from Bastia where the gunboats drew the enemy's attention, how long could the Corsican guerrillas, now under the command of Frediani, prevent French sorties, how long before the first English battery could be built to train a gun on the citadel? It was somewhat rash, perhaps somewhat visionary, but it was under way.

On the fifth night when every seaman's muscles felt permanently wrenched, feet blistered to blood, eyes aching for sleep, Captain Nelson sat writing his reports to Lord Hood by the light of an exhausted candle. The glow did not even touch the near slopes of his tent, but danced over its melting cup of tallow, making more smoke than flame. Captain Nelson looked up wondering where he would find another; was about to send for Frank when something whined over his tent, smacked the sentry rock above it, sending down a shower of rubble and rocks.

"Beat the alarm!" He blew out the candle, ran out.

With the rolling of drums, men stumbling to their stations, it came like a spring gale. Enemy shots ripped the tents, tore up freshly dug breastworks, gouged holes in the new roads. Shot they could not answer; the first battery still was not done.

"No one hurt, sir," Lieutenant Andrews, his eyes red from sleeplessness, announced at daybreak.

But no Englishman had slept that night. "Take an order to Captain

Hunt to send more men up here." Captain Nelson handed Andrews
a paper as the enemy guns slowly ceased fire, and the men went to
work lugging sandbags in long slender lines, bringing up powder.
"Stow that cigar, for God's sake!" he shouted at a Corsican who had
come into camp and was reclining against a tree, watching the powder
go by.

"Begging pardon, sir"—Lieutenant Andrews had still hovered—"but
may I suggest you word that, 'Captain Nelson *requests* Captain Hunt
to send more seamen'?" Andrews's face was slowly turning red.

"All right, request. Our battery opens today. Mr. Weatherhead, tell
John Corse over there—no smoking in camp. Let him chew if he must
have the filthy stuff."

"Aye, aye, sir." Weatherhead sprinted off, grinning to himself. If
the Captain had his way seamen would have neither rum nor tobacco,
just a nice light wine now and then. But that would cause mutiny
more quickly than hanging and flogging.

Captain Nelson had taken the paper from Andrews and was fumbling for a pencil. "Andrews, what the devil did you mean? Has
Hunt countermanded my orders?"

Andrews turned even more red. "Captain Hunt has hinted, begging
your pardon, sir, that he—" Andrews swallowed—"*he* gives the orders
to the seamen, sir. He, well, he blew up, sir, to me, making it clear,
sir, that while you are, as he says, 'attached to the batteries,' he commands the seamen."

"Well, I'll be damned! Very well, humor him, Andrews. We shall
say, 'Captain Nelson *requests*—'" He rewrote the order, paused.
"And what about my own ship?"

"He claims that, too, sir. . . . He's after all he can get, sir," Andrews
snorted.

"Indeed? Very well. Only let us get on with this war!" Handing
Andrews the new "request" the Captain stalked away. He'd have a
word with young Hunt, his junior in rank, if ever Hunt came ashore!
And a word with Lord Hood if need be. But as Hunt never came
ashore and Captain Nelson stayed "attached to the batteries," and as
Lord Hood replied cordially to Captain Nelson's delicate and circum-
spect query that, of course, my that Nelson commanded Hunt . . .
well, that seemed to be that. He would not give Hunt the opportunity
to run to Lord Hood to say Captain Nelson was bickering over a
matter of form; in fact he'd keep clear of Hunt so long as Lord Hood

knew which man commanded. And in a corner of his mind he recalled Sir Gilbert Elliot. He had a witness: though it was not his place to summon so exalted an emissary of the King, still it pleased him.

❊   ❊   ❊

From Admiral Lord Hood, commander in chief aboard H.M.S. *Victory,* to the Town of Bastia: a last ethical summons to surrender before firing commenced.

A reply from the French: "We have hot shot for your ships and bayonets for your troops. When two thirds of our troops are killed, I will then trust to the generosity of the English." Signed: "Le Combe St. Michel, Commissioner appointed by the Paris Convention."

As the small French truce ship sailed back into Bastia having answered Lord Hood, the Admiral's red flag broke from the main topgallant mast of *Victory.* A blinding, red, raging signal carrying across the water.

Colonel Villettes and Captain Nelson were watching intently as Lieutenant Duncan, with the patience of a born engineer and artilleryman, pointed the last 24-pounder cannon, just sweated into position. He elevated it higher and higher. At last knocked the quoin out altogether. She could now fire her extreme range: somewhere between 2500 and 2800 yards.

"Got it, sir." He stepped back beaming.

"Lord Hood has hoisted his flag, sir!"—Weatherhead saluting.

"Give the order to hoist ours on the rock, Mr. Weatherhead!" Captain Nelson started to smile. The battery had been finished exactly on schedule.

And as the red flag burst over the gray rock, waved its answer to Hood, there was a roaring "Huzza!" that bounced echoes from slope to slope.

The first battery opened: howitzers, mortars, carronades or "smashers," five 24-pounders, three 12's and a field piece saluted the besieged town.

The siege of Bastia had begun, and with luck and with vigilance and respect to the arts of siegecraft as laid down a hundred years before by a wise old Frenchman, Vauban, the French in Bastia were doomed by the rules of their own arts, printed in all siege textbooks.

❊   ❊   ❊

That evening in his tent, poring over the journal he kept for Lord Hood, a day-by-day account Lord Hood sent home to the Admiralty, Captain Nelson laid down his pen. Stood up. Sat down again. Flung himself on his cot. Sat up again. Clasped his hands and thoughtfully thrust out his lower lip.

A Corsican spy out of Bastia had brought the news there were two thousand more French soldiers in Bastia than had been taken into their calculations. Twice the force they thought they were tackling. Should he tell the Admiral? Or did he dare withhold it? That was the question, for the spy's information did not trouble *him*. He went back to his table, wrote out his report, made no mention of the spy's news. He smiled to himself. Responsibility was like a tonic to him.

❋　　　　　　❋　　　　　　❋

Neither side slept well after that. Yet it was a beautiful Corsican spring. The hillsides were abloom, Corsicans ran into camp with violets tucked in their sashes. Camp women slinked round the dark edges of woods smelling of the shrubs and the herbs they had traveled through. Sometimes bringing a rooster—stolen—or a sack of vegetables to cook for their men. Strange women mixtures of all the nations that had ever "liberated" Corsica.

There was a bracing lift in the breeze off the sea, balmy evenings studded with stars, and blast after blast of cannon in two streams, one arcing out from the town, one arcing out of the batteries. For the batteries seemed to grow up with the eternal urge of all moving things. The growing batteries knocked down outposts. Trenches were dug forward. Up cropped a new battery, closer, like the sudden spewed earth of a gopher. Batteries demolished by the town. Rebuilt. And so, mathematically calculated in engineer's parallels and definitions *ad infinitum,* proceeded a siege. At a cost.

A chance shot from the town blasted English guns, blew gun crews to atoms. Lieutenant Andrews fell, was hospitalized to the fleet. The fire was returned to the town with interest. However, so long as the town and the citadel held outposts the English advancements must be made coyly in the dark. Night was the best time to work, to make the enemy blink in dawn at the new guns coming closer and closer, the fire concentrating harder and harder.

And Frediani's Corsicans co-operated, combing the hills, preventing the French from throwing up new works nearer the English.

Teamwork. An efficient siege, considering that Colonel Villettes and Captain Nelson had the stern disapproval of an army general and an army colonel and two thousand idle Englishmen.

✳   ✳   ✳

Aboard *Agamemnon,* with almost all the senior officers on land, the midshipmen were taking their responsibilities very seriously—most of them. After all it was considered good form to almost hope that one's commanding officer would be killed—honorably that is—so his subordinate might take his place. The mids were very proud to report their efforts to the Captain when he invited them ashore to dine during an occasional lull in the shooting.

But Josiah was cracking his brains, having been assigned to memorize his Step-Great-Uncle Suckling's admonitions to young officers. He had crawled off to his berth in the gunroom having announced he intended to study. The Chaplain had beamed, for he had been feeling uneasy about the five pounds he collected yearly from good Captain Nelson to try to teach lazy-witted, swaggering Mr. Nisbet. It was also the Chaplain's duty to see that the boys did not drink, swear or learn sex perversions. Until they were fifteen the boys were berthed in the gunroom under the supervision of a secretly supervised gunner. After that they were men and moved into the cockpit. Even powder monkeys were not supposed to be allowed to fall victim of seamen's insidious vices. So Josiah, blessed, and apparently reformed, settled himself to study:

To keep a Ship of War in that state which is understood by the expression commonly made use of, "Being in very high Order, or really being a Man of War," the following rules are necessary to be strictly observed by the commanding offi—

Josiah took a deep breath, and another delicious bite of the sacred plum cake he had filched from Hoste's sea chest, washing it down with some tea. He had ordered hot tea from the ship boy who served him, some dirty beggar about his own age who had just received a kick in the stern for serving Mr. Nisbet cold tea, though the galley fire was always out between messes.

"Rule number *one*—" Josiah let out a groan of exhaustion and slept. The next minute something stung him. He leaped up howling, cupping his nose with both hands. A ship biscuit, harder than a rock, was rolling and rattling across the deck out of sight.

"Your watch, Mr. Nisbet," Hoste smiled, eyeing his open sea chest, his beloved cake reduced to rubble, cold tea awash on his clothes.

"Son of a bitch—" Josiah leaped for Hoste's throat.

Hoste left him clutching air as he disappeared up a ladder, gained the main deck, Josiah after; leaped into Jacob's ladder and shot aloft.

Josiah was right on his heels, bawling, "I'll kill you!"

And around and around on the platform of the top they darted, dodged behind the mast, peering this side and that, and around and around again while the ship rocked below and the top tilted like a tray in the hands of a drunken waiter. With a whoop Hoste sprang into the rigging, and shot down a stay, Josiah still after him. Now below, down through the tiers into the stench of the hold, up again to the lower deck. Hoste vaulted the great pipe that ran athwartship, pumped water, but a waister who was swabbing the deck left a slippery patch just then, and Josiah's leap fizzled into a sprawl.

"That'll be watch and watch by the God of War, you—*you*—Mr. Nisbet!" The boatswain's silver whistle chirped as he spoke, for it was still in his beef-red face. While the waister had quietly stowed his mop, sprinkled a few drops of vinegar in the vicinity of the dazed mid, and strolled off to sick bay in the forecastle, where he stayed tending the wounded out of Bastia, and hoping no one would dream he had anything to do with Mr. Nisbet's unfortunate fall.

And Mr. Nisbet stood watch and watch for a week, wondering why everyone in the navy was a potential villain, except himself.

❊   ❊   ❊

Deep in a wood filled with green sunlight, red coats and blue moved under flecking shadows. The general staff: Colonel Villettes, Captain Nelson accompanied by Lieutenant Duncan from the army and Lieutenant Clarke of *Agamemnon's* marines strolled softly together behind the faithful Corsican guide with the green teeth.

Colonel Villettes had been schooled in England, the son of a French-Huguenot family that had been forced to flee France during one of the religio-politico outbursts. Having adopted England, Villettes was more studiedly "English" than Captain Nelson, who was glancing aloft, taking a deep breath now and then, smiling to himself. He was in all his glory, and showed it. "Beautiful day, isn't it?"

"Hhmmmm." The Colonel did not even glance at a leaf.

Between the black-brown trunks of the trees Bastia's walls, her citadel and square towers and stone outposts, lay shroud white, occasionally brushed with golden brown shadows of smoke from her guns.
The peaks of the highest mountains in the distance still held threads
of last winter's snow. Behind, the sea was idly rolling, and over all
streamers of clouds drifted, fringed with sunlight, against the dark
Mediterranean sky.

A whine. A gash opened in the woods. Trees rending to the crash
of a cannon ball.

The party walked on. "Beautiful island!" Captain Nelson mused, as
if they were on a picnic, as they stepped over the still shivering
branches of a broken sapling oak. "I never saw such romantic views!
I wish Mrs. Nelson could see it."

Colonel Villettes nodded. "Any place would look romantic if the
ladies were here. Can't see these diseased mix-breed camp followers
myself either. If the army stays idle much longer we'll have to bury
it."

And another whine. This time a shower of rock tattered the leaves;
one ripped Duncan's coat, did not draw blood. The Corsican guide
swung farther to the right, through the underbrush, putting the top
of a hill between them and the town.

"Take these poor beaten wheat fields," Captain Nelson went on,
"and these untended vineyards. Think what a steady, well-controlled
government will mean. They'll build new roads from the interior.
Their timber is excellent for our ships."

"I understand our agreement provides for a parliamentary setup
similar to Ireland," from Colonel Villettes.

"Yes. That's the plan," from the Captain. "Calls for religious freedom, no new taxation other than their own laws require."

"Irish lot of trouble. Always grumbling about high tariffs. Want to
put a Catholic block in Parliament. Can't appreciate religious freedom
by itself; don't understand us. Impudent," the Colonel muttered.

They had begun to climb, occasionally stopping to consider the best
slopes for laying a new road to bring up supplies.

The Corsican guide lifted his hand. "Now we close." He pointed
ahead. "We come out on ledge—over there."

"Good!" Duncan exclaimed as they stepped from the cover of the
hill to the doubtful protection of the shadows from surrounding trees.
"This ledge must bring us a thousand yards nearer the town."

"They know it good," the Corsican grinned. "They fire here if mouses creeps."

They paced it and studied its possibilities. "We'll need a big breast-work—" the Captain turned to the Colonel—"besides the gun crews we'll need at least a hundred men ready to ward off attack."

The sun was beginning to set. The blue shadows from the hills seemed to promise a safer return than the full light of afternoon.

"We'll have an excellent opportunity to reduce the redoubt of their Camponella from here. What do you say, Clarke?" Captain Nelson stretched out his right arm, pointing at an enemy tower not very distant.

Sputters of smoke and fire came from the tower, brightening in the dusk. Musketry and the deadlier balls and chains of grapeshot, and the vicious langridge (tin canisters of nuts, bolts, scrap iron, and broken links of chain), cracked branches and twigs overhead. Lieutenant Clarke, who was a good head taller than Captain Nelson, had hunched over to sight down the Captain's outstretched arm. Captain Nelson could feel Clarke's breath on his ear. The guide stepped up behind. "Not safe, back."

"From where you are standing, sir, with a long 24-pounder at five degrees elevation . . . yes, it must be nearly two hundred and fif—"

There was a thud; a crack. Clarke slumped on the Captain's shoulder. Nelson, turning, caught him, eased him down to the ground. Clarke cried out, then lay groaning and writhing, his arm and a chunk of his side blown off. The Corsican guide lay dead at his heels, a hole through his chest.

Captain Nelson saw Clarke's blood on his hands, soaking the cuffs of his coat. Overhead the constant snapping and rattling of leaves and twigs; the distant baa-ing of wild sheep.

Colonel Villettes and young Duncan were staring at Captain Nelson, expecting to see him crumple. He returned the stare. A long minute that stretched into infinity; back again.

They were bending over Clarke. "We've got to stop his bleeding—"

"How?" There was just a big bloody hole, nothing to get hold of. Between them they tore up their shirts, and Duncan figured out a make-shift tourniquet. And in all the dark hell of sending for stretchers, seeing Clarke, half mad with pain, carried down to camp, of ordering the Corsican buried, of writing daily reports, of ear-splitting constant fire,

Captain Nelson would start now and then. Why? Why had he—out of those three—by what freak of fate? Fate? No . . . Providence! He said his prayers more gratefully than ever before, and he thought of his wife.

But time drove the shock out of mind.

To the men at the guns it seemed as if nothing would break the siege. Yet guns did move forward; the methods of siegecraft were deadly as days went by to the monotonous timing of steady fire. The French were starving and the English were edging forward.

❀   ❀   ❀

Late one night, Captain Nelson had crawled onto his cot, exhausted but content. The siege was progressing on schedule.

"Frigate afire, sir!" Frank roused him. He sat up groggy. Frank held a lantern. The light blinded him. He shook his head, started up; sleep vanished.

Tumbling out, scrambling up on the sentry rock, they could see a globule of fire rushing at the shore. Flames streamed with the wind; silhouetted the masts and the spars like three crosses that suddenly hurtled down. The fire stood still. The ship had been run aground.

Captain Nelson and his men were running down the beach. The frigate crew was floundering in the surf. Men were wading out, leading them in. The crew was blistered and scorched; eyebrows and cues missing. A tall angular officer staggered ashore. His face was grim.

He stood in the surf staring at his frigate. "Hot shot—out of Bastia—" he gritted to Captain Nelson.

And then she went up like fireworks into the sky.

❀   ❀   ❀

The angular officer turned up in camp a few days later, cleared of blame for losing his frigate. He saluted Nelson.

"Captain Serocold, reporting for battery duty—and if you will, sir, put me as close to those bastards as possible—"

Captain Nelson shook hands, nodded.

And another young captain came ashore. Young Captain Ralph Miller. He had a frigate intact, but he liked to keep busy. Captain Nelson would spy Miller now and then, hunched in the most forward batteries, trying to convert the gun crews to flintlocks and lanyards.

He loved guns. He didn't stay ashore long at a time, but Captain Nelson noticed the gun crews worked better on the days tall, damn good-looking Miller appeared; and each time with some new notion about the powder or the shot.

※ ※ ※

On another ironically beautiful spring afternoon, not long after Andrews and Clarke had been wounded, yet so intense was this time it seemed they had never been there at all, the sentries spotted a flurry of redcoats on the exact spot, high on the strategic ledge overlooking the town, where young Clarke had fallen.

"General d'Aubant and his staff and field officers, sir, and a Corsican guard."

"Damn. . . ." Captain Nelson leveled his glass. He could see his brother Englishmen laughing and chatting together, obviously criticizing the sailor's siege as they pointed here and there.

When the town opened fire on them they retreated, back down the mountainside, across the island clear back to San Fiorenzo. But the town fired on the heights all day and all night.

"Just when we were finishing the road, ready to build our battery up there!" Captain Nelson turned away.

And by the next day the French had desperately pushed forward, thrown up new works in the night, to train closer on the heights the English had hoped to command.

"The natural consequences of the parade of reconnoitering yesterday," Captain Nelson snorted to Colonel Villettes and Captain Serocold over their lunch of warm wine, moldy bread, watery boiled asparagus and a resiliently muscular rooster. "I'll tell you exactly when our brave General d'Aubant will attack the French." He shoved aside his plate. "The day Bastia falls to us! But I'll tell you what I think." His face grew calm, his eyes straight in the Colonel's. "A brave man dies but once, a coward all his life long!"

Serocold stared at his plate. Colonel Villettes grunted, "Great man— Shakespeare. Damn good," as he wrestled with a drumstick clamped between his teeth.

Captain Nelson had not even been aware of misquoting Shakespeare; there are times when thoughts transmitted become return. Captain Nelson went on half to himself: "And we cannot escape death. Should it happen to me in this place, I'd know it was the will of God!

I would not be one of those redcoats over there—I could not be—for anything on this earth!" Suddenly he grinned, and began to eat again. "Sermons! Damme, Colonel, but won't our work be a page in history! Let them sit in their camp! The more glory for our good men."

"Ummm. . . ." The Colonel finally wrenched the meat from the rooster's bones; swallowed it whole. But big, bony Serocold was picking at his plate. There were womanish tears in his eyes. He took another drink.

❄️   ❄️   ❄️

Day after day shells pounded Bastia and Bastia pounded the batteries, but with less effect than before. In the stealth of dark, in a high wind, a small boat had dashed off from the shore. Corsican spies brought the word:

Le Combe St. Michel, the French Commissioner, and two aides had escaped to Capraia, a tiny island not far from Corsica belonging to neutral Genoa.

Bastia then was doomed. The rats had left. But still the town held out, and the English pounded it until Corsicans brought word the town was afraid to give in. Afraid of vengeance. They had put the English to the necessity of taking the walls apart stone by stone, almost, as Johnson once urged Boswell, to crack them with their teeth. The townspeople knew, by the rules of war, that the English whose first summons to surrender had been rejected by Le Combe St. Michel were now under no obligation to spare the inhabitants—man, woman or child. What then? Mass starvation? Suicide? Or prepare to be massacred?

On another dark night, another small boat was not so lucky. Galeazzini, the brother of the mayor of Bastia, fell into English hands along with a boatload of wounded being sent out of the city. Lord Hood returned the wounded to the city with a week's supply of food. A gesture. While Galeazzini was quietly informed that if Bastia surrendered to Hood, neither the Corsicans nor the army would be allowed to plunder the city.

Captain Nelson was on his rounds, going from battery to battery, when he saw the first flash of white. A flag of truce from the citadel.

A weary line of French soldiers marching out of the Camponella and Colonel Villettes and Captain Nelson stood watching, having sent their officers forward; Serocold among them.

A bow.

The French were unarmed.

Handshakes. Weary smiles.

"Bastia is yours."

"Well fought, gentlemen. May Corsica prosper."

And as Serocold reported it to Captain Nelson, Serocold smiled, the inner torment gone out of him.

Below the drifting impeccable clouds on the edge of the black-green mountains, a scarlet speck, another and then another. In the brilliant May sun the whole ridge was abloom with redcoats.

"General d'Aubant, sir, leading his army," from Lieutenant Noble. He did not conceal his sneer.

"And look at them, Noble. Like eagles peering over the edge of the hills. And exactly on schedule. Bravo, General!" Captain Nelson clapped his hands together, smiling exultantly.

And in a delicate still May dawn, in the heart of the conquered white town, the strains of "God Save the King." The French Tricolor drooped, fell slowly, and England's colors were hoisted.

To a "Hip! Hip! Hurrah! Hip! Hip! Hurrah!"

To the march of the British Grenadiers.

Captain Nelson, his heart nearly bursting with glory, stood at attention while four thousand five hundred men laid down their arms to the navy's twelve hundred. . . .

His Excellency, Sir Gilbert Elliot, immediately went to work as H.M. Viceroy to Corsica. He had a warm spot in his heart for young Captain Nelson. He appointed Brogio his adviser on Corsica; Paoli brooded in his eyrie, uninvited to witness or to counsel.

❊   ❊   ❊

From Lord Hood to Captain Nelson: "The Commander-in-Chief returns his best thanks to Captain Nelson, and desires he will present them to Captain Hunt, Captain Serocold . . . as well as to every officer and seaman employed in the reduction of Bastia, for the indefatigable zeal and exertion they have so cheerfully manifested, in the discharge of the very laborious duties committed to them, notwithstanding the various difficulties and disadvantages they have had to struggle with: which could not have been surmounted but by the uncommon spirit and cordial unanimity, that have been so conspicuously displayed; which must give a stamp of reputation to their characters not to be effaced, and will be remembered with gratitude by the Commander-in-Chief to the end of his life."

❋ ❋ ❋

Captain Nelson was on *Victory's* deck waiting for Lord Hood to send for him. He had rowed over from *Agamemnon*, the first time he had been at sea since the beginning of the siege eight weeks before. As he walked he felt the old queasy seasickness threatening him. He must get back his sea legs. There was work to be done. The *Agamemnon* had immediate orders to take on stores and ammunition: to reduce the last fortified town on the island of Corsica—Calvi.

At last Lord Hood appeared on deck instead of sending for him. "Well, my dear Nelson, my heartfelt thanks to you!"

"Thank you, my lord. We shall, my lord, join heart and hand to take Calvi." They paced off the deck together. "May I presume to ask your lordship not to forget young Duncan; he is an excellent officer."

Lord Hood nodded. "Come, that's the hundredth time. No, I shan't forget any of your protégés, my dear Nelson. Eternally grateful to you. And good news! You shall have a new general to work with. D'Aubant is going home!"

"The new general, whoever he may be, will have my most hearty co-operation, my lord." Captain Nelson wanted to ask a favor. An important one. He wanted to ask Lord Hood to give him a Distinguishing Pendant, as was customary for captains on detached services. It would make his next command better understood among his captains. He was entitled to one. He did not dare broach the subject to Hood.

"The new general will be Charles Stuart, the fourth son of the third Earl Bute," Lord Hood announced.

And Captain Nelson winced. "Very good, my lord."

"And I'll send Serocold and Hallowell with you; both excellent captains. You will have complete command of the naval force on shore, just as you have had at Bastia."

"Thank you, my lord. I hope I may always merit your esteem."

"I'm sending young Hunt home with the dispatches—" Lord Hood added just as they parted.

So that as Captain Nelson returned to *Agamemnon* and his proud eyes followed the leaps and tosses of the Union Jack flying over Bastia's citadel, he wondered . . . To carry dispatches was an honor, and it meant a reward of five hundred pounds if the news was of victory, a vacation at home and then reappointment to a new ship, for Captain Hunt. Not that he resented the man, but he had been hoping Lord Hood would give him the chance to pick up some money for once. . . . Anyway, Hunt was gone. Yet as he went aboard *Agamemnon* he still mused. His own situation was not to be described. He was doing the work of a commodore, but he had no pendant, no acknowledgment. Why? And he wrote home: "I am everything to these sieges, yet nothing ostensible."

Never mind. He was grateful for the opportunity for action. Actions could not be hidden. In another month all England would be reading how he commanded the seamen, fought the batteries—with Colonel Villettes, of course—took Bastia from the French.

It would all be in the Admiral's dispatches, published in all the gazettes. And now he was off to command again. He was thankful Lord Hood was once more his friend.

❊   ❊   ❊

Captain Nelson to his wife: ". . . Josiah is very well. He is rough; but I love him. . . ." And not many days later: "I have invited him and Hoste to dinner; *that* lad is a charming boy. . . ." Unfortunately Fanny had lots of time to read between the Captain's candid lines and wonder why her son seldom got more than five words in any one of his stepfather's letters, over and over again: "rough, but I love him. . . ."

I V. Calvi

Summer, 1794

IN FRANCE that summer the Terror was still supreme. Even Robespierre had been guillotined.

Off Corsica, the *Agamemnon* lay alongside the mole at Bastia. It was night and her lights at each quarter were of a macabre blue; like sight without sense, they distorted the shapes they focused upon: turned living flesh gangrenous, made the conn and the binnacle loom like specters. The lights played over the straining windlass, the straining sleepless crew, lending an illusion of mold and decay, heightening the eternal musty smell of slowly rotting timber, rats and food. The lights threw their anemic glow toward the mastheads: the black sky and the stars were all laced together in the network of rigging.

Agamemnon was taking on the last of the stores for the next siege. The davits creaked, their curved arms threatening to break as the last of the ordnance was swung aboard. A bell clanged four times. Midnight.

On the wings of a small frigate, cutting a white wake in a black sea, night signals burning: the French fleet was at sea, heading for Corsica.

A boat rowing alongside *Agamemnon*.

An officer from Lord Hood with instant orders: the English fleet had been summoned from Bastia and San Fiorenzo.

"Avast!" from Captain Nelson. "Overside with the gun!"

One look of dismay passed over the crew, but the long cannon was eased back overside to the mole.

"Clear decks! Overside with the ordnance, Mr. Hinton."

"Aye, aye, sir!"

"Clear the between decks. Signal *Dolphin* to relieve us of stores. Prepare to weigh in half an hour."

As officers and crew scrambled, a soft mutter: "Two hundred tons to unload—like that—"

" 'Alf an hour—that's Nel."

"There's the ordnance in the hold, sir."

"Let it stand!" Captain Nelson dove back in his cabin. All day and all night he had been loading supplies . . . but an imminent battle at sea. He must get under way! He would have to clear the two gun decks in order to fight, but the rest of the ordnance he would take along with him. It might slow up *Agamemnon,* but, with a little skill, she would just have to overcome the difference.

At daybreak, the *Agamemnon* was unmoored and short on her other anchor as Captain Nelson watched the *Victory's* sails fill, and after her, one by one, five other ships of the line.

The six battleships sailed away. Like mountains of ice closing together, sterns flashing gold glances of light toward the shore; all sails set for the chase.

And still *Agamemnon's* winches unwound, the davits groaned as the last of the ordnance went by the board; the ship emptied again, and the fleet sailed to fight without Captain Nelson.

At last the anchor was a-peak.

"Pipe all hands—make sail, ahoy—let fall—sheet home and hoist away!"

"Brace the yards for casting to larboard and heave and aweigh!"

In the warm bright sun a sleepy drummer and a sleepier bantam of a fifer began: "Coil away the hawser" to the steady tramp about the capstan.

"She's aweigh, sir." The officer of the forecastle, the boatswain, to Lieutenant Hinton, who turned to report to the Captain fuming in the lair of his poop cabin. Hinton was wondering whether he would hear blame for inevitable delay, or praise for a really Herculean night's work.

"She's aweigh, sir!" worked wonders on Captain Nelson's stormy face.

"Very good! Won't you have some breakfast with me, Mr. Hinton?"

✳   ✳   ✳

By midafternoon, Lord Hood on *Victory* was listening to the seagoing gourmet's favorite tune: "The Roast Beef of Old England," preparing to leave his quarter-deck to dine, when the *Agamemnon* broke up over the horizon. Like a white feathered arrow shot from a bow she soon ranged within hail, alongside the *Victory,* and taking in sail slowed her pace to the Commander in Chief.

"Good," Lord Hood nodded. "There's Nelson." He turned to his captain. "What do you suppose he did with those stores, Captain Knight?"

"I can't imagine, my lord, but I think he would just as soon eat them as miss a fight."

"Captain Nelson's very impetuous," mused aging Rear Admiral Sir Hyde Parker, First Captain of the Fleet, whose duty it was to oversee all the captains on matters of routine.

Captain Nelson to his wife:

. . . we are now alongside the *Victory,* I pray God we may meet this fleet.

If any accident should happen to me, I am sure my conduct will be such as will entitle you to the Royal favor: not that I have the least idea but I shall return to you, and full of honor; if not, the Lord's will be done. My name shall never be a disgrace to those who may belong to me. The little I have, you know I have given to you, except a small annuity. I wish it was more; but I have never got a farthing dishonestly; it descends from clean hands. Whatever fate awaits me I pray God to bless you, and preserve you for your son's sake. I think always in the most affectionate manner of my Father; tell him so and ever believe me your most affectionate husband.

At peace with the world, Captain Nelson went on deck hoping for a battle.

A calm sea. A light wind. In the pale of the distance, the peaks of the Alps. Astern, the rock tip of Corsica. Not an enemy ship to be seen.

If ever the wind played pranks it was now when two fleets were just within reach, yet unseen to each other: one hiding, one hunting.

The wind puffed here, the wind puffed there around the rosettes of the compass. The wind was a minion of the devil today, all notions of dancing mischief. No wonder the seamen suspected it, whistled it, cajoled it, pampered it, solemnly cursed it. Two days went by, yachting days just off the Riviera, two days wasted.

At last, "Deck there, strange sail to southward!"

A flurry of signals from Hood. The strange sail answering. It was Vice-Admiral Hotham's division of the fleet coming to join the main body of the English. And Admiral Hotham regrets: although his seven of line were close to the enemy some days ago, he had not been able to get close enough to attack.

A frigate now, flying: "The enemy sighted!" The French seen last night twelve leagues off the island of Santa Margarita, lying with their heads off shore.

Aboard *Agamemnon:* "Deck there, Lord Hood making signal to chase northwest, sir."

"Stretch our canvas to the wind, if you please, Mr. Hinton." Captain Nelson smiled as he gave his orders, and continued to smile as the *Agamemnon* dug into the sea, spewed the first taste of brine, then setting her teeth ranged ahead, leaving the larger of line in the cream of the golden wake reflecting her copper bottom.

But nary a ship sighted, though the wind blew sportingly until sundown. As the light drained over the surface of the sea, following the sun into the water, the thirteen great battleships closed around their Commander in Chief in the towering *Victory*. A tight squadron. While the cruising eyes of the fleet, the swift smaller frigates, searched everywhere in the night.

At daybreak the frigates rejoined the fleet, flying the signals: "No enemy sighted!"

Aboard the *Victory,* Lord Hood sat shaking his head, his jaw set, disappointment tracing sleepless circles under his eyes. Vice-Admiral Hotham was there, hands folded over his stomach, a bit sleepy from so much to-do, but smiling amiably.

"I believe, my lord, that we did very well in driving them home."

Lord Hood coughed, did not answer Hotham but turned to Captain Nelson who had just come in, gray and haggard from anxiety and exasperation. His eyes were bloodshot from peering the summer sea for the enemy. He caught his breath in disappointment as Hood said:

"I'm sending you back to Bastia, Captain Nelson. Here are your orders." He handed him a packet. "Convoy the troops and stores to Mortella Bay in San Fiorenzo, and stand by to land them at Calvi as soon as I return. We must resume preparations for the siege of Calvi. I will join you as soon as I have ascertained what I fear has happened: that the French have put back to the mainland, into Gourjean."

"Aye, aye, my lord." Captain Nelson bowed, but his voice was bleak. Ordered back when at any moment the French fleet might . . . "Aye, aye, my lord, and may we hear a glorious account from your lordship soon."

He rowed back to his ship. England had made one of the gravest mistakes of the war when she failed to destroy the French fleet surrendered to her at Toulon. Listened to the Spanish allies who suggested they wait . . . Lord Hood had waited too long. The Spanish were not sorry, for although France was their mutual enemy, the destruction of a French fleet would have given the English navy greater superiority at sea than her Spanish allies wished her to possess. So after blaming the Spanish, and Lord Hood for listening or the Admiralty for not waking soon enough, the man to blame was Captain Sir Sidney Smith who had lulled England into a sense of false security by publicly announcing he had successfully accomplished what he obviously had not done. The sense of security still lingered, in spite of later official announcements that the Toulon fleet was intact, and that French-built battleships were scaled to much greater proportions than English battleships. A French 80 was about the same size as an English 100-gun ship. The French still had *Sans Culottes* of 120 guns. . . . Too late for recriminations? It sounded cowardly for an Englishman to admit that the French ships were finer than theirs, so the two fleets were judged by the number of their guns and not the destructibility of their bulk. And Captain Nelson hoped that Captain Sir Sidney Smith would never be given a chance to make such a costly boast again.

As *Agamemnon* turned stern to the fleet, Captain Nelson stood rooted to his quarter-deck, still hoping for some signal to recall him to fight. There had not been one decisive sea battle so far this war, and that, *he* felt, was not as it should be.

But *Victory* shrank into the water until only her topmasts were visible.

"Masthead?"

"Nothing in sight, sir."

Agamemnon sailed with the seas to herself, and Nelson, with nothing astern to recall him, let his mind play ahead. Once he had convoyed the troops as far as San Fiorenzo he would meet this new General Stuart. Could he persuade him—this fourth son of a third earl—to get on with the fight?

❄   ❄   ❄

From Bastia on the east coast, north around the peninsula, the *Agamemnon* convoyed twenty-two transports with fourteen hundred and fifty men exclusive of officers, and two of His Majesty's frigates: *Dolphin* and *Gorgon*.

The sun was already shining over the mountains, flashing on the round cups of the sails, casting long shadows astern, as the convoy took in sail, nosing into San Fiorenzo on the west coast of Corsica. Captain Nelson was on deck ready to put ashore, storm the General's camp, as *Agamemnon* clewed up her sails. And as the sun burst ablaze on the deck a boat shot off from shore, oars dipping smartly.

"General Stuart, Captain Nelson. . . ."

The head that appeared over the side was red: hair and face and eyebrows. The hair also reflected some gold, while the skin had the appearance of more red under it waiting to burst its purple network of veins. The eyes sparked at Captain Nelson, bright blue. The rest of the man was spare, strong, quick. Red man in a red coat: battle array all in one rig.

He shook hands with a grasping jerk.

"I have been expecting you, sir, for a *long* time!" he snapped. "Several precious days waiting—waiting for *you* to turn up! Well? Are you willing to get on with the war?"

Taken flat aback, Captain Nelson could only grin. "With all my heart, sir! Ready to proceed when you are, sir."

"Good, I had presumed you were waiting for some damned naval tradition—some order to trickle down. You're ready? Well?"

Captain Nelson blinked, and within the space of it considered his orders from Hood: *stand by,* for there was not another ship of the line to protect them till Hood got back.

"Ready, sir, and more than anxious to start."

"Good!" The General nodded brusquely.

As the General returned to the shore, Captain Nelson caught Josiah by the collar, gave him a hug. "Well, son?"

For a moment they laughed together, then Josiah shrugged. "What's the difference? You never let any of us mids come ashore."

"And get your foolish head shot off? What would I say to your poor dear mother who sent you to sea, not to soldiering?"

Josiah snorted. "There's nothing to do here."

"I tell you what. Sometime—if it's safe—I'll invite all my mids to come ashore and have dinner with me!"

"Oh, thank you, sir!" Josiah smiled mockingly. He had been permitted to come ashore at Bastia, thought he was going to fight, only to learn it was to witness the glory, the day it surrendered.

❊   ❊   ❊

The sun was setting as the convoy ranged down the coast. Aboard *Agamemnon* was another captain, Cooke, Hood's naval representative at San Fiorenzo, who had practically lashed himself to the mast in his ardor to go along. Captain Nelson took an instant liking to him, for everything looked better at the start of this campaign, until the General who had been studying the coast gave a snort.

"Damnedest shore I ever saw!"

He was pacing the quarter-deck with Captain Nelson. It was quite a parade. Captain Cooke and *Agamemnon's* lieutenants, and General Stuart's aides. A *petit élite* corps, with hardly room to maneuver. A wide aisle must be kept for the commanders.

"We will have a beach, sir, opening to larboard in a few minutes." Captain Nelson was listening to the soundings called from the bow. Deep water: sudden rocks. To the General's damnedest shore he was tempted to agree and add damnedest anchorage, but the army was so easily disconcerted he kept his own problems to himself.

"Take a native billy goat to get up those cliffs," from General Stuart.

The coast of Bastia had been comparatively easy, but the west coast of Corsica reared a ledge of rock in some places sloping up three quarters of a mile from the sea. And below seethed the foam of suicidal breakers dashing white, shooting up from half-submerged rocks.

"How soon do we land?" General Stuart drew himself up as if measuring his height against the wall he must conquer.

"We are sounding close on an inlet, sir, where there is some shore for our boats. Calvi is three miles to southward. There is a better anchorage somewhat closer, at Cape Revellata, but it is under fire from their guns. I hope that once our landing is established we may push forward batteries to release Revellata to our boats."

"And your men will drag guns up those cliffs, Captain Nelson?"

"Aye, sir, they're good stout lads."

The General whistled. Suddenly he took Captain Nelson aside. "You understand, I intend to go through with this!" His face blackened. "You understand, I intend to take Calvi!"

"I'm with you, sir." Captain Nelson shook his hand. "I expect to go ashore by dawn to reconnoiter and study the landing and if I may have the honor of your company, sir . . . ?"

General Stuart nodded. But he did not say any more. Perhaps he felt he had gone too far with a mere naval captain, for he began to grow distant once more, turning away to speak to Captain Nelson's old acquaintance, Colonel Moore.

❋   ❋   ❋

Though it was only three o'clock in the morning, it was already hot when General Stuart and Captain Nelson stepped out of the boat onto a meager beach. They were met by a Corsican guard that had come overland.

"Not much of a landing place." The General craned his neck at the cliffs. The Corsicans were watching the English sharply.

"Where's the road you promised us?" Captain Nelson to a guide.

"You stand upon it."

It was no more than a rut, whether it had been made by goats or accident or man made little difference. It led straight up a mean defile, sometimes no more than a corrosion on the rocks. It wound around, twisted on itself like a cat chasing its tail; hitched and inched up and up.

"God!" General Stuart's breath came in puffs. Below the ship's boats looked like clam shells tossed on the beach. "This may be a sailor's masthead, sir, but I have an army to land! Do you realize I have an army shipped clear from England without a horse or a wagon! My men have nothing to work with."

"Forward the slope seems gentler, sir." Captain Nelson had been watching for the first sign of weakening. Whatever qualms he had, he kept to himself. And some things he saw that the General fortunately did not: those sunken rocks twenty feet off shore, the heavy swell setting in with the sea breeze. There would be times when the ships would be cut off from the detachments on shore. But he was not one to propose difficulties.

The General squared his jaw and paced on. He did not speak again until, having been cooled by a small stand of oaks, they spied the first enemy outposts, and beyond them the high thick walls of Calvi.

They compared what they saw with the maps they already had: The Mollinochesco was about twenty-two hundred yards from the town, on the southwest side of it. The Mozelle fort was west from the town about nine hundred yards. The Fountain battery was in a shoulder of the hill, between Mozelle and the San Francesco battery which stood on a rock on the north side of the peninsula, washed by the sea. The town itself was apparently well fortified, with its great walls, but fortunately without any ditch or moat.

"Ah," said the General and clapped his mouth shut, eyeing his maps again.

Captain Nelson, who was dying to divulge his opinion, began with a cautious, "There's an excellent possibility of erecting a battery over there where the fire from Mozelle would hit its own batteries in aiming at ours."

The General did not answer. At last he rolled up his maps. "We'll need more troops before we can take it. Much more difficult than I suspected. More troops, Captain Nelson."

"I'll send Lieutenant Gibson's *Fox* cutter to San Fiorenzo directly, sir, with your orders."

"And more artillery and more stores!"

And with that a shadow brushed over the landscape. The General paid no attention, but the Captain glanced up, eyes narrowing on the sea. The heat seemed to grow more intense, yet the glare on the water was fading into dark patches, like steel, under the clouds. He said nothing to the General, but began to calculate how he would land the troops before the promised storm.

With the shifting shadows, the changing mood of the General, he must establish the landing now, ere a gale blew all thoughts of warfare right out of the General's mind.

❋   ❋   ❋

The storm gathered slowly, piling up for twenty-four hours, promising in the increasing swell of the sea surging into the inlet; moving mountains of water; sudden bared rocks rearing up in the hollows. The boats crawled up, the oars strained over the peaks. Sledding down, boatload after boatload of troops grinding at last on the sands. The

soldiers shook the surf from their feet, faced the land, glad to be anywhere after the half-rations and crowding in the transports.

Almost on the heels of the last man came a crackling flash; thunder;
a roaring of wind.

❋   ❋   ❋

"Pull, lads! Pull!" Captain Nelson stood outlined halfway up the
cliffs. The streaking fire snapped down through the clouds like a whip
laid over the bare backs of two hundred seamen staggering inch by
inch up the rock, jerked back by the insensible weight of the cannon.
The line blended in one sweating surge of taut muscle, bare feet
gashed open, blood on the rock; pulling till their eyes started from
their sockets, chests heaved, legs quivered. And down from above the
lean whips of lightning, the boom of thunder, at last a curtain of
water over them.

"And pull there! Heave! It's a ration of wine when it's up, lads!
Pull! Throw your weight in there!"

The men must burst veins and break hearts forever dragging up
guns behind them, harnessed like mules to their guns; as if the rock
cliff were not steep enough.

Leaving his seamen to his lieutenants, Captain Nelson slid down
the rocks, ducked under a flap of sail stretched over the powder.

"Pass the word for Captain Cooke!"

"Aye, aye, sir!" And Captain Cooke, soaked to the skin, groped
under the canvas beside him.

"You're drowned. Have a drink."

"Thank you, sir." Cooke helped himself to the bottle eagerly. "I'd
be grateful to you, sir, if you'd persuade Lord Hood to let me stay
on."

"God bless you, I need you. I have written," the Captain nodded.
"You've done the work of ten. But there'll be no more boats, Cooke.
Signal the transports to put back to San Fiorenzo. Let the others get
under sail, work for a safe anchorage. Get them off before they part
from their cables and blow on the rocks."

"Aye, aye, sir." Cooke darted out.

And thank God the powder was dry!

Up cliff, the gun lay sleek and still on its sledge, like some mammoth corpse. It jolted again, lurched, slid back, stopped, and the long
line of seamen labored on hour after hour all day and into the night.

Beyond the foaming mouth of the inlet, ships heeled over, sometimes a mast, sometimes a bottom pointed shoreward, as their cables frayed strand by strand.

"The navy's pulling out, sir." Colonel Moore smiled grimly at General Stuart.

"What the devil?" The General churned the mud with his heel; dove into his tent.

"We're stranded, sir. The ships are gone and not a gun set up. The usual naval co-operation." Moore's voice was pitiless. "Our poor men will be wiped out."

"Orderly! My writing case!" Stuart bawled and the gale bawled back at him with a "Heave, men, heave!" from the line of seamen struggling up the rocks.

And under a quaking lantern made fast to a swaying tent pole, to the chanting of the wind, the General hunched over his paper. His pen screeched, and Colonel Moore watched him. Moore's shadow thrown up the slanting side of the tent forebodingly higher than Stuart's.

"Captain Nelson will have to answer for this!" Stuart's face was mottled with purple patches. "For Captain Nelson!"

He thrust the paper into Captain Duncan's hand.

Duncan, Nelson's favorite artillery lieutenant at Bastia, hitched his coat around his ears and pushed down the beach to the navy encampment. A fresh gust of wind blew the rain and Duncan straight into Captain Nelson's tent.

"Well, Captain Duncan! I'm glad to see you again. Let me congratulate you on your promotion." Captain Nelson had glanced up, suddenly smiling, from the litter of reports, orders and invoices. He held out his hand.

"Thank you, sir! From General Stuart, sir." Captain Duncan laid the papers in Nelson's outstretched hand with the receipt for his signature. Captain Nelson scribbled his name. Duncan bowed and left.

A flicker of hurt had lit the Captain's eyes. His face turned slowly red. What had come over Duncan? Perhaps he no longer needed friends now he had his advancement? Captain Nelson stared at Stuart's letter without reading it; at last, with a quick toss of his head, he laid it out on the table before him.

All the devils in hell were unleashed tonight. Even the General's penmanship looked like a madman's, but as he made it out, the wording was strictly impersonal. What had become of the ships?

Captain Nelson couched his reply in the same official form:

I was in a great hurry to send these vessels away, as their cables were much cut by the rocks, and it had the appearance of blowing weather. If the weather put on a better appearance, abundance of shipping will remain here to hold the troops in case any unforeseen event should render re-embarkation necessary. It is right to inform you, sir, that if the present weather continue, it will, I think, be necessary for every vessel here to put to sea. I can only assure you that every exertion of mine shall be made to comply with your wishes on every occasion, for I am, with the highest esteem,

Your most faithful servant,

HORATIO NELSON

He signed his name a half inch high in his impatient simplification of letters; a bold right-hand slant illegibly run together. He started to fold it, then added:

I wished to have paid my respects to you this morning but really have been so anxious to get a 24 pounder in the road, that I trust you will excuse me. The work of the day being over, I shall do myself the honor of seeing you this evening.

Signed it again. And went back to other letters while waiting for the sentry to pass the word for a messenger.

A last paragraph in his report to Hood: "I not only have the greatest pleasure in having Captain Cooke with me, but his assistance to me has been very great. . . ." And a postscript:

General Stuart requests me to say that nothing particular has happened since our landing, and that he is really so busy that he cannot find time to write your Lordship; but begs to refer you to me for particulars.

And it took two hundred men to move a cannon capable of firing 24-pound balls. It had taken those men all day to get one cannon up the cliff. How long, O Lord, before Calvi discovered them?

He sat very still for a moment, after he had sent Lieutenant Noble off with his answer to Stuart. Duncan had chilled him. He felt again the workings of many men all at cross-purposes; an intolerable feeling as he listened to the wail on the cliffs:

"Heave till your eyes pop! Break your backs! Pull, my sweet hearties, pull there, you son of a sea cook—"

Captain Nelson stood up, pacing his tiny square of tent. England was at war with France. Wasn't one enemy enough for these gentlemen? He paced outside. A flash of lightning blinded him, then his eyes found his men straining above him.

"Pass the word for Lieutenant Andrews," he snapped at his sentry. Andrews, white and thin from his wound at Bastia, saluted.

"See that the men get an extra ration, Andrews. Their fag requires the best food we can find."

It was heretical. Unprecedented. It might have to come out of his own pay to increase their rations. He felt better.

Duncan! Nothing like kicking down the ladder a man rises by. He smiled suddenly, having pigeonholed Duncan with a phrase. He took one long breath of air and rain and went back to work.

"And the seamen want shoes, three hundred pairs. My men are barefooted . . ." and so on, reports and orders and, "as Cooke is anxious to remain, I hope he will be allowed by your Lordship to stay with me. . . ."

❊ ❊ ❊

And up went the guns by man power and man will alone; day after day after day. And after the gale: the sun like a maniac eye staring them down.

"How in the name of—" General Stuart glared at the report in front of him. His Engineers had been given explicit orders to finish the battery against the Mozelle last night. They proudly announced this morning they had finished—against his orders—the other battery. The wrong battery against the Mollinchesco! His own Engineers!

He stared morosely at the ground. Was there a man anywhere he could trust? Moore was a clever officer, but a cagey politician. Nelson was Hood's hireling. And he had told Captain Nelson the Mozelle battery would go forward last night. What would energetic Captain Nelson tattle to his Commander in Chief, Lord Hood, about this? And the thought made him boil. Hood had been highhanded right from the start, detailing a captain to transport the army, never coming near shore himself. And Stuart would be damned if he'd communicate with Hood after that. Captain Nelson had taken the hint; ceased asking him if he had letters to send to the fleet.

He ran his hand over his face. He had fever. Chills. The devil take everyone and get on with the siege. The poisonous swamp vapors were everywhere. He swatted a mosquito as he took up his pen, swallowed his pride, and wrote once again to Captain Nelson a hundred long paces down the beach waiting on Stuart's orders to go ahead with his seamen and guns. Stuart wrote out his note: he was sorry, but the battery would not be ready for the seamen's guns for another night. . . .

❄   ❄   ❄

It was dusk on the cliffs. A pregnant stillness. Captain Nelson's voice—low:

"Serocold?"

"Aye, sir, ready."

"Hallowell?"

"Aye, sir, my men are ready."

"Come into the lee of this rock." The two men stole up beside Captain Nelson, crouched down. They peered at the distant town and then more intently at the outpost of Mollinochesco. Silence. Then like a heartbeat in the stillness, slow, measured, more of a vibration than a sound: to a trained ear—soldiers on the march.

A white vapor hovered over the marshland and the sulphuric rotting smell filled the night air with the dread malaria while the mosquitoes pestered them with their stings. After a while most men got used to the stings, but never the insinuating fever vapors.

Now the tramping grew into a sound.

"There they go, sir," from Serocold.

Below the rock marched General Stuart and his men, silent as specters, closing in to attack.

Captain Nelson spoke softly. "As soon as the General begins his sham attack on the Mollinochesco the Army Engineers and their workmen will move forward to the new battery. As soon as they move we can bring up the guns. We should open our new battery at dawn, trained square on the Mozelle fort. The chances of the enemy finding us when Stuart is drawing their attention are so remote we will have our work accomplished in no time."

"It's a little light for the attack, don't you think, sir?"

"Aye . . . patience—they say—is a virtue." He had caught the tense expectancy in Captain Serocold's voice, seen Captain Hallowell's mountainous shoulders hunch forward. Captain Nelson tried to put his words to practice, sitting back against the rock. "Twenty-eight to thirty-five and Admiral Lord Howe only took six of the French!"

"That was great news, wasn't it? The Glorious First of June! Old Black Dick Howe is still doing business!" Hallowell had suddenly caught Captain Nelson's mutterings; decoded them.

"With twenty-eight of our battleships? A game of touch and take. Aye, but Howe's a grand old gentleman." He suddenly changed his tune. It was downright indecent of him to criticize or think to improve upon the first sea battle of the war fought by one of his first patrons. Howe had presented boy Captain Nelson to King George III—before the King lost interest in him. "Ah, well, if Corsica were in the English Channel, we'd be applauded, too. Never mind, I still have hopes our good Lord Hood can override the veto of his wise flag officers and fight a battle right here in these seas."

"What do you think of Hood's calling a council to vote on his plan of attack when he discovered he had chased the French fleet into Gourjean?" Hallowell, a Canadian, still had the ring of self-assured new worlds in his voice.

"Well, Ben, thank God we didn't sit at that council table and vote as they did. I would have gone into Gourjean!"

Hallowell laughed. "Sure you would. But perhaps Lord Hood was right. If his officers are scared and the wind fickle."

"They should not be unwilling!" Captain Nelson snapped. "The wind they cannot control. But don't forget Captain Miller volunteered to go in *alone* and burn their fleet! That he failed after those six hair-raising attempts is no disgrace to *him* . . . and don't forget Miller did the same at Toulon when it fell, and he fell wounded. That Miller, one frigate captain *alone* . . ."

"I took a liking to him at Bastia," Serocold agreed. "But Howe's First of June has everyone cheering at home. Completely hides our taking Bastia in the *Gazette*. But maybe that's just as well, considering who got the credit *you* earned, sir."

They lapsed into glum silence.

They could not see one another's faces; perhaps that was just as well, too. Like passing ships were these naval officers. They might have known one another for years, meeting occasionally, yet sailing on, ranging all over the seas. They seldom met for long; gliding in and out of each other's sphere; in and out of the main focal points of the war. It was hail and well met and how are the others? A murmur if some name were gone: a chance of war. God knew whose chance was next.

Now in the dark, drawn together, camaraderie; tomorrow—at the least, they might be scattered again.

"I hated to lose Cooke," Captain Nelson muttered, not ignoring Serocold's last remark about Bastia, rather letting it fall in with the train of their thoughts. "I begged Lord Hood to let him stay. He worked like an angel."

"Cooke's a good officer. Too bad his name wasn't Hunt." Hallowell tried to stretch his legs, succeeded only in scraping his shin. At last he settled his immense foot on something soft.

"Avast!" Serocold grunted. "Your heel's in my stomach."

"Sorry."

"No army games, Ben," Nelson chided.

"By the way, Nelson, I hear Captain Collingwood's coming out to this fleet soon."

"Coll? Bravo!" Captain Nelson sat forward. "He and I were stationed out in the West Indies. Remember his brother Wilfred?"

"No. I never knew he had a brother. Was he in the service?"

"Captain. He died. Overnight. Wilfred was—" He broke off. "He had a lot of promise." He and Wilfred Collingwood had thought of each other as much alike: not quite strong enough physically for the grueling fatigue of their profession. The memory of Wilfred's death, here with the smell of malaria everywhere, had stabbed him again. It still shook him almost superstitiously. Lots of men had died, that was nonsense. He wasn't superstitious. Take that gypsy just before he married: "At forty you will be at the top of your profession." Small chance of that at this rate. "And then—?" he had asked her. But that was all, and he had gone out of her dirty hut a condemned man. Why in the devil did he have to think of it—or Wilfred? "Have you heard from Troubridge?" he asked Hallowell. "He went home almost a year ago, wasn't it?"

"Haven't you heard, Nelson? His frigate was captured off Newfoundland. Lost his convoy to the French. But we got him back."

"Aye, I heard. . . . The French will regret the day they took him."

"I hear he's not changed a bit. He always was gravely astute. Never was exactly tender. Fierce. Great fellow!" Hallowell said.

"Can't blame him," from Serocold.

"Troubridge?" from Nelson. "I love him like a brother. Known him ever since we were mids in the East Indies."

"Jolly fellow," Hallowell grunted. And for a few more minutes they indulged in scuttlebutt—who was where, until somehow Captain Serocold came up with:

"Hunt, the hero of Bastia, who, according to Lord Hood, was 'on shore in command of the batteries, from the hour the troops landed to the surrender of the town, will be the bearer of this dispatch, and can give any further information you may wish to know respecting the Siege'!"

"Footnote to dispatch: 'Captain Nelson commanded the landing of the seamen. . . .'" Nelson tried to laugh it off, failed to sound very convincing.

Glum silence again while the tramping of soldiers grew in their ears like the pulse of a rising fever.

"Well, nobody cares about Corsica anyway after Howe's battle," Hallowell laughed dryly. The talk had come full circle again as it usually did when men tried to kill time.

"Yes, Ben," Serocold persisted. After all he had fought on the batteries; and he, too, had lost a ship, though Lord Hood seemed very uninterested. "But what got into Lord Hood putting Hunt ahead of you, Captain Nelson?"

"I've been trying to remember when Captain Nelson was on shipboard during that siege. I *thought* I was ashore."

"We wouldn't have Bastia if you hadn't been," Serocold nodded.

Hallowell had taken a cigar from his pocket; he rolled it between his fingers, sniffing it longingly. "Politics! The Right Honorables and m'lords have stunk up the navy. A man's reputation, as far as the public knows, hangs on the dispatch. Take Duncan—he was active, volunteered, all that, but Hood gave him a whole paragraph—what the devil?"

"Lord Hood said he would remember my protégés," Nelson laughed again curtly. "Lord Hood's words may have put me in the rear and put Captain Hunt in the thick of it, but my men know where I was— and my conscience! And I'm proud of our fight!"

"It just wasn't justice." Serocold stood up to stretch. "Well, I hope Hunt enjoys his new ship . . . small chance of me seeing one. It's dark enough now for the army attack. God! It's black as the hand of fate!"

"It's the country that counts after all," Nelson said soberly. And perhaps he was too ambitious. There was Serocold, no patronage either. Ambitious as sin. He tried to curb his thoughts. But he wanted to chisel his name in history, honorably, gloriously. Those words meant something more tangible to him than money or life itself. They lit that light all around. Odd? He sat conjuring it. There it was, like a soft moon, glowing through heavy fogs, and he felt nothing was too hard to do. He no longer even resented Hood. There was always the future.

"I'm going to write a history of our campaign in Corsica," Serocold announced. "Like Drinkwater's *Siege of Gibraltar,* you know. I always wanted to write and never had anything that I felt couldn't be said by someone else—and a lot better. Would you object, Captain Nelson?"

"I'd be much obliged. I'm no hand with a pen. Just an honest account of the siege."

"That's right."

"Serocold will write your gazette and I'll write Serocold's and you write mine, Nelson!" Hallowell laughed quietly. "We'll make us a trio of High Lords of the Admiralty yet! What's the Corsican method? Murder your enemies and bribe your friends. You should have cut Hunt's throat before he cut yours. That's the game, isn't it?"

"Aye, but who'd fight the French, Ben? Penny-wise and pound-foolish, dear boy."

"Well, it appears there are those who hesitate to fight the French. Take Hotham when he joined Lord Hood in June after sighting the French. Everyone knows now why he couldn't get near 'em. He thought they were nine to his seven. Imagine his mortification when it was announced there were only seven of French—an even number!" Serocold shook his head.

"Hotham's a dud!" from Hallowell.

"I don't think Hotham has much sporting blood in his veins." Nelson stood up. Suddenly he leaped up on the rock, his heart beating faster. "There they go!" And all resentments sloughed off at the first musket shot. The Captains watched tensely.

A blast of thunder and light from the Mollinochesco, then howled huzzas!

"Like Indians," Hallowell grinned.

"Good. Right in our trap!" Captain Nelson swung around. "Now where are the General's Engineers?" He peered back in the direction of camp. His seamen were taking their ease beside their cannons and munitions, his lieutenants pacing their ranks. He had been ready since sundown, but until the Engineers prepared the ground the guns could not be set up. This was a co-operative siege.

Below them the musketry flashed and the enemy forts opened up to repulse what sounded like a furious attack. The General's tactics were perfect; not a gun in the town or outlying posts fired on the site of the real night's work where the new battery was to be built.

"There's Captain Nepean of the Engineers now, sir." Serocold pointed to a shadow moving against the light of firing.

"Stand by then." And along the ranks of seamen went the first alert. But the shadow came to a halt, finally drifted back toward camp.

Captain Nelson began to pace the rock anxiously. Every minute that passed meant a minute closer to dawn when the enemy would see their position.

Below them the sham battle went on, a tactical feint, but measured in drops of blood. Unless the battery were erected tonight those poor devils would have fought for nothing, for the English were not strong enough yet to take the supposed objective. Though the General certainly had no intentions of bleeding his men, children who played with fire . . . Captain Nelson took out his watch, reading it by the reflected light of the battle. "Nine o'clock!"

The three naval captains paced the rocks. The attack seemed to be going on well in earnest. The soldiers were close on the Mollinochesco and the frantic town had opened fire on its own outpost rather than let the English have it! But no Engineers; no battery was being built.

"*Ten* o'clock!"

The tactics were working miraculously well. Every gun in the forts —and every gun that could bear from the town—pointed on the General's attack.

"If this were the navy command . . ." Nelson suddenly snapped, "if I weren't under that General's orders . . . I'd be lugging those sandbags myself!"

"Ten-thirty!"

Now a swift shadow. General Stuart's voice like a pistol crack. "Not an Engineer to be found! Not one damn Engineer! That *you*, Captain Nelson? You ready?"

"Yes, sir!"

"They'll push it now, by God!" The General strode off, could be heard yelling all the way back to camp. "Up there with your men!"

And up went the Engineers with the workmen to prepare the ground.

"Eleven o'clock." The seamen were leaning on their ropes, the guns going forward. "Avast!" Captain Nelson called out bitterly. The General had ordered it all carried back. The night was too far gone. The tactics, brilliantly and wholeheartedly executed, had not accomplished the strategy!

Captain Nelson eyed General Stuart as his men started hauling the cannon back once again. The General's red face was peculiarly drawn as his right fist pounded the palm of his left hand.

"When *I* say delay, sir"—the General spun on Nelson—"I suffer! My temper—my temper can't bear it!"

Captain Nelson suddenly felt a deep sympathy for him. "I understand, sir. We'll go through with it yet."

General Stuart studied the Captain. "You did your share." For the first time his face looked friendly. Then it darkened, hovering between hysteria and apoplexy. "My Engineer, Mr. Nepean, complains that my reprimand has brought on his gout again!"

❋   ❋   ❋

And all to be done over. For two nights moving forward, the barefooted, half-naked seamen hauling the cannon in silence.

And another attack. The bright spark of firing, the blasting of cannon. And as the seamen could curse aloud as they hauled, so the guns moved more easily.

"Push forward, lads!" Captain Nelson shouted to his seamen as the army began the new feint on the enemy.

Inch by inch in the dark came the guns.

"Come, lads, pull with a will," from Serocold. He was everywhere, urging his men; they liked the confident ring in his voice; his face was hidden in the dark.

Inch by inch came the cold, dead weight of the cannon.

"It's closing on dawn, sir!"

"Then heave lads, heave, we'll salute them with the sunup!"

Silence again. The covering fire had ceased. In the still pale hours, the last minutes of night, there was but one will: get the guns in position. With the sun all would be discovered, and they were well within range of enemy guns. Not a thought but for work. They were fighting time, faces set, eyes on the guns.

And up from the marshes the evil miasmas—the poisonous vapors rising like clouds of some shrouded host. The insinuating hum of mosquitoes. The first faint pink light breaking free of distant peaks.

"Damn the sun! Stay the night!" Serocold whispered. The air came alive out of the gray of the dawn, with a shimmering of light, like life itself. A sudden bird call.

"Stow that!"—hissed through clenched teeth. Not a creature must breathe as the light, gathering up the shadows, began to reveal their position to the enemy.

"Faster—there—" The platforms not finished. The guns not mounted.

"Dear God, the sun!"

It swelled up over the peaks, flashing down on the sweating backs, the long silent guns.

One gun inside the battery! "E-e-a-s-y there," Captain Nelson groaned with the men as they sledded it close to its platform.

One gun mounted: one of *Agamemnon's* 24-pounders.

Not a stir from the enemy yet. When would they, scanning the English position, discover the new battery built right under their noses?

"Five o'clock."

The cannon drew closer; to the creaking sledges, the panting of the men. Guns and more guns. Five guns inside!

And still the dawn grew as the light seemed to shift, then out of curiosity focus down where they struggled against split seconds of grace. Any moment some roving lookout eye would spy them, beat the town alarm.

"Six o'clock!" Luck so far.

Captain Serocold was waving his men up—up. "Come, lads, heave." His lips framed the words, but he kept the silence, glancing around. No man under the sun and the guns of the enemy was an entity unto himself. Now if ever in their mean useless lives, they must be their brothers' keepers! There was Captain Nelson, there was Captain Hallowell. Good men pull together. The prey and the kill. "Come lads, pull! Pull for your lives, lads!" Had the dark only lasted a little longer.

The ground jumped at them, dust rose, something peppered the cannon, made it ring.

"They've found us! Pull, pull, no mind the shot! They can't shoot straight! Into the battery there!" Serocold's cry.

"Give them a cheer and a salute from *Agamemnon!*" Captain Nelson shouted. And they all shouted in one pent-up howl, for enemy grape was on them, the deadly chained balls raining out of the air.

"That does it, lads!" Captain Serocold's face caught the full light, he grinned at Captain Nelson, his eyes brilliant, as death blotted the sun for Serocold, pinning him prone as the cannon. There was no head left on his tall angular body.

"Oh, dear God . . ." Nelson turned away; saw a man's leg shot off.

❋   ❋   ❋

The siege of Calvi had really begun.

Captain Nelson sat on an empty powder keg, using another for a writing desk as he wrote out an order for more powder to be sent up from camp. He was awake with that almost ecstatic awareness that fatigue brings after forty-eight hours without sleep.

Time had not stopped, nor the firing day after day. He and Hallowell, alone, were left commanding the seamen on shore, and though Hood wrote he had a dear young man who wanted some action, Hallowell and Nelson declined further protégés, they could handle it themselves. So day after day on the battery. The army did not fight the batteries, soldiers were reserved for last-minute storming, but General Stuart was there. And Nelson and Hallowell agreed Stuart was a damn good army.

On top of battery duty, Captain Nelson handled all stores from ship to shore, kept the army supplied, kept Lord Hood informed of progress by the Admiral's messenger at ten o'clock every morning.

"Captain Nelson, will you look here a moment?" General Stuart motioned him across the battery, behind the breastwork of sandbags. He skirted the gun crews.

Captain Nelson was shivering in spite of the broiling sun. A touch of ague. Hot climates always touched off old fevers. He brushed a mosquito from his face. God, how he hated their sting—sting—sting all day and all night! He had hated them all his life. They drove him madder than the fever itself. He followed the General, swatting here and there, a gleam in his eye when he got one. And when they bit through his clothes, it was an insult clear to his soul. They were like the French . . . he remembered he once accused the little devils of being sent to sting him for his sins. As he whacked one an awful blow, General Stuart almost grinned at him. Captain Nelson held it up by one leg, tossed it toward Calvi, as the General said:

"I'm considering erecting a battery to the left. That will advance us about—"

There was a whine just over their heads. "Look—" And they threw themselves flat on their faces. A hundred men hugging the ground, trying to burrow like worms. The explosion knocked their noses flat into the dirt, while everything seemed to soar slowly up.

Captain Nelson picked himself up carefully, lest he find he was missing some limb. And one by one the others stood up. General Stuart was brushing his sleeve very soberly—his dirt-caked face expressionless.

"They got our magazine . . ." someone said in a hollow voice.

"No one killed, sir!" From a lieutenant. "A miracle!" Just as the injured began to wail. They were lifted up, carted off to the surgeon two miles away on the beach.

❋   ❋   ❋

"Post, sir, just arrived from England!"

It all seemed rather remote. Captain Nelson shuffled his letters looking for one handwriting. The magazine had blown up. . . . Could it be? He ran through the letters again. Not a scratch of a pen, nothing from his wife.

"Well," he smiled suddenly at General Stuart, who had just finished dusting himself, though his face was still black. "As you were saying, sir, about that new battery . . ."

❋   ❋   ❋

And snatching a moment that night, he wrote off one of his stilted, self-conscious, but brotherly letters to his wife: to the enigmatical black-haired lady from the West Indies who, when she wrote, hoped her dear baby Josiah would always tell his stepfather all his "little secrets" and that so-and-so had a new bonnet that was not pretty, and his brothers and sisters were not always as considerate of her nerves as they should be, for "my mind and poor heart are always on the rack" . . . just like a woman, he felt.

MY DEAR FANNY,

I long to hear from you, for a post has arrived without any letter. Our batteries opened and it is possible you may have heard that a Captain of the Navy has fallen. . . .

He paused. He'd written Lord Hood that the grape blew Serocold's head off; and to old navy friends in England that Serocold was going to write a history of Bastia . . . but to Fanny, prey of her own inability to face anything, dear poor timid little creature, what could he say? Not what was in his mind . . . So he went on very carefully:

To assure you it is not me, I write a few lines; for if such a report should get about, I well know your anxiety of mind. We shall take Calvi in due time; and I hope without much loss of men. I am very busy yet I own I am in all my glory; except with you, I would not be anywhere but where I am for the world. I am well aware my poor services will not be noticed: I have no interest: but, however services may be received, it is not right in an officer to slacken his zeal for his country.

Your faithful and affectionate husband

He set the letter aside. There had been a letter for Serocold in the packet. . . .

He turned abruptly to his report to Lord Hood. He hoped someone at the Admiralty read this journal that Hood forwarded. Odd that with this journal in their hands—if they read it—they had not noticed the discrepancies in Hood's Bastia dispatch. . . . On the other hand . . . He scowled at Lord Hood's latest letter. The Admiral was displeased that Captain Nelson had mentioned the failure of the Engineers to go forward when ordered the first night. Why? He sighed, wrote: "I have just received your letter of last night, and have to request that any part of my Journal which may relate to the misconduct of any Officer, you will alter as you please. I write yours as my own, which contains nothing but the truth. . . ." But why should Lord Hood desire to spare Captain Nepean of the Army Engineers at the expense of blaming hard-working General Stuart? Nepean . . . Oh, yes, Nepean was the beloved nephew of the Secretary of the Admiralty, Evan Nepean, Esq., to whom all reports were forwarded. Ah, well!

Captain Nelson continued his dispatch, his head ringing with fever, aching from the steady booming of cannon up on the battery. But as he finished, his temper rose again: "Everything mentioned, your Lordship may rely is most strictly correct; only we must recollect the truth is not spoken at all times, but with your Lordship I have no reserves."

And on the tag end of another letter home, to old friends, one last burst of temper at Hood's Bastia dispatch: "I can forgive, but I cannot forget!"

❊ ❊ ❊

Summer was the time of the Corsican Lion Sun. King over all creatures; pitiless and merciless.

"Beastly hot!" Captain Hallowell climbed down from his post on a heap of sandbags. His face was white. His giant frame seemed to be melting away inside his clothes. They hung limply, coated with dust, patched with sweat. He looked weak as a newborn baby; and frightening. For sickness always seems more insidious when it debilitates a mountain of vigor than when it constantly haunts a frail man.

"You better see the surgeon, Ben."

Captain Nelson, who looked indecently fresh, washed and shaved, to Hallowell's haggard eye, had just come on battery duty. But Captain Nelson's eyes were sunken with sleeplessness. For he had taken his rest by wrestling with the landing of fresh guns. The windlass on the davit cast had broken in hoisting. More delays. But guns must go forward. The enemy had knocked up three of *Agamemnon's* 24-pounders, and if the visible breach, that nice hole made in the enemy fort, was to widen, they must have guns and more guns. And new batteries pushed forward.

"We're holding the superior fire, sir." Hallowell's step was limp. "The breach has been widened."

"Good."

As Hallowell stumbled off toward the beach, Captain Nelson took over.

It was only just dawn, yet the heat seemed to spring up with the sun. The men at the guns moved slowly, wiping the sweat from their eyes, glaring sullenly at the defiant town. They were phantoms of the jacks of a few weeks before. Too exhausted to complain; just alive enough to fight. Most of them shivered and shook while their backs blistered, their brains cooked.

Every few hours one of them dropped in a heap and did not get up again: Lion Sun and the mysterious fever killed more than the enemy guns.

From the town and the enemy batteries came the first morning shots. The night sheltering their position had been comparatively quiet. Now the thick hot air was shrieking with fire; the battery shaking as shell after shell struck uncomfortably close.

It was a routine beginning. Like any other day in the week. Captain Nelson went from crew to crew, but with his keen eyes on the heartily resented artilleryman sent up by Stuart. Captain Nelson had forbidden him to lay a finger on the seamen's guns lest the clumsy fool, who was so afraid of premature firing he used twice the necessary wadding and wasted precious stores, wreck the delicate perfection of *Agamemnon's* cannon! Captain Nelson took a certain pride in his crews trained to hit a target from a rolling deck. But co-operate he must!

He was close to the breastwork of sandbags, examining the havoc of a gun knocked off its balancing trunnions, one of which was broken off. It lay on its splintered platform, split to the ringbolts, a fine cannon burst open like a ripe fruit. The enemy fire was unusually accurate today.

He left the cannon and was studying the town as a geyser of sharp pebbles and sand shot up from the breastwork. His eyes caught the glint of it, and before he could throw himself flat, a shower of darkening blood poured down his face.

His hands cupped his eyes. And other hands gripped him.

"Are you badly hurt, sir?"

"I'm blind! Blind!"

And his hands were wrenched from his face. But he could not see who was holding him; who was half carrying, half walking him very slowly, very gently, down the two weary miles into camp.

With the warmish evil-smelling wash water trickling over his face, a faint light broke through the terrifying dark. He opened one eye. The other was too painful.

"I can see!" he told the surgeon, and the joy almost nullified the agony in his head. Sykes, his coxswain, was standing beside the surgeon, peering anxiously down at him, while Tom Allen brought fresh water to the surgeon, and went off to cheer his brood of patients. Just another waister tending wounded; he had graduated from pigs. Captain Nelson followed him with his good eye. Tom had given him a cheering grin and a "How do," disrespectful, but awfully welcome at the moment.

"No, no harm to your left eye, Captain Nelson," the surgeon said. "But there's a gash through your right eyeball. 'Twill probably mend." The surgeon did not look at him. He was busy with something on a table.

He clapped a few folds of linen dipped in olive oil over the eye, and holding the bandage in place with his thumb gave the linen a loop about the Captain's head. Knotted it and stood back washing his hands. He leaned forward, dabbed at the deep cuts and spongy bruises on the Captain's chest, sprinkling clean lint into the deepest cuts. "Just a few scratches. How do you feel?"

"Thankful I'm not blind."

"Leave that bandage on. I'll dress it again tomorrow. No doubt you'll see as well as ever in a few days." If Captain Nelson's head had not felt so battered, he might have noticed that the surgeon's reassuring smile twisted into a sad grimace.

"Give me your arm, Sykes." Captain Nelson sat up, slid off the operating table and took a step gingerly.

"Better take it easy, sir," the surgeon warned. "You must have bled a good quart."

"That was quite a slap those devils gave me"—the Captain smiled grimly—"but I won't be in their debt for long—I promise you that!"

"Do take it easy, sir," the surgeon called over his shoulder as he moved across to a seaman just brought down from the battery.

The surgeon swore to himself as he shooed the flies from a table. "No keeping clean here. . . ." He chose his instruments, dunked them in a bucket of water, and calling for Tom to bring the rum, a mouth pad and a couple more strong men, he began a slow amputation.

Closing his ears to the hoarse uncontrollable screams behind him, Captain Nelson ducked out of the foul-smelling tent. He took a breath of air. It tasted of marshes. Brushing the assortment of insects from around his bandaged head he muttered, "Steer for my tent, Sykes."

"Aye, aye, sir. And begging your pardon, sir, I hope you're all right, sir?"

"Thank you, Sykes."

He walked dizzily down the beach. He was too weak to go back on the battery. He'd have to call Hallowell just when the poor man was getting some sleep. Stumbling into his tent, he sat down and mechanically looked at his reports.

When his man, Frank, peered in to see how he was, there was the tedious scratch of his pen and no other sound. His face was gray.

❈   ❈   ❈

And the breach in the Mozelle fort widened. Hammered in day after day.

Captain Nelson had just stopped by the General's camp. He could see, before entering the tent with its flaps flung back for air, the General laughing with Colonel Moore. When Captain Nelson was announced, he walked in on a sudden cool silence. The first bit of cool air he'd found, for there was nothing cool in the air on the sweltering batteries. That, he realized, smiling at them, was probably not funny, yet the sudden quirk of his humor put him at ease and on guard.

"We've breached the Mozelle, sir." He addressed General Stuart after making a perfunctory bow to both men.

It was Moore who answered. "What do you call a breach, Captain Nelson? A crack? I have men to consider, y'know, not a mere technical phrase!" Young Colonel Moore leaned back in his camp chair, crossing his legs.

Captain Nelson squinted at him with his left eye. He had not yet become accustomed to seeing the world flat, after seeing it round for so long. Something about Moore made life not only flat; he saw Moore as a man deliberately distorting perspective.

"You will, of course, judge for yourself, sir, what you may or may not be able to attack—" He broke off. There was a lot more on the tip of his tongue, but a letter from Hood had warned him: "Beware of that Colonel. If you do not get yourself into a scrape by *talking,* you may depend upon it I shall not do it, as I shall know nothing to the General of what you have ever written to me. . . . The situation in which Duncan is placed makes *silence* highly prudent. Warn Captain Hallowell also."

"Have a drink, Captain Nelson," the General nodded; his orderly was proffering a glass.

One glance at the General's tired face told Captain Nelson that Moore had gained political ground if not enemy territory since the siege began. He took the glass, bowing to Moore. "The breach shall be widened exactly as you desire it, sir."

"Thank you, sir." Moore replied evenly.

The General smiled wanly. "Well, good news, Captain Nelson. We *are* going to storm tomorrow night." He heaved himself up, unrolling his map of Calvi on the camp table. He began to trace his plans.

"Colonel Wemyss with the 18th is to proceed by the left of your six-gun battery, with two field pieces drawn by seamen, and with fixed bayonets to take possession of the Fountain battery."

"Fortunately the Fountain's near knocked up now, sir, by our batteries." From the Captain, but as usual his optimism pleased no one.

"Having carried it," Stuart went on, "he is to direct his force against the San Francesco, if it fires. Now the troops under Colonel Moore, with two fieldpieces drawn by seamen, will move forward under cover of the three-gun battery, and carpenters under Lieutenant St. George are to go before to cut down the palisadoes. . . . Now, Major Brereton will advance by the right of the Mozelle, and cut off the enemy's retreat from the town. Colonel Moore's party will be supported by the 51st; and the 50th, having finished their work at the battery, will remain under arms."

It seemed clear and positive. Captain Nelson felt a weight lifting, as he looked forward to an end of the long-drawn-out battle against the French and the sun and the fever. As he bade them good night he had a friendly smile for Moore. If the man would fight, all would go well.

Yet three nights later he was back in the General's tent, trying to appear easy and to keep a check on his all too eager tongue. Nothing had gone forward!

"We have now made *two* breaches in the Mozelle, sir. Two."

"May I see you outside a moment, Captain Nelson?" Stuart rose as he came in. Colonel Moore made no pretense of more than a curt official nod, and Duncan looked like a piece of wood as he watched Colonel Moore flicking at the insects about the lantern with a small chart rolled into a wand. Moore watched without a twitch of a facial expression, though Duncan finally dropped his eyes and turned red, as Captain Nelson and General Stuart walked off in the dark.

It was a choking humid night. The air seemed filled with sticky winged creatures. The mosquitoes hummed in swarms from the marshes.

Captain Nelson had removed the bandage from his eye. It was blind and it pained. The surgeon said it "looked fine" and luckily there was no visible scar; just a widening of the pupil. He would never scare people, or have to wear a patch like a pirate. At first glance no one would guess it was blind. The only trouble was that his other eye bothered him, as if it were strained.

He and the General continued to walk slowly until they were out of earshot of the tent. The General's face was ghastly pale and the hand he rubbed over it shook.

"You got me in a scrape, sir!" he said finally, wearily, without looking at the Captain, who stopped, faced him in surprise.

"A scrape, sir! I? Pray how, sir? It's been my one aim all these months to assist you with all my heart."

The General's blue eyes were tired, his face wan. "You wrote Lord Hood that we planned to attack the other night."

"Aye, sir, I most certainly did along with my daily report; and indeed, sir, if I'm not mistaken, you told me that was the plan."

"Very odd that a Corsican colonel who had been on the *Victory* came into my camp. He knew all about it, Captain Nelson. Said it was talked of generally aboard ship."

"Talked of generally! I know nothing of that, sir. The truth is as I told you, sir. I naturally communicated with my Commander in Chief; but I am sure my communications get no further than Lord Hood."

"Then it is strange, isn't it?" the General murmured stubbornly, but his tone was polite.

Captain Nelson felt as if he were being turned slowly on a spit. "Perhaps not strange at all, sir," he replied thoughtfully. "We know that every man connected with us has been saying the storming would take place, as they say, 'tonight,' and they have said it every night since we landed, sir. 'Tis but part of their wish to get done with the business, no doubt, not understanding the amount of time necessary for such proceedings. That, sir, is what I would consider the answer to the Corsican colonel. Lord Hood has assured me time and again that his greatest desire is to co-operate with you to the end."

"Ah." The General rubbed his face again. Whether he believed Captain Nelson's solution or not, he appeared no longer suspicious of the Captain.

"Well, I must ask another favor of you."

"Certainly, sir."

"I must ask that your men exert themselves even further. Though I'm aware that *your* efforts have been all I could ask and more . . . But widen the breach in the Mozelle, sir, widen it, if you please."

"Aye, aye, sir, both of them shall be widened." Captain Nelson bowed. "May I bid you good night, sir, for I'm due on the battery to relieve Captain Hallowell. I'm worried about him. He looks worn-out."

General Stuart looked at the Captain, growing thinner and paler every day, and then thought of towering Ben Hallowell. "What about yourself? How's your eye?"

"Oh, I'm the reed among the oaks, sir. And my eye is quite well. Though it's blind, I still have t'other aimed at the French!"

General Stuart stood nodding as the Captain sauntered off. At last he shook his head and paced back to his tent.

Walking toward the battery, Captain Nelson tried to resolve the problems: the army, the navy—and Paoli? Yet Sir Gilbert Elliot ruled Corsica, and Paoli's Corsicans had helped fight. Not the force they had hoped for, but they had fought. Corsica had a Parliament now, and except for the town of Calvi, all Corsica was at peace and better off than in many years. England had already sent money for reconstruction. Then where the devil did Moore come into the picture? Stuart and Hood both honestly wanted to conquer Calvi, but their enmity or misunderstanding seemed to go deeper than the time-honored army-navy feud.

He paused at the top of a rise, getting his breath. The fever had weakened him so, he felt old suddenly.

There stood the ghostly walls of Calvi; not a town with people living in it, but like some weird white elephant rearing up on the cliffs overlooking the sea. The immediate military objective in this war with the revolutionary French; this strange war where neither side seemed anxious to win. Yet there was the enemy, was it not? To the guns then and have done with it! And God give the world peace!

But Stuart held back—or was held back. Whichever it was, the time lost was the same and the seamen died of fever on the batteries. And Captain Nelson began to eye even Stuart suspiciously. Everyone's mind began to feel warped for only the sun did not slacken its fire. Men dropped of it alongside their guns.

And back and forth from ship to shore came the supplies, more powder, more guns, more wine.

"It looks like Woolwich Warren," Captain Nelson said; "must they have bigger arsenals than at home?"

Captain Duncan was walking toward him, past a continuous line of men moving up the cliffs. A human chain loaded with powder and shot. The chain of men, working like mules, seemed never to stop, yet the army did not go forward.

"Our wine, Captain Nelson, has not arrived yet?" Captain Duncan asked; very smart in his powdered peruke and immaculate red coat and white breeches.

Captain Nelson, who had not had time to shave, and whose coat was dusty from being on the battery all night, held a sheaf of papers a little to his left, eyeing it distractedly. "Wine? That comes from the transports. These boats just brought guns from the cove at Cape Revellata. The wine is ordered for next trip."

"The order went in some time ago for the wines, Captain Nelson."

Wine or guns! "I'm well aware, Captain Duncan," the Captain smiled archly at Duncan, "but boats coming from the cove do not come from transports."

"Obviously not, sir." Duncan marched stiffly away.

"He's grown into such a great man!" Captain Nelson marveled. Then, catching the eye of one of his friends, a lieutenant sent ashore from *Victory,* he heaved a sigh, grousing: "If we make one trip from the ships, then what we ought to have brought was things from the shore—or vice versa!"

The Lieutenant flashed a smile that made his young face boyish. "May I tell you something, sir?" He vaulted a barrel of powder and crossed the sand.

"Pray, Moutray, what's on *your* mind?" He watched the youngster affectionately. For an instant his mind darted back to an island hilltop overlooking the Caribbean, to a tamarind tree and a pretty young woman with this youngster romping about on the grass. All of nine years ago! And again he felt old. And dear Mrs. Moutray was wid owed now, too late. Oh, but she and her husband had treated young Captain Nelson more like a son than the utterly devoted slave that he was—to her anyway. She had come the nearest to being his ideal of a woman, this lad's mother. He had been lost, miserable without her—ah—that is, until he met Fanny Nisbet, who had made life so much happier by reminding him of Mrs. Moutray with her little son.

"Well, Moutray?"

"I asked Colonel Moore a question, sir." Moutray was beaming, a mischievous light in his eye.

"That was daring of you. Hasn't your godfather taught you to watch your tongue? He's taught me."

"Aye, sir, Lord Hood gave me a speech on silence, but I couldn't resist asking Moore if he thought the pair of breaches we'd made in the Mozelle would fit the army. And Moore said, 'Why don't Lord Hood land five hundred more men to work? Our soldiers are tired!'" Moutray burst out laughing.

"He's answered our riddle! That does explain all!" Captain Nelson laughed rather quietly. "He's very considerate of his men. But my jacks are tired, too!" His eyes narrowed.

Moutray had doubled up laughing. Suddenly he said very quietly, "Moore's after Stuart. They're bosom friends now, it won't take him much longer. We're just a minor objective."

Captain Nelson nodded. As he turned away he realized Moutray was feverish, even a little delirious to be talking so much. He must watch out for that boy, his adored Mrs. Moutray's only son.

It was a few more days before all went forward with a glorious flashing of scarlet under the Lion Sun just as General Stuart had planned. Captain Nelson and Captain Hallowell looked up now and then from the new battery they were erecting, to cheer themselves hoarse. "I wish they had let me go too!" Captain Nelson shouted over the din. "Even if they just let me set up the ladders and take them down again!"

Hallowell shook his head at him. There was the least bloodthirsty man he'd ever met . . . yet the light that came into his face when the shooting began! Like an old war horse with his ears laid back! "It wouldn't become your rank, Nelson!"

"Who cares!"

The French fled the battered Mozelle as the sharp wooden fence of the palisadoes was wrenched down by the carpenters and the English troops stormed.

The Mozelle fort fell to the English. The loss: five killed; eight wounded. The seamen had softened the fort very well.

"Is he badly hurt?" Captain Nelson asked Lieutenant Moutray, who came wriggling down slope into the new battery which the seamen were just finishing.

"Surgeon says Colonel Moore's wound is not dangerous, sir. A rock fell on him."

"Send our sympathies to the Colonel," the Captain replied, avoiding Moutray's eyes.

Hallowell took a deep breath, eyeing the six guns trained now to the right of the ruined Mozelle, square on the town. "This ought to finish Calvi."

❊   ❊   ❊

And General Stuart's thanks to his troops for their daring attack, and to Colonel Moore, hero of Calvi. But no thanks—not even one customary word—from the army to the seamen who had dragged the artillery under the same fire as the soldiers.

"I shan't forget that!" Captain Nelson raged to Hallowell, angrier than when he himself was overlooked. "My men get little enough for their efforts!"

But patience. The siege had bogged down again.

A letter from Lord Hood to Captain Nelson: Urge Stuart on. For unless the town fell very shortly, Lord Hood must recall all his men from the shore. The French fleet was stirring again, threatening to land troops in Corsica.

Captain Nelson swallowed the news, determined to minimize its importance. He knew Hood's announcement would not spur Stuart, but dishearten him.

He joined the officers' soiree in the General's tent, as was customary. Yet again, after the first round of drinks, Captain Nelson was asked to step out in the dark, to stroll with the General to the zing of mosquitoes, the perfume of the swamps. His ears were ringing, and he shivered.

"Will you write Lord Hood, Captain Nelson, that I have summoned the garrison at Calvi to discuss terms for surrender?"

"You *have* summoned to—*discuss, sir?*" Captain Nelson could not hide his surprise that Lord Hood as joint Commander in Chief had not been consulted. Hood would be outraged. He had already written to Nelson to find out why Stuart snubbed him, but Captain Nelson had not dared to ask the mountain why he expected Mahomet to go to him. He had replied to Hood that all he knew was that Stuart had said he was busy.

"Will you write Lord Hood tonight, sir?" Stuart had repeated his question.

"If you'll pardon me, sir, it hardly seems proper for one of my rank to represent you on a subject of such great moment. Would it not be best, sir, for you to write his Lordship? Lord Hood wrote me today that he is most anxious to finish before the French fleet puts to sea again and he is forced to recall his seamen."

The General did not answer, but quickened his step. He was well aware that these final decisions were matters for commanders, not captains, and that he had acted without consulting Hood, against all military etiquette. But if Lord Hood chose to stay on *Victory,* Stuart would remain in camp. It was a strange time to begin to communicate directly when the two of them had refrained for months from making a bow. Stuart ignored the fact that Hood was blockading, preventing the French from bringing assistance to Calvi, and that in the navy a captain on shore was considered at least as competent as a brigadier general, so in Hood's eyes Nelson ranked almost as high as Stuart. But the army thought a captain was a captain, something very much below a major. Besides, what went on at sea was beyond a general's sphere of interest and Lord Hood might have called once.

"We need more working men, Captain Nelson. My troops must and will be spared for the assault should the summons fail."

"Aye, sir, we'll do our best."

"My soldiers cannot work and fight. So I'll be obliged to your seamen."

Captain Nelson had stiffened. His jacks were heartbroken ghosts working and fighting day after day. "We will fag to the death, sir, before any delay may be laid at our door."

"So Lord Hood wants me to go ahead or he'll pull out on me!"

"That is not exactly what I told you, sir."

"That's what I hear, Captain Nelson, if not from you."

Captain Nelson swallowed. Those leaky communications again. "Lord Hood is most anxious for the siege to be won, sir, for the French fleet takes advantage of his presence here."

But the General broke in very brusquely: "Then as long as the enemy sea battery as well as the Mozelle is destroyed, it would be but a matter of a few hours for Lord Hood to lay his fleet alongside the wall and batter it down."

Nelson turned it slowly in his mind. The General, who had refused any naval suggestions regarding a siege because naval men tended to bypass the traditional army methods, was himself flouting the very basis of the theory of siegecraft, which lay in closing on the besieged, leaving nothing to chance as the batteries were moved forward. Vauban, the master of some forty odd sieges, would spin in his grave. So it was more work for the navy? Asking the impossible to match Hood's threat? "Wood against stone, sir?"

"It would save our sapping forward from the Mozelle to blow up the outer town wall, Captain Nelson," the General said without looking at the Captain. It was the final sapping, the last trenches, the very works that made this kind of warfare deadly.

"May I observe, sir, that this business of wood against stone is much altered of late? The Spanish fleet was defeated ten years ago at Gibraltar, you recall, in that very way. Burned. The French have hot shot, sir, to burn our ships before we could stay long enough to batter the walls. Fire from a rolling ship wastes ammunition, of which we are running short. It could be more accurately aimed from our own batteries, sir. Had we no shore batteries, sir, the situation might warrant our making such an attempt in order to cover a landing. Lord Hood fought and took Bastia from the shore, sir."

"Thank you, Captain Nelson, you put your case very clearly. So I will be frank with you, sir!" And as they drew closer to the question, their civilities rose to a pitch of courtesy bordering on sarcasm. They were both sick and angry. "So that you may make it perfectly clear to your Commander in Chief, this is my intention, Captain Nelson: If the navy cannot keep us supplied in our needs in men and matériel, then, sir, before wasting more time, *I* shall decide whether to abandon or continue the siege!"

There was a long silence. The words had an ugly sound in the stinking hot air that vibrated with the steady hard fire of the seamen manning the guns on the far-off batteries. Captain Nelson had stopped, his face white. He began to speak very quietly, but with a hard assurance in his tone that made Stuart listen. "May I assure you, sir, that even if every odd that you mention were to be enforced against us, the batteries might still be held, and Calvi taken? I assure you, sir, that it is very unlikely that we will be forced to face that condition, when I have every assurance daily from Lord Hood that he will give every assistance in his power to further our cause, sir!"

"I have no complaint against you, Captain Nelson."

"Thank you, sir. My only thought is to be at your service."

"Thank you, Captain Nelson. The decision has not come to the crisis. Meantime, sir, I have a request to beg of you."

"Your servant, sir."

"About that battery which your good men are finishing tonight to the right of the Mozelle: may I trouble you, sir, to move it from the right to the left, by the tower? I am now convinced it will be more effective there. If you please."

"At once, sir. Good night." Captain Nelson drew a long breath. Two nights' work wasted! He was grateful for the dark, lest the General see there was no drop of humor left in his feverish half-blind face.

Time was against the English. Time meant sunstroke and fever. It took two nights more to comply with the General's change of mind.

"Easy now, lads, she'll come." Captain Nelson had gone himself to urge his men, for they had a sullen glance in their eyes when they saw what had to be done. "This is the last of it."

There sat a solid fat mortar in the soft dirt, among crazily pitched rocks, gaping like an idiot at the sky and weighing all of a ton.

"More plank to starboard."

The men heaved again. A cable snapped, slithered away through the wooden pulley, and the mortar lurched forward with what appeared to be calculated cunning: slid from the planks; fast among two rocks.

"Come, lads, we piloted it through these channels just t'other night . . ." And Captain Nelson strolled off almost out of earshot.

"Aye, and she'll go again." The men hurled themselves on the mortar. "And again if the army goes mincing and yawing ten points off the wind."

"All this tacking starboard and larboard. Thought 'twas forward we was to go."

"For all the General knows forward is aft and aft forward."

"Aye, he's put his stern to the town and don't know't."

But the talk was not loud, just a word here and there. Most of the men were silent, gasping for breath, their arms shrunken like ropes, their faces gray.

"We'll soon make an end to it, men, pull along, we'll have down the walls."

"Aye, Jericho . . ."

"This she-devil ain't no Ark of the Lord," a jack whispered as he fitted the cables round the mortar once more.

"Quit yer trumpeting and pull there, Joshua!"

"Pull you—" A boatswain's mate leaped on the man who had been fixing the cable. The man had slumped forward. "Stretcher," the mate snapped. Another man collapsed; more work for the living.

❊   ❊   ❊

A white flag of truce flew over Calvi.

And during the lull Hoste and Josiah came ashore to learn about sieges and partake of the Captain's dinner.

But Hoste had a headache, then typhoid. Josiah remained strong as a bull and as implacable. Hoste lay gaunt, given up for dead, and the white flag flew over Calvi.

Captain Nelson stood on the silent batteries shaking his head at the town. Calvi wanted to treat for terms. She would surrender in three weeks provided that French succor and reinforcements did not succeed in running Lord Hood's blockade; relieve the city.

"Three weeks. Madness." The Captain turned away. "Sheer madness." He looked about at his men. For three more weeks they must stay at their posts, waiting. Lord Hood, too, was dissatisfied. The truce offered all the advantages to Calvi! General Stuart was quite pleased for he wanted to act humanely toward the inhabitants.

Captain Nelson looked from the shadeless dreary batteries toward the town. Two days had already gone by, two days of watching his men die of fever. "Humanity . . ."

Now for the first time Hood and General Stuart clashed openly. The General strode down the beach, set foot in a boat, rowed to meet his joint Commander in Chief, thrash out their troubles.

As dawn of the third day came the seamen suddenly looked up, turned their heads. Stuck their fingers in their ears, shook them. But the sound grew. Behind the walls of Calvi: shouts, cheers. As if the walls spoke.

The white flag was wrenched down and the Tricolor fluttered alone. Captain Nelson and Captain Hallowell looked at each other wearily. "That's what they wanted, Ben. Time! Four boats ran our blockade last night. Calvi is stronger than she was three days ago. And we're weaker."

A blast from the town garrison, a hearty blast. Then as time crept by, the firing from Calvi grew spasmodic once more; shots fell haphazardly through the night though the seamen answered with a monotonous blast every three minutes.

"An officer of the 18th killed, Lieutenant Byron." Captain Nelson was reading over his reports. "They say he was heir to his grandfather's title, poor fellow."

"Oh, they'll find some cousin male to make a Lord Byron again. Titles don't die so easily as men—his grandfather was tried by his peers for murder once, remember that? Acquitted, of course . . ." Hallowell's voice trailed off.

"I think we have Calvi now." Captain Nelson was watching flames spurting up here and there as the battery pounded the town.

"Avast! Damn their tricks!" Hallowell pointed to a series of black flags suddenly fluttering up over the walls. "Hospitals! So they have shifted their hospitals within range of our guns! Cease fire!" Hallowell waved his arm.

❋   ❋   ❋

Truce again. General Stuart would not break the laws of war: hospital areas must be respected. The truce continued.

And once again day after day with the Lion Sun rampant high in the sky seamen must wait on the batteries under the layers of sweltering air. Immobile but alert. Captain Nelson and Captain Hallowell fagged with their men in the long dreary twenty-four-hour shifts. It helped morale, but could not cure fever.

"Far be it from me to cast a reflection on the General's humanity: I admire it." Captain Nelson looked up as Hallowell came on the battery. Hallowell was shivering and sweat rolled down his face as he prepared to take over. "But," Captain Nelson went on, "there are times, and I think the present is one, when it would be more charitable to our troops to make the enemy suffer more than have our brave fellows drop every hour—four and five dying a day!"

"The General's a strange man. He doesn't ask opinions—he gives 'em." Hallowell's voice was faint, his lips cracked. "But *they* know their climate." He jerked his thumb at the baked white walls of Calvi. "Climate's the weapon they're using now."

"Half the army's down sick, Hallowell. Our jacks are stronger in spite of their fag. . . . I don't see why the General does not send notice that they must remove their hospitals or else we destroy them flags and all! They'd move." Captain Nelson shivered until his teeth rattled and he wondered if he would go into the next stage of the fever: the rage, as the doctors called it.

He forced himself to stand; to walk. The ground seemed to pitch like a deck in a gale. He had to stay conscious. He knew this old fever of his and its course. But his men's lives depended on his staying conscious. For if the town fell and those poor fools got the chance they would commit suicide in the lust and thirst of plundering. He must get them back to the ship. "To the ship . . ." He caught himself, realized he was muttering. "The General sends a bullock every day for *their* sick," he told somebody, thinking it was Hallowell. It was young Moutray, Captain Nelson realized, while his head felt as if it were spinning around in widening circles.

"Come here." He motioned to Moutray, who looked like an old man. "You better rest while you have the chance, Moutray. I'll need you to keep a level head over these men when the town gives up. There'll be French ships in the harbor."

"Aye, sir, you could use a little rest yourself, sir." Moutray's voice was weary.

Captain Nelson shook his head. He was an old hand at these fevers. It was these healthy growing youngsters it killed. "Peruvian bark's what you need, Moutray. Bitter as gall. South American Indians used it for fever. Surgeon's run out of it."

"Dried spiders and cobwebs the old wives give you, and they say the mosquito carries the fever. Superstition . . ." Moutray tried to laugh, but he was too tired.

"I wouldn't put it past a mosquito, Moutray, but the doctors all say it's the swamp vapors. We had Peruvian bark in the West Indies. Remember the Indies?"

"Aye, sir. I must have been all of twelve when we left. I liked it. Mother and Father never went out there again."

"March, 1785, when they left," Captain Nelson muttered suddenly.

"Remember we used to walk up that hill, you and Mother and I, sir? And sometimes Captain Collingwood came along—I think he was in love with my mother. Don't you, sir?"

"Do you? It never occurred to me—except that we all were enchanted."

"You'd tell us stories about that polar bear in the arctic and the King's navy—"

"Ah, did I, Moutray?"

❋   ❋   ❋

And so day after day in the sun.

The new terms were: Calvi would surrender on August 10, 1794, provided no succor arrived. Meantime the seamen must still man the batteries, man them till they dropped of the fever or sunstroke.

One thought haunted Captain Nelson's malarial rages: should succor arrive for the enemy, would the English have the strength left to fight on? That was Calvi's last card.

It was the third of August. Seven more days. There was a rumbling in the murky yellow sky. The Lion Sun dropped for cover behind a black cloud.

The seamen stirred and raised themselves on their elbows.

"The wind!" The impassionate wind that had launched them in storm on these shores over two months ago.

And rain making mud pellets in the dust!

"Signal the transports to anchor in the bay under cover of camp."

"The *Victory's* under way, sir."

The blockading wall of the fleet was bearing up, vanishing over the horizon, storm staysails stiff: scudding before the wind. And clap after clap of thunder. Now, if ever, Calvi would be relieved while the blockading ships were hulls down, topmasts drawn after, vanished. But with a parched grin and a face lifted to the cooling wash of the rain an old sailor knew: no vessel dared challenge an entry to Calvi. Founder she must, whether friend or foe of the town.

"Let her blow!" a jack hollered. "Let her blow for a week! O God! Let her blow!"

Calvi must tear up her cards; hang out her last white flag.

"Moutray!" Captain Nelson shouted. "Get the men to the beach!" They were whooping and cheering and the Captain stood laughing at them till the tears ran down his cheeks. He had not felt so young in months. It was all over. "It's as easy to keep a flock of wild geese together as these seamen," he wrote the last lines of his journal to Hood.

Corsica belonged to England. The fleet would remain in the Mediterranean Sea.

❄   ❄   ❄

In the church of San Fiorenzo in Corsica, carved on a plain slab:

Sacred
to the memory
of
LIEUTENANT JAMES MOUTRAY, R. N.
who, serving on shore at the siege
of Calvi
there caught a fever,
of which he died,
sincerely lamented,
on August 19th, 1794
aged 21 years
This stone is erected by an affectionate friend, who
well knew his worth as an officer, and his accomplished
manners as a gentleman.

H. N.

❄   ❄   ❄

Parliament voted its thanks to the officers, seamen, marines and soldiers. While both Lord Hood and General Stuart failed to thank Captain Nelson in their dispatches; each sure the other would do his "unremitting zeal" full justice.

Lord Hood went home for a rest and upon preparing to rejoin the fleet was ordered to strike his flag and come ashore for having too peremptorily demanded too many ships, too many stores, of a most overworked Admiralty.

So the mantle of leadership in the strategic Mediterranean Sea had fallen on the stooping, somewhat tired shoulders of Vice-Admiral Hotham, who had in his sleepy way once seen nine French of the line when there were but seven.

So England took over Corsica, and the French on the mainland interned English officers and confiscated English transports that were carrying the French from Calvi under a flag of true into Toulon. Captain Nelson chalked one more black mark against the French.

In his white villa in Corsica, Sir Gilbert Elliot, Viceroy of Corsica, was comfortably settled with his wife and annually increasing family. He liked Captain Nelson very much. And Sir William Hamilton and his lady were delighted to congratulate their favorite protégé for his latest efforts.

The Viceroy of Corsica looked forward to a great prosperity in the island, for after so many years of bloodshed in France, what was left of England's enemy? One vicious gang after another had grappled the power until now a comparatively "Moderate" group sat in Paris, slowly stirring the troublesome stew. They were not friends of the Terrorists, having grasped the rule from them; nor were these Moderates friendly toward the Royalists, having helped overthrow them.

So they sat stirring the country's disorders, allowing various factions to simmer slowly, trying not to scorch the bottom nor boil over the top, calling upon the army now and then when the whole thing needed to be lifted off the fire to cool.

V. Vice-Admiral Hotham's Minuet

March 8 – 14, 1795

CAPTAIN NELSON sat in his barren cabin, once more master of his own ship, if not the proclaimed hero of Bastia and Calvi, nor the master of his own destiny. And he was more than usually restless. Months of fevers had made him prey to his hated old twosome: mosquitoes and melancholies. He'd known them in the West Indies. Now, he had at least left the mosquitoes in Corsica, but not the fever. The melancholies he tried to escape temporarily by seeking the company of his officers, inviting them to his table, for he dreaded dining *solus* aft in state and depression. But there were so many hours when the routine of the ship ticked on like clockwork—Lieutenant Hinton was very efficient—and the Captain crammed those hours writing long, long letters to everyone he knew. Then there were the hours in the night when he could not sleep because he could not breathe. He woke up, struggling for air. Had to get up, go on deck, pace. And brood.

After two years of war England's Mediterranean fleet had taken and lost both Toulon and the French fleet; then established a base in Corsica. But naval stores must still be purchased through Leghorn and sometimes the Barbary pirates sold good beef at ten dollars the head. Corsica, then, was a fortress only. Secure in it, Admiral Hotham had settled down to sit out the war for all of six months following the conquest of Calvi.

Captain Nelson had spent the first three months of that time repairing *Agamemnon* at Leghorn. Gloomily contemplating gloomier palaces; dining occasionally with the Pollards, an English merchant family there, and other merchants who invited him, mainly, he suspected, in hopes he would assign them the opportunity to handle his prize ships—if he ever took any. And he wrote more moody letters, complained time had stopped, *Agamemnon* would never be repaired. He never mentioned a woman, or allowed any mundane, chance gaiety to break the spell. The only woman he had ever mentioned in the last two years had been in his letter to Fanny when he met the Hamiltons that one time. Fanny might wonder till doomsday if her husband were faithful. He said he was—that was about the ultimate expression of love in his letters to her—and even his worst enemies, if he had any, never dreamed he was otherwise. Before he had married he had admitted, "You will say that Horatio is always in love" and proposing marriage to someone, if not in the process of being forcibly deterred from proposing by more prudent friends. He said, and no one denied it, that Fanny was the only woman in his life. Besides he had to set a fatherly example to the nosy young stepson eternally at his elbow. And he took even step-parenthood very seriously.

After Leghorn he had spent the rest of the six months cruising aimlessly, battling foul gales when the fleet should have been anchored, or lying at anchor during fine cruising weather until he wrote of San Fiorenzo: "I hate the damned place."

He had even approached the Walpoles and a few of his old naval friends with the hope of getting into Parliament—even if it meant as a Whig—though he stipulated the party must conform to his beliefs. After all, if men like Colonel Moore could get elected to Parliament . . . why, even old Admiral Rodney had gone broke keeping his elections bribed and holding his parliamentary seat. . . . All Captain Nelson asked was a chance to guide the country that he felt was steering dangerously close to rocks. But no one was interested. He had no money.

He felt he was drifting again. The three months *Agamemnon* was being repaired were to him three mortal months thrown away. And his health, which really had been damaged by fever, continued to decline in direct proportion to his rising boredom. He expected to die any day.

Corsica had absorbed him until it was achieved. Now he wrote: "What I have got at present is nothing: what I have lost is, an eye, three hundred pounds, and my health, with the satisfaction of my ship's company being completely ruined: so much for debtor and creditor."

He did not even find satisfaction in a letter from Hood, that sounded very much like the young Captain Nelson of a few years back. Lord Hood wrote him: "Look upon myself as thrown upon the shelf forever!"

No, much as he resented Hood's slights personally, he still loyally admired him as a fighting man. That distinction was always clear, especially after six months of Hotham. It was just as well Captain Nelson could make distinctions, conceal his true feelings from his superiors. For Fanny had written excitedly that Lord and Lady Hood had entertained their dear Nelson's wife, treated her "like a daughter." That was nice—for Fanny.

But Captain Nelson was growing neither famous nor rich. And when Fanny gently prodded him on these two tender spots, gently alluding to others' successes, he told her shortly his name "would be remembered after the rich were forgot." She could take consolation from that—as he did himself. For his belief was unshakable, and the present inactivity, the seemingly accepted stalemate in the war, was all the more intolerable. He toyed with applying for the West Indies station—he'd have more fun chasing smugglers than sitting in San Fiorenzo. . . . Time! He was now thirty-six years old, life was slipping by. And sometimes when he watched the master's mate turning the minute glass to time a tack, the suspense became insupportable and his mind would swing from the intensity of drive of a few moments before to utter despair. Why didn't he give up! Ask to be recalled. Even the doctors told him his health was bad enough for retirement. Go home. Take an ox and a plow . . .

Well, if England would just win the war . . . but war had a peculiar way of fluctuating like the sea, rising into small peaks, resolving again into hollows. Where and how was it drifting? There were facts to be grasped, like so much lumber washed up after shipwreck.

Revolutionary France was starving. Last year's crisis in France had been eased a little by the corn shipment bought from America. Lord Howe's battle, the Glorious First of June, had been to prevent the corn from reaching France. Howe had scattered the French fleet but not sunk the corn. Yet this year France was more hungry—more desperate.

It was that thought which absorbed him, though he found no one above him among the vice-admirals and rear admirals who worried about it. Not even Vice-Admiral Hotham in the *Britannia*.

Their orders regularly came down from the High Lords of the Admiralty, so even a commander in chief had limits to his sphere of supposed knowledge as laid out in his dispatches. Obviously, Lord Hood's curt dismissal did not lend wings of inspiration to another admiral's initiative.

Spheres of supposed knowledge! Captain Nelson scowled.

There was France. There was a French army even now along the Riviera, threatening to take it from the King of Sardinia who was not putting up much effort to hold his territory, but relying on Austrian armies. Beyond the Riviera lay Italy with the greatest harvest in years!

A multitude of little jealous states: rich and corrupt. They hated each other more than they hated the French. Just as they had three hundred years ago when France, led by a stupid but lucky adventurer, Charles VIII, marched, thanks to the betrayal of one city-state and another hoping to strengthen themselves at the expense of their neighbors, clear to Naples; caroused, ruined his army and still marched back again by the same methods.

Now France aggressive, her wits sharpened by hunger, would try to conquer Italy for food. The Allies had summoned a Council to Milan to discuss the prevention of it. The Council would not meet till June, but Austria would probably agree to stand like a wall. . . . Yet for two years England had poured millions in sterling into the Continent to assist her allies in stopping the French, and there had been but a halfhearted defense.

Captain Nelson heaved a sigh. He was tired of war. There ought to be plans. He was ill. Night after night waking up, struggling to loosen what felt like steel bands buckled round his chest. His thoughts were suddenly broken by a knock. Hoste appeared, thin as an oar, but alive.

"*Meleager* frigate signaling, no enemy sighted, sir."

"Very well, William."

So the English fleet now once again in Leghorn went ahead leisurely taking on stores.

❋   ❋   ❋

"Admiral making signal to fleet to get under way, sir! *Meleager* signaling enemy fleet sighted heading for Corsica!" Josiah tumbled into his stepfather's cabin before dawn; found him already awake, beaming at the news.

"What a beautiful morning it is, son."

March 8, 1795, was a clear bright morning with a cradling swell on the water, as if the sea had been swinging in its deep hammock. Now on waking was still idly dreaming, unperturbed by the bits of cloth at the English mastheads relaying the news that the French fleet was out again.

The *Agamemnon* with the rest of the fleet began easing out of Leghorn. They were all being towed by their boats past the twin rocks on either side of the bay. Harbors, awkward for big ships, must be worked with the diligence of sailors rigging ship models in old rum bottles.

Captain Nelson, pacing the quarter-deck, was happily absorbed in the immediate problem of putting to sea. While the men swung like gibbons aloft in the rigging unbending sails, forward on the main deck, nearly hidden by the shadows of the gangways and ship's boats, was an incongruous herd of seven fat bullocks in a cattle pen lined with fresh straw. They were switching their tails and now and then eyeing the crew aloft, not curiously, but indignantly; faintly lowing as the ship gently dipped or lifted her prow to the tide running out. A rooster crowed rather dismally, trying to cheer his hens in their lashed chicken coop.

While *Agamemnon* inched forward, avoiding fouling some sister ship, and the bay rang with the orders of officers bawling through their trumpets, the whistling and piping, the howls of profanity, the groans of timber and the tramping at the capstans as wet cables hissed dripping through deadeyes, the Captain watched the progress with an eye that had, he reminded himself proudly, piloted the Thames estuary, dogged the Mosquito Shore off Honduras, taken over from a nervous pilot to put into Quebec. The only time he had ever been run aground was when the "damned pilot" left his *Boreas* high and dry on a sandbar at Portsmouth. He had paced around her in rage at low tide. That was the time he went ashore to relax . . . take a girl riding. . . . So. His "blackguard horse" ran away with him, in one gate and out the other. Both horses ran away, and while he hurled himself on cobblestones to avoid being crushed between a cart and a wall, some "gallant" dashed out and rescued the girl. . . . He had been younger then. . . .

"Helm down a-larboard!" And *Agamemnon* avoided a Neapolitan battleship, *Tancredi* 74, which came fouling *Agamemnon's* course. Captain Nelson removed his cocked hat, made a polite bow to Commodore Caracciolo, who returned same. The *Tancredi* had been sent from Naples for the enlargement of the British fleet. But such a big man in such a little navy hardly need worry about fouling ships; did the Sicilies have even three battleships? Captain Nelson sneered through his long nose.

His heart was lighter than it had been in months as *Agamemnon* broke free of the harbor.

The wind blew a fine breeze from eastward as one after the other the ships cleared port and sails unfurled in a cascading of white pouring down from aloft till the wind snapped them stiff; bore the fleet away.

Captain Nelson was beaming; now perhaps they would actually meet the French fleet, rumored to be fifteen battleships and several smaller ships to Hotham's fourteen battleships. From Captain Nelson's point of view, the numbers were about right to total a French annihilation.

Hoste saluted, a telltale crumb of plum cake at the corner of his mouth. Did midshipmen ever stop eating? Hoste swallowed, coughed on a raisin, and announced: "*Meleager* making signal for enemy's fleet, sir, eighteen of sail."

"Take our position astern *Princess Royal,* Mr. Hinton." That was Vice-Admiral Goodall's ship, to whose van, or foremost division of the fleet, *Agamemnon* belonged.

But where were the French as the ships lilted over the sea? The sun climbing higher showed the boundaries of the water. Leghorn astern, a dark line; the tip of Corsica to larboard. To starboard: France.

That was all they saw for twenty-four hours cruising together except for a frigate flying sudden bad news: The English battleship *Berwick* 74 had tried to join them from San Fiorenzo. The French had captured her after her captain, Littlejohn, was killed. One less ship for England when she had none too many.

There was a quickening of Captain Nelson's stride, a hardening in his gray eyes as the quiet day slipped away to the rustling wake, the hourly bell on the forecastle, the lengthening shadows cast behind Hotham's fleet.

Morning. The crew on watch were sanding, then holystoning the decks; slopping about barefooted, trousers rolled up above their knees. The sweepers came after them, brushing the wet sand into the scuppers, leaving the decks white as bleached bones. In another hour there'd be the call to breakfast: "burgoo" (coffee) and "skillagolee" (oatmeal boiled in God knew what water) and for which the pigs in the manger were already grunting—as that's where most of it went. Then plenty of sea air to wash the foul breakfast taste away, unless some pious and envied jack had traded his grog for last night's salt junk. There were men who lived like Persians, doubling their rations of weevil biscuit and dogbody by not taking grog. As the men scrubbed and contemplated eating again after fifteen or sixteen hours, their minds traveled very little further. Maybe they'd meet the French and have a good fight before the master-at-arms called all hands up for punishment after breakfast. It was a tossup whether it would be better to have a leg shot off and pay stopped by the government for being so careless, or to hear the Captain read the Articles of War and order one's grog stopped for a week. Drunkenness was the most common offense and the Captain, instead of flogging a man every day, had the strange notion it was better to stop the source of the evil, for a while anyway. There hadn't been a good flogging for weeks. Beyond punishment and breakfast and the possibility of a battle, was noon grog. If a man had the restraint of an angel, he'd save his grog, then drink it plus his ration at suppertime and hope to stay sober long enough to pass muster and turn in. So on their hands and knees peering out of the ports, as they scrubbed under the gun carriages, the men could see there was still nothing in sight but the shores and the English fleet in close company.

The ships rode like a flock of great white birds, floating over the swells to a facetious wind that puffed the ships as a child puffs a feather; caught them aback, puffed again.

Captain Nelson had appeared on the quarter-deck, master-at-arms had called all hands up for punishment, some men who couldn't hold their double ration of grog long enough to pass muster and fall into their hammocks last night were ordered to do without, and the Captain had clapped his cocked hat back on his head and begun to pace.

Still no enemy sighted.

Was this war? Of course, this was the modern way. The French navy was schooled in the art of defense: to fire at English masts, run away, fire again at the oncoming English who could not bring their broadsides to bear when chasing; and so on, until the English masts were too crippled to follow. The English were baffled by it. So the navies seemed to exist as mere symbolic threats. How force the French fleet to fight? Lord Howe on his First of June (a running affair that had really lasted off and on for a week) had ordered his fleet to puncture the French line anywhere, and lay aboard, duel with whatever they found. It had won them six battleships by the end of the week. But the English had wasted much of their strength by not being able to concentrate their whole fire on one portion of the French. Still, it had been a battle. Even so, Captain Nelson thought it might be possible to attack less haphazardly.

War had become a civilized art in a highly civilized world. For all the world, except France, proclaimed its civilization. The French profession of liberty and freedom, while stirring dreams that lurked in every common man's heart, was losing the compassionate sympathy it had once roused, in the torrents of its visible bloodshed. Yet this was not the era of brutal hand-to-hand carnage. Not the time of unemployed soldiers roaming in bands all over Europe, plundering at will. It was not the same as a hundred years ago when Dutchmen and Englishmen wrestled all over the Channel for four days. When England's young Admiral Berkeley had to be pinned to his cabin table by a sword through his body, before he lost his ship.

Evening came. Still no enemy sighted.

❋ ❋ ❋

On the third dawn: "Enemy sighted." But only by outlying frigates. Captain Nelson was standing on a gun, leaning over the hammocks, watching the elegant barges of the flag officers lowered from various battleships; rowing smartly, flags fluttering, to confer with Admiral Hotham. There went Vice-Admiral Goodall, Rear Admiral Sir Hyde Parker and "too damn many others for one fleet . . ." he muttered, jumping down and beginning to pace. All the admirals going to hear Hotham's plans to lead England to victory, while the French came slowly into sight, but still far away, near France.

Captain Nelson glanced about his own ship, saw it was in fighting order. He'd been through it, white-gloved, on inspection day, and come back with few smudges on his fingers. But he could not bear to think of the conference going on at this moment. This was no time for conferences. Plans should have been laid to cover all emergencies months ago. The fleet ready to fight on sight, yet conferences were going on now with the enemy sighted. The wind might change. Or fall calm. The enemy escape while . . . oh, but he'd give his soul to tell Hotham. . . .

On *Agamemnon's* main deck the bullocks stamped and lowed mournfully. Dumb beasts going to slaughter while the worthy admirals went to plan battles together. Captain Nelson came to the forward end of his walk. He watched the bullocks; then through the open ports the diminishing admirals' barges. He half closed his eyes, pursing his lower lip. It was not the custom for admirals to consult captains.

After a leisurely hour the barges rowed back. And signals flew: General chase! He gave his orders to Hinton. This was it. He went quickly into his cabin. In another hour he might be dead.

March 10th, 1795

DEAR FANNY:

We are just in sight of the French Fleet, and a signal is out for general chase. We have but little wind, and unfortunately the Enemy are inshore of us; however, I hope the Admiral will *allow* us to go on, and if the French do not *skulk* under their batteries, I trust we shall give a good account of them. Whatever my fate, I have no doubt in my own mind but that my conduct will be such as will not bring a blush on the face of my friends: the lives of all of us are in the hands of Him, who knows best whether to preserve mine or not; to His will do I resign myself. My character and good name are in my own keeping. Life with disgrace is dreadful. A glorious death is to be envied; if anything happens to me, recollect that death is a debt we must all pay, and whether now, or a few years hence, can be of but little consequence. God bless you, and believe me your most faithful and affectionate husband.

He folded the letter. He had a new lease on life now, as if he had said his prayers and written his will again. And perhaps today his King would once again notice him.

It was a sharp gleam that darted from his eye: humble, devout, yet proud and ambitious, as he came on deck.

He glanced aloft, studied the fickle wind, then down at the daily scoured decks, the men hauling up buckets of water to wet down the sails, hold the wind: the commotion that was routine. The jacks were laying their bets on how much prize money they would earn . . . joking and laughing, but their faces were tense.

And the general chase was under way. It was luck that *Agamemnon* was small, swift and ahead, for even she barely moved. It was like sleepwalking, without any wind, or, when it blew, from east and hardly enough to flutter a scarf. The master conned the ship. It was a delicate chore, keeping the sails filled when the wind played tricks of hide and seek; promised easterly, lulled away, squalled round the compass, struck again several points off, dropped, flew back to easterly.

But the wind died down sleepily with the dark: the French were still out of reach and also becalmed. The English ships were signaled to close around their leader.

Hotham went to bed. It was not demanded, or even expected of him, that he should attempt the almost impossible: find a fleet, battle it in the dark.

❀   ❀   ❀

And another bright day. But the fleets had drifted apart. Distant cruiser frigates signaling through the blank, tense day: The enemy sighted here. The enemy sighted there. While the decks were holystoned again and jacks contemplated the chronic ulcers on their knees, and, as it was shaving day, nudged a pal, asked him if he would cue a mate's hair and in exchange have his cued afterwards. And there was a sewing bee between the gun carriages on the lower deck.

And another calm spring night with the wind starting up now and then, dancing around the compass and dropping again to nothing; the air lying heavily on the long swells rolling in from the southwest. The English fleet scattered, listless. And another night passed.

Sunday to Friday play cat and mouse. Captain Nelson began to lose weight as if the whole game depended on him. His pride was wounded. The French were again in sight. The wind which kept the English from reaching the enemy also prevented the enemy from reaching whatever objective they had been ordered to take. Probably Corsica, for they were not trying to put back to France, nor were they trying to fight.

But as the wind freshened:

"Deck there, Commander in Chief signaling: Form line of battle!" Even in capricious winds, a line must be made, so the book said. And tacking from hither and yon came the ships, or stood still becalmed on glassy surfaces ringed with waves and a breeze just out of reach, while the Admiral waited for them. He might have tried some other tactic, but that was only Captain Nelson's idea. The book did not require it.

"I have the horrors, Andrews, lest those devils make good their escape!" Captain Nelson turned to his lieutenant as *Agamemnon* slid into line behind *Princess Royal*. The wind was so light she hardly cut any wake, but sledded with the swells.

The French fleet was now in sight from the deck, like a flock of white gulls, doing the same as the English: forming the first position of battle: the Line. Was it possible they had come out to fight? Captain Nelson marveled, but he continued skeptical.

Next, as was written, would be to close—and duel, though a Howe or a Hood or a Rodney might have done better than this. But it was hard enough for Hotham to keep his ships together and the enemy knew the plan of battle, the final culmination of the art of sea battles . . . except it had never been properly tried wholeheartedly on both sides. So it remained mostly theory based on a doubtful hypothesis: that two navies wanted to fight a tournament to the death on the seas.

"One *week* wasted in maneuvers!" The Captain groaned to Andrews, who looked at him politely, but a little surprised at his expecting anything else. "Andrews, no day is long enough to maneuver and fight a battle!" The Captain strolled off thinking, How bring on a battle? How force the French to stand, wind or no wind, day or night? How prevent them from fleeing? By confusing them? By doing the unexpected . . . what would that be in this case? How bring the most guns to bear for the greatest effect with the least possible damage to his own fleet? *His* fleet? He glanced up as the signal finally flew:

"Prepare for battle."

He had been prepared for a week; slept in his clothes. The bulkheads were down, his furniture stowed below. Now he leveled his glass at the French and snorted. "The French have been all day at it and no line yet, Mr. Hinton. But they're still trying. They may fight."

"We've made a better show, sir, with our line!"

"A better *show*—ah—yes!"

"But with this crazy wind, sir?"

"Humph," from the Captain.

It was apparently a good show. The Italian shores were lined with black masses of sightseers watching the spectacle as one might the choreography of a gigantic ballet. It was beautiful! Like a massing of angels those twenty-seven great ships in their miles upon miles of lines, gilded and haloed in the waning sunset. The fresh-scraped copper bottoms casting gold lights over the sea, the black hulls and masts of the French glistening with fresh paint. The brown of the English with the paler yellowish stripes marking the gun tiers, broken by the red squares of open port lids. The English masts were freshly painted white to distinguish them from the French quickly in the thick of a fight; and also it helped make them less visible to the French trick of hitting them.

Then the wind fell stark calm.

"Oh God! Oh God!" Captain Nelson groaned.

With the night, the lights of the fleet bobbed like a water festival. Till the wind got its dander up: blew in earnest. Captain Nelson came on deck. Now strike? But no signal from Hotham. They must wait for the dawn in precision of order, if possible. Hotham's only signal before turning in had been: Keep in line and keep toward the French fleet.

Captain Nelson took those orders seriously, and *Agamemnon* dogged the signal lights and the signal guns of the French fleet in the dark.

❄   ❄   ❄

Dawn at last. The English line was still quite orderly except for *Agamemnon*. An officer aboard the *Britannia* to Admiral Hotham: "Captain Nelson has kept overly close to the French, wouldn't you say, sir? Shall I signal, Recall, sir?"

"He is very young," Hotham mused. Captain Nelson's position not only spoiled the perfection of the battle line, which was not very good at best for some ships seemed to have misjudged the direction the enemy would take in the night, and with Captain Nelson off there someone might have to assist him if he got overly zealous so close to the enemy. "Ah—" Hotham sighed, struggling with the demands of honor and the desires of his own cautious judgment.

❄   ❄   ❄

Aboard *Agamemnon:*

Josiah shooting down a stay, grinning as he gasped: "Admiral making signal to fleet for general chase, sir. It's hard to read, so far away. But that means us, doesn't it?" And Josiah astonished his stepfather by rubbing his hands and setting his hat raffishly for a fight.

"Acknowledge." Captain Nelson looked about. He had tried to anticipate the French maneuver during the night; not let them escape. But now there was not another English ship within hours of him. Very odd. He had merely obeyed orders.

So again it was each man for himself. "Make us fly, Mr. Hinton."

And Hinton was shouting: "Slack the stays—knock up the wedges, and give the masts play—start off the water and pump the ship!"

The wind, sportive until it was bored, blew squally and very fresh.

Agamemnon, pushing forward far ahead of the others, was still outdistanced by the French, who had, during the night, crumpled their line, turned and fled as Captain Nelson had suspected they might. The maneuvers of yesterday—of a whole week—were gone by the board.

Captain Nelson was poised on a companion watching the enemy through his glass. "Masthead! What's that white—smoke or canvas?"

"Deck there! Two enemy ships have run afoul, sir!"

The last two of the enemy ships had collided in the scramble to get away from the oncoming English. The flash of white had been a collapsing cloud of canvas.

"Deck there, one of the French of line falling behind. Her topmast's been carried away by the impact. They're deserting her, sir! Those dogs are deserting her!" And in the distance, tossed like a bird with a broken wing, the French ship was struggling to follow the soaring flock; she fell back at last, sails shuddering: abandoned.

"Bear down on her, Mr. Wilson!" And again the bawling of orders began.

Almost as Captain Nelson spoke one of the English frigates which had been cruising ahead of the slower body of battleships came about, heading down on the huge French ship.

"Deck there, *Inconstant* closing her, sir!"

"Freemantle would!" Captain Nelson was leaning out over the water, waving his hat. "Go it, old boy! God bless you!" Howling across miles of water. *Agamemnon* was still a good hour's sail from her prey.

After some several more minutes of what must have been hot but logical arguments, two more of the fleeing French fleet far ahead in the distance shivered, bore up, turning back to assist their crippled sister. Freemantle's frigate *Inconstant* was ranging within gunshot of the crippled ship. He fired, hovered, fired again, for the full hour that *Agamemnon* sailed in and the two sister French closed down closer and closer on the *Inconstant*.

Agamemnon pushed forward, her masts tilted rakishly, bearing down one against three, farther and farther from her own fleet.

"Clear the decks for action! Beat to quarters!"

Like so many pieces of loose lumber, overside went the seven fat bullocks.

"Clear the decks!"

Young Hoste tried to emulate his taut Captain; pretend he did not hear the drowning groans of the beasts. Someone groused: "There goes good meat . . ." and Lieutenant Weatherhead wrote it casually on the log slate. Seven fat bulls, like seven fat years gone by. This was not the time to philosophize. The drums were beating to quarters.

Captain Nelson had draped himself halfway out of his ship in order to see; was calculating his maneuvers. It was his ship and his men against three French giants. His eye picked the prize he should like: a massive black hull with three tiers of guns, a hundred twenty in all. A pyramid of canvas towering into the deep blue-bright sky. He spun around. Where was his battle support?

"Masthead, locate our fleet."

"Deck there, not a ship yet within several miles, sir."

Captain Nelson shook his head. The enemy prize would swallow *Agamemnon* as the whale swallowed Jonah. Still, if his crew were willing to give it a try . . .

But the best bet for *Agamemnon* was to strike the nearest, the disabled ship, a mountainous foe of eighty guns even with her masts crippled, for in her condition, he could outmaneuver her.

"I itch to go after the big fellow, Andrews. Looks like the old *Sans Culottes,* doesn't she? Shall we take her? What do you think?"

"My opinion is we couldn't do her enough damage without another ship to support us, sir! She's too big! But if we tackle the smaller crippled ship we may hold all three of them back long enough for our fleet to come up; support us. What do you say, Mr. Hinton?" Andrews turned to the 1st Lieutenant.

"That's my opinion, too, sir," Hinton told the Captain.

The Captain nodded. It was his also. But he had wanted to make sure no one ever said he shrank from a Frenchman of whatever size. 'Twas a point of delicate honor. "Oh, the crippled one's a good opponent," he agreed as her hull grew, darkening the sky above them. "I never saw such a ship! She's big enough to take us in her hold. You're right, gentlemen."

"I'm for fighting the big one!" Josiah interrupted without ceremony and his stepfather eyed him lovingly.

The Captain paced a moment thoughtfully. "The French fleet would hardly abandon an eighty to a sixty-four. I think they'll come back if we tackle her. . . ."

"Look at that pretty little corvette, sir, alongside the eighty. Isn't she a beauty?" Josiah pointed at a tiny sleek craft hovering like a wasp, just out of gunshot. "Can I have it if we hit it?" He winked at his stepfather, who studied the little craft without answering. She was taking no chances of falling to the English. She veered off, came about, sailing swift, teasing circles about the battleships; loyal to the crippled French ship. Captain Nelson's eye leaped back to the *Sans Culottes* 120. One of the biggest ships in the world, he had coveted her when she lay surrendered to Lord Hood at Toulon. Well, he might have to spar with her yet as she came slowly toward him. . . . If only he had support he would have all three. Alone he could only play tag—and play seriously. Until his support, even one ship, arrived, or Hotham flew his "Recall," he must tease these giants, keep on teasing them.

Meantime the crippled French eighty-gun ship was being taken in tow by a French frigate that had also put back. The *Inconstant* had hauled off, no match for so many battleships, while the two other French ships of the line stood off just about gunshot, to windward of *Agamemnon's* bow; neither coming nearer nor going away.

Captain Nelson smiled. They were giving him an advantage in spite of his being alone.

The French ships formed a long triangle on the sea, the apex of it, pointing at *Agamemnon,* was the crippled eighty.

As *Agamemnon* drew closer on the triangle of French ships, the seas made an empty blue ring all about her, the sails of the English fleet were no bigger than whitecaps on the rim. David strolling toward Goliath had nothing on *Agamemnon.*

"I intend to cross her stern, touch it, before I fire a shot, Mr. Wilson." The Captain called to the master without turning his head. He would sail head on, toward the enemy stern, then bear up, bring a full broadside to bear on it. Thus he would fire some thirty guns to the Frenchman's two stern chasers. That was crossing the T, an exquisite maneuver, for sterns had no guns comparable to a full broadside. Bows and sterns were the soft parts of any ship. In that way he would take and try to keep the advantage, bring the most guns to bear with the least possible damage to his own ship.

As the space dwindled between the ships, the French seemed to rise higher and higher out of the sea. The crippled ship's carved and gaudy gilt stern loomed above *Agamemnon's* bowsprit. A flash from the enemy stern chasers.

Splinters showered down on *Agamemnon's* deck. Every enemy shot had struck a spar or a sail! Her canvas was peppered. Just as always, the French wanted to cripple the English, then conquer or get away at leisure. Another blast, devilishly accurate, from the Frenchman's stern chasers. *Agamemnon* shivered. A wooden block crashed to the deck, a spar cracked, as she shied like a spirited filly.

The *Inconstant* was passing her, tacking at a tangent to *Agamemnon's* course, rejoining the English fleet. Freemantle and Nelson waved their cocked hats. *Agamemnon* was now alone. And the enemy fired again. Should the French cripple her here and now, it was a French prison or be blown to the clouds. The English fleet was coming slightly closer, though still several hours away, and if the wind fell calm. . . . Only one other English ship, the *Captain,* seemed to be getting nearer and she was about the distance that *Agamemnon* had been over an hour and a half ago. From Captain Nelson:

"Helm a-starboard! Brace up the driver and aft sails!"

The enemy fire was getting too hot for niceties. He'd have to start firing at a longer range, but he was still crossing the T.

Now *Agamemnon's* bow rose and slowly she swung around. The gun crews stood ready. A tension throughout the ship as she began to bring her first broadside to bear, square on the enemy's high soft stern. And as she began to rise on the starboard side, her lieutenants were running the gantlet of guns.

"Cock your locks. Take good aim. . . . Fire!" The ship rolled to the hammering recoil and a black cloud blackfaced the crew. "Stop your vents!" Her guns had been double-shotted, two balls instead of one. The gun crews cheered their shots.

"Hard a-larboard!"

As the smoke swirled away and the enemy stern gaped like a broken mouth, the *Agamemnon* swung slowly around, her bow dead astern the enemy; gained the distance she had lost in delivering her broadside. Then, "Starboard!" again.

One long, yet staccato blast as gun after gun discharged, shattering the name *Ça Ira* painted across the French stern. *Ça Ira* was helpless, some of her stern chasers already silenced. And after each broadside, *Agamemnon* slowly closed on her, then "Starboard!" again. And again and again. Part of her crew aloft tending sails in spite of the spattering enemy shot, while the starboard gun crews reloaded the guns in the minimum possible time. After each broadside there was the sullen lull, while *Agamemnon* came up for the next blow, and in the lull they could hear the French crews shouting. Minutes crept by. The battle was all *Agamemnon's,* with the whiff of her choking black powder smoke, the flashes and thunder of recoil. Until the rest of the

French masts went down and her sails hung in shreds, or drifted white bubbles on the water. Her yardarms were awry, stern crushed in. And still, as if hypnotized, the two French ships, the *Sans Culottes* and her sister, an eighty, edged the fight, warily watching without taking the slightest advantage of their windward position to sail in, drive off the lone Englishman. Only the tiny corvette darted in and out while the two French allowed *Ça Ira* to take all the beating, a monotonous beating, the same tactic over and over, for two solid hours; and still *Agamemnon* suffered only from *Ça Ira's* stern chasers which no longer fired accurately as *Agamemnon's* broadsides crushed the decks under them.

Captain Nelson saw that none of his shorthanded crew had been killed. The *Ça Ira* was helpless while her frigate tried to tow her, bring her slowly about so that her broadside guns could bear on *Agamemnon*. So *Agamemnon* would be thrown within range of the two other ships if she tried to cross *Ça Ira's* stern any more.

As *Agamemnon* ran across *Ça Ira's* stern one last time, *Ça Ira* at last came about. Her full broadside loomed like a wall above *Agamemnon's* decks; ready to cross *Agamemnon's* T, smash her bow to bits if she tried her old tactic again. Captain Nelson's eyes narrowed.

"Bring me in close alongside her, Mr. Wilson!" Instead of wearing, running away, *Agamemnon* scudded next to the wall of *Ça Ira*. Her gun crews were not grinning as the *Ça Ira's* shadow darkened the gun ports. "Point-blank, mates!" The quoins were nudged higher into place, the cannon horizontal. Sighting through the ports, *Agamemnon's* gun captains saw nothing but the wall of *Ça Ira,* her cannon run out, within half pistol shot.

"Her guns are still elevated!" Andrews crowed as the ships closed. That was what the Captain had seen. Now they ran the gantlet of thunder, broadside to broadside.

"Merciful God! Not a shot touched us!" Captain Nelson was shouting, and waving his speaking trumpet, face exultant. His crew howled their cheers.

"Hove in stays!" And *Agamemnon* came slowly about again. Her lieutenants were yelling, "Less powder!" And the gun captains' ladles measured short. "Let the balls go easy point blank!" The crews grinned grimly. One slow cannon ball raised a shower of knifelike splinters; a fast shot might cut clean through a hull—not kill anyone.

And *Agamemnon* came again, right under the big ship's sides, while *Ça Ira's* guns, all pointed skyward for hitting masts at a distance, were still not lowered to hit *Agamemnon* snuggled against her hull. *Ça Ira* was half crazed with her dead, the blood staining her sides as it ran thickly out of her scuppers. Her masts stumps, all shattered limbs; she fired full broadside after broadside and missed the low *Agamemnon*.

"Bring her around." Captain Nelson was grinning. One more broadside. He looked toward *Sans Culottes* . . . umm . . . they were closing on him. "Masthead! Locate our fleet!"

As the smoke cleared for the lookouts: *"Captain* is within a very few miles, sir." Could he hold on till the *Captain* arrived? And once more *Agamemnon* sent her curdling smoke and balls toward *Ça Ira*.

"Deck there, *Captain's* rejoining the fleet, sir. Admiral making *your* signal, sir, general recall, van ships to join him. *Captain's* rejoining, sir, rejoining."

"Acknowledge!" Captain Nelson scanned *Ça Ira*. She would be very slow making port. But why the recall just when *Captain* was closing to support him? But as the smoke cleared again:

"Deck there! French fleet to windward, sir, bearing down on us in line of battle!"

It was time to be off! "Wear ship!" He had held *Ça Ira* long enough to bring the French fleet back again.

And there they came, steering to give *Agamemnon* all their broadsides. But *Agamemnon* was already off, and the enemy fire only dotted her wake with the steam of red-hot shot seething up from the sea. "Someday they'll burn themselves up with their dirty tricks," Captain Nelson smiled.

※   ※   ※

And once more the two fleets began forming their lines of battle. "That held them," Captain Nelson mused, "they'll never make port tonight without abandoning one of their best ships."

And his ship's company were still cheering themselves, discipline relaxed by high spirits. Not one of them had been killed or seriously wounded. They were invincible.

Agamemnon was back again in her subordinate station behind *Princess Royal* and Hotham breathed a sigh of relief. Heroics were not for him, and he was not a little provoked for he felt he had flown the recall quite a while before *Agamemnon* had seen and acknowledged.

Agamemnon, midget of the fleet, spent the night repairing her rigging for the now certain battle tomorrow. Today had been but a solo performance, one to be proud of, that out of a fleet of fourteen English battleships, but one had taken her orders so seriously as to get into action. Odd? Very odd. Captain Nelson pondered that in the night. Ah, but tomorrow! Tomorrow! His hopes were high for a real shooting party!

❉   ❉   ❉

Morning found the French fleet still at sea, though somewhat separated from the battered *Ça Ira* and her one guard, *Le Censeur* 74.

The English had a fresh wind from northwest as close in their stations the English line was tacking, bearing down to divide the French fleet from the two isolated French battleships.

Captain Nelson presumed Hotham was challenging the French to stand in and prevent their crippled ship from being cut off. He could not believe Hotham only intended to capture two ships with his fourteen. To cut off a portion of the enemy with a concentration of one's own ships was correct, but to cut such a thin slice as two with fourteen seemed unsporting. Would the French accept the challenge? And Captain Nelson still wondered why the great *Sans Culottes* had allowed almost three hours to pass yesterday before she closed in on him. His opinion of the French sank even lower than his opinion of Hotham, as *Agamemnon* frolicked along astern the fine *Princess Royal,* whose ninety guns gave a prettily named ship a whale of a hull and made Nelson's Greek king look like a minnow.

Signals flew from Hotham's *Britannia:* Two English ships, *Captain* and *Bedford,* ordered to pair off, secure the *Ça Ira* and her supporter, *Le Censeur* 74. Why duel? Captain Nelson looked for more signals, why send only two against two? That had been the trouble yesterday: no battle support. But if Hotham would send three against two and take his eleven against part of the remaining French twelve he might win a smart battle. But eleven against even part of twelve was not Hotham's favorite number. He had eyes and the French ships were enormous; barring only the Spanish which were designed by an Irishman, there sailed some of the handsomest, best-sailing ships in the world. Works of art and understanding of the sea. Not, as was said of the English, "built by the mile" and cut off every so many feet. Perhaps Hotham had been too far distant from the smoke-screened action of yesterday to observe how those big beautiful ships hesitated to support each other. He must have been unable to see, for his last night's dispatch had forgotten to mention that *Agamemnon* fought alone for nearly three hours, though ships' logs recorded it . . . whatever it was Hotham was playing cautious.

But aboard the sleek, fragile *Fox* cutter carrying six 9-pounder guns was an English chief of a different mold: graying, gay Lieutenant Gibson, a dispatch courier for the fleet. His cutter was similar to the pretty French corvette that had hovered so daringly near *Ça Ira* yesterday.

The *Fox* was standing off from the fleets as *Captain* and *Bedford* bore down for the two French of line. While they plowed their slower wakes, Gibson made sail and in perfect form cruised under the towering stern of *Ça Ira*. From high on the battered poop, Frenchmen grinned down at him as if he were a fish, laughingly waved him away.

"Ahoy!" Gibson yelled through his trumpet, and his voice seemed faint from so far below. "Haul down your colors or I'll sink you!"

The French motioned him to go away, turning their heads from him.

There was a flash, a bang like a half-dozen firecrackers. The *Fox* veered off in a cloud of smoke, her crew cheering. Left the French ruing another gap in their stern.

Small heroics stood out where there were no greater ones. But there was nothing Captain Nelson could do about it. He must follow the intricate steps of the war dance as Hotham should call them. And what a flurry of signals Hotham made. They bobbed and tossed like bright scarves, all part of the ritual.

Now slowly, the two enemy lines drew toward each other, while in an isolated patch of black smoke two English ships closed with two French ships: battled to death, ordered ignored by their brothers.

Hotham's line, having cut its two victims from the main body of French, now appeared to pause, as a gentleman would, toe pointed outward in the slow dance. Hotham was honestly wondering what to do next. . . .

The French fleet, seeing their two ships were lost unless they attacked the English line, their numbers almost matched, veered away, hesitated wistfully, like a bevy of beauties. Then bore down on a parallel path to pass the English line; rake it distantly as they fled for home.

Captain Nelson groaned. The French should be cut off from home, forced to stand. Now a whole maze of signals from Hotham kept officers' fingers pasted in code books, translating:

"Admiral making signal to come to wind on larboard tack."

Captain Nelson gave the order and *Agamemnon* was thrown by it close to Hotham's *Britannia.* Twenty minutes passed.

"Admiral making signal to annul same." Captain Nelson shook his head. And meantime four ships were fighting alone; slowly battering to pieces. . . .

But this was a flustered old gentleman's battle and neither line drew close enough to do any great harm to the other. Captain Nelson's face grew haggard with disgust.

"Admiral Hotham making your signal, sir. Go to aid of the *Captain* and *Bedford* engaging *Ça Ira* and *Censeur.*"

"Acknowledge. Make all sail, Mr. Hinton."

The *Agamemnon* rippled with glee, bearing down. The two English ships were like logs on the water, nearly wrecked, having fought broadside to broadside, nearly to death, while the fleet maneuvered, not permitted to break the line to give assistance sorely needed. *Ça Ira* still had no masts rigged and both she and *Censeur* were shattered, but their flags were not struck, and the two English so crippled in their masts they could not close to lay aboard, take them by storming.

"Now we'll have our property, Mr. Wilson." Captain Nelson to the master.

"Aye, sir, *Ça Ira's* our bird, sir!"

"Deck there, *Princess Royal* to starboard, hailing us, sir, to keep astern!"

Captain Nelson, trumpet in hand, leaped on a gun, hung out over the hammocks howling, "Oh, *Princess Royal,* ahoy! *Agamemnon* ordered by Admiral Hotham to go to the *Captain* and *Bedford!* May I go ahead of you, sir?"

"*Agamemnon,* ahoy! Keep your station! And that's astern *Princess Royal!*"

"Aye, aye, sir!" And to himself, "I'll be damned. . . . Keep us astern *Princess Royal,* Mr. Wilson!" The Captain hopped down from the gun, pranced away in a fury. The *Agamemnon* fell back, sails sighing. Admiral Goodall was the Captain's immediate superior, and he was countermanding Hotham, who should have sent orders through channels, of course. . . . Meantime *Captain* and *Bedford* were two sad-looking ships. While the one Neapolitan, Caracciolo's

Tancredi 74, dropped as far as she could to the lee—out of gunshot of anything.

While the line of French came down on the English line, steering just barely within the maximum range of their guns. Nothing smashing, *s'il vous plaît.* Now *Agamemnon's* gun captains blew on their matches . . . and a long cloud of black smoke settled in the valley of sails as the English van ranged between the duel on one hand and the first of the French van on the other. The smoke made the targets even more inaccessible, yet for a brilliant flashing few minutes *Princess Royal, Agamemnon, Illustrious* 74 and *Courageux* 74 fought both sides at once; trying to strike the French fleet and give the knockout to the two lone French ships.

And all hell closed on *Agamemnon* as fire and recoil, her sixty-four guns crashing . . . and Mr. Wilson, the master, his eyes every instant on the sails, dropped in his own blood. Master's mate took his place. A gunner snatched one of the tourniquets handy by each cannon, patched him till the cockpit crews came, carried him off. A splinter three feet long javelined into a naked chest, the jack leaped in the air and Tom Allen was sent to replace him at a main deck gun. "Now prove your boasts, farmer!" someone jeered. And he did.

Sudden bloodstains oozed over the deck as if *Agamemnon* were made of flesh. The red paint looked slippery—black puddles were absorbed in the decks sanded for battle. The smoke was rending, no fresh smoke replaced it. The fire was already slackening. The French fleet had sailed by. Captain Nelson shouted to the masthead for signals from Hotham. There were none. He scrambled up, stared at the fleeing French.

"*Ça Ira* and *Censeur* have struck their colors, sir!" Lieutenant Noble was shouting as the smoke dwindled to drifting puffs.

"Mr. Andrews, board the prizes." Captain Nelson spun on his heel. "My boat!" The boatswain's whistle sounded emasculated as it piped through the dwindling boom of the guns.

❆   ❆   ❆

And Captain Nelson rowed off, not to receive French swords from surrendered ships, but to board the 100-gun *Britannia,* confront the holy of holies: the Commander in Chief on his quarter-deck.

The battle was *not* done!

Captain Nelson sprang up the gangway, saluted abruptly, still breathless. Hotham looked up from the armchair he had ordered set out on the quarter-deck, nodded to Captain Nelson to speak.

"With your permission, sir, may I suggest we leave our prizes and *pursue* the French fleet?" The Captain's words were polite, the tone commanding.

Admiral Hotham smiled up at him, laid a fatherly hand on Captain Nelson's arm. "Ah—what was that again, Captain Nelson?"

"The *Ça Ira* and *Censeur* have struck, sir. I propose leaving them with our two crippled ships and three or four frigates to guard them— and have after those devils! The whole French fleet is getting away— sir!"

Admiral Hotham continued to smile. He was breathless, leaning back heavily in his chair. His face very red from all the commotion of this last week. Captain Nelson paced back and forth, almost hopping, running his hand over his eyes, shaking his head.

While the French sailed like phantoms toward the harboring shores of France.

"Come, come, Captain Nelson, we must be contented." The Admiral's indulgent drawl stopped the Captain in his tracks.

"Contented, sir, when—" Captain Nelson speechlessly pointed at the vanishing sails. At last he rasped out, "Contented?"

The Admiral's smile faded, then reappeared as he glanced about at his fleet, counted his brood intact. "Yes, indeed, Captain Nelson, *I* think we have done *very* well!" And the Commander in Chief of the Mediterranean fleet turned away to speak to someone else.

That was that. Captain Nelson sprang down the gangway, leaped in his boat, almost capsized the crew. "Pull, damn it! Steer for *Princess Royal!*" He boarded her more desperate than ever, repeated his request to Admiral Goodall.

"You're absolutely right, my dear Nelson—theoretically." Admiral Goodall paced with the Captain. This admiral was a pleasant, rather facetious man, known as an excellent raconteur of high humor. He had led the only ships, the van, which had been in the scrap at all. "But we can't warp out of line against orders. Unprecedented. Court-martial. All that. Remember Admiral Byng?"

"But, sir, in this case—"

"He was shot."

"But, sir—"

"Shot dead. Dreadful disgrace."

"Then will you *write* the Admiral a letter, sir, demand that we chase those cowardly dogs? If councils of flag officers can deter a fight, sir, they should be able to encourage one!"

"Oh, right. I shall certainly approach him on the subject," Goodall smiled. "You're right, of course." He was amused beyond words to see Captain Nelson darting back and forth like a hornet. Usually the young man was charming good company. This must be what Lord Hood and some of the others had hinted. "Consider yourself appreciated, my dear Nelson. Every man in the fleet gives you the credit for keeping the French at sea yesterday. Between us," his voice dropped, "Admiral Hotham means well. . . ."

"Aye, aye, sir. Thank you, sir." Captain Nelson turned anxiously toward the French: mere white ghosts now, flitting away. "A smashing battle might have changed the whole course of the war, sir! Stopped France in her tracks! I beg you will write the Admiral."

Goodall nodded. Captain Nelson's voice had sounded close to outraged tears. The man was convincing. "Captain Nelson, Admiral Hotham's the best-hearted man in the world . . . ah . . ."

"Aye, sir."

✻   ✻   ✻

It was no use approaching the other admirals, Captain Nelson realized, if today was the outcome of their weighty council. "Best-hearted man in the world!" He ran up *Agamemnon's* ladder. "All he needs is a new head!" He barely nodded as Andrews crowed, and *Ça Ira* and *Censeur* flew Union Jacks.

"You'll be pleased to meet an old adversary, sir. Le Combe St. Michel, Commissioner of Bastia, was on his way back to take Corsica. And we got back all the officers who surrendered on our *Berwick,* sir."

"Very good." Captain Nelson stalked straight aft to his cabin, sank down on the battered old window seat under the stern windows. The guns were still hot, no furniture was set up. Frank, his manservant, was lying dead drunk in a corner. And Captain Nelson was heartbroken.

✻   ✻   ✻

Admiral Hotham to the High Lords of the Admiralty: "It is difficult to specify particular desert where emulation was common to all, and zeal for His Majesty's service the general description of the Fleet . . . it became impossible for anything further to be effected. I have, however, good reason to hope, from the Enemy's steering to westward, that whatever might be their design, their intentions are for the present frustrated."

From Sir William Hamilton to Captain Nelson: "I can, *entre nous,* perceive that my old friend, Hotham, is not quite awake enough for such a command as that of the British fleet in the Mediterranean, although he is the best creature imaginable."

From Sir Gilbert Elliot to Captain Nelson: "I need not assure you of the pleasure with which I constantly see your name foremost in everything that is creditable and serviceable; nor of my sincere regard and affection."

While the wind, disgusted with so much to do and so little done, now blew a gale and sent all fleets for haven. And all arrived safely except the *Illustrious,* Captain Frederick, whose ship had been in the van, taken much of the brunt of what fire there was, lost her masts, finally went ashore. *Illustrious* had to be burned, but no reflection on Frederick, who had fought hard.

So the score rested at the end of the week, Hotham gained two enemy battleships, lost two English: the *Illustrious* to storm, and the *Berwick* which the French had taken earlier in the week. The battle stood plus two, minus two for the English; and plus one minus two for the French in this battle of twenty-nine ships.

❋ ❋ ❋

Back at San Fiorenzo a few weeks later, Captain Nelson wrote to his wife:

SAN FIORENZO, *1st April, 1795*

I am absolutely, my dearest Fanny, at this moment in the horrors, fearing, from our idling here, that the active Enemy may send out two or three Sail of the Line, and some Frigates, to intercept our Convoy, which is momentarily expected. In short, I wish to be an Admiral, and in the command of the English Fleet; I should very soon do much, or be ruined. My disposition cannot bear tame and slow measures. Sure I am, had I commanded our Fleet on the 14th, that either the whole French Fleet would have graced my triumphs, or I should have been in a confounded scrape. I went on board Admiral Hotham as soon as our firing grew slack in the Van, and the *Ça Ira* and *Censeur* had struck, to propose to him leaving our two crippled Ships, the two Prizes, and four Frigates, to themselves, and to pursue the Enemy; but he, much cooler than myself, said, "We must be contented, we have done very well." Now, had we taken ten Sail, and had allowed the eleventh to escape, when it had been possible to have got at her, I could never have called it well done. Goodall backed me; I got him to write to the Admiral, but it would not do: we should have had such a day, as I believe the Annals of England never produced. I verily think that if the Admiral can get hold of them once more, and he does but get us close enough, that we shall have the whole Fleet. Nothing can stop the courage of English seamen.

I may venture to tell you, but as a secret, that I have a Mistress given to me, no less a Personage than the Goddess Bellona; so say the French verses made on me, and in them I am so covered with laurels, that you would hardly find my sallow face. At one period I am "the dear Nelson," "the amiable Nelson," "the fiery Nelson": however nonsensical these expressions are, they are better than censure, and we are all subject and open to flattery. The French Admiral is to be tried, and some of the Captains are under arrest: it is reported that the Captain of the *Sans Culottes* has run away. . . .

While Fanny learned naval history his father learned: "If you see Hoste's father in your travels, I beg you will say what a good young man—I love him dearly, and both him and Josiah are as brave fellows as ever walked. . . ."

Killed aboard *Ça Ira* during the duel with *Agamemnon* the day before the battle, as told to Captain Nelson: "The French Captain paid me the highest compliments—much more flattering than my own fleet, as they must have been true. We killed on board *Ça Ira* on the 13th, one hundred and ten, whilst only seven were slightly wounded on board *Agamemnon*. . . ."

V I. "Brigadier General" Nelson

July, 1795 – May, 1796

At ANCHOR in San Fiorenzo, Corsica, Captain Nelson and Captain Thomas Perrin Troubridge of *Culloden* 74 sat in the main cabin of *Agamemnon*. The cabin was bare as a prison. Carpets and curtains were for invalids or admirals. The idly swinging lantern lit the Captain's rack of small arms, his dirty-weather clothes hanging within snatching distance of the door, his spyglass, and the table, and a few battered chairs that had been hurled into the hold too many times when the deck was cleared for action.

The two men in the stark cabin were the same age: thirty-seven, though Nelson was much the senior in line for flag rank. They had seen very little of each other since boyhood.

Troubridge threw a large shadow by the lantern light, while Nelson, thinner than ever, cast hardly any at all. The light touching Nelson's face slid down his nose paralleling the lines of fatigue, darkening the hollow under his full lower lip, sliding off his plain ordinary chin onto his badly knotted cravat.

The light paused on Troubridge's great Roman nose, lit his high cheekbones and left the lower part of his face in shadows, out of which his chin loomed like a thundercloud. His hair was dark and unpowdered. There was something stormy about his eyes, though his face was neither brutal nor sensitive. The Articles of War were written the height and breadth of him.

Troubridge's almost glum appearance of reserved force may have been partly due to the fact he lived in a muffled world of deafness, for he contrasted strangely to Nelson's animal alertness, and his silences seemed heavy beside Nelson's occasional brooding stillnesses.

Troubridge looked angry when silent; Nelson thoughtful.

Perhaps it was only the light and the elemental uncertainty of the cabin rocking to the heaves and tosses of the restless water that suggested the tensions of a subconscious duel between the two men as they sat and talked casually, at first of old times and then, skipping the lapse of years, sought more immediate interests, now and then pausing as if each were still trying to reconcile the past friend to the present embodiment of the childhood frame.

Differences between the two men showed in the superfluous aspects of their standard uniforms.

Lean, attenuated Nelson had been painfully surprised to see that the slender Troubridge of boyhood was, in spite of his fighting countenance, already expanding toward middle age in the vicinity of his equator.

Troubridge was discovering that all Nelson's fighting strength seemed to lie now in his direct, flashing glance, that reached out and found what it sought with the positiveness of a streak of lightning. The rest of Nelson might have belonged to a clerk lost in the drab monotony of some London office.

On the other hand, Troubridge scowled at Nelson's slapdash dress. His coat appeared to have been cut for someone else, but Nelson's worn-out uniform with its tarnished gold braid was put to shame by a huge topaz ring set with brilliants that flashed on his right hand as he talked. A bit gaudy, somewhat cavalier. While it was a perfectly fashionable indulgence, Troubridge found it typical of Nelson's financial witlessness: buying a handsome ring when he needed a new coat.

Troubridge gave thought to his appearance; his coat was decently cut, and though worn it had been cared for, proof of Troubridge's self-conscious desire to conform. Nelson's total unself-consciousness of appearance made him almost embarrassingly conspicuous.

But nearly twenty years of drifting apart made each indulgently assume that the other was growing just a little set in his habits. Nelson still saw Troubridge through the eyes of a boy given up for dying: watching his friends take seemingly insurmountable obstacles in casual healthy strides; while Troubridge could not find the Nelson he had known—that East Indian fever had obliterated the husky, red-headed boy Nelson once and for all, except for the feverishly brilliant mind and ingratiating personality which Troubridge had always admired. The Nelson he knew was therefore disembodied. So they had both turned with secret relief to professional talk, as the eternal common denominator of their existence.

"Tell me, Nelson, how long has this sort of slipshod command been going on?" Troubridge poured himself another drink and helped himself to another biscuit, tapping it thoughtfully, brushing the weevils on the floor before he bit it.

"Ever since Lord Hood left. The French have twenty of line at Toulon and they want Corsica back."

"The conniving little bastards!"

"Aye. And I don't think we can afford to lose it. You should have seen Corsica a year ago, Troubridge. Every man armed. The other day I took a long walk into the country, carrying only a cane. Now their fields are tilled, their crops prosperous. Swords into plowshares. I'm grateful I had a hand in it."

"You've had all the luck this war."

"Luck?"

"I was riding around in a dirty French tub instead of reaching Newfoundland. Go on."

"On the other hand, Troubridge, while the mass of the Corsican people are friendly, they give us a lot of bull. Their leaders are bandits. By the way, and off the record, you heard all the trouble we had with the army?"

"I'm still hearing about it."

"After the shooting was over, Sir Gilbert gave Colonel John Moore twenty-four hours to get out and stay out of Corsica!"

Both men threw their heads back, roaring with laughter. At last Nelson sobered. "And Sir Gilbert has issued an invitation to Paoli to go visit England. There's a pension waiting for him. So—everything's battened down unless the French get saucy."

"Saucy! Oh, my God! Do you know what it is to be confined on a French ship? To be forced to the humiliation of sitting and eating at the same table with those villains? To listen to their gibberish. By the God of War, Nelson, I'll never insult my mother by fouling my mouth with their language—I *know* the lies they're telling! While I was staring—staring at the sea—waiting—and wanting to hang myself —thinking how can I blow their ship to hell!"

Captain Nelson's face had gone almost white at the rumbling wrath in Troubridge's voice. "My dear boy . . . by God, there'll be a good many spare hats among them when your *Culloden* lays them aboard!"

Troubridge grunted. He swallowed another biscuit, for he had continued to eat regardless of his tale of mental agony. He smiled grimly as he washed the biscuit down. "Did I tell you what those bastards did to me?"

"No. If they tortured you, Troubridge, I'll—"

Troubridge held up his hand. "It was the morning of the Glorious First of June." He sat forward clasping his hands around the plate of biscuits, while Nelson's face relaxed into a smile of anticipation. "I was aboard their *Sans Pareille*—what a name for that hulk—with Rear Admiral Nooley. I looked out and there was Lord Howe drawn up in battle order—beautiful sight. I nearly wept with joy. He was making signals while these French idiots were running around and forgetting to serve *my* breakfast! So this Admiral—Nooley—called to me. Would I tell him what Lord Howe was signaling about? Where were the English planning to strike? I told him."

"Troubridge!"

"It was the signal for the fleet to eat breakfast, like Christians, before battle."

"They probably didn't believe you."

"By God, they did, and it was. And I got some breakfast. Then that Nooley rattled off something—*brrrrr la la*—just the sound spoils my appetite, and the one officer that could talk like a Christian profaned the King's English by telling me that Nooley was ordering my breakfast because he didn't believe Lord Howe meant to fight! I dropped my whole loaf of bread yelling 'What!' and I laid hold of Nooley, and I told him, 'Not fight? Stop till they've had breakfast. I know John Bull damn well, and when his belly's full, you will get it.' But before I could finish eating I was ordered to the boatswain's storeroom with a guard. And all through the Glorious First of June, Nelson, I had to lean and listen against a French foremast. But I told that guard, I called him more dirty names than a sergeant of marines can muster for a raw recruit. And when I felt the jar of the foremast going overside above my head, I made that guard *dance* with me, by God! When they hauled down their flag I had the ship ready for Howe in short order."

Nelson leaned back in his chair laughing. "Have some more wine, Troubridge?" He slid the bottle over the table toward his friend.

"Thank you! So. While you conquered Corsica, I had to associate with the French. God, what food. But tell me—" Troubridge sat forward, eyes growing judiciously pensive—"I thought this Paoli was the George Washington of his people. What happened?"

Nelson shook his head slowly, recalling a tower and cries of *"Nostro liberatore—Paoli!"* He pursed his lips. "I expected great things of him. He wanted Corsica freed of the French. He invited us in. He signed an agreement. Sir Gilbert Elliot says flatly that Paoli has lied about him. That Paoli still hankers after the crown."

Troubridge snorted. "George Washington and the Corsicans. You wait. Washington will be crowning himself emperor or Caesar as soon as his so-called elected term as 'President' expires!"

"Troubridge, I couldn't give credit to such apparent absurd conduct on Paoli's part."

"Why not? He's a foreigner. No. You've been deceived, Nelson. But I'm not sentimental. Never trust a 'savior' or a 'hero.' . . . The world's full of thieves, Nelson!"

"Oh, but I gave Paoli credit for superior intelligence."

Troubridge's eyes narrowed. "I tell you the world's going to the devil, this dry rot of republicanism. There's no honor left!"

"Except me and thee?" Nelson smiled slowly. There were times when Troubridge, God bless him, reminded him of his old grandmother.

Troubridge grunted and subsided slowly, but his eyes smoldered.

"Now, I'll tell you what worries me." Nelson regained the offensive. "If we don't watch out France will move into Italy! Our merchants are already ruined for want of convoy and now the French have more ships than ever before concentrated in Toulon, thanks to our bold Swedish Knight—I mean Smith."

Troubridge raised his hand as if to twirl a black mustache. "He has rats served for dinner. I guess he got left over from Elizabeth's time."

"Rats? No!"

"Aye, baits a fishhook, has it lowered into the hold—fresh meat every day. Says they're tenderer than salt junk."

Captain Nelson swallowed. Suddenly he jumped up and threw open all the cabin windows. "He should have burned that fleet or kept still. But tell me, is it true he's been captured right in the Channel?"

"Aye. Right after he left London—right after all that crowing about destroying the French navy—the Frogs nabbed him. Been in prison with his sins ever since."

"If they were not our enemies, I would laugh," Nelson said soberly. "But tell me, Hotham *never* leaves port—not even for exercise?"

"Not if he can help it. He's content to let the months go by, happy if he does not lose a ship. Three months now we've skulked here in San Fiorenzo. And now there's a rumor that the Dons are treating for a separate peace with the French! The villains are already selling supplies at Marseilles. Not that one of our ships couldn't take three of them, but the time, Troubridge! If we had destroyed the French fleet last March the Dons would still be talking business with us. Now we may have a combined enemy fleet to contend with. That will scare Hotham to death. He'll demand reinforcements which the Admiralty won't send. Oh, God!" Nelson paced off the cabin like a caged lion. "Pray for a wind tomorrow to take me out of this hole!"

"I hear the French have offered Spain peace for fourteen sail of the line fully stored," Troubridge said.

"I take for granted not manned, as that would be the readiest way to lose them again!" Nelson paused in his pacing to refill Troubridge's glass. Then he filled his own with water and added a veneer of wine.

"What do you call that? Mouthwash?" Troubridge stared at the desecration of an excellent vintage.

"I've had that damned fever again. I'm alive and that's all, and— well, Hotham does not cool my temper. We have power here to do great things, if we know how to apply it. Hotham must get a new head: no man's heart is better, but that will not do without the other. If we are going to finish this war we must not be disposed to stop at trifles! It has already continued much too long, more by an opposition, and fear of an opposition at home, than by any want of power in England!"

"Well, there's the rumor of a change in our command."

"More than a rumor, I hope!"

"Sir John Jervis may be coming out soon. He's been out in the West Indies. Know him?"

"I met him once—was presented to the old—ah, they say he is very good."

"He's a Whig and he hates Pitt"—Troubridge shook his head— "but from what I hear, he doesn't let home politics interfere with the war."

"Aye, Jervis's name brings long faces to some of our officers who like Hotham's easy ways, and the fleet anchored alongside the Corsican ladies and those beautiful English damsels in distress who have fled the Continent. Freemantle's in love. Saumarez makes them swoon.

You know Cockburn of the *Meleager?* They love him, but fortunately for his career, he is poor. Can't board a ship without stumbling into a tea party . . . not that the ladies ever bored me, but I'd rather be at peace in a cottage with my own wife."

"Jervis will break up the tea parties. He says any man who marries is a damn fool."

"Yes and no . . . is he married?"

"Aye." Troubridge grinned slowly. "But what happens to the home fires, Nelson?"

"That's what I was thinking. Captain Littlejohn—of the *Berwick*— left a widow and four small children. If the government gives them anything to save them from starving they'll be lucky."

"From what I hear, Jervis isn't worrying about the orphans, Nelson. He simply visualizes the navy as a kind of priesthood." Troubridge hurled himself back howling at his own joke while Nelson's eye twinkled gleefully.

"Ah, well, I expect to be going home as soon as my promotion comes through, so I am not even expecting to meet Sir John."

"What? You?"

"I have no one to influence the Admiralty to keep me in active service." Nelson shrugged. "I've made up my mind not to worry if I am retired. I shall just take it easy, let what will come. I'd return to the farm—the ox and the plow—with no small degree of satisfaction," he finished rather hollowly, sitting down at last.

Deaf Troubridge leaped forward like a mule tormented by flies. He bellowed: "On the eve of promotion, you sit there and tell me you're going to *retire?*"

"I have made up my mind." The voice of a condemned man.

Troubridge leaped up, his head grazing the deck beams, kicking over his chair. "For God's sake, Nelson, don't do anything rash!"

"Rash?" Nelson laughed dryly, then raising his voice to make himself understood, shouted, "It's beyond my control, I said! I've determined on a cottage! I *won't* be sorry!"

But Troubridge was making so much noise as he crashed about the cabin, waxing passionate, his face turning red, that Nelson's words were lost. "If I had one thousandth part of your brains—nothing would be beyond my control!"

Nelson was on his feet too, beginning to laugh. He laid a placating hand on Troubridge's arm. "Our friendship has prejudiced you. And

happy happy shall I be to return to a little but neat cottage!" He
smiled, having outwitted the heartbreaking perversity of fate by accepting it.

But Troubridge had no truck with such subtleties. He glared at
one of the few men to whom he had always applied the word
"sterling." And now the damn charlatan was meekly hauling down
his colors to plod behind a plow. He swept up a fistful of biscuits,
washed them down with a whole glass of wine. Choked till tears stood
in his eyes. "You can't mean what you say, Nelson!"

Nelson started at the honest wretchedness in Troubridge's tone.
"No, Troubridge. . . . Oh, God knows there's no end to ambition!"

And as Troubridge collapsed satisfied, it was Nelson's turn to spring
up, pace back and forth. But he said no more.

❊   ❊   ❊

A few days later, the Commander in Chief, Admiral Hotham, sat in
the sleeping cabin of the *Britannia* congratulating himself on two
things: the French had not given him trouble for months, and now
he had seen the last of Captain Nelson for a while, that amusing
young upstart who had the audacity to board him in battle, issue
orders.

So Captain Nelson was off to carry on diplomatic negotiations with
the Austrians, who were lining the Riviera ready to strike at France and
bothering Hotham to death for support. Captain Nelson's reproachful
eye had brightened, delighted with the singular and detached service,
and Hotham had come close to embracing him in his thankfulness to
see him go.

Admiral Hotham dozed, still smiling.

A knock. A breathless mid at the door: "Captain Nelson—ah—
Agamemnon in sight in great distress, sir! The whole French fleet is
chasing her, sir!"

"Very well . . . no!" Hotham sat up. His dispatches had assured him
the French fleet was at Toulon. What had that young man done?

"He appears hard-pressed, sir. They have seventeen sail of line on
Agamemnon's wake, sir."

"Very good," Hotham said dismally. There was nothing for it but
to go on deck. He creaked and stood dizzily catching his breath. He
would not be able to carry on much longer; his illness was no longer
concealed by his good-natured calm.

He might have saved himself the laborious climb up the ladder to the deck, he realized, as soon as he stepped out in the open. He could see nothing. The closed harbor hid the wild chase. But the cliffs above were thick with Corsicans cheering and leaping and pointing to sea. It was like trying to follow a play by watching the audience, for knowing the Corsicans, Hotham grunted, it was a moot question whether they cheered the lone Englishman or the French.

"Signal fleet to put to sea," he said wearily.

But there was little the English fleet in San Fiorenzo could do, for the wind—when it blew at all—pinned them in port. Hotham's signal to put to sea hung limp at the masthead, or ironically lifted and pointed straight on shore; dropped again, shivered, hangdog.

The watchers on the cliffs and the ships nearest the entrance to the harbor watched *Agamemnon* neither lose nor gain. She looked like a tiny brown hare before black and white hounds. However the wind did favor her escape, when it blew.

She rose on the swells, just out of gunshot of her pursuers. So she had fled for seventeen hours after sailing right into the French fleet, on the course Hotham had said would be safe.

At last the watchers from San Fiorenzo saw *Agamemnon's* boats lowered; row ahead. Saw the oars rise and fall, yet *Agamemnon* seemed to stand still, while with a puff of fresh wind springing up from another part of the sea, the French closed on her.

Agamemnon still lolled on silky smooth water, no wind having reached her. Her boats slowly hauled her about, her sails hung listlessly, until as the ruffling water surrounding the French suddenly spread, the wind touched her. She hauled in her boats, sails snapping full, and flaunting a petticoat wake, danced out of reach again.

The sightseers on shore roared and hugged one another while sweat poured down the stern face of Captain Troubridge watching Nelson from the deck of H.M.S. *Culloden*. He groaned when the wind fell and bawled for his boat crews to get him free of the harbor. And sometimes he gritted orders to *Agamemnon,* far beyond any hearing, for among fanatically technical seamen, Captain Nelson had the dubious reputation of being "no seaman."

In the bay behind *Culloden* was the old *Victory,* back with a new Rear Admiral, Man, who was trying to get the van ships under way. (Goodall had gone to the Continent, disgusted at not being appointed Commander in Chief.) So hour after hour went by as the unwieldy ships edged out and the French hovered over Captain Nelson who was working *Agamemnon* toward port, using all the means within his grasp at each given moment. For once, even the saltiest captain who tended his ship as if it were an ailing infant agreed that Captain Nelson seemed to be concentrating on his navigation and not on the outcome of the whole war.

But the day seemed endless. The seven long hours that Captain Troubridge of *Culloden* watched were by the immediacy of the experience longer than the Biblical seven lean years in Egypt; or the first seven hundred in the life of a dead patriarch.

At last with a sudden savage puff of the wind *Agamemnon* lifted her bows till her bottom showed. She seemed to leap for the shore, while the French held off, tempted, but cautious. Not daring to come any closer lest the wind favor the English or becalm the French, wash them ashore. So there they rested as the sun went down and the English fleet continued trying to put to sea.

❋   ❋   ❋

Morning. Six of the English led by Rear Admiral Man, including Captains Nelson and Troubridge, sailed within gunshot of the fleeing French, who with a change in the wind were going home. After one raking fire, the wind began to flutter again, and Hotham signaled the English to come back.

"And thus has ended our second meeting with these gentry!" Captain Nelson threw up his hands, while his friend Troubridge was spied with his hands full: the wind, not the enemy, had carried off one of his masts. He limped home.

A few days later Josiah rushed his stepfather, hugged him. "Colonel!" he saluted, and waved a newspaper under the Captain's nose.

Captain Nelson had just been appointed Colonel of Marines; it was a naval award, and it came for his work in Corsica, plus the salary that went with it. Captain Nelson immediately wrote Fanny to give his father two hundred pounds, forgetting in his delirium that he had been begging her to buy a house with the first money that came into their hands.

On then to the Riviera where the French and the Austrians faced each other to see what could be done to spur an old Austrian general's horse!

❋   ❋   ❋

Captain Nelson to his wife:

OFF VADO BAY, *24th July, 1795*

What changes in my life of activity! Here I am, having commenced co-operation with an old Austrian General, almost fancying myself charging at the head of a troop of horse. . . . The service I have to perform is important, and as I informed you a few days ago from Genoa, I am acting not only without the orders of my Commander-in-Chief, but in some measure contrary to them. However, I have not only the support of His Majesty's Ministers, both at Turin and Genoa, but a consciousness that I am doing what is right and proper for the service of our King and Country. . . . I have eight sail of frigates under my command.

The Austrian army is composed of 32,000 of the finest Troops I ever saw; and the General when he gets to Nice will have the baton of a Field Marshal: what shall I get? However, this I can say, that all I have obtained I owe to myself, and to no one else, and to you I may add, that my character stands high with almost all Europe; even the Austrians knew my name perfectly. When I get through this campaign, I think myself I ought to rest. I hope to God the war will be over, and that I may return to you in peace and quietness. A little farm, and my good name form all my wants and wishes.

Yours,

HORATIO NELSON

❊　　　　　❊　　　　　❊

To his father:

July 29th, 1795
(Blockading neutral Genoese)

I am now co-operating with the Austrian Army under General de Vins . . . if Admiral Hotham will support the measures I have proposed, I expect, by the middle of September, we shall be in Nice, and of course, have the harbor of Ville Franche for our Squadron. But Hotham has no head for enterprise, perfectly satisfied that each month passes without any losses on our side. I almost, I assure you, wish myself an Admiral, with the Command of the Fleet. Probably when I grow older, I shall not feel all that alacrity and anxiety for the Service which I do at present. . . . From the vigorous measures I am taking with the Genoese, I am most unpopular here. . . . All war or all peace is my idea. . . . I am now pointed out as having been this war *one hundred and twelve* times engaged against the French, and always successful to a certain degree. No officer in Europe can say as much. . . .

That was the beginning.

Vado Bay was a mere bend in the land, a safe anchorage in fair weather and a trap in storms. By the Council at Milan it had been agreed upon for the Allied Headquarters. Captain Nelson's frigates had fanned out along the Riviera coast to prevent the enemy and the neutrals from supplying the French army.

Leaving Vado one evening, *Agamemnon* set out on a routine chore.

❊　　　　　❊　　　　　❊

Closing in along the coast of a dawn-streaked night, *Agamemnon* and six of her frigates hovered hawklike over a sleepy Genoese outpost which the French army had captured. A rumor had reached Captain Nelson that a convoy of provisions for the French army was due there.

As the sky cleared, and the Mediterranean flashed with the summer sun:

"Deck there, twelve sail inshore unloading supplies!"

Captain Nelson had been thoughtfully pacing the quarter-deck in the still cold shadow of the high curved bulwark. He leaped on a gun, peering shoreward.

"Beat to quarters. Make signal to squadron to cut them out. Mr. Andrews, call your boarders and take command of the boarding!" While the drummers beat the call to quarters, the boatswain piped the boarders away, and Captain Nelson studied the shore.

A flag fluttered slowly up over the small shore battery: Genoese; neutral! He tightened his jaw. . . . Then from across the water came faint shouts and the clattering of hoofs. Like little toy soldiers, a company of cavalry charged along the shore and flying over its leader: a Tricolor.

Swiftly and surely the boats closed on the small enemy sail, putting them between the seamen and the firing from the cavalry on shore. The Captain could see young Hoste, proud as an admiral in full charge of one of *Agamemnon's* boats, cheering his men and steering for an enemy brig.

Back and forth the French cavalry dashed, churning clouds of bright spray. The horses' wild neighing, high-spirited tosses of sleek necks through the gauzy drifts of smoke from the cavalry fire. All show. They could not hit the English, still grimly rowing toward their cherished supply ships.

"We'll hold our fire," Captain Nelson to Lieutenant Noble, "unless they start any real trouble. . . . But I want that corvette." He pointed down the bay toward a beautiful sleek black polacca hull. "She's the very one I spied when we took *Ça Ira!*" But she was cutting her cables, drifting wisely under the protection of the town and the batteries. "Signal Captain Freemantle to send a boat for a message." Captain Nelson eyed the sweet little corvette once more and went to his cabin.

Agamemnon, ALASSIO, *Aug. 26, 1795*

To the Commander of the National Corvette

SIR:

The French having taken possession of the Town and Coast of Alassio, I cannot but consider it as an Enemy Coast; therefore, to prevent destruction to the Town, and to avoid the unnecessary effusion of human blood, I desire the immediate surrender of your Vessel. If you do not comply with my desire, the consequences must be with you and not with

Your very humble servant,

HORATIO NELSON

While Captain Freemantle sailed off to procure the corvette, which lay at the western edge of the bay, *Agamemnon* lay, within half pistol shot of the battery, her ports yawned, her cannon run out, silently contemplating the sweeps and rushes of the frantic horsemen. Now and then a musket ball pinged through her sails. Still she lay, rolling slightly. The sun striking her rounding sides made the shadows of her port lids move slowly, as if she blinked now and then when the sun lit the muzzle of a cannon, like the iris of a giant eye peering out. For all the cries and clatter on shore there was infinitely more threat of death in her silence, so close that if she woke she could turn the creaming surf to blood in a wink. Still she rocked and dozed.

Captain Nelson's eye ached from studying the shore trying to decide how to wipe out the French and not wipe out the miserable Genoese villagers in the hovels ranged behind the French show. All he wanted were those illicit ships and he wouldn't mind taking the French along with them, but to fire point-blank on a half-starved mass of fishermen who were neutral would be pitiless; rouse more bitter neutral hatred of his blockade. He was already starving these people to death for not being able to resist the armed French who occupied their towns. His eye lingered on a flashing of French bayonets: soldiers marching down on the beach behind the cavalry. Still *Agamemnon* slept, and the musket balls from the shore seemed no more than fly stings on the hide of an elephant.

Captain Nelson focused his glass on his boat crews now laying in their oars, grappling the convoys, leaping for the decks.

Two of the convoys were galleys; their oars, manned by naked criminal slaves, lashing the water in measured strokes. Like centipedes. Then immobile: cornered by Captain Plampin's frigate, *Ariadne,* closing on the shore. A shot from *Ariadne:* galley oars broke like straws. A gap where the oars had been and the maniac cries of slaves, chained in the stinking dark. Howling in terror of the next shot. The galleys' flags struck.

Captain Nelson started. "Signal *Ariadne* she's running into danger!"

Captain Plampin was skirting closer and closer to shore intent on his next prey, jubilantly waving his hat at *Agamemnon.*

"Deck there, *Ariadne's* ashore!"

Captain Nelson groaned. "Signal boats to assist Captain Plampin," he snapped. "In his zeal he has done too much!" Through his glass he could see the surprised anguish on Plampin's face as he dashed his cocked hat to the deck. He had struck the insidious shallows that ran out, unsuspectedly, for yards and sometimes a mile beyond the water's edge.

The cavalry on shore was galloping down the beach, pouring their fire into Plampin's ship, spurring their horses into the surf, breasting the waves. As the English boat crews rowed toward *Ariadne,* the cavalry opened fire on the seamen.

Captain Nelson studied the position of his frigates. *Meleager* lay at a tangent to the town. "Signal *Meleager* to fire a few shots."

There was a blast, horses and soldiers fell back in the water as *Meleager* raked the beach at an angle, avoiding the town. Once, twice. The French retreated.

Captain Nelson nodded thoughtfully.

At the west end of the bay he saw Freemantle's *Inconstant* returning; the French corvette he had so long admired was lilting down the bay with Lieutenant Andrews aboard. So far so good.

One by one the convoys were being cut out, towed or sailed. The picture of Hoste commanding a boat suddenly darted through the Captain's mind. Where was he?

❉   ❉   ❉

Hoste had ordered his boat to steer for a brig. This was his hour to prove himself to his Captain. His heart was beating time to the pounding of the brilliant cavalry on shore as he leaped into the chains, swung himself onto the deck, pistols drawn for a death skirmish.

A Frenchman met him unarmed by the conn. He shrugged his shoulders to Hoste. Why fight? He pointed toward *Agamemnon*, still rocking and blinking quietly in the sun. The brig surrendered.

Hoste took a breath, somewhat dashed.

"Tom Allen"—he turned on one of *Agamemnon's* best gunners— "prepare to weigh." But what else should he do? Check her cargo? She might have explosives! Musketry from the shore was pelting her; she heaved underfoot and he felt as if he were gone! Then she settled again. But if she did carry powder . . .

Having set the crew to getting her under way, Hoste clutched his pistols, went to check the brig's stores. Some maniac Frenchman might be hidden below ready to blow her to bits as soon as she got in the midst of the English squadron. He ran down the main ladder, stumbled, groped. Below deck the brig was a dirty black cave. Half crouching under her low beamed deck he groped forward.

There were two pistol shots. A howl.

Silence. Then from very far down, near the bottom of the bay a faint, "Allen! Oh, Allen! Tom Allen!"

❋   ❋   ❋

Captain Nelson checked his watch. One hour since his boats were lowered. He closed his watch. Excellent.

In a sullen line alongside his squadron lay: the corvette, 206 tons, ten guns, eighty-seven men; one gunboat, six guns; three galleys; two brigs; one bark; one tartan, and on shore he could see three hulls, three bonfires made of three more barks.

And as one by one his crews reported "no killed, no wounded," he felt more and more pleased.

The last boat alongside. "Ahoy! Hoist out a grating!"

Lieutenant Noble ordering: "Quartermasters below to sling a wounded man!"

And slowly up the side came the litter. Hoste was on it. "Oh God!" Captain Nelson's heart sank. He'd just seen that youngster through typhoid. He ran forward.

"Where are you wounded, William?"

Hoste, his face ashen, opened his eyes. "Down the scuttle, sir. It was wine, sir, not powder. . . ."

Captain Nelson stared at him in bewilderment. "What happened to him? Easy, lower him slowly. Pass the word for the surgeon."

"He busted his leg, sir." Tom Allen, his face anxious as a crone's, shook his head. "He fell down a scuttle, sir, checking the cargo."

"Just wine . . ." Hoste groaned.

Captain Nelson turned away, facing months of anxiety all over again. If Hoste had been his very own child he couldn't have felt worse. "William"—his voice was almost angry as he walked beside the litter the men were easing toward the cockpit ladder. "William, let me know if there's anything—*anything* you want—any time!"

He glared at Allen and stalked back to the quarter-deck.

"Pretty soft." Josiah's face had turned scarlet, jealous of his step-father's attention to Hoste. He had never been trusted to take a boat crew. "Well, he asked for it." Josiah was still grumbling as he fell into step beside his stepfather. For a moment they stared at each other in unadulterated hate, then both of them smiled, both ashamed.

"I say, Father, when can I command a boat?"

"Any time you volunteer, dear boy. . . ."

❋   ❋   ❋

At San Fiorenzo, Vice-Admiral Hotham, whose admiration for Captain Nelson increased with absence, added a note when he transmitted Captain Nelson's dispatch on the capture of the convoy at Alassio to the Admiralty: "His officer-like conduct upon this and indeed upon every occasion where his services are called forth, reflects upon him the highest credit."

❋   ❋   ❋

Within a few nights Lieutenant Andrews and Lieutenant Spicer received orders to capture a small ship reported to be anchored at Oneglia. The two lieutenants each commanded one of the enemy galleys, now rigged for sailing only. Elated they slipped out of Vado and, keeping close together, scudded over the shallows till they spied three larger vessels with lateen sails, black and angular as bats' wings on the horizon.

"Shall we take the Captain a present?" Andrews hailed Spicer through the dark.

"They look very pretty . . ." from Spicer.

❋   ❋   ❋

Captain Nelson to his wife:

Vado Bay, 1st September 1795

. . . I have not been so successful. I detached Mr. Andrews to cut off a ship from Oneglia: on his passage he fell in with three Turkish Vessels, as it has since turned out, who killed and wounded seventeen of my poor fellows. Seven are already dead, and more must be lost by the badness of their wounds; and I am sorry to add, that the Turks got into Genoa, with six millions of hard cash: however, they who play at bowls must expect rubs; and the worse success now, the better, I hope, another time. . . . Collingwood I hear is arrived in the *Excellent* 74, with the Convoy from England. I am almost afraid that the campaign in this Country will end in a very different manner from what might have been expected; but I will do my best until it finishes.

❋   ❋   ❋

Within the Allied Headquarters of General de Vins at Vado Bay, Captain Nelson waited with Mr. Drake, the English Minister to Genoa, for some kind of decisive answer. At last De Vins appeared: a desiccated, weary, but dapper little man whose protestations of patriotic energy had begun to sound merely glib to Captain Nelson's ears. For two months the Austrian and French armies had faced each other, both, so De Vins claimed, in impregnable positions.

The room shrank as it filled with the clanking of swords and sabers at the sides of debilitated princes, tired generals, suave aides-de-camp, all of them terribly impressed but terribly bored by that zealous young Captain Nelson.

De Vins smiled, and his thin brittle face looked as if it would crack. "Now, Captain Nelson, I have dwelled on your plans. You desire a better anchorage for your ships than Vado and therefore you desire I lend you five thousand men to move in farther west at San Remo. Captain Nelson, I am not a seaman, but I understand San Remo is worse than Vado Bay. By the Military Commission held at Milan the Allies decided to make Vado their base where the English *fleet* could remain during the winter and prevent an enemy attack on Italy." De Vins smiled to the Captain to present his rebuttal—if any.

Captain Nelson had stiffened. The old devil with his half-truths had twisted his plans, made an idiotic shambles of his proposals. "Indeed, sir, San Remo is not so good an anchorage as Vado, nor was that my reason for possessing it, sir. The possession of San Remo, as headquarters for magazines of stores and provisions, would enable *you,* sir, to turn your army to the eastward or westward; the enemy would be cut off from provisions. And Nice, from the vicinity of San Remo, would be completely blockaded by sea."

The General had nodded thoughtfully to the Captain's reply. He knew very well that Captain Nelson wanted to attack the whole French army in its rear. That Captain Nelson wanted action, marches, battles—in short, a shooting war between the Austrians and French! But General de Vins was not too pleased that the Commander in Chief of the Mediterranean fleet had sent Austria *one* battleship when the Milan Commission had agreed on a fleet!

"Captain Nelson, would the Admiral Hotham assist, and cover the landing of six to ten thousand men on the coast of Provence? And will the Admiral Hotham undertake to prevent the Toulon fleet from molesting us?"

"I will communicate with him directly, sir; we are expecting his fleet any moment to appear off Vado."

❋ ❋ ❋

On a bright September afternoon the low scudding clouds on the horizon took shape: "Admiral Hotham in *Britannia,* with twenty sail of line, sir."

And Admiral Hotham signaling *Agamemnon:* he regrets he cannot stay to receive General de Vins, who had put on his best sash and boots for the occasion, but must proceed to Leghorn to water the fleet.

And Captain Nelson's boat crew rowing like men possessed; leaving an enraged and humiliated Commander in Chief of the Allies on shore to curse the arrogance of the British Commander in Chief afloat! Captain Nelson once more boarding his admiral: demanding action.

Hotham, his face chalky white, his eyes black-rimmed and slow to move, was smiling more wanly than usual as he shook hands.

"Will I return to Vado from Leghorn, the General asks? Ah—that is uncertain, my dear Nelson, I rather think I shall not have an opportunity of returning. My presence is necessary in another place."

"Aye, aye, sir."

"And then this General asks, will I assist and cover the landing of six to ten thousand men on the coast of Provence? Ah—*no, my dear* Nelson, but to his last question: Will I undertake to prevent the Toulon fleet from molesting his operation? Why, yes, most certainly. And how have you been? Well, I hope?"

"Thank you, sir . . . Frankly, sir, my only reason for approaching you about ships to assist De Vins is this: the General has no intention of moving, I fear, though I have been led to believe Nice was the objective of his campaign. But he means to go no further, sir, than Vado and he means to lay the miscarriage of the enterprise against Nice to the non-co-operation of the British fleet and the Sardinian army. To leave General de Vins no room to insinuate such a want on our part has been my object in proposing the movement into San Remo. I had enough ships to move five thousand men in myself without asking you to give more, sir, but the General has a new delay—a better idea perhaps—and again, by asking you to protect the landing of ten thousand men he lays the blame at our door if we refuse. May I, sir, have your permission for enough ships to land those ten thousand?"

"My dear Nelson, I cannot!" Hotham was still smiling. "For I must even beg some of your frigates . . . four ought to be enough for your work here. I'll take the rest. And while I am at Leghorn *you* will keep an eye on the Toulon fleet for us, as well as along the coast."

Captain Nelson stood stunned. "Aye, aye, sir."

❈   ❈   ❈

General de Vins and the King of Sardinia wrote the Court of Vienna that they were certain the English navy was receiving bribes from the French. And the complaint was forwarded to London. . . .

While English Ministers in Italy were writing Captain Nelson that the Austrians were probably accepting bribes from the French! But the complaint by the Court of Vienna cut Captain Nelson to the soul, though it did not disturb anyone else; not even the man to whom Nelson addressed a protest:

To the Right Honorable Lord Grenville, Secretary of State for Foreign Affairs:

MY LORD,

Having received, from Mr. Drake, a copy of your Lordship's letter to him, enclosing a paper highly reflecting on the honor of myself and other of His Majesty's Officers employed on this Coast under my Orders, it well becomes me, as far as in my power lies, to wipe away this ignominious stain on our characters. I do, therefore, in behalf of myself and much-injured Brethren, demand, that the person, whoever he may be, that wrote, or gave that paper to your Lordship, do fully, and expressly bring home his charge; which, as he states that this agreement is made by numbers of people on both sides, there can be no difficulty in doing. We dare him, my Lord, to proof. If he cannot, I do most humbly implore, that His Majesty will be most graciously pleased to direct his Attorney-General to prosecute this infamous libeller in His Courts of Law; and I likewise feel, that, without impropriety, I may on behalf of my brother Officers, demand the support of His Majesty's Ministers: for as, if true, no punishment can be too great for the traitors; so, if false, none can be too heavy for the villain, who has dared to allow his pen to write such a paper. Perhaps I ought to stop my letter here; but I feel too much to rest easy for a moment, when the honor of the Navy, and our Country, is struck at through us; for if ten Captains, whom chance has thrown together, can instantly join in such a traitorous measure, it is fair to conclude we are all bad.

As this traitorous agreement could not be carried on but by concert of all the Captains, if they were on the Stations allotted them, and as they could only be drawn from those Stations by orders from me, I do most fully acquit all my brother Captains from such a combination, and have to request, that I may be considered as the only responsible person for what is done under my command, if I approve of the conduct of those under my orders, which in this most public manner I beg leave to do: for Officers more alert, and more anxious for the good, and honor, of their King and Country, can scarcely ever fall to the lot of any Commanding Officer.

For myself, from my earliest youth I have been in the Naval service; and in two Wars, have been in more than one hundred skirmishes and battles, at sea and on shore; have lost an eye, and otherwise blood, in fighting the enemies of my King and Country; and, God knows, instead of riches, my little fortune has been diminished in the service: but I shall not trouble your Lordship further at present, than just to say—that I have had the pleasure to receive the approbation of the Generals of the Allied Powers; of His Excellency Mr. Drake, who has always been on the spot; of Mr. Trevor, who has been at a distance; when I expected and hoped, from the representations of His Majesty's Ministers, that His Majesty would have most graciously condescended to have favorably noticed my earnest desire to serve Him, and when, instead of all my fancied approbation, to receive an accusation of a most traitorous nature—it has almost been too much for me to bear. Conscious innocence, I hope, will support me.

And to his wife:

Vado Bay, *Sept. 15, 1795*

I am not, Fanny, quite so pleased as I expected with this army, which is slow beyond all description; and I begin to think the Emperor of Austria is anxious to touch another four million of English money. As for German Generals, war is their trade, and peace is ruin to them; therefore we cannot expect they should have any wish to finish the war. I have just made some propositions to the Austrian General to spur him on, which I believe he would have been full as well pleased had I omitted: in short, I can hardly believe he means to go any farther this winter. . . .

While Admiral Hotham, "whose presence was necessary in another place," went to Naples to spend the winter, recover his health and enjoy the cultured friendship of Sir William Hamilton and his lady. Captain Nelson closed his eyes in disgust. Only to open them on an order from acting Commander in Chief Sir Hyde Parker:

Send all the frigates except *Inconstant* and *Southampton* back to the fleet. Two frigates were all Sir Hyde could spare Captain Nelson. And would Captain Nelson continue the British navy's hearty cooperation with General de Vins according to his orders dated last June (when he had eight frigates)? And would Captain Nelson continue to keep an eye on the French fleet at Toulon, as well as continue to blockade the Riviera as far south as Genoa? In short: Captain Nelson would please keep *Agamemnon* stationed in or near three different ports at one and the same time.

Captain Nelson sat down very slowly, contemplating his orders. His hand groped for his bell. He must go ashore at once, spur De Vins to do something before some half-wit took even *Agamemnon* from him; left him to swim his blockade duty from Toulon to Genoa.

No one answered his bell. He rang again. He could hear the watch on deck passing the word for Frank to get the hell into the Captain's cabin. Still no Frank Lepee appeared. The bell again. More yells. Bawling, "Stop him—he's mad!"

A crash. "Damn you, make way!" Frank kicked open the door, stood in a fog of rum, his eyes bloodshot, leering at the Captain.

"Get out!" Nelson was on his feet.

"Did ya ring or didn't ya?" Frank's eyes were murderous, but somehow, in a corner of his mind, he was still functioning as he staggered toward the Captain's locker, fumbled to open it.

The Captain snapped out: "Sentry, arrest Frank! Confine him till he sobers up and never let me lay eyes on him again!"

Frank had turned slowly around as the sentry ran in. His face went all slobbery as a baby's. "After all the years I tended you? You won't let Frank go? I'm sober, sir, I'm sober!" He was crying, then howling like a banshee as the sentry prodded him out.

Captain Nelson sat down again as the door closed, cupped his aching head in his hands. Then he rang his bell louder than ever. "Pass the word for Tom Allen."

Allen, just as lumbering and ungainly as the day he left Burnham Thorpe, but blackened by sun and stronger now than a bull, saluted at the door. He was grinning as usual. "Aye, aye, sir, what'll it be, sir?"

Captain Nelson stared at his Caliban. Impudent, disrespectful, churlish, incapable of assuming even the rudimentary polish of holding his tongue until addressed, stubborn, willful . . . braggart . . . strong, honest and, "You may be my *valet.*"

"What's a walley?" Allen came in, looked around suspiciously.

"Frank—without the rum."

"Oh, I can do better'n him. All right, sir." Allen beamed, "A walley! Well. What's first, sir?"

"Full dress," but as Allen still looked dumb, "full fig—" And between the two of them they did a frightful job of it, but Allen's self-confidence, and his manly refusal to bend his neck to any yoke, sent the Captain ashore in good humor.

Winter set in very early that year. A steady sleet peppered the seamen as they crawled aloft over icy yards to tend sails, a knife-cold wind that would send Captain Nelson's two frigates scudding; even *Agamemnon* could not always stand up to it, but had to ride bare poled, while snow drifted on her decks, helpless till the storm whistled itself out.

After so many years of constant service, *Agamemnon* had grown rotten. She lay like a tub, cables were served round her hull in a makeshift corset. Her copper was loose in places; the toredo worm would soon eat her. She creaked and complained. Pieces fell out of her. She disintegrated. Her decks had the spongy softness of age without strength. There would be a crash in the night: another water cask fallen through her tiers, threatening to plunge right through her bottom; sink her. And the sea seemed to seep through the copper into her bilge. The clanking of the pump chains and the measured tramp of the men at the pumps threatened more disaster: men swore the vibration alone would have caused her to fall open like a ripe nut, but for the cables. Some swore she'd disappear sometime on the recoil of a broadside.

To the French on the Riviera she was a phantom looming up of a dawn, cutting their supply lines, disappearing in a fog . . . sometimes she was rumored to have been seen two, even three places at the same time. But except for Captain Nelson and his rotten old ghost ship, the French were watching intently the diminishing size of the British force blockading them. They would send their supplies in small boats, alongshore where neither *Agamemnon* nor her two frigates nor even her smaller brigs, could navigate; French supplies running in small swift polaccas that could outsail the *Agamemnon's* boats.

Captain Nelson wrote in vain for lighter craft, for gunboats. And days of howling winds would pass when he did not even see his frigates. When word would be brought to De Vins's headquarters that Austrian sentries, fully uniformed, had been frozen to death during the night.

The French soldiers had only rags on their bodies.

Still neither army moved from its "impregnable" hold on the coast of the Genoese Riviera, while Captain Nelson slowly added his score of enemy convoy craft taken to forty-seven, which did not include the innumerable neutrals he had turned back, refusing them entry.

November 13, 1795, General de Vins requested Captain Nelson to leave his frigates at Vado and take *Agamemnon* to Genoa where the French were running inshore, taking neutral Genoese fortifications behind the Austrian lines; threatening to land troops.

Captain Nelson shook hands with the weary ailing Austrian General, gave his orders to his frigates to guard Vado from any attempt of French ships to run in, and reminded the army once more of his arrangement to sound signal guns along the coast in the event of trouble.

Agamemnon steered for Genoa through biting gales.

❄   ❄   ❄

At Vado: orders from acting Commander in Chief Sir Hyde Parker: frigates *Inconstant* and *Southampton* to rejoin the fleet at once at San Fiorenzo. Captain Freemantle wrote a frantic message to Captain

Nelson far beyond recall. Then in compliance to the orders of the Commander in Chief, *Southampton* and *Inconstant* weighed anchor, left the Allied Headquarters unguarded at Vado.

All that were left were two tiny brigs which set sail with Captain Freemantle's letter, blew all over the seas before they finally reached Genoa, and Captain Nelson stared horror-struck at the news.

No one fired the signal guns, no one had time to give the order, for the French gunboats had moved into Vado.

And General de Vins sent word that under no circumstance should *Agamemnon* leave Genoa, for if she did, the *retreat* of the "impregnable" Austrian army would be cut off. . . .

❄   ❄   ❄

Two months later, and now all of three years out from England, the old *Agamemnon* had the pathetic appearance of a poor pensioner's widow in a clean but threadbare shawl as she dropped her anchors once more in San Fiorenzo. She had just come from a hurried overhaul at Leghorn. After much carpentering and debate, the cables had been removed from around her hull, and by a miracle she held together once more. She still creaked and moaned. *Aggie* was old, even her chivalrous Captain admitted it.

Thus she must make her salute to the new Commander in Chief, Sir John Jervis. Captain Nelson had taken pains with his dress. Allen had wrenched his cocked hat into some kind of shape, and Captain Nelson had buckled on his Uncle Suckling's small sword. It had been carried in his uncle's small but victorious battle between French and English frigates back on October 21, 1757. Both the sword and the date, October 21st, were therefore considered especially lucky by the sometimes superstitious Captain.

He felt a little conscious of the glittering epaulets on his coat. Until a recent whim of the Admiralty, epaulets had not been worn by Englishmen, being considered a French affectation. Now they were regulation, the Captain rather liked the gold braid. But nothing seemed to change Captain Nelson's appearance of having battled a gale as he struggled into his clothes. Allen, the valet, still defied cultivation—or dismissal. Allen now had charge of the Captain's keys to his plate and jewelry. But as Captain Nelson came on deck and the boatswain began to pipe, he spun on his walley. "Where's my writing case—the red one?"

"In the boat whar yow ast for me to stow it, naturally—sir." Tom eyed the Captain, indignant at being called to account.

"Show me. . . ."

Tom lumbered off, while the Captain waited. Tom had misplaced every valuable document he possessed a few weeks ago, caused a furor until he found where he'd forgotten them. Now Tom held up empty hands. "That's peculiar," he muttered.

"Beast . . ." from the Captain as Tom went back to the cabin, produced the writing case. "Huzza! Huzza!" Captain Nelson muttered softly, and with a "Very well, Thomas Allen," went overside while Tom cringed at being called Thomas before the whole ship's company. To have been cursed and flogged would have been nothing by comparison.

But the wind soon cooled the Captain's temper. This had been the coldest Mediterranean winter he could remember. He turned, eyeing old *Agamemnon,* as he pulled away from her. A paternal glance: *Agamemnon* was as fit as a rotten ship could be!

He faced forward again, a little defiantly. There lay *Victory,* and Admiral Sir John Jervis's St. George's banner flew at the masthead. There was the man whom rumor held to be somewhat of a hybrid: half devil—half god.

❋   ❋   ❋

Ushered at last below deck, to the cabin where he and Lord Hood had thrashed out the problems of Bastia, he faced Sir John Jervis:

An ugly, medium tall man, square-shouldered, he did not look his sixty years. His limbs, powerful in themselves, lacked proportion to each other, and to the body. Yet there was no doubt in Captain Nelson's mind, from the moment he laid eyes on him, that he was in the presence of a *man.* Jervis had unflickering, at first glance Nelson would have said ruthless, eyes, and the rugged elemental defiance of a granite cliff in the carriage of his roughly carved face. His nose was clumsily hooked, his mouth straight and hard, and his chin jutted forward divided into twin peaks by a deep, Mephisthophelean cleft.

His force seemed to lie behind the cold eyes, inside the cranium rather than in the muscular strength—which was in itself nothing to sneer at—of his body. Hands must involuntarily jerk upwards to salute, hearts quail. He might have trained men at the point of a gun in his youth; shot a reef point of a topsail out of the hands of a scared and fumbling seaman; or he might have yelled, "Heave that lubber overboard," if some jack had clumsily fallen out of the tops, killed himself. . . . He looked as if he could handle anyone or anything. Though, with the mellowing of age, his reputation was of less physical violence, and increasing ungovernable rages.

Captain Nelson saluted, making his bow *en garde,* but feeling armored by the consciousness of never having crossed this man's hawse till this moment, when Jervis thrust his hand straight out and no nonsense.

His handshake was cordial. "How do you do, Captain Nelson. I'm delighted to meet you and your gallant ship. Sit down, won't you?"

Captain Nelson's prize smile flashed. Disarmed utterly, he sat down in amazement. The man had sounded friendly.

He even looked friendly—or gave a rough facsimile of a good-humored nod—to the Captain's trusting smile. The fact that anyone had dared to smile so innocently at first meeting had rather disarmed Jervis.

Captain Nelson had found his voice. "Thank you, sir. It is a privilege to be at your service, sir."

"Umph," said Jervis.

He studied the Captain shrewdly, like a wise old watchdog, and his glance betrayed nothing of what he was thinking. He did not even blink at Captain Nelson's haphazard uniform though he was known to break others for so much as a loosely dangling button. Perhaps he was surprised to see a small, slender, rather frail-looking young man who was senior in rank to and yet younger than most of the captains in the fleet, and who sat looking at the Admiral with his gray-blue eyes unwavering, and an expression of friendly attentiveness on his rather wan face. The Admiral at last looked down at the papers on his writing table. An intelligent eye and a tender mouth responded to a light rein? The Admiral sat back, ready to try Captain Nelson's paces, see if he had any vice in him.

"I've read your reports and I am satisfied. Have you heard any more of De Vins, Captain Nelson?"

"They say he is dead, sir, from chagrin."

"Hmmph. The damn fool. Go on, sir."

"Sir." Captain Nelson sat forward, smiling wryly. "I have just received ocular demonstration of the futility of continental alliances! There they were, both armies remained to see who could stand the cold longest. The French naked, the Austrians fully equipped. And it was intense; weather that could not have been expected in this country. By November when I was sent down to Genoa by General de Vins to stop French privateers that were running in behind the Austrian lines to take Genoese fortifications and close the Vado road, Sir Hyde Parker took my two remaining frigates off Vado.

"The French followed with their coup. It was all over in a matter of days. . . . Sir, retreat it could not be called! The French, half naked, half starved, were determined to conquer or die. The only part of our allies that made any attempt at order were nearest Vado Bay, on the army's starboard quarter—right rear—facing the fire from the French gunboats. So the excuse of the gunboat fire does not hold for the rest of the army.

"For the rest, sir, it was the devil take the hindmost! I had my purser on shore at Vado. He ran with the Austrians eighteen miles without stopping. The men without any arms whatever, the officers without soldiers, women without assistance. My only gain in being forced to remain at Genoa was that by laying *Agamemnon* alongside the shore, I kept the great road from Vado to Genoa open. That road saved eight to ten thousand men including the General!" Captain Nelson stood up, began to pace. He turned full on Jervis, throwing up his hands, and his gaudy ring caught the light—almost blinded his Admiral. "Thus ended my campaign, sir, and I fancy from what I hear: *no defeat was ever more complete!*" He sat down.

"Never," Jervis agreed after a few moments' silence. "But you were put in a cleft stick. One battleship to defend an army at three points. It was a bungling insult."

"Sir, if you will forgive my saying it, the Austrians will lay the blame for the whole campaign right there. They say, and true, they were brought to it, at the express desire of the English, to co-operate with our *fleet,* which fleet or Admiral they never saw! There certainly are other and much better posts to prevent the invasion of Italy than Vado. I don't say they would not have been beat without the French gunboats; months ago I apprized them of what would one day happen; but they believed themselves invincible."

"Captain Nelson, I have sent word for the Austrians to name the day and place for me to consult with their chiefs. I have received no answer, but if France takes Italy . . ."

"Aye, and I tremble to hear of the want of bread for our poor at home, sir. If our loan to Prussia, which was swallowed whole, without one moment's hesitation at the time when the Prussians were actually withdrawing from this war—if that money even had been used on our own people."

"Captain Nelson." Jervis sat forward, eyes hardening. "Mr. Pitt is a congenital idiot! I have been in Parliament and I know, sir, that we are paying dearly for the millions we have loaned to our 'allies.' And we will pay for our broken promises."

Captain Nelson mused dryly, continuing the vein of their thoughts. "All I can say, sir, is that thanks to this last campaign, *we,* the Allies, have established the French Republic, which I think but for us—I verily believe—would never have been settled by such a volatile changeable people! And so, sir, if our purpose in going to war was to restore the crown"—Nelson smiled, and then turned down the corners of his mouth—"we might as well make peace. . . . However, as the French have gone into winter quarters, I am more convinced than ever the French will this spring make a greater exertion to get into Italy."

"The King's speech to Parliament precludes peace"—Jervis's lip curled—"'until we have the means of concluding, in conjunction with our Allies, such a peace as the justice of our cause—'" He snorted. "Until Pitt bankrupts the country, he means!"

"Sir." Captain Nelson decided to steer his course clear of politics; it was one thing for Jervis to speak his mind, but how could Nelson be sure Jervis was not merely leading him on? "The French have a great armament at Toulon which may be used to support an attack on Italy. They *must not* be allowed—" He caught himself, appalled. "Pray, forgive me, sir! I have allowed myself the privilege of thinking out loud. Pray, Sir John, believe, I have not the slightest intention of over-stepping my bounds as an officer under your command."

"Ah—I understand you were awarded the Colonelcy of Marines. Sir Gilbert seems to rely on your opinions. . . . Did you know the Paolists are trying to bring the French back and our army is suspected of having sold supplies to the Corsicans?"

"Aye, sir."

"And *you* advise *me* not to allow the French to move into Italy?" Jervis suddenly smiled, a big uncut diamond of a smile, as Captain Nelson shriveled.

"I seem perhaps to have taken a liberty to so freely communicate of my knowledge, sir, pray for—"

Jervis only smiled more broadly. "Of course, France means to conquer Italy. I also know that our recent fiasco on the Riviera has helped most damnably to secure a new *coup d'état* in Paris. Someone by the name of Barras has completely put down the 'Moderates' just when they were on the verge of dealing with us, had we been successful. The Moderates were dickering to restore monarchy. You heard about that?"

"Vaguely, Sir John. I never know what to believe in French newspapers, although"—Nelson smiled, realizing that perhaps he was not in Jervis's black books after all—"I have acquired the habit of believing in their victories—on land."

"This Barras called in the army; had quite a battle right there in Paris. The army supported Barras and the new government—or Directory—as that band of brigands now call themselves. It seems Barras's Directory carries more weight than ever. As a kind of plum, Barras has given the command of the French army on the Riviera to the young officer, some outlandish Corsican, I believe, who led the Paris uprising. Same young devil, the French papers say, who led the attack on our poor martyred garrison at Toulon just three years ago!"

"I thought General Dugommier was the chief of the French army at Toulon, sir?"

"Oh, he was in command, but this young officer claims he, though only an artillery captain at the time, planned the attack. Dugommier's dispatches did not credit him, but fellow officers did and Paris calls him the 'hero of Toulon.' Good God! The fall of Toulon was brutal and brilliant enough! Hardly Dugommier's type of war. So it goes on, Captain Nelson. Now, have *you* heard anything more of your promotion? I understand your name's climbed nearly to the top of the lists. You're in line for your flag."

"No, sir, I have not heard a word."

"You need a bigger ship, a ninety or a seventy-four."

Captain Nelson hesitated. He had made up his mind he would be retired; been writing to his wife he was coming home. And somehow he wanted to go home. He was sick of commands, such as the last, doomed to fail for want of proper means. If he went on, he wanted more. He was ill and he was weary of war. "I don't know how to thank you, sir, but I have been out three years now from home without one moment's reprieve. If you will excuse my mentioning it, the doctors all say I need a rest. So, sir, as *Agamemnon* has been out longer than any, she must soon be recalled to refit. With your permission, I will go home with my ship to be refitted myself, sir." And just as soon as he had gotten his woeful tale off his chest, seen a flicker of rage in Jervis's eye, he took a deep breath, smiled. "Sir, perhaps just a week ashore in Italy. I think perhaps the doctors are wrong. I will think so, Sir John, for I don't like what I just said. I very much believe that England, who commenced the war with all Europe for her allies, will finish it by having nearly all Europe for her enemies. Fear and bribery govern these states, Sir John. Fear of the French . . . so, I should like to *finish* the war, sir."

"I can understand your fatigue. Perhaps we can send you to Pisa for a few weeks." Jervis now seemed all sympathy. The Captain was obviously tired, thin as a ghost, but . . . Jervis knew he could use this man. "Tell me, should you have any objection to serving under me as a rear admiral?" Jervis's voice was roughly indifferent. He was not used to asking favors of captains.

Captain Nelson had straightened up. His eye blazed. "I should be proud, sir, to hoist my flag under your command."

Jervis looked pleased. "Very well. I shall write home at once that I may keep you when your promotion comes through, and have your flag sent here. Meantime you shall continue on detached service, blockading the French. Co-operating with the Austrians."

Captain Nelson's face lost a little of its first ecstasy. "Aye, aye, sir."

"And as you understand what is expected of the command, I will not tie your hands with written orders and I hope to give you a Distinguishing Pendant, something to impress these generals."

The Captain's eye flashed again. "I don't know how to thank you, Sir John, but I hope my actions may prove how grateful I am."

"Therefore, Captain Nelson," Jervis went on lightly and gently coaxing and flicking the reins, "you *must* have a larger ship, for we cannot spare you either as a captain or as an admiral!"

❋   ❋   ❋

Captain Nelson to his wife:

The fleet was not a little surprised at my leaving them so soon and, I fancy, there was some degree of envy attached to the surprise; for one of the Captains told me, "You did just as you pleased in Lord Hood's time, the same in Admiral Hotham's, and now again with Sir John Jervis; it makes no difference to you who is Commander-in-Chief." I returned a pretty strong answer. . . . My health never was better.

But First Captain of the Fleet, Captain Calder, was musing to his friends, feeling his honor required some public repairs, that someday someone was going to take a reef in their little "Brigadier General's" sails. . . .

While within a week, Sir John Jervis was writing to the Minister, Mr. Trevor, in Turin in answer to Trevor's letter recommending Captain Nelson to Jervis:

I am very happy to learn that Captain Nelson whose zeal and enterprise cannot be surpassed, stands so high in your opinion. I have only to lament the want of means to give him the command of a squadron equal to his merits.

And Captain Nelson let off further steam with one of his usual fond sermons to his nervous ailing wife:

Had all my actions, my dearest Fanny, been gazetted, not one fortnight would have passed during the whole war without a letter from me; one day or other I will have a long gazette to myself; I feel that such an opportunity will be given me, I cannot, if I am in the field of glory, be kept out of sight. Probably my services may be forgotten by the great, by the time I get home: but my mind will not forget, nor cease to feel, a degree of consolation and applause superior to undeserved rewards. Where there is anything to be done, there Providence is sure to direct my steps. Credit must be given me in spite of envy. . . .

But Fanny was inconsolable. For three years she had waited for the day when *Agamemnon* would come home. And now he was only waiting to transfer to a bigger ship, just when she had pinned all her hopes on only a few more months. Would he ever come back? He was seeking "the field of glory" when every other naval husband she knew was seeking some nook, as a naval representative or governor of some microscopic possession, where he could live in domestic comfort, peace and colonial pomposity. No, her husband would rather risk being killed than live ashore. She rubbed the sore, for she had nothing in the world to compel her to do anything else. So back to her treadmill: her visits to his relatives whom she did not care too much about, to resorts for her health, to dutiful visits with his father who secretly grumbled that her constant nervous anxiety had destroyed her health and soured her temper. . . . So Fanny tried to bear up, though she could not even read a book to distract her mind, but pathetically pinned all her hopes on the time when she would live again, when she would be secure: on the hour when her husband retired to enjoy her company.

❋   ❋   ❋

Agamemnon, however, was lifting her prow with a new dignity, in spite of her waterlogged state, for she flew the Distinguishing Pendant of Commodore Nelson, who was sitting at the moment at his desk, struggling through the twenty letters he must write today. The rank of Commodore was not a permanent step up. It was a courtesy from an admiral; it distinguished a captain as having a command detached from the fleet. Upon rejoining a fleet a commodore might be requested to strike his pendant, resume the title of captain if there were captains senior in line for flag rank in the fleet; or if the admiral chose to order it.

Commodore Nelson was just finishing a letter to Sir William Hamilton, who, with his lady, never forgot him, nor failed to beg him to come back to Naples to visit them. As usual Commodore Nelson wrote he hoped someday to take them by the hand with news of another victory, but "I cannot bear the thought of showing myself in a foreign port, without it being known that the British flag is triumphant." They had been too gracious that one meeting, a victory was needed to sustain the mood of a second visit. Finishing that letter, he dipped his pen in the ink, thinking of the French. They had pushed into Italy, gone on like a flood; the plains lay ahead.

With that to strengthen them, the Spanish had definitely withdrawn from the English alliance. A rumor had it that Lady Hamilton, with the aid of Queen Maria Carolina, had purloined a letter addressed by Spain to its son, King Ferdinand of the Two Sicilies. This scuttlebutt rumor had it that it was Lady Hamilton who had warned Jervis of the coming break with Spain. She was quite a patriot. Even old woman-hating Jervis grinned and grew weak in the knees when her name cropped up. Commodore Nelson smiled to himself. No, Jervis was *wrong:* marriage such as his own wise attachment kept a man's mind where it belonged, strictly focused on his *career.* So deciding, he applied his half-dreamy eye back to his papers.

So: Spain might soon declare war, send her fleets against her former allies. But Jervis was making a fighting instrument of what he had.

And Commodore Nelson's job was a nightmare of legalities, but he enjoyed it. The French and the neutrals supplying the French hated him and his blockade as much as—or more than—the West Indian businessmen had in their day. He had made one awful discovery: that England often used natives of the countries in which her consulates were situated to run her affairs. The result in Genoa had been that the "English" Consul registered a complaint against Nelson for the Republican Genoese Marquis of Spinola. Nelson had raged and laid down the law to the Consul, and fortunately his government had realized the situation and not broken and hanged Nelson at Spinola's request. The Commodore's latest success had been a letter addressed to "Horatio Nelson, Genoa," and the grim explanation that there was only one of him in the world.

His duties as Commodore were made doubly wearing because a commodore was entitled to a captain under him to assume command of his ship; leave him for larger spheres. He had no captain as yet. He was waiting for Captain Ralph Miller; the man's reputation pleased him. Meantime he had a new first lieutenant, Mr. Edward Berry, who acted as captain. Lieutenants Hinton and Andrews were both gone, made captains of small craft of their own. Andrews's sad attack on the Turks had been bold enough for a promotion.

The Commodore's willingness to wrangle and beg for his officers' promotions gave his ship a good reputation among officers who dreaded serving time and time again and being passed over for lack of patronage. And it gave the Commodore the pick of the more ambitious officers.

Even Josiah was ready to be made lieutenant, though he still aped the forecastle and refused to become a gentleman. Hoste had lost time, could not be made lieutenant for a while, thanks to typhoid and a broken leg, and a stretch in Leghorn recovering from another attack of fever. That reminded him he must write Hoste's father just to tell him William was well again and how much he loved that *gentle* and courageous boy!

There was a clatter on the companion. Voices singing down from aloft. 1st Lieutenant Berry's proudly pompous young voice from the quarter-deck: "Call the Commodore. Turn the hands up. Out with the reefs and loose the topgallant sails!"

The next moment, Josiah's surly face appeared at the Commodore's door. He snarled (or so it seemed to the stepfather, still thinking of Hoste):

"Convoy of small enemy vessels in shore, steering to eastward, Father."

❊　　　　　　❊　　　　　　❊

"Signal for general chase." And Berry was passing the Commodore's orders in lieu of any captain, as Commodore Nelson peered at a small line of white sails and black hulls frothing the green sea. They were hugging the rocky shore on which, he knew, though he could scarcely make it out at this distance, there stood an enemy battery.

"Deck there, they've run up Danish colors, sir!"

"Show them a Tricolor."

"Deck there, they're showing a Tricolor now, sir, and making signals of some kind, sir, not ours."

"Hoist the Union Jack."

"Deck there. They're hauling as close to shore as they can. Their Tricolor still hoisted, sir."

"Tack and close on them, Mr. Berry, if you please."

And Berry passed the order to Mr. Wilson the master, who was still at his post; aged from the battle scars on him.

Astern *Agamemnon,* but now pushing forward, were the four frigates of the Commodore's squadron. Two were in fairly good condition, the third, *Blanche,* Captain Smith—no relation to Sir Sidney—was lagging. The Commodore's eyes narrowed. She was not taking proper advantage of the wind. Smith had gone steadily from poor to worse of late. His other frigate captains showed no love for the man. Was he drunk again as they hinted? He had never caught him drunk, but his ship was beginning to show signs of it. "Make signal to *Blanche* to close. . . ."

She made only a token acknowledgment and finally, to Nelson's disgust, let the wind put her in irons.

The fourth frigate, the *Meleager,* Captain Cockburn, had been with *Agamemnon* so long she was the Commodore's favorite; and she matched *Agamemnon* in creaking and complaining, groan for groan, but she was leading the others in spite of herself. Cockburn was an excellent seaman, as well as a lady-killer.

Agamemnon was slopping along to the spirited beat of her drums; the running of feet to quarters. Her marines were drawn up smartly.

There was but faint wind, and the French convoy of small light vessels was taking advantage of it; making for the shelter of the shore batteries. Even so, old *Aggie* swam on, closing in, for the shallows were not wide here. She was pinning the French to the shore with her skirting brood of smaller frigates barring the retreat.

"Try the range from the lower deck, Mr. Berry." The Commodore was studying the batteries as, a few moments later, one of *Agamemnon's* guns went off.

"It goes over." But the second shot hit the mark.

Forward in *Agamemnon's* chains the leadsman chanted, "Five fathoms. . . ."

"Let go bower anchors! Mr. Berry, guns of main deck abaft the beam trained forward, and those before the beam trained aft—throw our fire into one focus."

Agamemnon still had a kick, as bearing up, patched sails luffing, anchors splashing down, she let go her first blast with a precision of direction and purpose that made the shore seem to leap and the battery crumble.

"Out boats and board the ships. Mr. Noble, call your volunteers."

The slim young lieutenant shouted: "Small arms men and pikemen forward to board!" More than enough ran forward.

Boatswain's whistle, "Boarders away!"

Agamemnon was silencing the shore batteries, preventing their fire from being directed at the longboats rowing shoreward; drawing the fire to herself. Shots arced over the water and *Agamemnon's* genteelly impoverished sails were once again tattered, her soft wood crumbled, her spars cracked.

Commodore Nelson watched his boarders through his long glass; rowing steadily, easily. Men should not be winded just before battle. Easy. The flashing of oars laying in, boats grazing. Cutlasses flashed against the black hulls. One man fell back. Through the curdling smoke one vessel's Tricolor fell—and another, while the batteries seemed to shrink, their fire growing sporadic.

He nodded, pleased, to Lieutenant Berry. "You have brought us luck."

"The pleasure is all mine, sir." Berry, who had the reputation for having been in almost every major fleet action since the beginning of the war, including Howe's First of June, smiled.

But this was routine to *Agamemnon*. For over a year, convoy after convoy had been taken this way. "This ought to put a nice crimp in the French army besieging Mantua, waiting supplies," the Commodore mused.

"The devils have cut their cables, sir, and are letting their ships drift on shore!" Young Berry groaned, and he sprinted off, directed the firing closer to silence the batteries before the enemy could get under the shelter of them.

But the English boat crews had manned the French ships and were rowing out, towing them off shore, spreading their canvas as they left the shallows, while the frigates stood in so close they threatened to beach.

One longboat rowed back to *Agamemnon,* shouting for a grating to be slung. Lieutenant Noble was gasping in the bottom of the boat. A bullet had gone through his throat.

❀   ❀   ❀

It was just dawn when *Agamemnon* weighed anchor and, with her squadron of frigates and seven small enemy ships in tow, showed her stern to the Riviera for the last time; steering for San Fiorenzo. Her last chore under Commodore Nelson was done.

The shabbiest, fightingest little battleship in the fleet going home; her Commodore moving on to the *Captain* 74.

Most of *Agamemnon's* men and her officers were transferring with him, except Mr. Wilson, who had a wife and big family and was plain sick and tired of war, and one midshipman who had inherited an estate. Hoste's family wanted him to come home, he had had so much bad luck. Hoste decided to transfer to *Captain* with the Commodore. The rest were a bit fickle about *Agamemnon.* That was the way with women and ships. They grew old and podgy and complaining. Though the jacks really had nothing to say about transferring or not, they went fairly willingly. Even if they sailed home in *Agamemnon* they knew they would not get ashore, but be transferred to some outward-bound ship within sight of home. So they followed the Commodore, rather than take the chance of a worse superior. In fact, aside from the probability that no seaman in his right mind liked his job, the Commodore did try to make their life bearable. He was sentimental about his crews, and already there were those other captains in the fleet who thought his references to his "old *Agamemnons*" smacked too much of snobbery; as if a jack who had served *Agamemnon* were the same as an "old Etonian." But the Commodore was not sentimental about the sea that made him sick, and as to the ship: "She sits like a tub," he laughed, even as he said, with more pity than love, "poor old *Agamemnon*."

❊   ❊   ❊

But before *Agamemnon* reached San Fiorenzo, Commodore Nelson made a quick visit to sick bay. There in the most decent quarters of the ship, smelling the vinegar and linen sheets, he found Lieutenant Noble was not expected to live. He went back to his cabin, sorry for Noble but elated over yesterday's loot. Captain Cockburn of *Meleager* had just come aboard with a baffled expression in his eyes, his neatly cut features scowling. He had been all night getting one of the obstinate enemy transports off the sand. His face was still unshaven and his uniform wrenched awry. The English girls in San Fiorenzo would have shuddered to see him, but to the Commodore, Cockburn looked perfection.

"I've been through the transports, Cockburn. What beautiful artillery those French make! And all of one hundred and fifty Austrian prisoners of war going home again with us. And see! A whole library of—*books!* So congratulations on a nice piece of work." The Commodore had turned from heaps of boxes and chests he had ordered brought into his cabin, to shake hands.

"Thank you, sir, but it seems we've run into some kind of trouble again with these damn neutrals!"

"These ships neutral? Not at all. I can read French. And by the look of the artillery we took, the French are in debt to us."

"I think so too, sir, but I spoke a Genoese master in a neutral ship an hour ago. He claims the one hundred and fifty Austrian prisoners of war. He was on the way to pick them up. He says they're neutral property because the French *sold* them to the neutral Swiss."

The Commodore had reluctantly folded an enemy chart, giving Cockburn all his attention. "Is he mad?"

"This Genoese claims them by right of neutrality."

"A Genoese claims that Austrian prisoners of war taken by the French and sold to the Swiss belong to *him*? Let us have one or two brought aboard, Mr. Berry." The Commodore turned to his 1st Lieutenant. "And send Lieutenant Pierson with them. We will hear what they have to say." He turned back to Cockburn as Berry went out.

"Good news. Sir John has at last promised me that you shall have the first frigate available, Cockburn. After all our fag together, I couldn't leave you in *Meleager*. I've picked out *La Minerve* for you— I hope."

"Oh, the forty-two our *Lowestoffe* 32 snatched from under their noses? She's a beautiful ship, sir. How am I going to thank you, sir?" Cockburn was laughing, a little overwhelmed at the luck of having the Commodore acting his angel.

"Aye, she's beautiful," the Commodore nodded as Berry returned with Lieutenant Pierson. The latter was a dark, polite young Neapolitan by birth, who had replaced Lieutenant Clarke, wounded and permanently disabled at Bastia. A few minutes more, and a sentry brought in two strapping young Austrians, half naked, filthy, bearded, but still so young they looked healthy in spite of themselves.

The Commodore sat down at his writing desk as Lieutenant Pierson gabbled away and the men gabbled back, watching intently as if by the flicker of an eye he might catch something. The men heard Pierson and looked anxiously at Nelson.

"They are Austrian grenadiers, sir," Pierson began, "captured in the last Austrian rout at Voltri."

The Commodore nodded. His latest bit of co-operation had been a farce. This time he had been ordered to protect an advance from a specified rendezvous. When he arrived to lay *Agamemnon* along the shore well ahead of time, he found nothing. The Austrians had attacked in a different place the day before, been routed again, possibly for good. That Austrian general was gone to Vienna for court-martial, suspected of having accepted a bribe from the French to lead his army into a trap. How else could the Austrians explain these sudden mysterious French victories at the moment when the world had decided the starving, naked French would disintegrate?

"When were they taken prisoners?"

"In the first storming, sir. They aren't deserters. They were taken to a French prison, then they were marched to the ships. Given thirty sous apiece, and were told they were going to Spain."

"To Spain! Ask them who gave them the money."

"They say it was against their will, sir. They were bought from the French by the Swiss, who will send them to Spain as one of the usual Swiss regiments of mercenaries."

The Commodore shook his head. " 'Tis not the first time I've heard these pious 'neutrals' whimpering when we turn back a shipment of their goods. The 'freedom-loving Swiss' . . ."

"They say, sir, the Spanish Consul deals through the Swiss Consul in Genoa. They are bought and paid for as 'Swiss.' Where the men were 'recruited' does not enter the agreement."

"It's as bad as the African slave trade, sir!" Berry gasped. He had an almost beautiful face, a great deal of dignity, and very little humor which he made up for by paying sincere attention to his orders. "Selling men like so many sacks of flour. Forcing them to fight their own people!"

Pierson spoke again. "They ask to fight with us, sir, until they can go home. They're begging me to ask you not to send them to Spain, sir."

"They shall be returned to their army as soon as we can make arrangements." The Commodore nodded to the men. They were just the material he could use, for his ship was shorthanded as always, but while it was perfectly good form to impress British merchant seamen, this would involve a temperamental allied government. "Cockburn, dismiss that 'neutral' Genoese vessel chartered by Spain to take these 'Swiss' Austrians purchased from France to Barcelona!" Tears came in the Austrians' eyes as Pierson translated and the sentry ushered the men out.

The Commodore went back to the enemy papers. A tall stack of books teetered on the corner of his desk as *Agamemnon* rose, groaned, fell, wallowed, rose again.

"I say, Berry, you have two eyes, perhaps you can spell out the name these articles are addressed to." The Commodore laid his ringed finger on the outside of a packet taken from one of the enemy transports.

Berry took the paper, studying it very conscientiously. "May I, sir?" He carried it to the light of the slanting cabin windows. "Buona—" He paused.

"I got that far myself." The Commodore was poring excitedly over a chart he had unrolled. "But what was the next letter?" he asked over his shoulder. "A script *s* or an *f* or a *p?* These French write such indecipherable scrawls! And such bombast and oratory! It looked to me like a capital *P,* but what's the rest of it?"

"I'd say it looks like a capital *P,* sir. Buona Parti."

"General Buona Parti. Never heard of him," the Commodore laughed. "And look at these books the Directory thinks he should read in his leisure hours!" He picked them up one at a time from his writing desk. "Maillebois's *Wars in Italy.*"

"Sticks close to his subject, doesn't he, sir?" Cockburn was looking over the Commodore's shoulder.

"And Vauban—ah! Vauban's *Attack and Defense of Places.* What excellent plates! There's the old arsenal at Toulon. Vauban designed it. Thank you, General, I shall keep this one. And what's this? Prince Eugene's *History;* and *Memoirs* of Marshal Catinat, Duke of Vendome; come, aren't we indefatigable?"

Cockburn slapped his thigh. "What a general! One eye on the book and the other on his artillery!"

"Oh, I say, how do you account for his rank, Cockburn?" from Berry, as Nelson and Cockburn exchanged a sly wink. "Do you suppose he's just another musician or surgeon like the ones at Toulon—that is, before we lost it?"

"Ah," the Commodore went on, *"Mémoirs Politiques"*—his accent was stoutly Anglo-Saxon and no Parisian nonsense—"the Life of the Duke of Berwick—by the way, we owe the French something for taking our *Berwick* last year. And what's this?" The Commodore glanced at the next book, tossed it aside. "He has no use now for *Hannibal's March Over the Alps!* The more's the pity. . . ." He ran his hand down the stack of books. "All from the Directory, gentlemen. Proof of their attention to details. . . . General Buona Parti. That doesn't sound French, does it? I spent a few miserable months in their outlandish country once, long enough to say that is—I wonder what the devil it is? Pierson! You are a linguist par excellence, pray tell us what nationality—if any—is Buona Parti?"

Pierson studied the packet, thought a moment. "Oh! Buonaparte was an aide-de-camp to old General Paoli years ago. But he's dead. Buonapartes lived at Ajaccio, Corsica, sir, I believe. Big family. Sons studied in France, if that's the same family, sir. I've heard that General Brogio loathes them—the Buonapartes and Brogios had a feud I understand."

"So? A Corsican! *Banditti!* I might have known it. An incorrigible people. So *he* is the one who claims to have planned the masterstroke for General Dugommier at Toulon? The villain who wiped out our poor garrison at L'Aiguillette. Hmmm. . . ."

"What about his clothes, sir, in this chest?" Berry asked.

"They're too small for me," Cockburn smiled, eyeing the Commodore, who had turned his back, examining his favorite trophy, the Vauban.

"Much too small, Captain Cockburn—" Berry swallowed, having at last caught Cockburn's measuring eye moving from the clothes to their chief.

"His clothes? I'll send them back by the French Minister in Genoa. Put them with his personal letters and papers. Who knows what hardship this General Sans-Culottes may endure without them!" Nelson beckoned Pierson. "With my French and their miserable scribbling translating is not easy. *Tiens,* Pierson, *voulez-vous?*" He held out more papers.

"The army when Buonaparte took command was effective thirty thousand eight hundred and seventy-five men, sir."

"That's *less* than we've been led to believe by the Austrians. . . ." The Commodore cocked his head on one side, frowning slightly, as Pierson paused, trying to decipher before translating further. The Commodore went back to the chart that intrigued him. "If this Buona Parti is ignorant, the Directory, it appears, wish to instruct him. . . ." He ran his forefinger down the chart of all Italy. "Pray God he remain ignorant, gentlemen!"

V I I. Sackcloth and Ashes

June, 1796 – February 13, 1797

IT WAS THREE O'CLOCK of a summer night. Commodore Nelson was on the quarter-deck of his new ship with her smart name and seventy-four guns: H.M.S. *Captain*. He had been asleep, wakened, choking for breath. Restless, full of new plans, he had come on deck.

The *Captain* lay hull down below the horizon, only her tops could spy into the closed port of Leghorn. Nearby, but unseen, were her frigates, *Meleager* and *Blanche*. The waning night was still so black, the ships and the sea seemed to have joined in listening for the heart-beat of a sick continent. Now and then the mechanical "All's well!" sounded from the sentries, meaning merely that the watchers were awake.

"Deck there. Signal light!" rung down from the masthead.

"Where away?" from Nelson.

"To eastward, sir, three points off the larboard bow. Making our signal, sir. It's the fisherman Neri, sir."

On time as usual. But when the Commodore strolled forward, perched himself high to peer for it, there was no light. The quick flare had been doused. The Commodore drew a breath of relief.

He heard a sudden drunken whoop across the water, faint but recognizable: Captain Smith in *Blanche* was carousing again. A degenerate captain, a mutinous, arrogant crew. Smith's officers had at last dared to rise against him, been clapped in irons, while the crew and the Captain grew more intimate.

This was his last night. The Commodore was sending him up for court-martial: probably disgrace and dismissal. He frowned. That an officer in his squadron would so abuse his rank, abuse himself as a man, had stunned him. He had refused to believe even Cockburn's reports of what went on behind his back. He had called Smith aboard, told him quietly and in private that there were ugly stories afloat, asked Smith to deny or explain them. Smith, in the torpor of a hangover, had damned his lieutenants and laughed off their charges. But he had not denied them. The Commodore had tried reasoning; been eyed with amused contempt by the man he wanted to help. That finished the business. *Blanche* must have a new captain. Smith was going before the Commander in Chief, Sir John Jervis, charged with gross immorality, degenerate conduct, consorting with his crew against his lieutenants. He was having his last fling. What still bewildered Nelson was that he felt heartsick when Smith did not care. . . .

Just as well then to be rid of him; some poor jack might have hanged for talking back to an abusive officer. Even Nelson's old favorite, Admiral Sir Peter Parker, who had nursed him through fever, and whom he thought of as the soul of consideration, was known to flog a man senseless for failing to salute a mid. . . . "By the God of War, I'll see the man's backbone!" And when Nelson dared say, "We seamen are a neglected lot . . ." few of his equals understood how he could bother to identify himself with a jack. Old Collingwood understood. Collingwood was hard as nails, and inclined to snub his officers, yet he had better discipline and less flogging than any other officer. Collingwood had just joined the fleet, but Nelson had not seen him yet, though he had greeted his arrival with a huge basket of choice green vegetables. Ten years Nelson's senior, Coll was his junior captain, and one of his oldest friends. Coll's face, like a stone cherub's, drifted through his mind. Coll drawing a hideous picture of Nelson in a frightening wig which he wore after having his hair cropped for fever; Coll showing that picture to Mrs. Moutray as the three of them sat on a hilltop. And Nelson drawing a worse picture of Collingwood, aggravating in that there was a slight resemblance, until Mrs. Moutray clasped the pictures to her heart, nearly weeping with laughter, and promising never to part with such rare examples of artistic genius. Then Coll reciting verses to her, for he had been to school longer and knew how to make verses:

> To you belongs the wondrous art,
> To shed around you pleasure,
> New worth to best of things impart,
> And make of trifles—treasure!

While Nelson, no poet, sat dumb, and when she was gone wrote: "I went once up the Hill to look at the spot where I spent more happy days than in any one spot in the world. E'en the trees drooped their heads, and the tamarind tree died: all was melancholy: the road is covered with thistles; let them grow. . . ."

Confound it! He turned restlessly in his tracks; Captain Smith's ruin still haunted him; disgusted that he must be the one to start proceedings to make a fellow officer's ruin public. Tomorrow *Blanche* would be off to face Jervis, unless Smith chose to shoot himself, expatiate his crimes, receive honorable burial. The Commodore doubted it after seeing Smith's face, grown devoid of any thought but his vicious obsession.

He listened to two young mids of the middle watch whispering together, probably only too conscious of the Commodore's presence.

"It was about time you left those girls in San Fiorenzo," the Commodore's chance shot hit the mark. There was an amazed silence, the youngsters exchanged glances. The Commodore was clairvoyant!

"Oh, I was just—ah—challenging a race to the masthead when this watch ends, sir."

"You'd better plan to have breakfast with me, instead. I'll have no more mids breaking limbs. That's an order, Mr. Hoste."

"Aye, aye, sir."

And as he turned away he heard them bursting with the joke. And, of course, the prospect of eating at the Commodore's table; free.

Now he glimpsed the master-at-arms and the corporals making their half-hourly rounds. His fisherman seemed to be taking forever to reach him. He watched the master-at-arms going forward to check the brick-lined galley, the only place safe for smoking on shipboard, then disappearing below to make sure no lights and no smoking went on anywhere else.

"Deck there, the fisherman's circling us, sir."

Well, in good time the Commodore would hear the worst, the last and latest news of Buonaparte's invasion of Italy, and on that he must weigh his proposal to Jervis; his plan to oust Buonaparte's army from Leghorn.

A pain in his chest caught him aback; he took a short breath, keeping well within those steel invisible bands circling him. He was sick and sick of war! He had been too busy to take that vacation, indulge the doctor's orders for a few weeks at the baths of Pisa. Too late now. For a moment he ached for home, the luxuries of existence: sleeping with his own wife, facing her across a breakfast table; and he could

see that table. There would be the delicate china. Why did a fighting
man yearn for porcelains, the delicate things? To go to Drury Lane or
Covent Garden, oh, some place gay every night! To have the pleasure
of falling asleep in the middle of Mrs. Siddons's Lady Macbeth, to take
quiet amusement in Fanny's shocked face as she prodded him to wake
up. To watch Hamlet worry himself to death for a change with that
hair-raising ghost of his. If he were Hamlet he would believe that
ghost just to get on with the action. . . . His nerves were straining,
as the mortal minutes of his life ticked away.

The fishing boat must have sunk! Now he glimpsed it: lateen sail, a
black triangle aslant the mast. It rose up against the night sky, like
the fin of a shark, disappeared. The same daring voyage made sometimes before daybreak, sometimes at dusk, day after day, week after
week.

He thought of the letter this week's mail packet from England had
brought from his former headstrong student, H.R.H. the Duke of
Clarence: "When I compare the want of energy in the old govern-
ments, the treachery and blunders made by the Austrians, with the
enthusiasm and activity of the French I can see no end to their conquests on the continent. . . . We cannot say dear old England is as we
could wish it: however we are better off than any other nation. . . ."

No end to war! And that from the son of George III, from Clarence;
more of a jolly sailor than one noted for his perspicacity! If Clarence
could see it, then God only knew what was ahead! England was still
trying to form coalitions, snug on her island, while time drifted by
and the French armies swarmed into Italy. Well, he smiled to himself, perhaps he could put a crimp in this Buonaparte's plans. Jervis
had agreed to give him much of the army from Corsica . . . with the
army from Corsica. . . .

He heard a creaking low on the water, the hiss of a boat's wake.

From the deck: "Ahoy, Neri?"

A grumble from the water: "*Sì*, Giovanni Neri."

Commodore Nelson went to his cabin. At last!

※   ※   ※

Seated now in the cabin he watched them shuffle in, tried not to
mind their aroma of garlic and old fish; nor to give way to the queasy
upchurning in his midriff.

What a crew! From co-operation with bristling Austrian generals in spanking uniforms the English were descended to this: smuggling news through Livornese fishermen in exchange for a loaf of bread!

"Well met." He rose as a woman's hand shoved Neri half across the cabin, and a volley of Livornese chatter preceded the mouth, still hidden by the shadow of the doorway. "Ah! My lady has come! She will tell me all!" He bowed, and with his most arch and beguiling smile, that threw his lieutenants, Berry and pale, still wan, Noble, nearly into convulsions, offered his lady a chair. He hovered, soberly near, occasionally turning away for a breath of fresh air.

The crosshatchings of her lined face wreathed and wrinkled. Her black eyes rolled. Her smile gave way her toothlessness: a crone's head on a whale's body, all muffled in rags. She let out one last comfortable wheeze, wriggled her bare toes over the Commodore's brand-new self-indulgence, a carpet, and waving both hands in the air launched once more into her incomprehensible cackling.

The Commodore watched while Lieutenant Pierson, as usual, absorbed it for him.

Beside the old lady stood Neri, clutching a damp black hat. His brown face was lined as the rocky shore. His eyes darted from the woman to Nelson, to Pierson, to the few luxuries that must have seemed riches: the gold-hilted sword hung high, the decent furniture. The commodore of a squadron was not much lower than God in his omnipotence over these people. He had the power of life or death in his hands: one loaf of bread made the difference.

Neri took a bundle of greasy newspapers from inside his shirt—the kind he wrapped fish in—handed them to the Commodore without a word. There would be messages from friends of the English inside the French lines.

"They have pillaged," Pierson began to translate as the Commodore's favorite old fishwife paused for breath, fanning herself and nodding her head. "When Buonaparte dashed into Leghorn following the first troops, the gates of the city were locked and the great boom stretched across the harbor. Buonaparte was welcomed by the Grand Duke himself at a dinner and lavish reception. The Duke, she says, fired the *feu de joie* acknowledging the French 'liberation' of the internationally recognized free port of Leghorn! The Governor of Leghorn who helped Captain Freemantle to embark the English merchants an hour before Buonaparte arrived—"

"Buonaparte arrived the same hour as I did?" The Commodore interrupted. The boom had already been stretched across the harbor when he, having been ordered to go there from Genoa, hauled up. "Well . . ."

"The Governor, sir, dared to declare Leghorn was still free by the international agreement. He has been our friend. And he dared to remind Buonaparte that he had promised to maintain its neutrality. She says Buonaparte flew in a rage, lashed about with his whip, calling the Governor a scoundrel and a—" Pierson, the good Neapolitan, swallowed—"he called him a *macaroni eater,* sir! The Governor stood it very well, but he asked permission to leave Leghorn as long as the neutrality had been broken and Buonaparte agreed. He could leave as his prisoner!"

Pierson paused for breath as one of the Commodore's servants, Coulson, poured wine. The Commodore had passed the word for Coulson, rather than take a verbal beating from Allen for being up so late.

"Where's the Governor now?"

"Imprisoned at Florence, sir; his family was sent after him to share whatever his fate will be. She says the French have ransacked the houses; trained guns on every street; undermined the town walls with powder and will blow it all up if the Livornese do not respect the Tree of Liberty the French have planted and hail when they parade their Liberty Goddess through the streets."

"But where's this fellow, Buonaparte, now—ask her that." The Commodore smiled again at the woman and her eyes danced as she tilted her wineglass and smacked her lips, and rubbed her feet, one, then the other, on the carpet; like a satisfied cat.

She heard Pierson's question. Scowled. Shrugged, almost crushed her wineglass in her paw, and then spat out imprecations that made even Neri wince. Pierson rolled up his eyes, thought a moment before translating to his pious commanding officer.

"She says this—ah—this Buonaparte demanded the shortest road to Rome. He wants to conquer the Pope! He dashed out of town with his cavalry. She says some say he fell off his horse. Some say he was killed in a battle. Everyone says he is dead, sir; they've been celebrating his death all week."

The Commodore waved his hand, his face sobering, trying to conceal his impatience. She had said that last week and he had believed it until more news proved it was only wishful thinking! The latest "facts" would be in Neri's papers and letters; even they would not be accurate. He must weigh the smug Austrian propaganda against the bombastic French and then try to *guess*. . . .

"Ask her how my plans have progressed among the fishermen."

The woman's eyes narrowed.

"She says they will fight to the death. All the people will rise when the English move in. She says the shoemakers, bricklayers, fishermen, all the different tradesmen have agreed to the assigned points from which to attack the French. They have already taken sticks to the soldiers—told them to go away!"

The woman sat silently shrugging her shoulders and shaking her head as Neri suddenly mumbled out a few words.

"He says that the Governor appointed by the French will lose his head"—and as Pierson spoke Neri ran his finger across his throat, patted the knife in his belt—"when the English move in. He says many Italian nobles were bribed by the French, told they would not be harmed. The nobles want a revolution to wrest the power for themselves. . . . And the Genoese minister now in London, he is friends of the French. Spies on English."

The Commodore nodded. "The Marquis of Spinola? We know him."

"Spinola's a rat," Neri hissed.

"She says," Pierson went on, "the fighting is great in the north. That everyone says this Buonaparte cannot push ahead. There has been a great battle for three days. The Austrians are said to be pouring in reinforcements."

Three days of fighting! The Commodore's eyes brightened. Ah, but until he knew what had happened on the *fourth* day . . .

Suddenly the old woman leaned forward, clasping her hands, talking earnestly to the Commodore.

"She says there are Corsicans in Leghorn, sir, ready to reconquer the island. That accounts for the enemy privateers collecting in these waters. She says the Corsicans make so much trouble with the French and with the Livornese the French have said, 'Go then, back to Corsica, take it for us—' and behind their hands the French say, 'If they succeed very well—if not, we are rid of a set of scoundrels.' "

"The French say that?" The Commodore laughed.

"And she says the Livornese spit on the French and their liberty. The people say war is war. It was hard under the Grand Duke, but the port of Leghorn was open. Now shops are closed. Nothing comes in by sea or land. There is no trade. The French take what they please —clothing, food. She says the Grand Duke tells them Buonaparte respects Leghorn—he will go away. She spits on the Grand Duke. She laughs at their *liberté*. She says the French bring their tall guillotines with their trees and their goddesses. They cut off the heads of their own soldiers, they cut off the heads of the Livornese. It's the guillotine that impresses the people."

Pierson suddenly grinned, "She says she is too old, sir, for *fraternité*, but already half Leghorn is with French child. As to *égalité?* She says it means she gives her mattress to soldier and then he doesn't shoot her dead. She says all wars are the same. She says she wants to fish and she will fish. She pays taxes no matter who conquers. In short, sir, she repeats, she spits on the French!"

"Tell them I rely on them to spread the word: 'Resist.' Tell her she is a brave woman and tell Neri I'll give him a paper—like a passport. No English ship will ever harm him. You may dismiss them." He passed the slip of paper to Neri, with a friendly nod. And he made a slight courteous bow to the old woman. In spite of her filth and her stench he felt she deserved his respect. He admired her, wretched excuse for a human that she was, recognizing that stubborn dangerous spark of temper he owned in himself.

"Coulson"—he motioned to his servant—"give these people the bundles of bread to take back, as usual."

The old woman sidled close a moment. "You feed the poor. They don't forget their friends," Pierson translated.

Watching them shuffle out of his cabin, he turned, dashed for the window, and drinking in air felt the waves of seasickness recede.

"Yow ot to be abed!" Allen startled him, as he leaned on the window seat, waiting for the garlic and fish to leave his cabin.

"Good morning, Allen. I'll have a stroll till breakfast."

"Yow ain't been to bed," Allen grumbled, grudgingly thankful that the Commodore had not stolen the march on him: waked and dressed himself.

The Commodore did not answer. Having got off very lightly, he walked past his "walley" to the deck where he found Berry and Weatherhead, seeing the last of the Livornese off in the dark. The mountainous woman lurched down into her tiny boat. They could hear the slipping of waves; their voices floating away.

"What a plague war is!" the Commodore muttered to his lieutenants. "When we went into Toulon it was on the promise that the Royalists would rise—overthrow the revolution! When we went into Corsica it was at the request of Paoli. Now we are in they consort with the French to 'liberate' them. Here, in Leghorn, are the French, and the Livornese cry to us. Well, by God we won't fail them!"

"That old woman, sir," Weatherhead said, "the French will cut her to pieces the size of tunny fish if they even guess where she's been. But tonight her people will eat."

"She has nerve," Berry said thoughtfully.

"Now there's something glorious, Berry, in that old creature leading her fishermen. How many nights has she come? But how is it"—he included Weatherhead in his sudden wry smile—"we always attract such *old* lady informers!"

"The young ones earn their bread from the French perhaps," Weatherhead mused.

"Will human nature ever change, sir?" Berry sighed.

"The poor, my dear Berry, ye have always. . . . And sometimes I hope and then despair of getting these poor starved Livornese to cut the throats of that French crew!" He caught himself up with a gasp. "Good God! What a thought for a Christian! Oh . . ." he stood shaking his head, "let us hope there is great latitude for us in the next world!" He turned away and then back again on his tracks. "Yes, Berry, I *am* wicked enough to wish their throats cut tonight!"

"Aye, aye." Weatherhead was used to the Commodore's occasional struggles with his conscience by now.

But Berry, being newer, though he and the Commodore got on very well, thanks to Berry's discovery that the Commodore responded to kind words, was rummaging for an answer. "Well, the Lord marketh the fall of a sparrow, sir, no doubt He will look out for us, sir!"

"But there's something strange in the wind. These mad Frenchmen rushing upon the world. Do you know what astonishes me?"

Berry answered slowly. He was something of an "aye, aye" man, and furnishing opinions of his own rather worried him. "Their quick thrusts, sir? Their, well, I must say, extraordinary progress?"

"No. Although I admit their progress has astonished me; that young boys defeat trained armies, but more so the *imbecility* and *fear* within the Italian states! Leghorn is taken, yet Genoa, next door, still demands from us the rights of neutrality to furnish these French devils with arms and allows the French to establish their garrisons on their territory! Imbeciles! Had they expended half the money to preserve their territories which they have paid to the French for entering them . . ." He stalked moodily beside his lieutenants. "When, I would like to know, will they have enough of these French fraternizing with their women, their churches and their olive trees!"

❊ ❊ ❊

They never saw Giovanni Neri nor the old fisherwoman again. New informers took their place. No one knew what had become of them when they sailed away in the night; all anyone knew was they had last been heard of leaving the *Captain.* . . . But the new informers brought news for bread, and distributed the slips of paper the Commodore wrote out to be handed to the people: Resist.

Commodore Nelson to Sir John Jervis:

We know the jealousy of the army against the navy, but I am by the King's Commission a Colonel in the army from June 1st, 1795. . . . If I landed as Colonel, of course, I should command the whole . . . if my character is known, the internal regulations of the troops should rest by order under the Major, Duncan; and I should only interfere in the great scale. . . . It has pleased God to prosper all my undertakings and I feel confident of His blessing on this occasion. I ever consider my motto, *Fides et Opera.*

N.B. Twenty four hours will do the business. Send an active Officer.

And again to Jervis: "If I write too much, say so, and I will hold my pen. . . ." But Jervis did not say so. He was anxious to let Nelson go ahead.

Commodore Nelson writing to Sir Gilbert Elliot, Viceroy of Corsica:

I have satisfied Major Logan that there is no danger in the attempt. . . . What is our object? To dispossess the French of Leghorn; not to keep it, I suppose, but free the Leghornese from a foreign garrison. This is the point . . . I suppose the French will, as is usual with those gentlemen, determine to die in the works—at least they say so; a mortar battery will probably bring them to reason. A regular siege I take to be entirely out of the question. Every house that is destroyed must make all the Leghornese urgent with the French, and probably the rich may pay the commander well for a capitulation; which, if I know Frenchmen right, he will not be averse to; so that he can say mortars, shot, fire, etc. in short, to hold out long enough to make a letter. . . . Our only consideration is the honor and benefit to our Country worth the risk? If it is (and I think so) in God's name let us get to work, and hope for His blessing on our endeavors to liberate a people who have been our sincere friends. . . .

❊   ❊   ❊

Commodore Nelson to his brother, the Reverend William Nelson:

I may tell you as a *secret* that probably the next letter you see from me will be in the *Public Gazette*. An expedition is thought of, and of course, I shall be there. . . .

P.S. I'm sorry to tell you the Austrians have had a check in Lombardy by fancying themselves too powerful. It disappoints my hopes for the present.

Commodore Nelson to Jervis:

We are anxious to receive news. All our expected hopes are blasted, I fear. . . . Austria, I suppose, must make peace, and we shall, as usual, be left to fight it out. . . .

❊   ❊   ❊

So Colonel-Commodore Nelson was declined the pleasure of crossing swords with the French army in Leghorn. And worse: Spain declared war against England, having followed her suspicious way of adhering to the nation offering the most immediate show of strength. Prodded by a jubilantly conquering France, Spain now hoped to regain the ascendancy she had long ago lost to England and Austria. The internal French Revolution was apparently ending, but the force of it now began to spill farther and farther over French boundaries. A starving impoverished people, just liberated from one form of tyranny, were tyrannically striking out everywhere. The French armies were supporting themselves by war and the French treasury beginning to prosper, and a prosperous treasury was gaining greater power for the new government. The war had become self-propelling.

From Jervis to Commodore Nelson: an order to commandeer a right to establish a garrison on the Genoese island of Elba preparatory to the evacuation of the English army from Corsica. Done. Bloodlessly. The next orders had come through from England; withdraw from the Mediterranean Sea! Prepare for a war with a combined France and Spain.

❊   ❊   ❊

The first autumn gales were blustering down from the Corsican mountains. Through the high surf pounding Bastia, the Commodore's launch mounted a long green swell, caught the first teetering crest of a breaker; slid shoreward, grating the sands.

The Commodore and Lieutenant Noble leaped out. Nelson cast one glance seaward. His ship was still beating against the wind, coming to anchor. Then with a determined step he crossed the beach.

A line of redcoats guarded the white villa of the Viceroy. Beyond their leveled bayonets roamed a skulking, knife-brandishing mob. These were the people who had once laughingly cried, "First we kill the French, then Maggiores. . . ." Now, "First we kill the English, then—"

Without so much as a second glance for them, the Commodore passed through the line of redcoats to the villa where only a few weeks ago he had arranged the evacuation of Lady Elliot, *enceinte* again, and her brood. Elliot's once prim little English children had war whooped aboard the frigate and given their mother, with her thoughts once more on England and civilization, a turn. Her children had grown brown and wild as the Corsican goats. Well, they were gone, halfway home by now, the Commodore hoped, and for the thousandth time, prayed Lady Elliot would take his emphatic advice to stay in her cabin; not go having that baby somewhere between Gibraltar and Plymouth. . . . All thoughts of the lady were banished as he stepped inside the entrance hall.

It was swarming with refugees. A mass of bundles and white faces. Everyone talking at once. Some were English merchants; some were English travelers who had fled northern Italy; some were English families that had always lived abroad; some were French Royalists hounded forever from pillar to post. Displaced. Welcome nowhere. Some were Corsicans who remained loyal to the English.

The Commodore went through the hall with an "Everything is under control. Pray just be patient . . ." and on into the Viceroy's study.

Sir Gilbert Elliot was slowly pacing the floor, unwigged, mopping his forehead and hopelessly turning from the window to his desk and the crates, half packed, standing around the room. His face was worried and sad.

"How glad I am to see you, Nelson!" He shook hands quietly. "What a bother this is."

"I am happy to be at Your Excellency's service. How do things stand, Sir Gilbert?"

"Oh, splendid! We've had the best wheat in years." The Viceroy smiled bitterly. "Corsica never was more prosperous. If it were not for the orders from home, those wretched Paolist beggars would be quiet."

"Indeed, sir, may I ask where our General is?" the Commodore broke in, too impatiently, he realized. "The French, Sir Gilbert, are on my heels. I have only two frigates left at Leghorn to prevent their coming and those French privateers are swifter than my frigates. Forgive me, sir, if I seem hurried, but I hope to embark you without bloodshed."

"The General is in the Citadel."

"I must see him at once—"

"Ah, but the Corsicans have mounted guard with our army, man for man, Commodore. The ringleaders call themselves the Committee of Thirty. They moved in on us the moment I announced our probable evacuation. Their haste was indecent! And with this gale of the last three days I hardly expected you'd get here; how did you? I thought you would go from your blockade to San Fiorenzo. That's where I sent my message to you."

"I had a hunch, sir, and picked up your message halfway between."

"The Committee of Thirty didn't expect you either. They have stolen all English property; locked up our warehouses. A band of thieves. But it breaks my heart to leave. The mass of these people are loyal good Englishmen. They see us going, what will become of them? Commodore Nelson, if we could only wait . . . I've written a hundred letters home not to give us up! I can't *believe* the orders from England!"

The Commodore had spun toward the window staring at the men with whom he had helped to conquer the French: to turn Corsican swords into plowshares . . . "A band of thieves all of them! They'll regret having no more silver harvest from England."

"Oh, they're only children, Nelson. They want the moon."

Commodore Nelson was staring at the Corsican mob manning new guns mounted along the mole, pointing them seaward at their brother Englishmen's ships. "Pray, sir, your effects? Papers?"

"I will send them aboard. We must obey orders. If only the people at home . . . As a secret, Nelson, my brother-in-law is on his way to

Paris now to discuss peace terms with the French! So why give up Corsica when the war is all over?"

The Commodore turned away from the window. "No one could regret it more than I, Sir Gilbert. . . . We will get your valuable effects off right away. Mr. Noble." He motioned to his quiet lieutenant. "Make our signal to anchor our ships abreast the town."

"It's all quite fantastic!" The Viceroy shook his head. "Would you believe it, they even announce they will take me prisoner. They say they will murder me tonight. Nonsense!"

"Good God! They dared to threaten your life, Sir Gilbert?" The Commodore threw up his hands. "The bandits! May I have the use of your carriage, sir? I must see the Citadel." The Viceroy's inability to believe his eyes and ears staggered him. And as for the Viceroy's brother-in-law making peace with the French who were just getting under sail with their conquests . . . He had a low opinion of peace talk—now with Spain thrown into the scale.

"Oh, you will find the Committee of Thirty has been there ahead of you. Out of a clear sky, these French!"

"Pray, Sir Gilbert, your carriage?" His orders were to evacuate the Viceroy *alive*. . . .

The Viceroy pulled a bell rope, gave the order. "Miserable wind. Pray, have you had any lunch?" He spoke hollowly and the Commodore realized Elliot's unusual loquacity was trying to hide wounded pride; postponing the inevitable.

"Thank you, sir, but the French are expected to land any hour."

"I pray they will land before you leave! It's all bravado! My people will rally to me when they see that Tricolor."

The Commodore weighed his answer. It was painful. He and the Viceroy did not agree, apparently, on the true designs of the Corsicans. "It would mean a battle, Sir Gilbert, useless bloodshed when the Commander in Chief's orders from home are to evacuate Corsica. If you will forgive me, I will return very shortly. I must see what I can do about embarking the British army."

Sir Gilbert sank down in his chair, his hand fell heavily on his desk. He had all the faith in the world in his brother-in-law's peace mission. Lord Malmesbury could not fail him!

❋   ❋   ❋

Riding along through the narrow, hostile streets with four of his "old *Agamemnons*," including Sykes and Allen, the Commodore felt his resentment rising. The very beauty of the island now seemed like a lingering delirium. He had given his whole heart and mind to liberate Corsica. Been willing to lay down his life—like Serocold—like Moutray. And he would do it again, but he would remember this time that his first impression had been correct. They would cry, "Long live the conqueror!" to all conquerors. He had been deafened by their cries of "Paoli!" What was the man he had admired so much he could not credit him with such absurd conduct as a lie? Living now, quietly in London, was he Machiavelli or martyr? Neither? Both? No matter. England—and Paoli—were through with Corsica . . . and good riddance! But he would not abandon the island like a quailing rat. He had taken the island, and he would leave it in good order—and not one penny of English goods would be left behind for the French!

The carriage jolted up through the wide-open gates of the Citadel. The Commodore raised his eyebrows ever so slightly. The Citadel gates were wide-open while the town was in revolt. No sign of activity here. The army was, no doubt, as usual.

Alighting from the carriage he made his bow stiffly to General de Burgh, who had replaced Stuart. The Commodore noticed only that, like all the rest of the army, the General was well dressed and powdered.

"I am here to evacuate the Viceroy, sir, and the army. I believe that your co-operation may facilitate the removal of all ordnance and stores belonging to us."

The General shook his head. "Impossible, sir. They have attached everything. As you see, we hold the Citadel merely by tacit agreement. Our guards are matched man for man by the rebels."

"May I suggest, sir, that as long as my ships are here to protect and embark you, *close* the gates of the Citadel to prevent any more getting in and overwhelm what you have?"

"Your ships will stay to protect our embarkation?"

"Aye, and though I propose to leave amicably, I will moor my ships opposite the town and batter it down if I must, sir. May I see the lists of store and ordnance we will evacuate?"

"An impossible quantity. Tons of it," the General muttered. "All in all, it comes to about two hundred thousand pounds sterling in value. I hate to leave it." He held out a sheaf of papers.

The Commodore ran over them quickly. "We won't leave it . . . twelve hundred barrels of powder, three hundred tons of stores—all kinds, fifteen hundred troops, baggage, hospital staff—sick—to say nothing of the six hundred *émigrés* who can't afford to leave a rag. . . . We will inform the Committee of Thirty the English still rule the island until the last boat shoves off."

The General was smiling when they shook hands. From the Citadel now, back to the Viceroy. As the carriage threaded the moody streets with their glaring white plaster houses, their shutters closed but for eyes peeking through cracks, Commodore Nelson looked out over Bastia's harbor.

Here, a little over three years ago, four thousand five hundred French laid down their arms to one thousand seamen and marines. Now he, himself, must see that the hard-fought Union Jack flying over the Citadel was *struck* in good order.

The wind had fallen, as these land gales often did for an hour or two at a time, and his ships lay just out of gunshot, unfortunately. But far out he caught a flashing of white, a battleship hung on the faint air. Jervis was sending him reinforcements. That looked like Collingwood's *Excellent* by the cut of her. Between them they would have this work done.

He found the Viceroy's villa once more in a weeping uproar, and the Viceroy secluded for his lunch and afternoon nap.

A swarthy-looking villain burst into tears at the sight of the Commodore; clutched his hand. "I have a privateer, sir, I'm an Englishman. If the Corsicans keep my ship I'm ruined!"

Suddenly a merchant wrung his other hand, threatened to kiss it. "They have taken our trunks, sir, even our shirts!"

And a general outburst: "Our furniture! We have nothing left in the world!"

"Gentlemen, please. We will evacuate you in good order. Nothing will be left undone."

But the merchants and privateers and the refugees continued to weep. Prosperous people yesterday, they fought for his attention like dogs in the gutter—which was what they feared would be their lot, unless they were mercifully murdered. It was the panic that must have once gripped Toulon.

And round the corners of the house the gale began to howl again. The Commodore caught the roar of it above the hum indoors. His face relaxed. "Mr. Noble! Signal our ships to summon the Committee of Thirty we will blow up the town if all English ships in the harbor are not released within fifteen minutes."

And now for the Viceroy again, for Sir Gilbert, while he remained, had power over both the General and the Commodore. The Commodore entered the cool darkened room, found the Viceroy far from asleep, yet pitifully inert, his eyes half closed. Two servants were just carrying the last crate, fully packed, to the hall. A diplomatic pouch lay sealed and weighted on the desk.

"May I have your consent, Sir Gilbert, to allow me to assist you on board just at dusk?"

"Fantastic," the Viceroy answered as a vision of diplomatic ruin welled up with his poorly digested lunch. "If they see me go . . . Come, what's that?" The Viceroy turned to the window. The dark high hulls of the English ships had closed in on the town.

Lieutenant Noble smiling as he saluted: "The Corsicans have quitted the mole, sir. Captain Sutton in *Diadem* pulled out his watch and gave them fifteen minutes."

"Nelson! Now you see?" The Viceroy's face lit up. "It will all blow over."

"As long as my battleships lie abreast the town, Sir Gilbert, yes."

"The Corsicans downed muskets and ran, sir, when they saw us," Noble said. "But begging your pardon again, sir, the Committee of Thirty still refuses to give up our goods in the customhouse. The merchants are in tears again, sir."

Casting a haggard exasperated glance at the Viceroy's back, the Commodore snapped: "Go to the Committee of Thirty. If the keys to the customhouse aren't delivered instantly and all other English goods turned over to us, say Commodore Nelson will open fire."

Within ten minutes Noble returned, still smiling angelically. "The keys, sir, have been turned over. They looked like ghosts, sir, when I mentioned your name."

A hush had fallen over Bastia. The mobs had scurried away like mice. There was not a soul to be seen on the streets. "I never saw Bastia so peaceful . . ." the Commodore grinned.

❋ ❋ ❋

Sir Gilbert Elliot and General Brogio were crossing the beach for the last time. They were wrapped in dark cloaks, hidden by the very dark that was to have murdered Sir Gilbert, while Commodore Nelson, with delicate energy, popped out of the shadows, politely touched the Viceroy's elbow.

"If you will sit there, Sir Gilbert, I think you will be most comfortable . . ." and he signaled the launch to shove off. Now. He turned back, free of the Viceroy's power, to finish the evacuation as he intended.

Seeing frigates as well as two battleships, Collingwood's *Excellent* and Lieutenant Berry commanding *Captain,* both seventy-fours, laid abreast Bastia, General de Burgh took heart. Wresting the Citadel from the Corsicans, he sent out the small detachments of troops to guard the seamen loading the ships with the two hundred thousand pounds' worth of English stores.

And oddly enough, Sir Gilbert Elliot, reluctant as he had been to give up, sent word he would take nothing from Corsica that had not been landed there for the English. A quixotic gentleman in his dark cloak and snowy peruke, he stood at the head of the *Captain's* gangway, clutching the brass rail that glistened in the dark. He peered back at his lovely white house, enchanting in the night; at the long lines of seamen lit by wind-tossed torches; glimpsing the army redcoats here and there. And he peered through hard bitter tears.

"My poor Corsica!" The Viceroy broke down and wept.

On shore inevitable news: the French had landed, were marching on Bastia.

The Corsicans, watching the English, began to weep, now they had won their demands. They blessed them and cried in their arms. No, Corsica had never been so prosperous. They *had* been happy. So they hugged them and cried through the night while the Committee of Thirty sat behind barred doors, minus the English money, but still triumphant.

It was too much for the mad island, this fighting and weeping. The wind rose from the mountains, scattering boats, lewdly whistling through the narrow back streets. Making the farewell to Corsica, as the beginning, desolate.

"And there they come!" Commodore Nelson turned on his heel, from the sea and the army to be embarked.

For now on the heights above Bastia, where vacillating redcoats had once appeared, marched the young French with their taunting Tricolor.

The Commodore drew himself up, eyes narrowing, his face lined with the three mortal years of war that he was undoing tonight.

❅ ❅ ❅

By midnight of that nineteenth of October, 1796, with a flourish of arms, stepping smartly, the last troops of the English army of liberation marched out of the Citadel down to the shore where General de Burgh and Commodore Nelson stood, directing the embarkation.

Between the shore and the ships the surf rose in restless breakers; like the echoes of yesterday's guns, they broke, swirling up on the sands. Over them darted the black boats, tossed about, up, down; oars like drowning arms clutched the spewed foam, rowing out.

As the night wore away, the English army dwindled with the outward tide on the sands, pulling off for the new post Nelson had secured for them, the last English garrison in the French dominated Mediterranean Sea: Porto Ferrajo, on the little island betwixt and between the mainland and Corsica, hardly worth their attention—Elba.

The last boatload of troops shoved off. It was dawn of another day. The General and the Commodore watched the Tricolor soar, once again, high over the Citadel. It stretched flat with the wind, haughtily waving them seaward.

"After you, sir." The Commodore bowed the General into his launch. The General sat down uncertainly between the last two pieces of artillery kept to cover their retreat. The shadowy crowd of Corsicans who had wept in their arms now edged forward, cheering the Tricolor, fingering their knives.

Commodore Nelson stood eyeing them; they waited and his head came up: "Now, John Corse, follow the bent of your detestable character—plunder and revenge!"

He took his time stepping into the launch and did not look back. He was the last Englishman to leave Bastia.

❅ ❅ ❅

It was not far from Corsica to Elba in distance measured in miles, straight sailing, port to port. But measured in time, it had taken the English all of three years to cross over. It might take other warriors somewhat longer.

With the fresh wind out of Bastia, in only an hour, the army, convoyed by *Captain,* hove to at Porto Ferrajo, Elba, and on the quarterdeck, Nelson took the Viceroy's outstretched hand, pressed it warmly.

"I wish you were coming with us, Sir Gilbert, though this is a beautiful port and may save our last convoys still coming down from the Levant."

"We shall meet again. For the present, I'm going to southern Italy for a little rest." The Viceroy was pale, very tired. He made no effort to smile. "I can't believe we have given up Corsica!" Tears started to his eyes again.

"They'll soon learn, Sir Gilbert, what a friend they lost in you. It would take the patience of Job and the riches of Croesus to rule that crew!"

"Can't thank you enough for all you have done, even to getting Lady Elliot safely off to England. War can't last much longer . . . my brother-in-law . . . but if it does"—the Viceroy eyed the Commodore pensively—"I know who ought to command these seas."

The Commodore shook his head, doubting his ears, as he watched the man go slowly over the side. With a sharp order to Berry, the *Captain's* guns saluted the ex-Viceroy of Corsica, smartly, nineteen times.

❖   ❖   ❖

Now the *Captain* was free of her last chore, and lifting her bows bore down for the fleet, saluting the Commander in Chief.

Jervis had pulled out of San Fiorenzo, in reluctant obedience to the orders from home to evacuate. He had postponed it for months, on the pleas of the Viceroy—and the persuasions of Commodore Nelson—but he could wait no longer. Now Corsica was completely evacuated of English.

The Mediterranean fleet stood off San Fiorenzo, still waiting for a straw: for all battleships to join, and pondering the news that the Spanish had sent eighteen battleships into the Mediterranean to join the French. While Nelson joined from Elba, Troubridge reconnoitered Toulon.

But the English fleet was outnumbered, without harbors, even without water. As the fleet grew thirsty off San Fiorenzo, a small midshipman named Parsons, who belonged to Vice-Admiral Waldegrave's *Barfleur,* watched open-mouthed when Jervis himself led watering parties back up Corsican cliffs, fought hand to hand for water for his fleet. Still they waited, for a whole squadron from Jervis's fleet was missing under Admiral Man, who had been sent to cruise in the Atlantic. He had been ordered to rejoin Jervis months ago. He had not been heard from.

Still Jervis waited for Man to make the Mediterranean fleet whole, Jervis hoped to beat the enemy now at the eleventh hour.

Corsica, evacuated by the Ministry's orders, loomed jagged and hostile as the sun set and a dispatch ship from England bore up:

If Jervis had not already carried out the Ministry's previous order for the immediate evacuation of Corsica sent out months ago, the government was now annulling that order, and Jervis was to hold Corsica! If he had evacuated Corsica as ordered, then retreat.

"Do they know their own minds, Sir John?" Nelson gritted as Jervis sat raging.

And Admiral Man would never come to rejoin the fleet. On receiving Jervis's orders, he had sailed as far as Gibraltar to obey, then at a council of captains turned back, and sailed straight home to England! Left Jervis without reinforcements while the Spanish and French were rumored to be pouring their ships into a Combined Fleet.

At last Jervis signaled his order: Retreat. And pray for reinforcements at Gibraltar.

Now Jervis in *Victory,* Troubridge in *Culloden,* Collingwood in *Excellent,* Nelson in *Captain* and eleven other of line, sails spread, bows pointing west for Gibraltar; in a long slow line, leaving a sighing wake.

"In sackcoth and ashes! Why?" Nelson was writing home, gazing from his stern windows aft at the miles of ships. Their clouds of canvas billowing in the silver November sky, hulls creaming the green water of the Barbary Coast. Day after day sailing west until at last the tawny Rock rose up guarding the legendary Pillars of Hercules: the end of the ancient mariner's world. The place where men had once paused, reading the warning signs, and turned back, not daring to challenge the edges of the ocean. But Captain Nelson was writing to Fanny: "As soon as we have defeated the Spanish Fleet, which I doubt not, with God's help, we shall do, I have two or three little matters to settle in Italy, and then I care not how quickly I return to you. Do not flatter yourself that I shall be rewarded; I expect nothing, and therefore shall not be disappointed: the pleasure of my own mind will be my reward. I am more interested in obtaining yours and my father's applause than that of all the world besides. . . ." But Commodore Nelson was a modern man at Gibraltar, and while the word "Combined Enemy Fleet" made long faces among the English, he assured all, including the flag officers: "England's fleets are equal to meet the whole world in arms!" And Vice-Admiral Waldegrave mused wryly that Nelson seemed to have glory burning and raging within him.

Yet after so long a war there seemed to be nothing definite ahead. No schemes for offensives. Yet Commodore Nelson pondered a letter from the Minister at Turin which he had received and mulled over for months: spies reported that France intended to invade England. . . . His answer was simple: "I suppose England will be the last to make peace; and whilst she trusts to her Wooden Walls she will be more successful than any other power. . . ." And the great mass of the navy was kept at home, inactive unfortunately; the Wooden Walls. While Jervis's orders were to cruise off Spain, await a meeting with the French and the Spanish. His fleet, already diminished by Admiral Man's betrayal, was minus now Ben Hallowell's *Courageux* which had been the last coming down the Mediterranean: disappeared in a gale. Ben Hallowell bobbed up, shoulders and head hulking above the tiny jolly boat that saved him. The fleet cheered; it was better to lose a battleship than to lose Ben. And surely some reinforcements would be sent from England. Jervis's fifteen could not be expected to fight double its odds alone.

Yet there was not a man in Jervis's fleet but hoped to restore England's place in the world. They had witnessed the skyrocketing power of France; knew the name of a new genius: Buonaparte.

❋   ❋   ❋

Even in England the news of the French invasion of Italy began to penetrate the Channel fogs. Thoughtful minds that had so far held aloof from breast-beating patriotism, their intellects pained that England should combine with decadent old monarchies to crush France's new panacea—liberty; these minds that had sought liberty when they joined the revolutionary forces in England, fought against the war, not for the more obvious gain that the ringleaders sought, but because they believed England was wrong in opposing France, now cried out in disillusioned anger. France had violated the neutrality of the "freedomloving noble Swiss!"

And the violation of free Switzerland struck the spark of anger that the declaration of war against their own country had not kindled three years before. One knows the faults of one's own country—or parents—so well! And men who had wept sentimentally at England's violation of French liberty could be just as sentimental about the liberty of the Swiss. For once an ideal captures hearts, it becomes the motivating force regardless of nationality. Perhaps Coleridge, the poet who had

> . . . blessed the paeans of deliver'd France
> And hung my head and wept at Britain's name . . .

expressed his bitterness most clearly during that winter of 1796–1797 when he wrote:

> When France in wrath her giant-limbs uprear'd,
>   And with that oath, which smote air, earth, and sea
> Stamp'd her strong foot and said she would be free,
>   Bear witness for me, how I hoped and fear'd!
>
> *   *   *
>
> "And soon," I said, "Shall Wisdom teach her lore
> In the low huts of them that toil and groan!
> And conquering by her happiness alone,
>   Shall France compel the nations to be free,
> Till Love and Joy look round, and call the Earth their own."
>
> *   *   *
>
> Forgive me, Freedom! O forgive those dreams!
>   I hear thy voice, I hear thy loud lament. . . .

And while Coleridge pondered his disillusionment, declaring freedom never "breathed thy soul in forms of human power," but was "the guide of homeless winds, and playmate of the waves . . ." poet Wordsworth was on his way home. His revolutionary spirit sated, Wordsworth was impaled at last by the other horn of dilemma. He had taken the vows of an arch conservative. . . . Dr. Priestley still studied gases and electricity though the new age of expanding industrialism had jolted to a halt. Money had to be poured into the war. England was going in debt and Priestley was still preaching that Christianity had been corrupted.

❋   ❋   ❋

GIBRALTAR, *December 10, 1796*

From the Commander-in-Chief to Commodore Nelson:

You are hereby ordered and directed to hoist your Distinguishing Pendant in *La Minerve* frigate, to take *Blanche* frigate under your command and proceed from Gibraltar to Porto Ferrajo in Elba. Upon arrival there, or meeting with them, you are to take under your command the seventeen ships or vessels named in the margin, and to carry into execution His Majesty's commands relative to the disposition of the troops and stores lately removed to that garrison from the island of Corsica. . . .

He read swiftly; no one in the fleet had known, but him, that he was expecting this order, and that he was going because he could be quick. Jervis had told him he must travel as fast as he could for on his return he would find Jervis off Cádiz, if the battle between England, France and Spain had not already occurred. His emotions had been divided. To leave the fleet *now,* on the very edge of the field of glory . . . but Jervis had soothed him:

Having experienced the most important effects from your enterprise and ability, upon various occasions since I have had the honor to command in the Mediterranean, *I leave entirely to your judgement* the time and the manner of carrying this critical and arduous service into execution.

The Commodore wrote off a line to his wife:

I am going on a most important mission, which, with God's blessing, I have little doubt of accomplishing: it is not a fighting mission; therefore be not uneasy. I feel honored in being trusted as I am by Sir John Jervis. If I have enough money in Marsh and Creeds hands, I wish you would buy a cottage in Norfolk: I shall follow the plough with much greater satisfaction than viewing all the magnificent scenes in Italy. . . .

That should cover every detail of their relationship. But would she buy that cottage? He doubted it. He wished she were anchored somewhere instead of roaming so mournfully, charting the rises and falls in her health and spirits according to how well his relatives understood her symptoms. Poor Fanny! But she was virtuous! In that he had begun to consider her as unique and himself wise for anchoring to so much moral perfection, contained as it was in someone whose brain was so light and so—ah—feminine as Fanny's. But why didn't she buy a *home?* He had money now.

And feeling virtuous himself, having helped maintain her health by assuring her there would be no *fighting,* he sealed his letter. "Coulson!"

He spied his servant peeking to see if the sleeping cabin were clear so he could remove the Commodore's effects to the frigate. "Send off this letter and then tell Allen to shake a leg."

Once on deck, the Commodore sent for his Captain, Ralph Miller, who had come aboard just after they evacuated Corsica, and given the Commodore a nice opportunity to catch up on his reading of naval history. Now, after all this time with Lieutenant Berry acting as a captain, the Commodore had one . . . now when he was leaving his ship with the fleet.

He stared for a moment along the white decks. It was wash day, the whole ship domestic with clothes hung up in the rigging. The *Captain* was the finest ship he had ever commanded, and not once had he had an occasion to test her alongside a worthy opponent. Captain Miller had tried out her paces coming down from Gibraltar and found where she was wanting; made the allowances for her idiosyncrasies. She had faults, of course, for she had taken a pounding during Hotham's "battle," but she was repaired.

The Commodore nodded abruptly as Captain Miller appeared. He had been caught off guard, been examining the bow personally, not expecting the Commodore to leave so soon. He came leaping nimbly along the companions of the waist, a handsome man only two or three years younger than the Commodore. He would still be sailing about in a cruiser had Nelson not spotted him. He was proud of his rise to a battleship and though he looked like some of the dashing young naval officers in the gazette engravings, only good for having their pictures painted, there was an energy in his grace, and he sailed the ship with the sharp and keen-eyed gusto that the men loved in a captain, and a commodore could trust. He had saluted and fallen nimbly into step with the Commodore, who, regardless of etiquette, was wandering where he pleased—as usual. Yet as Miller paced silently and attentively beside the Commodore his eyes had shown a spark of annoyance that anything about his ship should not be exactly squared and regulated. The annoyance resolved into inner amusement however, for he had expected tart discipline when he came aboard this fire eater's ship, only to be told, airily, "Do as you please, Captain Miller. . . ."

"I trust you will give a good account of the *Captain* should the battle occur before I get back, which I fervently pray will not happen, Captain Miller. Those devils have held off this long—they might just as well wait for me!"

"I will, sir, for I shall fancy you still on the quarter-deck. And I hope you will be there, sir," Miller smiled. "I've arranged to paint her, sir. She's due for refit."

"Good. Paint her while I'm gone and have her *dry* before I get back. . . . Miller, do you think you could find black instead of red? And if Sir John will permit, paint her black outside as well, except for the gun tiers. But have her *dry*."

Miller, who was no longer amazed that paint fumes made the Commodore seasick, nodded. "Aye, aye, sir. And there's a hint of a sprain in the knee of her head, sir, but we'll have her fit in no time. I've my eye on that new mizzen topmast in the mast pond, sir, in the storehouse. They haven't another one in pickle. They're scarce as hen's teeth and every ship wants this one, but she'll have it if one is to be had for the fleet. And with your permission, sir, if we put to sea before you're back, I'd like to experiment with some new shot. I think I have worked out the right amount of powder to effect a faster triple shot, sir. You take more powder and—"

"*More* powder?" The Commodore had been nodding to all Captain Miller said, but that brought him up short. That was a trick of this former American, Miller, he had not foreseen. The man not only loved guns, he could not leave explosives alone. "Take care of yourself, my dear Miller! You're worth more to me and to this ship than any number of broadsides. In fact, one good captain is equal to one French ship of the line! Come, what's keeping that lubber Allen? Where's my launch?"

"At your service, sir." Miller did not point out that the launch, with a grumbling Allen casting glances their way, had been ready for some time, for the Commodore's overwhelming compliment had just sunk in. Miller's face grew serene at the thought of having the ship to himself. "I hope to have her exactly to your taste, sir."

"I am confident you will. And as to Berry, he'll make himself useful until he goes home for promotion. He's the third lieutenant I've had made captain this war. He brings luck. And Hoste—"

"Oh, he's tops, sir! I wouldn't trade him for the world."

"Aye, Hoste gets on everywhere . . . but take care of my boy, pray, Captain Miller, if anything happens to me!" The Commodore's voice had grown suddenly hollow.

Miller glanced at him in surprise, that tone wasn't like him. "As I would my own two, sir."

"Two? Two *boys?*"

"Girls," Miller smiled.

"No matter. I congratulate you . . . Josiah *means* well, Captain Miller. You will not humor him, but he's a good boy—at *heart.*" With an impatient flourish of his hand, as if waving ghosts out of mind, the Commodore sent dazzling sparks from his ring; shook hands. "God bless you, Miller." And he was gone with the shrill pipes through the stiffly drawn aisles of his men. After him went his quiet, dog-faithful Lieutenant Noble, having volunteered as an aide.

❅   ❅   ❅

Aboard *La Minerve* frigate, forty-two guns, Captain Cockburn and his officers stood at attention as the Commodore's launch approached. The boatswain's pipe manned the sides and as Nelson's quick step touched the deck, his Distinguishing Pendant leaped to the masthead; the jacks bent on the capstan bars. The Commodore smiled. Cockburn, too, knew his tastes: no wasting time once he came aboard.

"How does *La Minerve* suit you, Cockburn? Better than old *Meleager,* I hope?"

"Thanks to you, sir. And she's sleek and fast as the French make them and we sail 'em, sir." Captain Cockburn shook hands.

"Pray let us try her!" The Commodore spun on his heel, watching the towering Rock begin to recede, but slowly, too slowly. How long did it take to reach Elba? An instant would be an age. He turned back to see Cockburn taut in his station, warping his ship out of the harbor, conscious of the Commodore's eye.

Astern was *Blanche,* with her new captain, Preston, cutting into *La Minerve's* wake.

And from Gibraltar, Jervis watched. At last he smiled and turned on Ben Hallowell, who was aboard *Victory* since losing his ship. *La Minerve* and *Blanche* were standing clear of the Rock.

"Hallowell, the way *Minerve* spreads her sails is magical! Cockburn is splendid!"

"Damn good, sir," Hallowell boomed.

And then the frigates were gone.

Two small cruiser frigates, alone, to run a round trip of a thousand miles through the lonesome French seas.

❅   ❅   ❅

Toward the end of the fifth day from Gibraltar clouds lowered, rending in shreds on the sharp chopping sea, raising mists. The ships were enveloped in one element: water. The frigates heeled over, decks pitched at all angles while the masts leaned like branches, dizzily over the waves. The men perched on spars; clung in the rigging taking in sail; bringing to, to ride out the night just off Cartagena, Spain.

Below deck, cramped at best in a frigate, Captain Cockburn had cleared his own cell of a cabin for the Commodore, and doubled up his officers like so many African slaves.

As to the crew in the forecastle, they were used to slinging their hammocks in a foot of space, where if they walked between decks, it was like apes. They could be thankful for all that, hove-to for the night. Most of them could count on some sleep unless the Levanter blowing straight for Spain grew wilder and tumbled them out to beat back should the ship threaten to blow ashore. But Spain was several miles away. The men on watch were soaked to the skin, but the rest were just damp as they slept.

In the Commodore's cabin the conversation had died a natural death after the last rummer of punch. As the ship pitched about, the Commodore propped himself on his cot, reading a volume of Charnock's *Biographia Navalis,* skimming the pages like a gull searching food, pouncing now and then on a paragraph, flipping the pages on. He had begun to nod somewhere between Admirals Blake and Rodney.

Lieutenant Noble, distinguished by the white scar on his throat, was stubbornly trying to write a letter home while the shadow of his hand and the quill moved over the page like the line on a sundial marking time. The Commodore had insisted that he and Noble double up, give Cockburn more room; the cabin was crowded.

The lantern swayed overhead like a bludgeon, as a massive lieutenant who would make two of the Commodore looked in to report the frigate was now lying bare-poled. He was a frankly plain-looking fellow, in his mid-twenties, yet there was an agreeable easiness about him as he stood swaying in calculated counter arcs to the lantern to avoid an accident to his skull.

"Pray, what time is it, Mr. Hardy?" The Commodore closed his book. He lay cocking his good eye at the telltale in the beams overhead, checking the ship's direction.

The massive lieutenant swayed back on his heels as the deck sloped several degrees; he saluted. "Just ten, sir."

There was a knock on the door. A mid's face peeped in, wet as a mermaid's risen out of the deep. *"Blanche* making urgent signal to speak us, sir. Captain Cockburn requests your presence on deck, sir."

Up they all started. Noble spilled the ink. Hardy, pivoting on his heel, crashed the lamp as Nelson flipped from prone to his feet and Allen shoved in, so no one could move, to dress his master, who was already casting off his dressing gown, reaching for his warmer coat.

❆   ❆   ❆

"Bear down on her!" And the Commodore was giving the orders before both arms were in his coat sleeves.

The hatches hurled back. "All hands make sail!" And aloft went the crew. The wind tried to pluck them, drop them into the sea. With a shivering creaking the masts leaned forward as the wind caught the sails, threatened to rend the ship apart till her bow rose.

There was only the dim signal light ahead, glowing and vanishing in the dark as the mists swirled between the two ships. Men on *La Minerve* strained to see, lest they crash *Blanche* in a sudden cloud bank.

As they drew close, *Blanche* rose up like a bird outstretching her wings; her sails reflecting her lights in a halo of fog.

The Commodore was balancing on a wet gun, leaning over the bulwarks. "Oh, *Blanche,* ahoy! Commodore Nelson hailing Captain Preston."

"La Minerve, ahoy!" Captain Preston shouted back. "Sighted two Spanish ships to leeward."

"Deck there, strange sail!" from *La Minerve's* tops almost as Preston spoke. "There are three lights, two ships, sir."

Nelson through his trumpet: "Captain Preston, ahoy!"

"Aye, aye, sir?"

"I'm bearing down on the ship which carries the poop light. You will bear down on the other. Good luck and God bless you!"

"Aye, aye, sir."

The Commodore jumped down from the gun, waved his trumpet. "Clear for action, Captain Cockburn."

"Beat to quarters!"

And as always the rolling of drums to warm up the blood; dry the fo'c'sle damp from the bones.

La Minerve flew with a rushing smack across the rough water; her rigging a-hum to the steady beating of drums.

"Bring me under her stern, if you please, Captain Cockburn. I wish to hail her."

The Spanish ship was a handsome dim silhouette, her sterncastle luxurious, for officers, all her proportions perfect. She looked about the same size as *La Minerve* of forty-two eighteen-pounders.

Lieutenant Noble discovered a broken quill in his hand; dropped it. 2nd Lieutenant Hardy strolled with the ease of a retired admiral as he bowled along the deck, issuing his orders loudly and to the point. Lieutenant Culverhouse seemed to be everywhere. Allen came across the deck, planted himself resolutely between the Commodore and the enemy so that the Commodore snapped "Stand aside," and Allen grudgingly allowed his Commodore to see his enemy objective.

The Commodore was studying his attack. In coming up under the Spaniard's stern, putting himself between the enemy ship and Spain, he would sacrifice the weather position, give his opponent the wind, considered the best for maneuvers. But in gaining the wind, the Spaniard must sacrifice the chance of racing past Nelson shoreward; to run in the other direction would be difficult, against the wind. The English would gain by crossing the Spaniard's T, bringing a broadside to bear at once on her stern, even while hailing in case she would surrender without fighting, and if not, holding her there to do battle. Pros and cons weighed in in an instant, so close to the subconscious that it came almost as naturally as breathing. The longest time for offensive planning was now. Once action commenced, the Spaniard would try to have his say, outwit any foreseeable tricks, so if Commodore Nelson's first moves were not perfect . . .

"Down helm to starboard!"

La Minerve closed under the Spaniard's stern. The gun crews stood ready. Hardy was bawling, "Hold it, hold it . . ."

Commodore Nelson through his speaking trumpet; sharp, imperative: "Ahoy! This is an English frigate. Surrender or I will fire!"

Back through the dark in peculiarly stilted English with a highborn cavalier ring: "This, *señor*, is a Spanish frigate. And you may begin when you please!"

"Go ahead, Captain Cockburn." And off went *La Minerve's* first broadside with a bursting of light and a roar, followed as she rolled steady by wood crashing down on the Spaniard's stern. "Keep on her stern, Captain Cockburn."

But the Spaniard was no easy prey. She was ready to match move for move though she had lost in the first maneuver. She came about like a tiger, wrestling broadside for broadside, falling away; each ship was after the other's most vital parts.

Cockburn was howling his orders above the cannon and the raging gale, while his men ran aloft tending the sails, lost from view in the smoke, lighted once and again by the flash of a touchhole, the spurts of fire as the cannon leaped.

La Minerve's decks shuddered and splinters flew. Allen was trying to spread himself, shield the Commodore, who constantly eluded him, in order to watch his battle.

In smoke and in fire with the wind blowing hard. A black sky full of storm clouds; the black sea all ups and downs made aim wild.

La Minerve crossed the stern again, heard timber cave in, while the Spaniard, hauling up, shaken and shattered, came round, and with a cunning shift in her plans bore obliquely away, scudding for shore.

"Wear ship!"

La Minerve seemed to rear up on her stern, her sails shaking, then snapping full as she plunged about, fell off toward the shore and brought up again across the Spaniard's bow, raking her, stopping her, turning her back to fight. The Spaniard lay momentarily dazed by the blow athwart her figurehead, like an animal struck on the nose.

"Oh! Ahoy! Do you surrender, sir?" Nelson through his trumpet as the ships fell apart, each trying to bring her broadside guns to bear.

"No! No, *señor!*" But again the crazed dash for port.

La Minerve cutting her off, another blow on the nose, laying open the tender bow with a full broadside.

"Kick 'em—hit 'em on tha head!" Allen was cheering.

As the wind caught up the smoke, rolled it away, there was an odd sucking, a crack, like a tooth coming out of a jaw. The Spaniard had lost a mast. Nelson turned to cheer Cockburn and saw Noble doubling up; saw blood splattered as if the clouds rained it. "Get Mr. Noble below!" The cockpit crew lifted him.

This was no haphazard duel, but now at last the Spaniard was dragging a wing.

The Commodore again: "Do you surrender, sir?"

"No! No, *señor!* Not while I have the means left to fight!"

"Then hammer her till she does, Cockburn." Until she lay like a carcass asprawl on the water; her guns still firing, but there were silent gaps on the gun decks. In the lull, coming up for the kill, the Commodore spied the flashing of guns far away: *Blanche* was hard after her prey, his battle was going well.

One last clumsy, stubborn flutter from the Spaniard; one last weary turn for shore. One more full broadside from *La Minerve.*

As the recoil ended, the Commodore raised his trumpet, but before he could summon, the same Spanish voice cried out: "Surrender! Ahoy! Surrender! I surrender, *señor!*" and a Union Jack was shoved over the Spaniard's stern.

From Cockburn: "Mr. Culverhouse, take possession."

There was a strange ringing silence after the deafening cannon; at last they could hear the mortal sounds: the wounded and dying; the screams from the cockpit cutting through the planks from the bowels of the ship.

"Put the men to repair ship, Captain Cockburn," the Commodore ordered. A gun crew was heaving the body of a mate through the gunport. They heard it splash, sink without any ceremonial. The Commodore gritted his teeth. Necessity. To work. *La Minerve* must sail on to Elba at once. He peered through his glass. No sign of *Blanche* at the moment.

"Masthead! Locate *Blanche!*"

"Deck there, no sign of her, sir!"

Men were running past the Commodore, and below deck he heard them running the cables out to take the Spanish ship in tow. At that moment the Captain of the surrendered ship came aboard. He stood still a moment, a tall man with a long haughty face, dark eyes half closed with exhaustion.

The Commodore drew himself up as the Spaniard came forward, bowing and proffering his particularly beautiful sword. "Don Jacobo Stuart, Captain of His Majesty's ship *La Sabina, señor.*"

"Well fought, sir." The Commodore accepted the sword, then shook hands. "From the moment you answered me nobly till the last gun."

Don Jacobo bowed again. He was weary. "My officers are *all* dead, *señor.* Out of my two hundred and eighty men, *señor,* I had perhaps a hundred and thirty left. It was impossible to continue, for which I am sorry."

Captain Cockburn had listened in amazement. *La Minerve* had two hundred and forty men, but nowhere near that many casualties. He must send word to the surgeon for a count of them, while the Commodore and Don Jacobo went through the grave ceremonial, the controlled polished civilities like two high-tailed long-spurred fighting cocks. But the crew on *La Minerve* eyed the Don with healthy respect; his name was familiar and they were proud of the Commodore who had happened on one of the toughest young captains out of Spain.

Meanwhile Lieutenant Hardy stood by watching the men volunteer to go with him to man the Spaniard's ship, help Culverhouse, already aboard, to make her fit to sail on. Coulson stepped forward and one after the other until there were twenty-four. The boatswain piped them away.

It was after two o'clock in the morning. The carpenters were hammering and sawing; the seamen splicing ropes.

"Deck there, strange sail to westward standing toward us, sir."

"Good. That must be *Blanche.*" The Commodore left Don Jacobo for a moment. "Captain Cockburn, give the men bread and wine. That may not be *Blanche.*" And he returned to his guest. "Pray, sir, you were saying?"

"I am descended from the Duke of Berwick, *señor,* and your noble King James II."

"Indeed?" The Commodore made another bow. "I am doubly honored, sir." Though James II had been run out of England, royalty was royalty. ❊   ❊   ❊

It was still dark. The night seemed to have lasted a year, but the jacks bent to their work. No man chose to sail enemy seas in a crippled ship. Behind *La Minerve* yawed *La Sabina,* and aboard her, men were cutting away her wounded mast, making her other two fast, the ship navigable. Lieutenants Culverhouse and Hardy and their men were working what was left of the Spanish crew.

Aboard *La Minerve,* the Commodore, having given the order for his prisoner's honorary confinement, was quietly preening with Cockburn, exulting over the capture.

"We got off miraculously, sir. Only seven killed and thirty-four wounded," Cockburn said.

"But what does the surgeon say about my poor Noble?"

"Very serious, sir."

The Commodore shook his head. "And he begged to go with me! Just got over one wound! Well, *you* fought a beautiful duel, Cockburn! *La Minerve's* discipline reflects it."

"Why, thank you, sir!" Cockburn smiled. Commodores usually considered that they themselves had won. "I can't take all the credit, sir."

"But I give it to you." The Commodore turned away. He had found fresh pleasure in Cockburn's surprise. He had a feeling he would even give Cockburn Don Jacobo's sword. It was a nice sword, but think how Cockburn would feel! Subconsciously, perhaps, the Commodore was building—in a very small way, of course—the kind of leadership he would like to see practiced; the kind of navy he thought England deserved. For within his own mind, his own pride told him that he himself had taken *La Sabina,* and conquerors could afford to be generous. Yes, he would give Cockburn that sword—and he would make a handsome ceremonial presentation.

"Deck there! Strange sail bearing down on the prize ship, sir!"

It was still much too dark to make her out. "Captain Preston, I presume," the Commodore muttered, rather piqued that Preston had fallen so far out of sight during action and had apparently returned without any prize. But for the sake of precaution: "We will not presume the ship is *Blanche*. Clear the decks, Captain Cockburn, prepare for action!"

It was not so easily accomplished this time for *La Minerve* was cut up from her last duel. The men stopped repairs to clear her somehow, though they grumbled because they knew it was *Blanche*.

Then through the night, a hail in Spanish! The dark looming hull of the stranger closing on captured *La Sabina*.

A puzzled silence. Then with an explosive thunderclap the stranger's broadside lit three ships: a smoking spanking fresh Spanish frigate; the crippled *La Sabina;* limping *La Minerve*. There was no sign of *Blanche*.

"Beat to quarters. Cast off the prize." And the two battered ships, *La Minerve* and *La Sabina,* separated as the Spaniard passed *La Sabina,* ranged alongside *La Minerve*.

And once again broadside met broadside. But this time *La Minerve* was cranky as Cockburn maneuvered her, though her men fought her guns with the same precision: three times to the Spaniard's one. The stakes: a second prize ship or a Spanish prison for them.

The wind had calmed toward midnight, now toward morning it

squalled all around the compass, dwindling out in baffling puffs of light air. With a last raking broadside aimed at *La Minerve's* rigging, the Spaniard surprised everyone by wearing. She stood off out of gunshot, a dark skulking shadow against the gray dawn. *La Minerve's* crew drew breath, then:

"Deck there, strange sail astern! She's of the *line,* sir!"

Nelson and Cockburn exchanged glances. Their eyes ached from straining to see in the dark. Now they knew their opponent was merely awaiting reinforcements.

"*Two* strange sail of *line*—and a frigate!" a mid yelped as the three new guests came nearer.

"Let us hope the frigate is *Blanche!*" The Commodore gazed anxiously toward his prize ship, *La Sabina.* The whole situation reminded him fleetingly of teasing a hornets' nest. "Mortifying, isn't it, Cockburn?" He smiled tensely.

And Cockburn nodded, heartened for some reason by the extremity of the understatement.

La Sabina had fallen away, was now only dimly in sight; making her clumsy way eastward—toward Elba. As the daylight at last began to filter over the sea the enemy battleships grew big as life.

"Deck there, *Blanche,* sir, just come in sight to northward!"

A faint dot coming toward them. Where had she been? She might just as well have remained at Gibraltar for all the good she had done. And now, definitely, the four strange sail knotting closer together astern *La Minerve* were all enemy Spanish. "Signal *Blanche* to join!"

A moment later: "She doesn't answer our signal, sir."

"Damn her!"

❈   ❈   ❈

As day broke their chances looked very slim before the oncoming sails: two Spanish of line and two frigates.

The men were again repairing *La Minerve,* swearing they would give the enemy a run for their money.

Carpenter shaking his head: "Those lower masts are badly wounded . . ."

While down came the Spanish, slowly, thanks to the light wind. Even so, they were an overwhelming number.

As Commodore Nelson paced the deck, turning it in his mind, the men worked without looking up just as they had worked and fought since ten o'clock last night. And *La Minerve* began to show signs of sailing.

Far off, all on her own, lay the prize, *La Sabina;* her makeshift rig managed to hold her up with the wind. Culverhouse and Hardy meant to keep her. Perhaps they could get away if the four Spanish tackled *La Minerve*. Cockburn and Nelson looked at each other again.

It was the carpenter and the crew now that might save the ship by making *La Minerve* fit in the shortening minutes as the Spanish came slowly down, rising and falling, steadily over the brightening morning sea.

The wind was still toying with the compass, now here, now there; stiffening for a minute as if promising east. Falling. Rising, now promising a westerly. While the Spanish came down with clean un-shot canvas catching the mistily diffused sunlight. The dazzling scroll-work, the reds, blues, golds of the bows, flashing like jewels, rising and falling, the wind and the sea. As if the seven ships were lying in giant scales: heavenward—hellward only; no haven promised but these.

La Minerve lay at the center of the Spanish target. *Blanche* was too distant for them to chase, while *La Sabina* lay just out of the Spaniard's reach.

"Oh God, Cockburn!" Nelson gasped, his glass to his eye. *"Sabina* has hoisted her colors! She's standing to fight them!"

There she lay, falling sadly behind *La Minerve,* minus a mast, but with a taunting Union Jack flapping jauntily from her crippled fore-top. She was challenging the Spanish as she spread all that was left of her miserable canvas. Like a crafty old mother fox, *La Sabina,* com-manded by Culverhouse and Hardy, began tempting the Spanish to chase her instead of *La Minerve*.

She no longer steered for Elba, but farther and farther from *La Minerve;* drawing closer in the path of the Spanish battleships.

The Spanish sails shivered uncertainly as *La Sabina* lumbered just within their reach.

With the hasty decision of men without too much tactical foresight, the first Spanish of line bore up, too tempted to resist: plunged down on the small *Sabina.*

Culverhouse saluted the battleship with a spirited but incomplete broadside.

The Spanish of line answered with a full blasting of guns. For a moment it seemed there was nothing but smoke left of Culverhouse and Hardy. Then a spitting from inside the smoke as *La Sabina* fought back; but the sound told that some of her too few guns were knocked up. And high over the smoke cloud on the sea, the Spanish masts soared, as coming about she raked *La Sabina* again and again while the other Spanish ships hesitated. . . .

"Steer for Elba, Captain Cockburn," the Commodore said grimly. "Signal *Blanche* to bear east." And *Blanche* and *La Minerve* stood off once more for Elba.

This was again too much for the Spanish. Capturing English was more like a fox hunt than a bullfight! So the second big ship of the line and two frigates once more began the slow, the tantalizing chase, leaving *La Sabina* to be devoured by one battleship.

Nelson and Cockburn were watching *La Sabina* across the widening sea. She was clouded in smoke, wallowing hopelessly, as down came her last stick of mast. Their sight blurred when the Union Jack was not hoisted again. Cockburn was swallowing hard. Hardy and he had been messmates when Hardy was only a master's mate and he just a mid. And Culverhouse was the best officer he had.

There was not a thing they could have done to save *La Sabina*. Frigates could not conquer battleships. As it was, they had lost but few men, still made their escape. Neither Cockburn nor Nelson tried to speak, for those few men were going to prison.

"I'll never forget . . ." Nelson muttered; he was pacing slowly. "But we still have Don Jacobo, Cockburn."

"Aye, aye, sir," Cockburn answered automatically, thinking of the immediate: in spite of *La Sabina's* bold sacrifice, three Spanish were still after *Blanche* and *La Minerve*.

The Commodore, however, had sent word that if Don Jacobo cared, would he join him on the quarter-deck before breakfast? Don Jacobo appeared. Cockburn suddenly looked wise. The Commodore was fattening their prize rooster, that he might crow the gallantry of Englishmen—perhaps reciprocate?

Cockburn eyed the Spanish astern. They were not gaining on him, nor falling away. If the wind continued even so lightly as it blew now, he had more than a sporting chance to outsail the enemy, for if frigates could not conquer battleships, their protection lay in their speed.

The voice that sang down from the masthead had a very monotonous tone: "Deck there, strange sail of line to larboard, due north!"

"A new turn to the day." The Commodore raised his glass with a polite, if somewhat weary smile to Don Jacobo, who had stiffened excitedly. But the Commodore could see nothing from the deck.

He tucked his glass under his arm, though his step was no longer exactly light.

"Deck there, fourteen sail of the line—Spanish!"

"Bear southward, if you please, Captain Cockburn," the Commodore said quietly, and back he turned to his prisoner, who had the decency to show no visible interest in the fact that the English were having the pleasure of counting fourteen Spanish battleships. While *La Minerve* and *Blanche* pulled their topmasts down over the horizon, out of sight of the Spanish fleet.

A new question was teasing the Commodore: where was the Spanish fleet bound? Sailing northeast . . . to join, perhaps, with the French before leaving the Mediterranean? If so, perhaps he still had time to reach Elba, fulfill his mission—not more than two or three days for that—and return to Jervis off Cádiz in time for a real fight.

Still the three Spanish ships chased *La Minerve* and wayward *Blanche*. Gradually the frigates outdistanced even the foremost of the Spanish frigates. By sundown, with a freshening wind from the west, the Commodore knew they were free of the Spanish, who would never stay on his wake through the night.

On the day after Christmas, 1796, ten days from Gibraltar, *La Minerve* and *Blanche* dropped anchor at Porto Ferrajo, Elba. Captain Preston had sent an account of his action to the Commodore. He had not done too badly, after all, the night he met the Spanish. He had forced his opponent to surrender after very few broadsides, but before he could board he had been chased, being closer to Spain, by the Spanish that were after *La Minerve*. He had lost no men. The Commodore forwarded the Captain's report to Jervis without one word of praise or blame; completely without comment; after all, he had in his own dispatch sounded no trumpets of joy at the battle, though he had recommended Cockburn, Culverhouse and Hardy—and Noble—to Jervis. "This is, Sir, an unpleasant tale, but the merits of every officer in the *Minerve* and her Prize, were eminently conspicuous through the whole of this arduous day." Commodore Nelson was the only officer or man who did not think he "had done very well" but he was something of a perfectionist: What was a battle good for, if the enemy lived to fight another day?

"Oh, that little minnow, my dear Freemantle?" Commodore Nelson shook hands with the young Captain who had just come aboard to greet him. He waved his hand ruefully at a deadly little ship made fast to a cable astern *La Minerve*. "Ran across her off the south end of Sardinia. Her name is *Maria,* just six nine-pounders, French privateer. I wish you could have seen the fish that got away from me, Freemantle."

"She's a sweet little prize, sir." Freemantle saw nothing wrong with the Commodore's catch.

"Has Sir Gilbert seen Sir John Jervis's dispatches he sent out? Is all ready ashore? I'm in a great hurry, Freemantle."

Freemantle, whose frigate *Inconstant* had been left at Elba as a guard, opened his mouth, eyed Nelson, and then closed it.

"What's wrong? Is he ill?"

"Sir Gilbert is still touring Italy, sir, now all the states have made peace with France. He went to Rome to confer with the Pope, who still regards this Buonaparte with some doubt."

"Gone to Rome?"

"We expect him back any day, sir. He's due, I believe, in Naples now to visit Sir William Hamilton. He expected you would meet him there, he said, according to Jervis's letter. He said, too, he would be ready to leave there by New Year's. After that a French minister is coming to Naples with a party of three hundred, a printing press and a troop of comedians. Sir Gilbert feels diplomatic society is going to the dogs, sir, so he would hardly stay after that."

The Commodore stood staring at Freemantle. "You say Sir Gilbert has received his instructions from home?"

"Aye, sir, but he said he would have plenty of time to go to Rome and get back to Naples. Sir John's dispatches said—"

"I have nothing to do at Naples."

Freemantle looked surprised. He need not have, for it was not the first time Commodore Nelson had rearranged Jervis's plans about Naples. Last year Jervis had suggested Nelson run down to Naples, drum up some ships for him, but Nelson had replied he saw no use in the idea at all, everything could be handled by letter just as well, and when Jervis had broadened the hint, Nelson had replied in the same. On the third hint from Jervis, Nelson had repeated his opinion but agreed that if Jervis *insisted* he would, of course, go at once. Jervis gave up, and Nelson obtained the ships by letter. "No, I shall have my hands full *here,* Freemantle. So off you go! Bring the Viceroy back the moment he arrives at Naples. The Combined Fleet is out!"

"Aye, aye, sir, but Sir Gilbert is not one to be pushed, if you will forgive my mentioning it." Freemantle smiled ruefully.

"I'm relying on you just the same. And keep a close check on your tongue. Not a word at Naples about this evacuation. We don't want a swarm of enemy ships out looking for our convoys."

"Aye, sir, not even to our Ambassador, sir?"

"He will know about the Viceroy leaving, but not about the convoys! Not to anyone," Nelson suddenly smiled, "not even to the Ambassadress, Freemantle, charming though she may be."

"Aye, sir. And she grows more charming every day, sir. And consider her beginnings, sir!"

"She must have a great soul to overcome so many difficulties. I am aware she does honor to the station to which she is raised, though I met her only once." He had spoken more woodenly than usual. He caught himself staring fixedly through the open ports at the calm bay. In those three days the Hamiltons had bewitched him; among no other people had he ever felt so much—*at home!* But he loved his wife too much to even try to remember Lady Hamilton's face. He and Fanny would have a home like that someday—and minus the string quartets and shallow society! He turned brusquely to Freemantle. "Naples is full of intrigue; no doubt even the Embassy servants spy."

Freemantle had not noticed the break in the conversation, for he too had been staring at the water and scowling. "I shan't say a word, sir." He took a deep breath, and then began to speak very fast. "May I have your permission to take my fiancée with me to Naples tomorrow, sir? You see, sir, Lady Hamilton has it all arranged. The wedding is—well, that is—I think she has it arranged. She's been softening the enemy and with your permission, sir—I want to get married."

"Congratulations. Pray, who is the enemy?"

"Ah? Oh, the enemy? Miss Wynne's parents. Lady Hamilton writes to come now while they're softening to the tune of eight thousand pounds marriage settlement, sir! Isn't Lady Hamilton wonderful?"

"And what then? Are you going to carry your poor wife about in a frigate? That little bit of a creature I saw you with in San Fiorenzo? She's just a child, have pity on her."

"She's ready to go with me for better or worse until I have her safe home in England." Freemantle searched the Commodore's face for assent, saw nothing even resembling sympathy. He swallowed.

"Oh, it is done, I suppose. However, I sent *my* wife home in a transport," the Commodore said loftily. He did not mention that he and Fanny had tried honeymooning on a frigate in the Indies, and that her female refusal to be hurried in getting every last damn ribbon aboard had made him *three days late* weighing anchor to obey a summons; and then there had been her pianoforte . . . He eyed Freemantle's crestfallen gaze with the maturer judgment of experience.

"In a *transport?* Aye, sir?" Freemantle whispered.

"No. I do not believe in women on ships! I warn you, I never knew a woman to obey an order! Sir John Jervis's opinion, of course, you know?"

"Aye, sir. But the Ambassador and his lady have made all the arrangements, sir, flowers and—sir?"

"That Jervis has transferred captains from here to the West Indies at the threat of marriage—anchoring themselves—always wanting to go home?"

Freemantle turned red; choked back his rage. These Spartans who never thought of women! He was so mad he did not at first register what the Commodore was saying next.

"You sail in the morning, Freemantle, with little Miss Wynne. I will give you three days to bring back the Viceroy—and Mrs. Freemantle. . . . General de Burgh, is he here—I hope?"

"Oh, Betsy will love you forever, sir, forever and— De Burgh? Oh, yes, sir, he is here!" Freemantle was beaming deliriously.

❊   ❊   ❊

The Commodore found the General as polished and pleasant as usual. He was just dismissing an aide with whom he appeared to have been in deep conference.

"Ah, my dear Commodore Nelson! Just in time for our ball to-night!" The General rose from behind his desk, and stepping forward bowed till the top of his wig appeared.

The Commodore returned the bow somewhat summarily. "That

will be a most pleasant diversion, sir, provided it will not delay the embarkation of the troops."

"Not at all, sir. Tonight we dance and celebrate the conquest of *La Sabina!*"

The Commodore smiled involuntarily. "Thank you, sir, and the embar—"

"*Tomorrow* we will discuss the whole situation—that is—ah—" The General motioned the Commodore to a yellow satin settee. "And how have you been since I last saw you? What news?"

"I left the fleet on the eve of great actions. So you will understand if I appear anxious to be done with Porto Ferrajo. How soon, sir?"

The General had taken a turn about the room. He paused, head back, studying the candelabra. Pursing his lips he adjusted a taper that had fallen somewhat aslant. "I have received no army orders to evacuate this garrison."

"No orders!" Nelson bounced off the settee, took a step here, there, like a trapped animal.

"No. And therefore I feel a certain diffidence, placed as I am in this situation." The General faced the Commodore with a very hot and uncomfortable glance. He knew this eager young man and rather dreaded him. "The troops were placed here by army orders and there are no army orders for their departure."

"But *His Majesty's orders* to Sir John Jervis!"

"Oh, I am convinced that such a plan is obviously intended."

"Definitely, sir. The King of England has ordered it."

The General was lighting a cigar. He puffed slowly, turning it in his fingers. "Will you have a cigar?"

"No thank you, sir, and now, pray, how soon?"

"You don't smoke? Snuff?"

"*No,* thank you, sir. And now, sir—"

"Now in my opinion, Commodore Nelson, you are perfectly right. And the signing of peace by all Italy with France ought to be our signal of departure. However, I must have my proceedings sanctioned by an order. I have every right to expect that."

"You are covered by His Majesty's orders, sir."

"Army orders, I mean. You understand. Orders are orders, sir. Can't disobey. Rank insubordination. Death penalty, sir. Terrific humiliation. Inconceivable. Though I won't say I believe I assist the service by staying here, here I was ordered to stay!"

The Commodore's head came up. "What could be clearer than the King's orders to Sir John Jervis? The fact they come through the navy does not appear to me to change the clarity of their intentions one tittle, sir!"

"Of course. Absolutely clear, but as they did not come through army channels, sir, as a soldier, I cannot disobey my army superiors, sir. I must obey them and them only! Discipline, therein lies the invincibility of the British army, sir."

The Commodore pondered the intricacies of the situation. To obey orders was, of course, all perfection! Yet it was impossible to become angry with De Burgh. His case was clear, if one confined one's mind to the narrowest of limits. He tried a new tack:

"Sir John Jervis's dispatches, which you have seen, sir, were for the removal of the army from Elba to Lisbon. There the army is expected to assist in warding off a threatened attack upon Portugal from France and Spain. If Portugal falls, sir, then not only the Mediterranean, but the entire continental Atlantic seaboard will be governed by the enemy: from Italy, sir, to the North Sea!" He allowed his tone to become acid. "However, what the political consequences may be of leaving Porto Ferrajo or of not having sufficient troops at Lisbon does not, of course, come within the 'sphere of *my* supposed knowledge'!"

The General beamed. "Exactly, sir! Nor mine either. Orders are orders. I'm delighted you understand, sir."

"As an officer, yes, sir. Therefore, I can only offer myself for embarking the troops and ordnance, and should you decline quitting this port, I shall then remove only the naval stores and proceed down the Mediterranean with the Viceroy and with such ships of war as are not absolutely essential for keeping open communications with the Continent."

"I am afraid, Commodore Nelson, that is how it must stand," the General replied quietly. "Come, we shall not be fit to entertain the ladies if we worry all day. You dance, of course?"

"Of course," the Commodore answered gloomily, and then, "I have found it is as much a prerequisite of being an officer—at times—as knowing how to fire a gun. . . ." And he smiled wryly.

"And the ladies have worked for a week on the decorations. We must pretend they are beautiful. Can't disappoint them. Brandy, sir? Good. . . . Besides, sir, there's talk of peace everywhere."

"Talk? Yes."

"Oh, more. Sir Gilbert's brother-in-law, Lord Malmesbury, must have reached Paris by now. He and his lady visited the Hamiltons for a while, you know. And what have we to gain by fighting these French?"

"Commerce. . . . Lord Malmesbury will return as he has come." The Commodore had risen, paced restlessly to the window. And all he saw from the windows were English frigates and small transports, no battleships in the Mediterranean after nearly four years of war. He turned away. "No, sir, I fear the war is *not* done. The French will want peace on their terms alone, as they have in conquered Italy. Are we willing to pay them tribute, to pay them to stop fighting us! Lose the right to trade with the Continent! And such tributes! This Buonaparte not only demands money, he demanded the Apollo Belvedere, sir, from Rome! What a race of people! He has robbed every state of its treasures. He is worse than the filthy pirates. And, sir, I am ready to take a ship against the French or the Barbary pirates any time. Much as I hate the French, I have never understood why we pay tribute to those beggars in Algiers, Tunis and Tangier!"

"That's another consideration altogether."

"I see no difference."

"The pirates, for a nominal sum, do not touch our convoys. Some countries do not find the tribute a nominal sum. Our merchants prosper, sir, so you see?"

The Commodore nodded. "Only too well. And at home there are complaints about the *black* slave trade! Do you mean to say there is such an advantage in paying tribute to Buonaparte?"

The General laughed. "The only advantage is in having peace."

"But the price, sir! What will our merchants do when that Corsican controls the Continent?"

"That, of course, does not come within my 'sphere,'" the General smiled. "After all, it is up to Lord Malmesbury. Come, I have a story that *will* amuse you." The General held out a round brandy snifter that reflected their uniforms, the blue and the red, as if they were caught in a translucent soap bubble.

"By all means. What's news?" Nelson was still frowning.

"Remember Corsica, that hauntingly beautiful sink hole of corruption, sir? It reminds me of the Dons at times, when they revolted at a decree to install sewers, sir, saying filth in their streets attracted filth and therefore purified the air. When the decree became a law they compromised as best they could, they installed their privies in the kitchens to keep the air about the food pure . . . does that recall Corsica?"

"Aye, and I hate the damn place!"

The General laughed again, and the Commodore noticed he seemed eager to be amusing, so the Commodore scowled the more the General laughed.

"It may please you, Commodore, to know the French party is losing popularity in Corsica. The Paolists—now, come, you mustn't miss this—the Paolists are revolting against the French and refer to the English as their friends. The *bahstuds!*"

"May they be damned the whole lot of them," the Commodore muttered. But he had started to smile as he set his glass down and held out his hand. "I must bid you good day, sir. I am expecting the Viceroy hourly so I shall begin evacuation of the naval stores immediately."

"Until tonight then, my dear Commodore, at the ball—as my guest of honor."

"Why, thank you, sir, with pleasure."

"And don't hold your breath waiting for Sir Gilbert," the General said dryly. "These politicians have no conception of orders, sir. . . ."

The Commodore's face registered pained surprise as he bowed again. "Until tonight, sir."

✿ ✿ ✿

But a lot of nonsense it was, being feted when there was work to be done. He stalked moodily out of the General's headquarters. The best-laid plans, when left to others . . . The orders of the King of England could not move a general. Sir Gilbert would have something to say about that, he hoped! Meantime he would send the convoys off as soon as possible. And he must not forget Don Jacobo Stuart!

Back aboard *La Minerve,* Commodore Nelson and his officers were drawn up on the quarter-deck before Don Jacobo.

"It gives me great pleasure, Don Jacobo," the Commodore bowed, "to *return* this sword to a Captain of such unquestionable gallantry as yourself. May I wish you a pleasant and speedy voyage home."

The Spaniard's face came alight; close to tears, he bowed low. "Sir, it was an honor to have been your prisoner. Such a duel was never before known on the seas."

They shook hands, and the Commodore gave him two letters:

To His Excellency Don Miguel Gaston, Captain General of the Department of Cartagena.

SIR,

The fortune of war put *La Sabina* into my possession after she had been most gallantly defended: the fickle Dame returned her to you with some of my officers and men on her.

I have endeavored to make the captivity of Don Jacobo, her brave Commander, as light as possible; and I trust to the generosity of your Nation for its being reciprocal for the British officers and men.

I consent, Sir, that Don Jacobo may be exchanged, and at full liberty to serve his King, when Lieutenants Culverhouse and Hardy are delivered into the garrison of Gibraltar, with such others as may be agreed on by the Cartel established between Gibraltar and St. Roche for the exchange of prisoners.

I have also a domestic taken in *La Sabina;* his name is Israel Coulson. Your Excellency will, I am sure, order him to be immediately restored to me, for which I shall consider myself as obliged to you.

I also trust that those men now Prisoners of War with you, will be sent to Gibraltar. It becomes great Nations to act with generosity to each other, and to soften the horrors of war.

I have the honor to be, with the most perfect esteem, your most obedient servant,

HORATIO NELSON

And another to Admiral Don Juan Marino, Don Jacobo's immediate superior.

SIR,

I cannot allow Don Jacobo to return to you without expressing my admiration of his gallant conduct. To you, who have seen the state of his ship, it is needless to mention the impossibility of her longer defense. I have lost many brave men; but in our masts I was most fortunate, or probably I should have had the honor of your acquaintance. But it pleased God to order it otherwise, for which I am thankful. I have endeavored to make Don Jacobo's captivity as easy as possible, and I rely on your generosity for reciprocal treatment toward my brave officers and men, your prisoners.

I have the honor to be, with the most perfect esteem, your most obedient servant. . . .

So off for Spain sailed the tiny *Fortuna,* a bit of a thing commanded by a lieutenant, but with a flag of truce at her masthead.

"And I hope that does it, Cockburn." The Commodore watched

her go, recalling the promise he had made to himself about Captain Cockburn: now he would have to *buy* Cockburn a sword. Never mind, it wouldn't cost a hundred pounds.

As *Fortuna* wafted out of sight, Cockburn said, "That ought to do it, sir. I never saw a Don put up a better battle, nor anyone more grateful than he was when you returned his sword. I bet that sword was an heirloom."

"Do unto others, Cockburn, and your lieutenants better *be* at Gibraltar, by God! But come, war or no war we must go to the General's ball!"

✿   ✿   ✿

And it rained that night at Porto Ferrajo. Mud filled the streets as the Commodore went to the ball.

Mounting the stairs in the local theater where the army chose to dance, he felt a sudden renewal of spirits: this was his first social appearance as a commodore flanked and attended by captains. And much more! At the moment, Commodore Nelson was the highest ranking naval officer in the Mediterranean Sea—by virtue of no one else being there. He knew he was vain enough to be deeply impressed with himself, yet he was not vain enough to assume anyone else would even think of it. He would show these people he remembered at all times his mission to Elba and the necessity of rejoining the fleet off Cádiz.

He and his Captains had paused a moment in the high doorway at the head of the stairs overlooking a room, amateurishly decorated in a wistful attempt to make a barnlike theater look like a palace. The blue-coated Commodore and his Captains presented a darkening warlike cluster, in spite of their frothy white cravats, gold braid, white knee breeches, silk stockings and dancing pumps. Nelson was in front, as became his rank; lean, spare, eyeing the throng down his long nose with all the *sang-froid* of the quarter-deck. Thus he stood ready to parry any low army snub.

There was a hush, a small flurry of multicolored gowns among the redcoats, a step forward: radiant smiles turned up the stairs to him! So—of course—he smiled back, spontaneously, sincerely pleased. Thus partially disarmed he discovered General de Burgh at his elbow, receiving him as the guest of honor, just as the orchestra burst out with the strains of:

"See the Conquering Hero Comes!"

Totally disarmed, flattered to death! The army had won the Commodore for the evening. And the ball rolled gaily on, for the only man whose energetic sense of "duty" might have spoiled it had not a moment between toasts to his recent battle with *La Sabina* in which to mutter "immediate embarkation." While on the side grateful eyes praised De Burgh (another earl's son) for his witty judgment of character; his amusing conquest of the conqueror.

One lady mused, "Would you have guessed that the dreadful young Commodore possessed an Achilles' heel?"

It was a standard garrison ball, somewhat dull; very boisterous to hide the boredom. The usual gentlemen were getting visibly drunk and the usual ones growing amorous. They had been garrisoned together so long they could expect nothing new. The wives and daughters and nieces had already picked their targets by the cut of a uniform, or the abandon with which an officer hurled his heart at their feet. And the men had taken their time to size up the females, relish them for the salubrious effect sex had upon the health, despise them for their constant desire to be protected and saved from anything that interfered with their pleasure whether it was an officer who spoiled a party by talking war, or the enemy French. If tomorrow a man died for them, well, *c'est la guerre*. So the ball was just as basic underneath its superfluous decorations as the people in their best frocks or full-dress uniforms who danced it.

Freemantle and his fiancée whirled by dancing the saltarello. She nodded and smiled to the Commodore, for Betsy Wynne, bird-brained and seventeen, had just realized that her future husband's commanding officer might be a human.

"Old Nelson's very civil and good-natured, isn't he?" she said brightly, "but he doesn't talk much, does he, dear?"

"Smart." Freemantle smiled.

"Lady Hamilton could make him talk," Betsy went on, in a dream. Tomorrow she sailed for Naples and for her wedding at the British embassy.

"I doubt it." Freemantle continued to smile, not wanting to talk about anyone except himself, or his Betsy. "He never has women on his mind. He sent his *bride* home alone on a transport!"

"Oh . . . oh?" from Betsy.

And from the crowds as they glided out of hearing:

"Not bad! She brings eight thousand pounds, they say. Old Freemantle did very well."

"Damn good bargain."

While the Commodore was telling the General, "As ever a young miss longed for a husband—I long to get back to the fleet!"

But someone motioned the orchestra to strike up "See the Conquering Hero . . ." and then "Rule Britannia."

The Commodore was so amazed that they should play it so often he resolved to tell his family about it in his next letter.

"Isn't he nice? Such simple straightforward manners," a lady told the General, as if the Commodore, who had lapsed into one of his silent observant moods, were both deaf and dumb. Then directly to him: "I was terrified by the name of Nelson, but I am not any more," she minced, dragging him away to pass him around like an *objet d'art*.

There was a young lady, some colonel's niece or major's daughter, he didn't know which, who wore two miniature frigates on the crest of her coiffure. One named *La Minerve,* the other was shattered. Very pretty. But as he looked twice he saw there was something too anxious in her smile, too willing. He deplored whores.

He passed her by. Marriage was like a moat, and he slowly retired behind the recollection of his as he looked over the different ladies. The ones he would have picked were, of course, the ones someone else had already spied and married. That was always his luck.

And some of their dresses were different, he realized, after a while. Styles must be changing. The bolder ones even permitted an ankle to exist. That was a step in the right direction. Their dresses were diaphanous white, seductively so, of some kind of strange cobwebby stuff, covered with shorter, bright—well, he would have called them shifts, but that didn't sound right exactly. Groping for the name, he asked Freemantle, who asked Betsy.

"It's pseudo-Greek, this new style," Betsy chirped, "*à la française,* Commodore Nelson."

It would be! The new age had conquered England—through the ladies, who would not be caught unacquainted with Parisian modes, war or no war!

As he had not answered, Betsy, who was very young, thought she must elucidate: "In Paris they even wear leopard skins."

"What for?"

Betsy, whose big eyes had been darting about the room, suddenly blushed; on and then off again. It rather charmed the Commodore, and he almost envied Freemantle's trip home, but only *en passant*.

Freemantle, sensing that Betsy would say more and worse, whirled her off, and she was still laughing like an elf as she vanished.

The General in the Commodore's ear: "They say they wear their evening dresses up to their—*knees!* Those French!"

"That's *rather* extreme, but what can we expect?" from the Commodore.

"Then here's to peace and may we all go to Paris!" from a horsy-looking Major who was getting slowly but steadily soused. The Commodore had another drink, and told the General it was a very nice party. And the decorations really did look less artificial as the night wore on.

And they still danced the minuet between "See!" and the dull English country dances and lively Neapolitan dances. The minuet: to the civilized precision of Vienna's venerable old Papa Haydn and the late Mozart.

"I heard an amazing performance in Vienna." One lady silenced the group around Nelson. "A first piano concerto. It was at one of those charity concerts for poor artists' widows one feels obliged to attend. But what horrified me was the state of music in this world. It's gone. A perfectly dreadful young man who looked like a revolutionist played his own work. Parts of it were indecent—they call it syncopation. I wouldn't allow my daughters to listen!"

"What was his name?" someone asked, because that seemed to follow.

The Commodore was staring off into space. He liked music and he liked to dance, but he hated chamber music, or a concerto, whatever that was.

"His name? I made a point of not remembering." The lady smiled as if she had consigned the young composer to oblivion. "But it began with a 'beet'—try as I will—I can't forget that. They say Papa Haydn is simply inconsolable over this man's work. Says he's muddled. No one can take Mozart's place."

"The new *Lieder* songs are charming," a milder lady put in.

"They are only for the populace," the musical authority snapped.

"Gad!" the horsy Major exploded. "If you want to hear music and see real dancing you should go to Naples! See Lady Hamilton dance the tarantella!"

"She's very forward and she sings without any tremolo," from the musical lady.

"She's magnificent! Statuesque!" from the Major.

"Of course," the musical lady smiled, ready to do Lady Hamilton to the death as she had the young Beethoven, "but she's a type. There are those who have delicacy and breeding, and those *actresses* who are too tall, have too much of themselves, off stage, don't you know? She does not waft, she exudes her charms!"

There was a silence, while the Major rallied his forces. "Madam," he said, "Sir Joseph Banks—the chap who sailed round the world with Captain Cook in the old days—saw her last year. He has seen the distant islands of the Pacific, the glories of Otaheite . . . and he was *enchanted* right there in Naples. Lady Hamilton was up at dawn ready to accompany Sir William and Sir Joseph on *horseback* on one of their scientific field trips. Madam, Lady Hamilton can ride like a trooper, talk intelligently about—about fish and volcanoes and *flora* and—and the Duchess of Argyll was her best friend!"

"What a pity the Duchess is dead. . . . *She* was a lady. Have *you* been to Naples, Commodore Nelson?" The lady tried to muster a defense.

The question came like a blow. The Commodore, who had taken no part in the conversation, suddenly remembered Lady Hamilton's face so vividly he could hardly remember Fanny's. That was terrible! His answer was crisp:

"Just once. I thought the view of Vesuvius was magnificent."

The musical lady gave him a poisonous glance and retired, sniffing, "How naïve . . ."

"I wish Porto Ferrajo was Naples. . . ." The Major stared gloomily at his drink. "It's the only place to live."

"Old King Ferdinand's a monstrous fool. Takes sport in pushing people over cliffs, diving into the sea after them. Then poses the hero. The Queen rules. As wicked as she is beautiful!"

"Oh, she's pitiful," from another, "think of her poor sister."

The Commodore edged away. Their talk pained him. The King and Queen of the Two Sicilies had been charming to him that one visit to Naples. He did not think it was right to speak so familiarly of the lawful heads of a country in these revolutionary times. Especially crowned heads.

And he met the colonel's-niece-or-major's-daughter again. Rather than be cornered by the lady or the devil he asked her to dance. They joined a group as the music began.

As he stepped forward and bowed to the lady she was talking very earnestly: "And you know the Neapolitan nobles have all joined the French Jacobins? It's fashionable to be revolutionary in Naples. And all the scientists and philosophers and literati are writing the manifestoes for the nobility—who never bother to learn to write." She curtsied, and he marveled that she could talk and not miss her step.

He bowed again. "In Naples, madam?" She nodded. "Why, pray?" But he had to wait till the final steps for her answer. As they walked slowly, she said: "It's the mode, I suppose. Only the *lazzaroni* and the masses love their macaroni King. That's always the way in Naples, you know. The *lazzaroni* and the poor love their foreign rulers because they hate the nobility more than foreigners. And the nobility hate the people and the King more than they hate the French. It's the custom, dates back forever. . . . And in France, Commodore Nelson, can you imagine, revolutions aren't fashionable any more!"

"Volatile people," he mused, neither interested nor bored, but finding her rather amusing after all. Not as obvious as he had first thought. He smiled encouragingly at her flirtatious efforts and she chattered on:

"If you are anyone you nod your head quickly—like this"—she demonstrated by bobbing her headdress of frigates five times—"as if it were rolling off! Shows you are really noble. And if you can't prove you had at least one relative guillotined, you simply don't count socially." She allowed her glances to become less transient.

"Indeed?" And he let his eyes linger.

"Oh, yes, so all the *nouveau riche* fishmongers and hairdressers and what you will are taking old titles. And the poor, Commodore—".

"Ye have always." He smiled at more than her speech.

"How witty you are! Oh, and it's *gauche* to wear a big revolutionary cockade in Paris. Just a tiny one tucked in a buttonhole. And, of course, everyone simply *laughs* at little General Buonaparte on his big horse!"

He drew himself up. "The French don't know what they want. . . ." He was not tall himself.

"Oh?" from the lady, as the slow dance ended. "But does anyone, Com-mo-dor-re?"

"Indeed yes, madam," and still smiling he passed her on to Captain Preston, who passed her to a lieutenant who walked her away, just as the Major cornered the Commodore again.

"Sir," said the Major, "an old Mediterranean man like you only been to Naples once? Then you must hear my theory." The Major drew the reluctant Commodore aside. "I'm waiting for Naples to capture Buonaparte, sir! It'll end the war! He will disintegrate. Forget his campaigns."

"He isn't going to Naples." The Commodore started to turn away.

"Sir? Not going? Then he must be a colder villain than even I suspected. Confound it, sir, he must go to Naples to rot in the tradition of conquerors!"

"What makes 'em rot?" from a drunk propped behind a potted palm.

The Major studied this newcomer to the conversation, at last went over and putting his arm around his shoulder said, "I'll tell you. Aside from the lush women—those black-eyed and black-haired milk-white human pillows—"

"I want the truth!" from behind the potted palm.

"I'm telling you, sir! Beside the women and the climate they say it's due to some damned mythological legend or curse!"

The Commodore took another drink and extricated himself. That was one drink too many. Allen would probably try to give him castor oil tomorrow. He set his drink down. He would rather stay sober than face Thomas Allen. But it was a nice party and someone had signaled for "See the Conquering Hero Comes!" once more. It began to pall on him. And someone was giving a breakfast somewhere; he followed wearily; Betsy Wynne was *still* chattering as they whisked him through rain-soaked streets, insisted he eat on top of that last drink.

But it had been a very nice party.

In the morning Freemantle and Betsy sailed for Naples and three days later they returned to Porto Ferrajo without Sir Gilbert Elliot. He was still rumored to be on his way down from Rome.

However, Freemantle and Betsy had married at Naples under Lady Hamilton's motherly guidance, and they came back overflowing with praises for the Ambassadress who could mend social disasters, bring enemies to clasp hands, arrange marriage settlements for young captains. She was noted for slipping pound notes into impoverished midshipmen's pockets. No one gossiped about her past any more. Her marriage was so respectable that Sir William often laughed at her outcries against the immorality of the Neapolitans, for he said he knew "Emma never rolled on the floor" with the Neapolitan Dukes and Duchesses.

People even whispered that she had really been married to Sir William secretly, long before they had announced their marriage. So Lady Hamilton had not only attained a pinnacle of success but she balanced upon it remarkably well.

Once back at Porto Ferrajo, however, Captain Freemantle left his bride pouting on his ship while he accepted Cockburn's and Nelson's invitation to come aboard *La Minerve* for a belated bachelor's party.

That night, Allen set his cot alongside the Commodore's and laying a string in the groaning Commodore's hand, said, "Pull it, sir." And Allen lay down on his cot.

"No." But the Commodore pulled the string. Allen leaped up.

"In case I'm sleeping too sound, sir, and yow need me. The string's fixed to me collar, sir."

"Go away, Tom. I'll just sleep this off. Take your cot out."

"Aye, aye, sir." But Tom lay down on his cot, careful to put the string in the Commodore's fingers again. "Next time yow won't have more than four glasses of wine, sir."

"No, Tom."

Recovering from the bachelor's party the Commodore began to grow ill with anxiety. Haunted by the thought of the action he had probably missed. It had been his bad luck all his life to be one of the countless officers who risked their lives in little known places, although he had done his best to make major actions occur wherever he had been stationed. Now, perhaps Jervis would defeat the Combined Fleet and this war would end. He had no opinion of the peace talk in Paris unless Englishmen had turned cowards or could make terms backed by a victory.

The war would end—and thank God for it—but he would be left one of the minor casualties of circumstance: retired and reduced to a captain's half-pay again. At just thirty-eight. Without any money to speak of, and very little hope of any other profession. Ambition still taunting him!

He had done all he could at Porto Ferrajo, all hinged now on the arrival of the Viceroy.

It was New Year's Day, January 1, 1797. He had written a gloomy letter to his father, listing the duties of officers to bolster his drooping spirits. And he had seen Freemantle's eyes all afire with genuine adoration of Betsy, as he spread out an array of fine shawls and bright silks he had brought from Naples for her.

"I'll buy some for Fanny . . ." And the Commodore sent off an order to the English merchants in Naples to spend ten or twelve pounds.

He was always sending home presents as sailors had since time began; fragile eye-catching things from faraway places that looked as garish and pathetic as broken butterfly wings when unpacked in London.

And still there was nothing important to do but wait . . . *Pazienza.* He had never thought when he commandeered the right to establish this garrison on Elba with a threat and a summons—no bloodshed— that he would have to waste long mortal days in it. Sir Gilbert was expected hourly. It probably did not matter anyway, no doubt the battle was won.

And he hated to sit in an anchored ship!

He went ashore in a black cloud of anxiety, determined to cheer up young Noble, who was still close to death.

He found his lieutenant in a hideous little room in the house commandeered for a naval hospital. Noble was out of his head with a hole in his belly and his shoulder shattered.

The Commodore sat for a while by the bed feeling more helpless than ever. The doctor had said the fever must run its course, and he hoped for the best unless the incurable occurred: infection.

Once Noble opened his eyes and tried to greet his superior, but Nelson motioned him to be quiet; took hold of his hand. He held it thinking of how long Noble had served him, how he had accepted Noble's devotion, his self-effacing presence, and how much he had grown to rely on him. He cursed the fate that let men suffer endlessly like this and himself for losing his most devoted lieutenant.

Could he have fought *La Sabina* differently? If *Blanche* and *La Minerve* had fought together, secured one prize in half the time with perhaps half the damage to themselves, made off: they would have taken one half their opposing force. Instead they lost both surrendered ships by fighting according to tradition, ship to ship. And his mind played heretic with tradition. Teamwork . . . how effect it?

Young Noble groaned and then glanced up apologetically.

"Oh, pray be easy, my dear Noble. I've written for your promotion. You'll have a ship of your own before long."

Noble tried to understand, perhaps he did for a moment. Anyway he clung to the Commodore's hand.

The doctor came in, all bustle and fine frock coat. He did nothing except lay his hand on Noble's forehead, look knowing and murmur, "I think the surgery has saved his life. Very trying of course."

"Haven't you a better room? One with light and air?"

"Light and air?" the surgeon asked, aghast.

"Yes."

"Certainly, sir, if you think I should risk it."

"Immediately."

"Your servant, sir." And the doctor retreated. These English with their baths and air!

The Commodore went back to brooding. If Sir Gilbert did not come very soon he would send the convoys ahead, two convoys, small enough for frigates to guard and elude the enemy. If one were captured at least half the naval stores would reach Gibraltar in the other.

He felt Noble's hand relax, sliding out of his hand; glanced anxiously at the drawn face. Noble had fallen asleep.

❋   ❋   ❋

One more day went by without Sir Gilbert. Two days, three, four, five . . . six, seven, eight, nine . . . twenty-nine days passed before *La Minerve* lay with one anchor up, short on her other.

Sir Gilbert had arrived! He had harangued and exploded with De Burgh, who still refused to obey the King's orders until they were confirmed by the army. It meant the navy would have to send another convoy after the army when word finally reached London that De Burgh awaited army confirmation. Months of delay. Though the naval stores had been sent ahead in two convoys.

At last the Viceroy and his suite came aboard *La Minerve*. Beside Sir Gilbert was General Brogio, Paoli's former friend, going into exile in the footsteps of his betrayed or betraying leader. And Lieutenant Noble, white, but walking gingerly, reported for duty.

So at last *La Minerve's* sails unfurled, leaving De Burgh and the army at Elba, she steered not due west, but northward toward San Fiorenzo, Corsica. The Commodore's haggard face relaxed at dinner. Raising his glass to the Viceroy: "I am sure of a pleasant party; let what will happen!" While Tom Allen, who was serving and listening and mumbling over the table, raised his eyebrows and shook one finger at the Commodore.

"Glass one," he whispered, loud as a gale.

Sir Gilbert had lifted his glass to the Commodore's cavalier toast. "Can't say how much I appreciate having you to conduct us, my dear Commodore, and the heartening news you brought me that Lady Elliot was home. It's so very important I get to London immediately. How soon will we be at Gibraltar?"

Elliot was eyeing the all too familiar coast of Corsica in surprise.

"Not more than ten days, I hope, Sir Gilbert. I shan't detain you. We are merely peeking in on the enemy at San Fiorenzo, Toulon and Cartagena as we fly by. Might as well reconnoiter as we go along."

"Ah—" but Sir Gilbert ate very little lunch. He no longer ruled his own destiny. Here the Commodore's word was law.

❆   ❆   ❆

Luck and Cockburn's skill with *La Minerve* were with them as they peeked into enemy ports. There were no enemy fleets to be seen. Perhaps the battle was over. The Combined Fleet of Spanish and French must have left the Mediterranean! But when?

It was a brisk breezy afternoon when the towering hulk of the Rock reared out of the sea and *La Minerve,* exactly ten days from Porto Ferrajo, shortened sail to enter the Bay at Gibraltar.

The Commodore was on deck, anxiously studying three ships of the line through his glass. They were anchored just outside the port of Algeciras, Spain.

"Dons . . ." He knew he could get into Gibraltar without an attack, for the ships were making no signs of sailing, and by the time they spied him, got under way, he would be safe.

"Perhaps our Cartel has been arranged, Cockburn." He turned to his Captain. "We will find out immediately if our lieutenants are on those ships. But let us keep a weather eye on those Dons . . . Bravo! Our convoys are in!"

"Exactly as you promised, Commodore!" Sir Gilbert Elliot had come on deck, dressed to perfection, ready to go ashore.

Nelson eyed him anxiously. "May I beg of you, Sir Gilbert, if it will not inconvenience you, to recall that the *Minerve* will be but a few hours in port; just long enough to effect the exchange of our officers. We will sail with the lark in the morning."

"With the lark, by all means!" Sir Gilbert nodded. "But I cannot get used to your nautical time."

"How is that, Sir Gilbert?"

"I came on deck this afternoon, now, only to discover that it is already tomorrow morning! Therefore I am late and should be coming aboard ship, shouldn't I?"

"Our dates run from noon to noon, sir. But morning is tomorrow morning. Although I should advise coming aboard tonight."

"I give up!" Sir Gilbert laughed. He was delighted at the thought of setting foot on land again. " 'With the lark.' That must guide me through your mysteries."

❊　　　　　❊　　　　　❊

By afternoon of the following day, Captain Cockburn, watching the Commodore pace up and down, saw trouble brewing. Nelson's face was white with rage, his good eye snapping. The Viceroy was still on shore and *La Minerve* still ready to sail.

Lieutenant Culverhouse and Lieutenant Hardy were roaming about, taking in the free air. The Spaniards had turned them over as agreed. The seamen would be exchanged soon.

Coulson was below, laying the Commodore's table from the officers' galley; furious to see that Allen, the bungler, had in spite of broken glasses and misplaced belongings of the Commodore managed to ingratiate himself even more with the Commodore during Coulson's heroic absence.

"So, *you* captured *Sabina?*" Coulson snarled.

"Me and the Commodore," Allen admitted.

"And who was't stepped for'ard to man *Sabina,* Tom Allen?"

"Yow may desert the chief but not me," Allen grinned. "I shielded him with my own body. He might be dead but for me!"

"I don't see no wounds on yer," Coulson sneered.

Allen shrugged. "Oh, me I heal quick."

"Lemme see yer scars."

"None o' yowr business."

As time passed, the Commodore's temper rose. It was based on hard fact: from Gibraltar he had learned that the French fleet had gone through the Straits weeks before, by-passed Jervis, and made port on the French Atlantic coast, but the Spanish Grand Fleet had been

sighted sailing through the Straits into the Atlantic only *four days ago!*
A battle was imminent while he was anchored at Gibraltar.

"And that does it!" he shouted to Cockburn, pointing a quivering
finger at the ships shifting on their cables. "The tide's turned! Yet . . .
if the wind holds we may make the weather tide tonight."

"Aye, aye, sir," Cockburn said quietly. Unless the tide and the wind
were flowing in the same direction—out—it was well-nigh impossible
to get out from under the Rock and through the Straits into the Atlantic. "There's the barge now, sir."

But it was not the Viceroy. Only a letter from his secretary in-
quiring if by any chance *La Minerve* were ready to sail?

The Commodore plunged down into his cabin and Allen fell out of
the way, dropping an armload of linen and tramping on it as he tried
to pick it up. The Commodore, with a weary eye on his "walley's" inability to learn the art of a gentleman's gentleman, wrote his reply to
the Viceroy's secretary, Mr. Hardman.

DEAR SIR:
The *Minerve* was most certainly ready for sea, and it is as true, that had
Sir Gilbert been on board, the *Minerve* would have been at sea before the
lee-tide made. . . . Now the tide is made against us; therefore, I most
heartily wish you all a good appetite, and only beg you will be on board
as early in the evening as possible—say eight o'clock—for I shall sail the
first moment after; but I fear a *westerly* wind.
Yours most truly,
HORATIO NELSON
P.S. I took my leave of the Governor, and refused to dine on shore.

Back on deck, the Commodore met a new passenger, Colonel Drinkwater, an aide to Sir Gilbert, who had come down from Elba on the
Blanche. The Commodore's gloom lifted slightly, for Colonel Drinkwater was one of the first army men he had met to whom he had
taken an instant liking. They had both been disappointed that the
Viceroy's suite absorbed so much room aboard *La Minerve* that Drinkwater could not make the trip with them. Now *Blanche* was staying at
Gibraltar for a while and room must be made for Drinkwater.

The Commodore invited him below, where they sat in the main
cabin, lulled by the quiet lapping of the water in the Bay. Through
the stern windows the Rock stood like a wall against the sky. Like a

lion couchant. So obviously so that one scarcely dared admit it for fear of being trite. Yet there it lay, a lion. Golden brown in the late afternoon sun. A giant lion. There was no denying it. Generation after generation had recognized its shape, tried to ignore it, but the word still said itself: lion.

Colonel Drinkwater and the Commodore had their backs to it as they sipped punch. The Colonel had witnessed the Spanish siege of the English garrison at Gibraltar from 1779 to 1783. His authoritative history, *The Siege of Gibraltar,* published in 1785, had described those harrowing four years. They began discussing it now, here in the shadow of the liberated garrison.

"His Royal Highness the Duke of Clarence was serving as a midshipman in 1780 when Rodney forced the entrance to the harbor, Colonel."

"And a magnificent battle he witnessed. Were you there, sir?" young Drinkwater asked.

"No, unfortunately. But I had the honor and privilege of tutoring His Royal Highness in the West Indies—about ten years ago, and he often spoke of it."

"What subject did you tutor?"

"Tactics," the Commodore said blandly. "Naval tactics."

The Colonel smiled. "Then you are not responsible for his tactics ashore!"

"His Highness is an excellent seaman and I think he should have a ship," the Commodore said very positively. The Colonel nodded.

"Perhaps then His Highness wouldn't uphold divorce, slavery and the Prince of Wales's debts in Parliament!"

"He's restless." The Commodore apologized for his favorite student, who was still at sixes and sevens with George III, and who now lived permanently and faithfully with his mistress.

The Colonel laughed to himself, sitting forward. "But the more I hear of your career, the more I am amazed. Now something should be written about Corsica."

"Thank you, sir, but it would have been the most gratifying experience could I have served under Rodney."

"He killed initiative," Drinkwater said.

"So I have heard from Lord Hood. But I have diverted you from the siege."

"Where were you at that time, Commodore Nelson?"

"I? Besieging the fort at San Juan, Nicaragua."

"Oh, my God! Were you with that murderous expedition! I've heard the tales of the boiled monkeys you were forced to eat."

"Oh, not I—have you ever seen a monkey boiling? No, I escaped the monkeys. But I did drink water from a spring which some mischievous Indians had poisoned with manchineel bark. Some of us died from it, but I've only suffered a corroded stomach ever since."

"But haven't I heard from Sir Gilbert that you served under Lord Howe? You must have seen the finish of our siege here."

"Worse luck. By that time I had recovered from Nicaragua and I was back in the West Indies."

"But you were with Lord Howe when he moved into New York?"

"When Lord Howe moved into New York, Colonel, I was cruising alone in a bit of a frigate off Cape Cod . . . so you see, though I have been in over one hundred and forty actions, I have never witnessed a major battle between two fleets. Unless our brushes under Hotham may be called that. So I have nothing of interest to compare with your siege. Pray go on."

"I'll pin you down yet," Drinkwater smiled. "But one interesting fact about those years we were besieged was the wonderful improvement in our artillery. We had to experiment. Necessity, mother of invention . . . As a naval officer you would have relished how we met the Dons' great battering ships. They were armored and roofed with wood so impenetrably thick that when we saw them closing in after three years' holding out we appeared doomed in a matter of hours. Horrible sight. Our solid shot would not penetrate their armor and we were taking a drubbing from their guns. By midnight of that very day when it looked as if this old Rock would return to Spain, we had furnaces going under the newly invented grates . . . within twenty-four hours red-hot shot from our batteries had blown up every battering ship!"

"And now those French devils carry furnaces for hot shot aboard ship against our international agreement not to use such terrible weapons in war. But we invented it . . ."

"It's very effective," the Colonel smiled.

"But the main thing is to outmaneuver a Frenchman, Colonel. The trick is to force him to fight. As for the hot shot, they burn themselves up more often than not."

"But with their long-range artillery, how can you outmaneuver them?"

"I am convinced it can be done," the Commodore said, and as he had never fought a major fleet battle his self-assurance amazed Drinkwater.

❊   ❊   ❊

Eight o'clock came and went. The Commodore's first temper had boiled away, leaving nothing but the charred remains of his hopes for being with Jervis in time for battle. The enemy was at sea. And what about those three battleships anchored at Algeciras? True they had brought the officers as arranged, but were three necessary? Would they chase him?

The tide was flowing out again, the wind from the east blowing straight for the Atlantic; now was the time. But he could not desert Sir Gilbert even though his whole future in the navy depended on being with Jervis.

Gibraltar had never looked so insanely gay as it did tonight. The lights winked facetiously at him. Everyone was having a very nice time, why worry about tomorrow?

Oars splashed near the ship. He spun about. Yes, he could hear the Viceroy's voice at the bottom of the ladder, slow, plowing through some anecdote.

"Let me tell you the story about Dr. Johnson," he was saying, probably to Brogio. "Apropos of Charles V who was reputed to know no fear: The man who did not know fear, Johnson cried, that man had never snuffed a candle with his fingers!"

The guests were laughing politely.

Now the piping began. The Commodore glanced about to see that Cockburn was giving the orders to weigh. But as the Viceroy's head came into sight, the Commodore felt the wind slap his other cheek. A tug underfoot. The wind had blown foul again!

❊   ❊   ❊

By morning *La Minerve* was under way, on the last lap of her obstacle race to rejoin the fleet. It was nearly noon when with a fitful fickle easterly wind, *La Minerve* nosed from the Bay, and found the three Spanish ships of the line standing off—waiting to chase.

La Minerve's crew was coaxing the wind into every inch of canvas as the Commodore smiled at Lieutenant Hardy. "They're after you again, Mr. Hardy. We must give them a race."

"Aye, aye, sir. May I suggest they are after the Commodore who gave *Sabina* a beating? They knew your name, sir, only too well from the French."

"Indeed?" The Commodore smiled in spite of himself. Life was hard and praise rare. But at the moment the enemy's attentions were inconvenient.

Sir Gilbert Elliot had been watching the Dons anxiously. "Are we in any trouble, Commodore?"

Nelson furled his temper, took a quick turn. "You see the Rock, Sir Gilbert, acts as a barrier to the wind, and until we are far enough out of the lee off it, the Rock will cause the wind to be light, perhaps baffling. Oh, but they'll have their troubles, too." He nodded toward the Spanish. "Though they are standing off farther than we are and have a little more wind, if we can hold out till we're free of the Rock, I dare say we'll give them the slip."

Sir Gilbert and his suite tried to appear at ease. They were not cowards, but the Dons' battleships looked very big; very near.

"And so, Sir Gilbert," Nelson came back from another turn on the deck, "may I suggest that Mr. Hardman makes sure all your papers are weighted? In case we think it advisable to throw them overboard."

Sir Gilbert motioned sadly to his secretary to be prepared to consign all the valuable documents he had obtained in Italy—to the deep.

In the whimsical gusts that puffed over the sea, first the Spanish and then *La Minerve* seemed to be gaining. While the sun flashed swords' points over the chop of the Straits and the slumbering beastlike Rock loomed so high it dwarfed the play. Small boys were running along the shore, and soon swarms of people were lining the cliffs; their faint cries as they watched the chase were like the wails of gulls over fish.

The Commodore, however, appeared less concerned than he had in the harbor, fretting over delay. Seeing this, Colonel Drinkwater stepped forward with an apologetic landsman's smile.

"I have heard so much of your exploits in fighting, sir, do you suppose we'll be privileged to witness it here?"

"Quite probably we shall have action." The Commodore frowned. This was no time to display heroics, with a King's Viceroy in his charge. "But before the Dons get hold of that bit of bunting—" he jerked his head, glancing aloft at his Pendant—"I'll have a struggle with them. . . ." He eyed the three enemy sail of line following his cruiser frigate. "And sooner than give up the frigate, I'll run her ashore!"

Small consolation, that. His guests tried to take it all in as the towering Spanish hovered astern like three angels of doom, their arrogant prows turning the water to show the white anger beneath.

The very slowness of their movements lent a sense of delirium, of disease; of trying to run away in a dream. There was a slowly warping madness in the scene. For as minutes went by as hours, the seamen's minds, used to being turned out to fight guns or gales on an instant, day or night, accepted the reality, left their worries to fate. The landsmen guests were not so inured to sea warfare.

Sometimes all four ships stood still. Hours went by like years. Only the cries on the shore and the shifting sun overhead seemed free of the hunt and the kill.

Yet each moment that passed was a gain for *La Minerve,* for the wind blew more steadily the farther she crept from the Rock. Two hours passed . . . three . . . four.

It was midafternoon, and the officers' dinner was served.

"Well, gentlemen, shall we dine?" The Commodore bowed the Viceroy down the hatch. Landsmen with their hearts already in their mouths must now find room for meat and wine; swallow it. Forget their lives were hanging in the balance of the wind, as much a quarry of the Dons as any fox that ever leaped aquiver to survive the hounds of hunting men.

Though the Commodore, some of the officers and all the guests left the deck, the ship plowed on slowly. Her jacks still made their precarious way aloft, tending the sails, pampering the wind; teasing it into every possible scrap of sail.

No one ever knew exactly what happened, aloft there a hundred feet above deck, among the white cups and shifting shadows, high in the maze of rigging, until a screaming sprawling dark mass hurtled down; struck the sea.

"Man overboard!"—the bawling of horrified shipmates. The next instant the sentry by the taffrail swung an ax, cut the line on a life preserver. And dozens of voices yelled·

"Out boat!"

Up from the cabins below, like a whale breaking surface, came

Hardy. He was overside in a moment and his jolly boat fell astern *La Minerve,* rowing for the spot where the jack had sunk. There was only the sparkling of reflected sunlight; an empty life preserver bobbing slowly away toward the steady white glare of the Dons' spread sails: the seaman was gone; stunned or killed by the fall.

Hardy's crew began the pull back toward *La Minerve,* which had not slackened her speed for a moment; was still pulling slowly away from the Dons.

The men on *La Minerve,* and the officers from their dinner, watched in silence as the backs of the jolly boat crew bulged, glistened with sweat; facing them sat Hardy, behind him were the Dons: hunters and the hunted.

For a minute or two the jolly boat seemed to be gaining on the frigate which was sailing on and on—but slowly. Then with a churning of oars the jolly boat slowed, almost stood still. The oars bit deep in the water, but Hardy and his crew seemed to lose ground, drift back toward the enemy.

"The Straits current flowing east!" Cockburn muttered, as the little black shell hung, drifted back, pulled forward, but no longer overtaking *La Minerve,* which was gaining more and more speed as she left the Rock. Hardy began receding slowly toward the Dons and prison.

The oars clawed frantically into the current. The Spaniards drew closer, and *La Minerve* sailed on.

The Commodore's eye suddenly glittered as he watched Hardy.

"By God! I'll not lose Hardy! Back the mizzen topsails!"

The order rang from lip to lip: *La Minerve* fell back, waiting, while the Dons seemed to spring from the water, gaining on her.

Hardy was trumpeting profanities, cheering his crew. The jolly boat staggered ahead to his chanted curses, kept staggering ahead as the men broke their backs now to gain *La Minerve.* Astern they could hear the Dons' prows cutting through the water until with a snap the leading Spanish battleship bore up: stood still. Puzzled by Nelson's obviously insane maneuver; his challenge to stand and fight them.

As the jolly boat caught the line astern *La Minerve,* "Make sail!" Nelson yelled. *La Minerve* gave a toss of her bowsprit up—bore away, spreading her sails in her magical way. While the Dons, topsails still shivering, waited another moment, apparently peering ahead to see if by any chance Nelson had sighted English reinforcements. Sensing the trick at last, their sails filled to chase once again.

The jolly boat crew lay panting on the deck. The veins standing out on their necks, their eyes bloodshot. It was a warm handshake Commodore Nelson gave 2nd Lieutenant Thomas Masterman Hardy. They were out of debt.

At last, breaking free of the Rock, *La Minerva* tilted and with all her sweet grace caught the steady easterly wind and soon left the heavier Spanish of line in her laughing wake.

By dusk the Dons were but froth on the curve of the ocean.

❊   ❊   ❊

They all went to bed early that night, doubled up in the cabins, cots set in every corner, for *La Minerve* was even more crowded than on her trip out to Elba. Colonel Drinkwater bunked next to the Viceroy. There were as many cots as each cabin could hold.

The Commodore had ordered *La Minerve* to sail southwest, keep before the wind till they lost the Dons. It was a roundabout way to Cádiz, but the surest. As he threw himself onto a cot fully dressed, he was thinking of the danger of the light fog in the night air. But Lieutenant Culverhouse was on watch.

Captain Cockburn lay sound asleep about six inches away from the Commodore. Some idiot had failed to latch the water closet door. It slammed to the roll of the ship, until one of the servants came threading the cots of the great to close it. The Commodore heard the Viceroy snoring in the next cabin, his snores seemed to rise and fall with the ship. He heard Drinkwater turning restlessly, coughing, trying to sleep; damned to count the Viceroy's wheezes. Brogio was a lump in the dark, too silent to be asleep; he must have been listening also.

The Commodore rolled over, slept, until he and Cockburn sprang up together to the cries of the lookouts in the tops:

"Deck there! Strange sails bearing due west. We're surrounded by sail!"

There was a tense stillness in the midnight as the Commodore and the Captain went on deck. The muffling silence of heavy fog pressing down on the Atlantic swells *La Minerve,* herself, seemed to have lost both bow and stern in nothingness; her crew hazy ghosts.

"What do you make of it, sir?" Cockburn's voice was hoarse, filled with fog.

The Commodore turned slowly, without answering. For as far as they could see through the mist, to north, to south, east and west of them, there were the dark forms of immense battleships hissing through sea, all sailing west.

"Deck there, there seem to be more than twenty, sir!"

And now and then the faint glow of signal lights winking from masthead to masthead. Silently. Knowingly.

Then a bell here—one there. Now a muffled signal drum.

"No, those are not our signals, Cockburn." The Commodore's voice was tense.

"No, sir . . . but can it be . . . five days ago passing the Straits?"

"It is the *Spanish Grand Fleet,* Cockburn! We're in the midst of the Spanish Grand Fleet! It must be . . ." And the Commodore kept staring about and about. "But what are they doing so far south? Sailing *west* . . ." He began to pace slowly.

"We're in a spot, sir, shall we try to veer north?" Cockburn asked. Culverhouse and Hardy were both there now. Hardy was grinning.

"I'm jinxed . . ." softly to Culverhouse.

But the Commodore had not answered Cockburn. He was pacing slowly. It was like a dream, a shadowy foreboding nightmare. At last he turned to his Captain. "They don't appear to notice us, Cockburn."

"Perhaps we can fall back, sir, extricate ourselves?"

"No. Not yet . . ."

Cockburn: "Aye, aye, sir?"

"No. Follow their maneuvers. I think we had better find out where they are bound."

"Aye, aye, sir." Cockburn's job was cut out. No questions asked.

"Can you sail like a Don, Mr. Culverhouse?"

"We can try, sir. But will *La Minerve* make a fool of herself? She's that proud, sir."

The shapes were like something unworldly; like ghosts of armadas, were it not for the sounds they made: wood creaking, occasional hails, the slow-timed thunder of signal guns on the hour.

"We have perhaps four hours till dawn, Cockburn. Time to see what they intend. *West.*" The Commodore stopped in his track. "The Indies? Are they after our West Indies Colonies?"

"West Indies, sir!" Cockburn stared at the ships as if his eyes could will them to turn back.

The Commodore was pacing faster. "I must warn the Viceroy he

may have a trip. If those Dons are going to the Indies we must outsail them, Cockburn, warn the Colonies!"

"Across the Atlantic tonight, sir! Aye, aye, sir!" Cockburn was instantly measuring rations, and water, calculating such a trip on no
notice at all.

The Commodore nodded. "We shall see," and he went below, too
engrossed in his plans to notice Cockburn's jaw drop as he stared after
him.

But the Viceroy still snored. He was a happily married man nearing
the end of a satisfactory mission to Rome. Drinkwater was in love and
given to acute hearing. He sat up as the Commodore's shadow cut
into the dim light from the forward cabin.

"Colonel . . ." In whispers they debated the issue. Nelson was determined to cross the Atlantic if the Spanish fleet did not change its
course. They both knew the Viceroy was determined to reach London.
The Viceroy continued to snore. And they decided to let him continue
doing just that. If, tomorrow, he woke heading west, he would just
have to rage. The Commodore nodded to the Colonel and went back
on deck.

Drinkwater lay tensely listening to the enemy ships. They sounded
nearer; sleepless Drinkwater envied the Commodore his immediate
responsibilities that allowed him no time to contemplate *La Minerve's*
helpless position if she were discovered.

On deck, the Commodore had been studying his watch by the binnacle light. He closed its cover reluctantly, as if regretting he could
not make time stop; hold the hour.

Delicately, with an eye to the enemy's every move, Cockburn ordered *La Minerve* to tack when the battleships tacked.

"I think they are changing their course, sir," he said after a while.
But they moved tauntingly, seeming to hover neither due west, as before, nor due north.

"We had better begin to veer northward ourselves, Cockburn. We
must be out of sight before dawn."

La Minerve worked herself gingerly, idling in her wake. Once
while they watched, ready to throw her helm down, two great hulls
bore down on her, passed, one on either side, within a few feet. The
voices of Dons high above on the decks. And one by one, *La Minerve*
let the ghosts of the Dons slip west by north past her. Again they
shifted.

"But they sail so cranky, sir, it's hard to tell if they are changing their course or—" But *La Minerve* followed, and the needle of her compass traveled slowly around:

West northwest—northwest by west, coming about. Northwest by north—north northwest—northwest—northwest by *north*—steering at last *north*. *La Minerve* watched the last of them sailing by.

The fog muffled their distant signal guns, their lights vanishing through the layers of mist. And again the black shadows, now far ahead, came about: north northeast—northeast by north. . . .

Last seen, heading *northeast*. Toward Spain?

"We will keep to westward of them, Cockburn, just in case they come about again."

When day broke they were gone, as if in the night the Commodore had only dreamed. Now, more than ever, he was anxious to join Jervis, yet: "We will steer to westward, Cockburn, make sure they did not come about again, are not striking the Indies." *La Minerve* ranged far out on the Atlantic, but the Grand Fleet had vanished.

By late afternoon, Nelson was satisfied. "You may steer for Cádiz, Cockburn. Apparently they are trying to circle our fleet."

❊   ❊   ❊

The next morning, the thirteenth of February, 1797, two months since Commodore Nelson left Sir John Jervis, *La Minerve* sighted the small English fleet, and saluting, bore up alongside the Commander in Chief in the *Victory*.

"The news, Sir John? The Spanish Grand Fleet seen two nights ago southwest of the Straits, sailing northeast!"

The Commodore's Pendant rippled out from the masthead of the *Captain* once more, while the long-awaited signals flew through the grim English fleet:

"Prepare for action!"

V I I I. St. Vincent

February – July, 1797

ALL THROUGH THE NIGHT of the thirteenth of February they heard the far booming of the enemy's signal guns. But dawn of the fourteenth, the vision was blurred by light fog; nothing in sight!

The dawn lengthened into pale misty daylight, the gray, heaving Atlantic rolled like a monster in pain; winter cold. Far off, on the curve of the sea, the English cruiser frigates winged back toward the fleet. Their signal flags hard to read . . . The fleet waited in close order.

The ships' crews were filling powder, fitting freshly oiled gunlocks into cannon. Deep in the hold of each ship, within the two magazines, lanterns flickered behind the double glass, lit the cautious slippered men on the felt carpeting, silent, entombed with the explosives. Those were the men who philosophized during battle. No one to speak to. Not a word.

On deck the crews were slinging the lower yards with chains, raising the nettings. Lumber and loose fittings stowed, the ships grew sleeker and more purposeful. The lower deck ports were yawned, so many red mouths opening, and with a low rumbling the cannons were run out.

Some of the hammocks were carried to the tops, and with the blankets were built into barricades; a breastwork for the lookouts who must stay at their posts aloft.

Commodore Nelson and Captain Miller had come on deck right after breakfast. And the crew had eaten better than usual this morning. As the dark cleared away the Commodore and the Captain stood like two shadows changing into human shapes with the light, as if they had stood there all night waiting for Valentine's Day; to shoot hearts in the morning.

The *Captain* was in fighting trim. Miller had more than kept his promise. Both men peered ahead, Nelson thoughtful, heavy-lidded eyes focused beyond his own ship, with the controlled intensity of a cat. Miller elegant, dash without affectation, all eyes for his ship, his third child: his sphere in battle. Captain Berry joined them, pacing pompously, in a way that had begun to amuse his inferiors, as if nothing could jolt him. He was still waiting to go home for reassignment to a ship of his own. He was on the *Captain,* now, merely as a "supernumerary"; he could sit back and watch the day if he chose.

"Two months, and you're back on the dot, sir." He turned to the Commodore who had greeted him with a nod. "Your proverbial luck, sir."

"I told them to wait for me—" from the Commodore, as the cruiser frigates drew nearer from three different points of the compass.

They had been searching for the enemy all through the night while Jervis's fleet had kept tight order, sailing slowly through the dark, so close and so ready the Captains could hail one another from their decks. With the daylight they had spread out again.

Still the morning lengthened. Still nothing.

"Deck there! *La Bonne Citoyenne* frigate signaling twenty-five ships of the enemy to south of the English fleet bearing east, for Spain, sir."

The three officers on the quarter-deck of *Captain* exchanged glances. Josiah, his face crimson with excitement, his eyes possessed as he saluted:

"Admiral making signal, 'Prepare for battle,' sir." And as the Commodore faced his stepson, Josiah's face suddenly changed, a deep possessive affection in it. "I'm glad you're back, sir, terribly—glad—" and he turned away, setting his hat fore and aft on his head.

Jervis's fifteen ships of the line were strung out in two columns convenient for sailing, moving slowly down the Atlantic, southward, parallel to the Spanish coast. On the gray winter swells, in a gray haze, seeking the battleground: fifteen sought to meet twenty-five.

Yet the hours dragged on, as the English hunted.

Signal flags. Hoste sliding down a stay, his eyes bright and big.

"Enemy sighted, sir!" He drew himself up. Aside from his eyes he looked as calm as his superiors. But, "This—is—it—this—is—it—" he was whispering unconsciously under his breath. The Commodore winked at Miller, and turned away pacing thoughtfully. A little faster and a little faster.

Now Jervis's loose double line must be tightened; now the moment of decision was come. How force the battle? How overwhelm? How overwhelm one portion of the enemy, take the offensive, and keep it?

Aboard the *Barfleur,* Vice-Admiral Waldegrave, Captain Dacres:

The signal lieutenant bawling from the main yard: "I have a glimpse through the fog of their leeward line and they loom like Beachy Head in a fog, sir! By my soul, they are thumpers, for I distinctly make out four tiers of ports in one of them bearing an admiral's flag, sir!"

"Don Cordova in *Santissima Trinidad."* Waldegrave turned to Captain Dacres. "We'll reduce this mountain into a molehill before sunset!"

And while the heroes spoke, Mr. Parsons, a mid, who had just the last week leaped into a boat square on Dacres's cocked hat, and only escaped reprimand because Dacres was paralyzed in his rage, now crept past the Admiral and the Captain: this was the moment for a hungry boy to pilfer the Admiral's cabin of fruit. . . .

❈   ❈   ❈

Aboard *Victory:* signal officers to Commander in Chief, who walked with First Captain Calder and Captain Ben Hallowell:

"There are eight of sail, Sir John!"

"Very well, sir."

A pause for a fresh look at the enemy.

"There are twenty of sail of the line, Sir John."

"Very well, sir."

"There are twenty-*five* sail of the line, Sir John!"

"Very well, sir."

"There are twenty-*seven* sail of line, *Sir John?* Nearly *double* our numbers, sir—"

"Enough, sir, no more of that. The die is cast and if there were fifty of sail I would go through them!" Jervis's ugly cleft jaw squared, he threw his shoulders back only to have one shoulder nearly shattered by a blow from lusty Ben Hallowell, his frontier blood roused.

"That's right, Sir John! By God, we shall give them a damn good licking!"

Captain Calder's eyebrows rose, but Jervis grinned for once.

And again aboard *Barfleur:* Midshipman Parsons, his mouth full of stolen fruit, choked as he peered this side, then that, from the Admiral's windows. The fog had lifted: the Spanish were in sight at last, in two groups, that apparently had become separated in the night. The group nearest Spain, to larboard, was small, like a flurry of distracted white hens trying to rejoin the larger mass of the Spanish fleet to starboard that was coming like a white cloud rolling up from the west, covering the horizon.

Aboard *Captain:* "Admiral making signal: 'Form line of battle. Divide the enemy fleet.'"

Now the first step, as certain as sunrise and sunset, birth culminating in death: a battle begins with a single line. It is the custom. Form line and await further orders, as circumstance presents.

The *Captain* swung into her place, third from the rear, her flying jib boom nosing the taffrail of the ship ahead. Admiral Sir John Jervis's *Victory,* as customary, in the center, while Captain Troubridge in *Culloden* led the processional; in the post of honor once assigned Nelson, before he left for Elba. Now Jervis, who was growing increasingly fond of forthright, hard-talking Troubridge, had made other plans. Nelson peered ahead for his friend Troubridge, so far ahead he was almost out of sight.

As senior Captain in the fleet, it was painful to Commodore Nelson not to lead, but never mind, let the battle but begin. The wind from the west favored the Spanish, blowing full in their sails, sometimes falling to southwest, still favoring the Spanish, while the English must tack, lose distance, but hold their position inshore, to prevent the mass of sails to westward from reaching port.

How strike to secure a victory? How force the Spanish to meet? By overwhelming the smaller cluster, would that bring the flock in? Or did Jervis only wish for a small bite?

As the long line of English, like a white javelin, aimed to sever the enemy, and the cloud from the west drew closer, it seemed but a matter of time . . . hell was inevitable, off Cape St. Vincent.

Culloden, bearing down like a bludgeon, threatened to crash the first Spaniard lumbering into her path. It hauled up. Troubridge did not waver.

The ships must fall together and duel to death. But Commodore Nelson was eyeing them anxiously. The enemy knew its greatest advantage lay in the threat of its being at sea even though the English were determined to take the offensive. The inevitable had not been forced yet. The Dons still had time. Too much time to change their minds.

There was a stiff wind, and two fleets drawing together. The hiss of the wakes, hulls creaking, the groans of whole forests uprooted, carved into masts.

Now battle flags soared to the mastheads flaunting their colors.

Flags looked liquid in the mists, transient and breath-taking against the gray fog and gray sea. The gold and red of the Spanish. The red, white and blue Union Jack of the English, and Jervis's flag: the St. George's banner, white with a red cross. The Vice-Admirals' and Rear Admirals' ships, a flag each, down to the Commodore's red swallowtailed Distinguishing Pendant.

Taunting their boasts and their different beliefs—the English crosses of St. George and St. Andrews; while the Spanish were hoisting out their great wooden crosses of Jesus from their booms—they swung rhythmically over the water, casting distorted reflections obliquely over the waves.

And those Spanish ships built of Inca gold! Ships that had once played host, wined and dined the English fleet: now mortal enemies. Like dreams of Midas gone mad: beautiful hulls, haughty prows and high sterns, lavish quarters for officers; whole fields of canvas; ships that startled the world—the biggest afloat.

Santissima Trinidad 130 guns; *Mexicana* 112; *Princepe de Asturias* 112; *Concepción* 112; *Conde de Regla* 112; *Salvador del Mundo* 112; *San Josef* 112; *San Nicolas* 80; and nineteen other ships of the line, all handsome 74's: *Oriente, Glorioso, Atlante, Conquistador, Soberano, Firme, Pelayo, San Genaro, San Ildephonso, San Juan Nepomucino, San Francisco de Paula, San Ysidro, San Antonio, San Pablo, San Firmin, Neptuno, Bahama, San Domingo, Terrible.* . . .

And the fifteen hard-working, long-humiliated, undecorative English with their lines of a Dutchman's clog, barren officers' quarters? Sir John Jervis had the *Victory* 100 guns, Captains Calder and Hallowell; Vice-Admiral Thomson, Captain Foley, the *Britannia* 100; Vice-Admiral Waldegrave, Captain Dacres, the *Barfleur* 98; Rear Admiral Parker the *Prince George* 98, Captain Irwin; then there was Captain Frederick with his new ship *Blenheim* 90, Captain Whitshead, the *Namur* 90; and exactly nine others, eight of them standard 74's—*Captain,* Commodore Nelson, Captain Miller; *Goliath,* Captain Sir Charles Knowles; *Excellent,* Captain Collingwood; *Orion,* Captain Sir James Saumarez; *Colossus,* Captain Murray; *Egmont,* Captain Sutton; *Culloden,* Captain Troubridge; *Irresistible,* Captain Martin; and one little fellow: *Diadem* 64, Captain Towry.

The Spanish then had twenty-seven ships and two thousand two hundred and eighty-eight guns mounted in hulls of well-nigh unsinkable size.

The English had fifteen ships, one thousand two hundred and thirty-two guns, about one thousand less than the Dons. Did Jervis mean victory or valiant suicide? If sheer weight of numbers, matched ship to ship, gun to gun, were all that counted—as was custom—then Spain would rise mightier than ever before, cripple England, become an asset to the new conquests of France. Guns cast from slave gold must rule the world. But slave gold was tempting the wits of men who recalled the great days of England, of Hawkins and Drake. New men, no longer pirates—though the Dons said they were, and heretics, too —these gentlemen of His Majesty's Fleet.

As Commodore Nelson watched the fleets, sure of Captain Miller, his mind ran free to think how he would fight were he Commander in Chief. To confuse, confound and overwhelm? Had Jervis a master stroke up his sleeve? He had made his line so fine one might not guess the high discipline Jervis had injected since Hotham's time. It looked so easy one could not expect it to have sailed otherwise though they were but fifteen to twenty-seven.

From the *Lively* frigate which was standing off, waiting, to witness by the special request of the Viceroy, before going to England, Brogio, Elliot and Drinkwater were watching. God knew what they were thinking as they watched their side go into battle. It was perhaps one of the first times in history that a sea battle was about to be witnessed by noncombatants at a close range. Jervis had not wanted it, but the Viceroy had been adamant, ready to die watching.

So the line sailed in perfect order. What Jervis commanded he ruled—except his Commodore whom he pampered—from the quarterdeck on the *Victory;* but he kept his plans to himself. He preferred dictation to instruction.

And Troubridge, the envy of all, was sailing splendidly, conscious of his position; handling his ship so brilliantly Jervis cried out to long-suffering, jealous Captain Calder who was growing daily more touchy directly under the Admiral's cold eye: "Look at Troubridge!" and Calder eyed without smiling as Jervis said, "As if the eyes of all

England were on him!" And Jervis stepped off to avoid another blow from Hallowell, whose face was radiant, his big frame seeming to grow with each breath he took.

Behind Troubridge was Captain Frederick in *Blenheim,* and so on through all the admirals of the fleet, down to *Captain,* with *Diadem* and *Excellent* in her wake. All eyes ahead were watching the Dons and Jervis's *Victory,* while Commodore Nelson brought up the rear.

Lines lengthened into miles. The fleets covered great masses of ocean. Space and the wind and time passed by, yet the obvious conclusion, a complete battle, hung on the assumption that the Dons seemed willing to fight.

At last the first of the long English line raked the smallest cluster of Dons, while *Captain* was hours behind. As the battle began far ahead, sparks and thunder and black smoke rose up from the ocean.

Aboard *Barfleur* little Midshipman Parsons's eyes grew bigger and bigger. His stolen fruit stuck in his throat. He dropped a beautiful orange—but he wasn't hungry. The light from the stern windows blotted out—a flash like lightning. The cabin crumbling around his ears.

Parsons turned, clutching two oranges, ran and ran and ran and did not seem to move till he burst like a rocket onto the quarter-deck, all eyes, face white, saw men die, ran on and on right into Vice-Admiral Waldegrave and Captain Dacres.

"Here!" And Parsons gave each one an orange. Smiled timidly.

Yet with the first promising broadsides, the opening guns of the battle for which England had waited four years, the pattern crumbled to pieces! The small cluster veered away, while the great cloud of Spanish coming down on the English hauled up, paused out of gunshot, came about and began to flee north to join the small cluster behind the English line. The Spanish had scattered in two directions. One Spaniard from the small cluster to leeward came raking down the English line, alone; her sisters had fled.

Nelson started, glanced at Miller, then peered ahead anxiously for Jervis's signal. There it flew, and he clenched his jaw as the signal lieutenants translated. Jervis—*Jervis* had blundered! He was signaling not a general chase, nor even for all to come about instantly after the Dons; no, Jervis flew an iron, composed: Fleet to tack in succession. One ship tacking after another, to catch the main body of Spanish sailing north. A beautiful, tragic scene of a disciplinarian, his plans smashed, unable to let go the reins even for victory. There was the stern line of English sailing south, the great mass of Dons sailing north. Two fleets passing each other far out of gunshot. But tack in succession meant no ship might tack to turn back after the enemy until she reached the point where the ship ahead of her had done so, and still they must keep the line.

One after the other the disciplined English followed Troubridge in *Culloden.* The line began to make a smart V, and Nelson in horror on the right prong must sail south to the apex of the formation before he could tack and sail north after the enemy. Perhaps the battle would end, or the Spanish join, or worse still escape, while he was still following, performing his duty, obeying orders governed by court-martial and hanging.

And while the English line formed its magnificent disciplined V, the Spanish in no form at all were tacking up the Atlantic just out of reach. The ships that had been the rear of their fleet now led all the others in flying retreat. Still their northerly direction was not favorable to their escape until with a gust, like a maniac's laugh from the sky, they started to come about, and scud before the wind straight for Spain—behind the long English V.

Nelson pivoted on the deck, eyes peering ahead for Jervis—for some instant signal. The Spanish would cross behind him, perhaps join their sisters, and be out of reach before Troubridge got into battle; make port in Cádiz, while Nelson must by order sail south and then north and then east—a matter of hours! The smart English line was still making its V, but not gaining on the Dons. No line could be broken. The fleet that hated Jervis's dictatorship but submitted to it was carrying out his signal to the letter: Vainglorious discipline. Still, for a split second more the *Captain* sailed south and Nelson's eyes stared back at the Dons, then ahead at the damnable V formation.

There was Troubridge's *Culloden* just coming up almost opposite him in the other direction. Nelson and Troubridge were nearly poised on the prongs of the V.

"Wear ship!" Nelson shouted at Miller, his voice crackling.

Miller yelped out his orders—unquestioningly. . . . The *Captain* broke the sacred line. The ship in her wake, the *Diadem,* rushed on by, eyes forward, uninfluenced by Nelson's madness, and the *Excellent,* with Collingwood gaping and then waving both arms at him, was coming up, but there was a space in the line: *Captain* shot across *Excellent's* bow.

"Steer for the enemy center, Captain Miller!" And *Captain* was down on the fleeing Dons, holding them there to fight, plunging into their midst, until the fleet could arrive. The last of the English line was now first into battle, hurled on the heels of the Spanish. The last of the Spanish, that had been the first, now challenged *Captain's* 74 guns. They were: *Santissima Trinidad* 130; *San Josef* 112; *Salvador del Mundo* 112; *San Nicolas* 80, and three others held by the *Captain* slipping her leash.

Aboard *Barfleur:*

"The *Captain* has put her helm down!"

Waldegrave was eating young Parsons's orange; he spoke as he swallowed a mouthful: "Only in the wind, she will box off directly."

But she did not.

Aboard *Victory,* Calder to Jervis: "Sir! The *Captain* and *Culloden* are separated from the fleet and unsupported; shall we recall them?"

Jervis: "No! I put my faith in those ships; it is a disgrace that they are not supported and separated. Signal *Excellent* to assist Commodore Nelson!"

And Ben Hallowell winked at Calder.

The *Excellent* wore, the instant the signal flew, as the *Captain,* all guns firing, disappeared in the canyons of Spanish, among the baffled Goliaths. And at last, Troubridge in *Culloden* came smashing through to join the self-made leader; put his ship between Nelson and the biggest Spanish, moved on, after giving *Captain* ten minutes' respite. Then Collingwood's *Excellent*. Three ships lost from sight of the disrupted V; swallowed in smoke and in glory.

❋   ❋   ❋

First *Captain,* then *Culloden,* then *Excellent*. But separated. Then Frederick in *Blenheim* came; all surrounded with Dons, broadsides to broadsides, both sides at once, with other Dons lying off, firing into them when they could. Until in the smoke no one knew if the first two, *Captain* and *Culloden,* floated.

The blast and the crashing jar of recoils. And the masts toppled down. Ropes and sails vanished from spars and yardarms; chunks of lumber seemed to float in the air. The high screams of the wounded, the low penetrating groans of the dying, to the slam of the cannon leaping back on their breechings.

Aboard *Captain* a ball took half a marine and his blood geysered. A splinter slit an arm like a sleeve, showed a white bone, hid it in a flood of red.

And the Commodore, pacing his deck, knew he had brought on the battle, but might drown with his ship, hammered to pieces under his feet. And the hoarse cheers of the gunners, yelling and yelling, hardly conscious of it. The sudden quivering leap of a wounded man, and more sand on the deck. More sand to prevent slipping in blood. The Commodore doubled up.

Could not breathe. While someone grabbed him, started him toward the cockpit, he straightened up. Caught his breath. Something had hit him in the belly, but he wasn't bleeding. He brushed anxious hands off; went on pacing.

Closing down on the *Captain* was the *San Nicolas* 80, almost pushing her was *San Josef* 112, while circling round but more distant— three others. In sulphurous fumes, black powder-streaked faces, whole walls of smoke hiding targets. Something lifted the Commodore's cocked hat from his scalp. Miller returned it to him. There was not much left to it, but back it went on his head.

And thunder and recoil the *Captain* fought back until the helm and the men at the helm disappeared, blown God knows where; leaving a trail of blood as they smashed through the bulwark; wood and flesh all together.

The *Captain* wallowed but her guns still held off the Dons, though her men dropped, smears of red. No time to count. They were replaced. The Commodore nodded. And then the replacements were wiped out.

Time stretched out of all reason, life had always been now. No past. No future. Now.

"There's Coll!"

In a rift of the smoke, a flash of the Union Jack and *Excellent's* bows. She was raking as she rolled in; knocked one out on her way: *San Ysidro* hauled down her flag. Collingwood did not stop for prizes, but bore down to rescue his friends.

The Dons farthest from *Captain* fell away as the *Excellent* came. Only two ships, *San Josef* and *San Nicolas,* hung on their English prey; sure of one victim between them.

Prow around came the *Excellent* aiming for *San Nicolas,* where her guns might bear full without striking Nelson.

Excellent came like a sled through thick woods. Grazing *San Nicolas,* Collingwood hauled up: the water disappeared between ships. *Excellent* fired her broadsides, muzzle to muzzle, ten feet from *San Nicolas;* sailed on, picking the bird she would wing: Collingwood's *Excellent* 74 attacked *Santissima Trinidad* 130.

The *San Nicolas* had heeled over, staggered by *Excellent's* blow, sails luffing, wind shaken out, caved in on her larboard side. She rolled, and *San Josef,* bearing down to strike Nelson, crashed the *San Nicolas.* Rigging and spars and bowsprit locked in a grinding smash.

"Lay us aboard!" The Commodore whirled on Miller. But there was no wheel and the order was howled down into the depth of the *Captain* where men grappled the relieving tackles below deck. And *Captain,* with rags left to sail her, rolled around.

"Volunteers stand by to board!" as her grappling hooks laid into *San Nicolas's* chains.

Nelson and Miller sprinted to the side, leaped on the bulwark. One of Pierson's marines swung the butt of his musket, shattered the glass in the Dons' quarter gallery window. Nelson and Miller both lunged for the hole.

"No, Miller! *I* must have the honor!" The Commodore went ahead. Miller stood stunned, left behind. Turned, rounded up crews of fresh men, had them ready to reinforce Nelson.

And leaping down from the window sill into the Spaniard's soft polished cabin, a sudden muffled stillness. Enclosed. The battle thundering overhead, Nelson, sword in hand with his marines and his old *Agamemnons* armed with pistols and flashing pikes, cutlasses dangling from the beckets on their wrists, rushed the door. The cabin was locked.

The Spaniards were firing through the windows and down through the skylight. A jack crashed dead, shot through the head.

"Sykes—Fearney—down with the door! Westminster Abbey or Victory!" the Commodore chanted again and again as bare shoulders crashed the door.

Nelson stood face to face with the Spanish Commodore commanding his ship. A pistol cracked; the Spaniard fell dying, rolling convulsively across the deck, while the other Spanish officers retreated and

a storm of bullets spattered in all directions. Step by step the Spanish
retreated and more of Nelson's jacks fell.

Still the Commodore and his picked jacks advanced. The *Agamemnons,* half naked, barefoot, discharged their pistols, hurled them down,
swung their cutlasses and their pikes like reapers.

And an English "Huzza!" above them. Nelson jerked his head up.
There was Berry! Commanding the Spaniard's poop deck! His beautiful face flushed with glory. Berry had crawled up the enemy mizzen
chains; first on board. He was hauling down the Don's flag. Had an
armful of it clasped to his chest. All glimpsed in an instant. "Bravo,
Berry! Forward, lads!"

Nelson and Pierson pressed on. They must take the whole ship. The
marines and the jacks rushed the larboard gangway over the waist to
the forecastle. Met another cluster of English jacks who had come up
over the side, stood holding the ladders, keeping the Spaniards below
deck. They had three Spanish officers surrounded, waiting and bowing to the Commodore; extending the hilts of their swords. *San
Nicolas* was Nelson's.

"Post sentinels at all ladders."

But the *San Josef* 112, all entangled in *San Nicolas's* rigging, was
still firing on the deck; she had not struck yet. Her sides rose like a
fortress above them as she shuddered and rolled, grinding against *San
Nicolas;* pounded on the other side by every English ship that passed
her.

Her muskets ran out her gallery windows, raked the English on
San Nicolas. Allen fell. Nelson hailed *Captain:*

"Ahoy! Oh, Captain Miller, send more men to hold *San Nicolas!*"
He spun back, and flashing his sword at the wall of *San Josef,* "Come,
lads, board her!" And he led them.

Berry was beside him now, dashing for the next ship. Berry loped
past the Commodore! Leaped in the ship's chains, clung there, leaning
back, caught Nelson's hand, pulling him up. Nelson's face was gray
and fleetingly he remembered he had been hurt, that something had
hit him back on *Captain* ten thousand years ago. But Berry, all monkey, was scrambling up ahead of the Commodore. Their hands and
feet slipped on the chains, but they seemed to be someone else's hands
and feet, they were only watching themselves in a dream of thunder
and hell, as their stranger hands gripped, clambered on.

"We surrender!" A Don leaned out above them, and they thought he was going to shoot, but he was holding up his hands.

"Thank God!" Nelson gasped as Berry and he made the deck and saw what a giant ship they had tackled. The decks swept away forever into the clouds of smoke, the masts soared to heaven. But their crew! Men cringing against the bulwarks, hands clasped on crosses, or clamped white to a cleat, sobbing in terror. The Spanish officers were bowing stiffly, faces set. One officer stepped forward, held out a short ornate sword with a rectangular hilt; a corner of the Commodore's mind noted it was somewhat Arabian. "Pierson, talk to him."

"He says the Admiral Don Xavier Winthuysen is dying below. This is his sword, sir."

But the Commodore could scarcely believe that a ship which carried a thousand men was his. "Ask him on his honor if the ship surrenders?"

"*Sí, señor.*" The Captain, his face tragic, bowed once again. The Commodore shook hands with him.

"Ask him to summon his officers and ship's company and tell them this ship has surrendered."

The Spaniard bowed, then stiffened as they came up from below. A dark, terrified, bewildered crowd falling over each other, misunderstanding their orders, turning about. They heard the news without understanding the agony on the Don Captain's face. "Snatched up from anywhere just two weeks ago. They know nothing." An officer turned sadly to Pierson. "What could we do? Some were willing but couldn't obey even if they tried. When the first guns were fired they went to pieces, down on their knees begging us, *señor,* not to send them aloft to tend sails! We have eighty old seamen in the whole crew."

He spoke wearily as the thunder of battle went on beyond the clouds of smoke. Orange lights burst against the gray winter sky. Commodore Nelson, turning about, saw English ships everywhere. There came the *Prince George,* Rear Admiral Parker. They hailed each other, as high on the deck of *San Josef* he looked back: down upon the *San Nicolas,* down upon the *Captain,* stump masted, wallowing: the fightingest ship of the day. Behind him his jacks drew their breath, watched him; some grinned through big splashing tears, the old ones who remembered *Agamemnon.*

As the Spaniards stepped forward one at a time, bowed to the small, thin young man with the brilliant gray eyes; one eye staring slightly harder, darker than the other, out of a smoke-streaked face. In his dusty tattered blue coat and what was left of white breeches and stockings. He was not smiling as they held out their swords to him. Taking them, he gave them in turn to his bargeman, Fearney. Suddenly the Commodore's lips twitched into a smile, life swung back to normal. Fearney's *sang-froid!* The bargeman was tucking the swords under his arm; holding out his hand for the next, as if it were nothing to see two battleships, a one hundred twelve and an eighty, surrender to his Commodore.

Leaving men to hold *San Josef,* Nelson started back to the *Captain.* A rough hand caught his, wrung it.

"Begging your pardon, sir." It was John Sykes, his coxswain. "I may never have another chance to take your hand; and hearty glad I am to do it now, sir!" And he wrung it again and again, trying to snuffle back his tears as he smiled. "Forgive me, sir, but God bless you!"

That was sweeter than surrendered swords. He had won his men. Down he climbed to the *Captain* to see what could be done to continue the battle. But *Captain* could not sail till repaired.

There was Miller, glued to the quarter-deck, obedient if his heart broke. Nelson caught his arm, impulsively led him down to his cabin. He took up one of the surrendered swords, pressed it in Miller's hands. "I'm under obligation to you, Miller!" He stepped back as Miller, speechless at the present, stared up in surprise. Had it not been enough? The Commodore wrenched off his ring and put it on Miller's finger. "I can't thank you enough, Miller!"

Now there came cheers as they went back on deck. The last of their fleet going by . . . There came Jervis in *Victory.* Had the time been so long? Or so short? But it was late afternoon.

And the *Victory's* crew was waving at *Captain,* cheering her and her two mighty prizes, and one by one the rest of the ships went by cheering *Captain,* as if each ship held a voice in her, singing out, fading, and the next coming up took up the exultant chant.

But the *Captain* was done for the day. The crews were sloshing buckets of water over the deck, washing the blood away from the cannon. Nelson gripped Miller's hand once again. Now *La Minerve,* a courier in the battle, was ranging alongside, sending a boat to take Commodore Nelson to the *Irresistible,* which could still sail. It was, perhaps, only then, that gazing about on the dead and the dying, knowing he'd lost a hundred and forty of them; staring at the slippery blasted deck, hearing the wails and the shrieks from the surgeon's cockpit, the Commodore remembered he was mortal. But he was alive and the spell of glory was strong: victory heady. Life was transcended! With the music of thundering cannons and enemy flags hauled down. His face was mystical, ecstatic.

"Will you patent it, sir?" Captain Berry, once more deliberate, held out his hand.

"Patent what, my dear Berry?" Nelson suddenly clapped his arm around Berry's shoulder. "Berry! My lucky Berry! First to board, God bless you!"

"Your new bridge over *San Nicolas* to the *San Josef*, sir. I think we should call it Nelson's patent bridge for boarding First Rates."

❈ ❈ ❈

It was too late to continue the battle, even from the *Irresistible*. The Spanish were fleeing, and rather than chase with his ships in battered condition, Jervis decided to secure the enemy ships already taken. It was done and that Valentine's Day near an end.

As the firing ceased, Commodore Nelson, his face still blackened except for his eyelids and his teeth flashing now and then in a smile, his shirt and coat mangled, only half a cocked hat perched athwart his blackened white head, was conscious again that he had received an awful blow in the abdomen. It might have been a chunk of wood. Iron would probably have disemboweled him. And he wasn't bleeding, though the doctor checking the bruises said he might be injured internally—but that didn't count. So he crawled wearily up the gangway, boarding the *Victory* to present the Commander in Chief with the swords he had taken. Yet as soon as he stepped on *Victory's* deck the excitement was on him again, bruises forgotten.

Sir John Jervis was there, blood-soaked and black as a slave, exultant among his officers. He stepped forward with drunken impulse of victory, caught Nelson in his arms, hugged him to his clammy blood-spattered shirt front.

"You're wounded, Sir John!"

"Not a bit! Stood too close to some poor devil marine . . . My dear Nelson, how can I ever thank you! *You,* you alone saved the day!" And once more Jervis's ape-strong arms bathed his protégé in his red embrace, nearly lifted him off his feet. The Commodore felt a twinge like a knife where he had been hit, but it was worth being mauled like a puppy to find Jervis so jubilant.

Ben Hallowell was there, wringing his hand with all the strength of a Canadian lumberjack, pounding him on the back.

And as Commodore Nelson presented the swords with all the dignity half a cocked hat and a black face could command, his Admiral put the swords back in his hands. While around *Victory* lay the English fleet, honorably tattered in the waning light, a bigger fleet than at dawn with its four beaten prizes in tow.

"No, no, my dear Nelson, you must keep the swords!" And over and over again for all to hear, the words of the disciplinarian: "My dear Nelson, I cannot sufficiently thank you!"

The words still rang in Nelson's ears as he went overside, back to his temporary ship.

It was just as well he did not hear the chill voice of Calder turning on Jervis, for Nelson would hear soon enough from his friends: "But was not Commodore Nelson's action, sir, in direct disobedience to your prescribed mode of attack?"

The other officers looked at each other, no one spoke, as Jervis studied Calder. Excitement, exhaustion and jealousy in Calder's intelligent but not brilliant eyes.

"It certainly was so!" Jervis's twisted face smiled inwardly. "And if *you* ever commit such a breach of *your* orders, I will forgive *you* also!"

Calder bowed, tried to smile, as he turned scarlet, cut to the heart when he had only meant to cut Nelson's throat.

But the moment had reminded Jervis of duty. He went to his cabin to write his report to the Admiralty.

He was Commander in Chief again, camaraderie forgotten. He thought for some time, quill over the paper. Here before him, on this piece of paper, he was about to recount the first naval victory of the Mediterranean fleet since the war started. Fifteen battleships had attacked twenty-seven and taken four Spanish of line, including two First Rate battleships!

Salvador del Mundo 112, *San Josef* 112, *San Nicolas* 80, *San Ysidro* 74.

Santissima Trinidad was reported to have flown a white flag, but rehoisted her colors as soon as the English stopped firing into her, and escaped.

The English had not lost any ships. But two of the Spanish ships had surrendered to one man. And that man had disobeyed orders, broken the English line, held the enemy to fight when his, Jervis's, plan had failed.

As a mortal man, a proud man, as a disciplinarian, what could he say to do justice to Nelson and still be Commander in Chief of his fleet: mainspring of victory? Words of praise for Nelson had been flowing from his pen since the first day they met, and harsh condemnation of other officers had flowed just as freely. He usually said exactly what he thought, in detail, without mincing matters or sparing his listeners. Tonight his pen sputtered even as he wrote the date. He took a fresh sheet of paper.

This victory meant a peerage for him. He was ambitious and he loved power. He was getting old. Perhaps he would not have an opportunity to fight again. Soon he must retire into, he hoped, the Admiralty. . . .

As Commander in Chief he wrote his dispatch in emulation of Caesar. How he found the enemy, then:

. . . His Majesty's Squadron . . . happily formed in the most compact order of sailing in two lines. By carrying a press of sail I was fortunate in getting in with the Enemy's Fleet at half-past eleven o'clock, before it had time to connect. . . . Such a moment was not to be lost; and confident in the skill, valor, and discipline of the Officers and Men I had the happiness to command, and judging that the honor of his Majesty's arms, and the circumstances of the War in these seas, required a considerable degree of enterprise, I felt myself justified in departing from the regular system; and, passing through their fleet in a line formed with utmost celerity, tacked and thereby separated one third from the main body, after a partial cannonade, which prevented their re-junction till the evening; and by the very great exertions of the Ships which had the *good fortune* to arrive up with the Enemy on the larboard tack, the ships named in the margin were captured, and the Action ceased about five o'clock in the evening. . . .

Captain Calder, whose able assistance has greatly contributed to the public service during my command, is the bearer of this, and will more particularly describe to the Lords Commissioners of the Admiralty the movements of the Squadron. . . .

And that was that. He had written a masterpiece, for he neither lied nor told the truth, but hid in a fog of honorable obscurities. And

he gave no thanks, not one word of praise, except the standard intro-
duction of Calder, to any officer or man in his fleet. Not even to his
Vice-Admirals and Rear Admirals! For he would take victory as he had
taken Nelson, into his arms, and keep it there.

As he folded and sealed the dispatch he was satisfied: he had
washed his hands of his officers. It would temper Nelson, if anything
could, to find rank insubordination, however heroic, unapplauded officially. It would temper the storm in Calder's nature to find himself
mentioned. Discipline. His mind relaxed, for once he had a peerage,
plus all the prize money from his command which he always considered his alone, refusing to comply with the ridiculous custom of
sharing it with his flag officers, he dreamed of becoming a Knight of
the Garter as other men dreamed of women.

In a private letter to the Admiralty, not to be published, he might
guardedly mention his newest favorite, Troubridge, who was not a
nerve-racking prima donna, like Nelson, and, of course, he would
mention Nelson. That young man was remarkably useful to him.

❋   ❋   ❋

While Nelson, with the sword of an Admiral Don across his writing desk, tried to write Fanny; gave up. He was too sick from his
bruises. He went to bed. A few days later: "I shall come laughing back
to you, the Admiral's dispatches will tell all, I am sure, so I need not
relate it. . . ."

And Tom Allen lay in the cockpit of *Captain,* groaning from the
wounds he sustained trying to keep close to his headstrong master.

But Captain Miller, somehow, found time the night of battle, and
the imperturbable spirit, to make a drawing of *Captain* laying aboard
San Nicolas and *San Josef:* for posterity. For without anyone sensing
it, other than in his constant creative attention to his command,
Miller too had a sense of destiny—a desire to record what he did in
minute and exacting detail. So he made drawings and wrote very long
letters to his wife, cautioning her to keep them always as *his* record,
for someday . . .

Captain Miller bent to his drawing, lovingly rebuilding the battle,
in a visual pattern, massing the ships; to the last shred of canvas,
masts gone by the board. As if in all the turmoil of commanding, there
had been an inner eye watching the whole. . . . When he showed it
to the Commodore, Nelson marveled that Miller had so many talents,

and he begged it from Miller to send it aboard the *Lively* frigate, to Sir Gilbert Elliot.

And aboard the *Lively* frigate that night there was exuberant talk as she waited for Captain Calder to come aboard with the dispatches for England.

Colonel Drinkwater sat taking notes as the others talked and gasped again at the sight of one lone English ship wearing out of the line; attacking a whole fleet of the enemy.

Sir Gilbert turned on the Colonel, almost annoyed at his silence. "Colonel, drink to our glorious victory!"

The Colonel tossed his notes on the table. "To have been an eye-witness, Sir Gilbert! An eyewitness! It calls for another history! With a new hero."

Sir Gilbert smiled. "I'll bear you witness. I've known Commodore Nelson for several years. . . . It will amuse me to tell it again and again. What an anecdote! It utterly annihilates what Johnson said about Charles V and the candle!"

Brogio's head came up slowly, as if a voice had suddenly spoken in his ear. "Did I ever tell you, Sir Gilbert, Paoli's philosophy on death: 'It is impossible not to be afraid of death; those who at the time of dying are not afraid, are not thinking of death, but of applause, *or something else,* which keeps death out of their sight: so all men are equally afraid of death when they see it; *only some have the power of turning their sight away from it. . . .'*"

But no one remembered old "Coll"—except Nelson, who wrote Collingwood immediately: "A friend in need is a friend indeed!" And Collingwood wrote back:

MY DEAR GOOD FRIEND,
First let me congratulate you on the success of yesterday, on the brilliancy it attached to the British navy, and the humility it must cause to its enemies; and then let me congratulate my dear Commodore on the distinguished part which he ever takes when the honor and interest of his Country are at stake. It added very much to the satisfaction which I felt in thumping the Spaniards, that I released you a little. The highest rewards are due to you and *Culloden; you formed the plan of attack,*—we were only accessories to the Dons ruin. . . . You saw the four decker [*Santissima Trinidad*] going off this morning to Cádiz, she should have come to Lagos [Portugal], to make things better, but we could not brace our yards up to get nearer. . . .

And on the day after battle, the Commodore went to the *Lively* frigate to say good-by to Sir Gilbert, but not finding him, for he'd gone to the *Victory,* Commodore Nelson was not in the least sorry to give an interview to Colonel Drinkwater and Colonel Drinkwater's notebook.

And while the English limped toward Lagos, Portugal, and the Dons limped into Cádiz, a few of the officers in the fleet who in the moment of victory shouted their cheers to Nelson as they, too, fought hard began to talk among themselves, band together, although the majority, like Hallowell and Collingwood, sang high praises and thought Nelson's insubordination was a damn good joke on old Jervis. Still, some began to suspect that Nelson's heroics would overshadow them all. They admitted what he had done was amazing, and it was not the fact that he boarded two ships, with the help of his friends' broadsides, that secretly annoyed them, but the fact, the very thing Calder had pointed out, blustered to Jervis: disobedience. Nelson had dared what none of them dreamed of daring: he had risked more than his life—which all of them risked every day—he had risked the disgrace of court-martial, perhaps hanging, to bring about victory for England. They admired it, marveled, but they felt cheated. They had obeyed orders, the first principle of being an officer, and had been ready to die, honorably applauded. It was that difference in Nelson, that something more than death, they could not understand. And they resented it, for in spite of being officers and honorable Englishmen, they were born men.

❊ ❊ ❊

But the nights following the battle kept every man taut. Fifty years later, Midshipman Parsons, grown old and retired, could still repeat the scene that had been etched in his brain:

We anchored in Battle order in this open Bay and in the evening a gale of wind came in from the sea . . . most of the ships with their sheet anchor down and some with the spare one. In the *Barfleur* we were pitching bows under, with three anchors ahead; one mile astern of us extended a reef of rocks on which the sea broke frightfully, and through which there appeared no opening; half a mile within them lay a populous village of fishermen and they expected a Godsend by the wreck of the whole fleet, they had gone through the trouble of collecting wood and burning fires through the night.

"Ship ahead driving," called the forecastle lieutenant.

"God help us!" I heard the Captain piously ejaculate. "Lower-deck, there, stand by, to veer on the three cables at the same time—place the helm hard a starboard." . . . And the Commander-in-Chief, *Victory,* passed our starboard side close, driving fast upon the rocks to leeward, which shook off the heavy sea, throwing its white spray to the clouds. There was an agonized cry of horror, and, "O God! Save her!" as this beautiful fabric hastened on destruction. We heard her last effort, as her spare anchor flashed in the briny flood and, thank God, she brought up with four anchors a-head. Never shall I forget the sight, as I caused our stern and top lanterns to be relighted. The roaring of the wind and rain, the bellowing noise of the officers' trumpets, the booming of numerous guns of distress, the roar of the breakers so near us astern, and the ghastly reflection of the surf and fires ashore—all, all are imprinted on my memory to the year in which I write. . . .

❀   ❀   ❀

There was always a lull following a battle and a gale, a vacuum in time when both fleets reeled off to recover. As if a giant hand had disarranged an intricate puzzle and for a little while both sides must scurry about, seeking the pieces, putting them back that they might begin again.

As the pieces were tossed back into the heap, first one and then another seemed the key piece wanting to finish the game. Until as the weeks went by and so many new clues, new points and distractions appeared that disappointment set in; a feeling that all that had happened was a disruption that had had nothing to do with the game in the end. And that was an illusion also, for the Battle of St. Vincent was more than a valiant show, though less of a strategic victory than the exaltation of the moment had made it appear. But it opened eyes. It proved that numbers, when inspired by genius, did not need to be matched ship for ship.

"When I think what I did . . . I am astonished; it absolutely appears a *dream* . . ." Nelson wrote again and again.

And Fanny wrote one of the sweetest letters of her life, all aflutter and slightly mixed as to who had been wounded in the battle, herself or her husband:

My dearest Husband,

Yesterday I received your letter of February 16th. Thank God you are well and Josiah. My anxiety was far beyond my powers of expression.

Maurice Nelson and Captain Locker behaved humanely, and attentive to me. They wrote immediately, Captain Locker assuring me you were perfectly well, Maurice begging me not to believe idle reports, the *Gazette* saying you were slightly wounded. Altogether, my dearest husband, my sufferings were great. Lady Saumarez came running to tell me she had Letters from her husband—all this was on this day week. He speaks generously and manly about you, and concluded by saying, "Commodore Nelson's conduct is above praise." You were universally the subject of conversation. . . . I shall not be myself till I hear from you again. What can I attempt to say to you about Boarding? You have been most wonderfully protected; you have done desperate actions enough. Now may I—indeed I do—beg that you never Board again. *Leave* it for *Captains*. How rejoiced Jo. must have been to have seen you, although it was but an absence of two months. Tomorrow is our wedding day, when it gave me a dear husband, my child the best of fathers. . . . Do come home this summer, or in the autumn. It is said a change in Administration would certainly have taken place, had not this wonderful and fortunate victory taken place. Admiral Parker, it seems, had written the *Captain* and *Culloden* bore the brunt of the Action. This instant have I received a letter from Lord Hood, telling me Sir Robert Calder was gone to Portsmouth. Thank you my dearest husband, a thousand times for your letter. God bless and protect you, and my Jo.—crown all your endeavors with success, and grant us a happy meeting. I can bear all my extreme good fortune.

Your affectionate Wife,
FRANCES H. NELSON

So the battle began to take its place as part of the game: one corner of the puzzle had been scattered and resolved in a different pattern.

But on the crest of success and Jervis's selfish dispatch came laurels: An earldom for Sir John Jervis, now to be known as Earl St. Vincent. Three staggering leaps in the peerage. And baronetcies for the flag officers. And a knighthood for Captain Calder, First Captain of the Fleet. And for Nelson, for he flew a Distinguishing Pendant? He was offered a hereditary baronetcy, but refused, explaining to the wife who had borne him no children and to his family:

I have declined all hereditary Honors, and as to entailing a title, unless you have a good estate to send with it, you send misery . . . until now I had not made both ends meet . . . chains and medals are what no fortune or connection in England can obtain; I shall feel prouder of those than all the Titles in the King's power to bestow. . . .

For Nelson then: the coveted recognition of knighthood—the star and the ribbon to wear. A "Sir" for himself, and a "Ladyship" for his wife.

But a vision of what he might do if he were to command a squadron in battle, or a whole fleet, for so long just a man's promise to his wife, had now become a reality. His name had finally crept up through the lists, his promotion to flag rank, and the promise of continued active service, had been on its way to him at the time of the battle.

Rear Admiral Nelson, now.

But what had the battle accomplished besides Jervis's earldom and the delirious love letters from English ladies: "Jervis—my Valentine!"

The Spanish fleet was crippled at the very outset of her alliance with France, shut up in Cádiz instead of reinforcing the French fleet. Very good. But the French were rumored to be sending reinforcements to Spain! Threatening Earl St. Vincent with a combined force of forty of line.

Home in England the battle had raised the spirits of people when they were cold, hungry and discouraged, impoverished by the long and, so far, not very victorious war. Raised all but the Irish who were already up, threatening to open their harbors to a French army of "liberation." And something was rotten in the idle fleets around England. Mutiny at Spithead. Outside of that all was contentment at home, though as Fanny's letter had pointed out, Pitt's ministry had been tottering and Jervis's battle had strengthened him. It was a bitter pill: Jervis hated Pitt.

And the French? That young Buonaparte, not even thirty years old, was having the audacity to close on Vienna. England no longer hoped for Austria to remain allied.

So the Battle of St. Vincent was but part of the game; it had given England a chance to catch her breath, but the stakes were as high as ever, unless Lord Malmesbury did effect a peace: either a satisfactory peace must be made, or England or France must fall, for until England fell France would have difficulties ruling a continent, and until France fell, England had announced she would not stop fighting to hold her place in the world.

But above all, the battle gave the English people a focal point for their emotions: a hero. Colonel Drinkwater and Sir Gilbert had kept their promises, told the truth; they were too impressed with having been eyewitnesses to withhold it. And they liked Nelson after that trip down from Elba.

And Nelson, who had held his peace for four years, except to his friends and his family, now took one look at Jervis's dispatch, sat back crushed. It was too much. Not trusting Sir Gilbert or Drinkwater to do any better by him, he wrote his own account of the battle, sent it to Jervis—who approved it! Then Nelson planned to send it to his old Captain, Locker, with a hint that, if he chose, he might publish it by changing the "I's" to "the Commodore." . . . First, though, Captain Miller must sign it.

So the English people heard from all sides that their hero was born at St. Vincent. The man, they said, in the first flush of enthusiasm, to stand beside Hawkins and Drake, for the people still talked wistfully of England's past glories, and deplored the present of hard work, hunger, poverty and toil and more toil. England had been great once, and they were glad to revive their memories; she would go down fighting in the spirit of her past. Some even revived the old legend that a hero always arose when England faced a crisis.

"Sir H.N. and his brave Captain Miller who took the Dons on St. Valentine's Day!" They sang it everywhere. The great could have their Earl St. Vincent, but the people had Sir H.N.

In Spain the Dons eyed him shrewdly: *fiero terror del mar!*

❊   ❊   ❊

"Until the next battle!" Rear Admiral Nelson spun a gold Spanish dollar on the table in his cabin; tossed it to Troubridge. "Take the mobility there in Spain."

"I beg your pardon?" Troubridge was examining the gold coin, polishing it with his palm.

"The mobility, Troubridge. The mob on the walls of Cádiz at this moment jeering their fleet to come out and fight us. Yet we saw what those Spanish officers were given to fight with."

"It's their own damn stupidity—declaring war on us," Troubridge glowered. "Did you read their dispatches to their King? 'The battle being fought in such heavy fog: when it cleared at the close of the day they could count but fifteen left of the English: therefore, may it please His So-and-So, the Spanish might justifiably claim they had sunk at least ten of the great English fleet.'" Troubridge leaned back in his chair guffawing until the chair creaked and the whole cabin quaked. "The lying cowards!" Troubridge, being deaf, made much noise.

Nelson nodded. "Ah, they were shooting at ghosts. Never mind, it isn't their honor that mortifies the mob and the merchants of Cádiz, it's those—" and he pointed at the gold coin. "Seven million pounds in gold, Troubridge, coming from Vera Cruz, Havana, Lima, and Manila while we blockade their fleet in Cádiz. Seven million pounds in three galleons all alone on the ocean!"

Troubridge held the dollar to the sun setting through the slanting windows that gave Rear Admiral Nelson's cabin a feeling of greater space than the small floor area warranted.

"Right on the King's neck." Troubridge pointed at the image of George III newly cut on the King of Spain's throat, for England's treasury was depleted; England was now issuing foreign specie to bolster her shortage of minted coin; calling for contributions from the people to be able to go on fighting.

"What's the new jingle? How does it go?" The Admiral thought a moment, then:

> The additional head on the dollar impressed
> Is to circulate Jervis's fame;
> To his valor, 'tis owing, it must be confessed,
> England made an impression on Spain!

He clapped his hands together, rubbed them, and did a quick turn about the room laughing.

But Troubridge only scowled at Nelson's capers. His friend was very high-spirited since the Battle of St. Vincent, and becoming a Rear Admiral and a Knight to boot. He hadn't been knighted yet, but it had been announced, and they were so far from home his friends had already started calling him Sir Horatio; for no one knew when a ceremony could be arranged, even with Jervis, Lord St. Vincent, acting as King's proxy. St. Vincent hadn't gone through his ceremony yet either. Troubridge's scowl deepened. There'd be a lot of pomp and fuss. "A lot of good the treasure ships will do us! You didn't find them when you took that quick running search a few weeks ago, and now if this special squadron sent out from home under Lord Seymour intercepts them not one penny of prize money will come to our fleet for guarding his way. Someone pulls a string, seats or unseats someone, and is given the chance to sail out, make a fortune, while we hold off a Combined enemy rumored to be more than double our numbers. I never thought they would do that to Sir John—Lord St. Vincent —or *you*, Sir Horatio!"

Nelson had winced slightly. He had been given a chance to hunt but been recalled to blockade before he could do a thorough job. Even so, it goaded him to have missed the ships.

"Very handsome of them, Troubridge, leaving us to spend our blood in opposing so superior a force. Let them share with us our dangers, share our honors, and share with us the wealth that may come forward. What a mark of favor to our good fleet! On the other hand, Troubridge, I have been thinking. Let them seek . . . There is a persistent rumor out of Spain that the Dons' treasure ships gave this privileged squadron sent out to get rich—the slip. The rumor is that the treasure has gone to the island of Santa Cruz de Teneriffe down off the African coast. They say they have put in there rather than risk running our blockade. If so, Captain Troubridge . . . ?"

Troubridge stood up, rubbed his hands. "Would we undertake a small expedition?" He caught himself. Nelson was no longer an equal. "Forgive me, sir." He was so blunt by nature, and even grown a little fatter, yet he said it so obsequiously that Nelson was hurt.

It had never occurred to him that on rising in rank he would leave old friends behind. The solitary splendor of absolute power meant nothing to him; he was too sensitive to enjoy it. Here was his *boyhood* friend scraping to him, the next thing friends would be hating him and that was unbearable. Being a hero meant winning acclaim— and acclaim meant being loved—didn't it?

"My dear Troubridge! You're my right arm! I depend on your judgments more than you realize, my friend! Who else could have led so magnificently as you did on Valentine's Day!"

"You're too generous, sir!" Troubridge had smiled slowly, his face turning red.

"Would we attack Santa Cruz, Troubridge? Aye, providing Lord St. Vincent says we may go ahead. I've practically got his permission, and you talk to him too. He thinks the world of you!"

"If Hardy could sail in there t'other day, we can!" Troubridge had relaxed.

"Hardy? What would you have given to have seen Lieutenant

Hardy row into Santa Cruz right under the Dons' fire, cut out a prize, and sail out of Santa Cruz: Captain Hardy of the *Mutine* brig! God bless that man, he's splendid!"

"That's one way to rise in rank. Steal an enemy ship for yourself."

"Troubridge, Hardy's made his own way. Hallowell, Cockburn and I have been trying to get him promoted. Now Lord St. Vincent writes me Hardy has no debt to any of us for promotion, 'He has got it by his own bat!' "

"Did Hallowell and Cockburn bring back any information after reconnoitering Santa Cruz? The force there?"

The Admiral had been leaning in the window smiling to himself over Hardy. "Not much we didn't know already. They had no one there to speak of when he attacked." He turned back to Troubridge, face sober, all business. "I'll tell you what we would do—" He sat down, drawing his chair up to the table, just as Allen came thumping in to light the lantern.

Neither Nelson nor Troubridge looked up till Allen thundered, "How do, that was a good beating yow and us gave the Dons, Captain Troubridge."

Troubridge, insulted by the audacity of a servant addressing him, turned purple, clenching his fists.

"You may *go,* Thomas Allen!" Nelson gritted.

Allen gave the last touch to the lantern and with a querulous glance at Troubridge shuffled out. Troubridge still could not speak.

"That monster is an excellent fighter, he was wounded in the battle; he doesn't steal." Nelson smiled slowly at Troubridge. "But he is an incorrigible farmer, my dear Troubridge."

Troubridge suddenly threw back his head. "The fleet's heard of him."

"I ought to get rid of him . . . but I haven't the heart . . ." Nelson raised his eyebrows, shook his head again and bent over the table.

The smoky yellow light of the lantern and the reflection of a golden sea rippling on the beams overhead as the sun went down lent an air of conspiracy to the two heads engrossed in the charts. They made an odd pair: two extremes of determination, counterpoints, like two different types of weapons.

"Back in 1657, you recall," Nelson began, pointing his right forefinger at the chart, "Admiral Blake had a similar problem." He glanced up; the lantern threw a dark shadow over the chart as the golden sunset outside deepened through a bronze gloom into total darkness. He shifted his chair.

"Things have changed in a hundred and forty years. Better ships. Better guns. I wonder how they sailed those little old cockleboats in those days?" Troubridge said.

"But the problem is the same, I believe. Blake went after six Spanish galleons laden with silver—and ten other ships which had put into Santa Cruz. He sailed in, burned them. The treasure went to the bottom of the bay, but if I recollect, Troubridge, he was much obliged to the wind coming suddenly off the land to carry him out again, more than to any exertions of his own." Nelson ran his finger around the chart outlining the bay. "Now I don't pretend to be Admiral Blake, neither do I care to leave success to a chance wind. We do know the Spanish ships generally moor with two cables to sea and four cables from their stern to shore—"

"Cut them adrift, sir? Sail them—oh, but the wind might blow foul," Troubridge said.

"Aye. Although we might get to be masters of them, should the wind *not* come offshore it does not appear certain we should succeed so completely as we might wish. As to any impediments other than the wind . . ." He shrugged.

"A small enemy garrison . . ."

"And Cockburn and Hallowell found nothing there but the usual cannon on the wall when Hardy went in. Captain Thomson's *Leander* has been cruising off there reconnoitering. Thomson's something of an authority on the place."

"And luck was with Blake . . ."

"And Fortune may smile again. True, Troubridge. But let's study the approach: the anchoring place is under very high land, passing three valleys. Therefore the wind is either in from the sea, or equally with calms from the mountains. Sometimes, in a night, a ship may get in with the land wind and moderate weather . . ." The Admiral leaned back, folding his hands. "So much for the sea attack."

"Would you risk it, Sir Horatio?"

"Gamble on the wind?" Nelson sat forward again, shaking his head. "I haven't told you my plan. My plan, Troubridge, could not fail." He tapped the chart. "This is what I have in mind: a plan so perfect that it would immortalize us and ruin Spain!"

"The merchants in Cádiz say better lose ten of their battleships than their gold, sir. But 'twould not be an even exchange. I wouldn't give a tuppence for their filthy ships."

Nelson's smile had grown bigger as Troubridge spoke. "With you as my second, we'd ruin Spain! And raise our country to a higher pitch of wealth than she ever yet attained! For that we must have a master plan."

"An army, sir?"

"Aye—an army. I need an army of thirty-seven hundred men. I need the army from Elba! They could do the business, for with the pressure on Portugal lifted a little by France moving on Vienna, De Burgh is free."

"By God, sir, that would take Teneriffe! See the shore, sir. It's not easy of access from the sea, but it drops off steep—here—so we could run transports right in and land the army—"

"In one day!" Nelson agreed. "Before the Spanish know what we're up to. Surprise and force will mean everything. And I know this: the town water supply runs in wooden troughs from the hills; we cut it off—as an inducement to surrender. We'll make good terms: no molestation whatever providing they give up the treasure." He pursed his lips. "Otherwise total destruction if one gun is fired."

"It's perfect, sir. With our ships laid across the harbor, an army on shore and their parched throats croaking surrender . . ." Troubridge's face was hard as he spoke.

"Ah, but the more powerful and complete our exertions, offering them no alternatives, they would surrender at once. Now we must approach De Burgh. A few redcoats have their use in dazzling the eyes of the enemy. But the army must have some inducement other than public gain, Troubridge. We navy men risk our fame and our lives every day to serve England, but a soldier obeys orders and no more. We will ask St. Vincent to persuade De Burgh. After he presents all the public and honorable inducements to the army to assist us in taking the place, then perhaps we might offer them half the prize money."

"A *whole* half?"

"Aye, make it a generous offer. I know the army. But even if De Burgh, who is due here any day, won't go with us, perhaps we can persuade our naval marines stationed at Gibraltar under General O'Hara. I think he has six hundred Royals . . . We'll drum up a thousand more men somehow. Teneriffe never was besieged before, therefore the hills are not fortified to resist any storming. There is just one battery by the harbor and the Citadel on the other side." Suddenly he laughed. "Who would not fight for dollars, Troubridge?"

"Ah—it's a matter of *honor,* sir, that we take those ships!" Troubridge said solemnly.

Nelson glanced up; his careless joke had been misunderstood. He looked Troubridge in the eye. "I lay my hand on my heart, Troubridge, it *is* the honor and prosperity of our country we wish to extend."

There was a knock on the door. Captain Miller came in, and the uncomfortable moment was forgotten. The Admiral motioned Miller to sit down. "Hear more of my plans to take Teneriffe, Miller."

As Miller folded his elegant length into a chair he mused, "What was it Milton said?

> '. . . Satan alarm'd,
> Collecting all his might, dilated stood,
> Like Teniff . . .' and something else
> And something else, then:
> 'His stature reach'd the sky, and on his crest
> Sat horror plumed . . .'

Nice place, eh?"

"You sound as literary as dear old Collingwood, Miller!" The Admiral smiled. "Yes, the mountain is about twelve thousand two hundred feet. That's back of the town. We don't intend to scale it. Ring the bell, will you please, Miller, for some wine?"

As Miller rang, Troubridge rubbed his face and turned gloomily toward the windows thinking that all Yankees were alike, even loyal New Yorkers like Miller were beyond understanding at times.

As Allen, humbled and silent as an oyster, brought wine, set it down and stalked out, the Admiral took another turn about the cabin. "Meantime, I wonder if De Burgh has left Elba? This old *Captain* ought to be good for one more trip; we can't let thirty-seven hundred men fall into the hands of the French. Then when we get a new ship, Captain Miller, and as soon as we hear the treasure is *safe* in Santa Cruz, then the sooner we take Teneriffe, gentlemen, the sooner we will all be immortal!"

❊   ❊   ❊

When Troubridge had gone back to his ship, Miller took a paper from his pocket and laid it over the charts.

"Berry signed this before going home, sir, and so have I, but you did ask if we had anything to add, sir . . ."

"I did, Miller. My writing always needs a sharp pruning knife." The Admiral picked up his paper: " 'A Few Remarks Relative to Myself in the *Captain* in which my Pendant was Flying on the Most Glorious Valentine's Day, 1797.' Well?"

"Begging your pardon, sir, but Berry was also the first to board the second ship."

"Oh, yes! Yes, so he was! I'm not so fast as Berry in running up chains. I don't think I'll ever recover from that blow in the belly, Miller. I think it wrenched all my insides out of place."

"Perhaps a poultice, sir?" Miller asked very practically.

Nelson eyed him as if for an instant Miller had turned French. He hated medicines. "I attribute my good health to having nothing to do with doctors, Miller!" As he wrote in that Berry had been first, scratched out his own name. "I didn't forget my old messmate Collingwood or my inestimable Troubridge. I've mentioned Fearney and Sykes—Pierson—all my old *Agamemnons*—I wouldn't miss any for the world."

"They won't forget it either, sir. No one will ever forget Fearney's *sang-froid*—and when you should be taking the credit yourself, sir."

"I'll never forget his face. But is there anything more? I *know* I cannot spell—Captain Locker can, however . . ."

Miller hesitated. Nelson had taken him from a frigate to a battleship on his merits alone, for Miller's father had lost his fortune fighting for England during the American war, so Miller was adrift, and Nelson had sent that drawing to Elliot; it would be printed . . . still . . . "Sir Horatio . . . there's nothing more to add, except that it may seem strange to some that I didn't go with the boarding party. Ordinarily it's considered the custom . . ."

"How's this: 'Captain Miller was in the very act of going also, but I directed him to remain.' "

Miller let out his breath. "I appreciate that, sir, a point of honor. And I'm eternally grateful to you for letting me read and sign the paper, sir. I treasure my sword and ring, sir!"

"I have found, Miller, by long hard experience, that if we don't advertise by wearing a star or make ourselves known the admirals have their own reasons—" The brand-new Admiral came to a jolting stop. Folded the letter with its bold, sliding, eliding right-hand slant.

"A thousand thanks for everything, sir!" Miller meant it, as he shook hands, bid him good night.

❈   ❈   ❈

Left alone at last, Rear Admiral Nelson sat down to read a letter from his father while his mind still toyed with the possibilities before him.

Blockade work, right under the Commander in Chief's thumb, was dull; men like Collingwood were more suited to it than himself. And even Collingwood hated it. There was the haunting thought of seven million pounds' treasure that would help stabilize England's treasury, and put himself out of the red for once. Could he persuade De Burgh?

He opened his father's letter: "My dear Rear Admiral . . ." He chuckled. His father and Fanny! Her latest decision about him, after thinking the battle over, was, "You have acquired a character and name which all hands agree cannot be greater; therefore rest satisfied." That's what Fanny had said since rising in rank, God bless her! He had replied to her in a vein which he hoped would quiet her: "Rest assured of my most perfect love, affection, and esteem for your person and character, which the more I see of the world, the more I must admire. The imperious call of honor to serve my Country, is the only thing that keeps me a moment from you, and a hope, that by staying a little longer it may enable you to enjoy those little luxuries which you so highly merit. I pray God it may soon be peace, and that we may get into the cottage" . . . but she still hadn't made up her mind on which cottage to buy.

He took a deep breath and plunged into his father's letter. "My dear Rear—" he had read that.

I thank God with all the power of a grateful soul, for the mercies He has most graciously bestowed on me, in preserving you amidst the imminent perils which so lately threatened your life at every moment; and amongst other innumerable blessings, I must not forget the bounty of Heaven in granting you a mind that rejoices in the practice of those eminent virtues which form great and good characters. Not only my few acquaintants here, but the people in general meet me at every corner with such handsome words, that I was obliged to retire from public eye. A wise Moralist has observed, that even bliss can rise but to a certain pitch; and this has been verified in me. The height of glory to which your professional judgements, united with a proper degree of bravery, guarded by Providence, has raised you, few sons, my dear child, attain to, and fewer fathers live to see—

The Admiral stopped to rest his eye, and instantly he was thinking: if the army would storm Teneriffe—or if not, just the marines—or if not the marines he could count on Troubridge who was worth a hundred soldiers alone, and volunteer seamen and ship's marines. Once he had established the beachhead—but he must finish dear Father's letter:

Tears of joy have involuntarily trickled down my furrowed cheek. . . . The name and services of Nelson have sounded throughout the city of Bath, from the common ballad singer to the public theatre. Joy sparkles in every eye, and desponding Britain draws back her sable veil, and smiles. It gives me inward satisfaction to know, that the laurels you have wreathed sprung from those principles and religious truths which alone constitute the Hero; and though a Civic Crown is all you at present reap, it is to the mind of inestimable value, and I have no doubt will one day bear a golden apple; that field of glory in which you have long been so conspicuous, is still open. May God continue to be your preserver from the arrow that flieth by day, and the pestilence that walketh by night! I am your affectionate father,

EDMUND NELSON

Come, that was splendid! A fighting man needed reinforcements; and he had three reverends in his immediate family blessing him, to say nothing of the more distant relatives, some nine or so connected with the Church in the last fifty years. He locked it away with letters giving him the freedom of Bath, London, Norwich and Bristol. . . . Freedom of cities. The Freedom of London usually came in a gold box. It was like Christmas! Only he hadn't had the freedom to live with his own wife in four years. The most lovely virtuous wife in the world . . . anyway, almost . . . anyway virtuous! And without that what was mere beauty . . . anyway . . . anyway she was his *wife*. And he loved her. Yes, by God, he did love her. He wished he were home. He wished home offered an outlet for ambition. No, he didn't wish he were home—just yet—but he looked forward to it. What home? He didn't have a home! He had a wife and no house. Why not?

He took the key out of his desk abruptly. And he recalled his father's letter: "that field of glory . . . is still open. . . ." That was what he thought, too.

And he never crossed his father. Only once anyway. But that was for dear sister Kitty's sake. He had not agreed with his father that girls should be apprenticed as milliners or seamstresses as soon as they reached their teens. Nor had he been surprised when his two older sisters fled the shops as soon as they worked off their time. He had simply supported Kitty, who broke his heart when he saw her growing up apologizing for her very existence, trying not to be in anyone's way. Given a chance she had married quite well. That was not crossing Father, and even if it was it was the lesser of two evils. And he felt he was *right,* when everything was weighed together. His eldest sister had died young and unmarried.

Now if he could persuade De Burgh . . .

❊   ❊   ❊

A few weeks later: Through the circle of the Rear Admiral's glass the block-shaped white houses of Cádiz seemed just within reach of the ten battleships of his inshore squadron. The houses stood packed together on a projection of land thrust out in the Atlantic, girdled by a massive white wall. Within the arm of land was the great bay, and the Dons' fleet.

"I say, Father, there's a beauty!" Lieutenant Nisbet was at his stepfather's elbow. Taller, more bearish than ever, but he had risen one notch in rank, having, thanks to miraculous health, fulfilled his time as a mid.

"All I see, Josiah, are the gulls and filth—and that cowardly fleet."

"Don't look so low, sir; up there, on the wall, see her?"

"No." The Admiral leveled his glass, raking the wall with it.

"The voluptuous one with the highest comb. She's flirting with you, sir, I'm sure of it. The bitch has a clever eye."

"Mr. Nisbet!" The Admiral groaned.

But Lieutenant Nisbet had managed a wink at Captain Miller, who became suddenly engrossed in the planks of the deck. Captains did not tease admirals, although, of course, Lieutenant Nisbet had privileges . . . Miller drew a long breath, held it, let it out slowly. For the first time since he had been appointed captain to Nelson, he felt the cramp of his position. Here was a new ship to command: *Theseus* 74, as fine as *Captain* had been before Nelson got through with it and she had to go home for complete overhaul. But there were disadvantages as well as advantages to being the chosen captain to a commodore or an admiral: the honor was great, but the work twice as difficult because of the constant personal relationships. Especially when the fleet was inactive, as now. It was as bad as two men trying to keep the same woman, even though the men might be the best of friends. Miller felt like the husband, for all the problems of the ship came to him, while the Admiral could disarrange all Miller's domesticity by a chance word.

"Ah! There she is!" The Admiral suddenly laughed, and Miller realized he had been standing staring at the deck much too long. He watched Nelson training his glass on one of the ladies of Cádiz out promenading the wall. "Well, I won't say she isn't tempting—to youngsters, of course."

"Good for you, sir," Josiah laughed. He was in one of his rare and painfully clumsy moods of affection. His manners and speech always plummeted too deep or soared too high, without any self-control. Most officers blamed his stepfather for not having smacked him about a few times. For the boy was not stupid. He could handle a ship. But he just never seemed to give a damn. And his stepfather had spoiled him, in so far as he had not broken him. Whether Josiah could or could not be broken into obedience was a question most officers agreed they would enjoy the privilege of proving, provided they did not have to answer for Josiah's broken body to the stepfather. So through the fleet the custom was to ignore the boy, and as he was at present, no one wanted him in any ship.

Miller realized now he had been studying Mr. Nisbet too long. He looked about for something to take him off the quarter-deck, away from the cluster of giggling mids and laughing officers, all ogling Cádiz. But it was Sunday afternoon, just before dinnertime. The ship's band had just finished playing "Spanish Ladies," everything was under control. There was nothing to do but stare at the wall, at the refuse rolling about in the dirty wash of the surf, for Cádiz was built too near sea level to drain into her sewers; nothing to do but listen to the screeching of scavenger gulls—with the ladies just out of reach.

Miller wished he were home, and yet he had not been out from England as long as the Admiral, who had been out since the war started over four years ago! Either that man took vows of chastity on leaving home, as Miller himself did, of course, or else he knew when to hold his tongue.

Miller liked him for that, for there was nothing in this lonely male naval world more tedious than a foul-mouthed superior repeating the old obscene anecdotes of his prowess.

"Come, Miller, have a look at her." The Admiral had turned around and Miller was suddenly glad to see that Nelson was as bored as himself.

The Admiral jerked his head toward Cádiz. "They're taunting their fleet to come out and fight, flirting with us to make their officers jealous, save Cádiz's gold—the whores." But before Miller had to answer, Josiah broke in.

"I think we cut a smart figure out here."

"Beware of the arrows and the pestilence." The Admiral nodded solemnly to his stepson, surprised Miller with a fleeting wink and did exactly what Miller had wanted to do: left the deck.

"He always gets those sermons mixed up." Josiah was laughing, and falling into step with Captain Miller instead of keeping his respectful distance. "I say, sir, couldn't we arrange a truce boat to run ashore for something this afternoon?"

Captain Miller gripped his telescope, then with a polite shake of his head turned away, feeling young Nisbet's fierce eyes boring his back. By God! He was Captain of this ship and he refused to be intimidated.

And there *Theseus* rocked, anchored just off Cádiz, while the tops of the enemy masts rocked in the bay, swaying together like dormant trees in the wind. Oh, to be home!

Yesterday was muggy hot. Today with the dry land breeze worse. The sun glared on the metallic sea. And there they were. The English with bulkheads down, the Admiral rowing every night to every ship in his squadron for inspection to make sure they were ready any moment to fight, while the Dons lay within at their ease. Blockade. The most nerve-racking thankless work in the world. Week after week. It was bad for a fleet, roused the devil in fighting men sick of dull routine under the constant rigidity of discipline that St. Vincent demanded.

Miller paced the deck, watch in hand, shook it. It had not stopped. It was life that seemed to stand still. Soon he could eat. He sniffed the heavy odor of Sunday pudding. He wasn't hungry. He glanced forward. The men were dancing together on the forecastle: as burly a pack of followers of Terpsichore as ever tried to keep time to music. But the Admiral had suggested it, and tonight the jacks would act out unbearable theatricals. Anything to keep them distracted—to keep their minds off mutiny.

The home ports were rotten with it. At Spithead the jacks had commandeered the fleet for a whole week, run their officers. Demanded decent food and pay when they were wounded. The government had handled it pretty well until the mutiny spread to Nore out of sympathy, the ringleaders had been considered pro-revolutionary, and all the sympathy for demands made at Spithead had been wiped out. Action would cure them. Let those idle jacks see a gun aimed at them.

Miller studied his men. A tough crew, but they looked all right. Yet you could never tell, not even Nelson. Right now there were two men in the fleet chained in irons on *Swiftsure*. Lord St. Vincent said they were mutineers feigning madness in order to talk more. Nelson had gone to see them and come back oddly shaken and mentally depressed in a way that had astonished Miller. And he had written Lord St. Vincent: ". . . even the sight of the two poor men in irons has affected me more than I can express . . . the youth may, I hope, be saved, he has intervals of sense, his countenance is most interesting . . . I will with pleasure pay fifty pounds to place him in some proper place for his recovery; the other, I fear, is too old." Miller scowled. The whole fleet of officers was laughing at Nelson's proverbial naïve generosity, his weakness for sympathy. Anyone could play on his emotions. St. Vincent said it was a waste of good money, and Nelson had waxed even more eloquent: "I hope for the poor men's sake that they are imposing on me; but depend on it God Almighty has afflicted them with the most dreadful of all diseases. They do not sham, indeed, you will find I am not mistaken, and all the Commissioners in the World cannot convince me of it. For what purpose can these poor wretches attempt to destroy themselves? For what purpose can one of them have spoken to me as rationally as any person could do? Do let Dr. Weir look at them. . . ."

But *now*, there were four more men suspected of mutiny . . . and Nelson was furious. He had been all for the mutiny at Spithead, but ready to sail a ship against Nore. Miller finally tucked his watch out of sight and turning about came face to face with young Nisbet again. The youngster's secretive high living was beginning to show already in his face, yet the Admiral apparently saw nothing.

"The Admiral would speak to you, sir." Nisbet's eyes scorched him, reminding Miller that the Admiral's Boy would like to run a truce ship in to call on the ladies. Truce ships went back and forth between the two enemy fleets. The English bought vegetables and newspapers and exchanged occasional prisoners; Admiral Nelson had sent in word a few weeks back that he did not wish to alarm the ladies, but the British fleet was going to fire a *feu de joie* for King George's birthday.

The Admiral Don had replied:

MY DEAR SIR:

I correspond to the urbanity merited by the letter with which you honored me . . . the Ladies of Cádiz, accustomed to the noisy sounds of salutes of vessels of war, will sit, and will hear what Sir John Jervis means to regale them with . . . in honor of his Britannic Majesty's birthday; and the general wish of the Spanish nation cannot but interest itself on so august a motive.

God preserve you many years. I kiss your hands.

Your attentive servant,

JOSEF DE MAZEREDO

Miller and Nelson had marveled over the expressiveness of the close. "A truce ship, sir?" Josiah wheedled again.

Miller refused to notice Nisbet as he went below, and the band played "Rule, Britannia!" and the ladies of Cádiz, who had listened to the *feu de joie,* strolled the white walls; noses high to their fleet, eyes and smiles for the English. And their black mantillas floated in the bright air.

Below deck, the Admiral was holding a letter as Miller came in.

"This was picked up on the quarter-deck during the night watch, Miller." He handed the paper to the Captain.

Success attend Admiral Nelson! God bless Captain Miller! We thank them for the officers they have placed over us. We are happy and comfortable, and shall support them, and the name of *Theseus* shall be immortalized as high as *Captain's.*

Signed: SHIP'S COMPANY

"Well!" Miller looked up in amazement, and his heart softened. "And this crew just came from the Channel Fleet—from the mutiny!"

"And now, Miller, I have less pleasant news. Apparently all we accomplished when we took *Captain* on her last cruise to meet the army convoy coming down from Elba was that scrap of good will to 'God's Children.'"

"You mean that Yankee convoy trapped in Málaga, sir?"

"Aye. What seamen! They measure their charts by thumb and sail by dead reckoning. Ask them where they want to go and—well, I can't talk like one, but they'll study their charts and then say, 'Well, it's only so many inches from here to here!' It is a small world, I suppose."

"The best use ever made of a Tricolor was when I saw it flying from one of your frigates, sir, and those twelve Americans, scared to death of the French privateers, following it like so many ducks."

"Aye, Miller, we can go out of our way to drum up a little international good will, but we cannot persuade an English army to attack Teneriffe! And General O'Hara also refuses to send his Royals. No marine general will go! In spite of the fact you and I danced attendance on that marine general's wife—what was her name?"

"Mrs. Pigott, sir," Miller grinned.

"Ah, yes, Mrs. Pigott!" Their eyes met and Miller threw back his head laughing.

"But we didn't jettison her, sir, though as we hoisted her out I had my doubts about the cables."

"You were more gallant than I when you said you hoped we'd soon have better weather for her next visit to a big battleship. I've prayed for constant gales. Women raise havoc with discipline."

"Aye, even Mrs. Pigott distracted the men, sir. Well, it's bad luck, sir, that the army and marines refuse."

"But I have talked to Freemantle, and he's anxious to go, though he wants to get his wife to England. And Troubridge. St. Vincent, however, thinks we'd better stay here. He needs us—unless we can force that lazy fleet out to fight, beat them. Then we can be off."

"What about Captain Bowen, sir, will he go?"

"If we go at all."

"He's a marvel, sir. He sailed a bit of a transport nearly all the way around the world and back once in less than two years. He says if Jervis hadn't gotten him his appointment to lieutenant after he had served four times his time and been abandoned ashore years on end he never could have gotten ahead."

"Jervis looks on Bowen like a son. Well, our only hope now of forcing the Spanish fleet out is to annoy their merchants . . ." The Admiral had walked to the windows, gazing out at Cádiz, letting his eye follow the rocky coast as it dwindled to the vanishing point toward Cape Trafalgar. "The merchants have a longer memory than the fleet, Miller. Cádiz has been one of our favorite targets for three hundred years. There was Raleigh under Essex."

"That was back in Cervantes's time. He was in Cádiz then. There was a sailor for you."

"I always understood he wrote a book."

"Yes. But he served in the battle of Lepanto. Lost an arm beating the Turks. Escaped from the Barbary pirates later . . . quite an adventurer."

"Lepanto! Very good. Since Essex, Miller, Cádiz had a taste of our fleet under Buckingham. Then Blake, then Sir George Rooke. I think it is time to remind them we have been too lenient these last fifty years. Our jacks need exercise."

"Gunboats, sir?"

"Aye."

Miller stood looking out the windows at the white wall of Cádiz and at the ladies whom Admiral Nelson had dreaded to alarm. Now what in the devil was it, he wondered, about Sir Horatio that reminded him of Don Quixote?

✳   ✳   ✳

GENERAL ORDER
July 3, 1797

By order of the Commander-in-Chief: All the barges and launches, without exception, with their carronades properly fitted, and plenty of ammunition and pikes, cutlasses, broad axes, and chopping knives, a clamp in each boat with spikes, a sledge hammer, and a coil of rope to tow off any armed brig, mortar, or gunboat that is carried, are to be with Admiral Nelson at half-past eight o'clock this night for a particular service. . . .

The white walls of Cádiz, mounted with seventy cannon, shone faintly through the dark as on muffled oars, long dark shadows moved in from the English fleet. The night was sultry. The nauseous stink of the refuse hurled over the walls added weight to the warm moist air. The only sounds were the constantly quarreling sea birds gorging in the night and the repeated boom of the breakers over the rocks. Of human sounds there were none.

Among the low black shadows were three faint sails hovering about a larger and blacker shadow. Closing in closer and closer to Cádiz. Suddenly, below the eerie white of the wall, the iridescent enameled white of the breakers, other dark shadows appeared coming out of port: Spanish guards.

Rear Admiral Nelson sat in the stern of his barge beside Captain Freemantle, who had just convoyed De Burgh from Elba. Miller had been left behind on *Theseus* in command of Nelson's inshore squadron of battleships while the Admiral attended to a "particular service."

The officers in the barge could not see the faces of their own men; just the faint warm outline of the ten oarsmen, and as always Nelson's shadow: young coxswain Sykes. In the prow of the barge was the faint shine of the barge cannon, the blunt light carronade.

There were barges and launches as far as their eyes could see, and each group of boats was commanded by a captain or a lieutenant from the fleet. The three flitting pale ghosts high above them were three small cutters guarding the main boat, the prima donna of the evening: the *Thunderer* bomb vessel, armed with mortars.

As the *Thunderer* moved in with her flock of guards, she gave her first roar and lit up the sea, roared again and again: spewing her bombs high over the wall into Cádiz, while the seventy Spanish cannon mounted to guard the city opened up.

The launches and barges rowed close to the *Thunderer* to prevent Spanish launches from boarding her. Their small carronades barked at each other's shadows across the water.

The bombardment went off like clockwork as bomb after bomb rained down on the houses of Cádiz; lively fires shot up.

"That should bring their fleet out." Nelson had just turned to Freemantle when the *Thunderer,* with a fizzling smack that landed a bomb far short of the mark, stopped firing. She began signaling, her mortar had jammed.

Now as the cutters moved in to tow her back, the shadows of the Dons' launches shot from the shore. The carronades flashed and the black English barges moved forward to ward off the attack. This had been foreseen, but not hoped for.

In the thick dark splashed with flame, the cannon on the wall making a tiara of fire over Cádiz, the barges closed.

"Oars, lay in, bouse forward the gun and load. Sykes, lay us aboard!" Nelson and Freemantle had drawn their swords, the oars in, the old *Agamemnons* snatched up their pikes with the steel points shining in the night, patted the pistols tucked in their belts, as firing lit a lean swift launch bearing down on the Admiral's. There were twenty-six flashing oars and four Spanish officers with drawn swords. Nelson's ten oarsmen fingered their pikes, a few had caught up axes for their left hands. The next instant the boats grazed. Men grappled hand to hand.

The barges rocked, shipped water over the gunnels as the Spaniards came, two to one, then the barges rocked apart, a pike dropped a Don in the gap and the boats struck again. Nelson's and Freemantle's swords whistled as the Dons tried to gain the boat the second time; they came with a spring like a storming of tigers; each for himself. A fierce slashing here—there—while the seasoned *Agamemnons* supported each other.

"Watch 'im, mate . . ."

"Get 'im." And two men whirled round and round, fell in the bottom while the others trampled over them, and someone brought an ax down on the Don's neck.

"Beg pardon, sir!" Sykes, with a thousand eyes, nudged the Admiral, parried a sword aimed at his back; fought all around his Admiral like a whirlwind, as Nelson hacked like a maniac at something with gold epaulets, and a jack's bare hand wrenched down a bayonet aimed at him.

With the slippery water, the uncertain footing, blades flashing from every side, the fitful light and the howling and grunting of madmen. To live meant to kill—and Nelson wrenched his sword out of the sudden warm sheath of a belly.

A Don spying his head turned; a dark arm swung up, a blade whistling down. And Sykes shoved the Admiral out of the way, took the blow on his own skull: dropped at the Admiral's feet; was trampled on.

The jacks stood their ground till the Dons gave a yell and dove into the water, swam for shore. And their officers slumped back in their boat. Eleven old *Agamemnons* and two English officers had killed eighteen Spaniards out of thirty . . .

Then row back weary but happy. A prize in tow, a city in flames; and other English launches rowing away towing two Spanish gunboats.

Sykes was lying in the bottom of the barge. Freemantle was bleeding, but alive, and his bride, Betsy, was waiting for him on his new frigate, *Seahorse*. Nelson, his eye still flashing, his face tense, had never had such a close fight. And in the sudden lull he discovered he had

been courageous—scared and brave all at once. They had done well
tonight. He had taken Cádiz unexpectedly on her soft side. Tomorrow
she would reinforce this soft side, and tomorrow night he would strike
on her hard side. Surprise. He began to smile grimly, as he bent over
to look at his coxswain. "Sykes?"

"You all right, sir?" Sykes rasped. And in the firelight Nelson saw
a slim, refined face worshiping him.

"God bless you, Sykes." The Admiral tried to smile. "The audacity
of them attacking my old *Agamemnons!*"

And his bloody battered crew grinned back at him.

❊   ❊   ❊

But no amount of bombardment would bring out the Spanish fleet
though Cádiz grumbled and crumbled, and Spaniards on a truce ship
exchanging prisoners complained that the bombardment caused the
citizenry of Cádiz to plunder and rob each other at the height of
the firing. Delighted, Nelson wrote St. Vincent: "A glorious scene of
confusion . . . destroyed several priests; that no harm done, they will
never be missed."

While the Dons saluted Rear Admiral Nelson by shooting all day
at *Theseus* riding at her anchors in her customary position well
within range of the town. The Dons fired and fired and missed her,
until the jacks hooted. *Theseus* was taking on charm.

And while the Dons fired so indelicately and inaccurately on this,
a Sabbath morn, the officers of the English fleet assembled aboard the
Commander in Chief. Stood solemnly and respectfully uncovered as
they heard the Articles of War read to a stony-faced company.

Four mutineers had been tried by court-martial, found guilty. They
must hang at dawn, regardless of Sunday.

After a while the men stopped jerking and leaping from the yardarm of St. Vincent's new ship, the *Ville de Paris.* The officers of the
fleet clapped their cocked hats back on their heads and rowed back to
their ships.

Vice-Admiral Thomson had dared to denounce St. Vincent publicly.
Not for hanging the men, but for desecrating the Sabbath, instead of
hanging them on a nondescript Monday. Thomson had been instantly
discharged from the fleet. Did anyone else desire to comment?

Admiral Nelson returned to his cabin aboard *Theseus.* He had summoned the ship's company. Now he stood, thoughtfully turning over

Spanish, English, French newspapers. There was only one name in it: Buonaparte. Italy had fallen to him. Genoa had a revolution. Lord Malmesbury was still discussing peace terms. All Europe would soon be at "peace" with France on Buonaparte's terms.

The Admiral tossed the papers aside. He had told St. Vincent: "I would rather see fifty of our men killed by the enemy than one of them hanged by us."

He went on deck to talk to his company. The Chaplain could give the sermons.

The men listened quietly, while the Dons' guns barked at them. The Admiral's theory was basic, and well illustrated by the noise, as he pointed out France and Spain were the enemies of England; that Englishmen had better stick together. It wasn't so much what he said, after the hangings at dawn, that impressed them, but himself.

"Nel's all right. He fights like a bloomin' angel!"

The Admiral went back to his cabin. The Sabbath had been pretty well profaned all around this morning what with the Dons firing out of Cádiz and the English yardarms weighted.

The Admiral had one more duty this Sabbath. Captain Sir Robert Calder desired to know how Rear Admiral Nelson felt about Thomson's dismissal. Did Calder recall, perhaps, the pleas Nelson had made for those two other men a while back, or just what was his motive for asking? Nelson had already written St. Vincent: "I congratulate you on the finish, as it ought, of the business, and I (if I may be permitted to say so) very much approve of its being so speedily carried into execution, even although it is Sunday. The particular situation of the services requires extraordinary measures. I hope this will end all disorders in our Fleet: had there been the same determined spirit at home, I do not believe it would have been half so bad, not but that I think Lord Howe's sending back the first petition [of mutineers for pensions and better food] was wrong."

Now for his avowed enemy Calder:

I am sorry that you should have to differ with Vice-Admiral Thomson but had it been Christmas Day instead of Sunday, I would have executed them.

We know not what might have been hatched by a Sunday's grog: *now* your discipline is safe. I talked to our people, and, I hope with good effect: indeed, they seem a very quiet set.

Ever your most faithful . . .

So a few days later when red flags of mutiny suddenly cropped out in the Dons' fleet at Cádiz, spread hourly from ship to ship, *à la* Nore and Spithead, the jacks were looking to their guns ready to meet the enemy if Spanish officers brought their ships out rather than put up with mutiny.

But the red flags continued to flutter over Cádiz, nothing brought the Spanish fleet out.

The dreary blockade went on.

So Admiral Nelson went back to his plans for attacking Teneriffe—without an army—writing to St. Vincent: "With General Troubridge on shore and myself afloat I am confident of success. . . ."

I X. Teneriffe

July, 1797 – April, 1798

CAPTAIN MILLER was alone in *Theseus's* poop cabin, reading before going to sleep. He liked these moments, off by himself. He heard the rush of water against *Theseus's* hull, felt her leisurely purposeful roll. The night was quiet. He was sleepy, his cot snug and ahead lay action; behind lay that damn blockade duty. The balance of time was perfect.

Theseus and her tiny squadron were steering for Teneriffe.

He yawned, turned a page in his book. Suddenly he pored over the page, felt himself drawn bolt upright. For a moment his sailor's soul shivered superstitiously. He closed the book, not too carelessly, and laid it on his writing desk.

Exactly two hundred years ago, in 1597, Essex had sailed to Teneriffe, and with him had sailed John Donne.

Donne had written:

> Doth not a Tenarif or higher Hill,
> Rise so high like a Rocke, that one might thinke
> The floating Moone would shipwracke there, and sink?

Miller lay back smiling; he knew how Nelson would scoff at his literary finds. The Admiral was either not superstitious at all or else defiant of superstition: the attack was planned for a Friday. The jacks would mutter and make signs to appease their jinx.

Day after day the squadron had sailed down the Atlantic:

Theseus 74, Rear Admiral Nelson, Captain Miller.

Culloden 74, Captain Troubridge.

Zealous 74, Captain Samuel Hood, a cousin of old Lord Hood.

Three frigates:

Terpsichore, Captain Bowen, considered one of the best mathematicians and navigators in the navy.

Seahorse, Captain Freemantle and spouse.

Emerald, Captain Waller.

With the sleek *Fox* cutter, under still gay Lieutenant Gibson, one of the few officers who were constantly invited around the fleet to lighten officers' dinners.

And as they had sailed they had drilled. Under the bright sails in the geometrical shadows red-coated ships' marines glowed fiery red, then turned somber dark as the ships rolled the shadows about. On calm days the gun crews fired at targets towed out to sea. There had been excellent spirit. The stakes were the treasure from *one* Spanish ship; the other two treasure ships had not been accounted for. The stakes, though lower than first expected, were still stimulating.

Lord St. Vincent had issued the order: take Santa Cruz de Teneriffe. It was entirely up to the navy and therefore some degree of risk must be expected without the army from Elba or the marines from Gibraltar. But as Admiral Nelson laughed, "I know it is my disposition, that difficulties and dangers do but increase my desires of attempting them . . ." he had accommodated his first plans to the reality. And he still had a more positive plan than Blake's mad dash in and out on a chance wind. Now surprise in attack meant more than ever if his force of nine hundred were to accomplish what he had planned for four thousand seven hundred to tackle. Leaving nothing to chance that could be foreseen, he trusted only the initiative of "General" Troubridge, whose desire to undertake the expedition had helped sway St. Vincent to allow them to go.

So of a saffron dawn when silk sea and gauze sky promised islands of riches near, a purple shadow grew on the horizon, blazed like a ruby scepter as the sunrise touched it.

"Deck there! Landfall dead ahead!" Cries from the sky like the welcoming calls of the land birds coming to light in the rigging.

The dark hulls on the bright yellow seas shortened sail, but crept closer, their topsails like clouds drifting high over the ocean. The island was still many miles distant; so high and so lonely was this mountain called Teneriffe, it towered out of the water, a stone monolith unperturbed by seven small specks drifting toward the town at its feet: Santa Cruz was still hidden below the horizon.

To Thomas Troubridge, Esq., Captain of H.M.S. *Culloden,* and Commander of the Forces ordered to be landed for taking Santa Cruz, dated, *Theseus* at sea:

July 20, 1797

SIR: I desire you will take under your command the number of seamen and marines named in the margin (900 exclusive of officers) who will be under Captains Hood, Miller, Freemantle, Bowen and Waller, and the marines under Captain Thomas Oldfield and a detachment of royal artillery under Lt. Baynes, all of whom are now embarked on board his Majesty's frigates *Seahorse, Terpsichore,* and *Emerald.* With this detachment you will proceed as near to the town of Santa Cruz as possible, without endangering your being perceived; when you will embark as many men as the boats will carry, and force your landing in the north east part of the Bay of Santa Cruz, near a large battery. The moment you are on shore, I recommend you first attack the battery; which when carried, and your post secured, you will either proceed by storm against the town and mole-head battery, or send in my letter, as you judge most proper, containing a Summons of which I send you a copy; and the terms are either to be accepted or rejected in the time specified, unless you see good cause for prolonging it, as no alteration will be made in them: *and you will pursue such other methods as you judge most proper for speedily effecting my orders, which are to possess myself of all cargoes and treasures which may be landed in the island of Teneriffe.* Having the firmest confidence in your ability, bravery, and zeal of yourself, and of all placed under your command, I have only heartily to wish you success, and to assure you I am your most obedient and faithful servant,

HORATIO NELSON

By four o'clock on Friday afternoon, Nelson was below deck in *Theseus* going over his plans for the last time with Troubridge. The Admiral had supervised every detail, down to the exact weight of his scaling ladders; to ramrods of iron, not wood, for wood broke in a hurry; to the exact size of the platforms for cannon. His favorite carpenter had made the sledges exactly to his specifications; every last detail of equipment had been indicated. Details were all the more important now his force was cut by four fifths.

He shook hands with Troubridge. "Good luck."

"I shall have the battery northeast of the town in our possession by dawn, sir."

"The surprise. Take them before they discover us. I leave it all to you. My ships will be down on the town to support you as day breaks. Santa Cruz will be paralyzed."

Rear Admiral Nelson was on deck to watch his three frigates carrying Troubridge and the first landing party as they pulled away from the battleships.

Now he must wait, keep the larger ships of the line hulls down, tacking to eastward below the horizon lest Santa Cruz be warned of their coming. In the night he would work forward, while Troubridge and his men stormed the battery, held it. When dawn broke tomorrow . . .

He smiled confidently to himself. The attack was under way. He went below satisfied, till with the dark, slowly tacking to eastward, the battleships peered for the first signs of firing on shore. The Admiral was back on deck, pacing.

It was a cloudy night, growing blustery. No firing yet. But it was early of course. A cloudy night was perfect for secrecy, but he did not like the increasing northwest wind whistling through the rigging toward the African coast just to eastward. There were strange birds wind-tossed in the sky. He ran up the ladder to the poop: nothing to be seen. Of course, the ships were too far off to see the beginning of action.

A frothing across the sea! His heart leaped and then fell. Stupid! After all these years to start at the gambols of porpoises.

He began to wish he had gone himself, just for the sake of his peace of mind. Now impatiently:

"Masthead, what do you see?"

"Deck there, nothing in sight, sir!"

Then something must have happened . . . no, not necessarily. Patience was just the least of his virtues.

At last he ordered the squadron hove-to. Hour after hour wore away. The watch changed. And the wind rose, but Troubridge's frigates would have anchored by now. The boats would be rowing in —perhaps landing.

Every barge in the fleet had been ordered to move in tied together. Every last detail he could foresee. It was past midnight: no firing visible. Silence and darkness everywhere.

1st Lieutenant Weatherhead had been keeping his respectful distance; he now stepped forward waiting to speak to the Admiral. For four years Weatherhead had come through action after action unscathed, rising slowly from lowliest lieutenant to this, tonight: acting captain of *Theseus* in Miller's absence.

The sky was beginning to pale, or was it still night? One fancied the worst.

"I expect Captain Troubridge's firing any minute, Mr. Weatherhead."

"Shall we make sail, sir?"

It was three-thirty in the morning. Should they be in full sight of the enemy when dawn came with no proof that Troubridge's all-important share of the attack was accomplished?

The sky was getting lighter, the wind perversely inconstant. The sun would rise soon. Already the peak of Mt. Teneriffe was beginning to glow like a coal as the sun, still below the eastern horizon, sent a tentative ray of light poking curiously into the sky. Still nothing. Two flying fish shot like silver sparks through the air. Silence.

"Make sail, Mr. Weatherhead, we will approach cautiously."

The big ships began to press forward and the sky lifted higher and higher above them; the stars receded and the sun loomed up over Africa. Teneriffe flashed like a torch, then grew dim, lost in encircling clouds.

Now for the first time they saw the town of Santa Cruz rimming the bay, while along the rock-walled shore, facing the sea, their barges pitched in the surf, and the sound of firing came slowly to their ears from the fire-spitting enemy battery!

The barges were shoving off, away from the enemy fire. Pulling out to sea, toward the three frigates riding bare poles at anchor. And at last as Nelson watched incredulously, one of the frigates was unfurling sail, moving slowly away from the island; coming to meet his battleships.

His heart sank.

He had made a mistake. If he had only been on the shore with the first landing party he would not now be wondering what had gone wrong. . . .

It took the frigate three precious hours to reach him, for the wind was now peevishly light, three hours before Captain Troubridge stalked across the quarter-deck saluting.

Troubridge's voice was angry but positive as he faced Nelson: "It was the damned current, the foul wind! It was midnight before we got the frigates within three miles of the shore. Dawn when we landed. By that time, sir, we were revealed, the enemy battery opened on us before we could storm."

"And you saw *no alternative* but retreat?"

"Captain Bowen and I have considered an alternative, sir. With your permission, sir, we will go round the fort; attack it from the heights in the rear. I only came for your permission, sir, to change the prescribed mode of attack, as I thought it advisable to consult you before altering any plans. May we go ahead now, sir?"

The Admiral stared at his Captain for a split second of unbelief. "Yes! Go ahead, by all means! I will attempt to bring the squadron as close inshore as possible to draw the enemy fire from you."

"We'll have the Dons groveling by sunset, sir!" Troubridge saluted smartly and went back. It took him three more hours to return to the frigates. Admiral Nelson felt no more than a passing anger toward Troubridge. Anger he could not sustain. It was Nelson's command, all his, right or wrong, and he, Nelson, had been *wrong!* He should have gone himself. Troubridge had been the perfect subordinate, done his best, and it had not been enough . . . "and you will pursue such other methods as you judge most proper for speedily effecting my orders . . ." Troubridge had judged proper to consult, relying on Nelson's superior judgment. Now the Nelson of St. Vincent—of Cádiz—of Calvi and Bastia—was cursing himself as he paced up and down, his face drawn, pride crushed.

And it was too late for Troubridge's next move. The battleships, as Nelson had foreseen in his first plan, were too unwieldy in the fickle wind to lay them inshore, with the chance of going aground.

But with his plans sanctioned from above, Captain Troubridge was boldly landing his men under slaughtering fire not only from the battery, but now from the very heights he had planned to possess. In the six hours he wasted obtaining permission, the Spanish had foreseen his next move. Still Troubridge charged the shore.

The Admiral turned to Weatherhead, snapped: "Make signal to Captain Troubridge, Recall." It was almost sunset. Santa Cruz could count his ships. He was revealed and repulsed in his first attempt.

Turn back? Tell St. Vincent Santa Cruz was invulnerable? But was it? He could not face St. Vincent until he was sure. He began turning the next move in his mind. How take an alerted armed city with nine hundred men?

He did not know that he could. But, by God, he would try!

❊   ❊   ❊

Two days passed of stark calm and sudden dead foul winds. Still the squadron hovered over Santa Cruz, Teneriffe, for Admiral Nelson was suffering wounded pride. His orders, the orders he had asked for, were to take Santa Cruz . . . suicide? So he gave his orders to the squadron: tonight they would take Santa Cruz de Teneriffe.

When Betsy Freemantle heard of it she thought it was about time. She was tired of ships, and "old Nelson" who had taken Elba with a threat and a summons seemed rather slow. When her British navy wanted something, it always took it—like that—didn't it? So Betsy Freemantle invited everyone to have dinner before the attack tonight.

Just before dinner, of the day named for attack, Captain Thomson, *Leander* 50, joined the squadron. That meant a couple hundred more men. Everyone felt better.

Admiral Nelson sat at Freemantle's table, a guest on the *Seahorse,* and tried to keep his mind on the halting conversation, to appear cheerful for the sake of his officers, and for the sake of teen-age Betsy Freemantle sitting near him. But her lighthearted chatter, her adoration of Freemantle, were just so much more trouble.

She seemed smaller, more fragile than ever, like a piece of porcelain among utilitarian pots. Her faith in the officers at the table, her talk about "their Teneriffe" . . . he wished she were anywhere but here.

He had given his order, storm Teneriffe. Tonight was the night to woo Fortune but without Blake's advantage of total surprise. Still Santa Cruz did not know when he intended to strike or how. To that he clung. They would strike at dark. He toyed with his dinner while his officers gamely kept up a pretense of conversation. Something about horses and Paris. He wished *she* would talk just one language at a time, but she had lived on the Continent and her words were likely to be anything. He gave up trying to follow sentences when the key words kept rippling off into French or Italian.

The more he had studied Santa Cruz the more his cool judgment told him he was ordering a gallant but desperate adventure, and the more he realized it, the more his pride demanded he make the point of honor. He had written a farewell note to St. Vincent: "This night I, humble as I am, command the whole, destined to land under the batteries of the town and tomorrow my head will probably be covered with laurel or cypress. I have only to recommend Josiah Nisbet to you and my country. . . ."

But honor was something tangible to him.

He picked up his fork and determined to swallow his dinner as he caught Mrs. Freemantle's eye. She was either sensing his mood, or reproaching him for one of his well-known silences.

He smiled and was rescued from having to say anything by Lieutenant Gibson, who had apparently been talking all along.

"Officers used to save their money and go to Paris," Gibson said, "because it was cheap."

"Boulogne was cheap. Full of English who were full of cheap wine. Most officers went to Paris to study the language and French naval tactics." The Admiral spoke rather touchily. He was at bay tonight. He wished he had not spoken when Gibson only smiled solemnly and left the conversation to him. He did not want it.

"Were you ever in France, Sir Horatio?" Mrs. Freemantle tidied up the conversation, smiling as if he had just knocked a glass of wine into her lap.

"Yes." The Admiral took the hint, for he had suddenly realized that if Mrs. Freemantle lost her faith in his invincibility she would probably have hysterics. The kind his wife had. That would drive him wild. "Yes, Captain Macnamara and I went to France during the peace in '83. You knew Mac, Captain Troubridge?" He raised his voice.

"Aye, aye, sir." Troubridge's refusal to learn French and his deafness had not made him the focal point of conversation before this moment. Now he declined to carry on, continued eating omnivorously.

The Admiral sighed. "Mac and I wanted to learn French. We had fixed on Montreuil, about sixty miles from Calais in the road to Paris. We set off *en poste,* they called it, though we did not get on more than four miles an hour. Such carriages, such horses! It would have made you laugh," he brightened slightly, "at the ridiculous figure the postilions made with their enormous jack boots and their rats of horses. Their chaises had no springs and the roads were generally paved like London streets; you may imagine we were pretty well shaken together before we had traveled two posts and a half to our first stop for the night—Marquise. Here we were shown into an inn—they called it—" he really smiled at last—"I would have called it a pigsty. We were offered a room with two straw beds, and with great difficulty they mustered up clean sheets and gave us two pigeons for supper, upon a dirty cloth with wooden-handled knives. The next morning we pushed on for Montreuil where we put up at the same house with the same jolly landlord that recommended La Fleur to Sterne. And his *Sentimental Journey* describes ours very well."

He started to sink back into silence, but Mrs. Freemantle's eyes did not let him escape saying more as easily as that. He went rambling on, while his thoughts were with his ships.

"But we couldn't stay. I believe there were sixty noble families in the neighborhood who owned everything and the other houses so poor as to be uninhabitable. So we pushed on for Abbéville. It was just what we wanted, but imagine our mortification when the minute it was learned in the place that two Englishmen had arrived, we were besieged and most unluckily. It seems two Englishmen, one of whom called himself Lord something or other, and another gentleman had decamped at three o'clock that afternoon in debt to every shopkeeper in the place!"

Lieutenant Gibson threw back his head, his smile flashing, as the Admiral went on describing his trip as if it had been a forced march: "It seems they had kept elegant houses and—ah—*horses*—and—so on—" He smiled chivalrously at Mrs. Freemantle. "We found the town in an uproar. On Mac's urgent advice we steered off—and finally settled in St. Omer."

"Oh, the English colony! Of course, Sir Horatio! *That* was civilized, was it not?" Betsy's eyes twinkled. She had lived in France and loved it. If it weren't for the stupid old war . . . England was going to be very foreign to her!

"It was all right except for some of our officers: two noble Captains, Ball and another officer, who went strutting about like great coxcombs wearing French epaulets."

Captain Bowen sat forward. "Captain Alexander John Ball, sir? That sounds like him, but he's a damned good seaman in spite of it."

"Oh, I dare say Coxcomb Ball keeps afloat."

"And did you ever find someone to teach you French?" Mischievously from Mrs. Freemantle, while her husband swallowed uneasily, for Nelson's French was atrocious.

"Oh, ah, *oui, oui.* Mac and I found lodgings with a French family. We used to play cards together, the two daughters, Mac and I—so you see we had to learn. The girls—oh, by the way, Freemantle, remember George Andrews? His father was the English clergyman at St. Omer. I took Andrews to sea with me when I went out to the West

Indies in the *Boreas*. That makes four of my lieutenants made captain this war. Berry and Noble were the last to go."

"They'll get ahead," Miller smiled.

"Yes, my lucky Berry. I miss him." He turned to Mrs. Freemantle. "I have taken up your whole party with one nonsensical story. Your dinner has been charming." He rose, and over the reflected light of the sea on the paneling, the shadows of the officers cast grotesque figures as they filed out. The shadows scurrying like hunted men. The masts were creaking, the ship groaning quietly.

But Mrs. Freemantle's face was gay as the officers went on deck to return to their ships. She had drawn old Nelson out; that was quite a social triumph, "Wasn't it, dear?" she asked her husband for the second time. She sighed when he did not answer. Now the cat had *his* tongue.

Forward, the élite of the ship's crew were grinding cutlasses. The sound put her teeth on edge. The muscle-gnarled seamen were squinting at the silvery edges of their pikes, choosing the best pistols, making sure they had locks and flints. Each man wore a patch of white canvas on his jacket for insignia.

Betsy Freemantle sighed. What a fuss for a threat and a summons. Men took themselves so seriously!

Her husband had glanced down at her. She looked even younger as a sudden equatorial gale blew her hair and her scarf, her soft skirt. She walked with her husband, hand laced in his, wondering why he gripped her fingers so hard at times. It hurt. And she wondered, too, if that strange feeling she had every morning was going to turn into a baby one of these days?

❊   ❊   ❊

The squadron was anchored a few miles off Santa Cruz. The ships were too big to maneuver within the small fortified harbor with its doubtful winds.

At six that night, the long black boats rowed off with oars muffled in kersey cloth or canvas. They bobbed about in the freshening wind, until they disappeared, and Betsy, who was tired after her party and the yelling and tramping and thumping of men, went to bed grateful for a little peace and quiet.

❊   ❊   ❊

No one in the barges spoke above whispers. The oars, lightly dipping, did not splash, even the oarlocks were wrapped. There was no moon. No stars. Only a milky curd lowering in the sky, a faint rain beginning to pelt softly down with the sudden buffets of wind.

There was a long pull of several hours from ship to shore. They must row slowly for fear of the splash of swift deep strokes. Their object was to land on the mole—carry it—rendezvous in the square; storm the Citadel, then summon the town to surrender. Bluff their way.

Troubridge, Hood, Thomson, Miller and Waller had charge of six divisions of boats as well as a small Santa Cruz fishing boat Hood had captured the day before. It was now manned with eighty seamen. Lieutenant Gibson and one hundred and eighty men moved in behind them with his pampered lovely, his sleek little *Fox* cutter.

With the Admiral's boats were Freemantle's and young Captain Bowen's. These three officers to supervise and command the whole.

They could not see each other in the dark as they steered for the lights of Santa Cruz; they could only feel the tug of their cables tying them together.

"I shouldn't have allowed you to come, Josiah, if we're both—" The Admiral broke off his whisper to his stepson.

"Why the devil not? I'll go where you go!" Josiah gritted back, his tone crushing any Ruth-Naomi tenderness that may have been lurking in his strange heart. Hoste had been left aboard *Theseus*.

His stepfather said nothing more. His restless eye caught the thin, eager profile of Lieutenant Weatherhead etched against the sky, and beyond it was nothing; as if the boats and his men were adrift in space.

"Now softly, easy . . ." from the coxswain.

As the boats drew into the harbor mouth the wind rose higher in baffling whirls. They could see the gleam of the surf breaking in long snakelike runs along the sea wall—or was that the mole?

Where in the name of God was the mole? The boats pitched forward as the gale blew them in, piling up waves behind them. Each boat a world of its own, enclosed in the night with the invisible cables pulling them into one scheme.

Still the town seemed to sleep; only here and there faint lights in the houses, and the rising white of angry surf; the sea rushing in with the gale, hurling the small boats forward, all caught in the incessant urge of the ocean. They listened for the enemy. They listened for each other, breathing softly. The oarsmen with their backs toward death, blindly trusting the senses of their night-blinded coxswains. Had a night ever been more malign, a wind more perverse, one proud man more desperate? The big calloused hands working the oars had just a few hours back been writing home. Saying good-by.

Still they pulled forward where they knew the mole ought to be and their hopes rose: the town was drugged with its sleep.

The waves lifted the boats on high crests, hurled them down into black pits, up again at the white surf; faster—faster—the mole nearly reached—

A bell clanged! Immense. Omnipotent. Out of nowhere! Clanging and clanging: sudden and everywhere. Like a fist in their faces. Echoing and re-echoing in their ears. The alarm bells of Santa Cruz pealing; ringing and ringing and ringing as the town woke: spat a circle of fire from shore.

Balls thundered close to the water. Rockets hissed into the sky. Burst. Spread light. Died. Soared again. Blue flares. The bay flashed with the fire of cannon aimed at the boats.

"Cast off boats and huzza!"

And a wild desperate cheer in the night. Now each boat pitched forward; all scattered.

The humming of sudden silence. The groping of flares. And again the stabs of light; cannon balls plowing the water sending up walls of spray. And over all the howling of wind.

"Steer for the mole! The mole! Pull for the mole for God's sake!"

But where was it? And the cannon again lit it an instant; blinded the searching eyes. Darkness again.

Another phantom blue flare suspended in space.

"The mole!"

The Admiral's boat grazed it, rocked, another landed. A mass of men out, cutlasses flashing, muskets leveled: facing four hundred Dons and the mouths of their cannon. . . .

And the Admiral running up the stone steps, sword drawn; and Bowen and Freemantle. No time to wait for the others.

"Spike their cannon!" The Admiral and a wild pack of seamen. The first men staggering, blood-splashed, quivering on the stone before they had struck a blow; but others came scrambling over them, rushing on.

Josiah, pistols in hand, trying to follow his stepfather, saw a red gash shearing across Weatherhead—and Freemantle—and Bowen. Josiah hurled down his pistols, caught his stepfather as the gash spread to him, and the deadly grapeshot spent itself in the water behind them. He caught up the Admiral, who was crumpling, going down, shifting his sword to his left hand.

"You back and you there—to the boat!" Nisbet yelled at the last men flying by. They stopped, lifted the Admiral and carried him back. His right arm dangled in shreds, his left hand clamped his sword till the knuckles showed white.

"To the boat!" Nisbet shouted. Five men obeyed while the others raced on, spiked the cannon till they all fell dead or wounded.

Without a glance for another, without hearing the cannon, Nisbet was jerking his neckerchief loose, bending deliberately over the Admiral, feeling for the severed artery. He found it, held it, began applying a neat tourniquet. But the tide had washed the boat on the sands while high overhead the cannon flashed. The men had laid the Admiral in the boat; he was fainting at the sight of his blood.

The men wrenched and hauled at the heavy boat, finally launched it in the surf.

"Keep close to the wall," Josiah yelled, and grabbing an oar threw his weight on it, pulled with the others, while the cannon balls roared above them. The Dons' cannon were elevated, aimed at the harbor entrance, leaving a narrow corridor clear round the bay, next to the wall, that was not under their fire.

Then all hell blew up. A thunderous shot struck the *Fox* cutter below water. Tore a hole clean through her.

"God help us! She's wrecked!" as she staggered, heeled over slowly; sank. Men shot, stunned, maimed, drowning. Blue flares lit a churning mass of heads, arms, clotted together. Screaming mouths filling with water. Strangling arms writhing like snakes trying to pull their souls out of the water; climb on the backs or the heads of others. Fists smashing friends. The mass knocked under by the waves. Up again. Men who could fight without blinking gone stark raving mad in the water. A scrambling for wreckage, and the fight to the death to cling to it. Hands broken by heels, slipping away, agonized eyes staring at uplifted broken hands; drowning slowly.

"Jack—for God's sake?"

"Sorry, mate. It's my life."

And Jack lives, another jack beaten off, and another. Tyranny supreme on a bit of wreckage; paddling for his life. Knocked senseless. Left to drown, and another man astride the wreckage.

And someone saving someone, pulling him up on the wreckage. And one man swimming slowly, holding up a stunned mate. Some murder; some save. Some die murdering; some die saving. And some were swimming, stopping to fight off the maniacs dragging them under, swimming on, fighting again, reaching a chunk of lumber. Exhausted. Only to shove it toward a friend. Swim on, sink finally.

"Help them for God's sake." The Admiral had finally struggled to sit up, and with his good left hand clasped a drowning arm, pulled one of his men up from the water. Reached for another. And instantly the sea swarmed with men. The boat lurched, shipped water. Crammed with men the boat threatened to sink; its gunnels barely above water.

An oar poised like a spear to ward off sharks.

"In the name of God!"

"No crowding! Or we'll all sink!"

So some had to be left behind.

"We're almost to *Seahorse,* sir," Nisbet told his stepfather, who was sitting bolt upright, forgetting his wound which was bleeding again like a fountain.

"Steer for *Theseus!*"

"Dear God! Father, you're bleeding to death! That's too far, you'll die. *Father!*" Nisbet's voice was breaking.

"Then I'll die, rather than face Mrs. Freemantle—and no word of her husband. Steer for *Theseus!*" The Admiral's white face was pinched, aged in the blue light.

❊   ❊   ❊

Troubridge's barge had shot past the mole, now with a long last pull it lurched through the mounting surf, crashing on shore right under the Citadel. Behind him came Waller.

Picking themselves up they turned to see how many boats were following; saw some boats hesitate, crazed men shouting, "Avast! Turn back! We'll be stove in that surf!"

Boats thrown broadside to the breakers: swallowed. They bobbed up empty, to splinter on the rocks; leaving masses of drowning men to struggle with the sea and each other.

Troubridge grappled a stunned lieutenant by the shoulder.

"Round up the stragglers! March!"

"The ladders are gone—powder wet—" Waller told him. "We can't storm the Citadel!"

"March on the square!" Troubridge roared down the surf and cannon. He had now all of eighty half-drowned men around him to take Santa Cruz; but at the moment he thought he alone had failed. "Nelson will be in the square."

As the eighty men drew together, a handful of Spaniards came out of the dark. Dripping seamen leveled their pikes, rushed the Spaniards, wrestled dry guns, took the Dons prisoners. A moment's success. They shoved on toward the square.

The gleam of a marine redcoat. A hail. "Who goes there?"

"Messenger, sir. Captains Miller and Hood landed southwest of the Citadel, are marching on the rendezvous."

"Very well."

The city was dark as they pushed along narrow streets, filling them from wall to wall. Where were the Spaniards? Troubridge thrust his head forward, big nose sniffing the way, listened. The cannon still fired around the harbor, but the rest of the town was suspiciously still.

"Avast!" He eyed the town square ahead. Not a man to be seen anywhere.

"Good God! Where's the Admiral?" Waller gasped.

"We'll take cover. Wait for the others," Troubridge answered. Every house was dark. Not a sign of life. Only the clouds piling higher and higher, and the hammering of the cannon on the sea wall.

One building caught Troubridge's eye: small high windows, heavily barred, one massive door. Some monastery or convent. He pointed it out to Waller. Stealthily they crept, hugging the walls, simulating shadows.

Troubridge detached a dozen men. They ran forward, smashed the old iron lock. The door flew open, echoing hollowly down dark corridors, answered by sudden hysterical screams. Sanctuary.

Troubridge loomed like the reincarnation of all their sins over a trembling, sobbing cluster of nuns hugging their Abbess.

"In there!" he grunted. They swirled off, choking their sobs, huddled down in the dark of the chapel awaiting the worst. But he bolted the door on them. Turned back to his men.

So far, all went well. He ordered a lieutenant to take inventory of his force: eighty men and a handful of prisoners for hostages—no powder—no ladders—everything drowned. No food. Troubridge strode up and down past the empty cells of the virgins. . . . He must wait for Nelson. The Admiral would think of something.

"Watkins!"

"Aye, aye, sir!"

"Go to the mole. Find out what happened. Try to get some word of the Admiral."

"Aye, aye, sir!" The man slipped through the door, disappeared.

A new sound in the streets. Quick-marching men. "Clear the decks!" Troubridge gritted. The men took a heartier grip on their pikes and fingered their few Spanish muskets. Posting himself by the convent door, Troubridge peered through the cracks at the square. He could see shadows rushing up the same street he had come. Who was it? His men had piled up wooden chests and heavy chairs, were balanced now, muskets aimed out the high cloister windows.

"Deck there! I heard a voice speaking English to northward, sir!" A man craned around from atop three chests.

They listened. The mass drew near. They heard a "What's this, Hood? Where's Nelson? Where's Troubridge?"

The convent door lifted back.

"Hood! This is Troubridge!"

"Thank God! How many of you?" The mass flowed into the building. Troubridge gripped Hood's hand, then Miller's; almost broke them. "Where's Nelson?"

"Not here?"

"No sign of him!"

"Not a man of them?"

"And Freemantle? Bowen? Waller? Thomson? Gibson?" Miller's voice.

"Waller's here."

"How many men have we now?" Troubridge watched them troop in. "Avast there! Up with a light!"

He took out his watch as a seaman with a gash on his cheek, his hair matted, came forward. His big hands were holding a slim white taper. Like some medieval saint carved out of wood, the jack held the candle over Troubridge's watch.

"We've an hour till daylight."

A beating of steps on the stones. "Watkins," from outside.

"What news?"

Watkins came in, his face haggard, catching his breath. "The mole *was* stormed, sir. The enemy cannon all spiked, but the Spaniards have taken it again. No word of the Admiral, sir."

The officers stared at each other. Their leaders, Nelson, Freemantle and Bowen, gone! Then all turned to Troubridge. He was clenching and unclenching his jaw. "He may have missed the mole," Troubridge said stubbornly. "He may come yet."

No one answered. For someone *had* spiked the enemy cannon; been captured or killed by a fresh storm of Spaniards.

"Beg pardon, sir. The count of our forces, sir." A lieutenant stepped up. "We've eighty marines, eighty pikemen and one hundred and eighty small armed seamen—total including officers now three hundred and eighty, sir."

"Very well." Troubridge lifted his chin, turning to the other captains, all junior in rank to him. "We'll give Nelson one hour and then—" He sounded resolute to the others as he turned away, paced up and down thinking, what then?

"Maybe we could summon the Citadel, bluff a surrender? They don't know how big a force we have still aboard ship," Miller said after a while.

"Bring up two prisoners," Troubridge ordered a sergeant of marines. And turning to a lieutenant, "Paper—ink—"

While the two Spaniards stood with their hands bound behind them, their eyes smoldering, the lieutenant dashed off and after rummaging through the convent found the Abbess's apartments, her small desk. He summoned a jack who brought it, on his back, to Captain Troubridge.

A pike thrust into the crack sprung the lock. Troubridge wrote his summons to the Citadel: surrender or be destroyed.

"Sam Hood, you speak Spanish?"

"Aye."

"Tell these men they are to take the sergeant with a flag of truce to the Citadel in return for their release."

Hood gave the orders. The Spaniards bowed, even smiled. *"Sí, sí . . ."*

Troubridge finished the paper. The sergeant saluted. He was armed, the prisoners helpless. Troubridge motioned them to be off.

Ten minutes passed. Twenty.

Troubridge paced up and down. Behind him the jack with the white taper trudged, sheltering the flame with his hand.

Slowly the convent began to glow, its dull stone walls took on light. The taper seemed fainter and fainter. Troubridge studied his watch. One hour gone. Nelson was either dead or a prisoner. He felt a surge of anger to the marrow of his bones.

"We can't stay here," Miller said slowly; his face was stony as he approached Troubridge. The sergeant of marines had never returned.

Troubridge's face was like a rock, his eyes burned. "We will march on the Citadel—as the Admiral ordered." The captains nodded slowly. Honor was all that was left them. They must march with three hundred and forty, without scaling ladders, cannon or powder.

The men had been sprawled wherever they could find space. Their fate was not in their keeping. Some had even slept. Now they drew up stiffly. They were tired, hungry and desperate.

The sun lit the square as they unbarricaded the doors.

But there were guns, the bright glare of sunlight on cannon newly mounted at the mouth of each street; all trained on the square. Behind the cannon, as far as their bulging eyes could see: French and Spanish soldiers marching in on them. Thousands.

"Avast." The door barricaded again. Trapped. Troubridge's face grew fanatical, his jaw clenched.

"Sam Hood, it's up to you. You must talk to them. Miller, help us write this." As Hood sat down again at the Abbess's desk Troubridge dictated:

SANTA CRUZ, *July 26, 1797*

TO HIS EXCELLENCY THE GOVERNOR:

I request that the officers, seamen and marines belonging to his Britannic Majesty shall embark with all their arms of every kind, and take their boats off, if saved, and be provided with such others as may be wanting; in consideration of which it is engaged on their part they shall not molest the town in any manner by the Ships of the British Squadron now before it, or any of the Islands of the Canaries—

Troubridge read it aloud.

"What about the Admiral?" Miller said.

"I'm coming to that," Troubridge growled:

And prisoners shall be given up on both sides,

Given under my hand and word of honor . . .

"You will not sign this, Hood, until the Governor signs it. And tell him that if this offer is not accepted in five minutes we will burn their damn town and kill every Spaniard in it—with bayonets!"

"Aye, aye, Captain Troubridge. I'll tell him." Sam Hood marched out under guard with a bit of the Abbess's wardrobe torn into a flag of truce.

❊   ❊   ❊

The Comandante General of the Canary Islands, Don Juan Antonio Gutierrez, was a tall man, rather stout-waisted, his body tapering toward a small head. He had a pale skin and green eyes, long black hair. The thin lips of a shrewd man. He made a courteous but reserved bow to Captain Hood and sat down at his desk to consider the Englishman's offer. Behind him stood his aides, all silent as wax-works.

He shook his head, smiling enigmatically as he studied Hood's square straight figure with its stubborn reddish straw hair. These Englishmen amazed him. The Comandante was the master of eight thousand soldiers, Spanish and allied French sent secretly to protect the treasure since last May when English pirates had begun reconnoitering Santa Cruz, their boatloads of pirates cutting out the French *Mutine* brig.

"There is one thing, *señor*. Your men, our prisoners . . . I do not think we should give up the prisoners." He was not much alarmed by an army that could be housed in one convent.

Hood did not blink. "Then, sir, much as we regret injuring innocent inhabitants, Santa Cruz burns! You have five minutes to make your decision!"

The Comandante General closed his eyes and his black eyebrows rose slowly toward his scalp. His fingers drummed the table. These men touched the chivalry in him!

Sam Hood had taken out his watch. It had stopped. He could see the salt water under the glass. But cupping it in his hand, he eyed it and began to count slowly.

The Comandante General's eyelids flickered. There were English battleships outside. They had been here nearly a week. Let them go? Let there be peace in Santa Cruz? He still had the treasure and who knew what these English pirates might hatch by tomorrow if they remained.

"Very well." He stood up. "I will sign."

Hood managed to close his watch reluctantly as Gutierrez signed his name. Hood took up the pen the Comandante offered him.

"Ah, but now, *señor*," the Comandante shook a few grains of sand lightly over the sheet, "I cannot permit you to leave us—as my guests —empty-handed."

Hood had swallowed each phrase slowly, wondering what tricks the enemy would play. Did they know they had the Nelson of St. Vincent prisoner—or was he dead?

"Come." The Comandante turned to his aides, who had stood immobile all through the meeting. He was smiling, for he was not one to be outdone by heroics. "Send bread and wine and fruit to refresh Captain Troubridge's valiant men! And our hospitals, Captain Hood," the Comandante General opened both arms, "are for the comfort of your wounded men. The boats you desire in which to embark will be at the mole, and should your ships need to victual or water, *señor,* as my guests," he bowed, "Santa Cruz kisses your hands!"

❊ ❊ ❊

As *Theseus,* with her long lists of casualties, began to work slowly back up the Atlantic, young Lieutenant Hoste and Captain Miller paused a moment outside the Admiral's sleeping cabin.

"He wouldn't let anyone touch him, sir"—Hoste swallowed—"when they finally reached *Theseus,* he ordered the boat back instantly to save others. He jumped out of the boat onto the ladder, just one hand to hold on. You know how quick he is, sir, he ran up the side calling for the surgeon to get his instruments. He knew the arm had to come off and the sooner the better. He's been like a second father to me." Hoste tugged at his vest, swallowing again.

Miller nodded. "Aye, *Lieutenant.*" He said that to bolster Hoste, who was mourning for everyone. To Miller's astonishment Hoste's eyes brimmed over.

"My commission *would* have made me happy—under any other circumstances, sir—" Hoste was speaking very evenly in spite of the tears running straight down his face. "But I lost my best friend in Lieutenant Weatherhead, sir." And Hoste marched stiffly away.

Somehow Hoste's story had brushed all routine reports out of Miller's mind as he knocked on the Admiral's door. Funny, nobody, even now, had a kind thought for young Nisbet.

Allen had opened the door a crack just as Miller started to turn away.

"Captain Miller, sir."

"Come in, Miller." The Admiral's voice sounded distant. The weariness of four years of war seemed to have struck him all at once. "You may go, Allen." And for once, Allen was mute and humbled. His eyes begged Miller not to stay long, as he slipped through the door; stood like a whipped dog in the corridor with his ludicrous string fastened to his collar.

The Admiral was sitting as usual at his writing desk, staring out the windows at the tantalizing last glimpse of his Teneriffe sinking back into dazzling waters. The right sleeve of his dressing gown swung empty.

"Pray, sir, let me call the clerk. You could dictate from your cot." Miller suddenly understood what Hoste had felt.

"I must learn to manage somehow, my dear Miller." The Admiral jabbed his quill at the inkwell, missed it the first time. "Did you send off the beer and cheese to the Comandante General, and pick up his dispatches for me to send into Cádiz?"

"Aye, sir, I did," Miller answered. Not to be outdone by the Dons' courtesy, Nelson had offered to carry the official report to Spain: Gutierrez's account of Admiral Nelson's repulse.

Miller frowned, watching hopelessly as the Admiral with a white face, forehead grooved in the throbbing agony of a fresh amputation, began to write in a shaking wiry backhand, so unlike his old scrawl. "If there is anything I can do, sir?"

"How's Freemantle?"

"Better, sir."

"And Weatherhead's gone after four whole days of—"

"He went very easily, sir. He seemed to be in no pain. Hoste nursed him constantly." Miller did not remind the Admiral that *Terpsichore* frigate had just committed the remains of her Captain Bowen—Jervis's "boy"—to the deep.

"Gibson's gone, too, in that—" There was an awkward silence.

"Pray, sir, won't you allow me to call the clerk? Isn't there something I could do for you, sir?"

"No thank you, Miller." The Admiral's pen spluttered. The paper slipped askew. He smiled wryly, laying down the pen, setting the inkstand on one corner of the paper to anchor it; picked up the quill again. "I must master this mutinous left hand. There. How's that?" He had written in the date in the strange round backhand, as labored as a child's first attempt to write. But it was legible.

"You're doing wonderfully, sir." But as Miller watched, the first effort began to weaken, the letters grew black and jagged. Illegible. And the more the pen threatened to waver, the blacker he made the slashes and angles on the paper. The words grew bigger. Miller turned away.

"You must have the clerk, sir. Then you'll be ready for anything by the time we're back with the fleet."

The Admiral turned slowly to look at Miller. Suddenly he snapped, "Nonsense, Miller, I'm *beached!*"

"I can't believe that, sir." Miller tried to smile. "I'll pass the word for the clerk." He bowed for lack of words and went out quietly.

The Admiral went on trying to write to Lord St. Vincent, and the empty sleeve of his dressing gown swung to the pitch and roll of the ship.

I am become a burthen to my friends, and useless to my Country. . . . When I leave your Command, I become dead to the world; I go hence and am no more seen. If from poor Bowen's loss, you think proper to oblige me, I rest confident you will do it: the Boy is under obligation to me, but he repaid me by bringing me from the mole of Santa Cruz.

I hope you will be able to give me a frigate to convey the remains of my carcase to England. God bless you, and believe me, your most faithful

HORATIO NELSON

You will excuse my scrawl, considering it is my first attempt.

Three weeks later *Theseus* joined the fleet and Nelson received the following:

MY DEAR ADMIRAL,

Mortals cannot command success; you and your companions have certainly deserved it, by the greatest degree of heroism and perseverance that was ever exhibited. I grieve for the loss of your arm, and for the fate of poor Bowen and Gibson, with the other brave men who fell so gallantly. I hope you and Captain Freemantle are doing well; *Seahorse* shall waft you to England the moment her wants are supplied. Your stepson is made Captain of the *Dolphin* Hospital ship, and all other wishes you may favor me with shall be fulfilled, as far as is consistent with what I owe to some valuable officers aboard *Ville de Paris*. We expect to hear of the

Preliminaries of Peace being agreed on every hour. I have betted one hundred pounds that they are settled on or before the 12th, and that the Definitive Treaty is signed before that day month. Give my love to Mrs. Freemantle. I will salute her and bow to your stump tomorrow morning, if you will give me leave.

Yours most truly and affectionately,

ST. VINCENT

It was a startled Commander in Chief who received word that the gaunt white ghost of his protégé had come aboard to thank him personally for that letter. But with St. Vincent's bolstering letter had come one from Rear Admiral Parker of the *St. George,* who had once, according to Fanny's letter, given *Captain* and *Culloden* full credit at St. Vincent. Now Parker, having read Nelson's exuberant account of the battle, was deprecating Collingwood's share, and demanding, politely, an accounting from Nelson of the exact time the *Captain* had been alone under fire. Parker was meticulous, and the breezy looseness of Nelson's "It seemed like an hour, but I do not pretend to say how long it was . . ." seemed to be a perfect loophole for making Nelson ridiculous. Parker's letter seemed rather futile now—as did Nelson's account.

Lord St. Vincent wrote a different kind of dispatch about Teneriffe; perhaps it made him a bigger man, for he took defeat as he had taken victory, on himself:

> I detached Rear-Admiral Nelson with orders to take Santa Cruz which I conceived was vulnerable. Although the enterprise has not been successful, His Majesty's Arms have acquired a very great degree of luster. Nothing from my pen can add to the *eulogy* the Rear-Admiral gives to the gallantry of the officers and men employed under him. . . . I have greatly to lament the loss the country has sustained in the severe wound of Rear-Admiral Nelson, and the death of Captain Richard Bowen, Lt. Gibson and the other brave officers and men who fell in the vigorous persevering assault. . . . I hope Rear-Admiral Nelson will live to render important services to His King and Country. . . .

Killed or drowned at Teneriffe, 230; wounded, 110.

❄   ❄   ❄

In a house at Bath, England, that summer, the Reverend Edmund Nelson had just sat down opposite Fanny to sip his late breakfast tea in the sunny little front room. It was nearly eleven, the hour when he would utter his first word for the day after struggling all night to breathe. He had "the asthma" the doctors said, and the time and the patience to indulge his symptoms. He was glad to discuss it, especially with others his own age who looked hale and hearty except for a red flush that he knew would carry them off, drop them dead overnight, while he carried on and on.

As the Reverend sipped his tea he nodded to Fanny over the rim of his cup. Age had mellowed his attitude toward life and toward young females, and though he had once dreaded his son Horatio's choice of a wife, feeling she would be a little too fine a lady for him, perhaps critical, he decided this morning, as he did almost every morning, that Fanny was a well-meaning child to be pitied and indulged. If she seemed abnormally afraid of living—like a child in the dark—it gave him the opportunity to lead her toward the light. She was the most patient congregation he had ever sermonized, though like all congregations she lacked the resolution necessary to follow his advice. Even so, she listened, and she did not stray. If she did not follow, she at least stood still. Only her eyes troubled him now and then: haunted. Perhaps she had loved her young Scotsman, Dr. Nisbet, too well. She did not mention him. She talked only of her present husband. And of him less and less, till today she was dumb. There were hideous rumors floating about Bath. She knew he had left the fleet for a small expedition; since then, not a word, only these tormenting whispers among navy wives.

"My dear," the Reverend Nelson found his voice, "your own understanding is a much better source of comfort than anything that can be offered by me or any of us who have your happiness at heart. How many times have rumors proved false, child?"

"Of course, Father, you are right." Fanny glanced up at the frail, crisp old man; she did not smile. Her voice was level, to a stranger it would have sounded mature and controlled, but to the old man it merely delineated the invisible line through which no one could pass, no one must find the little frightened creature in her lair.

The old man sighed. No man could relieve the rack of gossip that Fanny's circle of navy wives stretched themselves upon, like fakirs finding solace on their beds of thorns. Reason had no weapon to cope with one whispered rumor: an expedition had been wiped out. He could only try to alleviate her discomfort, for she would not relinquish the gnawing pleasure-terror of one single rumor. Yet on the other hand he recalled that when terror became fact she refused to believe it; she had brushed aside the fact that her husband was injured at St. Vincent as idle rumor, knowing that her husband was inclined to dwell on his health, even if it were only a scratch. The ways of the Lord and of women were beyond the tired Reverend.

"Shall we walk this morning, Fanny? Or what will make you happy, my dear? You are so indulgent of me, Fanny, I'm afraid at times, you will not be explicit. If I don't hit on what you want, forgive me, child. Poor substitute that I am, what shall we do with the day?" There was an almost servile discomfort in the Reverend's voice; he dreaded that Fanny might complain to his now favorite son he had not been good to her, just as Fanny complained—quietly—of his other children to him.

The Reverend had never devoted his thoughts to anyone, not even his dead wife, as he had to this one not-so-young lady from the West Indies.

"I could not bear to walk today, Father. But you go, you can bear news better than I can."

"But some amusement, child, to get your mind off your trials?" the Reverend coaxed. He had never thought gaiety belonged among the rights of his daughters, now he would have danced a jig if it would have made her smile. Perhaps the death of his daughter Ann had changed his mind. Ann had danced herself limp at a ball, run outside for a breath of air and died of pneumonia three days later. He had not realized that he loved his daughters until he lost Ann. Now he made up for it, to Fanny.

"Not even a little walk?" He smiled. "Very well, I shall stay home and write letters." Still Fanny did not smile.

To keep life on a dead level, without tears, without laughter; perhaps it was best for her. She alone knew the tensions within her, and how hard she must struggle behind her complacent wall to keep them from dragging her she did not know where, but she feared that wherever they led there would be nothing but loneliness. Even if her husband were here, holding her in his arms at this moment, there would be the ghosts of his ship floating between them, and the sails would always be just unfurling. "Pray do not trouble about me, Father," she said.

"Susanna will bring us all the news," he said as they heard the rustling bustle of the Reverend's second daughter, Fanny's sister-in-law, on the stairs; saw the shadow of Susanna's bonnet in the door. Susanna was always dressed and ready when she suggested strolls.

She came in, rather plump. Her hands threatened but never quite split her gloves. She was very efficient, knew the value of economics and the nonsense of anything else; Admiral Nelson's older sister.

"Good morning, Mrs. Bolton." Fanny eyed the bonnet (it was not one Fanny would have picked) realizing that her sister-in-law had defeated her. Susanna would walk and listen to gossip regardless of Fanny's delicate state.

"Good morning, Father—my *Lady*—" Susanna trotted into the room, and by her intonation of Fanny's new title she had cleverly destroyed any pleasure Fanny might have felt in hearing it. Susanna gave her father a daughterly kiss, but a kiss that still held resentments of her working apprenticeship. Work had made her a canny female, with her mind balanced to the hardships of the world: the necessity of steering her husband's finances with a firm hand; not allowing family sentiment to lighten her purse. "You're not walking, Father? Exercise will do you good."

"I am indolent today, Susanna." But his protection of his daughter-in-law did not escape Susanna's shrewd eye. She was on the point of answering when she whirled about.

"The post—there's a letter!"

As the servant opened the front door Susanna seemed to bounce a little, the plumes on her bonnet reared like a frightened horse as she took the papers. "Oh! Oh, dear! Oh, *dear!*"

"Is it from my husband?" Fanny's voice was oddly flat.

Susanna's hand went to her heart. She held out the letter. "Prepare yourself, Fanny," brusquely, like a surgeon about to cut.

Fanny took the letter with the angular black scratches:

"To Lady Nelson, Bath—" She held it without a quiver while her face went dead. Then she screamed hysterically, dropped it as if it were a snake. "It isn't his! It's not his writing!"

Then, with her face once more composed, she picked it up and laid it face down on the table; walked to the window, stood there staring at the crowds strolling the streets. She followed them with her eyes without seeing them.

Susanna and the Reverend Nelson, shaken by her scream, stared after her. At last the Reverend's fingers crept toward the paper, stopped. His lips began to quiver and he sank back in his chair shaking his head.

It was too much for Mrs. Bolton. "Aren't you going to read it?"

"I haven't the courage—I can't!" Fanny did not turn around.

The Reverend murmured, "God's will be done . . ." but Susanna Nelson Bolton gave an angry sniff. "I refuse to mourn till I know what is in that letter!"

"Do read it to us, Susanna," Fanny whispered. She had gone from hysteria into a somnambulant trance.

Mrs. Bolton took the paper, her temper sustaining her for the moment. But her fingers shook as she broke the seal. "It might be from anyone—perhaps he has a new clerk or—oh, Fanny!" and she burst into tears. Fanny walked very evenly to a chair; sat down very straight.

Susanna began to decipher the almost illegible words:

MY DEAREST FANNY,

I am so confident of your affection, that I feel the pleasure you will receive will be equal, whether my letter is wrote by my right hand or my left. It was a chance of war, and I have great reason to be thankful; and I know it will add much to your pleasure in finding that Josiah, under God's Providence, was principally instrumental in saving my life. As to my health, it never was better; and now I hope soon to return to you; and my Country, I trust, will not allow me any longer to linger in want of that pecuniary assistance which I have been fighting the whole war to preserve to her. But I shall not be surprised to be neglected and forgot, as probably I shall no longer be considered as useful. However I shall feel rich if I continue to enjoy your affection. The cottage is now more necessary than ever. You will see by the papers, Lt. Weatherhead is gone. Poor fellow! He lived four days after he was shot. I shall not close this letter till I join the fleet, which seems distant; for it's been calm these three days past. I am fortunate in having a good surgeon on board: in short, I am much more recovered than could have expected. I beg neither you or my Father will think much of this mishap; my mind has long been made up to such an event. God bless you, and believe me,

Your most affectionate husband,

HORATIO NELSON

Just joined the Fleet perfectly well, and shall be with you perhaps, as soon as this letter. Good Earl St. Vincent has made Josiah a Master and Commander. I shall come to Bath the moment permission comes from the

Admiralty to strike my flag . . . when the first you hear of me will be at the door. God bless you and my Father and ever believe me,

Your most affectionate,

H.N.

Mrs. Bolton's voice had steadied as she reached the end. "There! And he's—oh, Fanny, my dear!" And Mrs. Bolton ran to her sister-in-law, sobbed in her arms. But Fanny seemed like a dead thing, and when Mrs. Bolton had had a good cry she gave another sniff, secretly angered with her poor brother's stiff little wife.

And as the day passed Mrs. Bolton felt downright huffy. By the time evening came, Fanny still sat outwardly unmoved, listening to the Reverend Nelson's scriptural quotations.

It grew late, but Bath was gay tonight and the voices of fashionable strollers seemed hectic. Mrs. Bolton announced she was going to bed.

The living room had grown very still.

"So little Josiah is a hero," the Reverend sighed.

For a moment Fanny's face brightened. Suddenly she put down her embroidery, went to the window. Occasional carriages went by.

"Father!" She turned as if shot.

The Reverend started up from his chair. "Child, what—"

"It's his *voice!*" And Fanny's face turned slowly scarlet as they both heard a weary rasping order, pitched for a gale rather than a street:

"Right here, driver! This is the house!"

The Reverend had stumbled to the door. But Fanny stood rooted to the window listening to that almost forgotten, now intensely familiar sound.

Four and a half years had vanished. Gone where? She wanted to smile, to laugh. But you can't shake off torture just because someone has knocked aside the instruments. Tears came in her eyes, but beyond that she was paralyzed. And there wouldn't be any arm. But she must not notice it. It would be hideous. But he had said it was just a mishap. Thank God he didn't care; it would have been unbearable if he cared. Just a mishap . . . he was strong and he hated scenes. He would understand her.

But she was still standing alone in the living room. She heard his father laughing, and his laughter—and, of course, Susanna's. She closed her eyes, still as a column of stone.

"But where's my wife? Fanny, don't you *remember* me?"

She was too upset to catch the weary, almost petulant twist that changed his face from pure delight to wry laughter. He was different. He didn't look the same. And that sleeve. And there was his family everywhere.

"My dear—" as his arm went around her. "Oh, I should think—rather!"

And at last they were both laughing.

❋   ❋   ❋

And still the war did not end. Peace talks were in vain. France had a hero who promised her the boundaries of ancient Gaul, who had always done what he boasted he would do. Who had cried: "Soldiers of France, I will lead you onto the most fertile plains of the world. There you will find great towns, rich provinces. There you will find honor, glory, and riches. Soldiers of the Army of Italy, will you be wanting in courage?"

Buonaparte had conquered Italy.

Now, after four years and a half, the war had only begun. Peace-maker Lord Malmesbury, brazenly insulted, left Paris, and the world waited to see what would happen next. A defeated Austria made peace with France: Campo Formio; resented it sulking and smarting.

While all over the world, even in far-off, happily isolated America, the place where young Europeans all hoped to go and set up the new Utopia, shops displayed the latest toy: Give your children a new Christmas gift! Miniature guillotines, perfect in every detail, guaranteed to decapitate paper dolls.

And as for England's hero, by some whim of what was usually a fickle public opinion, no one blamed him for Teneriffe! He emerged from it England's "Darling." Even the opposition, while denouncing the Admiralty and St. Vincent for ordering the attack, and bewailing—and justly—the loss of so many lives, uttered no complaint against Sir Horatio, who had talked St. Vincent into it, and might have withdrawn when he saw his plans disintegrating. Quite the contrary, they applauded his pride, his do or die. Newspapers announced England was safer with Nelson to fight for them. They referred to him publicly as Nelson, as if he were a peer of the realm. Publicly then, Teneriffe had not hurt him a bit.

Yet in spite of his brave tone to Fanny, he had written St. Vincent: "I am not the least better than when I left. . . . I found my domestic happiness perfect, and I hope time will bring me about again, but I have suffered great misery. My general reception from John Bull has been just what I wished, for I assure you they never forget your name in their honest praises." But to the male members of his family: he only wanted "a hut to put my mutilated carcase in. . . ."

Three months had passed and he was no better as he sat in a big wing chair by the fire staring miserably at the grate. He had just tortured himself into reading a letter from Lieutenant Weatherhead's father:

I am conscious, Sir, that I ought long since to have congratulated you on your return to your native country, and to have offered my acknowledgments for the many and great favors conferred on my poor Boy. I have more than once sat down with an intention of making this offering of my gratitude—but have hitherto found my spirits unequal to the accomplishment of it. I now, Sir, though late, beg leave to present my most sincere thanks for the numerous and signal favors conferred on my son, from the moment he entered with you on board *Agamemnon,* to the hour of his fall. . . . To the last moment of my existence I shall retain a lively remembrance of all your favors. I would willingly flatter myself, and the hope affords some slight degree of consolation, that you did not find my Boy totally unworthy of the generous patronage you so liberally extended toward him. That you may live long to serve your country . . .

He had answered it, best he could.

DEAR SIR,

Believe me, I have largely partaken in our real cause for grief in the loss of a most excellent young man. Whether he is considered in his moral character, or as an Officer, he was a bright example to all around; and when I reflect on that fatal night, I cannot but bring sorrow and his fall before my eyes. Dear friend, he fought as he had always done, by my side, and for more than one hundred times with success; but for wise reasons (we are taught to believe) a separation was to take place, and we must, however hard the task, be resigned. With most sincere wishes for your future happiness without alloy, believe me, dear sir,

Your most faithful servant . . .

He chose a fresh sheet of paper, balancing his writing case precariously on his knees, and with more than a little relief turned his mind to addressing Hoste's father.

After mentioning Weatherhead:

Your dear son is as gallant; and I hope he will live long to honor Norfolk and England. I grieved to have left him; but it was necessary, and Lord St. Vincent will continue to be his kind protector and friend. His worth both as a man and as an Officer, exceeds all which the most sincere friends can say of him. I pray God to bless William. Happy father in such a son! As to myself, I suppose I was getting well too fast, for I am beset with a Physician, Surgeon, and Apothecary, and, to say the truth, am suffering much pain with some fever; but time, I hope, will restore me to tolerable health. Captain Ralph Willet Miller is Captain of the *Theseus*— one who loves William, *and is the only truly virtuous man that I ever saw.* I beg my respects to Mrs. Hoste, and believe me,

Dear Sir,

Your most obedient servant,

HORATIO NELSON

Lady Nelson desires her compliments.

And these letters had killed the afternoon—and nearly himself. He balanced the writing case gingerly with his one hand as he set it aside.

Today, with the cold London damp seeping in, with the jangling rowdy clatter of horses and carts and fast carriages on the cobbled street, would never end. Tonight he would not sleep because of constant pain. Tomorrow would be the same.

Perhaps he could take a walk. Some days he went calling from dawn to dusk. Today he just couldn't, though this was the kind of pain that did not stop when he sat still. He wanted something to lift him bodily out of his skin. It was the kind of pain that had to be wrestled with, worn out, till exhaustion let him sleep regardless of pain. He seemed to move more quickly, walk faster than before. Even so, he could not escape it; though sometimes meeting old friends, allowing himself to get wrought up in a political argument, he could forget it. No one quite understood how he "managed so well" or else they thought he complained a great deal over something that was not half so troublesome as it looked. But they did not look forward to a surgeon tugging at the ligature every day, a ligature that not only had been carelessly knotted around the artery, but had caught up a nerve with it.

So he would muster his will, sally forth. He had come down from Bath to be knighted, and the trip had done him in again. But he had felt the King's sword, heard George III, who had once announced he had a poor opinion of Nelson, now officially pronounce him Knight.

In fact the King drew him aside for an interview of half an hour, during which time Sir Horatio did most of the talking and the most pertinent statement His Majesty had made, for he was in one of his periods of mental health, was:

"I see you have lost an arm."

Sir Horatio, accompanied by Captain Berry, who had not yet persuaded the Admiralty to give him a ship, rose to the occasion with his one remaining eye on their future:

"But not my right hand, as I have the honor of presenting Captain Berry to Your Majesty."

George III had thought for a while. Recently he had even taken the trouble to allow his son, the Duke of Clarence, to speak to him. And Clarence, with an unselfishness not common to him, had used the opportunity to tell his King-Father all about Nelson. The Royal family was at peace internally. At the moment, then, old George III actually doted on his son's best friend:

"Your Country has need for a bit more of you, Sir Horatio."

Recognition at last! Surrounded by the centuries of accumulated custom and pomp the actors appeared expendable; the props were eternal. The King had permitted his newest Knight to identify himself with the symbolic immortal.

And he clung to that through the pain and fever, even when the infection flared and the doctors shook their heads.

Now he heard Fanny's light steady step and broke off his brooding. Fanny's mild voice, but not her words, came through the closed door. Who had come to disturb him? For a moment he rather perversely hoped it might even be the surgeon, for the room was morbidly still. At last he heard the landlady's voice and hoped Fanny would not bring her in. He had rather expected his old friend Alexander Davison to drop by. Davison had prevented him from marrying that beautiful girl in Quebec, taken him by the arm and walked him to his ship. But he had forgiven Davison, for Davison was the only man with the patience to handle Nelson's financial affairs. He was his agent, and more often than not it was Davison's money that Nelson was spending, but Davison said he had taken a long-range view of Nelson and hoped someday to at least break even.

Sir Horatio listened to Fanny's voice and stared gloomily at the rented furnishings in the rented lodgings his brother Maurice had found for them on Bond Street. The place was neither good nor bad.

It was impersonal. The furniture was light and simple. The natural reaction to the plush and carved Jacobean junk of the last century. But it wasn't home.

He wanted a home. For four years he had begged Fanny to have a home ready. Why, when she disliked his relatives, did she still prefer to visit them, annoy herself, rather than keep house? He had outwitted her. Sick as he was, he had already found and *bought* a house: Roundwood. He would see Fanny in it before he sailed away again. He wanted a garden of his own, and a wife under his own roof. He did not know if Fanny was pleased or not, she said she was, but she found so many obstacles to moving in right away while nursing him. Why? Why? Poor little creature, everything was so hard for her. Patience was Fanny's virtue.

Now the voices had ceased. Worse and worse. The house was more gloomy than ever. He closed his eyes. He would creep up on sleep.

The drawing room latch clicked. The flatfooted jarring step of Allen followed Fanny's conscientious tiptoeing.

"Horace dear? Are you asleep?" She whispered just loud enough to wake him if he were.

"No! How could I sleep!" But as he had not meant to snap at her, he did not open his eyes. He listened to the tray being set on the table by the fire; the faint infuriating tick and tiny clinking of china as Fanny did her best to prepare his tea without disturbing him. He could hear Allen breathing in soft grunts as if being a manservant and general butler and jack-of-all-trades about a house were infinitely harder than being a gunner.

The very faintness of the sounds they made annoyed him. There was the positive promise that Fanny was going through the ritual regardless. If she would only be brisk and be done! It was the stone-cold knife and slow amputation through healthy flesh all over again, high up above the numb shattered wound. "I am not asleep."

"No, my dear?" Followed by more slow ticking and chinking.

"Pray, Fanny, no tea for me." He opened his eyes, saw only her aged, but still familiar, nervous smile of indulgence that quietly reminded him he had snapped at her. And that made him more miserable—and short tempered. His arm twinged in recurring pulsations.

"It will refresh you, dear," and she held up the cup to Allen. "For Sir Horatio."

Allen hedged, but as the Admiral, to his disgust, said to her, "Thank you, my dear," Allen gave it to him only slightly slopped over in the saucer. And Allen withdrew, his faith shaken in his master's invincibility. And Allen began to hate Fanny. Fanny had sensed it before Allen knew it in himself.

"Frank was more of a gentleman," she sighed as Allen disappeared. "Poor Frank! I felt so badly about him."

"I got him into a hospital, didn't I? Thanks to your pity," the Admiral smiled. "And I know Allen is a beast. But he's nursed me, Fanny, and he's honest even if he does tell clever lies."

Fanny laughed outright, then as she heard Allen's footstep creaking away from the door, "Oh, Horace, he heard me!"

"No matter. The beast was eavesdropping."

But Fanny had turned pale, as if Allen could harm her somehow, just by knowing her thoughts. She lapsed into a cold studied silence. There was always something or someone to come between them, spoil everything!

She sat contemplating her tea, not knowing what else to say, feeling that anything she said on a day like today might irritate her husband. She knew she was not witty, could not keep pace with his quick, darting, allusive conversations until she made him stop and explain, and by that time he would be tired—and impatient. Men were such poor invalids, they were so accustomed to health they did not know the virtues of a chronic invalid's patience. They did not realize that to plunge back into marriage after four years' separation required a little patience and more understanding. For now she had sensed that marriage was stranger than absence. She needed time to get used to being made love to and then snapped at the next moment. He never snapped in his handsome letters, nor did he make vulgar love. As she gazed at the leaves in her teacup Lady Nelson unconsciously pressed her lips together; four years of that gesture had made her face appear closer to middle age than her thirty-nine years warranted. She lied all the time about her age now that she saw the lines, but still they did not disappear as she had thought they would when her husband came home. But he talked of going away again! How could she be happy with that hanging over her? If only he would retire now with all England singing his praises. He had done enough. They were socially acceptable, and their income, managed by Davison who some people said was unscrupulous because he was rich, but who was martyredly honest with them, was sufficient. They could have a carriage and small parties. Perhaps she could have a maid. Her husband agreed she needed a personal maid to do all the dull chores of keeping her smart wardrobe up to date. He agreed to everything, she could have the moon if she could reach it, but he would not resign his commission! As she sat there her eyes filled with tears, and her face quivered.

"I'll fire Allen if you wish it, Fanny, though you know how I feel."

"Oh, no! Pray, I—I'm just *so* tired . . ." and she trembled even more visibly. "More tea, Horace?"

"*No,* thank you." But there it was, brimming and steaming before him. For a moment he felt an exhilarating storm of temper focusing on that cup. On Fanny. For a moment he was sick of her. And the old West Indian toast darted through his mind: "To a sickly season and a bloody war!" And that was crowded out by the voice of Captain Pringle on the very day of his marriage: "The navy yesterday lost one of its greatest ornaments by Nelson's marriage. It is a national loss that such an officer should marry: had it not been for that circumstance, I foresaw that Nelson would become the greatest man in the service . . ." His fever was rising with his temper. And there was that abominable gypsy! "You will be at the head of your profession by the time you are forty . . ." And then? "I can tell you *no more!*" But he brushed them all out of mind, while Fanny, sensing she had done something wrong, cringed back in her chair, her face plain, old and anguished.

Not that a fine face and figure meant anything, he reminded himself, grappling with his temper. Then his arm twinged.

"Pray, my dear husband, have I upset you?"

"I'm not upset. I'm only very miserable, Fanny. *You* haven't dressed my arm today."

Fanny's face remained white. "I was waiting for you to feel equal to it," she faltered. "Shall I do it now?"

"Tonight will do. Then I'll take laudanum and enjoy a thoroughly miserable night."

"Whatever you wish, my dear." Fanny had not regained her color. Her first husband was dead and her second was being shot to pieces. And every day she must look at that arm and remember it. Why? He had called it a mishap. Why this sudden insistence that she dress it? To be rid of the doctors—he said . . . But Allen could do it, not that she objected to the work, but it required all the nerve she possessed to face that physical fact: his arm had been shot off in battle. Wouldn't it have been better if they had both agreed—as he had said at first—that it just hadn't happened—this mishap? "I'll do it this minute if it will make you easier, dear."

He was smiling at her. She felt better, just as horses came pounding down the street, pulled up on the muffling straw laid out before the door.

"Oh, I hope that isn't another caller. Your friends kill us with their attentions!" Fanny sighed.

But the Admiral looked up eagerly when their knocker was gently rapped.

Allen stomped in, announced, "Got an old friend. Colonel Drinkwater, sir. Looking pretty well, too." He had ignored Lady Nelson.

"Splendid!" The Admiral sat forward.

But Fanny had flushed. Terrified and infuriated by Allen's manners. "But are you sure, my dear, he won't talk politics and tire you?"

"Show him in, Allen." With a sudden jerk of his left hand the Admiral sent his blanket flying. "Stow that slop."

"Oh—" Fanny gasped until she remembered that was a nautical term for bedding she could not get used to. "Allen! Leave the blanket here—" she pointed at a footstool—"Sir Horatio must not be chilled." Her voice had a fanatical ring to it, for she had summoned every ounce of nerve to command her husband's monstrous valet. Allen looked from one to the other. The Admiral nodded to him to fold it and leave it on the footstool. Allen did, but the glance he gave Fanny made her blush to her eyes.

Sir Horatio was on his feet in the center of the room as Colonel Drinkwater came in with that cautious quiet step of a visitor to a sickroom. His face went blank, then beamed relief as he shook the Admiral's left hand.

"But this is splendid! What a wonderful nurse your ladyship must be!"

"She's an angel from heaven, Drinkwater." The Admiral smiled at his wife, and Fanny blessed him.

"He mends every day." Fanny automatically proffered tea, her nerves still jangling from her bout with Allen.

"Have you been to the Admiralty, Drinkwater? I didn't get out today—writing letters." The Admiral had paced the room once, then made his way back to his chair, grateful to be in it.

"That's what I came to tell you! Duncan's Channel Fleet is out—after the Dutch."

And at that moment the bells of all London began to ring out with their thousand voices. A gun went off, signaling a victory.

The Admiral was on his feet again.

"Oh, now—now, my dear, don't let it excite you!" Fanny jumped up to press her husband back in his chair.

He refused to be pushed. "Drinkwater!" His face was radiant as he stretched out his left hand. "I'd give this other arm to have been there!"

    ❊   ❊   ❊

That night, just as Fanny had feared, the hero of St. Vincent had to take laudanum, which made him speechless and drowsy though it did not relieve pain. While London went mad with joy at the newest success. A *feu de joie* lit the dome of St. Paul's Cathedral while horses reared and shied at the mobs, children were trampled, and hoodlums beat up any enemy suspects, and pretty generally imitated Duncan's battle in the Channel. It was considered French to sleep that night. The mobs rushed down the streets hurling stones at darkened windowpanes.

No. 141 Bond Street was dark.

"Beat in the door! We'll have no lovers of French asleep!" and a burly fellow, vest torn, coatless, rolled up his shirt sleeves while another fondled a stout cane. With a "Hip! Hip! Hurrah!" the crowd rushed the door.

A nightcapped head popped out. Two tough eyes squinted. "Wot's going on? Coon't a body rest? Or is the bloody town afire?" Allen bawled louder than the crowd.

"Lights! Lights! Wake up the dead! Hurrah for Duncan! Hurrah for the Victory of Camperdown!"

"On yer way, lubbers. Sir Horatio Nelson is badly wounded and he wants to sleep."

"And who's 'im?"—from the torn vest.

That did it. The man with the cane whirled around, several in the crowd snarled at torn vest:

"Who's 'im? Sir 'Oratio Nelson? 'Im what took two ships by 'isself at St. Vincent? Attacked eight thousand Dons at Teneriffe? Ask me that again. . . ."

The torn vest suddenly remembered. "You'll hear no more from us," he shouted at Allen. "Let the 'ero sleep, God bless 'im!"

Duncan was made a Viscount with a pension of three thousand pounds a year for having led a superior number of English against an inferior number of Dutch, and taking half the Dutch ships. Unfortunately it was necessary to court-martial one of the English captains for having failed to fight wholeheartedly. But it was a victory and right under Londoners' noses. England had gone to war, allied to the Dutch. France had beaten the Dutch. The Dutch had made peace with France, and therefore when the French sent them out to begin the invasion of Ireland, the English, also, beat the Dutch. The street singers strolled through London town singing "Lord Duncan and his Fleet" and still now and then, because the story of Jervis, Lord St. Vincent's fifteen against twenty-seven appealed to them, they sang "Earl St. Vincent and the Glorious 14th of February," and sometimes still: "Sir Horatio Nelson and the brave men who fought on board *Captain*." But time wore on, and as Nelson wrote to Miller, the last battle was always the best.

After a while men remembered that Camperdown, like St. Vincent, was still not a defeat of the French fleet.

St. Vincent had taken the Dons, Duncan the Dutch. What would Englishmen cheer if sometime someone beat that young Buonaparte's ships? Why, the man who did that must be loved like the King, God bless him!

But Nelson, unstrung by laudanum and opium, seemed never to mend though Sir Gilbert Elliot, dropping in, said he looked splendid, more rested than he had ever seen him. Elliot was in excellent humor in spite of his brother-in-law's fiasco at Paris, for Elliot hoped to pluck a diplomatic plum: the Ambassadorship to Vienna. But in good time, diplomacy ran through slower channels than ships.

"An old acquaintance of yours has been making quite a social lion of himself since his daring escape from prison, Sir Horatio. He's revived the celebration of his destruction of the French fleet at Toulon."

"Smith? The noncombatant Smith?" The Admiral smiled.

But Sir Gilbert suddenly frowned. "You want the Mediterranean command."

Nelson sat forward. "My heart's set on it, but," he added carefully, "only as a subordinate to the great St. Vincent. . . . Pray believe me, I am humble. All I ask is one ship for a left-handed sailor."

Sir Gilbert nodded. "Smith has a diplomat brother in Constantinople —named Smith—" Elliot's eyes twinkled. "And of course you know Smith's personality—a seagoing Buonaparte—all bluster and oratory but he is a great friend of Dundas, East India Company, you know— and Lord Elgin. I fear Smith is almost jealous of Sir Arthur Welles- ley's new appointment."

"No doubt he'd like to be Viceroy of India," Nelson mused.

"By the way, Captain Hunt's escorting Sir Arthur to India. Between us, Nelson"—Elliot's voice leveled off without any humor—"Smith would like very much to command the Mediterranean."

"He is only a very junior captain!"

"He works through Pitt, not through the Admiralty."

"But he can't!"

"I don't exactly say that he can." Elliot turned to Lady Nelson, who had, of course, lost the thread of the conversation. "Has your lady- ship read Colonel Drinkwater's *Narrative of the Battle of St. Vincent?*"

"As far as I could bear to, Sir Gilbert. But Sir Horatio promised me so many times there would be 'no fighting.' . . ."

And after Sir Gilbert left she sat very quietly. "Horace, what did Lord St. Vincent mean in his last letter to you?"

"About Pitt's refusal to raise a monument to Captain Bowen in Westminster because there was 'no precedent'?"

"No, about Josiah."

"What he said. The boy has done well convoying transports and protecting stragglers."

"He said 'marvelously well,' dear."

"Yes, indeed."

"But what did he mean by Josiah only *'wants cultivation* to render him a very good character . . .'?"

"Isn't that fine!"

"But Josiah has an angelic character, Horace!"

"Yes. I love him, Fanny. By the way did I tell you Hoste's a lieu- tenant? And Noble's a captain?"

"Yes, dear, you did."

Until December life went racketing on, or stood still paralyzed by drugs, or roared down the nights conjuring delirium. And no letup. A consultation of the very best surgeons: until the ligature, carelessly made of silk and more carelessly wound around the nerve as well as the artery, came away, the nerve would be irritated, the wound inflamed. A fresh amputation or leave it to time and nature? They toyed with both notions. While the patient fretted to be back in service.

"You have bought the house, Horace, aren't you content to live in it?"

"I wish nothing else, my dearest."

"Then pray be contented now that we have one. You have a right to a roof and a warm chair by the fire."

"Not one scrap of my ardor has been shot away, Fanny!" How old did she think he was at thirty-nine, for God's sake?

"But a house will be lonely. I don't know anyone in Ipswich."

"Invite our friends. I could not be a hermit either!"

"And it needs so many repairs before I can risk my health in it."

"You may do anything in the world you wish to make it comfortable. Your place is in our home, Fanny—my dear. Did you remember to send off that letter to St. Vincent with the gold sword for Cockburn, Fanny?"

Fanny nodded. That's where so much money went. But she did not say so. She began again at a tangent:

"Captain Andrews is home—retired."

"I know. Poor fellow, his health bothers him. I can't understand it, he was only wounded twice."

"And once in a silly duel in the West Indies, remember, dear? Perhaps he thought it wise to rest on his laurels."

"Oh, my God!"

But at last the stubborn silk cord binding the artery gave way. It was just before Christmas, 1797. The pain was over. The Admiral gave his thanks humbly to God.

And immediately presented himself to the Admiralty while Fanny held her breath. Would they have him?

The Admiralty had his name down for the *Foudroyant* 84, the newest and finest ship in the navy. Only she wasn't ready. The *Vanguard* 74 would be ready sooner, late February or early March, if he didn't mind taking a smaller ship.

Back to Bond Street jubilant: "Fanny, write Berry he's going to sea with me in the *Vanguard*."

Fanny, face pale, stiff in her armor: "But he's just getting married!" Even so, she sat down at the desk, took a sheet of paper.

"Tell him: 'Any event which has the prospect of adding to your felicity cannot but afford me pleasure; and I most heartily congratulate you on becoming one of us' "—he smiled at Fanny, but she was holding her feelings so tightly under control she made no response—" 'and we shall have great pleasure in being known to Mrs. Berry.' " Still Fanny did not smile. He waved his hand impatiently, took a quick turn, then: " 'I am confident nothing will alter you for the worse, and I wish you no better: therefore we will leave off complimenting . . .' "

Fanny suddenly lifted the pen, held it back. "I should think you would want Josiah for your captain."

"He needs the experience of being on his own bottom!"

Fanny raised pained quizzical eyebrows. So he translated:

"His own ship—he's not even a post-captain. He's very young, Fanny dear. He's still rough, but I love—"

"Lord Rodney made his son post-captain at fifteen, dear husband."

"I do not have his influence, Fanny! Berry was posted after St. Vincent, he's almost thirty and if it had not been for his gallantry—"

"I thought Josiah was a *little* gallant at Teneriffe!"

"He was! Pray, my dear, don't you understand?"

"Never mind, dear husband! I shall never ask it again."

He took a turn about the room, started to explain more. But explaining to Fanny was like trying to walk through quicksand. "My dear . . ." He gave her a kiss, eyeing the letter. "Tell Berry not to mention we're going yet, and—ah—"

But Fanny swept out of the room, head high, cheeks flushed; a moment later her histrionic sobs came through the ceiling. He sent Allen to fetch the doctor *again*.

❈ ❈ ❈

"And deck the halls with boughs of holly, fal la la, la la, la la, la *la!*"

"Beautiful!" Reverend Edmund Nelson leaned back in his chair as the family ended the carol. He was beaming upon them as if they were still eleven naughty little infants, coming to say their evening prayers, casting rather subdued and awesome glances through the darkening windows in the direction of their father's employer: Jehovah. But only six of the children still survived, and the five of them present now answered his benevolent benedictions with varying degrees of reciprocation: from the Admiral's alert smile to sister Susanna's snore.

"Come here, child." The father beckoned his son, who stepped over to him, sat down on the arm of his chair. The Admiral was looking fine. And on his coat he now wore a sunburst star of knighthood. His empty right sleeve was pinned dramatically to his chest; all in all he looked as if he had been through a war. It did not please him, he did not like seeing the ladies start and pale as if he were a crippled beggar, but he made the most of it and cut a distinguishing figure; even if it did spoil tea parties to have the war brought home! His family was different. Tonight he could relax.

"The Lord hath dealt leniently with me, my son," his father mused, "that I should live to see this day." Father was feeling like a sermon after the hearty dinner of Norfolk turkey. He folded his hands over his chest. "But what of the future you will say . . ." He raised his finger to silence his son's sudden protest. "The hairs on your head are numbered—a comforting thought."

"The future? I pray, sir, yours shall be endless." After all, Father said he had been dying for forty years. "You are like me, Father—at Calvi all the prevailing disorders attacked me but I had not strength enough for them to fasten on."

The father beamed at his son's appreciation of his long duel with death. "Ah yes. And I remember your dear departed uncle's letter to me, when you begged to go to sea: 'What has poor Horatio done, who is the most delicate of all, that he should be sent to rough it on the sea? But let him come, and the first time we go into action a cannon ball may knock off his head, and provide for him at once.' I dwell on that, how little we know of the future!" The father turned from one to another of his family, a rather strange lot, some wan, some well. Perhaps the ancestral cavalier blood refused to mingle with the Reverend's farmer stock. "I trust in the Lord," the father nodded, "that He will prosper your going out and coming in."

"And bring back a ship, Horace!" a new voice broke in. Eldest brother William, a Reverend also, pulled his chair closer. There was a strong facial resemblance in all the three brothers and two sisters scattered about the room with the usual air of sacrificing pleasure for a family gathering. But their physical resemblance and a certain animation of expression were all that bound them. They did not pay much attention to the brother, the Reverend William, until he coughed out a laugh, "Bring us a *lord*ship, Horace!"

"I think Sir Horatio has done quite enough." Fanny rose impatiently, left the cluster. She had moped through the evening, for now that her husband was well and with the prospect of active service, he was more delightful company than she had ever remembered him. She almost believed she had fallen in love all over again. They had gone to theaters and parties and concerts. Been entertained by some of the right people who thought her husband was at least a minor social lion, though being not too tall and minus an arm, he did not win the ladies as quickly as the black-eyed, black-mustachioed "hero of Toulon," Sir Sidney Smith. Yet it still seemed strange to Fanny to see her husband's exploits pictured in prints hung up in shop windows. Especially when the artists had used the only portrait available. The Rigaud, which belonged to Captain Locker, an oil of a rather charming wistful young Captain Nelson aged twenty-one. The artists had been faced with a lapse of eighteen years in his age. They improvised: etched in stern lines, sharpened the boyish face which, while not handsome, was certainly passing fair; lengthened the long-enough nose, straightened the mobile lips from a near-smile to a villainous sneer; succeeded at last in drawing a haughty young prig of unidentifiable age, totally unrecognizable to contemporaries who knew the subject, but promising to jolt posterity. Perhaps it was just as well, for it had taken the Admiral but one glance at the engraver's efforts to consent to have a new portrait done by Abbott. Now while Abbott was once more restoring the reality, slightly less boyish, but still rather engaging, the engravers were already plotting to continue the piratical character they had created for the public; some merely went on with the first picture by amputating the arm and fixing the eye. It was rather a fuss, Fanny thought, and almost frightening when she walked with her husband to hear the mob suddenly cheer him, recognizing him by the sleeve and the star, and sometimes she wondered . . . Was it too much ado? Sooner or later someone would surely discover he was only her lovable-laughable Horace!

She had emitted a long sigh for multiple reasons as she crossed the room slowly and sat down very wilted, beside Nelson's youngest sister, Kitty Matcham.

Kitty glanced up with a quick sweet smile, much like her brother's. She was more sprightly, more youthful than Fanny in spite of the fact that she was always just recovering from, or expecting a child. Fanny noticed that with a pang of resentment, for she knew her husband must notice it too, as Kitty said, "Horace was telling me you called on Captain Miller's little girls, Fanny. Were they cunning?"

"We did. What those people thought of the Admiral, a Knight of

Bath, sitting in the middle of the carpet with two little moppets, I cannot imagine!"

Kitty laughed. Laughed doubly, for she was thinking that it was just as well her husband, the worldly George Matcham, had not come to hear Fanny say that. Fanny was poison to George and vice versa. George respected and admired his brother-in-law but he could rave for hours trying to understand how a man of the Admiral's intelligence had ever picked such a lazy, indolent, indifferent, half-hysterical, dull—yes, and stupid wife! Kitty thought that was going too far. She could see the female point of view, though why Fanny should be so difficult over trifles, refusing to make a home, and yet so very faithful . . . "She's virtuous, George." But when he demanded she explain that, Kitty could only point out that she was faithful—George would nod solemnly—that Fanny was smartly dressed—George would shrug —that Fanny's health was terribly delicate—George would laugh—that Fanny hadn't always looked haggard, and settled from the neck down —to all of which George would finally curl his handsome lip, muttering, "You'll see . . ." That distressed Kitty. She wanted her brother happy, and virtuous.

"Of course, that's the way my uncle, the President of Nevis, found him—on all fours—" Fanny had been rambling on, but Kitty knew that story and was tired of the President of Nevis.

"Are you coming to Bath as usual, Fanny, when Horace leaves? Or going to Roundwood?" Kitty asked. George was already resigned to having Fanny, perhaps it perversely amused him to study her even while he swore he could not abide her in his house. He was always suavely polite. Kitty could count on that, and on the fact that Fanny, equally haughty, was suspicious of George's suavity. No one ever won that duel.

Fanny was now studying Kitty suspiciously wondering if she dared speak her mind to her husband's favorite sister. "I think perhaps I should have a little rest before undertaking Roundwood. It's physically impossible for us to move in before Horace goes, though he seems to think he could move into a house and onto a ship at the same time. Allon's behind it, Kitty. I dread that man's influence. Oh, dear, I mustn't *think*, Kitty, I'll go all to pieces. Horace didn't have to go to war again . . . Kitty, I *suffer* so!"

"Do come to Bath. George and I are counting on it!" Kitty suddenly felt a genuine surge of pity. For when Nelson left and Fanny went to Roundwood the Reverend Father had announced that he would look after Fanny; pay her a nice long visit. And the next moment Kitty saw her father's side of it. Horace expected him to be with Fanny, would have been hurt if he thought his father and Fanny did not get along; besides, when the war started the Reverend had even given Fanny money to fill out her husband's slim pay, though Fanny liked to say how she gave "our father" two hundred pounds when her husband was made a colonel of marines. It was all mixed up. "It's a nice house," Kitty said. "Horace has talked 'cottages' so long. I'm glad you worked him out of his mood for a 'hut.' He took Teneriffe very hard. . . ." Kitty frowned.

Fanny gasped. "A hut! He never mentioned any such thing to *me*. I assure you I have *some* pride—" But she was drowned out by a burst of laughter from William. The men about the fire were obviously reminiscing.

"No. I'll never forget that time!"

"Oh, he'll be safe, William. Remember he shot a partridge *once* . . ." from a slim, dreamy-eyed young man, the youngest of all the brothers, the Reverend Suckling Nelson. He was hauntingly thin.

"Come!" Nelson was laughing uneasily as they all laughed at him, even Kitty and Fanny. "Suckling, what a terrible memory you have!"

"I can remember more, old man . . ." Suckling smiled, gave a weary wave of his hand. He leaned against the classic Greek mantel, eyeing his family from the lofty heights of a Cambridge graduate who was the only member of the clan who had not had to suffer the torments of poverty while learning to preach. He had been financed, of course, by Captain Nelson of the *Boreas,* the one who had to borrow money to get married. Suckling, however, refused to be so dreary as to make his mark in life. "You did hunt desperately, Hor. When I recall how you used to carry your gun on the half-cock, banging away by *ear."*

"I admit it. Shoot I cannot. I always came home with a wet jacket and a bad cold. I never cared for hunting."

"Nor did we care to hunt with you!" William laughed bluntly.

"Be a fisher of men . . ." the Reverend droned, rather wide of the mark, while the Admiral caught Fanny's sympathetic eye. She knew William bored him; that Suckling was his white hope.

"But the most atrocious thing I ever saw was that bullfight—"

"Dear! Please! Not the details?" from Fanny.

"They called it a fine feast." He acknowledged her plea with a smile.

"You cheered the bulls, I hope?" from Suckling.

"I did. It would not have displeased me to have seen some of the Dons tossed by the bulls. Bullfighting shows a total want of humanity."

"'Thou shalt not kill' . . ." bemusedly from the Reverend, who was concentrating more on the digestion of his dinner than the conversation.

There was an awkward pause, as it dawned on all of them the words were doubly pointed, and the conversation might appear to take a personal turn.

"Yet he who lives by the sword . . ." The Admiral paced to the fireplace as his father spoke, having taken the remark as the family dreaded he would. "Very good." His head came up, lower lip thrust out. "I happen to be a *believer* in God! He will spare my life or take it as He chooses. Therefore," he smiled at them all, "may we die in our professions: a preacher praying and an officer fighting!"

"Nobly spoken, my heroic son." The father nodded sleepily. He was usually sharp-witted, but tonight, with the turkey, he swayed with the conversation like a rusty old weather vane. The family breathed relief.

Yet Fanny had turned bewildered eyes to Kitty, who pretended not to notice.

"Bravo!" from William. "And it was warrior David the Lord loved, was it not, my dear Father?"

Suckling's face had grown as pensive as Kitty's.

"It was David, my son. 'I took thee from the sheepcote, from following the sheep, to be ruler over my people . . . And I was with thee whithersoever thou wentest, and have cut off all thine enemies, out of thy sight, and have made thee a great name, like unto the name of the great men that are in the earth . . .' Think on that, children, and think on David's later years."

"Oh, he was terribly terribly Old Testament, rather," Suckling nodded.

"Can't you understand his dancing before the Lord?" William sneered.

"I can," Suckling waved his thin hand again, "I can see *him* doing it. But times change, brother, vain and indecent today, don't you think?"

"Bathsheba, ah! Bathsheba!" William laughed, and there was something gross in his laughter.

The Admiral was pacing up and down the room.

"David displeased the Lord when he broke another Commandment," the father said.

And blunt William supplied it. "Thou shalt not commit adultery."

"Yes, David did stray from the flock," Suckling smiled.

"And the French are the black sheep of the Devil!" The Admiral suddenly winked at Kitty, who winked back, knowing exactly how much he liked hearing three sermons simultaneously. Fanny only saw the wink. She thought it typical of the family, if not really polite.

"Impossible to turn the other cheek to the French," William said; "they're atheists."

Nelson nodded. "They laugh at you. Kick them and then talk to them. That's all they understand: force."

Suckling glanced down at the floor. He could see their conversation was putting his brother on his worst, his most contrary behavior.

"And there's no commandment to turn the other cheek!" the Admiral went on rather heatedly. "No doubt we should, but I'm not hypocrite to pretend *I* could. So I'm wicked! But it would be just as wicked to 'bear false witness'!"

William suddenly doubled up. "Who was it—*who* was it that smuggled his own wine into England after enforcing the Navigation Acts in the West Indies?"

The Admiral saw red. "It was *my* wine! I did not intend to sell it!" He started to say more, then laughed and turned away. He might have reminded his brother William of his long record as a Naval Chaplain. But he did not. William was just a boor—but he loved him! William had sailed to the West Indies and right home again, but he had prevailed on his brother to draw his pay, keep his name on the books "on sick leave" as long as possible.

"You never did know how to make money," William said.

"It is not my forte. But if I had not been wounded there on the mole at Teneriffe you would be applauding the acquisition of the greatest treasure ever taken for England!"

Suckling sank down in his chair. Here it came. William had done it. The Admiral launched into the details of Teneriffe. Why did his brother love to pose the hero? Was that his reward for being a hero? Gilding the lily a bit. Suckling closed his ears. It had brought the heroic back down to the human scale once more. From the ideal to the poseur. But he was not a poseur. Everything he said was true. And as Nelson finished his lurid description of how he switched his sword to his left hand as he fell, how he saved his men, Suckling chimed with the others, "Bravo, Horace!" And somehow he did not feel like a hypocrite. Who knew how the Admiral's next voyage might end?

Kitty had been watching Suckling. "Cheer up, Suckling. We have an Admiral, all we need now is a Bishop in the family!"

William was saying "Thank you, Kitty," just as Nelson cried, "Bravo, Kitty! Suckling, say 'thank you' to your sister."

William, feeling the most offended, was the first to regain the floor. "And what about my little Horatio?"

"He had better be a parson, too." The Admiral smiled. "Though I promise to do more for him than Horatio Walpole did for *me,* his namesake!" And he started to speak to Kitty.

"A parson!" William was after him. "With you an Admiral he ought to be in the Admiralty someday!"

Nelson shook his head. "He'd better be a parson. It's a much quieter profession."

"Come, I have hopes for *my* boy. I've already managed to get his name up for Eton."

"Eton!" And Susanna was heard from. She sat up, wide-awake. "Did you say Eton? How, I would like to know?"

"And why not, Mrs. Bolton? With a Knight in the family?" William glared at her.

She rolled her eyes up to the Admiral's. "If I had so much money, I'd invest it in something practical for the child. And that reminds me, Sir Horatio . . ." She managed to intrude herself between Kitty and her brother. Kitty drifted away laughing, went back to Fanny.

"There's a villain holding up the price of a piece of land that Mr. Bolton wants. Now a word in the right place would force that villain to sell! And you do know so many people, Dukes and—"

"I don't know anyone who would lift a finger for me, my dear sister," the Admiral shied, smiling. "That's why I chose glory. It was all a poor boy could aim for. And do you know," he grew suddenly serious, "I can still close my eyes and there comes that most beautiful soft mellow light"—he tried to turn back to Kitty, but Mrs. Bolton linked her arm through his, patted his hand.

"Yes, I know, dear. Now Mr. Bolton—"

"That light is your guide, Horace." William rescued him. "And by the way, about Eton, don't worry if it appears to you to be a terrible hardship for my little family. I feel I owe it to our whole family. Of course, if you could put in a word for me to one of your friends . . . there's a vacancy coming up at Canterbury."

"I can't make you Archbishop, William, much as I wish I could."

"God forbid that you should have such a wicked thought! No, dear brother, it's just the vicar who is expected to die and—"

"It's rather painful to wish the poor fellow dead. But I suppose that is no different from rising in rank when a superior officer's killed . . ."

"God's will be done, Horace. I shall try to carry on for him. Poor fellow. And, of course, if I had that living . . . by the way, how did your petition for wounded compensation go through?"

"I don't know yet. You see they have no record of Admiral Nelson losing an eye at Calvi, only of a Captain Nelson. I had to get a new surgeon's certificate to prove my eye was blind, besides the three I sent home from Calvi. I thought while I was about it, I'd get one for my arm as well. So I took the certificate for my eye to the clerk and told him I'd be back the next day for an arm, and then in a little time longer, God knows, most probably for a leg!"

William shouted with laughter, but Kitty turned white. Fanny pressed her lips together and Mrs. Bolton clucked like a hen. But it was Kitty who turned the conversation in spite of her shock, the way she would joke or humor a child that wanted her to know it had bruised its knee. She rather believed she understood her brother better than he did himself. "George says you have gained an advantage, Horace."

"How so, Kitty?"

"Your right hand will never know what that restless left hand is about, dear!"

Everyone laughed except Fanny, who leveled a javelin glance at Kitty, then turned toward her husband with a little chattering gasp of virtue outraged. His smile faded. Fanny would pry at Kitty's remark till it festered. He rather wished they would all leave a fighting man some illusions of peace at home.

It was Suckling's turn to prod the tortured conversation. "I almost forgot, Horace, there's a man by the name of Meeks wants to sign with you. He's a friend of one of my parishioners in Burnham."

"What is he?"

"Midshipman. He was with the merchant marine, got impressed into the navy—"

"Oh, no! I won't have an impressed officer! Even with the men, I'd rather not."

"But, Horace, you'd like him. He's crazy to serve under you."

"Absolutely not! I'm sorry, but I have plenty of applications for mids. I just *can't* take this—this Meeks, whatever his name is."

"I'll tell him. It will break his heart."

"I'm sorry, Suckling, but that's the answer: no."

"Come, my dear son, when you went away last time I prayed I would live to see you again and the prayer was granted. Let's forget wars tonight, if I should presume to say I hope to see you again, the question would readily be asked, How old are you? *Vale! Vale! Domine Vale!* And it will be as well—"

"Oh, Father, this is Christmas Eve!"

"Christmas?" The Reverend sighed. "So it is. Just thirty years since your dear mother died. And how you did cry, child, I thought your little heart would break. You have her eyes."

"Father, pray—" The Admiral paced off. That was something he still could not talk about.

"Is Buonaparte going to invade England, Horace?" Suckling asked very loudly.

"No. How can he?"

Mrs. Bolton's eyes grew round. "Why, dear, don't you know? With his army!"

"He cannot walk across the water, Susanna."

"But they say he will. He's marching now, right to the Channel. It says so in those dreadful manifestoes he publishes! Everyone says he's coming."

"He—" The Admiral started to speak.

But Fanny, coming up suddenly, laid her hand on his only arm. "My dear, aren't you tired? It's very late."

"Fanny, you talk to Susanna. Tell her that—"

She shook her head. "You've done enough! Why must you go! Isn't ambition sated?" Her voice was rising.

He studied her rather sadly. "Ambition? My dearest wife, it's my duty to my country."

Her face remained clouded.

"I go now only to secure those honors that you so richly deserve,

Fanny." His tone was so bland, she felt relieved. And she couldn't resist that kind of compliment.

"Thank you, my dear," and she held her head high for all the Nelsons to see.

But her smile faded as he went on, perhaps pushing his luck too far, "I shall carry the picture of you *settled* in our cottage wherever I go."

"Kitty insists I go to Bath, Horace. She's planned on it."

He threw up his hand. "Very well, Fanny, I shall not ask it again. A prophet is not without honor except . . . and am I *never* to have a place to lay my head?"

Fanny stared at him, then started to laugh. "Oh, my dear! You say the strangest . . . I'm glad you don't care, dear."

"I bought that cottage for you."

Mrs. Bolton's eyebrows went up. "Well I never saw a hut turn into a cottage as big as that ark before!"

"Ark! It's roomy, sister, but did you expect Lady Nelson to live in a hovel?"

And Fanny smiled at him again. What a pity he was going away, now when he was so gallant.

"It's a nice house," Mrs. Bolton said and was saved from having to praise it more as the door flew open and brother Maurice blew in, still cold and puffing the frost.

"Merry Christmas! How well you look, Admiral!" He flung an affectionate arm around his brother while managing a "Good evening, Father," and a gay wave to the others.

"I thought you were never coming, Maurice. Where's Mrs. Nelson? You never bring her to me." The Reverend Father peered about the room, then back at his son.

"She had a headache, Father." Maurice avoided brother William's disapproving eye and nodded to Nelson to come have a chat with him in a corner. Maurice's easygoing manner seemed a little dashed, as William cleared his throat, letting his eyes rove over the ceiling. Roundwood and Buonaparte were all forgotten at the thought of Maurice's blind common-law wife—not that they knew for sure she was only his mistress for he called her by his name, but they suspected the worst. Mrs. Bolton looked knowingly toward Fanny, and Fanny looked at Kitty. They were all agreed on that subject! Only the Admiral looked blank. He knew the worst was true; he was the only one Maurice had dared confess to.

"How's the Navy Board?" the Admiral asked.

Maurice shook his head, smiling. "From the viewpoint of a miserable clerk, it is bad as ever."

"If you had paid attention to your studies, Maurice, followed the Lord's way as two of your brothers have—or the sea as our hero has—you would not be regretting your life," the Reverend sermonized.

Maurice and Nelson looked at each other. "I'll get you into the Admiralty if it kills me, Maurice."

"Don't sacrifice yourself. First Lord Spencer isn't worth it. Anyway Buonaparte's supposed to be coming to wipe us all out. Boney—Boney —that's all I've heard all day long!"

"At the Navy Board?"

"Everywhere!"

"There, Horace, do listen to us!" Mrs. Bolton was alarmed again. She eyed her younger brother with an elder sister's indulgence. She could never forget that once upon a time she had to remind him to go wash his face. "We will all be murdered in our beds!"

"Not in our beds!" Maurice hopped up, winking at Nelson, raising his fists. "We'll be fighting from every hedge—like Englishmen!"

"Besides, Susanna, he has to cross the Channel," the Admiral reasoned. "He hasn't the force assembled to do it."

"He has ships, Horace."

"Then let us pray!" Maurice's eyes suddenly twinkled and they all looked abashed and upset. "Let us pray like the old Scotch divine who knelt on the beach to pray when that American pirate John Paul Jones was raiding our coasts twenty years ago: 'Now, dear Lord, dinna ye think it a shame for ye to send this vile pirate to rob our folk o' Kirkaldy; for ye ken they're puir enow already, and hae naething to spare. The way the wind blaws he'll be here in a jiffy, and wha' kens what he may do? He's nae too good for onything. Mickle's the mischief he has done already. He'll burn their houses, tak their very claes, and tirl them to the sark. And waes me! Wha ken but the bluidy villain might take their lives? The puir weemen are maist frightened out of their wits, and the bairns skirling after them. I canna think of it! I canna think of it! I hae been long a faithful servant to ye, Lord: but gin ye dinna turn the wind about, and blaw the scoundrel out of our gate, I'll nae stir a foot; but will just sit here till the tide comes. Sae take ye'r will o't.'" Maurice finished with a sober, "And the moral to that is: the wind turned and blew Jones's prizes ashore and did *blaw* the scoundrel out of their gate!"

"Sacrilege!" Susanna sniffed.

❋ ❋ ❋

Before *Vanguard* sailed from England Fanny had one more social triumph. Lady Spencer, wife of the First Lord, gave a dinner party especially to meet Lady Nelson. It was unprecedented, and Lady Spencer was amazed at herself, for when Sir Horatio had cornered her he had only asked her to "notice" his wife when he was gone and instantly aroused Lady Spencer's curiosity to discover what kind of woman that strange man had married.

Fanny had shuddered, turned clammy and then crimson at the invitation; finally composed herself and emerged calm and triumphant from her inner tussle. Even if Lady Spencer were noted for her scathing opinions of most navy wives, and for not recognizing the existence of anything lower, male or female, than a rear admiral, Fanny could boast her uncle had been President of Nevis. . . . And that might help Lady Spencer's opinion of Sir Horatio, who, as a very junior rear admiral, was probably just higher than a loblolly boy in Lady Spencer's eye.

And that steely appraising eye of Lady Spencer's actually found the haughty lady from the West Indies favorable. Armored in reserve after her first fright, Fanny's large dark gray eyes peered out of her almost sharp little face, though Fanny's black curls, her glory in the intimacy of her boudoir, had succumbed to the fashionable graying cast of powder. It made her look even more respectable in her rich dark gown. She often liked purple velvet . . . Lady Spencer perhaps thought Fanny's tastes somewhat regal for a rear admiral's wife, but she was truly amazed that anyone so totally unself-conscious, so appallingly thrown together as Rear Admiral Sir Horatio Nelson could have had the intelligence to persuade such a trim, decorous little lady to marry him.

But even as Lady Spencer was congratulating herself for having risked inviting Lady Nelson, she saw that unpredictable white-haired boy of an Admiral start, sweep the room with a strangely calculating gleam in his good eye; finally focus on her, the wife of the First Lord of the Admiralty, and begin to glow. Lady Spencer stood paralyzed with dread.

naking a sudden lightning decision as he began to steer for
s. He had realized that unless he acted with a stroke of diplo-
e would have to throw himself at the mercy of his dinner part-
rhaps that pallid viscountess eyeing him with revulsion, or the
hioness with her fixed smile who was trying to appear to see
ning, and apologetically beg her to cut his meat! She would do it,
d everyone would stare and stare, until he'd want to slam his fist
down on the table and shout "This was gotten honorably!"

He steered straight for the First Lady, made a diffident little bow
and put his heart in his smile. "Lady Spencer, I must beg the privilege
of escorting Lady Nelson to dinner—"

Lady Spencer's smile froze. Her eyes turned glassy. This upstart
whom she had condescended to be kind to by noticing his wife was
commandeering her dinner party! He was not a genius but an idiot!

He poured on his diplomacy. "I have so little time with her, I cannot bear to be separated—even for a moment."

Lady Spencer's lips moved slowly: "Of course . . . charming . . .
of course." She was still toying with the possibility of his idiocy while
to the amazement and amusement of everyone Fanny walked and sat
with her husband—and cut his meat. Fanny's pale face was flushed, a
little piqued that her husband had dared make her conspicuous, upset
Lady Spencer, and just a little flattered by the fact that Lady Spencer
was studying her with a dawning motherly curiosity usually lavished
on brides.

Sir Horatio, who had created the unprecedented scene, was as calm
and relaxed as a cat on the kitchen hearth and the guests went away
talking about his simplicity.

❋   ❋   ❋

To Lady Nelson, from Sir Horatio who had gone to join his ship:

MY DEAR FANNY,

At half-past five I arrived here, and what you will be surprised to hear,
with great difficulty found *one* pair of raw silk stockings. I suppose in
some place or other I shall find my linen, for there is scarcely any in this
trunk. The wind is fair and on Saturday morning I go on board, and with
the lark on Sunday I am off. . . . Kind love to my Father and Kitty,
and ever believe me, your most affectionate

HORATIO NELSON

My dearest Fanny,

I go on board at two o'clock, and, if possible, I shall sail early tomorrow morning. Mr. Marsh has given Allen no account of his money which you gave him to buy Funds—Get it.

God bless you all, and ever believe me,

Your most affectionate,

Horatio Nelson

I have opened the letter to say thanks for your letter. . . .

To Reverend William Nelson:

Portsmouth, *March 31, 1798*

My dear Brother:

You will not, I hope, attribute my not answering your two letters to any other cause than that of really being hurried by my approaching departure. I participate in your sorrow of G. Thurlow's deficiency of rent, and his determination to give up the farm, but all landlords are at times plagued with their tenants. In short, the times are big with events, and before the year gets round we shall either have a good peace or what I dread to think on. But God's will be done. The wind is fair: in two hours I shall be on board, and with the lark I shall be off tomorrow morning; therefore I have only time to say God bless you and yours, and ever believe me,

Yours most affectionately,

Horatio Nelson

April 1st, 1798

My dearest Fanny,

We put to sea this morning with the Convoy, but the wind at noon came to the Westward, which obliged us to return to St. Helen's: thus have I lost the finest East wind that has blown this year, and there can be no guess when we may have another; so much for Admiralty delays: however, I shall not go out of the ship unless upon duty, and get off as soon as possible. My place is tolerably comfortable, but do not shine in servants. A Captain Peyton, a fellow-traveller of yours [from the West Indies] is a passenger with me, as are two Land Officers for Gibraltar. Captain Peyton is going in the *Defence*. . . . The Matchams, I think, are getting to Bath sooner than they first intended; but whatever may be other people's opinions, I am clear it is right you should be in your own cottage. May God Almighty bless you, will ever be the fervent prayer of your most affectionate husband,

Horatio Nelson

St. Helen's, *April 3rd, 1798*

My dearest Fanny,

The wind still continues as foul as it can blow, but as I am now fixed on board, it is my intention not to move out of the ship, to which I begin to be reconciled. As to news, I cannot tell you a word beyond my own ship. If you look at Queen Square Chapel, it will tell you to write or not, but on the sealed side of the letter write,—"If the *Vanguard* is sailed, to be returned to Lady Nelson, *Bath.*" I can only, my dear Fanny, repeat, what I hope you know, that you are uppermost in my thoughts. With my kindest love to my Father, believe me your most affectionate

Horatio Nelson

I cannot find my black stock and buckle. I find the weights for *your* scales are on board this ship. Love to Kitty, my Sister, Mr. Matcham, etc.

St. Helen's, *April 5th*

Pray, my dear Fanny, did you put up the three Portugal pieces? for if you did, they cannot be found. If they are not sent, so much the better. My black stock and buckle has not yet appeared, nor are the keys to my dressing-stand sent. If they were left with the stand in London, the man has neglected to pack them up. I can do very well without these things, but it is a satisfaction to mention them. All my passengers are gone on shore till the wind comes fair; but I shall, if possible, remain fast on board. We have had very blowing weather, and there seems no prospect of a change in wind. My barometer [arm] told me the weather would be bad. So far it answers, and I find an amusement in attending to it. . . . God bless you, my father, etc.

Your ever affectionate . . .

St. Helen's, *April 7th*
Wind S.W.

My dearest Fanny,

I have looked over my linen, and find it very different to your list in the articles as follows:—thirteen silk pocket handkerchiefs: only six new, five old. Thirteen cambric ditto: I have sixteen. Twelve cravats: I have only eleven. Six Genoa velvet stocks: I have only three. You have put down thirty huckaback towels: I have from 1 to 10. Eleven is missing from 11 to 22, that is Nos. 12 and 21; therefore there is missing No. 11–22, and to 30:—Ten in all. I only hope and believe they have not been sent. I do not want them. Have you the two old pieces of gold which my Father gave me, for I have them not? and yet I am pretty positive I brought them home: if you have them not, they are lost. . . . My health never was better, and only wishing for a fair wind. God bless you.

Horatio Nelson

Have received only one letter: love to all.

St. Helen's, *April 7th, 8* p.m.
April 8: Noon, Wind S.W.

Many thanks, my dearest Fanny, for your two letters. From my heart, I wish it was peace, then not a moment would I lose in getting to my cottage. I wrote you this morning about my things. I have bought a *new* stock buckle at double the price of the old one, which eighteen years past, cost 1s. 6d., just one penny per year, and it was certainly now worth 1s. . . . Mr. Pitt will get money whilst it is to be had, and for this world I would not take a false oath. You will take care and secure a few hundred pounds, for if England to herself is not true, our funded debt must fall, and with it who can tell *what*. May God Almighty protect you is the most sincere prayer of your affectionate husband,

Horatio Nelson

Kind love to my Father, Kitty, my Sister, and Mr. Matcham.

❋   ❋   ❋

During the past winter Lord St. Vincent's fleet had stubbornly block-aded Cádiz. Now St. Vincent was pondering one thing: the young Buonaparte who boasted "I will go whithersoever I will . . ." had been very quiet since the signing of peace with Austria. Then why were there four hundred transports loading with troops at Toulon and Marseilles? Ready to strike where? Did they relate to the loud mani-festoes from Paris proclaiming the invasion of England? Or was that a ruse? Or were the transports at Toulon a ruse as they had been when Buonaparte struck into Italy? In the closed chambers of the Directory in Paris, twenty-eight-year-old Buonaparte's finger must have traced some map, paused, snapped the paper, and announced to his govern-ment: "We will strike there!"

St. Vincent still wondered: where was Buonaparte going to strike? North—east—south—or west? From Naples had come letters from both the Ambassador and the Ambassadress begging for England to protect Naples, for the Kingdom of the Two Sicilies was sure Buona-parte intended to strike them. St. Vincent wrote Lady Hamilton:

My dear Madam,

I feel myself highly honored and flattered by your Ladyship's charming letter of the 15th of April. The picture you have drawn of the lovely Queen of Naples and the Royal Family, would rouse the indignation of the most unfeeling of the creation at the infernal designs of those devils, who, for the scourge of the human race, govern France. I am bound by my oath of chivalry to protect all who are persecuted and distressed, and would fly to the succor of their Sicilian Majesties, was I not positively forbid to quit my post before Cádiz. I am happy, however, to have a knight of superior prowess in my train, who is charged with this enterprise, at the head of as gallant a band as ever drew sword or trailed pike.

The design Miss Knight [a friend of Lady Hamilton's and daughter of an Admiral, deceased] is at work upon will hand my name down to the latest posterity, coupled as it is with your fair form: pray say everything kind to her and the venerable lady mother, and be assured, my dear Madam, that I will avail myself of the first opportunity which places us within reach of each other, to pay you my homage in person; at this distance I can only say, that no one of your acquaintance respects and admires your Ladyship more truly, than

Your true knight, and devoted humble servant,
St. Vincent

On deck the aging Lord St. Vincent walked silently, staring out to sea. He needed a wiry, half-blind, left-handed right arm for a special and dangerous mission. He had, as usual, very few ships to spare at present. But England must be informed of what Buonaparte intended to do with four hundred transports. And who but Nelson would tackle the problem regardless of the odds against him?

And at last, like a twig on the horizon: a flash of white.

"Deck there! Strange sail to northward."

"Up with you there," Vincent roared at a mid who quivered like a rabbit at the first word. "What ship is it?"

"Deck there, the blue flag at the mizzen, my lord, Rear Admiral Sir Horatio Nelson's *Vanguard* answering our signal . . ."

St. Vincent turned on his heel. He would eat well today, listening to the booming salute of *Vanguard's* guns.

❊   ❊   ❊

To Lady Nelson (sent to their "cottage," Roundwood, but forwarded to her at Bath):

May 1st, 1798

My dearest Fanny:

I joined the fleet yesterday and found Lord St. Vincent everything I wished him: and his friends in England have done me justice for my zeal and affection toward him. . . . The Dons have, I find, long expected my return with Bomb-vessels, Gunboats and every proper implement for the destruction of Cádiz and their fleet. They have prepared three floating batteries to lie outside their walls, to prevent the fancied attack:

and lo, the mountain has brought forth a mouse. I am arrived with a single ship and without the means of annoying them. The Admiral is probably going to detach me with a small squadron; *not on any fighting expedition* therefore be not surprised if it should be sometime before you hear from me again. . . . God give us peace. England will not be invaded this summer. . . .

X. The Hunt

May 1 – July 31, 1798

LEAVING LORD ST. VINCENT, *Vanguard* anchored at Gibraltar. Here she was to pick up her squadron, meager as it was. Until St. Vincent's fleet received reinforcements from England, Nelson must make shift with whatever Rear Admiral Sir John Orde, who had recently joined the fleet, could reasonably spare from the squadron at Gibraltar.

Nelson remembered Orde from way back. A man much older than himself. He had met Orde in the West Indies, later Orde had been a governor of one of the islands out there, and more recently been acquitted for lack of convicting evidence in a London trial that had charged him with something slightly more elegantly stated, but which boiled down to a charge of blackmailing and similar abuses of the islanders. So he had come back to the navy, declining to return to the islands where his life was probably not worth a ha'penny. The navy casually remarked that excuses must be made for his insufferable personality, for he had "never been to sea. . . ."

Nelson had once mused that he had actually done that John Orde a favor when no one else would lift a finger; for even to associate with the man was to risk his finding some means of making trouble. He had a smooth insinuating tongue. But Nelson had purchased and transported some wine for Orde, and he had hoped, but dimly, that Orde would have the common decency to remember it.

Here at Gibraltar, Orde made his usual suave bow to Nelson, and then turned purple when he learned he must give up some ships to that upstart Nelson who was the youngest as well as one of the lowest ranking rear admirals in the whole British navy! St. Vincent was giving Nelson more important missions than any other officer in the fleet. And Orde's gout raised havoc with what was left of his temper.

❋   ❋   ❋

Aboard *Vanguard,* Nelson scanned the list Sir John Orde sent him: *Orion* 74, Captain Sir James Saumarez, that was fine; *Emerald, Terpsichore,* and *Bonne Citoyenne* frigates, *and*—he gritted his teeth:

Alexander 74, Captain Alexander John Ball!

"Coxcomb Ball!" His first expedition to reconnoiter the enemy transports assembling in Toulon and he had to draw that—that coxcomb from St. Omer! Replacing his lists in his desk he turned to the midshipman, a young man, not a boy, awaiting his reply.

"Have Captain Ball down here, Mr. Meeks."

"Aye, aye, sir."

The mid saluted smartly. Meeks was better than the Admiral had expected, even though he had been impressed in the navy at one time, and after all, dear Suckling had insisted. . . . The young man seemed quite capable—but Captain Ball! The Admiral sat down suddenly in his chair, for the roll of the ship was awkward to meet, one-armed. Perhaps he would get used to it, just as he had to being seasick.

A polite knock. Nelson waited a full minute before looking up. He had not laid eyes on Ball since the first violent impression fifteen years ago when two sensitive young captains in their early twenties had registered mutual contempt at first glance.

Now Ball stood before him, tall, broad, exquisitely appointed, untarnished gold braid glittering like the sun. His navy blue was of the best cloth—best cut—of course! His too handsome face seemed suspiciously smug as he bowed his respects to his new commanding officer.

Nelson looked him over a little longer. So Ball was still only a captain . . . ? And what a perfectly beautiful way Ball combed and cued his hair! The Admiral squinted, and then with a wickedly arch smile asked:

"What? Have *you* come to have your bones broken?"

Captain Ball bowed again. As he came up, his answer was studied, slow to be sure, perhaps almost halting, but absolutely correct.

"Sir, I certainly have no wish to have my bones—ah—broken, unless my duty to my King and Country require such a sacrifice, sir. Then, I promise you, they shall not be spared, sir!"

"Very good, Captain Ball." The Admiral picked up a sealed packet. "We shall not make sail tonight until dark. Our mission is gravely important. Here, sir, are your most secret orders."

"Thank you, sir." Ball bowed again. "May I wish your good health, sir?"

"Thank you. Good day." The Admiral coolly acknowledged the man's speedy—but dignified—retreat.

And Captain Ball, taking a deep breath as he returned to his ship, cursed Defoe for writing *Robinson Crusoe,* luring innocent boys such as Ball had been when he lay on a cliff in Devon and dreamed of the ships and the sea. . . . Under Admiral Nelson, who possessed the memory of a sadistic elephant, Robinson Crusoe's situation was now highly enviable. Ball had learned much of the world since he flaunted the sowing of his wild oats at St. Omer, snubbed that big-eyed, downy-cheeked, virtuous son of a parson.

❊   ❊   ❊

By the time Nelson's small squadron had secretly sailed from Gibraltar, taken its position near Toulon so that the French could not move without being sighted, he was glad, for the sake of his command, to admit that Coxcomb Ball sailed tolerably well—in fact, to be broadminded about it, Ball sailed as well as any captain and he kept his ship trim.

Be that as it may, Nelson gave him little thought as he lay in his cot late one Sunday night, for what concerned him more was the sudden twinge where his right arm had been, clear out to the tips of his nonexistent fingers, the warning ache in the stump: bad weather. It had proved an accurate barometer so far. But even that was of secondary importance to the major problem in his mind.

Here he was, in command of the only squadron, and without a fighting force, to be sent into the hostile Mediterranean Sea; reconnoitering the French fleet. The most important post in the navy at the moment and it was all his. He smiled to himself. He would vindicate himself this time, prove how indispensable he was to England. He knew his captains expected glory with him in command and he intended not to disappoint them. So far, all was well, and he meant to chasten Buonaparte.

Terpsichore frigate had picked up a small French corvette yesterday. Now Nelson lay in his cot trying to piece together the news he had gathered by astute questioning:

General Buonaparte, himself, had arrived in Toulon last Friday, over there just a few miles away. *No one*—not even the French naval officers—knew where Buonaparte was going. Nelson smiled again; only he knew that, for he intended to take Mr. Buonaparte to Spithead if he ventured upon the water! He turned the situation in his mind as the *Vanguard* rose and fell on the somewhat uneasy swells.

There had been a wet cast to the sunset and the wind tonight did not appear so promising, but Nelson had given orders to Berry for the topgallant yards to be struck and all small sail and lumber out of the tops. He had weathered these seas too many years to be worried. And he was sailing with his Lucky Berry once more!

He closed his eyes, about to say his prayers and fall asleep . . . But where was Buonaparte going? The French, he knew, had fifteen ships of the line in Toulon. Their flagship was *L'Orient* 120, the ship he had itched to attack back during Hotham's poor action. The old *Sans Culottes!* Rechristened since rabble revolutions had become unfashionable. *L'Orient* had been one of the ships Captain Sir Sidney Smith was still receiving credit for destroying at the evacuation of Toulon. That was too bad all the way around.

Now at Toulon, besides *L'Orient* flagship and its fleet, the cavalry and thousands of troops were reported already embarked in a convoy of two hundred transports; and there were rumored to be two hundred more transports in Marseilles. When and where bound? And was this Corsican—this Buonaparte—going with them? If they sailed, Nelson must warn the world. St. Vincent must know immediately. The fleets guarding England must know. He had a small problem in trying to decide how to warn the world and stop Buonaparte with only three battleships and three frigates, for he intended to follow that blackguard wherever he tried to go. But the very odds made for greater glory and he thought of Agincourt and Henry V's speech to his small band of brothers.

His arm twinged again and he became suddenly aware of a sharper pitch to his cot; of rising high in the air, plunging down—leaving his stomach up there. Standing almost on his head at one moment, on his feet the next. The wind was beginning to roar. He sat up, ringing for Allen. As the ship's stern rose again and then fell: a jar.

"Pass the word to ship the deadlights!" he yelled at the sentry. But water pouring through the main cabin stern windows almost drowned him out. What the devil was wrong? His ship had been pooped! The sea gurgled in, his cabin was awash. Someone was passing the word now for the windows to be shuttered.

He had better go on deck, see if Berry had the ship under control.

Allen ran in. "It's too stormy for yow! Yow coon't go on deck, sir, yow'll be blown away!" And Allen caught the Admiral in his arms, kept him from falling over the cannon mounted in his sleeping cabin. Stood him on his feet and tried to lead him back to his cot.

"Get me out of this damn thing!" The helpless Admiral jerked at his long frilly nightgown.

It was all an able-bodied man could do to keep his balance; so it was with difficulty that Allen got the Admiral's nightgown off, eased him into his clothes. "I told you I didn't want to go to bed, Allen!"

"Aye, aye, sir," Allen grinned. "There you are, sir, but yow got no business on that deck, sir!" Allen warned him again and again as he helped him up the ladders to the quarter-deck.

But the Admiral had scarcely realized Allen's presence; he was only an arm to balance on. For Nelson, alone, with three battleships and three frigates, had been sent to match wits with Buonaparte. He alone . . . and the wind was rising, blowing east. His mind was focusing closer to the sphere of his squadron. If anything happened to them. If Buonaparte gave him the slip, ran through the Gut past Gibraltar into the Atlantic . . . But not on a night like this with the wind blowing east! A convoy of transports would wreck if they tried to beat up the wind toward Gibraltar.

❊   ❊   ❊

A gale of blackness everywhere. The wind and the rain tore down on the ships, piled up the sea in peaks till it showed its teeth, sent waves churning over the decks. For a moment *Vanguard* heeled, losing her bearings, ran with her starboard gunnel near buried in water.

"Storm stay—" and the wind snatched the orders, lost them. Flattened the frail, crippled Admiral to the bulwarks. He clung to a belaying pin as the *Vanguard* plunged down, down a long wave, dove under a sheet of hard biting spray, rolled, shook, till the wooden figurehead rose up dripping; staring up, up, as the men clung to the steep deck. Then she heeled, shipping water over all, shuddered again and plunged down another black slope, till she lay surrounded by slithering shifting mountains of water.

Now faint pink lights flared closer and closer till the lightning played all around them, darting horizontally, burning serpents. Splitting their ears with its thunder.

And stubborn sails battled the men crawling like beetles in the rigging. Canvas held stiff, crammed full of wind; snapped, exploded, extended in streamers. The masts rocked.

Nelson eyed them uneasily as he barked out his orders to furl the sails! Was Berry mad or slow? And with each plunge down into black valleys, each lurch skyward, the masts seemed to lean more heavily upon the rigging.

Berry made a quick run across deck. A slant figure into the wind, reached the Admiral, pointed up, his mouth open, his words forced back in his throat. He gasped at last:

"The new rope's stretching, Sir Horatio!"

And as the men tried to take up the slack it was like tying knots in taffy. The ship had been out from England one month. She was not weathered yet. Her masts swayed in widening arcs as the rigging stretched, grew slack, while five hundred and ninety-five officers and men battled the gale.

Berry was shouting for Captain Faddy of the marines to lend a hand, and as Faddy yelled for a lieutenant, a naval lieutenant bawled, "Send marines forward to the main deck, secure stays on mainmast—"

And a mid: "Master-at-arms! Go below—send all idlers up! All idlers up!"

And the master-at-arms disappeared down the fore hatch howling: "All idlers up! All idlers up! Stewards and servants and barbers and sweeps, cook's mates, ministers, doctor's mates and loblolly boys! All idlers up! You're drowning, rats!"

And the carpenter saluting, his ax glistening wet: "Shall we cut, sir?"

When all eyes turned up. The jacks in the main top were clinging for life as the main-topmast bent like a pine on a cliff: snapped! A new mid sobbed like a girl as the men were hurled down with the wreckage. If the men cried the wind howled them silent. Berry went gray. His command would end in court-martial.

The mast dragged at the rail, booming against the ship's timber, ramming her bottom, while young Meeks ran out on the wreckage, and hands gripped the ropes. One after the other the half-drowned jacks were pulled back, up onto the deck, shouted up into the rigging again. One man was missing, washed into the sea. Another had lost his grip, fallen. He lay mangled, stark dead on the deck.

The Admiral's eye roved the deck. "Secure the guns, Captain Berry!" Hammocks, hawsers and cleats were soon holding the cannon, for should one of their bolts draw free of the planks, two thousand pounds would go smashing and careening across the deck.

While the sea rose like a monster, slithering, lashing, dove under them, over them; flashed its white, churned and thrashed. While *Vanguard's* mizzen-topmast curved like a drawn bow in the wind, the Admiral's eye was on the yardarm: a little globule of light—of the "electric fluid" that poured out of the sky—began to glow on either end.

Berry saw it, yelled, "Man the fire engines!"

At that instant the wind cracked the mast, it collapsed. No lightning struck.

Vanguard pitched, dove down, down again, her bowsprit under to harpoon the bottom; and wave after wave gushed over her.

And the constant boom of broken masts trying to sink her.

"Cut away wreckage!" But even as the carpenters ran forward, and *Vanguard* came up for her next thrust, bows spewing fountains, there came the ominous forewarning third crack.

"Look out for the fore-topmast," Meeks shouted, "stand from under!" As the men ran, Meeks waited, was the last to run.

The long death crash of timber. A lurch as the *Vanguard* plunged down again, and as the crash ended, a mortal scream knifed hearts through the thunderous quake that shook the whole ship: the fore-topmast broke in two pieces: stove the forecastle deck.

As Nelson shook the spray from his eyes, the stumps of three masts lolled in the limp, sagging rigging, while someone called out, "It was Mr. Meeks—poor Meeks killed!" as they crawled into the wreckage of the fore-topmast, hacking it: found his crushed body. Berry closed his eyes involuntarily: three dead. Opening his eyes he caught a glimpse of the Admiral's face set like a mask.

Now a new booming against the bottom: the best bower anchor had been knocked loose, was hammering against the ship. The carpenter cut it away.

"Captain Berry!" The Admiral still clutched the belaying pin. "Is there *any* sail left?"

"A rag of a spritsail, sir, that's all."

Berry's young face had turned old: *Vanguard* was being blown straight for the shores of France.

"Wales Clod!" The Admiral shouted to the master.

"Aye, aye, sir!" And the wind hooted louder at each new voice.

"Wear ship first favorable moment. We've a rag of sail left!"

"Aye, aye, sir!"

They waited while *Vanguard* tossed this way and that, like a crazed wounded animal, heeled over, groaned and wallowed. She might—she *must* catch the wind for a moment somehow in that scarf of sail, hold herself steady, until they could tack, claw off the lee shore, the enemy shore. Otherwise: shipwreck.

"Aloft there! Secure that stump of foremast!" An earl's son, Lieutenant Capel, was bawling like a fishmonger, while the master's eyes were glued to the ghostly scrap of canvas, a mere thread on the bowsprit.

He hung onto the great double wheel, bawling at the quartermasters grappling it with him, to hold it, hold it; trying to catch the wind, while wave after wave broke bludgeons over *Vanguard*: drowned the sail, filled it with water, reversed it, shook it like a handkerchief; all to the crazed jar of the wreckage pounding the bottom, the carpenters' frantic axes.

The Admiral's eye, too, was fixed on the sail. If that went—if the creaking bowsprit collapsed—if . . . "Coax it—easy—" One minute passed. Two . . . The bowsprit threatened to give way. Ten minutes. *Vanguard* pitched, rose: the sail snapped full!

The Admiral wheeled on the master. As *Vanguard* steadied . . .

"Down helm—" A dozen voices were yelling with him, every eye had been on that sail.

But already Wales Clod and his men, feet braced, faces grinning by the streaking blinding stormlight, were swearing and coaxing the great ship around: showing her high stern to France.

Done. The Admiral nodded. So far, saved for a little longer. But where was his squadron? Were they all wrecked? Had this night ruined him?

Dimly now and then he thought he could see first one of them, then another. Were they sunk or was he blind? He saw—then only thought he saw—then again nothing as *Vanguard* rolled crazily with no sails to guide her but the scrap on her bowsprit.

"Now it's time for yow to go below, sir." Allen had been hovering as close as he dared. "Yow're soaked, sir, yow'll catch another cold."

The Admiral did not answer. His hand was cramped on the pin,

his arm nearly wrenched from the shoulder. Had he lost every ship?
If *this* could happen to *Vanguard* . . .

Berry glanced around at him now and then for fear he would save
the ship only to see the Admiral blown away. No. There he clung
like the last leaf of autumn, with Allen behind him, reaching out
now and then to steady him.

Was this accident? The hyena laughs of the wind; the cracking roars
of the wreckage; all the devils from hell screaming aloft in the rigging?

Allen's constant grumbles went unheard, unfelt. The Admiral heard
nothing, saw nothing, but the catastrophe to him—to *Vanguard*—
perhaps to the world—as he waited for morning.

But the gale did not slink away with the dark and the dawn was
no more than a smudgy light brushed into a dirty gray sky where
funeral clouds encircled the wreck. His sphere had narrowed to one
maimed ship. Were there no others?

"Deck there! *Alexander* and *Orion* with *Emerald* frigate, sir, keeping company!"

"Thank God!"

"There now, sir, everything's fine and yowr breakfast served, sir."
Allen was beaming out from under his black forelock, proffering a
plate of very cold tongue and cold rolls. The galley fire was doused.
They must eat cold and stay cold till the storm quit. The Admiral
turned from Allen's offering, raising his spyglass.

But only *Vanguard* was shattered and mauled to the water's edge.
Alexander's and *Orion's* masts were intact. So were *Emerald's*. The
two other frigates were only faintly discernible as they lay-to among
the waves, their bare poles etched against the horizon. They were
making no signs of trying to follow. The last *Vanguard* saw of them
they still rode out the storm, acknowledging no signals!

Four ships left to stop Buonaparte's armada and one of them barely
able to swim.

And no letup. The wind blew straight east, hour after hour, day
and night, from Sunday to Monday to Tuesday. If ever a man felt
doomed, it was Nelson. His dream of glory turned to nightmare
disgrace.

His wet clothes sloughed off at last for a dressing gown, he was flexing his frozen fingers trying to get warm for the first time in three days over a brazier of coals Allen had brought to the main cabin. The Admiral watched Captain Berry rechecking the 1st Lieutenant's calculations of their position. Aft, were the stern windows opening on the Admiral's small private gallery overlooking gray nothing. Nelson turned from the coals, paced to the starboard, then to the larboard gun. The interior of his cabin was painted nerveless black and white. He paced back to the now welcome red of the coals.

He gave a short bitter laugh. "I can't call what happened by the cold name of accident, Berry."

His Captain steeled himself. Here came the Admiral's wrath after the storm. "Latitude 40° 50' north, Sir Horatio," Berry answered meekly.

The Admiral studied the chart. "Fire a gun and hoist signal of attention to the squadron, Captain Berry. We'll signal the squadron to try for Oristan Bay in Sardinia. If we can't make that perhaps we can reach the island of St. Peter's. . . ."

A mid at the door: "*Alexander* signaling she is going to take us in tow, sir."

"Signal I'll be much obliged to Captain Ball. . . ." He tried to smile, but that was all that was left to make his humiliation complete.

❋   ❋   ❋

Hour after hour the *Alexander* tugged at the beaten *Vanguard* while the *Orion* sailed ahead to sound anchorage. The gale had finally spent itself into a dying wind. Nelson and Berry stood together, tensely judging their last hope as Tuesday waned into sunset, lighting the rock coast of the island of Sardinia and, snuggled near it, St. Peter's.

"Now will the fickle wind *last?* Whistle it, Berry, whistle it."

Berry put on a faint replica of a smile. Would the wind last till *Alexander* could tow them into some port? "She blows and inhales!" Berry muttered.

"I cannot call what has happened," the Admiral began again, "by the cold name of accident." His face was wretched as Berry turned, still fearing recriminations. The Admiral smiled wearily. "No, Berry, I believe it was the Almighty's—" He stopped, head tilted heavenward, eye fixed on *Alexander's* rigging. Her sails had begun to flap stupidly.

"Damn!" He pivoted, pinned Berry with his glance. "Stark calm!"

He spun on his heel, began pacing the deck, lurching slightly, trying to balance one-armed.

Under the *Vanguard* he felt the insidious lift of a westerly swell. No wind. *Alexander* was useless to *Vanguard* now. The umbilical cable sank down in the water between the two ships. They stood still, while just a few miles up the coast were the island of St. Peter's and a calm bay.

Coming about, Nelson saw Berry's face caught unaware. Poor "Lucky" Berry had aged ten years in three days. He was weathered without any need for recriminations.

"And *no* frigates!" the Admiral snapped, making Berry and the lieutenants on the quarter-deck jump. "It seems very odd that they could all have left me by accident! No eyes! No eyes to watch Toulon! They're as bad as privateers; all they want is prize money! No eyes to watch while *Vanguard* repairs!" He turned away, still muttering something about hanging would be too good for them. The *Emerald,* last of the frigates, had made off during last night. "And if I ask where they have gone, they will tell me they were *blown* away!"

"Boney can't escape you, Sir Horatio," Berry ventured.

The Admiral nodded abruptly without answering, gazing grimly across the sea. Well, in another hour it might not make any difference what Buonaparte did with the world—to *Vanguard* anyway. The sun was gone now, behind them into the sea, and the swell from west was carrying *Vanguard* straight for the rocks of Sardinia. Sometimes she seemed hell bent on dragging *Alexander* in, with a swishing of cables rising out of the water, pulling taut, then with a lull falling slack again. But inevitably both ships drifted closer and closer to shore.

The leadsman was forward in the chains getting a cast of the lead every five minutes, another lead was being cast from the starboard gangway. Not that there was much they could do, even if the leadsman were to chant there was no water under them. Still there was always a chance till the moment they struck.

Now and then there was a sharp clap as the oars in the barges on the booms were thrown up by the sudden swell, fell back.

"The spare anchor will have to do, Captain Berry."

"Aye, sir, I think it will. I've passed the largest cable through the starboard quarter port, and bent it to the cable on the spare, Sir Horatio. Made a spring to cant the ship to larboard, sir. . . ."

"Beg pardon." It was Wales Clod, the master. "But with that rag for a sail?"

"It will have to do." The Admiral squinted forward, frowning.

"Won't matter if the spritsail's too light in a stark calm," Lieutenant Capel mused gloomily.

"Very good, Captain Berry," the Admiral said apropos of nothing but habit, and went below. Slept as the night came again.

There was quiet for a while, the signal lights of *Vanguard* and *Alexander* glowed like cat's eyes in the dark.

A howl from the lookout man on the bowsprit: "Breakers ahead!" and the catheadsman added: "Breakers on both bows!"

Captain Berry watched the unwelcome white edging the distance. He could hear the dull roar of treacherous surf carrying hollowly across the oily black sea.

The Admiral had come back on deck. They paced together, the grave handsome Captain a little like a priest; the tense, yet relaxed, enigmatical Admiral, by his presence reassuring, alert and yet quiet as a perfectly trained cheetah.

It was midnight perhaps when the Admiral ordered his speaking trumpet and leaving the quarter-deck stalked forward.

"Oh, *Alexander,* ahoy!" His voice magnified by the trumpet: crisp and imperative. "I'm obliged to you, Captain Ball, for the assistance you gave me. Now cast off the hawser! Shift for yourself. I won't wreck two ships if one can be saved!"

And Ball's slow voice booming back through the dark: *"Vanguard,* ahoy! With your permission, Sir Horatio, we will stay with you!"

"Shift for yourself, Captain Ball!"

"Thank you, sir!" came the answer.

Berry's face had grown more priestlike, more gaunt and esthetic, for Nelson was commanding their last hope to leave them. Without the dragging *Vanguard* in tow, the whisper of a breeze might save *Alexander.* Berry watched Nelson walking back toward him. How soon would he row off, hoist his flag on *Orion* or *Alexander?*

Nelson came slowly down the deck; as he swung his left arm what there was left of the right swung feebly, counterbalancing his step. The jacks who swore, "Our Nel is brave as a lion, and gentle as a lamb," already called the stump "Nel's fin."

Berry was watching him, his mind, haunted by the immediate danger about which he could do nothing, mulled over the words "lion" and "lamb" and "fish," until Berry forced it to seek some loftier pigeonholing phrase. He found none. Lion, lamb and fish. There was a cleft, or was it a scar, straight through the Admiral's personality: the lamb would never lie down with the lion though they lived side by side, always enemies, one seeking, one eluding the other. The lion would swallow the lamb, but the lamb would still bleat inside the lion. Captain Berry rubbed his face with his hand and the image of his bride floated through his mind: detached. Fighting men had to lead two lives perhaps. And tonight—in another hour—going down with his ship he would learn all the answers to life and death.

And Nelson's flag would fly over another ship. Should he suggest it?

But the Admiral had stopped beside Berry, linked arms with him, said nothing. They began to walk again. And Berry sensed the Admiral was leaning wearily. He was not as strong as he used to be. Teneriffe and long months of nerve-racking pain had taken some of the spring out of him.

And still could be heard the swish of the hawser suddenly bringing up tight: the tug of two ships together! A little hope began to creep back into Berry's face. Captain Ball was staying with them! The Admiral appeared to notice nothing, plunged in thought.

"Ball is a good man," he said at last, and Berry wondered why the words were sounded so solemnly.

"Aye, that he is, Sir Horatio." And Berry saw one of those almost angelic, sweet smiles light up Nelson's face, vanish, leaving his face grim and plain.

They made no pretense of sleep. If the wind did not rise they would wreck. Hour after hour they paced together. They had done all they could think of to prepare for whatever might come. The cables were bent in case they could anchor, or run out a lead, make a spring, keep off the rocks—somehow. But that best bower anchor lay at the bottom, somewhere off Toulon.

Berry wondered how long one night could endure. The surf shining brighter and brighter; the slow sure swell of the water was measured and soundless. While Berry thought of his ship and his personal ruin, his bride widowed, the Admiral thought of his squadron:

Yesterday three, now two ships of the line and one hulk for his flagship. No cruiser frigates to be watching Toulon. To be disgraced and dishonored was nothing to the anguish he felt for England should

St. Vincent wait in vain for some word! What if the French sailed? Skirted St. Vincent . . . and where would an armament strike?

"Thank God it's getting light, Sir Horatio," Berry said suddenly. With the first gray glimmer they could see *Alexander,* stubbornly tied to them, and beyond was the ugly white surf leaping high, and arms of land running out all around them like tentacles of an octopus. "Embayed," Berry muttered. It would not take much longer to founder.

The Admiral and Berry had just reached the end of their walk, pivoted for the turn, when the Admiral started. Something had brushed his cheek. He whirled on Berry.

"Did you feel it, Sir Horatio?" Berry was peering at *Alexander's* sails. They had not rippled for hours, just hung limp. "There!" And a sudden shout from the seamen.

One corner of a topsail shivered. Fell. It shivered again, and all *Alexander's* white canvas whispered, but still the ships drifted until the men could see the brown rocks, the fresh green slime, as the surf sank back, dashed forward again.

A sudden morning breeze.

A hiss of the hawser lifting out of the sea. As *Alexander's* sails billowed out, full of weight, full of life, she gave a gentle, a motherly tug at the *Vanguard.*

And slowly the *Alexander* came around, broadside to the shore. She skirted it delicately; a fine full-breasted lady lifting her skirts from a curb. *Alexander* towed *Vanguard,* with *Orion* still leading them up the coast, to a calm safe bay.

❊   ❊   ❊

The *Orion, Alexander* and *Vanguard* totaled over seventeen hundred officers and men with which to repair Nelson's wreck now anchored at St. Peter's. Still, as Nelson gazed down on a letter in his hand and then at the rickety old fort guarding the bay, he wondered. . . . The Governor of St. Peter's did not choose to receive His Britannic Majesty's ships in Sardinian waters—for fear of French reprisals.

"We will stay." But he sat down, thinking it wise to register his disappointment:

Having by a gale of wind sustained some trifling damage, I anchored a small part of his Majesty's fleet, under my orders, off this Island and

was surprised to hear, by an Officer sent by the Governor, that admittance
was to be refused to the Flag of his Britannic Majesty into this Port.
When I reflect that my most gracious Sovereign is the oldest (I believe)
and certainly the most faithful ally which his Majesty of Sardinia ever had,
I could feel the sorrow which it must have been to his Sardinian Majesty
to have given such an order, and also for your Excellency, who has to
direct its execution. I cannot but look at Afric's shore, where the followers
of Mahomet are performing the part of the good Samaritan, which I look
for in vain at St. Peter's, where it is said the Christian religion is professed.
May I request the favor of your Excellency to forward one Letter for
his Britannic Majesty's Minister at Turin, and the other for his Britannic
Majesty's Consul at Leghorn. May God Almighty bless your Excellency
is the sincere wish of your most obedient servant,

HORATIO NELSON

And he ordered his ships to move in and hang the Governor's
chagrin.

Already *Vanguard* rang with hammers as the Admiral ordered his
launch and made his precarious, clumsy way overside. A miserable
feat, one-armed on a swaying ladder; yet the pain of having to be
hoisted out in a chair—like a fat Mrs. Pigott—was infinitely worse.
His crew rowed him away. And again the embarrassingly slow crawl,
as he who had always gone skittering like a mid all over his ship
clambered up the side of *Alexander.*

Captain Ball was on his quarter-deck, calm as ever, his aisles of men
briskly drawn up to receive their Admiral as if they were home in
Spithead.

As Nelson appeared, Ball was studying him, wondering if anything ever pleased Sir Horatio. Ball decided he did not look pleased.
His face was set—until Nelson's glance met Ball's.

The Admiral's face lit up. He smiled disarmingly, chagrin written
all over him. "My dear Ball! A friend in need—" And the next thing
Ball knew the Admiral's arm went around his shoulder! Then, gripping Ball's hand, shook it.

Ball turned slowly red, outmaneuvered, momentarily baffled.

"No one could have handled a ship better than you did!" The
Admiral said that.

Ball smiled as it dawned on his sophisticated mind that the Admiral
was trying to "make up"—be friends with him. "Thank you, sir."

"And there I was on Sunday, my dear Ball, ready to lead the best captains in the world—" Nelson flung up his hand. "Pride goeth, Ball—"

"With your permission, Sir Horatio, I would like to offer my carpenter. He's itching to be at *Vanguard,* and he's a good man."

"Let's talk to him, if you please."

Ball sent for a stunted square fellow called Morrison who had a bulldog chin, snappish blue eyes and a lean long nose (much like the Admiral's if one dared to notice such things). He gave his salute smartly.

"Well?" The Admiral, the Captain and the carpenter stood staring at the poor ship. Her "trifling damage" amounted to stumps for masts, a sprung bowsprit, battered-in forecastle. "Well?" The Admiral spun about. The carpenter jerked himself rigid. "How soon can you have her fit for active service?"

Morrison did not move, but he rolled his eyes and swallowed hard. He had forgotten to stow his quid before addressing the gods and the heroes. " 'Twould take three months back at Spit'ead, sir." He swallowed again, squinting at the ship.

"Three months!" Nelson barked. "Three *months?*"

The carpenter touched his hat. "At Spit'ead, sir. But if you'd allow me, sir, for she don't look a bit crank aside from her wounds, I'd take a main-topmast for a foremast; a topgallant mast for a topmast—scale her rig down. Aye, that'd do it quick, sir."

"How many *days?*" The Admiral spoke the word very distinctly. If the Lord took but seven for all Creation . . .

Morrison pursed his lips, squinted again sullenly, then stiffened. Grudgingly he nodded his head. "Seven, sir, that'll do it, sir."

"Six at the most. What's your name?"

"Morrison, sir. Thirty years warranted carpenter, sir."

Four days later Nelson was writing a recommendation naming Morrison to Lord St. Vincent for the post of head carpenter at the Gibraltar yards, while *Vanguard, Orion* and *Alexander* sailed smartly out of St. Peter's Bay to return to the rendezvous off Toulon. No doubt the frigates were there on their post waiting, having no news to communicate.

After recommending Morrison, the Admiral chose another sheet to write Fanny, feeling the rise and fall of his ship as she cut through the sea with a joy unusual to his squeamish system. *Vanguard* was off again!

My dearest Fanny,

I ought not to call what has happened to the *Vanguard* by the cold name of accident. I believe firmly, that it was the Almighty's goodness to check my consummate vanity. I hope it has made me a better officer, as I feel confident it has made me a better man. I kiss the rod with all humility.

Figure to yourself a vain man, on Sunday evening at sun-set, walking in his cabin with a squadron about him, who looked up to their Chief to lead them to Glory, and in whom this Chief placed the firmest reliance, that the proudest Ships in equal numbers belonging to France, would have bowed their Flags; and with a very rich prize lying by him. Figure to yourself this *proud, conceited man,* when the sun rose on Monday morning, his Ship dismantled, his Fleet dispersed, and himself in such distress, that the meanest Frigate out of France would have been a very unwelcome guest. . . .

※   ※   ※

The Admiral was in high spirits, his pride restored to that pitch which his vanity required of it. He strolled on deck, smiling amiably to all.

The tops were hailing the deck with "Cape Sicie to starboard. . . ." And the *Vanguard* with *Alexander* stood in to join *Orion,* which had been sent ahead to the frigates.

"Deck there, *Orion* signaling, no frigates in sight, sir!"

Nelson, his glass to his eye, scanned the seas. "They have *deserted* me, Berry! Those blackguard pirates have deserted me!" And for the first time he regretted that he had failed to obtain forms for ordering courts-martial when he left St. Vincent.

"They may have put back to Gibraltar, sir, thinking *Vanguard* would go there to refit."

The Admiral did not—or could not—answer. "No frigates!" No eyes to reconnoiter his station. "Make signal we'll run in close to Toulon, Captain Berry, see for ourselves what the French are about."

"Aye, aye, sir."

It was a warm June morning. A glorious gala day with the sun flashing merrily over the water, the sky filled with the blue of the sea. *Vanguard* pushed forward; a born speedy ship, she could hold her pace in spite of her comical stunted new rig, and Berry was pushing himself and his officers to the limit, to prove himself worthy after that gale.

The arm of Cape Sicie where the English had once been wiped out of Fort L'Aiguillette by young Captain Buonaparte grew as *Vanguard* frothed ahead, almost capering in the fine breeze.

The Admiral beamed at Berry as the men hurled themselves on the braces for a new tack, and the ship came about in record time, lopping seconds off the usual allotted. The two hundred enemy transports and fifteen or sixteen battleships would soon be visible to *Orion* far in the lead.

Nelson was priding himself, and justifiably, that no other admiral would be back in fighting trim on his station so soon after the gale of last week. . . . He heard the first cry from the tops. It startled him before it fully registered.

"What do you see?" Berry howled. The deck seemed to reel.

"*Orion* making signal she spoke a neutral: They're flown, sir! *Boney's flown!* There are *no* ships in Toulon!"

❋   ❋   ❋

The sun shot white fire. The seas heaved. The Admiral tried to breathe as a sudden sharp pain stabbed through his chest. He ran below to his cabin, calling for his secretary, Mr. Campbell; dictated orders: listed the numbers of the code rendezvous to be called at. The three battleships must fan out; search. If only his frigates had stayed on the station; watched and warned him! Without cruising frigates, the eyes of the fleet, his battleships were stone blind.

Buonaparte had escaped him.

A mid at the door. "Strange sail to westward, sir."

As Nelson came on deck, Berry had ordered their private signal to be made. Was it even *one* of their frigates?

From the tops: "She looks French by the cut of her, sir. A corvette hull, brig rigged. She's running up a Union Jack, sir, but she looks— there it flies! She's answering us, sir! *Mutine* brig, Captain Hardy, sir!"

The brig flashed over the water, a swift little shell, only a quarter the size of even a frigate. She bore up under the high black and yellow wall of the *Vanguard*. Nelson clasped his friend's hand as Hardy, beaming, presented a packet of dispatches from St. Vincent.

"Have you seen my frigates, Hardy?"

"Aye, Sir Horatio. Captain Hope cruising in his frigate off Barcelona advised them to go down to Gibraltar. Took them off your station, awaiting *Vanguard* to come down to Gibraltar to refit."

"My God! My God! Hope should have *known* me better!"

"I have to report, sir"—Hardy's eyes were smiling in spite of the Admiral's crushed glance—"a squadron is on its way to join you, sir."

"What's that?" Nelson came out of his abject trance, looked up from the deck.

Berry, who had been clenching and unclenching his hands, almost dropped his glass.

"Lord St. Vincent sending you battleships, Sir Horatio, to take the French fleet. Eleven of line, sir, under Captain Troubridge in *Culloden.* They've been ready and waiting since the hour you left the fleet, sir. Lord St. Vincent signaled them to join you the instant he spied the tops of his reinforcements from England. They're flying, sir!"

The Admiral caught Hardy's hand, wrung it. A squadron—a whole fleet of battleships, all his to command. Fourteen now in all!

"Great news, Sir Horatio!" Berry's face had flushed red with joy for his commander.

"Eleven more battleships. We must signal *Orion* and *Alexander* we're off on a shooting party!" They were all laughing. "With fourteen battleships, my dear Berry— Hardy—" he slapped his thigh—"we can take any French fleet in these seas!" And he went to his cabin to read his dispatches while Berry and Hardy watched him go, then nodded to each other.

❊   ❊   ❊

By the Earl of St. Vincent, Admiral of the Blue, Commander-in-Chief: (Most Secret)

In pursuance of orders from the Lords Commissioners of the Admiralty, to employ a squadron of His Majesty's ships in the Mediterranean, under the command of a discreet officer (copies of which are enclosed, and other papers necessary for your guidance), and in conformity thereto, I do hereby authorize and require you, on being joined by the ships named in the margin, to take them and their Captains under your command, in addition to those already with you; and to proceed with them in quest of the armament preparing by the enemy at Toulon and Genoa . . .

The Admiral smiled—*preparing?* They were already gone!

the object whereof appears to be, either an attack upon *Naples* or *Sicily;* the conveyance of an army to some part of the *coast of Spain,* for the purpose of marching toward *Portugal,* or to pass through the Straits, with a view of proceeding to *Ireland.* On falling in with said armament, or any part thereof you are to use your utmost endeavors to *take, sink, burn, or destroy* it. Should it appear to you, *from good authority,* on your arrival up the Mediterranean, that the enemy's force, capable of being sent to sea, is inferior to what is reported by intelligence herewith transmitted, you are, in this case, to direct such ships to rejoin me as may not be absolutely necessary to ensure your superiority, the moment you shall find yourself in a situation to do so. . . .

Could he part with some of his fourteen (eleven of which had not yet arrived) and still count himself superior to fifteen battleships and two hundred transports? He would postpone that decision for a little.

You are to remain upon this service so long as provisions of your squadron will last, or as long as you may be enabled to obtain supplies from any of the Ports in the Mediterranean; and when, from want of provisions, or any other circumstance, you shall be no longer able to remain within the Straits, *or in the event of the enemy's* escaping to the *westward (which you will take especial care to prevent),* you are to lose no time in rejoining me, wherever I may be.

St. Vincent

Given on board the *Ville de Paris,* off Cádiz,
May 21, 1798
To Sir Horatio Nelson, K.B. Rear-Admiral of the Blue.

Additional instructions: In a private letter from Lord Spencer, I am led to believe, that you are perfectly justifiable in pursuing the French squadron to any part of the Mediterranean, Adriatic, Morea, Archipelago, or even the Black Sea. Should its destination be to any of those parts . . .

From Lord Spencer to St. Vincent (enclosed with Nelson's dispatches):

I think it almost unnecessary to suggest to you the propriety to putting the squadron under the command of Sir Horatio Nelson, whose acquaintance with that part of the world, as well as his activity and disposition seem to qualify him in a peculiar manner for that service. . . . The appearance of a British Squadron in the Mediterranean is a condition upon which *the fate of Europe at this moment depends.* . . .

The Admiral read that twice. The fate of Europe depended on *him.* His hour for glory had come, and with it the responsibility of deciding the fate of Europe!

After reading that it seemed but an irrelevant detail that St. Vincent's private letter warned him the Admiralty was split wide-open by First

Lord Spencer's appointment of Nelson. The wedge no doubt being helped into place by Pitt's protégé, Captain Sir Sidney Smith, who had spent the last few months making promises in high places. . . . Whereupon St. Vincent's flag officers, hearing of the Admiralty split, were making Nelson's appointment the focal point of another of their attempts to oust their Commander in Chief. Rear Admirals Parker and Orde had been sent home as the result and would no doubt talk very loudly about it.

But Nelson knew that though St. Vincent implied Nelson was the cause of Parker's and Orde's denouncement, he himself was really not the *basic* cause of their quarrel. St. Vincent high-handedly refused to share the fleet's prize money with any of his flag officers, claiming his share would not be large enough if the percentage of prize money above the captains' puny shares were split so many ways. It was greedy and uncustomary, and there was the root of the trouble every flag officer started against him. Nelson, who resented it as much as they did, had suggested to the flag officers, and unknown to St. Vincent, that they all join together, hire a lawyer to take it to court, like civilized men, and get on with the war. They had agreed and considered it until this sudden split in the Admiralty gave his fellow flag officers the chance to kill two birds with one stone: Vincent *and* Nelson. But as far as Nelson was concerned the quarrels in the fleet must iron themselves out, for he was in a bigger scrape: *Buonaparte had escaped!*

When he pounced back on deck a few moments later he found Berry and Hardy discussing the gale.

"But that means one thing, gentlemen." He cocked his head up at Hardy. "The French fleet with that madman aboard is here, somewhere in these seas. You came through the Gut, Hardy, and no word of him. But *where?*" He cried out to the wind. And he paced off, eyeing the seas: trackless as deserts; waves shifting as dunes.

A strange, fascinating medium on which to make plans, telling no tales, leaving no traces. Like a blank sheet of paper. Ships passing with the curve of horizon between them might have passed eons or seconds apart. A secretive place. A place for men of dazzling genius to play weird tricks. And all thirty-nine-year-old Rear Admiral Sir Horatio Nelson had now were his wits with which to track Buonaparte on the shifting crosshatch of waves. At least until frigates joined him or he picked up some scrap of news. Surely someone had seen those ships somewhere! But where had the French gone? Was there some clue to be found even here, on a blank sea?

"Well, gentlemen, what do you think?" He turned back to his captains.

"The talk in the fleet was, Buonaparte is after Ireland, as a means of invading England, Sir Horatio," Hardy said.

"But would he sail from *here,* with our fleets in the Atlantic and in the Channel?"

"They seem to think he means to circle them . . . Buonaparte intends to strike—"

"Everywhere!" Nelson laughed, waving his hand. "North, east, south, west. Every port in the world says, 'He will strike *here!*' But that is not the question. The question is where? And if he has not gone through the Gut— Oh, if Troubridge were only *here!*"

Meantime he must think where this Buonaparte would strike. Where would the stakes be the highest? While *Vanguard* and *Orion* and *Alexander* spread out, not too far from the rendezvous, trying to find some clue, but not daring to miss meeting their reinforcements.

❊　　　　❊　　　　❊

Two days later like a host of avenging white angels Nelson's battleships came, with their cannon saluting his flag, flying down out of the west. And Troubridge was far in the lead—first to reach him, grip his left hand.

Now for the first time since the English had retreated in sackcloth and ashes fourteen sail of the line were back in the Mediterranean Sea. All Nelson's! Did it matter if some leaked, some lagged? They were the élite of the navy, the most beautiful ships he had ever seen, all *his* to sail—*where?* Only his unshakable faith in himself stood to ward off the myriad black thoughts that one word brought winging into his mind. Where? Was he too late? And how could he win with the odds all awry? But he looked through his windows and saw *his fleet,* and his hopes rose with his pride. No matter where, he would find Buonaparte!

But his face, like Berry's, had aged ten years.

His fleet. These were his ships:

Culloden 74, Captain Troubridge, who must be, like Berry, the Admiral's right arm, since the night Troubridge's bold three hundred and eighty had marched out of Santa Cruz with their colors still flying!

Theseus 74, Captain Ralph Willet Miller, with young Lieutenant Hoste aboard. Miller's guns fired faster, he used lanyards—no matches and touchholes for him.

Alexander 74, friend Ball, Captain.

Vanguard 74, Rear Admiral Sir H.N., Captain Berry.

Minotaur 74, level-headed, bold Captain Louis.

Swiftsure 74, Captain Benjamin Hallowell. It had been a long time since Serocold died at Calvi. Had it been only *four* years?

Audacious 74, Captain Gould, a man who matched the name of his ship.

Defence 74, Captain Peyton, his recent young passenger on the trip out from England.

Zealous 74, Captain Samuel Hood, another gentleman from Teneriffe.

Orion 74, handsome, iron-featured, hot-tempered Sir James Saumarez who had tackled *Santissima Trinidad* with Collingwood at St. Vincent. Senior Captain of this fleet, Saumarez was second in command to Nelson; Troubridge third.

Goliath 74, Captain Foley, another old Mediterranean man from St. Vincent, and a tough one.

Majestic 74, Captain Westcott, a baker's brilliant son who had gone to sea as a lowly cabin boy; had shot up to captain high in line for flag rank.

Bellerophon 74, Captain Darby, a good-natured fighting Irishman, noted for social blunders and an acute professional sense.

Leander 50, with young Captain Thomson from Teneriffe.

Collingwood alone was missing from the lists. But St. Vincent needed to keep some good men off Cádiz. Coll was writing his "mortification . . . capturing cabbage ships!" doing small odd jobs when he had worked like a slave to have his ship in fighting trim, hoping St. Vincent would relent, let him go too. No. Collingwood had a reputation for being able to stand tedious routine. His *Excellent* would have been a better ship than tiny *Leander,* though Thomson was pleased as punch at his big chance, and spoiling for a good fight.

So that was his fleet: thirteen standard Third Rates, all seventy-fours, and one fifty, smaller than old *Agamemnon.* But *no frigate cruisers!* Nelson must sail without eyes on the biggest man hunt since the Spanish Armada challenged England. And as he stared at his list, he prided himself that the odds would break the heart of any other officer tackling his first great command.

❊   ❊   ❊

And as the battleships joined their Chief *the wind fell stark calm!* Sails drooped on fourteen ships, flapped dismally against the masts.

Alone in his sleeping cabin, Nelson was going over his orders again: find Buonaparte. Through the windows he could see the same trackless surface that Odysseus or the first Phoenicians had seen. The same inscrutable, glassy bright element mirroring air. Thus the seas had been before man lashed two logs together, thus they had been when only the fish fought other fish, though the primeval forests of Etruscans and Iberians had heard clashing of men. But since the first logs were lashed together and had met other logs lashed by other tribesmen the surface of the seas had known no peace. Before Hiram of Tyre sailed his merchant ships into Jaffa to barter the cedars of Lebanon with King David of Israel there had been rival ships. But great warfare had grown slowly upon the water. Battleships were the outgrowth of the guards who once sailed on the merchant traders. It had been centuries before the merchant marine and the navy were two distinct groups during a war: the merchants in convoys, the battleships exchanging no goods but death. Only once, perhaps, in a century did two battle fleets sail forth both equally determined; one to escape notice and reach its destination, the other to find and destroy it. How find the quarry? How discover a fleet whose destination had not even been known to its officers before sailing, determined as Buonaparte was upon conquest? The stakes on both sides must measure twice the height of Teneriffe.

As Spanish acquisitions in the New World had tempted England, so England, waxing strong and rich, had tempted France for over a hundred years. There was probably a clue in all this to Buonaparte's move. But which of the many valuable possibilities was the right one?

The world for this modern Caesar? He must never have the chance to weep like the young Alexander; or wax rich as Baber and Tamerlane.

The French had the First Rate *L'Orient* 120, and some Second Rates, eighties, besides their Third Rates, seventy-fours. . . . Admiral Nelson was frowning as he looked up to answer the mid at the door. The boy gulped, and Nelson smiled to himself, amused; only to remember that young Meeks who had begged to sail with him was dead, shrouded, leaded head and foot. Committed to the bottom with the all too familiar rites before the solemnly drawn-up men, some of whom Meeks had saved from the same fate. Gone overside and forgotten as quickly as possible. Twenty-four hours was considered lengthy mourning. . . .

"Captains have come aboard, sir."

"Very well." He got up. It would have been more impressive perhaps, considering his youth and the fact that many of his captains were older, for him to write tight little orders to his captains, signal his will: keep his thoughts to himself, hoard his command jealously. But there was too much at stake for vainglorious dictatorship.

He went into the main cabin where his captains were gathered, all talking at once, each trying to impress on the other the exact destination of Buonaparte. There should have been a few more rear admirals among them considering the size of the fleet, but St. Vincent had no rear admirals lower than Nelson. It was a big fleet for one man to handle alone. That merely pleased him.

"Ah—" and the captains stiffened, leaping to their feet.

"And where is he today, gentlemen?" Nelson smiled, taking his seat. They shook their heads. Silence.

The reflected light played over the paneling, rippled and shadowed a chart of the Mediterranean Sea, turned it translucent; mocked its outlines with distorted high lights; made the carefully engraved boundaries fluid. The light facetiously and ironically repeating the slow undulations of the becalmed sea.

"Stark calm and no frigates!" The Admiral smiled wryly. Only Captain Hardy in his small *Mutine* brig, to take the part of three cruisers! Hardy was to be the eyes for the whole fleet. An impossible task, for while Hardy was one direction, the enemy might be anywhere else clear round the compass.

"Now, gentlemen, since we are still uncertain as to where John Corse—or Buonaparte, I believe they call him—is gone, with the first wind we will scatter; rendezvous off Naples and Sicily, for they must be guarded until we have some definite clue. But with a calm, I will take the opportunity to say I am honored in leading this band of brothers."

These niceties set the tone he wanted. No mystery. No jealousy. No confusion of purpose. "So, where, in your opinions, has Buonaparte fled: north—east—south—or west?"

They drew in their breaths: "North, sir—"

"East, sir—" from Ball.

"West, sir—"

"That seems to eliminate south," Troubridge grunted. "Now if we only knew for certain when he sailed!"

From the Admiral: "We can be *positive* he sailed sometime between Sunday night, May 20th, and June 1st when we arrived back on this station. Today is the seventh, is it not? Then he *may* have a head start on us of anywhere from a week to eighteen days!"

"Damn the luck! Fate's a bitch!" Troubridge rubbed his face.

"We will find him wherever he is, gentlemen." The Admiral had thrust out his lower lip in a way they all recognized meant business. "Eighteen days could have carried them through the Gut, perhaps. Yet if he sailed in that gale—knowing French ships and their timidity in foul winds—" He broke off again.

"If Buonaparte commands as they say he does," Hallowell smiled, "we have to deal with an army man who might not know the difference."

"True, Ben, and it would be pleasant to think they had foundered, but, providing he did sail then, he must have sailed east. However, did he sail east as a ruse? Did he intend to loop, say, around Sicily before sailing west? Who knows what a general would do?" He paused. "I have received letters with arguments for every conceivable destination listed in my orders from every minister and consul in these seas. Every one of their arguments for their opinions appears sound, except for one thing: no two of them agree as to where he is going. Keeping this comforting thought in mind, we must weigh every argument for ourselves. Suppose he did not intend any ruse, suppose he sailed *east?*" The Admiral looked from one to the other. "Wherever he goes, our orders are simple: to take, sink, burn, and otherwise destroy."

Troubridge rubbed his hands. "A jolly sport, sir!"

"In my orders I am especially cautioned against allowing the enemy to get to *westward* of our fleet. He must not go through the Gut! Gentlemen, Lord Spencer says the fate of Europe at this moment depends on us."

After a moment he asked, "After we make sure of Naples, then what do you say?"

"It wouldn't be the first time they tried for Ireland . . ." from Troubridge.

"That was quite a gale of wind, Troubridge," Ball smiled; "he would have to sail east, as Sir Horatio suggested, or founder."

"But if he didn't sail in that gale?" Miller suggested.

"And what about Spain?" from Peyton.

"Or the Antipodes, gentlemen!" Nelson laughed dryly. "We must think on these things . . ." He had not one positive clue to guide him, yet he had an idea that Buonaparte was after greater stakes than anyone, even the ministers at home, guessed. Where would he strike if he were to try to wreck England without challenging the big Channel and Atlantic fleets? The wind had been westerly, blowing east, and as far as Buonaparte knew, France ruled the Mediterranean Sea. "We must try to think of every possibility. Don't forget French Kings once even coveted—India."

Ball glanced up, nodded, as if he had already been thinking the same. So did Darby. Most of the others took it as they had the Antipodes. Nelson of Teneriffe might be that rash and visionary, but a land genius like Buonaparte would not consider such a harebrained scheme: to transport an army thousands of miles, across water and without provisions, should he be cut off, except for what he could find in a desert! But at last Saumarez brought his hard face to bear on the Admiral's; scowled his approval with a stiff nod!

One week later, with fits and starts of light airs, Nelson's squadron lay along the coast of Italy without one scrap of news. All Nelson knew was that the French armaments known to have been preparing were gone. He had known that for two weeks. Nothing more. The French had vanished on seas empty of ships. As if Buonaparte had spreak a cloak, wished himself invisible, disappeared in the air. And so great had fear painted the man, there were those who would swear he had the power and the means to be everywhere!

Hardy's *Mutine* ranged alongside. "Oh, *Vanguard!* Nothing to be seen."

And the next day *Vanguard* spied and hailed a small Tunisian cruiser with a band of Barbary pirates aboard.

"Well, Berry?" Nelson's face was growing wan again as he paced his main cabin from gun to gun glimpsing the pirate through the stern windows: sailing away, cutting across *Vanguard's* slow, maddeningly quiet wake.

"The Tunisians say they spoke a Greek ship on June 10th, sir, who told them that on the fourth he had passed through the French fleet of about two hundred sail, as he thought, off the northwest end of Sicily—steering to eastward!"

"Eastward!" The Admiral laid his hand on Berry's arm, as he framed the one word again: India. Did not say it aloud.

"Signal Troubridge to come aboard!" He went to his writing desk. He was studying a chart of the Mediterranean Sea when Troubridge appeared. His finger was tracing the route he believed Buonaparte was sailing: up the Mediterranean to Egypt—to march across Egypt with nothing to bar the French army but a few Arabs, after all England's treasure. It had to be India! Yet until he made sure did he dare sail east; leave the west—leave England—unguarded? "Should the enemy escape to *westward* of you, which you will take especial care to prevent . . ." and then, not in the orders, but in the additional instructions, "the Black Sea . . ." But only if he were *sure*. And to be sure did not mean his personal hunches, but *facts*.

He looked up as Troubridge came in, but his forefinger was still glued to the chart, pointing to Alexandria, Egypt.

"You will go in *Mutine* to Naples, Troubridge, find out all you can. You must persuade them to send me Neapolitan cruisers. I must have eyes! I've written Sir William Hamilton and I am sure he will do all he can. The Two Sicilies are neutral, more than that we are led to believe they are friendly. In a few weeks we will have to have stores. They must open their ports. But bring me news of the French, Troubridge. You must stress this, that according to my dispatches, Buonaparte means to strike Naples or Sicily. That must bring us their support. We are sent here to defend them. Harp on it." He gripped Troubridge's hand. "And don't overlook Lady Hamilton. She has the ear of the Queen, who was, don't forget, the sister of Marie Antoinette. God bless her for she hates the French!"

When Troubridge had gone to scare Naples into assisting them, Nelson wrote to the Admiralty: "If the French pass Sicily, I shall believe they are going on their scheme of possessing Alexandria, and getting troops to India—a plan concerted with Tippoo Sahib, by no means so difficult as might at first be imagined. . . ." Tippoo Sahib was Sultan of Mysore, India, and he hated English domination. There was also a hint of trouble in Turkey, a pretender claiming the throne. Between Buonaparte, Tippoo Sahib and the pretender, what might not happen to India? And if Russia, who was watching the war very closely, trying to use her power on the side of the mightiest, if Russia who had always wanted Turkey and India—even tried for them in the days of old Catherine the Great—were to throw her weight with France . . . just when Mr. Pitt was trying to sway Russia to England's coalition . . . the fate of Europe.

Nelson signaled for Captains Ball and Darby and Saumarez to tell them his plans. Over and over and round and round they went, matching clues. This was the time to be cool, to use every atom of intelligence, leap at nothing, reject nothing until it had been picked to pieces. This was as important as a battle. The Admiral seemed to have lost all consciousness of himself, his will fed his mind, a disembodied intelligence.

"And that's your opinion, gentlemen?"

"Aye, sir, and the sooner we're gone the better; they have perhaps a month's start on us!"

So they agreed. Buonaparte's destination was probably India. On Nelson remained the responsibility of the decision; did he dare, with only the hearsay of rumor and his own wits, backed by his captains, sail east when he was ordered to guard the west? Columbus had once sailed west to find the east. Buonaparte was apparently reversing the procedure: sailing east to ruin the west.

Nelson was outreaching the "spheres of his supposed knowledge" to take such a risk. To leave Gibraltar unguarded without definite information. But he had made up his mind. If Buonaparte passed Sicily he would sail to Egypt.

Troubridge had come back in three hours, blood boiling, as he laid out the various letters answering Nelson's request for cruisers, news, and permission to enter Sicilian ports.

After the Admiral had glanced through them, looked up, turned white with anger, Troubridge nodded.

"Boney's been by. They say he has gone to Malta. That he is completely at peace with the Two Sicilies. Malta is claimed by the Sicilies—but apparently they're overlooking that little breach of promise. They say they are in no danger."

"They were crying out for our protection, Troubridge!"

"Boney's been by . . . they're paralyzed, Sir Horatio."

"Malta—that means east, Troubridge. And no cruisers and no permission to enter their ports!"

"The Queen listens to us, the King to the French. As Spain goes so goes Ferdinand—as Austria goes so goes Maria Carolina, but she's tough, sir. And the Sicilies take the hindmost. Our Ambassador could get nothing but a vague permit to allow us the usual neutrality: four ships in port at a time."

"Time! Four at a time. That's not good. Malta? I say India. India by way of Malta. Yet before I left St. Vincent I heard talk that Buonaparte intended to take Sicily by way of Malta! These letters from Naples leave us where we started!" The Admiral paced off the cabin waving a handful of papers.

"The Neapolitans are babbling idiots, Sir Horatio! Lady Hamilton went to the Queen while I talked with Sir William and the rest of that pack of fools. She's the only one who's kept her head, but I don't think she accomplished a damn thing. She wants to ship as a powder monkey just to have at Buonaparte!" Troubridge laughed like a thunderclap, scowled again.

"Did she really? That beautiful creature would have us all flustered!" And Admiral Nelson blushed like a girl.

Troubridge stared, unbelieving. Such *idiocy* from *Nelson!* And for a moment he saw something agonized in Nelson's face as his color returned to its normal pallor; a tormented struggle, revealing a man of irrevocable passion—of Teneriffe—shot through Troubridge's mind out of all reason. He did not like it.

"I had a letter from her, Troubridge. She says," Nelson fumbled about on the desk, extracted it from the heap, " 'the Queen desires me to say everything that is kind and bids me say with her whole heart and soul she wishes you victory. . . .' And that is all. There's no promise of help in that."

"And that misplaced Englishman who calls himself Prime Minister, Sir Horatio! Acton—the blackguard is neutral! Their Foreign Minister Gallo is scared we'll upset his plans, he means to wait to see what Austria will do."

"Then let us be off, Troubridge." The Admiral riffled the stack of useless apologetic letters, sick with disappointment.

Troubridge growled, brought out: "Aye, now the French Minister

in Naples knows how big an English force is in these seas he can't
wait to send word to Paris. . . . Oh! Let us but get sight of Buonaparte and his army! By God! We shall lick them!"

"Our only hope is that the Queen . . . that Naples will assist us
under the rose, Troubridge. Meanwhile we shall 'lick 'em'!"

The Admiral smiled at Troubridge, who saluted, left Nelson with
the fate of Europe gnawing like a cancer at his fast beating heart.

As *Vanguard* weighed anchor off Capri that afternoon a dispatch
ship hailed, pulled alongside. A young captain named Bowen of the
Transfer, who had recently brought St. Vincent's letters and dispatches for Naples, and who was staying at the English Embassy,
brought Nelson one letter . . . two letters.

One was on a small scrap of Lady Hamilton's stationery:

DEAR SIR, I send you a letter I have received this moment from the Queen.
Kiss it and send it back by Bowen, as I am bound not to give any of her
letters. Ever your,

EMMA

He scanned the Queen's letter. It promised that she would give
secret orders for his fleet to be watered and victualed in the big fortified harbor of Syracuse, Sicily, whenever he called there. And he sent
it back by Bowen with a:

MY DEAR LADY HAMILTON,

I have kissed the Queen's letter pray say I hope for the honor of kissing
her hand when no fears will intervene, assure her Majesty that no person
has her felicity more at heart than myself, and that the sufferings of her
family will be a Tower of Strength on the Day of Battle, fear not the event,
God is with us. God bless you and Sir William pray say I cannot stay
to answer his letter. Ever
                    Yours faithfully
                                        HORATIO NELSON

❊   ❊   ❊

And baffling light winds. Off the Faro of Messina, June 20th, more
news from the English Consul:

"All I can tell you, Sir Horatio, is that the Russian Minister just
arrived from Malta reports the French landed at Malta. On Tuesday,
the twelfth, they had taken the old city. Their fleet anchored between
Gozo and Malta. . . ."

"And that is all?"

"That is all, Sir Horatio. Would to God we knew more!"

Admiral Nelson watched the man go back overside. Absurd! Buonaparte was not done. Two hundred transports to take the little island of Malta? What then? Was the latest news gathered from paid French spies by the English Minister at Florence, Mr. Wyndham, correct? The spies swore Buonaparte was planning to attack Sicily by way of Malta. That Buonaparte's promise to Naples that he would not attack was merely a ruse. . . . Nelson sat utterly alone in his cabin. So the latest rumor was that Buonaparte would still sail west. No, he still believed Buonaparte was going to Egypt, through Egypt to Suez. In three weeks from the time Buonaparte re-embarked at Suez, with ordinary sailing, he would land on the Malabar coast: attack a totally unprepared India.

That was Nelson's theory. And still his squadron battled foul winds and calms trying to get clear of the tortuously narrow Straits of Messina, to be in a position east of Malta should Buonaparte sail. And Nelson was still convinced that he must sail east, yet as rumors had snowballed over his first small kernel of inspiration the decision had grown more complex. What had he to base his decision upon besides his common sense, his wits, his presumption that he could guess better than ministers of state, and his inherent distrust of spies—whatever nationality? His instructions permitted him to go to the "Black Sea," provided he had reasonable assurance the west was protected. But what of Sicily—Portugal—and Ireland? He had not one scrap of official proof to back his decision . . . yet if he hesitated waiting for proof and Buonaparte *had* sailed east . . . he could not bear the thought of it!

On circumstantial evidence alone, he must make his decision, and if he were wrong . . . But he was *right!* He knew it. And this was his evidence, gleaned by his wits:

First, as far as he knew, Buonaparte had left Toulon sometime during that gale, blowing east, and he had chosen to sail at a time of year when the westerly winds blew straight for Egypt almost unceasingly. Now for the obverse of this evidence. If Buonaparte were to sail west from Malta while Nelson sailed east, Nelson would give Buonaparte the overwhelming advantage of the weather position. Buonaparte would possibly sail through the Strait of Gibraltar while Nelson was beating back against the wind from Egypt.

Second scrap of evidence: Buonaparte had sailed on this adventure himself. No petty sally this trip. He had fourteen or fifteen battleships by latest count, forty thousand troops, two hundred and eighty transports, many hundred pieces of artillery, wagons, draught horses, cavalry, *and* this is what intrigued Nelson: Buonaparte had with him artificers, *naturalists, astronomers, mathematicians.* . . . Like a new Alexander this man!

Captain Berry reporting at the door of the Admiral's cabin: "The wind comes fresh westerly, sir."

"Steer for Malta."

Off Malta, June 22nd, 1798, one whole month since the gale blew *Vanguard* off Toulon, more news, the same news:

Malta surrendered June 15th and on Saturday the 16th, the French fleet left Malta *to attack Sicily.* A French garrison was left at Valletta, Malta, with French colors flying.

Sicily? But the wind was fair westerly.

"Signal squadron to make all sail for *Egypt,* Captain Berry."

And as the signal flew, Sir James Saumarez, who had agreed and still agreed that Nelson was *right,* now told fellow captains his opinion of the Admiral's orders to sail east in spite of all rumors to sail west, that right or wrong: "Did the chief responsibility rest with me it would be more than my irritable nerves could bear!" And his handsome face hardened. East or west, it did not matter to the captains, they were under orders, a court-martial would not find them guilty. Only Allen and the officers of the dark middle watch knew how little the Admiral slept, how often he paced alone.

Meantime in England, Fanny was writing her husband: "On Sunday, the 20th of May," which was the night *Vanguard* nearly wrecked, "we arrived at Roundwood. The satisfaction I felt was very great on being under your own roof. No thanks to any earthly being. Our Father was all for staying although the house had little or no accommodation. . . . The house is quite large enough. . . ."

And from Cádiz, St. Vincent was writing Nelson not to be dismayed by the gale. St. Vincent thought it was a blessing in disguise, for knowing that Nelson had only three battleships at the time, Buonaparte would have sailed anyway—though no doubt crippled. As it was, the gale gave Nelson time to meet the reinforcements under Troubridge. And St. Vincent was sending the frigates back, led by

Captain Hope, who had taken them away. They were on their way from Gibraltar. Josiah with them, for even St. Vincent had found he could not control the lad.

Also, three Portuguese battleships under the Marquis of Niza were soon to be assigned Nelson by the only *"man"* St. Vincent had met in all Portugal: the Portuguese Minister of Marine. But St. Vincent's letter would be a long time catching up with Nelson's squadron now sailing *east* on a hunch, leaving the west unguarded. . . .

And all of a week after Nelson had vanished from Naples, his frigates sailed into the Bay of Naples with a "Where's Admiral Nelson?"

"God only knows!"

And the baffled frigates, the eyes Nelson longed for, began to track him, here—there—finally found the code messages left for them at Cape Passaro: sailed on for Egypt three weeks behind Nelson's squadron, on a straight southerly course.

Then weeks after the frigates vanished from Cape Passaro, at a more leisurely pace came the three Portuguese battleships, firing a salute smack into Naples, scaring the hysterical Neapolitans and themselves nearly to death. They could not leave until they had made many profound apologies. The Portuguese even took a fancy to Naples while the Neapolitans begged them to be off. And they, too, eventually up anchored after more apologies and farewells. The Portuguese sailed off, found the messages left by the frigates, and began a wary, lonely cruise in the general direction of Egypt. Horrified at the thought of meeting Buonaparte.

But all sails in Nelson's squadron were set for Egypt. And Hardy's *Mutine,* the only eye Nelson had, was now sent on ahead to warn Alexandria to arm; that Buonaparte meant to strike *there*. And God preserve Hardy and his little ship on its long lonely trip, for that ship might still save India.

Nelson was positive. His decision for good or for evil had been made. And while his captains wondered, thanked God they were not in his place, the very fact he had made up his mind acted like a tonic on him. Still, in spite of his gracious smile, his mental certainty, he began to feel a tension about his heart. As the grim days crawled by, it grew into a pain. He cocked a sharp eye on the sun, let no officer make a false reckoning. Straight for Egypt, not one point off the shortest course, for if Buonaparte left Malta on the sixteenth he was still one week ahead of Nelson.

And every minute seemed time lost, yet those fourteen battleships, St. Vincent's élite, sailed as ships never sailed before. They were old ships, but their captains pampered them like poor winded race horses. If they could have flown, Nelson would have complained of the lag; if they could have pinned messages on the wind, it would not have been fast enough for him.

He spread them out, but not beyond instant recall. And they must chase nothing for prize money. They must keep together, ready to fight instantly, blindly straight for Egypt; they must make up that week's start of Buonaparte's.

If they could have tracked the trackless, followed some wake, but the wakes of their own ships closed as they passed, and the seas were as always.

And no frigates to see beyond the maddening enticing curve of the water. And Allen was grumbling constantly for the Admiral to eat *something*. But while his body wasted, his mind burned brighter and brighter. He had made his decision. The fate of Europe. . . . This was it.

He wasted no time that could be utilized. Over and over in his mind as he paced the now sweltering decks, while Berry's lieutenants drilled and drilled the men; under the African summer sun, as his eyes wept at the glittering surface of water, he planned one thing: His Battle.

And every day it was possible, he had his captains to dinner, hammering home to them every conceivable position in which ships might be found, whether anchored or at sea, in port or out of port, with or without transports, running free or standing to fight, and for each situation he tried to fathom how place his ships to deal them a master stroke. Then turning to each captain: "And what would you do in this case?" Listening patiently, then sharpening their wits, pitting them against each other, letting them hash out their suggestions, then clarifying their ideas with thrusts of his own, until each man not only talked Nelson's tactics, but thought they were his own. He was the young tutor once more, and this time he had fourteen brilliant and seasoned students, and he radiated his sublime self-confidence.

"There must be no position in which they can be found, that we have not taken into our calculations. I want no last-minute array of signals to distract you, gentlemen. If Buonaparte's convoy is still above water, ten of us must attack his battle fleet, whatever its number, and four of us close on the two hundred odd transports. . . ." Saumarez and Troubridge would lead the two divisions against the French fleet while the other four battleships must sink every transport. The captains knew that with their slim numbers the plan spelled annihilation for both fleets, but it would be an immortal battle. "If the transports get away Buonaparte might still succeed with part of his plan, make a landing somewhere. But wherever he goes, we will sink what we find, and if he has landed the French army will be cut off to starve. For when we get through, gentlemen, England will control the Mediterranean Sea."

He taught his wise band of brothers the safety of teamwork. Each man must know in advance, the moment the enemy was sighted, and their position judged in a glance, how Nelson intended to fight it. He taught them to look for Achilles' heels where none could expect to find one. And still he did not know how many ships his fourteen must tackle. No matter. "We will annihilate them."

But no ships joined him, frigates or Portuguese. They did not even spy one lone sail rimming the horizon. His squadron, like Noah, had the seas to itself. As if at the moment there were no other life anywhere on the earth.

Fourteen towering sails surrounded by nothing but water and air. And the intolerable heat increased. Awnings were stretched over the quarter-deck. The trip seemed endless.

Yet it took them, flying before the westerly wind, but six days from Malta to Egypt.

June 29, 1798:

Another clear, blinding dawn under the Egyptian sun; another blank lunatic reflection of nothing spread over the sea.

Land had been sighted hours ago, the white Pharos Tower of Alexandria grew in the circle of a hundred glasses: shimmering and shapeless in the harsh light, marking the mouth of the Nile, the long desert path to India.

Alexandria, Egypt.

Nelson felt his heart pounding dangerously fast as the bay opened, and the lookouts began to cry, "Deck there—"

His heart throbbed in mortal agony. He had made his decision. Sailed east when the world cried: Sail west! But he was positive!

Every eye in the fleet was on Egypt as the lookouts shouted: "I see one old Turkish ship of the line, sir, and four Turkish frigates. No French fleet here, Sir Horatio. Only a few tiny coastal vessels . . ."

The Admiral lowered his glass, his face ashen, as the full weight of the words seemed to crush the breath out of him, turn him sick. "Oh, God!" he gasped soundlessly, reeling. He heard voices far away, through the frenzied ringing in his ears, through the crashing of all his—of all Europe's—hopes!

"*Mutine,* Sir Horatio, making signal to speak us." Berry's voice seemed suddenly to be shouting in his ears.

"Well—Hardy—?" The Admiral's voice was even but dry.

"The British Consul, Mr. Baldwin, has been away on a trip for three months, Sir Horatio. No one here knows anything about the French expedition. They don't believe it, sir. They were damned rude and indifferent."

"We will run up the coast, Captain Berry. Circle this end of the Mediterranean. He must have got wind of us and changed his course!" And with a bitter smile, that was no more than a grimace, "The devil's children have the devil's own luck!" But only his pride kept his back straight, head up, as he left the deck—and staggered into his cabin.

Alone in his stifling hot sleeping cabin, he collapsed on his cot. His heart beat slowly and tortuously, everything seemed to be circling him, turning black, yet he knew the sun was pouring in his window. He could hardly breathe. He was cold as a corpse. He was ruined!

Like a damned blind Samson pulling down all Europe with him. His heart thudded slowly as he breathed with short rasping groans. His heart seemed to fill his whole body; threatened to burst out of it.

Had that damned dog Buonaparte outwitted him? The Admiralty, backed by the state, said: Naples, Sicily, Portugal—or Ireland, and he had sailed off to Egypt.

He weighed it again, every possible clue he could grasp, and with a gasp of exasperation covered his face with his hand. Where were the French bound? They were going to India!

Oh, God, he was *still* positive. Was he mad? Or had he outsailed them? Impossible, if they had left Malta on the sixteenth . . . had that rumor, too, been false? He had believed only half of it, only the fact that Buonaparte had sailed. He had ignored the rest of it. Supposing

Buonaparte *had* taken Sicily while he was off on a chase to save India —or gone to Ireland! The French had tried for Ireland only last year.

At this moment hanging would be merciful.

No! He believed it as firmly as ever, that Buonaparte meant to strike through Egypt. He must have veered off! He must have! Buonaparte had frigates. And if *one* French frigate cruising afar had spied Nelson's fleet of a night, or had even heard his signal guns, just as he himself had once blundered into the midst of the Spanish Grand Fleet and escaped undetected . . . Just one dirty French frigate. It might have tagged him for days. The thought nearly maddened him. To be blind in the midst of enemy eyes! It must have been that. And Buonaparte had changed his course, perhaps all his plans. At this moment he might be landing farther north, in Syria. . . .

He rubbed his face and his hand came away dripping with cold sweat. If he were to die at this moment, *want of frigates* would be written on his heart.

He sat up dizzily. The devils had broken his heart. He had felt it break . . . but that day at dinner, he smiled blandly at Berry whose face was pained. "We will have them yet, Captain Berry."

And the word went through the fleet: Nelson had no nerves.

So the English fleet vanished north, leaving a sleepy Alexandria, not even shooing off the eternal, but sacred flies laying blinding eggs in their eyes. Alexandria sank back into the lethargy of an Egyptian summer; drowsily amused by all lunatic Englishmen.

But there was nothing under the molten mercurial skies as Nelson searched the shores of the eastern Mediterranean, sailing north past Syria, Cyprus, and, at last, sadly west, skirting Caramania, Candia, the Morea. Nothing but waves laughing up at him. Not one word of the French. Buonaparte was invisible.

And no frigates or Portuguese battleships joined the English.

Six hundred leagues of a wild-goose chase. Back then to Sicily to see if it were safe, for his fleet had run out of stores. The water in the casks was green. The men thirsty, the salt beef growing saltier.

To Syracuse, Sicily, then on the Queen's promise. Perhaps the frigates from Gibraltar would join him there, or he would learn where they were. And every night, on his knees, before going to bed:

"And please God, I want the French fleet. Amen."

❊ ❊ ❊

That summer England knew terror. Not since the days when the Spanish Armada had sailed into the Channel, been wrecked by foul winds and Sir Francis Drake, had England known such sick panic as she did now. As weeks went by Buonaparte seemed to sail ever nearer and nearer, while they waited for some news from Nelson. None came.

On the streets, in the Parliament, in homes and coffeehouses—especially Lloyd's where the odds on insurance were wavering—every man posed as an admiral.

"Impeach Nelson! Break him! Throw him out of the service!" An M.P., his face white, turned on Sir Gilbert Elliot.

"Sir, I still have faith in that man. You forget he was not reinforced till after Buonaparte sailed!" But Sir Gilbert was tired of saying that.

"Who sent that madman off to Egypt?" Another voice.

"No one! St. Vincent's lost all control of him and he'll pay for it! Sending his lowest ranking Rear Admiral after a genius like Buonaparte!"

Sir Gilbert said nothing, yet he, for one, had recommended Nelson to Lord Spencer before Nelson left England and Spencer had laughingly told him he already intended to appoint Nelson, "his favorite young hero," to the command. Even the King had claimed he appointed Nelson—then. But no one in his right mind—not even the King—admitted having approved Nelson now. And the people who had hailed their "Darling!" even after Teneriffe, now turned on him. After all, what had he done? Taken two ships at St. Vincent, just two old Spanish ships, and hadn't he disobeyed orders? They hated their "Darling" now. His waywardness had become a threat to their personal security. And Sir Gilbert had other reasons for anxiety: his son George was on Captain Foley's *Goliath*.

"St. Vincent's ruined and about time," the M.P. went on. "He hates Pitt and he's done this to spite him. Two admirals charge St. Vincent with gross partisanship—dereliction of duty naming a crippled-up boy to hunt Buonaparte."

Sir Gilbert's sharp eyes snapped. "Orde has never done anything but draw his sword against his Commander in Chief! That is mutiny!"

"And about time, sir! Parker is a brave man and he, too, denounced St. Vincent. Parker was senior admiral to Nelson. He had a right to that command."

"No, sir, he did not. St. Vincent has the right to name his squadrons and send them where he pleases."

"And we must leave our lives—the lives of our families—in St. Vincent's hands alone? *We* will be fighting Buonaparte on our beaches and in our fields while fourteen of our finest battleships are vacationing in Egypt! How did Nelson ever get his rank so young? I'll tell you. It's all privilege. Orde says it is a political clique and Nelson's at the bottom of it. All he is after is prize money for himself and St. Vincent!"

"Well, the Admiralty is finished. And Mr. Pitt—oh, St. Vincent's done a good job of betraying his country. But the man who will hang is Nelson for sheer dereliction of duty. Egypt! So Nelson sailed *east* to save us! The answer, gentlemen, is simple: Nelson's afraid to fight Buonaparte. He's lost all his nerve since Teneriffe."

Thus Englishmen woke after five years of war, and like a sleeper starting up to a strange sound in the night cried out: "Invasion! Invasion is Buonaparte's next step!" They called up the farmers and the clerks and they talked of fighting from behind the last hedgerow. They drilled men armed with pitchforks and sticks and stones, marched them about the fields and the beaches, while the pro-French sympathizers in England thought now, at last, George III's crown would topple.

And poet Coleridge wrote his *Fears in Solitude* during the alarm of invasion, his ode to the country he had decided he loved in spite of her faults: "O native Britain! O my Mother Isle!"

> . . . Thankless too for peace
> (Peace long preserved by fleets and perilous seas),
> Secure from actual warfare, we have loved
> To swell the war-whoop, passionate for war!
> Alas! for ages ignorant of all
> Its ghastlier workings (famine or blue plague;
> Battle, or siege, or flight through wintry snows),
>
>   *   *   *
>
>   Boys and girls,
> And women, that would groan to see a child
> Pull off an insect's leg, all read of war,
> The best amusement for our morning-meal!
>
>   *   *   *
>
> Like mere abstractions, empty sounds, to which
> We join no feeling and attach no form!
> As if the soldier died without a wound;

As if the fibres of this godlike-frame
Were gored without a pang; as if the wretch,
Who fell in battle, doing bloody deeds,
Pass'd off to Heaven, translated and not kill'd:
As though he had no wife to pine for him,
No God to judge him! Therefore, evil days
Are coming on us, O my countrymen . . .

     *   *   *

                  Spare us yet awhile
Father and God! O! Spare us yet awhile!

     ❈   ❈   ❈

It was the twentieth of July, three weeks from Alexandria, having skirted the whole eastern Mediterranean, beating north and then west against the stubborn westerly winds, when Nelson's squadron bore down on the great fortified harbor of Syracuse, Sicily. Two whole months since Buonaparte had sailed from Toulon. And no news. Not even from Lord St. Vincent. All Nelson's letters which he had ordered left at Cape Passaro had been carefully sent up to Naples! Though Nelson, heartbroken, knew only too well what England—what Europe —must be thinking. And the thought mortified him.

As the English, counting on the Queen's promise of aid, sailed toward the outer island of the old town of Syracuse, longboats shoved off from the shore.

No admittance! According to the Articles of War only four enemy ships might anchor in the neutral port at one time, as was agreed on at Naples to Captain Troubridge. So the English must accept a delay of at least two weeks. Nelson sat stunned in his cabin. The Queen had not worked her miracle. . . .

Still the English ships closed in. Somehow he must get supplies or give up the chase. He sent Troubridge on shore to remind them that the Queen had given her word, and to present his demands to the Governor. And the Governor presented Troubridge with miles of red tape.

"I *know* the Articles of War, sir!" Troubridge, eyes deadly, stood over the small polite Governor, and through the windows fourteen battleships stubbornly edged in, right under the fortified walls. No shots were fired. "I have reason to believe, sir, that you have private orders to permit this fleet to victual and water at Syracuse."

The Governor's face became oddly blank. "That is impossible, sir. I can only repeat to you, Captain Troubridge, that according to the Articles of War, by His Majesty, King Ferdinand's treaty with France, only four ships may anchor at one time. Those are the *King's* orders, sir."

Troubridge stared the man out of countenance. "The Kingdom of the Two Sicilies demanded the protection of England. This fleet has been sent here, sir, to save you!"

The Governor nodded. "I can only repeat the King's orders: to order my cannon to fire should you force an entry, sir."

"And that is your answer?"

"What else could I possibly do, sir?" The Governor eyed the Captain enigmatically, while Troubridge foamed at the mouth. "The position in which I am placed . . . you understand. It is impossible to permit you to anchor. I have strict orders, sir, to protect Syracuse from any breach of neutrality." Even as he spoke his stone walls did not open fire on the wooden walls closing them. "And under no consideration will we sell you supplies or allow you to water by the King's orders."

And while Troubridge went back to the ships raging, the Governor of Syracuse, still announcing his intentions to resist, ordered the battle-ships, all fourteen of them, shown to anchorages, but scattered them about the harbor to give the breach of neutrality which he was determined to fight, he said, some resemblance of respectability in case some French ship nosed in, saw what was going on. To victual Nelson was an act of war against France.

The next morning the street boys followed the seamen to the fountain of Arethusa, gabbling the old legend: this was holy water, it came by underground springs from Jerusalem, and drinking of it, and filling their ships, the English were sure to be blessed. While the Governor put on a magnificent mask of outraged neutrality.

And food aplenty was sold, though of course it doubled in price, while the Sicilians followed the seamen laughing and weeping for joy, cheering them and wishing them victory, and the Governor repeated the impossibility of complying with any English requests for food or water or anchorage.

The masquerade drove Nelson wild. Hounded to death by King's orders, by having to pretend this and that when every minute he ought to be after the French. Yet his ships were being supplied in record time. Was it his determination or his friends' intrigue? Syracuse was a tough old town over a thousand years old, and the cannon on her walls were not rusty.

The three nights spent at Syracuse were like years. Nelson lay on his cot. Tossed and tossed till he got up and found his watch. Something was wrong with it. It said two o'clock. Only two . . .

"Sentry, pass the word for the Officer of the Watch to Declare the Hour."

The Officer of the Watch saluting: "Two o'clock, sir."

"It can't be! I heard six bells hours ago!"

"Begging pardon, sir, they just struck, sir. Two o'clock."

"Very well."

Nelson set his watch down, he had been on the verge of destroying it. He closed his eyes for another four or five hours.

"Sentry! Pass the word for the Officer of the Watch."

The Officer of the Watch saluting.

Nelson: "You again? Middle watch hasn't changed yet?"

"Two fifteen, sir."

"That's what you said before."

Embarrassed silence, then meekly: "Two fifteen, sir."

"Go verify that, if you please!"

The Officer of the Watch reappearing: "Two *sixteen,* sir, beg pardon, sir."

"Very well . . ."

And the fleet began to suspect that the Admiral did have nerves.

❈   ❈   ❈

In exactly three days the English fleet was ready for sea. Syracuse had supplied them and watered them in record time. Still not one scrap of news. One rumor: the French were supposed to have been seen sailing northeasterly from Malta. Was it false? The last rumor he had heard before going to Egypt had been that the French had sailed west. . . . He felt fairly certain that if Buonaparte had sailed west into the more populated area of the Mediterranean he would have heard of it, and it was obvious Buonaparte had not attacked Sicily. All of which proved one thing positively: rumors were likely to be false.

As the fleet unmoored awaiting the westerly breeze, he wrote Fanny: "It would have been my delight to have tried Buonaparte on a wind, for he commands the Fleet as well as the Army. Glory is my object, and that alone."

And as the wind freshened, he gave his order once more:

"Sail east!" Circle back, somewhere he had missed Buonaparte; once more he left the west unguarded . . . sailed east on his stubborn wits and one rumor.

❊   ❊   ❊

While overland from the gossipy English resort colony at Naples word traveled to London by way of Vienna and the German States, by post chaise: Nelson had gone mad! He was hiding! He would probably shoot himself.

London went crazy. Two months of sailing in a slow convoy would just about carry Buonaparte and his invisible armada to Ireland! No one sang "Sir H.N. and the Glorious 14th of February," it was like cheering the murderer of one's own mother. They chanted, "Hang him!"

Sir Gilbert Elliot, having recently been created Lord Minto, dropped his newspaper into his breakfast. "Egypt—*again?*" Lord Minto rubbed his head, trying to solve the insoluble. If Nelson did not succeed there would probably be no Ambassadorship to Vienna for Elliot, Lord Minto.

While Nelson's old commander at Hotham's "battle," retired and now disgruntled Admiral Goodall, the man of humor who had seen Nelson's fury at work, glowered at questioners who asked:

"What is your favorite hero about? The French fleet has passed under his nose!"

And Goodall lost his sense of humor utterly, roared his answer from habit of the quarter-deck: "I know him well! Something capital will be done! You will not hear from him until he has thundered in the storm and directed the whirlwind!"

His voice was not still and small, but it was lonely.

Lady Nelson was at Roundwood, secretly bored by the Reverend's eternal sermons. And the house was in the wrong district. And she could not bear the neighbors. But she stayed under her own roof, where she could escape the company she had once sought: the navy wives with their now vicious question: "What do you hear from Sir Horatio?" And Fanny sat staring at his portrait, the new one by Abbott. And it slowly dawned on her that he was the only friend she had left in the world. She wrote him the picture was her friend—on second thought, she might even call it affection she felt. Then out of habit she covered up such a bold unladylike admission with dull trivialities.

Off Cádiz, Lord St. Vincent grew more taciturn, more dictatorial daily. He had pinned his past and future reputation—his hope for the Garter and the Admiralty—on Nelson's genius. And he began to curse himself for a fool and Nelson for a charlatan. Troubridge, who could obey orders right or wrong, was the man to trust. But he was not a rear admiral. Troubridge, who was "capable of commanding the fleets of England," but no genius, was the man for St. Vincent, who hoped to retire from active service into the Admiralty still holding *all* the strings of power. Discipline. Nelson, the fool, thought *he* had to be right. . . . But Troubridge's wife had died and been buried in England. The word would not reach Troubridge, still writing to her, till his son's letter made its way always just behind Nelson's crazy fleet sailing east. . . .

While First Lord Spencer wondered how soon his reign at the Admiralty would collapse in disgrace, and Lady Spencer positively made up her mind that her husband's favorite white-haired boy-hero was an idiot!

❊   ❊   ❊

In Naples, two people who had been close to the whole scene of this struggle for the domination of the Mediterranean realized how hard Nelson had fagged and under what obstacles, and for how many years. They had only laid eyes on him once, for three days, but in those three days he had left the memory of his magnetic personality.

Lady Hamilton taught the Queen of the Two Sicilies to cry, "Hip! Hip! Hurrah!" like a drunken jack. No doubt it made the French Minister furious when he heard of it. Lady Hamilton hoped so.

But Sir William Hamilton sat wincing and muttering over a letter from Sir John Acton, the Prime Minister of the Sicilies, who had exploded when he learned that Nelson had been supplied at Syracuse against the King's orders, and that it was unfortunate the brave Admiral Nelson had miscarried, "notwithstanding the most energetic efforts to meet the French before sending an Army God knows in *what* direction, and what is their mischievous project. . . . We are now *open,* exposed for war directly on Admiral Nelson's account. You see fairly our situation. Are we to be left in this position? Will

Admiral Nelson run to the Levant again, without knowing for certain the position of the French and leave the Two Sicilies exposed?"

Sir William laid Acton's letter aside, with the same contempt he would have used to toss a "to be continued" paper-bound romance out the window. And he looked at Emma to rest his nerves. Her full-blown beauty had grown almost too voluptuous, too heady with the years.

She was walking restlessly from window to window, her scarf trailing carelessly, beautifully. Her long chestnut hair tumbled about her shoulders. Sir William suddenly chuckled to himself. God bless her! Of course! She was in all her glory. The heroine of a real drama had adopted a real live Admiral and a whole fleet of battleships! Somewhere in her past she had spent days on end, curled in a corner of some scullery, learning to read; glutting herself on melodramatic romances. So who but Emma would have put her reading to practice; flung herself at the Queen's feet, weeping, imploring aid for her countrymen—and obtained it? Emma Hart Hamilton playing the Goddess Bellona!

His antique statuary had come to life; she was almost as clever a scene stealer as poor dear young Nelson. Sir William picked up his pen, refreshed. There was his wife, his art, his secretary, his wheel horse, his faithful Emma. Looking up now and then as he wrote, he saw her reflected a hundred times in the wide mirrored room he had designed for her. Now and then she paused, rested her soft arms on the edge of the large glass aquariums set in each tall window. The glass reflected the glow of Vesuvius, while the sensitive little sea urchins Emma loved to collect were lost in the shadows.

Sir William finished writing to Admiral Nelson: "God bless you, my dear friend, it is late at night. May all your disappointments be at an end." Dated it August 1st, 1798, and wondered what Nelson had found since sailing from Syracuse, Sicily.

❄   ❄   ❄

Meantime, Nelson had plunged once again east, into the white hot sun, skirting the dusty pale shores of enslaved Greece—the Morea; and the Republic of Seven Isles; Candia. . . . Hunting everywhere, Nelson found nothing. The days seemed unending. Time had struck a rock, sunk barnacled and hoary. Yet there was not a sick man in his

fleet of eight thousand. He had bought the best food Sicily could pro-
duce. Miller on *Theseus* declared every day a meat day; fattened his
fighting men. Some of the other captains were pessimistic and did not
waste so much good food. But never had the days seemed so endless.
Had it been only four days since they left Syracuse? They flew and
seemed to stand still. But as ever, during these days, Nelson had his
captains aboard *Vanguard* to confer.

"Whatever their position, by day or night, fair wind or foul, we
will attack . . ." Yet while he talked bravely to his captains, he suffered the torments of the damned. He felt he had been *right* to sail
to Egypt, but no one would believe it. He wrote bitterly to St. Vincent:

The only question to be stated is, You should not have gone such a
long voyage without more certain information of the Enemy's destination.
My answer is ready, Who was I to get it from? . . . Naples or Sicily,
either knew not, or chose to keep me in ignorance. Was I to wait patiently
until I heard certain accounts? If Egypt were their object, before I could
hear of them they would have been in India. To do nothing was I felt
disgraceful; therefore I made use of my understanding, and by it I ought
to stand or fall. I am before your Lordship's judgement, which in the
present case I feel is the Tribunal of my Country; and if, under all circumstances, it is decided that I am wrong, I ought for the sake of our
Country to be superseded; for at this moment, when I know the French
are not in Alexandria, I hold the same opinion as before, viz.: that under
all circumstances I was right in steering for Alexandria, and by that opinion
I must stand or fall.

However erroneous my judgement may be, I feel conscious of my honest intentions, which I hope will bear me up under the greatest mis-
fortune that could happen to me as an Officer—that of your Lordship
thinking me wrong. . . .

He sent it to Ball for criticism, for he had developed an immense respect for Ball's cooler temper.

Ball read it and stared in amazement. What else could Lord St. Vincent think of Nelson after all these long weeks? And Ball marveled
at something else: Nelson had the faith of a mustard seed!

Ball wrote back: "I would never advise a friend to begin a defense
of his conduct until he is accused of error. . . . Your candour of mind
implicates you have doubts. . . ."

Nelson studied Ball's answer in pained amazement. Doubts? He had
no doubt that he had been right, he merely intended that St. Vincent

should understand. Not to be understood was agony . . . it was the same old problem. He had always been troubled with too keen a sense of honor.

In desperation he had scattered his fleet, made his battleships into cruisers.

Troubridge in *Culloden* had sailed off into the Gulf of Coron for news and Ball in *Alexander* bore off, both ships so far distant that time or a perverse wind might not permit them to rejoin in time for a battle.

By the morning of the twenty-eighth of July the Mediterranean lay like molten glass under a blue-black sky. The fleet was passing Morea. A flurry of signals from *Alexander,* and in another part of the sea the tops spied *Culloden* lumbering back with a prize in tow.

A ghost of an Admiral was on deck, an emaciated shadow of the laughingly confident man who had left England in April. The sun seemed to mock the knight's star on his coat, and yet his glance, as he watched the ships sailing back with their signal flags flying, was like the sparking of steel.

Culloden came first signaling she had taken a wine ship with news, and *Alexander* was signaling she had spoken a ship, same news:

Signal Lieutenant Capel's face flushed as he translated the flags bursting in succession: Enemy fleet actually sighted four weeks ago steering *southeast* from the Island of Candia!

The Admiral wheeled on Berry. "Bear up! Make signal: Steer for *Alexandria, Egypt!*" And again his heart ached, till tears stood in his eyes. But this time his heart ached with unspeakable joy.

❊   ❊   ❊

As *Vanguard* cut a scimitar swath in the sea, prow around toward Egypt, he stood still, staring across the water, catching his breath, his heart hammering. When, how, where had he missed them? Through Egypt to India! All the treasures of the East! A new Alexander was marching!

And he had been *right!* Dead right—and missed them! But now . . . slowly his face took on color again.

"We've found them, Berry! Thank God, we've found them!" And he started to laugh and the whole ship was rocking with the wild war whoops of jubilant laughter. To drill and to drill and eat heartily week after week.

And the jacks winked at each other. "Nel'll give Boney a piece of his mind . . ."

And that afternoon a white bird flew in the Admiral's stern windows, careened through the cabins into the dining room, perched on the back of his chair. Berry started.

"Good omen, Sir Horatio!" he whispered.

The Admiral motioned slowly for a crumb. The bird eyed it and eventually ate it. For a moment all protocol was forgotten, as the officers whistled and twittered and chirped to the little white bird cocking its head at them, but keeping his perch by the Admiral.

And the captains and officers who thought Nelson had no nerves —no sailor superstitions—noticed a satisfied gleam in his eye: A white bird—a promise of victory. . . .

On Tuesday evening, the thirty-first of July, 1798, Nelson signaled the fleet to keep in company. They could almost smell the Nile Valley in the season of flood, as in the dark, under a dagger of moon, the fourteen battleships clustered about their Admiral, ready to fight; sailing steadily down on Egypt during that night.

❊   ❊   ❊

It was dawn of the first of August and Nelson was on deck to greet it. "Signal *Alexander* and *Swiftsure* to look out." And the two ships swept off searching.

There was a wild fierce joy through the fleet, the first laughter hushed: hunters creeping up on a prize quarry. Still a few captains doubted they would find anything. Buonaparte had had too much time to march, send his fleet back to France. But the men on *Vanguard* grinned and nodded toward the Admiral with his blazing star, his pinned-up sleeve—and, yes, a most damnable toothache that had come on in the night. But the only recognition he gave the miscreant tooth was an occasional gentle fingering of his jaw. For he watched his company like some small proud hawk, as they put the battered *Vanguard* with her makeshift, stunted rig to test the wind.

Behind the main body of ships was *Culloden* doggedly clinging to her prize: a fine French wine ship for a parched English fleet. As the morning advanced, Nelson's ships gushed across the sea searching. Saumarez sat in his cabin; he believed as firmly as Nelson that on the first trip they had been justified, but he did not believe they would have a second chance. And again he thanked God it was not his command.

The hours crawled by and the Admiral paced off the time in the space of his quarter-deck and sometimes from gun to gun in his main cabin. After five years of war, and of staggering disappointments, he was closing on the crucial hour: his name would be immortal—or—

10 A.M. "*Alexander* making signal of land, Sir Horatio."

Ball in *Alexander* was sailing southeast seven or eight leagues away, the fleet following.

And scan Alexandria once more, through the circling glass: Once again the blinding white tower and at last, "Deck there, I see a Tricolor over the town, Sir Horatio! But no enemy ships!"

No ships. Had Buonaparte sent his fleet back to France? Saumarez thought so. Buonaparte was a genius.

Even so, the English were preparing for action, for now Nelson believed that at any moment they would find the French ships . . . unless . . . he swallowed the thought. They had to be here!

To the rumbling of loose fittings to be stowed for action, the ships continued to search as the sun passed the noon zenith. The surgeon, Mr. Jefferson, was preparing the cockpit, clearing the senior midshipmen's mess table for surgery, fighting to keep jacks from stowing loose gear in the one place for tending the wounded. And it had been the surgeon's first unprecedented order on joining ship: all surgical instruments must be kept in hot water in a hanging stove in the galley preparatory to use. The Admiral had learned about a stone-cold knife without opiates.

Yet, even now, the restless shimmering seas were empty of enemy ships. These were the longest hours that Nelson had ever lived.

There was a fine breeze of north wind, smooth water, fair weather. Troubridge's *Culloden* still brought up the rear, seven miles astern with her prize in tow like a drag anchor. And *Alexander* and *Swiftsure* were still quite far ahead, while the English peered into the tantalizing mouths of the Nile delta with its infinite inlets. Somewhere in there the French might have anchored.

The *Goliath* and *Zealous* were also in advance of the *Vanguard*, while the other eight, with their white canvas flashing high overhead, clustered in a casual, but deadly, posse about the Admiral; sailing about five miles an hour, comfortably, in positions "as convenient." From noon till midafternoon: only desert and sea.

Then Signal Lieutenant Capel yelling: "The *Zealous* gone crazy with signals, Sir Horatio!"

And as Sam Hood's signals shot up—unfurled: "French battle fleet sighted! Sixteen of sail!"

X I. And the Kill

August 1, 1798

As CAPEL'S VOICE paused, the Admiral gave his orders, and *Vanguard* was signaling: Prepare for battle!

Captain Berry caught the Admiral's eye as the signal flew. He had never seen so much happiness written on one mortal face, as Nelson gave orders to feed his men: fill John Bull's belly before battle.

Five years of war were focused on this moment: his lifelong ambition to command an English fleet in a battle was suddenly here, now. This minute.

Sam Hood continued to signal: French off larboard bow, lying in a bay at anchor close to land in line of battle.

"Haul our wind, Captain Berry!" The Admiral's voice crisped like sparks from a cat.

And almost the instant *Vanguard's* jacks tumbled up to furl the royals, catch the fine topgallant breeze from northwest, the whole squadron of sail rippled, following suit without any signal. Nelson nodded as his battleships came about, flung their dark shadows east, for he saw he had but one heart in his fleet: one instrument for his will. And for an instant he was conscious of a frightening tension around his heart, of exalted expectancy: here was his stage for glory. This, his first battle to command, must be perfect.

The ships sailed closer and closer to the bay with the northwest wind in their favor.

"The Bay of Shoals, Sir Horatio, Aboukir . . ." Berry was gripping a crude chart with no soundings as if it were Buonaparte's throat.

The Admiral was on the starboard companion, leveling his glass. "And there they are!"

The French battle fleet lay in a single close line, with bare poles, anchored. They were seemingly landlocked, surrounded by sandspits, out of reach! The Admiral's glass swept the bay, seeking some channel. The bay was roughly some ten miles deep and fifteen or twenty miles wide. There had to be a channel! The French had sailed in. Then the English would say a prayer and trust to their own navigation. The Admiral glanced back at Wales Clod, his master. Clod was squinting confidently at the French line, grinning into the sun, shading his eyes, chewing slowly on his quid.

"I piloted the entrance to the St. Lawrence, Mr. Clod, after the damned cowardly pilot failed me in a fog. . . . What do you say to this?"

Clod stiffened, but he was still grinning. "The channel's easy, if *they* durst it, sir!" He jerked his thumb at the French.

The Admiral nodded, satisfied.

No frigates—no Portuguese—now, no soundings of the channel!

The Admiral fixed his glass on the French again, as his ships closed on them. What next? His main plan was always to use a majority of his ships to engage a portion of the enemy, and in such a way that the enemy would be paralyzed, its ability to maneuver crippled from the start; forced to fight where his ships had already pared down the enemy numbers. That meant attacking enemy ships from both sides. He intended to conquer all, but not by laying his line parallel, ship to ship, in vain duels. First he must secure the victory, then conquer individuals at his convenience.

It seemed to Captain Berry that the Admiral had merely glanced at the enemy fleet when his good eye began to gleam confidently.

Nelson, sharply: "Make signal to fleet to attack van and center."

What he had grasped in a moment was this: The French were lying with their heads to the wind, to starboard off *Vanguard's* bow, on the west side of the bay. If Nelson's ships concentrated on the foremost enemy ships, on the French van and center nearest the entrance of the bay, the whole French line would be trapped where it lay in battle order. If the rear French ships broke the line—which was highly unlikely, for their line close to shore was a powerful defense—but, if they did, they could do only one of two things: the rear French could either flee to eastward down the bay, leaving half their fleet to certain destruction, or the rear might beat slowly up the bay, dead against the wind—so slowly, if at all, that the English would have had time to paralyze the van and center, and be ready for whatever the French rear tried. Thus Nelson hoped to grasp the offensive and hold it to the end.

The bay where the battle would be fought was shaped as if someone had punched an irregular oval on the land, leaving strands of reef and sand to mark the division between bay and sea. Thirteen handsome enemy battleships lay like black hippopotami basking in the apparently untouchable shallows, looming tremendous in the glare of water and sand. Towering up, dwarfing all others, was the great *L'Orient* 120, the center of the French line, matriarch of them all, with four frigates clustered near her. There were three eighties and nine seventy-fours besides the gunboats, and the bomb vessel that could snuggle under a battleship's tender, defenseless stern and create awful havoc. Twenty-two French sail in all. The French had also a land fortification on an island at the mouth of the bay, among the shoals: a mortar battery and a big gun, lying three quarters of a mile in front of the French van ships, pointing across the harbor mouth.

The French ships lay bow to stern, the thirteen battleships stretching into a three-mile line which was curved outward, following an irregular bulge of land within the bay. The French line was lying about north and south, curved toward the east like a great dam, or a drawn bow.

In the center, where the arrow would have crossed the imaginary bow, lay *L'Orient,* her fatal broadside ready to cover the entrance of the bay. The French position was excellent—for them—in perfect accordance with recognized naval tactics. They even seemed to have anticipated any naval heretics, such as Nelson, for by curving their line, their van ships lay from north to southeastward, diagonally to the entrance, so the entire van presented its broadsides to the harbor mouth.

The shore gun, the van, and *L'Orient* were all trained on that one vulnerable spot: the entrance. A black wall defending the pale shores of Egypt; intended to discourage any enemy fleet from even peering into the bay, much less trying to force an entry. Or, if an enemy fleet were so foolhardy as to try to get in, the French were anchored close against the shore, to prevent any enemy sailing inshore of them. The French intended to force any enemy to fight broadside to broadside against the French outer wall of starboard broadsides. The French would not even have to touch their larboard broadside guns now pointed shoreward.

Nelson's eyebrows rose and drew together. He had made two fleet signals, so far, almost before his officers could think twice, the "Prepare for battle" and the "Attack van and center."

In following those signals the English would attack France's biggest defense, their curved broadside wall, first. It looked like madness and suicide, yet in daring to do so, the English might wrest the offensive at the very moment the French would expect to annihilate them. . . . It was a risk. . . . However, in outnumbering the French van, and by grace of the wind blowing the English straight into the bay (unless the French fire was too strong, or the wind fell stark calm, or flew clear around the compass) the rear French ships would be powerless for some time. And on one point, both Nelson and General Buonaparte were in perfect agreement: no war could be fought without risks.

So in order to attack the French at all, the English ships entering the bay (provided they did not run aground) would have to turn their almost defenseless prows to the broadsides of the French van, the shore batteries and the long gun. The English must prepare to accept murderous, perhaps paralyzing fire, before they could answer with more than their small bow guns. The French van was in position to cross the T on any ship entering. The French Admiral had obviously, by his fleet's position, and the fact that the French gave no signs of trying to put to sea, counted on the English hesitating to run the gauntlet of obstacles he had prepared for them: try to navigate an unknown channel under full fire.

Nelson's mind had been made up on that point since the night Buonaparte slipped from Toulon: Nelson would fight 'em, hell or high water.

Still, as the English sailed closer and the French line grew immense, all the obvious advantages apparently lay with the French. But there must be an Achilles' heel, though the French had tried to foresee every possibility, the best laid plans . . . Nelson's eye never left them as he scanned that black wall again and again for some loophole. . . . The French had made their line so close to the shore. . . . Nelson measured the thin line of blue between the French and the shore with his eye.

"Captain Berry," he suddenly grinned, "where there's room for an enemy ship to swing there's room for an Englishman to anchor!"

Berry's face lighted. There was the Achilles' heel! Provided Nelson's captains dared to attempt the awful, hair-splitting navigation: the danger of running aground in that fingernail paring of water between the French fleet and Egypt. The tragedy of going aground, having to surrender without striking a blow. The risks multiplied to infinity, but Nelson was calmly calculating the tremendous advantage.

The French obviously did not dream he would dare to sail inshore of their line; probably did not conceive it to be possible, for the French always needed wider berths for their ships, never challenged reefs or sledded over shallows. And as Nelson calculated, his eye grew to pinpoint focus. The surprise he would give the French! And he clapped his hand to his thigh, nodding gleefully to Berry.

Let no one who hesitated in shallows attempt it. But was the water really deep enough between the enemy and the shore? Well, it had to be. It meant shaving the shore, trusting to God there would be no sudden variation in the depths, and relying on the congenital caution of French seamen toward shallow water. But if some of Nelson's captains could sail inshore of the French, he would sandwich their van between two fires: bring each French van ship between two of the English: force the French to fight both sides at once and fore and aft, a pellmell battle, in the tradition of Nelson's favorite bloody old Dutch masters. His captains knew what he wanted. It was a matter of cold calculating nerve at this point.

The Admiral turned away from the enemy, sizing up his own fleet which, having come about to pounce down on the French, had left Ben Hallowell's *Swiftsure* and Ball's *Alexander,* the two ships that had been leading, now almost nine miles in the rear, while Troubridge in *Culloden* was still seven miles away, casting off her prize ship, racing to join the fleet. No time must be lost waiting for them. He must attack with whatever he had . . .

The Admiral now gave his third signal, his final word; from now on his captains must concentrate on their work: "Form line of battle as convenient." Every man knew from those three laconic signals what moves were to follow.

The English ships came cautiously onto the shores of Egypt, checking their eagerness, their wakes idling. Foley in *Goliath* and Sam Hood in *Zealous* were jockeying to lead the van, while making the final decisions whether or not they could sail inshore of the French line. Foley in *Goliath* was slightly ahead and would not give way to all Hood's pleadings, or Hood's *Zealous* nearly nosing *Goliath*. Foley was sounding carefully, taking no chances of going aground in an unknown enemy bay; weathering the outer shoals with the dexterity of passion tempered by reason: at the end of the hunt, the kill.

The main body of English were now very close on the entrance of the bay. Dead ahead the treacherous water looked like a veneer of thin glass stretched over sand. But there was a darker line. Was it the channel that led to the French or was it one of the blinds in the labyrinth?

The Admiral in *Vanguard,* hailing Captain Hood, who was waving his cocked hat, exultant at finding the French: "Captain Hood, are we far enough to eastward to bear up clear of these shoals?" For there was the sand spit jutting out at the very entrance of the bay, a mean hazard to be weathered before heading west again toward the French line.

Hood: "Eleven fathoms, Sir Horatio. I have no chart but with your permission, I will sound with the lead and I'll carry you as close as I can with safety, sir."

Nelson doffed his cocked hat, beaming at Hood's antics. "I'll be much obliged to you, Captain Hood."

With a last triumphant toss of his signaling hat, Hood turned to lead Nelson, and lost his cocked hat to the chastening wind; watched it sail away in the water.

Now *Vanguard,* the flagship, hove to, and Nelson stood anxiously watching the first of his brood sail past him. Once his van ships were in, depending on what they had been able to do, he would direct *Vanguard* to reinforce them and lead the rest.

The sun grew yellow turning the sands gold as it dropped lower and lower, while the jacks who must soon man the guns ran aloft in the rigging tending the sails, to the monotonous chant of the lead being cast. *Vanguard* waited, sails luffing, like a bird resting for an instant. The water was idly slapping her sides. There was a strange stillness in spite of the human cries; that natural quiet of late afternoon on the seas, just after the brisk last ruffling flurry of wind, the sunset, and the seas calming while the wind blew fair, but high.

As the van ships moved in *Vanguard* waited . . . Captain Miller in *Theseus,* with young Hoste on the quarter-deck, rushing up. Her canvas suddenly towering beside *Vanguard,* hailing the Admiral: "Oh, *Vanguard,* ahoy! May *I* lead the van in *Culloden's* absence?"

Nelson, engrossed in the over-all battle, gave a quick shake of his head, left Berry to answer: "Second in front of the Admiral, if you please, Captain Miller!"

Foley and Hood were already leading splendidly, though they had stolen Miller's rightful position in Troubridge's absence. *Theseus's* sails collapsed, hauling up beside *Vanguard,* so as not to crowd the two self-appointed leaders now feeling into the channel. *Theseus's* sails sighed and sagged as *Agamemnon's* had sighed in her day, but this was not Hotham's battle, Miller told himself, as he paced up and down trying to calm himself, subordinate his ambitions, this battle was all little Nel's. . . . By the look of the French there would be laurels aplenty for every captain.

The French ships looked alive now, waking from their siesta. They were running out cables, springing in the water like boxers limbering up. By running out two cables, one from the bow and one from the stern, to an anchor, the ships, by hauling on one or the other cable, could maneuver against the wind, bring broadsides to bear more easily.

The French had not hoisted their colors. Without flags there was no distinguishing the two fleets, except in the beautiful build of the French and the yellow stripes marking the gun tiers on Nelson's ships. And the English port lids, black outside, blood red inside, checkering the yellow. The French were all black—and glossy—*L'Orient* was taking in scaffoldings that had been slung out for the afternoon painting.

Silence.

Foley's *Goliath* was drawing within gunshot of the French. Every eye in the English fleet was brimming with admiration as this the first, the test ship, challenged the broadsides of the French van.

A flash of blue, white and red at French masts. The Tricolor waved its welcome! Nelson nodded to Berry and up shot the Union Jack and St. Vincent's St. George's banner and Nelson's blue flag. "Nail a half dozen of mine to the masts!" Nelson shouted.

Still no shots were exchanged. Then a blast from the long gun in the shore battery. The first puffs of smoke.

Suddenly the black wall spoke: Foley's *Goliath* had "received the honor of the first salute" from the French.

Nelson drew a satisfied breath. He had done all he could in advance to make his instrument play by itself, make himself expendable if need be. That was his only secret. In fair wind or foul, daylight or dark . . .

The wind was fair, but the sun was low in the west. The battle would be fought in the dark.

❊   ❊   ❊

Meantime the French, having launched the romance-novel-loving Buonaparte against the great pyramids on the first lap of his journey to Suez, had worried and then laughed off this very moment, having reasons to believe it would never come. The French had sailed from Malta not six days ahead of Nelson, but only three, and they did not travel as fast as the English. Of a still dark night they had suddenly heard strange signal guns coming nearer. Silent as only the hunted can be they had frozen, then veered north and more northerly while their cruiser frigates reported the English fleet was one hundred miles off paralleling their course for Egypt! The night had seemed endless, Buonaparte's project had been discovered. But while the English kept on their straight southerly course, Buonaparte ordered his fleet to circle north, the identical move Nelson had suspected when he found Alexandria empty. When morning had come the French had put leagues between themselves and the hunters.

Their frigates had not seen one topsail of English again until the terrible day just one month ago when Buonaparte's far-flung frigates had swooped down on a stunned, aghast Alexandria, Egypt, and learned that the English battle fleet had been there, seeking the French, only forty-eight hours before! And that it had sailed off in a north-easterly direction. The French frigates had returned to their armada signaling once more that they were discovered. There had been the terror of expected doom in the French fleet, for forty thousand soldiers might go to the bottom with the flimsy transports. Buonaparte had paced *L'Orient's* beautifully decorated quarter-deck, made up his mind in an instant. He must attack now.

Fortune had always given the English the seas, but the land was for France! Fortune and his bright Star had saved him by forty-eight hours. And to the horror of navy men who expected the English any moment to return, he demanded they set him ashore with his army, announcing to Egypt:

"Buonaparte, the General of the French Republic according to the principles of Liberty, is now arrived; and the Almighty, the Lord of Both Worlds, has sealed the destruction of the Beys. . . . Tell the people that we are the friends of the true Mussulmen. Is it not us who destroyed the Pope . . . woe, woe, woe to those who shall take up arms in favor of the Mamelukes, and combat us. There shall be no hope for them, they shall all perish!"

And no English fleet returned. Then three weeks after Buonaparte had landed, the French fleet had sighted a flurry of English frigates—all alone—hauling up, apparently to reconnoiter them. From their strange actions and the news from a neutral vessel that put into Alexandria that the big English fleet had been spied far north after leaving Alexandria, circling the eastern Mediterranean and last seen heading westward, the French had breathed a sigh of relief. The more spirited of them breathed disgust. Apparently the English fleet's frigates were only keeping an eye on the French. "Which," wrote Admiral Ganteaume to Bruix, at home, "unhappily confirmed us in the opinion, that it had no orders to attack us. . . ."

The English frigates had not come very close to the French, but had borne off, all sails set, sweeping the seas, sailing away in the general direction the first English fleet had taken weeks before.

(No one, English or French, had sighted the Portuguese.)

The French transports had been anchored at Alexandretta, in tight shallows, out of reach of anything bigger than a gunboat, but at Aboukir was the French battle fleet:

L'Orient 120, a First Rate
Le Franklin 80, a Second Rate
Le Tonnant 80, a Second Rate
Le Guillaume Tell 80, a Second Rate
Le Généreux 74, Third Rate
Le Guerrier 74
Le Conquérant 74
Le Peuple Souverain 74
Le Spartiate 74
Le Timoléon 74
L'Heureux 74
Le Mercure 74
L'Aquilon 74
La Justice, frigate, 40
La Diane, frigate, 40
L'Artémise, frigate, 36
Le Sérieuse, frigate, 36
La Fortune, 18

Alerte, brig, 18

Railleur, 14

L'Hercule, bomb vessel, 8

Salamine, 8

Now the French battle fleet was here to defend the land forces, for Buonaparte had no intentions of being cut off from France, though some of his naval officers had thought he was risking too much to leave a big fleet anchored that would have been safer at sea, keeping the sea lanes open.

Early in this afternoon of August 1st, when for a month French armies had been pushing into territory without the world guessing it, the second division of the French fleet had sent a party on shore to dig wells. And every ship in the fleet had sent twenty-five men to protect the workmen from the attacks of the ungrateful Bedouins who persisted in creeping up over the dunes, sniping at the French liberators.

At two o'clock the French lookouts had signaled: Twelve strange sail west northwest!

And the French fleet had signaled: All boats, workmen and guards repair on board ship. The signal flew for some time. But the once splendid French navy, that only a few decades ago had threatened to wipe a lax English navy off the seas, had been the last to fall to the revolutionary doctrines, and was now the last to give them up to the strict discipline of the new order.

A few citizen sailors, tired of digging and possibly intimidated by vague recollections of the old school, climbed after a while into the boats. The rest shrugged, looked about for a bit of shade in the hollows of dunes.

By three o'clock the English ships grew like a nightmare before the eyes of desperate officers trying to clear their dirty unkempt ships for action. Someone forgot to stow the great barrels of black paint aboard *L'Orient,* left them standing in the open. But if anyone thought of it, there was no time left: Two more English ships were seen as the English all came about in a flashing white mass, as if drawn by one cable, instantly bore down on the bay.

Commander in Chief Brueys to his captain: "But the shoals! Unless they have pilots they will run aground. No, they cannot attack. They have deliberately run away from us for weeks. If they come, they will blockade us. We will give them the slip of a stormy night as we did from Toulon."

Commodore Casabianca and his small son were standing on the sunburnt deck of *L'Orient.* There was a galaxy of admirals in the French fleet.

"Another English ship!"

"Only a brig, citizen!"

Brueys: "We must draw them onto the shoals lying off the island. Signal our brig to decoy them."

But though the Lorelei of a French brig wheeled and flirted, the English fleet did not notice it, did not waver.

"They have pilots on board!" Brueys cried. "They have bribed the Bedouins! No ship could sail these channels without pilots!"

But there came the English, steadily, slowly, by the main channel, hauling well around all the dangers.

"Signal our brig to attack the English brig, draw them to rescue it."

The French brig attacked the *Mutine,* Captain Hardy. The English fleet appeared not to see it. A few slow puffs of smoke—from Hardy —a Tricolor down.

Admiral Brueys gave his order again: "Recall seamen on shore." His ships must get under sail, escape. But his seamen refused.

Ordinarily a ship such as *L'Orient* which had over a thousand seamen to man her could sail without twenty-five or thirty and not miss them. But Brueys hesitated. He knew his men were inefficient; whatever went on in his mind as he stared at the loose lumber piled on the decks around the larboard inshore guns which he did not expect to use, he hesitated, and then decided to trust to his great three-mile wall; to fight the English at anchor.

"Signal ships to send a hawser to the stern cables of the ship ahead, to make a chain." The French would stand, for they had taken the strongest position they could devise, and the English had not numbers enough to fight them broadside to broadside.

But no chain was made. The signal was not obeyed—in time.

There were heartbroken Frenchmen to witness this day: this squadron of oncoming English behaved as no Englishmen had before them. There were Frenchmen who could see in it the beginning of the end of the French navy. The navy with which Buonaparte already planned someday to invade England in order to conquer all Europe.

Admiral Villeneuve, a quiet, intelligent, well-bred man, was there, face shocked to see his liberated countrymen mutinous while the enemy English sailed down as if into home port. There was an almost hypnotic terror in it; the feeling of being paralyzed, devoured at leisure.

As the English came within range and both fleets hoisted their colors one of the English ships flaunted a half-dozen flags, nailed to its masts. Was it the English flagship? It made a fine arrogant target, but just out of reach, as it hovered, allowing the English van ships to pass by it. Everything the English did before the French eyes seemed mysteriously prearranged, and the French felt as naked as Adam when God called out his name.

Now a hysterical signal flew from *L'Orient:* Fire on the English bows. Prevent their getting into the bay. Fire in the name of the Revolution and all the forgotten saints! But no ship fired, for by this time the French had argued and logically decided to try to accomplish the chain of cables. Signal repeated: *Fire!*

And at last the battery on shore opened on the English. As the shells began to fall, the chain of cables to prevent English ships passing through the French line was left uncompleted in the sudden scramble to man the guns. Brueys had finally impressed on his fleet the need to grasp and hold their tremendous advantage: they must smash the enemy's defenseless bows and bring down the English masts with their broadsides before the English could bring their broadsides to bear on the French.

The French saluted: they were masters of artillery and they laid down their broadsides in earnest, elevating their guns, pointing straight on the harbor mouth, as the first of the English turned her bows toward the wall of the long French line.

❈　　　　　❈　　　　　❈

The sun was very low, sending blinding golden darts across the blackening dunes, into the eyes of the horror-struck French glancing back once more at the traitors on shore, then to the tall English ships with the last rays of sun pouring over the cups of their sails.

Like the first drop of blood, the sun touched the horizon. And on the undulating crests of the dunes, creeping closer, the silhouettes of Bedouins and Mamelukes with the black lines of their muskets. They stood like old prophets, robes billowing about, waving their arms, cheering the English fleet; cursing the French "liberators."

While frivolous heat waves blended the sea and the sand. And the

Arabs grew tense. They folded their arms, watching the great show begin.

The last rays of sun lit the St. George's banner with its bright red cross, and flashed back from the furling sails of the English pouring down on the three miles of French ships. The sun lit the English jacks racing down the rigging to man guns. The Arabs rubbed their hands, tugged at their beards, and leaped, crying out, as the first English ship, having run the channel, now bore down on the head ship of the French line, blazed with the last light, and shot across the baffled French bows, blotted the Tricolor from sight as it hauled up *inshore* of the French line! *Goliath* and *Zealous* came scudding like crabs in the shallows, behind France's wall! The prophets gnawed their beards.

The English would run aground! The *Goliath* and *Zealous* had sailed under the high arc of the elevated French fire which was still frantically pouring shots onto the distantly oncoming English masts. *Goliath* had swung clear inside the French line before her anchor began to rumble down. The anchor dragged. And *Goliath* passed the first French of line, brought up at last between stern and bow of two French ships, inshore of the second French line. Hood's *Zealous* followed. *Goliath* had proved the depth. Hood took the inside station on the first French ship which *Goliath* had passed. And as each English ship ran the gauntlet of French fire, and at last brought its broadside to bear, blasting both French bows and sterns, anchoring where the French chain of cables should have been, the stunned French could not bring their full larboard broadsides to bear on them.

Next came square-jawed *Orion,* Sir James Saumarez. Her copper bottom faintly scraping, she rolled in and around past *Zealous,* pushing farther along the line inshore, while even the English held their breath. A French frigate was barring *Orion's* path. *Orion's* high bow crashed the French frigate, knocked it, masts cracking, stove in, clear into the wash of the shallows where it rolled about like a pebble. And *Orion* sailed on, pulled abreast the fifth French ship: *Le Peuple Souverain,* whose citizen sailors were watching noncombatant, paralyzed arms on their shovels. And right on *Orion's* stern came *Audacious,* Captain Gould, skimming the shore like a sea gull, anchoring between two French, hitting both: stern and bow.

Followed by Miller in his trim *Theseus,* where Hoste sprinted along the main deck directing the gun captains. *Theseus* came hauling close under the still elevated French fire, and Miller gave *Le Guerrier* a

Miller special: cannon treble shotted, three balls at one blast, three blasts to their one, and moved on to the third ship, *Le Spartiate,* just as Nelson's *Vanguard* came into play.

Vanguard was nosing toward the French line through the smoke and the enemy fire concentrated on her vulnerable bow. Nelson's van ships had already sailed in perfectly: all safely inside the French line. Now was his time.

At this moment, Admiral Brueys on *L'Orient* looked about. Was there a chance—a maneuver left to him? In twelve minutes the English ships that had brought their broadsides to bear had knocked down the French van ships' masts, crippled their flight. But was the English line going to form all on the inside of the French line? If so, could the French cut their cables, drift off somehow, escape down the bay and put to sea—even join their rear ships right here?

But the *Vanguard,* her bow bleeding, the men at her bow guns just replacing a wiped-out crew, was bearing down now, *outside* the French line, clewing up her sails, hurling down her anchor: setting the seal on the master plan; outnumbering the French van ships, forcing them to stand and to fight both sides at once, while the rear of the French line could only watch helplessly, trapped though two and three miles away.

Passing outside the French line just as Miller had done on the inside, and at almost the same time, *Vanguard* attacked the French *Spartiate.* Nelson had put a pincer on the head of the French line, cut them off from their rear. Nelson had made the seemingly invulnerable French wall a trap for its own destruction.

Miller had fired one broadside into *Spartiate* when he saw English flags beyond *Spartiate's* masts: "Hold! Direct fire forward of mainmast on *L'Aquilon* and abaft on *Conquérant!*" Miller clenched his fists. "The Admiral *stole* my bird!" He could almost hear Nelson's voice, saying, "No, Miller, *I* must have the honor . . ." the day at St. Vincent when they both lunged for the same hole.

And *Theseus's* broadside cannon were pried around, the forward guns aimed at *L'Aquilon's* soft gilt stern, and the aft guns at *Le Conquérant's* weaponless, grinning gaudy figurehead.

But *Vanguard,* in setting the seal, had assumed the most hazardous station momentarily, for the whole starboard, seaward side of the curved French van now concentrated its fire on her. She shuddered, splintered, and wallowed in smoke. Nelson began to frown, turning to

Berry: "This is too hot! We may have to cut our cables, Berry, veer off . . ." He paced off in a cloud of smoke, came about. "But not yet." And as *Vanguard* rolled, English shots struck her also, for in trapping the French, fighting within pistol shot by night, errors were inevitable.

At last, behind *Vanguard* came Captain Louis in *Minotaur,* hauling up when he saw *Vanguard's* stubborn martyrdom, holding the outer wall of French all alone. *Minotaur* stood in to draw part of the enemy fire from *Vanguard.*

"God bless Louis!" Nelson's face relaxed, for with the dark slowing up the remaining English ships still hazarding the channel, *Vanguard* had taken the French fire too long.

Behind *Minotaur* had come *Defense,* Captain Peyton, then the *Bellerophon,* Captain Darby, and the *Majestic,* Captain Westcott, all swinging out behind *Vanguard's* shield, passing on down the line: the first part of the battle had been accomplished in a matter of minutes, the French had to stay and to fight at Nelson's dictation.

As *Bellerophon's* tough Irish Captain picked his bird, tried to bring his full broadside to bear on the bow of *L'Orient,* cross the T on the haughty French flagship, *Bellerophon's* anchor dragged . . . and in horror Darby saw himself drifting helplessly abreast the giant of the French navy. Broadside to broadside. *Bellerophon* was no match in this position to the towering pride of France. *L'Orient* cannon, like a thousand eyes, began to feel for *Bellerophon's* side: flashing madness the eyes came into focus and pulverized Darby's ship, shattering every mast. Darby fell wounded and his 1st, 3rd and 4th lieutenants fell dead. *L'Orient* threatened to wipe *Bellerophon* from the bay. Broadside after broadside from *L'Orient's* three starboard gun tiers, and other French ships taking shots at the mangled *Bellerophon,* till at last *Bellerophon* reeled off, dazed, still firing as she drifted crazily down the line, her flag nailed to the stump of her mast. A fighting hulk with a score to settle with Buonaparte.

Night had come. The sun had been swallowed in smoke as it sank: premature twilight; sudden night. A red and black battle flashed with orange light. The drum beats had crescendoed to steady cannon fire. And around and around on the sand rim of slaughter were the bearded shouting Arabs. And far inland men began to stare at the new glow in the sky. And in Alexandria, French soldiers climbed up on rooftops wondering . . . unable to see what was happening or where.

Thunder and smoke still blanketed the French van, while the French rear, ordered to hold the line, heard the enemy guns drawing closer.

And as the battle waxed, Nelson was praying for his own rear ships: be neither fools nor angels but for God's sake fly! The battle was still in the balance.

The rear English ships barely crept as they came in, feeling their way toward the channel, challenged by shallows and darkness, while the battle glowed dead ahead in a pit of blackness: a false beacon, for the shoals lay between Nelson's rear ships and the battle. If they were misled . . . Nelson fought back the thought. They must make it.

Within the bay, the *Majestic* had passed *Vanguard*: a flash of cannon fire lit the high wall of *L'Heureux* dead ahead of the *Majestic's* bows. Captain Westcott yelled, "Hard a—" choked, blood gushing from his throat. "Starboard!" screamed his lieutenant, leaping over the dead Captain's body. Too late.

With a grinding, splintering jar, the ships rammed. The *Majestic's* defenseless jib boom locked in the French main rigging, while the French poured broadside after broadside into *Majestic's* bows.

"Cut away wreckage!" her 1st Lieutenant howled. The carpenters climbed forward on the bow, faces set, as they crawled into the deadly French fire. An ax splintered and the head spun silver sparks through the air, all that was left of ax or carpenter. The other carpenters edged on over the slaughtered and quartered remains of their comrades, hacking like maniacs at the entwining cables that clutched them to *L'Heureux's* side.

A last broadside from *L'Heureux,* for on the lift of recoil the severed ropes fell like dead snakes in the water and the ships rolled apart. The *Majestic* swung around. Her 1st Lieutenant Cuthbert fighting eye for eye, tooth for tooth, as bringing *Majestic's* broadside guns to bear, Cuthbert laid open the tender bow of the first French ship in his sights: *Le Mercure.*

A wooden figurehead took to the sky, a winged Mercury soared, bright painted face expressionless. Dropped like a dead bird straight to the bottom of Aboukir; bobbed up—floated by, sightless eyes upcast.

On *Vanguard,* the tension had slightly eased as the other ships came into play. Nelson, relying on Berry to fight *Vanguard,* turned to watch his rear ship still hazarding the shoals in total dark. So far ten ships had come in. Little *Leander* 50 which Nelson had scoffed at when Thomson had once asked if he might not be counted on to fight an enemy battleship by himself, was just now sounding in, but not yet within range. When she came she was supposed to assist another ship, not attack all alone. Thomson was guiding her brilliantly. Nelson smiled. Thomson was sailing his baby battleship, trusting only his wits and not the deceptive firing. *Leander's* full sails cast back the battle light, as she came gliding over the water. Soon then, Nelson would have fifty more guns from her to replace *Bellerophon,* which was so badly crippled Nelson could no longer count on her to maneuver as she floated, mastless and rudderless, firing whenever a target happened her way. He had nine ships now, actively fighting the French thirteen of line and four frigates until *Leander* came within range, and *Culloden, Alexander* and *Swiftsure* arrived.

Where were they? Nelson tried to count the English signal lights breaking clean now and then through the smoke, like four stars across mizzen top yards. Three English ships were overdue.

Troubridge, Ball and Hallowell—three of his very best men! Where in God's name were they?

Nelson put his glass to his eye, tried to hold the focus while the organ music of balls whined past him, and the rigging was plucked like harp strings by the scrap iron of langridge and the deadlier grape. A jack fresh from the farm, face drawn with aching for home, anywhere but this hell, saw the Admiral standing cool as you please not minding the shot peppering the deck all about him. The jack's face grew bolder and when he watched the Admiral disappear in smoke, reappear, jaunty cocked hat and all, glass still pasted to his eye, he didn't feel quite so lonely.

And it wasn't until the jack went to reach for a match that he discovered three fingers were missing where he needed them. But the man next to him fell in pieces, and the jack felt he was getting off easy.

As bit by bit the wood disappeared, another knot of men liquefied into blood, men bellowed and screamed and cheered while in the blinding light of firing under the faint winking stars, between the blankets of smoke, Nelson watched tensely.

There!—at last—was *Culloden,* bearing down, just in the mouth of the bay. "Thank God!"

❋ ❋ ❋

In *Culloden,* Troubridge was hoarse from urging his ship in, his great Roman nose like a second prow thrust out, pointed straight for the center of carnage. His guns primed, his men ready, his eyes burning for revenge. He was coming, all sails set, not slowly enough to sound too carefully, but steering by the fire ahead. The leadsman was chanting:

"Eleven fathoms." Safe—deep. *Culloden* surged on: crashed. The masts leaned forward in the rigging, and then with a sickening lurch that sent the crew head foremost asprawl, *Culloden* settled back on her stern.

Troubridge was roaring as he picked himself up. The sails still bellied out, but *Culloden* did not move. He looked about: he was stuck. His valiant ship stuck in the sand—and there—*there*—just out of his grasp: the greatest sea fight since the world began!

"Out boats!" He was raging, and sobbing under his breath: "Shoot me!" Clenching his fists. "Somebody shoot me—" Crying in utter agony of hideous degradation; honor completely dashed. No one dared look at him as he bellowed his orders.

The boat crews strained, oars snapped, but *Culloden* stood like a rock at the mouth of Aboukir. "Like a Goddamn lighthouse!" Troubridge gnashed through his tears. Hardy nearly tore *Mutine* brig apart tugging; *Leander* put back, tugged. Anchors were lowered into the boats, rowed out as Troubridge tried to spring *Culloden* off. Nothing could budge her. She was stuck.

Nelson had dropped his glass as if shot, his face distorted with half-mad rage. Berry stared. That face would never leave him. Even in the midst of a battle, Berry stared aghast as the Admiral turned away, brought out at last a low groan, "Why didn't that damn fool sound!" And paced on, speechless, calculating his chances with his best friend, his best ship, utterly useless to him! *Bellerophon* was also practically useless, so the most he could possibly hope for now were twelve English, one of them a mere fifty—*Culloden's* accident might make the difference between complete and partial victory—if—if *Swiftsure* and *Alexander* did not follow *Culloden* onto the sands. If he lost them, too . . . "Oh, Troubridge! Troubridge!"

Berry, himself furious at Troubridge, held his breath as Nelson raged, "Like a lighthouse!"

Just that. *Culloden* suddenly blazed with lights. Troubridge was still doing all that he could. While *Alexander* and *Swiftsure* bore down from the sea into the treacherous bay. They hauled up to a heartbroken trumpeting:

"Oh, ahoy! *Tack!* Bear *east* for God's sake! *Fathom!* Fathom as you go in!" And then a groan, "I'm going *mad!*"

And *Alexander* and *Swiftsure,* with a backward glance for the *Culloden* lighthouse, gingerly swung out to skirt the submerged reefs.

Nelson was pacing *Vanguard's* quarter-deck, watching through the rents in the smoke. His face changed from fury to calm in a flash as he saw *Alexander* and *Swiftsure* were safe. Now, twelve English battleships against the enemy thirteen and four frigates.

His temper vanished, leaving his face almost compassionate as he turned to Berry. "My poor Troubridge! Think what he's *suffering,* Berry!" And Berry stared again, as a cannon ball grooved the deck, sent up a shower of arrowlike splinters to impale flesh; and blood trickled into the gaps on the deck.

Now down on the battle came the two fresh ships, healthy reinforcements, to attack the dazed, trapped French.

In the red-orange light of firing, the strangling black smoke, glistening blood oozing out of the scuppers, crippled ships groaned, drowned out human screams. A forecastle vanished from a French ship. Deafening constant thunder.

Nelson had relaxed again. All was well. So far, excellent . . . he staggered. The fire blacked out, the din whined away and he seemed to be falling forever and ever into a roaring hell.

Berry saw the Admiral's high forehead split open in a burst of enemy langridge; saw the blood obliterate the face, the skin hanging down over his eyes: caught him in his arms as Nelson murmured something about death and his wife.

❋   ❋   ❋

Aboard *L'Orient,* French Admiral Brueys, bleeding head and arm, had grimly turned away from the sight of shattered *Bellerophon.* A moment of success; saw success dwindle. Now well within the bay, shaking the breeze from their furling sails, Hallowell's *Swiftsure* and Ball's *Alexander* fell on *L'Orient* bow and stern.

Nelson's first eight had concentrated on the enemy's first five, crippled them, fought slowly on, eyes watching to support each other. But Nelson had been carried below; now, if ever, was the time to prove a leader completely expendable. Still no slackening in teamwork. No vain duels, boarding ships, one ship at a time. No boarding whatever.

While Admiral Brueys still stood on *L'Orient's* deck, reeling, looking for his ships to aid one another as they looked helplessly up to him.

On the ship astern was Rear Admiral Blanquet, deafened, shouting an order. Blanquet dropped, shot through the face.

Aboard *L'Orient* Brueys staggered about, saw the French *Franklin,* cables cut, drifting into English fire. Then with the audacity of a bulldog, Captain Thomson's *Leander,* having failed to budge *Culloden,* darted in to challenge *Franklin* 80 with her fifty guns. *Leander* had run out cables from her bow and stern to her anchor, making a spring. She was maneuvering against the wind, as she chose. And *Leander* hung on *Franklin,* brought her broadside to bear while what she could not put into *Franklin's* bow, Captain Thomson aimed at *L'Orient.*

Brueys, nearly fainting from loss of blood, ordered the impossible: French ships to hold their line, for the English must be kept under the tremendous fire of French broadsides. And *Vive la France!*

Brueys dropped, slashed in two. "I will die on my quarter-deck." And as Brueys played his last, most gallant act, the crippled French ship just ahead, *Le Peuple Souverain,* ironically reeled out of line; Nelson's pincers had broken the spine of Brueys's last possible defense. *Le Peuple Souverain* left a gap ahead of *L'Orient's* bows open to the English, as she swung slowly, drifted under the side of *L'Orient.* Double tragedy.

Ben Hallowell spied the advantage, crowded his *Swiftsure,* which was already pounding *L'Orient,* into the gap to offer whole broadsides to the stern of the drifting *Franklin;* and still *Swiftsure* struck *L'Orient,* while *Leander* still hung on *Franklin's* bow.

In the blaze of the cannon fire, the first Tricolor quivered; wilted and slid down the mast of *L'Aquilon. Le Peuple Souverain* was next. While *Vanguard,* with over a hundred of her company dead or wounded, her decks a slaughterhouse, hammered into her first opponent: *Spartiate.* The Tricolor flapping in the wind jerked at last, hauled down.

A moment of respite for *Vanguard.* A boatload of marines sent to hold *Spartiate* bobbed over the water, for the English were taking no chances with the French trick of striking colors for a rest; hoisting again. The boat sent back the first French officers.

Down in the caverns below deck of *Vanguard,* with the dark and the heat and the thunder, the dust sifting down through the planks, the Admiral had been carried down the steep blood-slippery ladder into the red screaming hell of the cockpit. Mere jacks lay in rows already ahead of him, awaiting the harassed surgeon whose arms were red to the elbows.

"Another glass of rum down his throat."

A groaning jack clamped his teeth on his mouth pad, gulped the rum; was sick. Drank more, while the surgeon probed for grapeshot lodged deep in his pelvic bones. Gave up. The chain would not budge. The man screamed and down went more rum. The surgeon gave him a harsh stare, turned away, his face more set, to the next man just as someone yelled, "Mr. Jefferson, the *Admiral's* wounded!"

The surgeon turned from a chest operation; the rule was "no precedence for officers, first come first served"—but the Admiral! Jefferson stumbled across the cockpit, and Nelson ordered him to go back to his business. He would take his turn with his fellows. The surgeon pivoted, hunched away, knees bent, ducking the low deck beams overhead, to finish the operation he had left. The men grinned, the ones who were able to—Nel was a tough character. And while some still howled helplessly, many grew quieter.

Nelson had already made up what was left of his dazed mind: he was dead. Shot straight through the head. He sent for his chaplain to pray for him.

Finally, in the glimmering light of the candles smoking in lanthorns, Mr. Jefferson arrived at the Admiral, heaved a sigh of relief. The Admiral was not shot through the head, as it had first appeared, but athwart it. The wounded jacks cheered but Nelson struggled up, insisting he was dead.

"Now just relax, Sir Horatio," the surgeon pleaded, "just lie quietly and don't worry—don't try to think about anything. Just relax"—while the surgeon, squinting in the dim light, could not see any crack he could lay a finger in, and tied Nelson's forehead back up into place, and implored the Admiral to try to sleep. The Admiral was carried out of the cockpit.

When they had laid him down carefully and set a sentry to guard his door, and his secretary to tend him, Nelson sat up, trying to get his bearings, figure out where he had been entombed. He could not lie still. His head was ringing, his teeth set with the agony of concussion; shunted off by himself, he could not even see his own battle, nor even his secretary for the blood pouring into his eyes. But he heard him, the man was also wounded. Nelson continued to sit bolt upright while his head throbbed with the din that drove a wounded man cold, then numb, then raving.

"Campbell! Take a letter!"

"Sir Horatio! The surgeon said—oh, pray, sir, you must rest and—and don't worry!" The secretary roused himself, peered at the Admiral through the gloomy fitful reflected light flickering down the companionway past the silhouette of the sentry.

"Where the devil am I, Campbell?"

"In the bread room, Sir Horatio."

Nelson let that sink in, trying to understand why he had been shunted off ignominiously. "Ready, Mr. Campbell? 'To Earl St. Vincent—' "

"Sir—I—can—" Campbell sickened, staring in horror at the wreck of his Admiral groping blindly about the tin-lined walls of the bread room, falling against one of the drying stoves, in the trembling shuddering dark. They were deep below water, in the safest place, not far from the sacred magazines.

" 'Having found'—no. Let me think. Oh, my head, let me think! I have seen the hand of God guiding us—*Campbell*—?"

But Campbell's finger shook the pen to the floor. He had fainted.

"Campbell!" Nelson groped, found the quill, the paper, at last the ink. It dripped over his hand, while in his big, quavering, left-handed scrawl, he tried to write. The paper crept, the ship shuddered, as he tried to find some words . . . never, *never* before in history . . . Glory? It was God! God . . . but the quill balked, the paper slipped. His hand was weak and stupid. He staggered up and nearly fell headlong. His head was stupid, too. Fuzzy, spinning. He'd lost his eye, his arm, and now his head! But not his will . . . he—he alone had led his fleet . . . *whose* guns were slackening? Suddenly a strange hand caught his.

"Sir Horatio, are you better?"

"Who is it?"

"Berry, sir. Do lie down, sir!"

"Well, Berry?"

"*L'Aquilon, Le Peuple Souverain, Le Spartiate, L'Heureux, Le Ton-nant* and *L'Orient* have struck, Sir Horatio!"

"Is that *all?*"

"That is all I know for sure, Sir Horatio." Berry pressed a cold French sword in the Admiral's hands. "*L'Orient* has caught afire, sir."

"Take me on deck!"

"But your head, sir. Mr. Jefferson said—"

"Jefferson bedamned! Where's your arm?"

Berry linked his arm through Nelson's, half carrying him, led him up, into a light more brilliant than day.

Nelson opened his eyes sticky with blood; rubbed at his stiff lashes. The French were roasting alive in their mightiest ship: leaping for the water. Wretches who could not swim clung like leeches to the sides, feet dangling, screaming for help that no one could render.

"Our boats—not *one*—all!" Nelson to Berry.

"That's the only one left, sir!"

"Out with it!"

"Aye, aye, sir!" And down she went and common English jacks risked their lives to fish common French citizens out of the bay. And from other ships, any boats that could swim, that were not already shot to pieces, rowed out while cables were cut and the battleships, both French and English, edged away from the most awful catastrophe that could happen at sea: fire in a wooden ship.

Aboard *L'Orient:* The paint barrels had burst into flames, could not be extinguished. Now a gaping furnace. Slowly, surely, planks grew hot, sank underfoot, trapped men below deck. And as the survivors scrambled forward, decks cracked, caved in. Left spiraling screams; arms clutching smoke, plunged into the furnace.

To the gleeful crackling of flames leaping from yardarm to yardarm; fiery banners of flame breaking out, streaming with the wind that howled into the hell, blew it bright, showered the shores of Egypt with its sparks.

And clots of men in the water. The ship spawning in abortive agony. Men gone mad with fear, or sublimely indifferent: dragging some half-drowned mate, shoving him into a boat, dropping back to save another. Dragged under, drowned by lunatics trying to walk on the water—on the heads and the bodies of others: all going under together.

And low on the waves, Frenchmen and Englishmen gripped hands, shook off the water, grinned speechlessly, for a moment not enemies but towering men trying too late to undo what was done.

The bay was brilliant with the torch of fresh paint, pitch, spars and powder.

Aboard *Vanguard*: "She's been burning for two hours already, Sir Horatio," Berry shouted as the light brightened and brightened till the color came back into men, showed the warmth of live flesh, the vital red of fresh blood; breathed no life in the dead, livid and still as the moon. The light sparked and danced on the cutlasses, guns and gold braid.

Now in the light, and by a glance, men could see St. George still flew at every masthead. Where was the Tricolor? Victory was secured! Mopping up must wait, for now . . .

All eyes on *L'Orient*. And rimming the shore the Arabs leaped high, their shadows stretching behind them. Sparks flew toward the arcing black sky. To leeward, at the rear of the French line, there was heavy firing still where ships not fascinated by the holocaust wrestled; their aim more accurate in the light.

Nelson clung to Berry's arm, swaying, dazed. Behind him the stumps of masts, his mangled men, blasted guns. His face was twisted in pain and in horror and in wild fascination at the hell he had finally dealt France.

Victory! Total war! All or nothing! *L'Orient* roared and hissed above the screams of mortals. The Admiral's face grew slowly ashen. This was more than enough.

"Oh, dear God! Save those poor devils!" But there was no saving them now, though his jacks rowed daringly close to death, back and forth, time and time again, disgorging stunned silent Frenchmen; ninety had been saved by *Vanguard* so far. *L'Orient* carried more than a thousand. And still the ships' boats scurried.

And now all *L'Orient* crackled in one lump of fire. Strings of flame licked her rigging, soared into the sky, shone out of her ports. And men who could not swim dropped at last, as her sides grew hot, like small lumps of burning tar: drowned. And now and then heat touched off a cannon, a crazy shot ricocheted around the bay; balls ringing like bells on metal, plowing through flesh, splintering wood.

And down on the water, a boy crying *"Mon père!"* and Commodore

Casabianca answering. Their cries carried far, yet their hands, as they struggled, could not reach each other.

"Vive la France! Vive la Liberté—vive Buonaparte!" To their dying breath: *"Vive Buonaparte!"*

And the Arabs on shore had drawn closer, mingled in with the men who had mutinied; while the light of *L'Orient* grew like the sun rising up in the night again. Roaring and crackling in her death throes. The fire eating its way into her vitals: her magazines . . .

And all eyes were hypnotized watching *L'Orient,* flagship and symbol of Buonaparte's mad strike for empires.

The flames gushed into her bowels, fed by the wind; licked powder, roared: flashed thunderbolts to the moon.

❀   ❀   ❀

Silence.

A curdling black cloud churned in the sky. Men gaped at it superstitiously for what seemed like hours till flaming bits of *L'Orient* began to shoot down like comets out of the night. A blazing mast crashed straight down, hissed as it struck through the strugglers in the water.

Silence. Men stood, eyes glassy, stunned, ears plugged, deafened: awestruck.

Not a gun was heard in Aboukir Bay. The explosion had stopped the battle. One minute. Two minutes. *Total silence.*

At last men tried to shake themselves, wake up. Aboard *Theseus* a childish cheer as men tried to shrug off the paralyzing trance.

"Oh, *silence,* for God's sake . . ." from Miller, and yet he began to smile grimly. The blast had shaken his brain in his skull. And his thoughts drifted like a rudderless ship. It was not honorable to cheer. Victors had always wept, that's what he had learned. It was probably in the Articles of War somewhere. . . . Then he saw the massacre at Toulon again. He had been there the night the mob rose. . . . Sorry, he could not weep. He didn't feel like cheering either. "The devil is beyond blackening . . ." His smile faded into indifference. Five years of hell paying off tonight. He was tired of war. He had two little girls. One he had never seen. He rubbed his eyes. Tonight ought to finish it once and for all.

And for another minute more two fleets in the midst of a battle were stunned into saluting the dead where *L'Orient's* skeleton was slowly dropping six hundred thousand pounds in ingots of gold and diamonds, the ready cash for the French army, into the sandy bottom of Aboukir.

It seemed like hours, but time is elastic. *L'Orient's* masts and rigging, bits of her hull, were still raining fire.

Alexander's fore-topmast burst into flame.

"That's Ball!" Miller jumped. "Get the fire engine into the boat! Go to *Alexander!*" And he glanced gratefully heavenward: he had wet down his furled sails. *Theseus's* canvas was soaked.

But Captain Ball, though bleeding, was still master of his fate. Bringing his ship about before the breeze, he let the wind tilt the blaze away from the rest of the rigging and doused it with his own fire engines pumping.

"Bravo, Ball!" Miller wiped his face on his sleeve. He saw without thinking: there was blood on him.

He drew a deep breath, blinking to reaccustom his eyes to the sudden dark as distant firing began again, and saw for the first time the moon had risen serene in a cloudless sky. Life had not stopped for them. The earth was still turning. He felt like a child waking out of a nightmare, hoping that when he opened his eyes there would be grown-up faces to reassure him. His head was still addled from the shock of *L'Orient*. He stared at the moon. . . .

But there! Casting broken spars athwart a long moonbeam: a French ship that had not struck!

Captain Miller: "Lieutenant Brodie, if she surrenders on hailing take possession. If not, burn false fires."

Into the boat went the lieutenant, putting the last mark of doom on the French frigate that *Orion* had knocked clean out of the bay at the very beginning: she surrendered.

But men were weary. The battle was ending. Miller glanced about once more. Nelson had vindicated his Teneriffe. They had won, and his men were falling asleep. They had been at their posts since dawn; fighting for life since sunset. *Theseus's* masts were swaying in the frayed rigging.

"Avast! There are some devils trying to get away! Mate, overside, fathom the bay, find the channel so we may get near them!" And Miller looked at his masts again. Would *Theseus* sail unrepaired?

The two rear battleships of the French line were warping out, slipping away to eastward, led by Admiral Villeneuve who had abandoned his own ship, was wisely trying to save something out of the wreckage.

With that, while waiting for the mate to find a navigable passage, Miller staggered into his cabin; slept dreamlessly till sudden orders came:

Admiral signaling: Secure rear enemy ships! This should have been done while Nelson was left in the bread room. He was angry again.

Miller roused his crew, and down the bay tottered *Theseus,* suddenly found herself alone, for no other English had obeyed the signal: *Theseus* lay facing five French with Tricolors rehoisted! Miller studied them, waiting for reinforcements. He did not fire. Neither did the five French. The six ships only eyed one another. Nothing happened.

The jacks looked dimly at the enemy, then curled up and fell asleep, heads propped on guns, on cannon balls, pillowed on splinters and unidentifiable iron; their legs sprawled as they slid down on the slippery deck. Dreamless sleep. Work well done.

While English and French suffered together, companions gripped in agony, the wounded with their bodies full of splinters, the armless and legless lay wide-awake or delirious; what laudanum and opium there had been was gone.

After *L'Orient* blew up, Berry had taken Nelson once again below. This time into the shambles of his cabin where the gun set up during battle still smoked and a red smear slowly spread along the beam overhead. And Berry stood over the Admiral till the gunner valet, Allen, put him to bed.

The Admiral's eye was glittering, his face flushed, but his mind was still in command of his ships when he was not helplessly and wretchedly sick. "Not a ship must leave Aboukir Bay!" But he was carried off again with the incoherence of "the rage."

Nelson, with a bandage holding his head together, could lie in his cot assured by everyone, if not by his inmost senses knocked around the compass, that he was doing very well. No one seemed to understand how very very tired he was. Perhaps he wasn't making himself clear. No one seemed to be obeying his orders. Didn't they understand that *no enemy* ships could be permitted to escape? They said something about masts being too weak. So he gave his orders again. He wanted them to obey and let him sleep—a victor. He was very tired and his ambition fulfilled. . . . No! It was just beginning. He tried not to think. He wanted to sleep. But he could not sleep! He could not rest any more than some of the crazed amputees who tore off their bandages, tried to walk without legs. To get away—or keep fighting— or talking—or crying. Some sang "Rule, Britannia."

"If it were mortal he would be unconscious," Berry and the other captains who had rushed to congratulate their Chief reasoned with their undamaged heads. Yet they watched over him tenderly; Gould had written him a letter of jubilation—just a note—in the midst of battle. Nelson had led them to glory; they would follow his flag anywhere!

He was more than human. He had made them immortal. He was England awakened, Drake reincarnate—greater than Drake! Berry answered Gould and all of the captains for Nelson—"We are but one heart and one soul."

So the Admiral lay babbling like a child, and when he came to: "Secure every enemy ship." And then he staggered up in a moment of clear cold consciousness. There was no one to replace him. The work must go on. The world must be notified. He must warn India, for captured French dispatches actually spoke of "Suez and India . . ." and he stared hopelessly at some of Buonaparte's letters, trying to read the man's scrawl, finally recognized two words: George Washington. Gave up dizzily, dropping his head in his hand. Buonaparte wanted to be a George Washington. Well. And for the first time he began to feel better, almost laughed aloud, and his mind cleared a little more.

Berry must carry the news of the victory to St. Vincent with Captain Thomson in *Leander*. That left a vacancy to be filled: Hardy must be posted, Captain Hardy of *Vanguard*. Poor Westcott was gloriously dead, then Lieutenant Cuthbert was Captain of *Majestic*. That still left *Mutine*. The little brig must carry duplicate dispatches in case anything unforeseen should delay *Leander,* for the world must know at once in order to act on this victory, make the most of it. Capel must be Captain of *Mutine*. He would go to Naples, then overland to London. That still left *Mutine* at Naples. Hoste would go with Capel, become Captain Hoste of *Mutine* brig when Capel went . . .

Nelson's head began to spin again; he fell back on his cot calling feebly for Allen.

The surgeon looked in on the Admiral. "The rage is passing off." He smiled at Berry.

But just as suddenly as Nelson had felt happy and clear-headed, black depression now closed down on him. His thoughts jumbled and blurred, or loomed clear and cold as icebergs floating out of a dark sea. Small worries tormented him; large thoughts floated away. As if his spyglass were turned around.

"My head is shook," he moaned.

"Aye, aye, sir. No wonder, sir," Allen said.

❋   ❋   ❋

As the sun had come up, Captain Miller tried to rouse his men.

"After those ships!" They staggered up, gripped the capstan bars, round and round like sleepwalkers, dazed. The anchor weighed, they slid down under the bars, while Miller yelled and his officers cursed them to their feet again.

But they moved like men in a dream.

The two French battleships and two frigates under Villeneuve had maneuvered away out of gunshot. Miller ordered his guns to fire on what remained. His masts were too shaken to chase.

And in the dawn of the second day, the battle went on till two more French battleships again hauled down their flags to the English, and a French frigate dashed herself on the shore—her masts toppling over her bows onto the sand. Her crew set her afire. Ran for the desert. A battleship tried the same: somehow, with a second wind, *Theseus* hauled it off, took possession.

The last of the battle fought slowly through fogs of exhaustion, under a burning desert sun, with flies settling down everywhere. The stench of yesterday's smoke and yesterday's blood, and the countless bodies washing up on the shores.

Only Sam Hood in *Zealous* could stay awake to chase the two of line and two frigates still edging down the wide bay.

Miller in *Theseus* kept a light fire playing around the captured ships, preventing the French from setting any more fires and escaping in small boats ashore. Small jobs. Weary ones . . . no one really cared if those last two battleships and two cruisers got away. It had been a great battle. Never anything like it in history. Only Nelson still raged, "Chase!" and Allen bending over him, bathing his head to keep it scrupulously clean, free of any deadly infection, said, "Aye, aye, sir!"

Sam Hood obeyed. Not enough. Hood was recalled. And on the third day the battle ended. On the third day Troubridge got *Culloden* off the sand and wrapped her stove bottom with canvas, set the pumps to dancing and clanging, then stomped ashore: took the French battery that had been deviling him.

The Arabs built fires and feasted for joy for a week, and Nelson ordered a day of thanksgiving and prayer. It was kept solemnly. It impressed the French as much as the battle.

Nelson had finally dragged himself to his writing table to make his reports. He was beginning to believe that he was not shot through the head. That he would live long enough for the peace and quiet of home which he suddenly craved. He thought tenderly of Fanny, how she had waited for him all these years.

Troubridge hunched in, stood head bowed. He had contemplated suicide, even gone to his cabin and stared at his pistols. Nelson might order a court-martial, hound him out of the service for *Culloden's* accident.

Nelson looked up, held out his hand. Troubridge gripped it in both of his, speechless, tears in his eyes.

"My dear Troubridge, your character is so thoroughly established . . . let us rejoice."

Troubridge only moaned from clear down in his shoes. Miller, too, had come in. He clapped his hand on Troubridge's shoulder sympathetically.

Nelson shook Troubridge's hand. "But for you we would have lost *Alexander* and *Swiftsure*." And he smiled like an angel which was perhaps just as well, for Troubridge went out, chin up again.

Nelson turned to Miller. "We couldn't have fought without you. As soon as you have the prize ships at Gibraltar, you must go home, see your family."

And Miller went out, his face joyous, tears in his eyes. The wish of his soul granted before he could ask it.

As Nelson slowly began to make out his abstract of the battle, the cold facts before him laid out in numbers, he began to realize for the first time how much he had accomplished. He had won the first victory over the French fleet this war, and as he collected the accounts from his various captains, he felt at last the exaltation of victory.

ABSTRACT OF SHIPS ENGAGED IN THE BATTLE OF THE NILE

ENGLISH	GUNS	MEN	FRENCH	GUNS	MEN	HOW DISPOSED OF
Vanguard, Admiral Nelson, Capt. Berry	74	595	L'Orient	120	1,010	Burnt
			Le Franklin	80	800	Taken
			Le Tonnant	80	800	Taken
Orion, Saumarez	74	590	Le Guerrier	74	700	Taken
Bellerophon, Darby	74	590	Le Conquérant	74	700	Taken
Defence, Peyton	74	590	Le Peuple Souverain	74	700	Taken
Minotaur, Louis	74	640	Le Spartiate	74	700	Taken
Alexander, Ball	74	590	Le Timoléon	74	700	Burnt
Audacious, Gould	74	590	L'Heureux	74	700	Taken
Zealous, Hood	74	590	Le Mercure	74	700	Taken
Swiftsure, Hallowell	74	590	L'Aquilon	74	700	Taken
Majestic, Westcott	74	590	L'Artémise	36	300	Burnt
Goliath, Foley	74	590	Le Sérieuse	36	300	Sunk
Theseus, Miller	74	590	L'Hercule Bomb	8	50	Burnt
Leander, Thomson	50	343	La Fortune	18	70	Taken
Mutine, brig, Hardy			Alerte, brig	18		Taken
			Railleur	14		Taken
			Salamine	8		Taken
Culloden, Troubridge (ran aground, not in battle)	74	590	Le Guillaume Tell	80	800	Escaped
			Le Généreux	74	700	Escaped
			La Justice, frigate	40	400	Escaped
			La Diane, frigate	40	400	Escaped
TOTAL	1,012	8,068	TOTAL	1,244	11,230	

Casualties:

English: 218 killed, 677 wounded, total		895
French on board ships burnt, sunk, taken		8,930
Escaped or sent ashore by cartel, including wounded		3,705
French taken, drowned, burnt, missing		5,225

❈   ❈   ❈

Nelson sat back astounded. In changing the whole course of this war, in this battle, he had lost *less* men in killed than he had lost at Teneriffe. The French casualties were gruesome. He could smell them, taste them in the thick hot air, where, if he turned his head, looked out his window, he could see the black line on the beach, not seaweed but corpses. They could not bury them as fast as the sea disgorged them. He did not look out the window, for three days and three nights he had thrown up all but his skin and his bones.

But as his head and heart rallied he realized, at last, how much he and his band of brothers had done. With the thirteen battleships, all inferior in size and number of guns to the French, which he had brought into action, he had beaten the French fleet to its knees, and captured eleven of their thirteen battleships! What would St. Vincent say! What would First Lord Spencer say! And Fanny—and his father! They would . . . why, Fanny would . . . she never had, but this time he knew she would give him delirious loving praise! Why, there'd be a *feu de joie* in London! He had kept that old promise to Fanny: now he'd have that gazette to himself! And he remembered the days of torture—just last year—when he had thought he was finished, watching London cheer Duncan. But Camperdown had been nothing to this.

His victory—why, he would go down in history—his name remembered—immortalized. The most astounding sea fight in history. It had political consequences reaching all over the globe. He had reconquered the Mediterranean Sea in one stroke! Saved India. Humbled that wretch Mr. Buonaparte. Pitt could call up all Europe to arms, form the new Coalition. . . . And as for himself? Why, if St. Vincent were an Earl and Duncan a Viscount . . . what would he be? And he wondered how it would feel to be called "m'lord." . . . He stood up, grinning at his own delight, half ashamed of his downright vanity. He made his shaky way to his shaving mirror hanging over his washbasin. He was not surprised to find a crack in the glass as he winced at his ghastly bandaged reflection. He'd make a strange-looking "m'lord" but an honorable one. He felt he'd earned it, by God!

Allen came in, stopped dead, then grunted for him to go back and sit down and that he ought to go to bed.

"I was contemplating the remains of poor old Horatio Nelson, Allen." The Admiral staggered obediently back to his chair. He held up the five thin fingers of his left hand. "An eye at Calvi," he bent one finger, "a belly at St. Vincent," he bent another, "an arm at Santa

Cruz and now my head—" he still had one finger raised. He eyed it wryly. "Tolerable for one war, Tom, tolerable."

And he sat back, feeling almost lazy for the first time in his life, listening indulgently to his Caliban's, "Aye, me and yow has done pretty well these last five years, sir, considerin'. And I hear through a friend of mine who's man to one of yowr captains—I won't say who —that they're forming a Nile Club, the captains are, and are going to give yow the handsomest sword in Christendom they can afford."

Nelson started, as surprised and delighted as a boy over the prospects of a new wooden gun. And his laziness fell from him. Life had only begun. "You should not eavesdrop and gossip so much, Thomas," he grinned.

"Me, sir? Why I—" Allen spluttered—"may I drop—may I—" but Tom eyed the sky and the Almighty's domain and subsided. As he went out to get water to dress the Admiral's head again, Nelson's cabin was still but for the squeaking of a quill in his wobbly left hand.

Thirty-nine-year-old Rear Admiral Sir Horatio Nelson had begun his triumphant report to the world:

Vanguard, off the Mouth of the Nile,
3rd August, 1798.
Almighty God has blessed his Majesty's Arms . . .

Bibliography

(*Note:* All the characters mentioned in this biographical novel actually existed.)

The author has used the letters written by Nelson as the foundation for this novel; whenever humanly possible he has spoken in his own words. Therefore the main authority referred to has been Nelson himself.

Among the books concerning Nelson which the author has read during the last twenty years, the following have proved most interesting:

The Dispatches and Letters of Lord Nelson, Sir H. Nicolas, London, 1845, 7 vols. In spite of the fact that Nicolas does not contain all of Nelson's correspondence, it covers so broad a field that little has been unearthed since which might add to or subtract from the summation of the man represented in these volumes. Not even Morrison's *The Hamilton and Nelson Papers,* 2 vols., 1893–1894 cracks the "literary monument" which Nicolas intended to create for Nelson.

Nelson, Carola Oman, 1947. Publishes many of Nelson's letters which were deliberately misquoted by historians Clarke and M'Arthur. Oman's biography contains a splendidly exhaustive bibliography on Nelson.

Clarke and M'Arthur, *Life of Nelson,* London, 1809, 2 vols. The authors of this book were hampered by two things: the danger of libel and exposing contemporaries; and their own lofty judgment of morality. They also "improved" Nelson's literary style abominably, dehydrating the man and his wife. The copy in the author's possession was once the property of the Reverend Dr. Scott, Chaplain and interpreter for Lord Nelson in *Victory.* The volumes contain Dr. Scott's marginal notes, as well as his heavy underscoring of the text, which reads: "In all his life he was never known to do an unfriendly act to any Officer about him: if they behaved ill, and he was asked to prosecute them, he used to answer, 'That there was no occasion for him to ruin a poor devil, who was sufficiently his own enemy to ruin himself' . . . the sailors say of him, 'Our Nel is brave as a Lion, and as gentle as a Lamb.' "

Life of Nelson, Southey, 1813, a handsome rewrite of Clarke and M'Arthur's fluffy style, and Harrison's *Life,* 1806 (Lady Hamilton's attempt to persuade the government to give her a pension).

Nelsonian Reminiscences, Lieutenant Parsons, 1843, republished and edited by Lang, 1905. A little-known classic of its kind: half fancy, half fact. It does full justice to Lord Nelson's *valet de chambre,* old Tom Allen himself.

Of contemporary works the following are considered accurate, though they are sometimes contradictory in details:

Nelson: *Sketch of My Life,* written in 1799 for M'Arthur, and *Remarks Relative to Myself* at St. Vincent, 1797.

Parker: Letter on the Battle of St. Vincent is in Nicolas, 1797.

Drinkwater: *Narrative of the Battle of St. Vincent,* 1797, and *Siege of Gibraltar,* 1785.

Dr. Moseley: *Treatise on Tropical Diseases* with Foreword on Nicaragua campaign by Lord Nelson, London, 1803–1804.

Captain Miller's drawing of the Battle of St. Vincent is to be found, retouched by engravers, in Clarke and M'Arthur, 1809.

Captain Sir Edward Berry: *Narrative of the Battle of the Nile,* 1798.

Chaplain Williams: *Narrative* of same.

Captain Miller: letter to his wife written August, 1798, minutely describing the Battle of the Nile is in Nicolas.

Admiral Blanquet: *Account of the Battle of the Nile,* 1798, contains an excellent description of the explosion of *L'Orient,* and the deaths of Commodore Casabianca and son. The French version is quite similar to the English, though understandably bleak and bitter.

Elliot, Lord Minto: Speech in Parliament, 1798, describes Nelson's work in Corsica, at the Battle of St. Vincent, and declares Nelson to be as great a statesman as he was a fighter. Reprinted in Nicolas.

Tucker: *Lord St. Vincent,* 1844, 2 vols., London.

The Naval Chronicle for 1790–1798.

Memoirs of Sir William Hoste.

Life of Admiral Collingwood, by Murray, London, 1936.

The *Monthly Mirror* for November, 1805, one of the many gazettes